I0822512

SUPPERS OF MANY DISHES

SUPPERS OF MANY DISHES

OLIVER OSITA AKAMNONU

Library of Congress Control Number: 2008903068
ISBN: Hardcover 978-1-940909-06-6
Softcover 978-1-949909-07-3
Ebook 978-1-940909-08-0

This book was printed in the United States of America.

To obtain additional copies of this book and/or other titles in Dr. Akamnonu's collection, contact:
AKAMNONU ASSOCIATES INCORPORATED
Email: droliver@akamnonuassociates.com
Phone: +1(413) 693-8428 or +1(818) 823-6830
Website: www.akamnonuassociates.com

Contents

BOOK 1

BOOK II

DEDICATION

To Mmadukibeya, my father, who always waited patiently for me in the railway station even under the rain, on any day I would come back from school, To that most affectionate and caring mother, Eliaba, my mother who showered equal love on all her children and who, despite failing health, always struggled to ensure our comfort.

To those my other seven mothers, wonderful wives of that great sage, the mothers who provided the dishes upon which background this book is largely built, the mothers who individually cared for each of the forty-six of us as their own.

To my first and only love, Chika, my dear wife, my confidant and best friend, for always believing in me and for always tolerating my lateness to events that I would attend with her,

To Olisa, Chibu, our loving daughter Somto, and Chuka—our children,

To my many brothers and sisters, participants in the suppers of many dishes, and beneficiaries of the unfettered paternal love that was richly bestowed on all of us.

To Cy, my brother and friend; to Obi, my childhood friend; and to my numerous cousins and friends upon whose moral support and good wishes I always relied for solace in times of uncertainty and near despair.

And finally, to that great school and her products, that great alma mater, the cornerstone of our character and our talent, for teaching us, even from our very beginnings, the attributes of hard work, honesty, and self-discipline, and for bringing home to us the great need—to "fear God and Honor the King."

ACKNOWLEDGEMENTS

I wish to thank Darcy Livingston and Leonard Dayao for their invaluable work in the typing of the manuscript. I also wish to thank my son Chuka, who started the initial typing job before he had to give up due to the compelling call of his studies. My thanks also go to my wife, Chika, who did the initial proofreading, as well as to Vanessa and Meg of Xlibris publishing for their patience in explaining to me the intricacies involved in the production of the book.

And to my boss, Lidia, and my childhood friend, Anthony, I say thank you for those very supportive words of encouragement during the early stages of this work.

Prologue

SUPPERS OF MANY DISHES

The tropical rain falls hard in large drops.
The goats in the stable bleat in protest against the splashing water invading their abode.

A woman is in labor on the floor of the open hall.
She rolls in pain off the raffia mat spread beneath her back and the banana leaves underneath her legs.

A male child is born into the bare hands of the traditional birth attendant
As she yells on top of her voice, urging the young mother to bear hard and not to stifle the baby.

The child grows up in the midst of scores of other siblings.
He learns to struggle and to hold his own.

A fight with a bigger cousin earns him a transfer to the city.
He learns to steal mangoes and to compete in class.

Through life's travails his memory still recounts
The suppers of many dishes, in the village of his birth.

Book I

An African child, the third of forty-six siblings,
The travails, the joys, a taste of the West

The Children, the Chores, and the Chickens

Okoli lived with his grandmother in a section of the village called Ikpa-umuoji. He often accompanied some big local girls, the *onusayas*, to hunt for snails after the rains. The snail hunting was often in the early hours of the night, and the young hunters used dim light from sticks laden with the oiled fiber of oil palm fruits called *akpulakpu*. Those were the days when neither the hurricane lantern nor the dry cell battery torchlight had made their debut in Okoli's village. The light bushes, wet from the rains and rotting vegetation, provided good breeding grounds for snails. The frogs that often came out at such times of the night to also hunt for food were sometimes themselves hunted. Occasionally toads would be mistaken for frogs and get picked up. The latter would however be readily dumped away from the hunters' bags and clay collection pots once they were identified. Once in a while, a species of snakes called *eke ogba,* which often came out at such times of the night, also to hunt for food, would send shivers through the young hunters. Mgbafor, the biggest of the girls whom Okoli often went snail hunting with, was never afraid of the eke ogba snake. She would use a thick stick to uncoil any eke ogba away from a big snail if she saw the former attempting to swallow the latter.

There was this amazing reverence for this snake the eke ogba by the much-older villagers. The eke ogba was said to be harmless, and it was a taboo to kill or harm it in any way. But the taboo went only as far as the elderly natives were concerned. This was especially so for those natives of the village who had not been converted to Christianity, and these were in the majority in Okoli's village, Ndiakunwanta. The converts and other settlers in the village did not share in the reverence for this stout and multicolored snake, which characteristically moved very sluggishly, had a small head, but could amazingly swallow large hens' eggs and occasionally the incubating hens themselves. Indeed some settlers from adjoining towns were known to secretly kill, cook, and eat these snakes with yam porridge, an act that would often cause serious rifts between the natives who revered these snakes and the settlers, who often saw the eke ogba dish as a delicacy. These settlers often said that the meat of the eke ogba tasted like chicken, but that it was certainly more delicious. Okoli once had the canning of his life when his grandmother discovered that he had accepted and eaten the meat of the eke ogba, which was given to him by Nweke, a wine tapper settler from an adjoining village.

On many occasions, Okoli saw his grandmother "talking" to one large eke ogba, which might be crawling at the foot of the mud wall surrounding Grandmother's yam barn. Grandmother would usually "tell" the snake that it should get back fast into the bush because *ndi uka* (Christians) were around. This was because Christianity was gaining grounds in the village, and the Christians were taught to disregard the pagan beliefs and myths about the sanctity of the eke ogba. Indeed the Christians would instantly kill any eke ogba at sight and bury it or throw it into the nearest bush. Some others, as earlier said, would make a feast of same. Coincidently (or could it have heard Grandmother), the eke ogba without physical prodding would, when so commanded or warned, often gradually crawl away from Grandmother's yam barn.

Okoli and his group often were careful during their snail-hunting trips to avoid the precincts of the nearby *okwara* stream with its adjoining thickly wooded *ohia ojii* which was the source of the okwara stream. Ohia ojii, whose translation means the *dark forest*, was famed to be home to black and bearded witches who had pendulous breasts extending to their knees. These witches were said to feed only on dead human bodies and on the fish from the okwara steam. These witches, who were called *nwanyi mgbalagada ala* (the giant-breasted maidens), were said to guard jealously the fish from the okwara stream to the present day. *Azu okwara* (fish from okwara stream) is not eaten by anybody in the village because it is believed that the witches led by Nwanyi mgbalagada ala will definitely come to attack anybody who harvests or eats the fish upon which they feed. Consequently, the fish in okwara stream are usually very large in size and surprisingly, to this day, do not shy away from visitors to the stream. They even occasionally swim into people's buckets as the people fetch water. They have to be emptied away from the bucket of water cautiously, and as they are emptied, the incantation must be repeated: "Nwany mgbalagada ala, biko azu gi-o-o" (Big-breasted maiden, please accept back your fish.).

It is only by so doing that one can escape the wrath of Nwanyi mgbalagada ala.

The settlers in the village do not share the reverence and fears of the villagers and consequently sometimes secretly go at night and harvest the large fish from the okwara stream, just as some of them secretly kill, cook, and eat the eke ogba snake. It was into the ohia ojii bush that dead bodies of criminals, people who hanged themselves and people who died from mysterious illnesses like swollen legs and abdomen (*anasarca*), were, in the past, thrown. It was believed that only the witches led by Nwanyi mgbalagada ala could deal with the ghosts of such "dangerous" people and that it was unsafe to bury such people inside their or other peoples' compounds as was the practice. The settlers in the village did not respect these beliefs and practices but would certainly not dare to manifest their contempt openly. The new Christian converts were also taught to disregard the practices even though most of the latter even with their new faith would still not eat the fish from the okwara stream.

Mgbafor, the big girl and snail-hunting team leader, was usually fearless. She had a deformity in her right leg (possibly from infantile poliomyelitis), but that never deterred her. On one of the snail-hunting expeditions, Okoli and his friends were so scared by a loud howl and a quick dash from a wild animal, whose eyes glowed brightly from the dim light sources from among the low bush. The little hunters fled, believing that a tiger or a leopard was on their prowl. The three or four snails Okoli had harvested that night along with his face cap, which was a Christmas present from his father, were lost during the escape bid. Later the following morning, word spread round the village that Mgbafor, the deformed young lady, had the previous night killed the beast which had terrorized the young snail hunters. She was said to have stood her ground while the rest of the hunters fled. She had flung the big stick, which she usually supported herself with while walking, at the animal which turned out to be a giant wild cat.

Mgbafor was never shy of dirt or dung either. Okoli had on more than one occasion seen her pull off a giant snail from among a pool of human fecal matter. Human feces was not an uncommon sight in the bushes in Okoli's village at that time since there were no public toilets for the villagers or passersby going to or from the farms or markets.

Okoli would, on many other occasions, see the earth appear to go upside down. These were the many occasions that he suffered from *eba*. Eba was the general name which people in Arondizuogu, Okoli's hometown, gave to a wide array of high fevers (hyperpyrexias) emanating from a wide range of infective and parasitic diseases. Malaria, typhoid, and all kinds of fevers were branded as "eba." Many children Okoli's age then in the village often played outside, either completely naked or at best scantily clothed in shorts, which were called "knickers." The naked bodies of the children often provided good feasting grounds for the ever-present mosquitoes, especially in the evenings. Childhood malaria consequently was very rampant.

On many occasions when Okoli had attacks of malaria, the palm trees and the plantain and banana trees which *surrounded* his grandmother's house would all appear upside down. On market days the stream of people walking past Okoli's house to Nkwo Isoku, the local market, would all appear to be walking upside down with the market wares on their heads all (apparently) upside down.

Okoli remembers faintly one occasion when he convulsed (febrile convulsion) and Eliaba, his mother, who also appeared upside down, was crying frantically while applying *ude aki*, a dark oil extracted from roasted palm nuts, all over Okoli's body and mouth and shutting the latter's eyes with her palms. The shutting of the eyes with the palms was to shut out the hallucinatory sight of the charging ram *ebune,* which was usually seen during the episodes of febrile convulsion. It was about sixteen years later while in the medical school that Okoli was to see scores of kids whose feet and sometimes hands were burnt in open flames by their mothers and grandmothers in similar well-intentioned but fruitless efforts to treat febrile convulsion, the type which Okoli often had. Okoli was lucky he was spared that aspect of treatment to drive out the devil of febrile convulsion. He probably might not have the fingers to write any later scripts. Luckily in his last fifteen years of practice, Okoli did not see a single case of foot or hand burns from this well-intentioned but misdirected practice, which must have gone extinct with better medical enlightenment.

The Wrestling Combat

Okoli's father, Nwankwo, also called Ogbuka, was the only son of his mother who had two other daughters. Ogbuka was also the second of the five sons of Okoli's grandfather who had two wives. Two wives were the much Okoli's grandfather could afford in a culture where a man could marry as many wives as he could afford. A man's wealth was assessed partly by the number of wives that he had as well as by the size of his yam barn. Okoli's grandfather, whose actual name was Obeki, had assumed the nickname Akamnonu, which means "am I stronger by words of mouth alone?"

Every name or nickname in Okoli's culture had a meaning or was associated with an event. A child who for instance was born during the new yam festival was named Orieji, implying that the child came to eat yams, a widely eaten tuber. Again the child who was born during a festivity that involved the killing of goats or chickens was called Nwaofulanu, implying that the child came out because it saw meat. Other names were associated with one of the four market days. The names Okoli, Okoye, and Nwoye for instance meant the male child born on Oye market day. Similarly, Okeke, Nweke, or Okereke stood for the male child born on an Eke market day. Similarly, Okonkwo, Nwankwo, and Osunkwo stood for the male, born on Nkwo market day, while Nwafor, Osuafor and Okafor, or Okoroafor stood for the male born on Afor market day. It was not uncommon in a large family to have two or more people bearing the same name based on the market day of their birth. Where for instance there were two Okekes in the same family, the name of the respective mothers would be attached to each of the two Okekes to distinguish one from the other. Thus, Okoli was occasionally called Okoli Eliaba to distinguish him from other sons of Ogbuka born on Oye market day

In the event of the same mother having two sons each born on a similar market day, seniority would be used to distinguish one from the other. The younger Okeke for instance would be called Okeke nta that means

"Okeke small." Other names were associated with deities, while others were statements of wishes, expectations, or abhorrence's.

There is no single name in Okoli's culture and native Igbo language that does not make a statement, in addition to the market day name which could be multiple in the same household since there are only four market days. The market day name is known on the day of birth, but the given name is made on the eighth day after birth. It is on the eighth day also that every child is circumcised, according to Igbo culture.

Okoli's grandfather was originally called Obeki. He was later to assume a new name. The origin of Mbeki's name change had emanated from a wrestling combat. Two communities had decided to avert an all-out war by agreeing to each presenting the strongest man in their respective midst to wrestle between themselves. It was decided that the champion's community would be the winner of the war with all accruing booties and spoils of war. The opposing community to Obeki's was said to have presented a huge intimidating and fierce-looking individual, called Diogu. Diogu's size struck fear into all the strong men of Obeki's community. The strong men of both communities were all out in the arena, the disputed long stretch of empty land separating the two feuding communities. The drums of war were beating. The leaders of the two feuding communities with their men all armed with machetes and wooden clubs were out facing each other. The "Goliath" Diogu from the opposing side to Obeki's had stepped forward. There was no match for him in Obeki's side as the man who had been selected to oppose Diogu had chickened out and fled the community at the last minute and failed to turn up at the arena. Diogu, the towering giant from the opposing community, had stepped into the arena amidst the reverberating drums of war, daring his opponent to also step into the arena. After some wait for a match, the drums went dead. The opposing side was about to be declared the unopposed winner as Diogu stood there in the arena with his fierce looks and intimidating size, apparently daring any challenger to step forward to be made a mince meat of. The heads were held high on Diogu's side, but the chins and heads were bowed in Obeki's side.

Then, suddenly from amidst the crowd on the apparently brow-beaten side stepped forward a stout short man, a Lilliputian when compared to the giant Diogu. Obeki elbowed his way through the crowd and leapt forward to face the giant. Each wrestler was clad in his traditional loin clothes, barely covering the genitals and nothing more. Each represented the interest and fate of hundreds of fighters from his community; but one did not have the height, mass, and muscles of the other. Obeki had presented himself apparently as a sacrificial lamb to redeem to any possible extent the image and honor of his community from the intimidation of a raging giant. He must have been driven either by daredevilry or by sheer naivety.

The resignation and sense of defeat from Obeki's side and the upbeat mood of the opposing side in a mood of assured victory was palpable. There was silence. Diogu, at the insulting sight of the challenging "Lilliputian" did not even wait for the war command to be issued. He charged menacingly at the tiny Obeki. The aim was to grab Obeki and tear him to pieces. The stout short Obeki dodged the massive outstretched hands of the giant and docked in between the giant's widely spaced legs, grabbing the latter's rear supporting leg. The move threw Diogu off balance, and in a move to rotate to turn around and grab the daredevil challenger, the giant slipped and went down. Obeki quickly leapt on top of the crash-landed giant. A local David had triumphed over a Goliath!

By traditional wrestling rules, once a contestant was down and the opponent leapt over him, a winner was declared. The battle was thus over. The incredible had happened! The applause was thunderous. The victory drums roared to the high heavens. The stout short Obeki was carried shoulder high. Exclamations of "*akamnonu, akamnonu*" rented the air from Obeki's group. "Am I greater by words of mouth alone?" Thus, the four hundred and forty-two descendants of Obeki got a new name, Akamnonu: "Am I greater by words of mouth alone?"

The Catholic Priest That Never Was

The five sons of Obeki were merchants. Guided and tutored by Papa Nke Ocha (the fair-skinned papa), the eldest and a very benevolent man, three of the brothers moved to Aba. They went into importation and sales. The last two of the brothers had secondary-school education, and all five lived in Aba, the largest merchant town close to and east of the River Niger. The River Niger is one of the longest rivers in Africa. Okoli and his friends used to recite aloud the names of the African rivers in school: Nile, Niger, Congo, Senegal, Orange, Limpopo, Zambezi. They used to repeat these ever so often that it almost became a song for them.

As earlier said, Okoli's father was called Nwankwo since he was born on an Nkwo market day. His given name was Ogbuka. Though he was the only son of his mother, Ogbuka had wanted to be a Catholic priest. He was said to have been told by the missionaries, after a week or two however, that he would spend twenty years before he would be ordained a priest. That was because he did not have the opportunity of an earlier primary-school education. When he could not cope with the required duration, Ogbuka opted out of the idea of becoming a priest. He thereafter switched from the one extreme of celibacy to the other extreme of marrying eight wives who bore him forty-six children, twenty-seven sons and nineteen daughters. Okoli was the third of the forty-six children. Okoli's father's fifth and seventh wives were sisters, being children of the same parents. He always told his children that his target was to have twelve wives. Okoli's mother, Eliaba, was the fourth wife. Ogbuka always told his children, whenever they asked him why he chose to have so many wives, that if he limited his marriage to only his first wife (who incidentally was married for him by his mother while he was still underaged), some of them might not have been born, at least not in their current forms. The eldest two of Ogbuka's brothers were also polygamists. The youngest two, who incidentally had the opportunity of a secondary-school education, were monogamous. Each of these younger two indeed wedded in the Catholic Church, and every wife had as many children as possible since there were no birth control measures in place. The tenth child of any woman was followed by a big celebration.

Polygamy was a very accepted and indeed often admired social norm in the culture of Okoli's people in Ogbuka's days. It is still practiced even though it is no longer fashionable, with the advent of Christianity. As earlier stated, it was another way of demonstrating how wealthy a man was, in conjunction with how big one's yam barn was. The two situations complimented each other as a wealth determinant. The more wives a man had, the more hands he had in his farm and reciprocally the bigger his yam barn. In Ogbuka's case, he was not a farmer, and so did not have yam barns.

Under tutelage from his elder brother Papa Nke Ocha, Ogbuka had been trained in the art of importation. He was an importer of bicycle parts and tools. He imported from Great Britain, Germany, Holland, Hong Kong, and Japan. One of the things Okoli and his siblings used to test their memories with when they were young was the recitation of the different companies that their father used to import from: Raleigh Industries, Hein de Windt, Brazendale, John Rieckermann, etc. A lot of people often wondered how a man who did not go to school could function successfully as an importer. How did he communicate successfully with his business counterparts in Europe and Asia? How did he deal with the volumes of mails? It was a big paradox which many of Ogbuka's friends could not understand. For his forty-six children, they grew up seeing Ogbuka reading letters and dictating replies through an assistant who did the writing. Ogbuka could read but could not write! He could sit down for hours, often far into the night reading through the volumes of letters coming from the companies from whom he imported goods. He would dictate replies to Hyman, his principal assistant for many years, or occasionally to any of his children, any who was around and who could write well. And he easily knew those who could write well. Ogbuka would readily correct any writer who wrote what he did not say or who omitted to write what he said or who misquoted him, maybe believing that he was illiterate. He dictated his letters in the native Igbo language, but could easily point out any misquotes written in the English language, a language he did not speak. He often told his children that many years before, when he had a big business downturn, he was almost continuously indoors for three months reading the Bible. He could quote the verses in the Bible ever so readily even though he did not go to church nor professed to be a practicing Christian. He was baptized in the Catholic Church and given a Christian name, which he retained throughout life. That was probably about the time he was considering becoming a Catholic priest.

After he dumped the idea of priesthood, Ogbuka became a firm practitioner of African traditional religion. He did not believe he was a pagan since he said he believed in the existence, the almightiness, and the infinite goodness of God. But he said he also believed that an individual's forefathers could intercede for him or her, just as, according to him, some Christians often pray that the saints should intercede for them before God. These forefathers and deities, as he said, could be represented by carved symbols in wood or stone.

The Resident Medicine Man

By the practice of his African traditional religion, Ogbuka also believed in native doctors many of who combined practice as herbalists with the more sinister practice of invocation of the gods, the dispelling of evil spirits, and often the invocation of good and evil spirits either to "protect" an individual or to wreck havoc on any individual whom the native doctor chose to visit evil on. Such native doctors who were called *dibia* were at once revered and dreaded. They often painted their faces with soot and chalk to confer a more dreadful look, and they would also often hang weird garlands around their necks for greater awesome looks. The powers of the native doctors varied as widely as the intimidating names which they often assumed. Some would answer Osimili, the never-drying sea. Others would answer Ogwudire, the medicine that translates into effect. Others still would answer Anya na fu uzo, the eye that sees beyond. Some others would answer names denoting their fields of specialization like Azu elu ana that means the back that never touches the ground. This latter medicine man would be patronized by wrestlers who would pay for the concoctions and or talisman that would ensure that the wearer's back never touches the ground, a big asset in wrestling competitions.

Many of these native doctors made a lot of money, especially if their concoctions happened to succeed, and they had more patronage and charged higher fees. Ogbuka was a very strong believer in the power of the native doctors. He consulted many of them from far and wide and later on had a resident native doctor stationed permanently in his house. Most mornings before he left the house, he would consult with Boki, the resident native doctor who hailed from a town called Aguleri. Those consultations were usually carried out in Boki's "sanctuary," the inner of the two rooms which Boki occupied in Ogbuka's house. During the consultations, Ogbuka would stretch out his palms, and Boki would spit into them. He would then momentarily place on Ogbuka's hand a short rounded but clublike wooden object shaped like a miniature baseball bat, which Boki called Okedibia. The Okedibia—which over the years had collected chicken feathers and the blood of slaughtered chickens, goats and rams—often looked dark brown and grotesque. Boki, looking attentively at the Okedibia as if very inquisitively, would then bellow at the top of his voice the following:

> Okedibia gwam okwu, gwam okwu,
> Okedibia gwam!
> Ndu Ogbuka, ndu Ogbuka,
> Okedibia gwam!
> [Okedibia, talk to me, talk to me, Okedibia, talk to me! Ogbuka's life, Ogbuka's life, Okedibia, talk to me!]

After a short pause, Boki would then in a low but consistent voice and still with a fixed gaze on Okedibia reel out the day's instructions, the dos and don'ts and the type of people and places to avoid for the day. It was only after he was done with his job that Boki would now collect the two pennies consultation fee, which the client would have placed on the ground prior to the commencement of the consultations. Even though Boki lived rent free in Ogbuka's house, the latter was never exempt from payment of the routine consultation fee before Okedibia would "talk." The gods must exact their fees even if the client was Boki's father or mother or even his wife.

If a client desired more extensive consultations, the client would have to pay more. In such an instance, Boki would proceed to call up a retinue of smaller gods. He would call each by name, salute each extensively, and proceed to make enquiries. As he called out each god, who was represented by a wooden or metal carving, Boki would extol the qualities and powers of the relevant god and extensively thank the god for not disappointing him in the past. He would then urge the god to "do as you always did in the past" and quickly convey his (Boki's) requests to Oseburuwa using the following lines:

> The god of gods
> The king of kings,
> The one who never fails,
> The one who sees the good and the bad,
> The one who sanitizes with lightning,
> The one who waters the earth,
> The one who causes the barren woman to conceive,
> The Amadioha of the universe,
> The god of our forefathers . . .

There was no end to Boki's salutations to the Supreme Being. There was no end to the exultations. And as he exalted the Supreme Being, Boki held his eyes tightly shut and repeatedly nodded his head in reverence. It was usually a very exciting event for Okoli whenever he accompanied his father to consult Boki.

Boki, before he would discharge any client, would warn the client that his, or her requests, would only be fulfilled if the supplicant maintained "a clean, just, and upright lifestyle." Ogbuka certainly always complied with these latter requirements throughout his life. He was to tell his children and all who listened to him that the tenets of his African traditional religion which abhorred cheating, oppression, and graft, if emulated by mankind would help solve a lot of the problems of humanity.

Boki also rendered many "protective services" to Ogbuka and to as many members of his household as cared to participate. These protective services were in the form of tattooed herbal markings on the foreheads, chest, wrists, and ankles of these clients. These herbal markings, many of which remained indelible, were said by Boki to protect the recipients from "any evil machinations of enemies and even evil spirits." Okoli himself was a recipient of many rounds of these "protective" markings. Initially he proudly displayed them to his small school friends as a mark of his invincibility and invulnerability to witchcraft. Later on as he grew up in school, when some of his schoolmates like Cletus started taunting him about these pagan tattoos, Okoli started to hide the markings with his polo shirts. Indeed he would occasionally opt out of a soccer contest if his team was the side that would play bare bodied. He would opt out to prevent the prominent tattoos on his bare chest from being seen by his other schoolmates, especially his major tormentor, Cletus.

Boki, a very huge man, was said to be a very effective dibia, and even though he was permanently retained by Ogbuka, he was widely patronized from far and wide. He, unlike other native doctors, was always neatly dressed, and he never painted himself with either soot or chalk unlike most other colleagues of his who would do so to look fierce or attract attention to themselves. He always prided himself with the assertion that he never practiced evil medicine, but he would always declare that any body who visited evil on any of his clients would "reap that same evil tenfold." He demonstrated this on several occasions after the traditional Ikeji festival when several enchanted young men would be brought to him speechless and morose looking after they were said to have tried to visit evil on some of Boki's clients. On two of such occasions which Okoli himself had witnessed, Boki had demanded that each of the offending young men would procure two rams and pay handsomely in cash before Boki would withdraw the spell on these young men who made attempts on Boki's clients. To the amazement of everybody present, after Boki's demands were met, the latter merely approached the young men and rubbed his hands on their faces and sat them down. Soon afterwards, the young men started to talk again and became completely normal. One surprising thing about Boki was that he would never participate in the eating of the meat of any of the animals brought as a fee for the withdrawal of a spell. He also said that he would never touch or utilize the money paid as ransom for such services. He would say that the latter was money from the result of a service for which he had already been paid and therefore the money belonged to the gods. He usually insisted that the money paid would be put directly by the payer into one of the many small clay pots, which Boki always had handy for such occasions. Each night after such "cleansing exercises" as Boki called those rites, the latter would be seen leaving the compound with the pot containing the money. He was never seen to return with those pots. It was said that he always emptied the contents of the pot into a nearby river and that he would break the pot and pour the clay pieces into the river.

Boki, despite the enormous patronage he was enjoying, never lived ostentatiously. He never bought a car nor did he buy or build a house. He remained unmarried for a very long time, and when much later in life he married, he never had a child. He always said that his numerous *agwu* (idols) were his children. He was hardly ever seen with women, and he always said that he would always need to sanitize himself for his medicine to be effective. He was scarcely seen talking loudly, and he would never get into an argument with anybody. He always insisted that before anybody would get into his sanctuary, which was the inner of the two rooms that Ogbuka provided for him, the person must wash his or her hands and face using *ncha ngu*, a local soap made from caustic potash, palm oil, and the ashes of palm fronds.

Boki was known to eat only once a day, and he was known to be very choosy about his food, which virtually always was cassava fufu, a very traditional diet made from fermented cassava which was then sieved in raffia baskets and thereafter boiled and pounded. Boki would roll the fufu balls between his two hands, and after dipping the very large balls in rich *onugbu* soup, he would thrust the large balls into his mouth and swallow the balls whole, his two eyeballs bulging out in the process. So much effort often appeared to go into the swallowing process, and the nearest attentive passerby would readily hear the loud gweee sound produced by the swallowing process.

Okoli often wondered why Boki would not make the *akpu* balls smaller. Boki was to explain later that he only felt the richness of the akpu balls if they were as large as possible. There was always that fear by people watching Boki for the first time as he ate, that the latter might choke as he swallowed the very large balls without chewing them. He never did. Instead, he would often gulp two cupfuls of water after the heavy akpu meal. He would then beat his chest loudly with his clenched fist and shout at the top of his voice, "Oseburuwa dooo."

It was always a feast for the residents of Ogbuka's house at Aba whenever Boki had clients who brought goats and rams as only a single drop of the blood of the slaughtered animal would be utilized by Boki "for the appeasement of (his) Okedibia," the chief of his carved idols.

Boki was later to train one of Ogbuka's wives in the art of native medicine practice. Even though he lived free in Ogbuka's house, Boki had insisted that he must be paid the full fees before he consented to impart some of the knowledge. The process lasted several years. As usual, he had collected the payments in a clay pot and had gone to the stream on the night of the full payment with the pot. He said that the money belonged to the gods and that if he touched the money, he "would lose (his) powers." He also always said that he would charge neither more nor less than the amount dictated by his idols, and that was irrespective of who the client was.

It was on the night of the full payment for Ogbuka's wife's training that tragedy nearly struck. Albert, one of Ogbuka's servants, had decided to secretly trail Boki to the stream when the latter left the compound with the pot containing the money. Albert possibly had secretly decided to recover his master's money should Boki, as was often claimed, decide to empty the money into the Waterside, as the local river was called. Boki came back as usual after midnight. Albert was however not seen. It was when the front door of the house was about to be locked for the night that somebody called Ogbuka's attention to the fact that Albert was not in the house. Throughout the night, Albert was not seen. A search party was organized. It was very early the following morning that Albert was seen, completely naked, and sitting by the side of the gutter along Asa Road, one of the major streets in Aba. When Albert was clothed and brought back to the house, he would neither eat nor speak. He could easily have been overrun by any of the heavy trucks plying the Aba Port Harcourt Road. It was only when Adoha, Albert's girlfriend, revealed that Albert had confided in her the previous night that he would trail Boki to the river to collect Boki's money that people got to have an idea of what might have happened to Albert. After the revelation by Adoha, Ogbuka was very angry with Boki for casting a spell on his (Ogbuka's) boy. Boki remained unperturbed and unapologetic throughout the time that Ogbuka was fuming. He maintained a straight face and through out the time that Ogbuka was reproaching him for what he did to Albert merely kept muttering in a low tone, "Wete ebune, Wete ebune. Wete ebune, Wete ebune" (Bring a ram, bring a ram. Bring a ram, bring a ram).

Ogbuka's anger and scolding of Boki was of no consequence. When he found that Boki was not even moved, and Albert remained morose and kept gazing into the sky, Ogbuka's anger turned into pleadings; but that made no difference, as Boki kept, almost inaudibly, muttering, "Wete ebune, Wete ebune," as if he himself was under a spell. Ogbuka had no choice but to dispatch two other servants to Ahia ofuu, the new market some four miles away, to procure a ram, which was handed over to Boki. The latter accepted the ram unabashedly and with no sign of remorse. He then took the ram into his house and came out a few minutes later with a piece of chalk with which he encircled the spot where Albert was standing. Then still holding the ram with his left hand, he made two other parallel lines across the circle and led out Albert through the parallel lines, muttering, "Agwu haa ya, ozo emena. Agwu haa ya ozo emena"

(Agwu let him loose, he will not tempt you again).

Agwu was Boki's bad god who wrecked vengeance on Albert for trailing Boki.

Albert stepped out of Boki's circle looking as one who just woke up from a protracted sleep. His first sentence to Ogbuka was, "Good evening, sir."

It was six thirty in the morning!

One of Ogbuka's wives, who was trained by Boki, turned out to be another successful practitioner of native medicine, even though she did not quite exhibit as much feats as Boki or Nganga, another traditional medicine man.

Boki and Nganga were reputed to be the superstars during the traditional Ikeji festival when a ram would be tied to a tree and any man or woman who felt that he or she "was strong enough" or "thoroughly cooked" in the art of native medicine would win the contest if he or she untied the ram and took it home without collapsing. The site for the yearly contest was known as "Produce Ndiawa." It was said that any weak contestant attempting to untie the prize ram during the Ikeji festival might even die on the spot from the spell, the flying needles, and enchantments which other contestants would continuously cast on the over ambitious contestant. These other competitors and spectators would usually stand in a circle around the prize ram to watch for who the strong man for the day would be. This practice has defied to a large extent the advent of Christianity. The exciting practice still remains a mystery to Okoli and most of the spectators during the annual Ikeji festival, which attracts thousands of tourists from all over the world to Arondizuogu Okoli's hometown. Some people condemn it as voodoo or black magic. To many others, however, it is African science, which probably should be further studied and put to the advantage of humanity.

Ogbuka had numerous wooden and metal carvings and symbols which he usually lined up as idols representing certain deities. These deities ranged from Ikenga, which was the chief god, to the least which was a kind of guardian angel. Ogbuka never accepted that he was an idol worshipper as he said he did not worship any of those carvings. He merely used them as symbols to focus his attention on an object while making his sacrifices. He contended that his carvings served him the same purpose which the statues in the churches served the churchgoers. Even though he no longer went to church, Ogbuka retained his Christian baptismal name. He still always prayed before and after meals, still called on God to supervise his family meetings with his household, still ensured he kept his hands clean and clear from any and all evil practices. He also always said that he would never be party to the oppression of widows, orphans, or the downtrodden. Indeed he was known throughout the village as the one man who, even at great risk to himself or his family, would always stand up in defense of the rights of the downtrodden. He always would throw his gates open to all and sundry to participate in the different dishes on his table any time he was home, and he seemed to derive special joy seeing people eat out of his table. He had also undertaken to pay the school fees of any primary school pupil who were unable to pay their school fees. He encouraged his sons and nephews to go into the Catholic priesthood, perhaps to compensate for what he missed. He indeed later successfully sponsored one of his nephews to priesthood.

During festivities, sacrifices of animals, usually chickens or goats, were made through Ogbuka's wooden symbols by sprinkling blood of the slaughtered animals on the symbols. Often the feathers or hairs of the slaughtered animals were also stuck on the wooden or stone carvings. After years of pasting of blood and feathers on them, these carvings often looked messy and bizarre. Even though Okoli and his peers were taught in schools and churches to disregard and boycott these practices, the children subtly enjoyed these ceremonies and indeed craved for them. The ceremonies provided a distraction from the normal daily chores. The children enjoyed shooting with rubber catapults at the lizards and birds that gathered the following morning to feast on the pellets of meat and food that adorned the *chi* and *nkwu* as the carvings were called. Above all, the children enjoyed the rare feasts of meat and yam porridge, which each of these festivities brought about.

Okoli remembered vividly the many occasions when a chicken would be sacrificed. These were usually native chickens which were often no bigger in meat content than medium-sized pigeons. What these chickens lacked in meat content they made up with in the sizes of their claws, which they utilized adequately for scattering heaps of garbage while foraging for food. Their food consisted of ants and kitchen waste. Commercial chicken breeding, which utilizes poultry feeds and which produces rich muscular chickens, was nonexistent. Thus the full meat content of the chicken which the family of a father, eight wives, and forty-six children shared might be no more than the equivalent of two legs and two thighs of a modern-day agricultural chicken. Sometimes when Okoli reminisces, he starts to wonder at how he and his other siblings managed to grow physically with such low-protein consumption in their early years of life.

But the children were always full of joy whenever the festivities that would warrant the slaughter of a chicken would be approaching. Such occasions included the Ikeji period when the harvesting of the new yam would be celebrated. Another occasion was the *iru agwu* period when each of the wives would be expected to get a chicken, also to be slaughtered before her agwu. The Agwu was the bad god, whom if not appeased might get angry occasionally and make the individual to behave abnormally or go frankly mad. The modern-day schizophrenic patient would have been told to go and appease his or her agwu, a process known as iru agwu.

The sharing of a chicken in the family of fifty-five (a father, eight wives, and forty-six children) was usually very orderly. Often there would be other children who lived with Okoli and his siblings in the family, and thus the number of people who would participate in the consumption of the one chicken could be as much as sixty. Certain parts of the chicken were traditionally owned by certain designated people in the family hierarchy.

The first son of the family would, as of right, take the head of what every animal was slaughtered in the family—be it a chicken, a goat, or a ram. The second son of the family would take the lower jaw. The first daughter of the family and the second daughter together would traditionally share the skin and muscles of the lower abdomen. The wives of the family would traditionally share the hip or pelvis of the animal. The *di bu uno*—that is, the father of the family—had the heart and gizzard of the chicken. In the case of a goat or ram, the di bu uno would have the heart alone. Any nephews and nieces of the family who were present would usually have the neck of the animal. Udor was Okoli's youngest brother at the time. Usually he consequently was left with the middle toe of the chicken as his share. The subsequent selection of shares after the first two sons and first two daughters had taken their traditional shares was done in order of seniority. On one occasion, someone else had taken up the middle toe of the chicken before the choice got to Udor. The latter broke down crying uncontrollably as he believed that someone else had taken what rightly belonged to him.

"Owelu na okem," (He has taken my share) cried the angry Udor.

He had over the years always got the middle toe of the chicken and had come to that wrong belief that the middle toe of the chicken was his right.

This process of designating certain parts of an animal to certain members of the family was known as *nze*. It was strictly adhered to in the family. It would be considered an abomination if a wife of the family slaughtered a chicken and did not reserve the gizzard for the husband. Such an indiscretion was usually punishable by a fine of a full hen. In a similar vein, the failure of a husband to reserve the waist of the chicken for the wife or wives of the family would constitute justifiable reasons for the wife or wives to threaten to leave the family until the situation was remedied. If such a situation arose, the in-laws would be summoned en masse, and usually the husband would make some reparations.

Even though the sharing of a single pigeon-sized chicken between some fifty-five people often left the size of individual shares to as small as the toes of the chicken, the amazing thing was that despite such infinitesimal shares, the entire family often looked forward to occasions where a chicken would be slaughtered. The remembrance of the aroma from the roasting of chicken, the smell of the burning feathers, and the expectancy of his share of the lower jaw of the chicken (which often boiled down to only the tongue and jawbone of a chicken) usually brought very happy memories to Okoli. Many years later when he was in secondary school, Okoli would remember these occasions with immense nostalgia.

Okoli always looked forward to the holidays when he would again go back home for a festivity where an animal would be slaughtered, and he would have his designated share of the lower jaw as the second son of the family. By the time Okoli was in secondary school, the family had gotten more affluent and had graduated to slaughtering a goat during festivities. Eliaba, Okoli's mother, would meticulously preserve by smoking to dryness whatever lower jaws of animals that were slaughtered in Okoli's absence. Such meat would usually be preserved for Okoli in raffia baskets hanging over the kitchen fires for as long as Okoli was away. On one occasion when Okoli came back, the mother presented him with three dried jaws of goats slaughtered during the former's absence. Okoli went back to school with one of the smoked jaws; and the sharing with his friends Aboni, Donald, and Livi was a great feast.

Okoli's father, Ogbuka, lived in Aba. All his wives but one always lived in Ndiakunwanta, Okoli's village at Arondizuogu. The wives took their turns to go to live in Aba with Okoli's father. The duration of each wife's stay in Aba ranged between six months and one year. Usually the youngest of the wives could stay in Aba for up to one year at a stretch. Each wife's stay in Aba was entirely at the pleasure of their husband. The duration was not governed by any particular timetable. It was Ogbuka's prerogative to decide. It was subtly understood that the timing was governed by the time that Ogbuka wanted any of the wives to make a baby. The younger and more recent wives always enjoyed longer durations and more frequent intervals of stay in Aba. It was almost entirely a man's world. The wives accepted the situation as it was the culture of the people. Any of them who felt aggrieved of course would complain to either Ogbuka's mother, who was highly respected, or better still to Papa Nke Ocha, Ogbuka's elder brother. A complaint to the latter was sure to be addressed and any anomaly rectified. Papa Nke Ocha's role as the patriarch and mediator in the larger family was usually never challenged.

Ogbuka's wife in Aba was usually engaged in petty trading often in retail trade of *garri*, the local staple food made from grated cassava tuber which was thereafter dried and fried often with a little palm oil. The trade in garri was usually for the pocket money of the resident wife. The family upkeep was usually financed by Ogbuka himself, who also ensured that bags of garri, yam tubers, and bags of beans and stock fish were transported home to the wives at home. Okoli does not remember any single occasion that there was shortage of supply of these items. One of the greatest joys of the wives at home was the monthly trips to Ama Edward, the closest bus stop to Okoli's village for vehicles commuting between Aba and Arondizuogu, a distance of some one hundred miles. The transportation of the bags of garri beans and stock fish from Ama Edward was usually done on foot by the wives. It was a monthly ritual, and the wives were usually the envy of the other village women as they were seen usually in a single file with loads of these items in metal pans on their heads from Ama Edward to Ndi Akunwanta. Many of these other village women would certainly love to be one of the wives of Ogbuka. Okoli could not remember any month end when the loads of food did not come. One of Ogbuka's trusted friends called *onye ka Ozulu, a* very famous transporter, always ensured that these items were safely packed in Mazi Onuka's stores at Ama Edward if Ogbuka's wives were not handy to collect them. The regular supply of stock fish (an import from Norway), a delicacy for the Igbo people of Eastern Nigeria, was particularly a thing of joy for the wives at home. Its availability probably compensated for the short supply of other forms of protein like chicken and beef. The near total absence of stock fish during the early days of the Nigerian Civil War possibly contributed to the high incidence of kwashiorkor (a disease emanating from protein-calorie malnutrition).

The Outward Journey Begins

About the time Okoli got old enough to start kindergarten school, he was whisked off to Aba to live with his father even though it was not his mother's turn to go to live in Aba. Okoli was however to live in Aba for only a very short time before his maternal uncle Cosi came from Enugu to collect him. Okoli's movement from Arondizuogu to Aba was hastened by his alleged bullying of younger children and constant fighting with his peers. He also often was said to confront much bigger children. The final straw was after a fight with Ikpeghe, his paternal cousin. The fight was allegedly provoked by Okoli on the way home from firewood-collection duties. Ikpeghe was an older and bigger girl, but during the fight, Okoli managed to give Ikpeghe a red eye and a bump on the face. Ikpeghe thereafter had chased Okoli back to the house, where Albert, Okoli's father's houseboy in the village, saved Okoli from what might have been an onslaught from Ikpeghe. Unfortunately, it was the weekend that Okoli's father was to come home. By Sunday night, Okoli was whisked down to Aba in spite of opposition from Eliaba, his mother. He was never to return to Arondizuogu on a permanent basis.

Okoli's movement to Enugu after a short stay at Aba was, on the other hand, motivated by the latter's mother's fear that her son might be maltreated by her cowife at Aba in her absence. Okoli however neither complained of any maltreatment, nor indeed could remember any single incidence of maltreatment at Aba. Each resident wife always looked after every child of the forty-six as her own child. It could of course not have been otherwise as the husband of the household would not have been indifferent to any such discrimination.

Okoli's mother had nevertheless persuaded her brothers living in Enugu (the capital of Eastern Nigeria at that time) to come and collect Okoli from Aba.

Okoli's short stint at Aba brought him into first close contact with one of his cousins, Ceewai, who was to be not just a cousin but a friend.

Ceewai's father, Nduburuiriro, a very amiable man, was the immediate younger brother to Okoli's father among the sons of Obeki. It was Ceewai's presence at Aba that motivated Okoli's spending his holidays at Aba, both when the latter was in primary school at Enugu and when he was in secondary school in Government Secondary School Afikpo.

Okoli's short stay in Aba prior to moving to Enugu was not uneventful. He could still recall the endless evenings when wooden cases of goods (bicycle parts) would be moved into their house from Port Harcourt. Okoli was usually spared the ordeal of participating in the rolling of those cases from the trucks into the stores, which were located inside the yard.

Okoli's father's compound in the village was a two-storey (two-floor) building located at the center, with eight other buildings each of two rooms for each of the wives forming a semicircle around the storey building. The family house in Aba on the other hand was a two-storey building with another single building of eight big rooms behind the two-storey building. Four of the rooms in the bungalow were used as stores for goods. The other four rooms were rented out to tenants. Another house of four tiny rooms was used as kitchens and kitchen store. Adjoining the four rooms were four other very tiny rooms, two of which were used as bathrooms and two as toilets. The kitchens were simply empty rooms, where the cooking was done on the floor with firewood. Unlike in the village where the cooking pots were placed on stones, the pots in the kitchens at Aba were a little more sophisticated. They were placed on metal stands called *ekwu igwe* and the firewood burnt from underneath the ekwu igwe. The kitchen stores contained wooden cupboards, and each tenant had the option of locking his or her cupboard with padlocks. The landlord (as Okoli's father and other house owners were called) had a separate kitchen store.

The bathrooms were also bare floors, and the bathing water was taken in with metal buckets. The single water tap in the whole house was located in a pit, which had steps leading into it. The tap had to be located in a pit; otherwise, the water pressure might not be sufficient to get water to the surface. The occupants of the yard were privileged to have a flowing water tap. Most houses were built without sources of water supply, and long lines of metal buckets were seen at every public water tap. *Ikwo mmiri,* which means struggling to fetch water from the public water taps, was a feat for the muscular and powerful. Often, not only would the metal buckets be badly dented but teeth loss, lacerations, and black eyes would be sustained during the process of struggling to fetch water at the public taps. The women and younger people would usually line up their buckets and metal pans waiting for sunset when the long line of buckets would have thinned down. The muscular young men often would not want to queue up and would jump the queue to slug it out at the trickling taps. Sometimes they would get a girlfriend or two by collecting the latter's buckets and knocking off the buckets of other weaker men at the flowing taps. Such strong men were called *Kill We* (a name taken from a popular strong man called Kill We, who was reported to pull loaded trucks single-handedly and could support six men standing on his abdomen as he leaned over backward). Indeed, the name Kill We for the strong man was said to have emanated from an incident in which the strong man was said to have had a fight with another young man. The opponent of the strong man, after he was beaten up, had gone to his village to collect eight other youths to attack his opponent who thoroughly mauled all nine assailants, breaking the bones of two of them. Two of the mauled assailants were said to have escaped further onslaught by running to the residence of the then British-born district officer (DO) shouting, "Kill We, Kill We."

The name Killi We thereafter came to symbolize strength, and any strong man who succeeded in pushing off others from the public water taps came to be called Killi We.

The chaotic situation in the "pumps," as the public taps were called, made the few houses with functional taps very attractive. A number of other houses with installed private taps were however not as lucky as Okoli's family was, since the pit that Okoli's father dug to install his tap ensured the house had water a good part of the time when other taps might go dry.

Occasionally, however, the taps would all go dry during the day only to flow at night when the pressure of water would be higher due to decreased general demand. On such occasions, the cemented pit would be filled up with water by morning if a careless person had forgotten to turn off the dry tap earlier on in the day. In such situations, the front door of the yard of Ogbuka's house would usually be thrown open for people waiting at the public taps to rush in to fetch the water from the flooded pit. Okoli had on one occasion flooded the pit by inadvertently leaving the dry tap open overnight.

The following morning, he, without being so instructed, opened the front door to the yard and invited people from the public pump to come and fetch free water from the flooded pit. The rush was so much as most of those waiting in the long line at the public tap all rushed over to Okoli's house. The clash of buckets was deafening. And, when the flooded water from the pit was exhausted, the remainder of the crowd who had not gotten water refused to leave the premises. They struggled so much for the trickling water from the tap in the pit until they broke the handle of the tap. Okoli got a taste of twelve lashes of "Mr Do Good" as Okoli's father's cane for his misbehaving children was called. "Spare the rod and spoil the child" was a well acknowledged dictum in Okoli's family. There was no question of the caning of a misbehaving child being labeled as child abuse in Okoli's culture. Some particularly misbehaving children had their special canes, each suiting the particular child's size. After that flooding incident and the subsequent taste of Mr Do Good, Okoli learnt to do good and never again forgot to turn off the tap even if water was not running. Okoli never again threw open the gates for people from the public pump to come to fetch water.

The Super Restrooms

The toilets in Okoli's house at Aba made spectacular scenes. They appeared to be the neatest toilets Okoli ever used in Aba. They consisted of two tiny rooms of about six feet by six feet. In each toilet, two steps led up a wooden plank at the centre of which was carved out a six-inch-diameter hole. The plank was placed across well-plastered raised blocks. Between the blocks and leading out fully and openly to the outside at the back of the yard was the bucket. To defecate, one would climb up the two steps and squat over the opening on the plank, which was many years later replaced by a concrete slab with a lid. (The concrete slab was introduced after one or two people had fallen into the bucket filled with human waste from the collapse of the decayed supporting plank.) The individual would then defecate into the bucket below. The first night Okoli was at Aba and had to use the toilet, he was so fascinated by the sophistication of having to ease himself from inside a room.

That was a sharp contrast to the system in the village, where most toilets were indiscriminately situated in the bushes. The only person in Okoli's village who had a toilet under a roof was Mazi Ogwumike, who reared pigs. He had a big tree trunk placed across two raised tree stumps across which he would usually squat to defecate. He had fat pigs housed in the mud house room under the tree trunks. The pigs roamed inside the mud-walled building with raffia palm-thatched roof. These pigs would usually struggle to feed on whatever came off Ogwumike and his household as they defecated. Ogwumike's father many years earlier was said to have had his genitals gulped en masse by one of the pigs, which was impatient to let the fecal matter drop off Ogwumike's father's anus. The toilet was said to have been shut down for sometime after the accident. It was however reopened some six months later by Ogwumike after the pigs got thinner following his father's unhappy demise.

The accident that led to his father's death deterred Ogwumike only for a while. He appeared to have been encouraged to reopen the pigs' sty by the number of people who often begged him for their convenience to reopen the *ogwe*, as the toilets were called. The convenience offered by the ogwe was particularly so during the thick of the rainy season when the bushes would be very wet and messy. Ogwumike did not however let the passersby use his toilet out of pure altruism. It was more of a symbiosis between the toilet users on the one hand and Ogwumike and his pigs on the other hand. The fecal matter deposited by the users fed the pigs in Ogwumike's toilet, and the toilet users benefited from the privacy and the shelter from the rains or scorching sun. Whenever there were loud grunts from the struggling pigs on any Nkwo market day, it was likely that some passerby, to or from the market, was patronizing Ogwumike's toilet. It was likely that the hungry pigs were struggling for the fecal matter from a customer. Both sides benefited from each other: Ogwumike's pigs would get the feces, and the passerby would get the shelter and privacy and the comfort. It was good business.

The second night Okoli went to use the bucket latrine, as the toilets in Aba were called, he was greatly frightened at the sound he heard from below just when he squatted to ease himself. Somebody was pulling the bucket from under and from the outside and in the darkness. Okoli ran out of the toilet back into the yard screaming, believing it was a thief. Raymond, one of the tenants came out to reassure Okoli that it must be the night soil man. Okoli knew nothing about night soil men. These were people whose occupation was to nightly collect the buckets filled with human faces, carry the buckets on their heads through dark alleys between adjoining rows of houses unto other bigger buckets stacked on hand-rolled wooden carts called "trucks." These hand-rolled carts were usually parked some distance from the buildings being served. Hence, these unfortunate individuals who were often paid so little would, even under thunderous tropical rains and sometimes in pitch darkness (as the lamps they often carried would go off under the rain), convey open buckets of human waste with no gloves and no masks. They would then empty the contents into collection buckets, clean out the service buckets with short stout raffia brooms, and return the buckets to the houses being served.

Okoli had heard stories of night soil men from his elder brother Mako, but he had never until that night, his second night in Aba, encountered one. Okoli had heard from Mako stories of how some night-soil men would thrust their brooms on a toilet user's buttocks if the latter came into the toilet oblivious of their presence behind the yard and attempted to defecate into a hole when the night-soil man must have pulled out the bucket for emptying. In such a situation, the night-soil man would be laden with the extra job of cleaning out the messed-up floor of the toilet pit. He would therefore punish the offender by inflicting multiple puncture wounds on the latter's buttocks with his short stiff brooms. The wound so inflicted would serve as a reminder to the offender to look well next time around to ensure that a bucket was in place before proceeding to use the latrine.

Okoli heard of the story of the man who was so wounded with broom sticks. When the victim opened the door to the back of the house to challenge the night soil man, the latter who was already waiting for the victim as he was opening the door immediately emptied the handy bucket of human feces over the victim's head, and the intended fight was over. The victim in addition to his anal injury thus had an unhappy "welcome" to the club of night soil men of Aba. He had to run back into the premises dripping with feces, used toilet paper, and urine that were the contents of the bucket. Even his best friends in the premises, at first sight of the victim, stepped back as he ran toward them for help. He was lucky the taps had flowed that night, and there was an ample supply of water in the buckets to be poured over him. He had a good bath thereafter with Omo, the popular detergent powder in use in Aba. Bottles of perfumes also had to be instantly donated to the victim to mask the "perfume" from the contents of the bucket.

There were no night soil men in Okoli's Ndiakunwanta Village at Arondizuogu. There was no need for them. The call of nature was usually answered in the many bushes around the houses. It was years later that pit latrines came into vogue. Septic tank system came much later, and even then, it was only for the few who had deep-drilled water wells called "boreholes" since it would be so cumbersome to fetch buckets of water from the stream only to empty same into the toilet tank when so many bushes were around.

Comrades in Mischief

Okoli made quite a few friends of some young boys in his neighborhood at Aba. It was from them that he learnt to make paper kites. It was also from them that he learned the art of attempting to derail a moving train by lining the rails with pins. Okoli's family in Aba lived some five poles away from the east-to-north rail line linking Port Harcourt and Enugu. Morning, afternoon, and night residents of the area would hear and see the trains roaring past. These were steam engines, and their horns could be deafening. Sometime before Okoli came to Aba, there was said to have been an incident of a train derailment. A goods train conveying groundnuts (peanuts) and some cattle from the northern parts of the country to Port Harcourt in the south was said to have derailed around Aba. A number of cows were said to have been killed, and bags of groundnuts were said to have been scattered all over the rail line. Damian, a big boy living around Okoli's house, had lied to Titus, Okoli's friend, that he and his friends had caused the train to derail by placing pins along the rail line. He said that when the train derailed, people around were allowed to collect free meat from the killed cows and that young children had plenty of free groundnuts to eat. Damian further said that the meat his father collected lasted them many months and that the cups of groundnuts which he personally collected lasted him many break-time snacks at the school for over two weeks.

Okoli and his friends had believed Damian's story. They fancied how pleasant it would be to repeat the feat so that they would have plenty of meat and peanuts. There and then, they arranged to meet at a lonely spot along the rail line to place pins along the rail line. That way they would make the trail to derail again; and there might again be plenty of meat, groundnuts, and perhaps other goodies. Titus had said that the train might also be carrying some *akwa ogazi*, the eggs of guinea fowls, which Titus particularly liked. His parents had forbidden him from eating akwa ogazi because he was once seen eating four guinea fowl eggs, which he bought from a nearby kiosk. His father caught him eating the eggs, and it was discovered that he had stolen the sixpence with which he bought the eggs from his mother's wallet.

On the appointed day, Okoli and his friends set out for the rail line. Titus provided the pins, about ten in number. They then lined the rail with the pins at about a ruler (a foot) intervals as directed by Damian. They then went some distance off the rail line to wait for the trains to come. They waited for so long, but the trains did not come. They had no idea of the train schedule. When it was getting dark, they collected back their pins and went home. The following day, they came back much earlier and lined the rails once again this time with many more pins as Okoli then provided a full packet of pins. In all, they lined up over sixty pins.

It was a Sunday, and the movement of people going to and from church prevented the boys from using up the entire packet of over one hundred pins. Soon after they had lined the pins, Okoli and his friends heard the sound of the train as it was leaving the nearby substation. They were all filled with expectation. As the train approached, they had to move a little farther away from where they were standing so that the train would not fall on them when it got derailed. As they stood with anxiety and expectation, Titus noticed that he no longer had his bag, his empty schoolbag which he had come with to collect groundnuts and possibly eggs from the derailed train. He had dropped the bag along the rail line as they lined the pins. He was tempted to dash back to collect the bag just when the train was under three poles away. Damian however held him back, thereby saving him from the possible danger of being crushed.

The train soon rolled by. Coach after coach rolled by, without derailing. As each coach rolled by, Okoli and his friends expected it to derail. All the over thirty coaches rolled by without a single one derailing. The expedition had failed. Even as the convoy rolled on past their pins, the boys still expected it might derail some distance away. They watched in great disappointed as the coaches rolled out of sight. What might have gone wrong? The boys all looked at themselves in bewilderment and utter disappointment.

Damian said it was because they lined the pins too closely together. He said that his friends who had caused the derailment during which they collected a lot of meat and groundnuts had lined the pins at intervals of about forty feet corresponding, according to him to the length of each coach. That way many coaches would derail simultaneously to pull the entire convoy down. He had earlier during the planning stages told his friends that he actually participated in the operation. The disparity between the two versions of Damian's story did not stir any doubts in the minds of his younger listeners. Their young minds were completely consumed by the imagination of how they would loot a derailed train.

The boys went back to collect their pins. The pins were all gone! Titus's school bag was gone too. They had lost it all, the pins, the schoolbag and the expected booty.

The disappointment on the faces of the young adventurers was palpable. On their way back home, Damian convinced the others that they should try once again with the new intervals in mind. Assurance was written all over Damian's face. His disciples needed no further convincing. They still believed him.

On that third appointed day for the new derailing job, Okoli went with Titus to collect Damian. The latter joined the duo with three pieces of metal, which when he placed close to any of the pins which Titus and Okoli again provided would pick the pins up. He said that those metals were called *magonets*. He said that he learnt that if those magical metals were placed beneath the groove of the rail line, they would hold the pins in place and ensure that the train got derailed. He assured his friends that the former attempts had failed because the force of the steam from the train easily blew away the pins, but that if the magnets held the pins in place, the train would surely be derailed. He gave the reassurance that they would certainly succeed that day and that they would certainly come back with lots of goodies by way of meat, groundnuts, and guinea fowl eggs. He was able to reestablish high morale among his two younger friends.

The three set out again on a Sunday morning. Okoli went with a raffia palm bag. Titus who had earlier lost his schoolbag came with an oversized jute bag, the size that *garri* (fried, grated cassava) was usually carried in. Okoli had teased Titus on their way that the latter might not be able to lift that bag if he filled it even halfway with groundnuts and that if he collected guinea fowl eggs in the bag, they would all break. Surprisingly, Damian did not come with any bag that time around. When Okoli asked him on their way what he would collect his booty with if they succeeded, he did not answer. Could he have lost faith in the plans, or could he be nurturing other plans?

The boys again lined the rails, but this time at much longer intervals. This time they did not have to use as many pins because of the longer intervals. They placed one magnet as directed by Damian under the rail's shoulder: one magnet at the beginning, one midway, and one under the last needle. Just when they were done with the last pin, they heard the train's horn indicating that it was leaving the substation and heading in their direction. The boys were certain that this time they would succeed. Titus and Okoli were upbeat. Okoli's heart was pounding in his chest, more out of anxiety and expectation rather than out of fear.

As was the case during the second trip, all the coaches rolled by with their deafening noises. None derailed. Again the boys lost all the pins save two that they found flatted out on the rails. The three magnets were also gone. The train-derailing effort had ended in failure. As the boys headed home with empty bags, Damian said that he bought the three magnets for ninepence and that Titus and Okoli should reimburse him sixpence. In the ensuing argument, Damian slapped Titus on the face, and a fight started. It took the efforts of a group of four passersby to separate the bitter fight between the two. There was no mention of the magnets or of the fruitless effort to derail the train.

Movement to the Coal City

Okoli and his uncle Cosi arrived at Enugu about 8:00 p.m. by rail from Aba. It was Okoli's first trip by rail. Indeed it was his first entry into anything with proper seats, as he had never for once entered a car nor had he ever seen an airplane at close range. The vehicle by which he came to Aba from Arondizuogu was the Onye ka Ozulu truck which, like every other mass transit vehicle in use at the time, was largely built with wood and had wooden benches spanning the entire width of the truck. Only the driver and the two front seat passengers faced the direction of the journey. The trucks had no kick-starters either. To get started, the vehicle had to be wound with an S-shaped metal winder by the guard who doubled as the fee collector. All the other passengers sat on wooden benches facing backward. Occasionally a demarcation would be placed between the driver and the middle of the vehicle, where people would sit facing each other. That section called "second class" attracted slightly higher fare and had a little more privacy. At other times, excess luggage which could not be accommodated under the passengers' legs would struggle for space with occupants of the second-class facility which because of its slightly higher fare was often not fully occupied.

Okoli's train journey to Enugu was largely uneventful as he spent most of the time surveying the inside of the train. He was greatly fascinated at the orderly arrangement of the seats. Unlike the truck on which he rode to Aba, each seat sat a maximum of four people, had back rests, and had knee space for people facing themselves. Also, Okoli was fascinated by the fact that there was a corridor between the rows of seats along which people could walk even when the train was in motion. He was fascinated by the fact that at the different stations there were lots of goodies being hawked around. Okoli's father had given him five shillings when he was leaving for Enugu. That was a lot of money considering that the largest amount of money Okoli had ever owned was about two shillings gathered over several months from gifts from his several uncles and aunts. When he got to Umuahia town, about midway between Aba and Enugu, Okoli's uncle Cosi, took him down to eat at one of the several food vendors in the station. The rice, stew, and goat meat served were such a delicacy for Okoli.

On the way back to the train, Okoli's uncle also bought him two guinea fowl eggs. As he was about to crack the eggs to eat them, Okoli's mind again flashed back to his friend Titus at Aba. Titus probably would have benefitted from one of these eggs if he were around since he loved akwa ogazi so much. As the train blared its loud horn to leave and the linesman waved his green flag, Okoli's mind also flashed to the three occasions that Damian, Titus, and he went out to derail the trains with pins.

Up till that moment Okoli still believed that even though he and his friends had failed in their attempts, it was still possible to derail the moving train with small pins placed on rails. Could some tiny schoolboys down the rail line be attempting on that train what he, Okoli, had attempted at Aba a couple of months back? If that was the case and the boys succeeded, Okoli felt he might even die, just as the cows in the earlier derailed train were said to have died. For the first time he began to regret those attempts he and his friends had made to derail some trains. His fear was actually motivated by fear for his own life rather than remorse for the contemplated action, since religion was not a serious issue for him, coming from a rustic and essentially African traditional religion background, with no formal religious teachings.

When Okoli and his uncle Cosi got to Ogui Road, the major road spanning the city, it was like a new world to Okoli. Double fluorescent tubes hung across the road suspended by poles from both sides of the wide road. One could virtually pick up a coin that dropped anywhere along the road. That was a sharp contrast to the best-lit road in Aba, which was Asa Road where the streetlight, though fascinating to Okoli when he first came down from the village, was nowhere to be compared to the Ogui Road experience. Okoli trudged on fast behind his uncle, who appeared very tall then since Okoli was tiny and Ogbuka, his father, was not on the tall side. The tallest man Okoli had ever set eyes on was one Bernard who was their neighbor in the village. Bernard was said to be more than six feet tall and people called him Alakuku. The name was derived from one giant Alakuku, who hailed from Umuahia, the famous railway town. Giant Alakuku was said to be well over eight feet tall and could not easily be accommodated in any vehicle.

When Okoli arrived, Zitti Chemist, the pharmacy shop which served as shop and residence for his pharmacist uncle, Okoli was filled with bewilderment at the dining table arrangement. He saw glass cups with serviettes sticking from them. He saw enlarged photographs depicting the Lord Jesus Christ and the Blessed Virgin Mary hanging from the walls. He saw rug carpet on the floor. His only idea of carpet hitherto had been the linoleum carpet, which some middle-class families had in their living rooms in Aba. The cushions in the parlor had white armrest and headrest covers. Okoli went from chair to chair, admiring them until his elder uncle arrived. Okoli had earlier seen his elder uncle only once when the latter came home to visit Okoli's grandmother in the village. Okoli had only very faint ideas about this uncle, whom people simply called M. O. Okoli could only recall memories of M. O. as a tall fair-complexioned man who wore thin-framed eyeglasses.

When he came into the dining room where Okoli was standing, still admiring the neatly arranged drinking glasses and the serviettes sticking from them, M. O. lifted Okoli up on his shoulders and called Matthew who doubled as cook and steward to get food for the latter. Matthew had a high wooden stool in the kitchen, and before long Okoli was munching rice and stew, perching on Matthew's wooden stool, his legs hanging midway between the seat of the stool and the floor.

Most things at Enugu were more sophisticated than their equivalents in Aba. This was probably because Enugu, being the capital of the region, had a lot of educated civil servants. These civil servants, even though they might not have as much money as the businessmen in Aba, had much more refined living conditions. The streets were cleaner; the houses were neater. Water supply was much more regular. There were not many public pumps, and most yards (premises) had central taps from where the landlords and tenants fetched water. People did not have to dig pits in the ground before they could have tap water since the water pressure at Enugu was quite high, unlike in Aba. Most families had rooms and parlor, as opposed to the situation in Aba where most houses were built as single rooms. A good number of the people used kerosene stoves even though some still used firewood. A few people used coal, as Enugu was a famous coal-mining city. Again this was in contrast to the situations in Aba and Arondizuogu, where all cooking was done with firewood using stone or metal stands for the iron or clay pots respectively.

The kitchens were less sooty, and the toilet facilities were neater. Even though most toilets were still the bucket system in Enugu, somehow the residents managed to keep away the flies by extensive use of Izal, a popular disinfectant. Once in a while however, a couple of blue bottle flies would dash across to unwanted places. Okoli never encountered any of the night soil men in Enugu. It was quite possible that they, too, were quite sophisticated and might have sophisticated ways of collecting the buckets of waste.

M. O.'s Chemist shop shared the same premises with a bank, which was one of the biggest establishments in Enugu at the time. Okoli's mind easily dashed back to the poorly clad traders who daily rolled their wares to and from the popular Eke Oha market along Asa Road in Aba either on wooden two-tire trucks or on their bicycles or on their heads. This was in contrast to the neatly dressed bank worker or secretariat worker in Enugu. The latter would come to work fresh from his house often finely perfumed, in a tie, or in a two-piece suit. Even the language was not as raw as in Aba. Even with people of Okoli's age group, the use of profane language was not the order of the day in Enugu as it was in Aba. The little boys did not come out naked to play under the rain, and the sight of children in dirty torn shorts, a regular sight in Aba, was a rarity in Enugu. Again, such diseases that accompanied abject poverty and lack of adequate medical attention like *awakonu* (angular stomatitis) or *abu nti* (purulent otitis media) were not easily seen among the preteen age group in Enugu as was the case in Aba. Obviously children in Enugu generally enjoyed better feeding and better medical care than their counterparts in Aba despite the famed riches of people in Aba as successful businessmen.

Okoli's first acquaintances at Enugu were the children on the yard where he lived. Anayo and Ebuka were about Okoli's age group, and it did not take long before Okoli struck new friendships. The holidays came on soon after Okoli arrived at Enugu, and so he had ample time to go mango-plucking with Anayo and Ebuka. Many of the mango trees were either in the surrounding schools or in the mission houses. Most were however located in European quarters, the section of Enugu where the colonial masters and a few top African civil servants lived. Most of the streets in European quarters were lined with mango trees, and because these were so plentiful and were largely located inside people's houses, the fruits on them outlasted those in the mission houses and the schools.

Most mornings Okoli and his newly found friends would set out for European quarters to steal mangoes. *Stealing* was the word because even though plentiful, the mango trees were designated to particular quarters.

Oftentimes the mango thieves, who were mostly very young primary school boys, would have running battles with the stewards of the owners of the premises in which the mango trees were located. Many of these owners were white British colonial officers or some highly placed senior African civil servants, who because of their status were allowed to live in the part of Enugu designated as European quarters.

There were a few of the houses that had dogs, and these boys always avoided those particular houses that had dogs. The most vulnerable trees were those situated in courthouses and offices. Most Saturdays and Sundays, groups of these boys including Okoli would descend on the mangoes in such premises. With time, the guards in such premises learnt to leave the boys alone, so long as they would only climb to pluck the mangoes and not throw sticks or stones to bring down the mangoes. Such sticks and stones often missed their gargets and landed on roofs of houses or on the glass windows of the houses. Often the culprits would not be caught, and the guards who were usually not armed would be held responsible. In a few quarters, however, there were occasionally groups of guards who had bows and arrows. It was said that the arrows were magically charmed to seek out and pierce the eyes of mango thieves, especially if the mango thieves were boys of Okoli's age. I was also said that even if the intruder threw sticks or stones on the mangoes and started running away, the arrows would follow the individual and seek out the eyeballs and pierce them. The arrows would still seek out and pierce the eyes, irrespective of the direction in which the individual was running.

The arrows of those guards were said to particularly love to pierce the eyes of young boys. With time, the boys grew to fully identify those few houses where the guards had charmed bows and arrows. Even the bravest of the boys always avoided getting to those particular houses to pluck mangoes. The neighboring houses to the bow-and-arrow-guarded houses were also immune to the mango-stealing escapades. There were often enough mangoes elsewhere to steal, rather than to risk losing an eyeball stealing from the dangerously guarded houses.

On the third day that Okoli and four of his friends had gone to one of the houses near the courthouse to steal mangoes, Okoli was to sustain an injury which was to remain a permanent mark on the bridge of his nose for the rest of his life. The young friends had attacked a detached mango tree, believing that it was not guarded. The mangoes on the tree were so ripe and so inviting to the young thieves, who soon gathered stones and sticks and started hurling on the fruits to bring them down. No sooner had the first stick hit a branch than the boys heard shouts of, "Menini! Menini!" (What is wrong! What is wrong!).

The shouts came from the far ënd of the court building. Soon a fierce—looking bow-and-arrow-wielding guard surfaced from the corner of the courthouse! The alarmed young mango thieves took to their heels, abandoning their stones and sticks. As they ran in different directions, Okoli remembered that the charmed arrows of the guards were said to have the power of seeking out the eyes of young boys. To guard his eye, therefore, Okoli immediately covered his two eyes with the palm of his left hand while clutching his schoolbag meant for mango collection with his right hand. He did not run far. Not seeing the direction in which he was running, he soon ran at top speed against another mango tree whose ragged branch pierced through his face, making a big hole on the lower bridge of his nose, barely missing his covered eyes. Believing that it was the charmed arrow that had actually caught up with him, Okoli fell to the ground in pain, and with red-hot blood spilling from the hole on the bridge of his nose, he started yelling, "Uta agbam, uta agbam!" (The arrow has hit me, the arrow has hit me!")

Anayo and Okoli's other three friends seeing their fallen colleague and in a commendable show of heroism were able to defy the arrows and rally to the aid of Okoli from whose wound blood flowed freely. They were able to carry the latter on their backs in turns for the nearly one-mile route back to the Chemist shop. The true story of the cause of Okoli's accident was never told to M. O, Okoli's pharmacist uncle. The perpetual scar on the bridge of Okoli's nose however remained a constant reminder of the events of that day. That scar was to remain there for the rest of his life.

Whenever Okoli and his friends came back from their mango hunts, Janti a cousin to Anayo would be handy to collect the choicest of the mango loot. Janti was a big boy. He must have been in his midteens. He was ebony black, very muscular, and usually had disheveled hair, which was never combed and which often stood out like the bristles from a porcupine. He often presented a fearsome look. He would never go on mango hunts with the younger boys who however did not mind letting him choose the best of the mangoes if only for the protection he offered them against other neighboring big boys. Those other big boys from neighboring houses like Janti were also in their midteens. Most of those big boys did not go to school. They were mostly apprentices in some trades like carpentry, welding, tailoring, or allied trades. Others were relations of landlords or tenants, who were brought from the villages to keep the homes. Janti belonged to this latter group, and Okoli and his friends were careful never to lose his friendship. His passion was pigeon hunting. He loved to trap pigeons, kill them, roast, and eat them after applying oil, salt, and pepper on them. Hardly would one go to the kitchen of the landlord who was Janti's uncle without seeing rows of pigeons being roasted on metal wire racks by Janti.

On one occasion, Janti had climbed into a neighbor's ceiling (attic) through the manhole situated in the corridor in pursuit of pigeons. While chasing the pigeons, he fell through the cement-asbestos ceiling boards into the neighbor's bedroom. He fractured his leg during the fall. It was a Saturday evening, and the neighbor had travelled to the village for the weekend and had locked the room after him. Janti was trapped inside the room. He crawled to the door in great pains and banged ceaselessly on the door, which the owner had locked from outside and left for home.

Most of the adult neighbors had also travelled to the village for the weekend as was the practice.

Janti remained in the room shouting in pains and was without food or water. The few adult neighbors who happened to be around were afraid to break the door to let Janti out. The apartment in question belonged to the bank manager who obviously would make a big case if his apartment was broken into in his absence. These neighbors were of course reluctant to involve the police for fear that they might be labeled as accomplices. Besides this, everybody wanted to avoid the "did you or did you not" and the "come today or come tomorrow" questions that at that time characterized even well-intentioned reports to the police. Janti lay in agony in the locked room till Sunday evening when the bank manager came back from his weekend trip to the village.

A lot of other neighbors were indeed happy that Janti was so trapped since he was considered a troublesome character, and most of the tenants considered him a nuisance. By the time Mr Sampson, the bank manager, come back to let Janti out, the trapped pigeon hunter appeared to have lost over 10 percent of his body weight, and his eyes were redder than ever. Thereafter there were fewer pigeons roasting in Janti's fireplace.

Janti served Okoli and his friends other purposes apart from his big-brother-protection role against the other neighboring big boys. Janti was a master in the art of making rubber catapults. Ready-made catapults cost as much as fourpence. The boys bought the Y-shaped sticks and the rubber band separately, and Janti would couple them and make first-class catapults for them, and the total cost would not be more than twopence. Again, if a catapult got loose, Janti had the strength and the expertise to retie it very well. The catapults were ready and useful tools for the boys in bird and squirrel hunting. These made good snacks for the boys in an environment where meat and other protein foods were a luxury, and growing children were forbidden from eating eggs for fear that if they enjoyed them, they might steal money to buy more eggs.

The boys also used the catapults to shoot and kill the big red-headed lizards, which they often threw to any cats in sight.

Janti did not fire catapults. However, when any of his catapults will be used by the boys in pigeon hunting, the killed pigeons will automatically belong to him. It was an unwritten pact, and none of the boys ever contested that. Even if he was not present, any killed pigeons would be kept for him, and he would always receive them as of right and without thanks. If Janti got to know that any pigeon that was killed by any of the boys was concealed from him, that particular boy would be in big trouble. Okoli and his friends soon learnt not to devote much time to hunting pigeons as these would all be surrendered to Janti, who would receive them without thanks.

Okoli Goes to School

Soon the school year began again. The nearest school to where Okoli's uncle lived was St Brigid's School. It was a Catholic primary school, and Catholic Church was the only church in Okoli's village at Ndiakunwanta. It was simply not a question of choice. If one went to church in Ndiakunwanta at that time, one simply went to the Catholic Church. Okoli's uncle used his influence to get Okoli enrolled into St Brigid's School even when the latter did not have any papers to signify completion of the kindergarten classes either at St Brigid's or at some other school elsewhere. M. O. (Okoli's uncle) owned one of the only two private pharmacy shops in the whole of Enugu. Okoli was registered into primary 1B. That was the first time he had a fully quarantined education even though he attended from home like other pupils—quarantined in the sense that hitherto he had no focus, no sense of direction, and indeed it never occurred to him that he should read. The breakable slate which was sometime bought for him at Aba along with the white chalks were often left anywhere Okoli went to. He had enough busy day hatching pranks with Titus and Damian, his friends. But at St Brigid's, for the first time in Okoli's life he had to handle the pencil, paper, ink, nib holder, and writing nib. He had to have books, and he had to read them. He had to have uniform and had to wear a shirt to and from school. He also had to wash these uniforms every weekend.

It was no longer a question of running out naked to play under the rain. It was no longer a question of having on his shirt and his shorts while going out and coming back to the house with neither a shirt nor the shorts. It was no longer a question of going to school without combing his hair or leaving his hair uncut for months. It was no longer a question of going to school without cleaning his teeth with chewing stick, displaying food particles stacked in between the teeth for weeks. It was no longer a question of leaving his fingernails sticking out like talons with mountains of blackened materials displaying at the nail beds. It was no longer the days for biting off his overgrown fingernails with his teeth. The time to tame the little ruffian from Aba was at hand.

Okoli's first few days at St Brigid's were very uneventful. He knew nobody, and nobody knew him. There was hardly anything exciting. The only thing that caught Okoli's attention was the presence of many mango trees. The trunks of the mango trees were so large that it was possible for two boys to hide on one side and not be seen from the opposite side. The trees must have been planted at the early days of the founding of Enugu with the discovery of coal in the city many decades back. What worried Okoli the most was that, with the sizes of the trees and the heights of the first branches being so high up, it must be very difficult to climb the trees to pluck the mangoes. The trees must really have been in place for quite some time. Over the following couple of days, Okoli was to find out that unlike the mangoes at the European quarters, there were no guards after school hours for the mango trees at St Brigid's School. Sticks and stones could therefore be used to bring down the fruits dangling from the high branches. There were no charmed arrows that might follow one's eyeballs to lodge in them, either.

The first Monday through Thursday presented no serious problem. The only class problem was to learn how to properly articulate the nib after it was dipped in the ink pot.

There were no modern-day Biro pens that were prefilled with ink. A writing nib affixed to a wooden nib holder was the pen. The ink pot was separate, and the nib must be dipped into the ink pot for one to write. If one should spend too long thinking about what to write, the ink would dry on the nib, and to be able to write again, the nib would need to be dipped back into the ink pot to have a fresh supply of legible ink. There were various types of ink in the market. As part of the list for one to start classes, Okoli's uncle had given him a bottle of Quink ink. Okoli was later to learn that Quink ink was considered the most superior brand of ink. The class teacher, Mr Ene, had come straight to Okoli's seat on the class bench to lift the latter's bottle of ink. When he confirmed what was written on the label, he stopped and took a second look at Okoli. Not many of the pupils used Quink ink. The teacher must have felt that Okoli must have quite some class. Little did the teacher realize that Okoli knew nothing about ink names nor their qualities. Okoli's uncle was of course the person who truly knew the quality of the ink. Lack of appreciation of the cost or quality of the ink was of course manifested by the fact that the ink which was expected to last Okoli over a month only lasted two full days.

By Okoli's third day in school, the ink had completely spilled from its bottle and soaked all the exercise books and few textbooks in the raffia-made schoolbag. Everything had been painted blue including the raffia schoolbag and Okoli's white shirt over which the schoolbag hung. Okoli did not initially notice the spill from the improperly closed ink bottle until he felt some rather soothing coolness at his back, coolness from the scorching heat from the sun on Okoli's way back from school. Okoli felt his back with his fingers, and his fingers were all colored blue. Of course, he quickly removed the blue-soaked shirt and folded it into his equally soaked schoolbag. The following morning, he used his spare shirt to school. He took the spare exercise book which he had left at home and headed off to school. In class, he borrowed some ink from Agu, the boy who sat next on the bench to him. (The pupils were initially placed in class in alphabetical order.) Many of the characters in the textbook were still legible, and so Okoli reckoned there would be no problem with the ink spillage of the previous day. The class recitation went on smoothly.

Then came the spelling classes. The pupils were then asked to turn to the things which they copied into their notebooks the previous day. Everybody else flipped through their exercise books. Okoli could not flip through any. He had left his previous day's notes in the house, since they were thoroughly smeared with ink. As the other pupils were spelling words aloud from their notes, Okoli was mumbling some incoherent words since he had no notes to read from. He kept moving his lips to give the impression that he was participating in the spelling recitation. As the pupils recited, Mr Ene was pacing to and fro between his table and the blackboard. His low-cut mustache and his thick-rimmed eyeglasses appeared to move incoherently as he recited the spellings for the pupils. Okoli's nonparticipation in that spelling class went unnoticed for some time because he had kept mumbling and moving his thick lips visibly after the rest of the pupils.

Agu was about Okoli's size. They must also have been about the same age. But Agu appeared to know a lot more and talk a lot more. He told Okoli soon after they sat down following the morning class prayers that a bigger boy in a senior class who was Mr Ene's pupil had told him that Mr Ene would not see beyond his nose if he removed his eyeglasses. Agu's information about Mr Ene's bad sight immediately flashed in Okoli's mind, and he started praying that Mr Ene's glasses dancing ungainly above his nose should suddenly drop and break. That way, Mr Ene would not see that he, Okoli, was not reciting the spellings with the rest of the class that morning. Okoli started wishing that the school bell would suddenly ring, calling the pupils out on the routine half-hour break. He just wished that something, anything would happen to distract Mr Ene or make him immediately change the schedule.

But none of these was to happen.

Instead, Mr Ene suddenly stopped pacing up and down and fixed his gaze in Okoli's direction. He adjusted his glasses. He now walked to the middle of the table maybe to see Okoli more closely. Then came the thundering words, "You"—pointing in Okoli's direction—"stand up."

Okoli turned his head sideways in a silly wish that Mr Ene might be pointing to someone else.

"I mean you there in wide slings," he thundered. "Stand up. What is your name? Why are you not reading? Are you sleeping in class?"

Of course, it was obvious he was referring to Okoli. Besides the fact that Okoli was the only person not reading the spellings, he was the only person in the whole class using wide slings, the belt like cotton or rubber bands tied or buttoned unto trousers. Okoli's father used to get a couple of them as souvenirs during Christmas from his oversea partners. He used to give them to local tailors to cut and join to match his sons' shorts' sizes. Okoli had about three pairs of them, and he used them on his school shorts. The other pupils in school all used narrow-sized slings made from cloth to hold up their shorts.

As Okoli stood up, the thundering commands and questions continued unabated.

"Spell me lines four and five. Do it fast before you sleep again."

"My name is O-o-k—" Okoli managed to mutter in between the commands.

Before he could complete the word *Okoli*, the other questions followed. "O-o-k . . . What? What are you eating? Are you sleeping, or are you eating? Everyone else is reading."

Of course, Okoli was not eating anything. Out of fright, he was merely rolling his tongue in his mouth and chewing his lips. He had always had the habit of chewing his lips whenever he was troubled or when he was under stress, and that habit had added some bumps to his already-thick lips.

Okoli was then summoned to the front of the class to read out the spellings from his notes. He came to the front of the class with his notebook, but it was a blank notebook. The actual notebook was at home. As Okoli could not read out anything, he stood there gazing, too miffed and too frightened to tell the story of the ink spill.

Mr Ene marched forward and bent down to Okoli's level. He apparently had wanted to help him read out the spellings. Even with Mr Ene's frightful moustache, Okoli could see some benevolence through the former's glasses.

But it was a futile effort. There was no way Okoli could be helped. There were no spellings to help him with. The exercise book was blank.

Obviously, to the best of Mr Ene's understanding, Okoli had not been copying the notes.

Mr Ene was miffed.

"Four days in school? And you have not been copying any notes? Get me your schoolbag. Quick!" Mr Ene ordered.

Okoli reluctantly brought his schoolbag to Mr Ene.

All that were in Okoli's school bag were three thoroughly ink-stained textbooks, a mouth organ (a present from Okoli's uncle Cos), and two big ripe mangoes!

It then appeared very obvious to Mr Ene that Okoli had either been sleeping or playing at the mouth organ or eating mangoes while others were copying notes. Any punishment was then justified, and Okoli knew it. Thus was Okoli welcomed to the real world of school discipline and corporal punishment. The six strokes of the cane that followed across Okoli's tiny buttocks signaled his initiation into the reality of school life for Okoli's age and time, the age where the dictum was accepted: "Spare the rod and spoil the child."

It signaled the consequences that awaited any carelessness, any misdemeanor, any school disobedience, any pilfering, or indeed any bullying that got observed or reported. It signaled the action that would whip out any misbehavior or harden the miscreant depending upon from which perspective one would see it. Okoli never had the opportunity of narrating the story of the ink spill. That had been overtaken by events.

Schooling Comes On Stream

After the first midterm tests, the pupils were rearranged in class in order of their positions of excellence in the class tests. The pupils in the class of forty-five were seated in eight rows of benches akin to church pews. The highest scorer in the class tests would sit on the first bench at the extreme right of the teacher facing the class. The fifth would sit at the front row extreme left. The least scorer would therefore sit on the last row extreme left of the teacher facing the class.

Okoli came sixth after the first test and therefore kept the second row seat for a while. Thereafter, following the weekly tests, his position oscillated between second and twelfth. Nwarime, one fat bright-eyed boy, who always kept to himself maintained the extreme right front row seat throughout that first year as he came perpetually first in the weekly tests. The extreme left of the eighth row had one permanent occupant, one Bartholomew who was nicknamed Banto. Banto was the biggest boy in the class. He was probably also the oldest.

Banto was a big bully, but he always did the bullying so subtly that it scarcely got noticed by any teacher. His victims, the much smaller boys in the class, were also usually too afraid to report. His favorite punishment for anybody who annoyed him would be to hold the person by the ear and twist the person's ear until the person screamed. He would thereafter kick the victim on the buttocks with his knee and push the latter off to run away and avoid further ear twisting. Banto did not talk much and hardly participated in games. He always had a dirty white bandage tied around the ankle of his left leg. It was later that the other pupils learnt that he had a long-standing leg ulcer, which had refused to heal. He spoke a dialect which, though Igbo the native language, was difficult to understand since it deviated appreciably from the Onitsha-oriented dialect, which was widely in use. Banto who spoke the indigenous Enugu dialect occasionally would get angry if one did not appear to understand him, especially if the person appeared to ridicule him because of his dialect which differed from the widely spoken Onitsha dialect. Okoli himself only learnt the Onitsha dialect from his association with his friend Anayo.

Mr Ene, the class teacher, did not appear to bother Banto either. The entire class was once put on punishment of four strokes of the cane each for noise-making. The caning however stopped short of Banto. The other pupils all started gossiping that Mr Ene was afraid of Banto because of the latter's big size. The truth of course was that Banto never participated in noise-making.

During the process of mark-reading for placement of pupils on the forms according to their positions, Banto would not wait for the conclusion of the mark reading. He would walk rapidly to the eighth bench and unilaterally take the seat for the fortieth position. He always suspected he would come fortieth. Invariably by the time the fortieth position was announced, it would be Banto.

The weekly form orders continued, and the seating positions in class continued to change. Only Nwarime's and Banto's positions remained constant in the first and fortieth respectively. Banto remained a constant occupant of the "position forty" seat, and he never complained.

As the term rolled on, the students got to understand Mr Ene better. They got to understand that in fact he could occasionally smile, as against previously held beliefs, especially if a pupil could fully recite the poem "Twinkle, Twinkle, Little Star" without any mistakes.

The pupils got to know that Mr Ene's cane was usually hidden across two nails behind the class blackboard. His dos and don'ts became clearer to the students. The first five of Mr Ene's ten commandments were the following:

> You must not sleep in class.
> You must not eat groundnuts (peanuts) in class.
> You must not fight in class.
> You must not spit on the floor.
> You must not copy from another pupil.

He instituted a prize of two colored crayons each to the occupants of the first and second positions in the class weekly tests. Within a few months, Nwarime's schoolbag was bulging with colored crayons. He was the undisputed champion of the class throughout the year. The new school year used to start in January. The duration was fashioned to fall in tune with the Christian church calendar. Thus, the first term would end just before the feast of Easter. The third term holidays was the longest and was fashioned to give as many as two full months for the Christmas holidays.

The end of terms was particularly busy periods for the pupils. Not only were the end-of-term examinations sources of worry for the pupils, there was usually a lot of grass cutting to be done. During the term, the pupils came to school with cutlasses only on Fridays for field grass cutting. Immediately after the end of the term examinations, each pupil was expected to come to school daily for the whole week with cutlasses to cut the football (soccer) fields, brooms to sweep the compounds, and wood charcoal for painting of the blackboards.

The fields were usually shared out for cutting between the different classes. The class monitor would supervise the work after it would have been shared out by the class teacher. One of the major privileges of the class monitor was that he was not required to have a share of the field cutting. This was a fair compensation for the enemies he incurred for submitting names for punishment when people made a noise in class. The monitors were appointed or reappointed on a term basis. Okoli never got to be a monitor in his first year in St Brigid's School.

On the last day of each term (usually a Friday), the different classes would gather and have the individual results publicly announced by the class teacher. A typical result would be read out as follows:

Okeke Nwankwo—Pass
Joseph Okoye—Fail
Bartholomew Agu—Fail
Nwarime Emenike—Pass,
Uche Nweke—Pass

As the results were announced, the report cards with the class positions were also handed over to each pupil to deliver to the parents or guardians. Those that passed would shout with joy, especially if they had very good positions. They would then race off home with their report cards. Those that failed would cry except for those like Banto, who had gotten used to failing. Most of the latter group would hide the results from their parents or destroy them and report that the report cards were yet to be issued. A lot of the parents had never attended any school and would often believe what ever their children told them about the school.

The first day of each new term was often filled with scores of parents who had come to collect the results of pupils who had not come home with any results. Most of such results had either been destroyed or hidden by the children who performed very poorly in the tests or examinations.

Once in a while, the absurd would happen. On his way home from school after the handing out of the second term's results, one of the big boys in the class whose name was Otigba had snatched Nwarime's result and had taken to his heels. After a short chase from Nwarime, the big boy handed back a report card to the former. Little did Nwarime know that Otigba had, during the chase, exchanged his (Nwarime's) first-position result for his own thirty-sixth-position result. It was not until the first school day of the third term when Nwarime's father came to the school to report the delivery of the wrong report to his son. The level of Otigba's intelligence did not go as far as to realize that each report card bore a particular name. Surprisingly Otigba's own parent or guardian did not come to report the handing of a wrong report to their son or ward. They were probably too overjoyed at their son's improved position to check for the name on the report card. They probably might even have rewarded Otigba with a new pair of shoes for suddenly soaring from a near bottom of the class position to a top position.

The first day of the new term just like the last day of the previous term was usually a very uncomfortable day for most of the students, except the class monitors. The fields were once again overgrown with grasses. The most troublesome type of grass was the type called "elephant grass," which was particularly difficult to cut. The main football field at St Brigid's was filled with elephant grass, and a number of the pupils often sustained blisters on their palms from pressure of the cutlasses during grass cutting after the first day of each new term.

The Christmas holidays following the end of the third term was usually very enjoyable and full of expectations of the Christmas and New Year festivities. Not only would most children have plenty of rice and meat (most families usually slaughtered a chicken for Christmas), there was hardly any child who would not have a jumper (a loose-fitting long shirt without collar and with two wide pockets at both lower sides) for Christmas. Many others would also have a cap and possibly a pair of sandals. In preparation for Christmas, groups of children in adjacent neighborhoods would often gather to form new dance groups and learn new songs. Many others would contribute pennies to purchase *ekpo*, the carved wooden face of the masquerade with openings on the carving for the eyes and the mouth. Loose cloth attached to the top and lower end of the carved wooden face would cover the head and chin respectively as the carving was secured over the wearer's face with a string or elastic band. The ekpo masquerade would dance while the handlers, the rest of the group, would beat metal gongs and sing the songs. The children would take their ekpo dancing group from house to house to sing, dance, and entertain people. In return, the audience would applaud the dancers, and a few would drop coins in appreciation. When the dances were taken to individual houses, the dancers were often given bowls of rice to eat. In the first ekpo dancing group that Okoli participated, the mask was worn by Anayo, who lived in the same yard with him.

They were about nine boys in all, and they collected a total of elevenpence during the first of the three days December 25, 26, and 27 that they sang and danced. They had all decided to give the money to Janti, the big boy who lived in their yard to keep for them. They had intended to collect back the money and share among themselves after singing and dancing one more day, on New Year's Day.

Janti was not a member of any dancing group. Okoli's dancing group nevertheless felt that their money would be safe in Janti's care since the latter was so much bigger and older than they were. On the evening of New Year's Day after the day's performance, the boys gathered to share the money. Okoli called Janti to return the forty-sixpence, which the group kept with him. Janti came out red eyed and grabbed Anayo, who was his cousin, by the collar, gave him a very hard knock on the head, and reached out for Okoli. The other seven boys fled. Janti never returned the money despite later complaints to the parents and guardians of the children. All that the boys were left with was the sixteenpence which they collected on New Year's Day, which they had not yet handed over to Janti. The boys had learnt their lessons. When they reconvened during Easter which was three months after Christmas, they resolved to share whatever they collected same day after each day's performance.

Maturing at St Brigid's

The classes were reorganized after each year at St Brigid's. The pupils who failed in primary 2 joined those who passed in primary 1 to make up the new classes of primary 2. This pattern was followed in other classes. Each class was subdivided into four streams: A, B, C, and D, each with forty pupils randomly selected. There was thus no strongest A class nor weakest D class. By primary 2, most pupils must have gotten used to the school system except for a few transfer students. Particular teachers were usually allocated the same class for several years. The headmaster, however, had the discretion of assigning the teachers as he saw fit. Only the headmaster and the catechist were not assigned any particular classes. The headmaster was the overall administrative head of the school while the catechist oversaw the moral and religious instructions. The catechist, however, occasionally took over the class of any teacher who was absent for the duration of the absence.

Only a handful of the former classmates in Okoli's first year remained with him in his new B class. The others had been assigned to classes A, C, or D. A few others were repeating primary 1. The new class teacher was a tall soft-spoken very fair-skinned man, who always wore baggy shorts and knee-length hoses. He had lots of freckles, and the pupils immediately noticed that his eye balls would suddenly dash from one side to the other.

Unlike Mr Ene in Okoli's former class, the new teacher, Mr Ude, did not wear glasses and did not nurse a moustache. The pupils also noticed that when Mr Ude would be talking to somebody, it would appear as if he was looking at another person. They learnt from those who were repeating the class under him that they had nicknamed him Anya Inegam, which implied that his eyes were scrutinizing someone else while he appeared to be looking at another. The pupils felt very relaxed with Mr Ude because he did not appear to scold them very much even when he would come in and meet the pupils making a noise. He would simply tap the blackboard duster several times on his table to quieten the class. The tapping of the blackboard with the duster often raised a lot of chalk dust.

The very first day in class 2B, the pupils observed that Mr Ude, the teacher, was fond of adding *m* before most of his words. He would for instance say *mbecause* whenever he meant to say *because*, and he would pronounce the word *because* as *mbukuz*. It did not take long before *mbukuz* replaced Anya Inegam as the new class name for Mr Ude.

A very pleasant thing in Okoli's new class was that the pupils quickly scrutinized the back of the blackboard and neither saw a cane nor even nails across which a future cane would be kept. Most of the pupils, especially pupils like Okoli who did a lot of talking in class, were very pleased with the apparent absence of an instrument for punishing noise making. Little did they realize that another instrument which would be unveiled later would be more worrisome.

Mr Ude did not immediately appoint a class monitor for the new class. It was only after the first Friday test that he announced to the class that whoever came first in the first test for each month would be the monitor until the next test. That was not a welcome news for the biggest boys in class who often were appointed monitors so they would supposedly use their intimidating sizes to enforce discipline. Incidentally the pupil who took the lead after the first test was neither the tallest in the class nor the most muscular. He was a slim, fairly tall boy who rarely talked much. He would never shout on any one to stop making a noise. He would quietly copy down the name as the noisemaker disturbed others, and by the time Mr Ude was back, the names of all the noisemakers and those who fought or quarreled in class during the teacher's absence would be on Mr Ude's table.

Mr Ude had a quiet disposition. The pupils hardly ever saw him in class using a whip. The only times he would be seen with a whip was when he was required to man the front gate of the school for latecomers. Every minute of lateness to school attracted one stroke of the cane. More than ten minutes of lateness attracted caning and grass cutting.

The method of punishment for disobedience or other forms of misbehavior in Mr Ude's class was to make the culprit or offender kneel down for varying lengths of time, ranging from minutes to hours. Any misbehavior in Mr Ude's class would attract such long periods of kneeling down that the individual would occasionally prefer to receive some strokes of the cane on the palms or buttocks and be allowed to sit down thereafter.

The first day Okoli got written up in class 2B was for eating groundnuts in class and scattering the shells on the floor. Groundnuts were usually sold with their shells. The dual "crime" of eating and scattering peanut shells carried double punishment. Okoli was made to kneel down for so long that his thigh muscles ached for days.

The sitting position in Okoli's new class was not done in order of academic excellence, unlike in his first year under Mr Ene. The pupils were rather seated in order of their heights. The shortest pupils sat on the front-row bench, and the tallest boys sat at the rear bench. It was a more comfortable sitting arrangement for pupils who were not academically superior. That way it would not be easy to detect at a glance the pupil who came last in the class test. Only the brightest student was easily detected since, being the class monitor, he was to sit right in front on the extreme right facing the teacher. This position afforded him the opportunity of alerting the class on entry of any visitor to the class. On entry of the teacher or any visitor to the class, the class monitor would immediately tap three times on the writing form. The entire class would then stand up and if the visitor was a male would say in unison, "Good morning, sir." (Or say, "Good afternoon, sir," depending upon time of day.) If a female, the class would say, "Good morning, ma'am."

The visitor or class teacher would then be expected to reply,

"Good morning, class."

The class monitor would then again tap three times, and the class would sit down.

One of the big boys in Okoli's class in primary 2 was Cletus. He had an even bigger brother, Raphael, who was in primary 4. Both Cletus and Raphael were almost always in company of each other outside the classroom. Cletus was a big bully. Even though he was not the biggest boy in the class, everybody was wary of getting across his path. Even the biggest boys in class avoided a fight with him because any fight or simple verbal exchange with him would draw the wrath of his brother, Raphael, and the duo would subdue even the biggest boy in school.

Okoli's first encounter with Cletus was on one Monday morning during recreation (break). Okoli had come to school with a penny and decided to buy a cup of *moi moi* (mashed bean cake sold in metal cups). Each cup of moi moi sold for a halfpence. The moi moi, groundnut, and biscuit hawkers often stationed themselves outside the school gates during recreation periods. Cletus was standing outside the school gate. He was gazing at the hawkers with his two hands in his pockets. Apparently, he had no money on him, and he watched the hawker give Okoli his halfpence change after the latter had bought a cup of moi moi. As Okoli sat down near the gate to eat his moi moi, Cletus walked towards him and asked the latter why he bought only one cup of moi moi. Okoli told him that he needed only one cup.

"Didn't you see that I was here?" Cletus queried Okoli, looking the latter menacingly in the face. He stood for a while in front of Okoli, who expected him to pounce at his cup of moi moi at any moment. In fact, Okoli thought of handing Cletus the cup of moi moi voluntarily if only the latter would leave him alone, especially as Okoli had another halfpenny in his pocket. Luckily Cletus did not strike, at least not immediately. He instead walked into the school compound apparently to confirm that no teachers were in sight. Okoli's worst fears were soon confirmed as Cletus again came back in under two minutes. That was even before Okoli was halfway through the cup of moi moi, which he had started gulping quickly before Cletus would change his mind and come back.

"Why are you eating here? People are not allowed to eat near the gate," Cletus barked at the visibly frightened Okoli.

Of course, that was not true. Many other people were busy having their snacks crouched on the floor near the school gate.

"Take that moi moi to that gmelina tree," Cletus ordered, pointing to a huge gmelina tree down the road outside the school fence and outside of view from the school gate.

Impulsively Okoli complied, even though Cletus, not being teacher nor even a class monitor, had no authority to issue such a command. Okoli simply wanted to avoid any confrontation with the ever-menacing Cletus, who nonetheless had his plans.

Cletus followed Okoli down to the shade of the gmelina tree away from the view of other pupils. As Okoli again sat down on the floor to eat the moi moi, having so far complied with all Cletus's orders, Cletus now did the unthinkable. He unzipped his shorts and starting urinating into Okoli's cup of moi moi! As Okoli was about to raise an alarm, Cletus told him that if he shouted or told anybody, he and Raphael, his brother, would deal with him and give him a black eye after school. Okoli had to hold his peace and maintain a feigned calmness, lest a more sinister punishment should follow. He abandoned the cup of moi moi as Cletus simply walked away with both hands in his pockets as if nothing had happened.

Okoli was never to forget that incident, not even after many years when he with Cletus and Raphael became among the well-behaved boys who got selected to serve at masses as altar boys. He was never to report to anybody, but he always wondered whether Cletus ever went for confession for his misbehavior of that fateful afternoon.

Entry into primary 3 was very smooth. By that time, Okoli and his friends had become fully familiar with the school environment. By then they had known the teachers who came to school with cane. They had also known the number of lashes each teacher was likely to give for specific offences. They had known who the wicked big boys were and who the kind ones were. By primary 3, they had essentially known the very bright boys who were likely to sit on the front row as the sitting arrangement had once more reverted to the order of academic excellence. They had essentially known that for one to be number one in the front row, one needed to beat the boy called Aboni if one were unlucky to be in the same class with the latter. Above all, those who at one time or the other got into the temptation of aspiring to come first in class had come to know that it was not easy to beat Aboni. The best one could do was to pray that if one were in B class that the boy called Aboni should be in the A class or the C or D class.

It was in primary 3 that the rest of the pupils began to acknowledge the academic wizardry of that slim, fairly tall boy who in primary 2B would, as class monitor, copy down the names of noise and troublemakers like Okoli and submit without uttering a word. In primary 3, both Aboni and Okoli often checked on each other's score for superiority after class tests. The two gradually became friends. Okoli never really beat Aboni in any subject except occasionally in English language, but excellence in that subject alone was never enough to turn the tide in Okoli's favor over all. If Julius Caesar "bestrode the world like a colossus," that boy called Aboni rode the academic waves like a jockey superstar, most of the primary school and all through the secondary school through which fate and some academic excellence were once again to bring him and Okoli together. Only once in a midterm test did Aboni have a challenger in Okoli, and that singular vaulting ambition earned Okoli six strokes of the cane on the buttocks. Aboni had fought Okoli outside of the classroom soon after the mark-reading, apparently for taking up his first position. Mr Ebo, the class teacher, wasted no time in calling in the two academic giants of his class, laying them simultaneously across the table, and unleashing six hot lashes of the cane on them simultaneously for disgracing him. As the strokes of the cane landed on the duo, Okoli who lay farther away from the teacher on the table screamed in pain. The apparently more stolid Aboni did not as much as utter a cry of pain. It was possible that, lying closer to the teacher as the latter stood against the table, Aboni experienced less of the force of the whip, and that the force of the whip landed more strongly on Okoli who lay farther away.

Mr Adinobi was the assistant catechist when Okoli came into the school. By the third year in school, he had become in charge of recruiting and coaching the young mass servers (altar boys). Among the qualities he searched for was the ability to memorize and recite well and fast. That included the ability to memorize and recite what one did not understand. Okoli was lucky to be among those selected from St Brigid's School. Okoli's erstwhile assailant, Cletus, and his brother, Raphael, were also among those selected. Those selected underwent weekend courses in memorizing popular Catholic prayers in Igbo, English, and Latin languages. Learning and reciting some intricate prayers in English was difficult enough for a boy whose language of upbringing was not English. Learning and reciting such prayers in Latin language was an uphill task. But the pupils were able, many of them, to learn even when they did not understand the meaning of what they recited. Many could not cope with the following:

> Confiteor Deo Omnipotentes
> [I confess to Almighty God and the]
> Mea culpa mea culpa mea maxima culpa.
> [Through my fault through my fault through my most grievous fault].

Even when they did recite these words, including the full version of Pater Noster Qui Est in Coelis (Our Father Who Art in Heaven).

The above was in addition to the many other Latin prayers, many of whose words might be too jaw breaking for any village boy. Those people who could not memorize were dropped.

Okoli even in spite of his rather traditional background fully believed in the power of prayers, and the experience of being a mass server did strongly change and redirect him from the unruly rascal who would want to derail a train to the child of God which he thereafter sought to become. He nevertheless always had nostalgia for the days of iru agwu and Ikeji when his father and the latter's eight wives would slaughter animals and sprinkle the blood and feathers against the carved *chi* and all powerful *ikenga,* the head of the gods, while at the same time reserving all reverence to Oseburuwa, the god of gods and the king of kings.

Despite the inner wish to be good and remain good, however, Okoli still found that, in the middle of other boys, through the rest of the primary school through the secondary school and even through the university, the frailty of human nature often prevailed. That was because he would not want his friends to laugh at him or to believe that he was a weakling. He did not make much attempt to extricate himself from peer influence. Unlike his father, he never considered becoming a reverend father, and the thought of marrying eight or twelve wives, or even marrying at all, was not yet one of the things under consideration for him. He merely enjoyed the exposure and limelight which being a mass server afforded him, as he daily perched on the steps of the altar to recite the first few verses of the Apostle's Creed, the Lord's Prayer, or the Hail Mary, as the congregation would complete the rest of the chorus.

Nothing fascinated Okoli as much as adorning the red and white altar boy's vests, especially during church festivities. Much as his being a mass server did not completely keep him away from a few pranks in school, it curtailed some excesses which his rather crude and rustic background from Aba might have led him into. As a mass server there were certain things that he would not want people to see him do. He would no longer, for instance, want to be seen stealing mangoes from European quarters nor would he any longer want to be seen trying, or planning to go to derail trains. Even the thought of fighting in school began to look like a big sin to him. But he never forgot that his fellow mass server Cletus once intentionally urinated over his cup of moi moi at school. The latter was also to later teach Okoli how to go to the nearby convent and obtain a few sandwiches and biscuits from the reverend sisters by telling a few phony stories of having kept awake all night at the sacristy, leading prayers, or participating in some other mission work. Such pranks and mischiefs often kept Okoli moody for days after he must have eaten the sandwiches and cookies, but he often found himself repeating many of those same pranks often, and again when he was with the rest of' the boys, especially when he was with Cletus and his brother, Raphael.

Okoli also never forgot that it was Cletus who introduced him into the prank of peeping through the side of the bathroom when ever Zisu, a boy who joined them in class 3 midway through the term, came to urinate. Virtually every other boy in the class was circumcised as was the custom of the Igbo people. Zisu however was not of Igbo extraction, and it was Cletus who mischievously told the other boys that Zisu was not circumcised and got Okoli and a few other boys to always nose around and pretend to go to urinate whenever Zisu went to the bathroom to urinate. Okoli always pondered within himself whether he should confess that prank or not. It was Cletus who convinced him that he should not, since if he did, then he would have to refrain from that pleasurable pastime. It was many years later that Okoli got to realize the folly of what he was doing and the greater folly of allowing himself to be so controlled by peer influence.

As a mass server, Okoli would usually out of necessity arrive much earlier at masses. He would help get things out for the mass. He would lead in some of the group prayers like the Rosary. The leader of the team was usually a sacristan, who was a full-time staff. Cletus, Raphael, and Okoli along with some other mass servers were to serve with boys from other Catholic schools. His four years as a mass server taught Okoli about the need for punctuality, dedication to duty, and respect for constituted authority. He would get up early every morning and do the nearly one-mile journey from Asata, Enugu, to the Catholic Cathedral at Ogbete, Enugu, and still come back early enough to prepare for and go to school at St Brigid's. His training and service as an altar boy must have greatly prepared Okoli morally and academically. Otherwise, how would he explain the fact that even with the full-involvement seven days a week in church activities, Okoli was still able to pass the leaving certificate examinations with distinction. How would one explain his ability to score high enough in the entrance examinations into Government Secondary School Afikpo as to be one of the five best candidates that were awarded full board and tuition scholarship after the examinations and interview process. Okoli often pondered over these and similar questions and felt convinced that it was not merely coincidental.

After Cletus and Okoli met again as mass servers, they served together for four straight years. The thought of Cletus urinating into Okoli's cup of moi moi at St Brigid's School always reared up in Okoli's mind whenever he saw Cletus, but he never discussed the issue. His subsequent attitude towards Cletus did not depict that either. Okoli was even to learn a few more vices from Cletus as time passed. He was to learn how one could sneak into the church store and quench hunger by devouring unconsecrated hosts. *Quenching hunger* was a description often used by Cletus to describe eating. A one-time attempt at drinking altar wine later got the duo of Cletus and Raphael into big trouble. The indefinite suspension handed to Raphael must have been the saving grace for the group from getting into deeper trouble.

The Friends Fight Again

It was in primary 4 that Aboni and Okoli met again in the same class and became very close friends. It was also in primary four, second term, that Okoli successfully, for the second and last time, had an edge over Aboni in class. The first time was after a weekly test. After the results were announced, on their way out of the school, Okoli had said to Aboni, "You now see you can be beaten twice."

What followed was another fight, this time with tearing of shirts. Again the two friends were called back to class by Mr Ebo, the class teacher. They were again laid across the table parallel to each other and simultaneously this time were given twelve strokes of the cane. Again, Okoli believed he must have gotten the raw end of the stick as the whip descended for twelve consecutive times, because as he kept screaming after each stroke while Aboni hardly cried, even though this time he was laid farther away from the teacher. The quarrel ended thereafter, especially as Okoli never again "smelt" the first position in any competition with Aboni.

In primary 5, the friends were separated: Okoli to 5A under Mr Ukome and Aboni into 5B under another teacher, Ms Oneabo, the only lady teacher in the entire school.

Primary 5 was Okoli's most difficult class. Each day on his way to school, the statement would ring repeatedly in Okoli's ears: "I cannot teach mathematics without flogging."

That was a marching statement for any one who came to 5A and who decided to disregard mathematics. Mr Ukome, the 5A class teacher, would drum that statement into the ears of each pupil on the first day of classes.

Nwodo and Ajenu, who were both Okoli's classmates in 5A and who disliked mathematics, did not appear to feel the pains of the strokes of the cane. They never cried during the caning. The pupils later found that they sewed pillow padding into the backsides of their shorts to absorb the effect of the whips each day the pupils had math classes. Of course, the gimmick did not always stand the test of time. After the first few strokes in each case, the dull sounds would give away the gimmick, and the bare buttocks suffered directly for every question failed. Before caning them for any failed question, Mr Ukome soon learnt to feel the buttocks of Nwodo and Ajenu to ensure they did not have any pillow padding sewn into their shorts. The slogan changed thereafter:

"You can not go through 5A without mastering mathematics."

It worked! The pupils who passed through 5A were the best in mathematics in the school. That, of course, was with the exception of Aboni who was the best overall even though he was in 5B.

By the time the pupils got to primary 6, the main focus for every one was twofold: sitting for entrance examinations into the secondary schools and sitting for the first school leaving certificate examinations. Every one of the four class teachers in primary 6 worked extra hard to prepare his or her pupils to pass the entrance examinations into the best secondary schools. It was the pride of every teacher to have pupils from his or her class pass the examinations to one of the three government colleges (secondary schools) or to one of the top mission secondary schools. They also each competed between themselves for whose pupils would excel in the first school leaving certificate examination organized by the Regional Ministry of Health. At the beginning of every school year, the headmaster (usually addressed as HM) would publicly announce to the students, parents, and guardians the name of the class teacher of primary 6 whose pupils did best in both public examinations the previous year. The presentation of the teacher was usually followed by a thunderous applause and a standing ovation. The names of the various teachers through whom these best students had earlier passed through was also read out for public recognition.

It was usually a thing of great joy for any teacher who was so recognized. The pupils were not in a position to know whether such recognition attracted any material benefits. Certainly such best teachers were usually well respected.

Okoli's primary 6 teacher was Ms Oneabo, a soft-spoken, very thorough teacher. She was earlier the class teacher for primary 5 and had taught Okoli's friend Aboni in class 5. As previously said, she was the only female teacher among the eight teachers of the senior classes, primaries 5 and 6.She had also won the Best Teacher Award for two consecutive years, two and three years previously. The thing she disliked the most was lateness to class. The pupils knew that early enough. She never carried a cane, and

Okoli could not recollect ever seeing her whipping any pupil even when she manned the main gate, which the teachers took in turns from week to week. If one misbehaved in class or came late for any activity, she would simply send the person out of class. If one came late to school, she would also send the person to cut grass. The school store was never short of cutlasses for use in such situations.

Ms Oneabo was not as crazy about math as Mr Ukome was. But she loved poetry. A great deal of Okoli's early flare for poetry he would give credit to Ms Oneabo, and later in secondary school to Mr Guorge. After the initial morning prayers before the start of classes, Ms Oneabo would make the class recite a few lines of poetry, which she had meticulously written out on the blackboard even before the start of the day's classes. Thereafter, the board which was usually mounted on a triangular wooden stand would be turned over for the day's classes to begin.

By the second term of primary 6, it was time to apply to the secondary schools of the pupils' choice. The headmaster assembled the primary six pupils and narrated to them the histories and merits of the top secondary schools, all government, mission, and a few private secondary schools. He told them that there were three government secondary schools for boys located at Umuahia (known as Government College Umuahia), Afikpo, and Owerri. He further said that there was only one government secondary school for girls known as Queen's School Enugu. Queen's School was inapplicable to the pupils, since St Brigid's was an all-boys school. Of the boys' secondary schools, the headmaster told the pupils that the most famous was Government College Umuahia, both on account of its long history and on account of its performance in the West African School Certificate Exams. He however said that Government Secondary School Afikpo, though a relatively young school, had maintained 100 percent passing rate in the West African School Certificate Exams throughout its existence.

"In my opinion, therefore, I would recommend Government Secondary School Afikpo on account of its excellence and consistency," the principal would say.

Of course, who were the pupils to counter HM's recommendation? Thus, every pupil from St Brigid's who sat for the entrance examinations into the government-owned secondary schools for that year chose Afikpo. And the pupils were not disappointed.

Among the mission-owned schools HM had recommended were College of Immaculate Conception Enugu, Stella Maris College Port

Harcourt, and Bishop Shannahan College Orlu. Okoli chose College of Immaculate Conception Enugu (because he had lived in Enugu) and Stella Maris College Port Harcourt (because it was close to Aba), where his friends Titus and Damian lived and where Ceewai, his cousin and best friend, also lived.

When Okoli got home from school and presented his list of choices to his uncle for approval (parent's or guardian's approval for the list was mandatory), the latter approved of Government Secondary School Afikpo and College of Immaculate Conception Enugu. He, however, disapproved of Stella Maris College Port Harcourt and substituted St Patrick's College Calabar. Okoli's uncle was a product of St Patrick's College Calabar. Okoli's final list therefore were for Afikpo, Enugu, and Calabar. The pupils were to find out many years later that in addition to the schools presented to them, there were many other top government-owned schools like King's College Lagos, Bayero College Kano, and Government College Ibadan. There were also many other top mission schools like Dennis Memorial Grammar School Onitsha and St Augustine's Grammar School Nkwerri. However, these other schools were not presented before the pupils at St Brigid's either because of their distant locations or because of sheer religious bigotry.

Religious patronage must have played a role in HM's presentation of the options because St Brigid's being a Catholic school, and HM, being an employee of the Catholic Mission, would not be expected to be seen promoting schools owned by other missions. Besides, at the time Okoli was in St Brigid's School, he was given the impression that everything St Brigid's was good while everything about St Barth's (St Bartholomew, the nearby Anglican School) was bad or, at best, not entirely good. Religious politics was so much played out that even as young as Okoli and his friends often sang derisive songs about Protestant pastors while the non-Catholics would on their part ridicule the white robes worn by the Catholic priests. They told Okoli and his Catholic friends that the *fada*, as the pupils from St Barth's called the Catholic clergy, wore long white flowing robes akin to gowns worn by women because "they were neither men nor women" and that that accounted for why fada did not get married. Some would further say that the reverend sisters were the secret wives of the fadas, and that the latter partially covered their faces with white robes because the fadas were keeping them in purdah and did not want other men to see the faces of their "wives." They would further translate the CSSP degrees which the Catholic priests attached to their names as "Common Standard Six Pass."

"Your fadas will marry all your sisters and use your AMC (annual missionary collection) to maintain them," they would taunt the Catholic pupils.

"All your pastors would collect all your tithe and church collections and give to their wives and their children, and they will laugh at you when your money finishes," the Catholics would fire back. They would further add, "Your tithe would enrich the pastor and his children, and when you get poor, they will laugh at you."

Luckily these derisive and discriminatory religious lessons drummed into the ears of young minds did not sink deep. Certainly, they did not influence the children's choice of friends. Certainly, when the children went to pluck mangoes in European quarters, they did not care who were Catholic or who were Anglican. And for those of them who were lucky to later attend the government secondary schools, religious affiliation was hardly of any consequence. It no longer mattered to them after primary school who was Catholic or Anglican or Baptist Methodist or Presbyterian or even Muslim or Buddhist or whatever. They got more concerned about who got the A and who came first in class after the class tests. And their choice of friends was not determined by religious affiliation either. And that was the beauty of Okoli's alma mater.

The results of the entrance examinations into secondary schools were soon released.

The result of St Patrick's College Calabar came out first. Okoli was overjoyed at the news that he passed the entrance exam.

"So I will soon be a student," Okoli said to himself. People in secondary schools called themselves students. They referred to those in primary schools as pupils. The students were very proud people. They were the chosen few. They would come home from holidays wearing their school sweaters even on very hot days. The seniors among them would wear the college blazers and perhaps the caps with the school badge engraved on them. It did not matter that the temperature might be constantly above 100°F.

A student would come back speaking English even after only one term in secondary school. Speaking in vernacular (native language) was a punishable offence in secondary schools. Of course, a student would never come out naked as he would occasionally do while in primary school. As a student, one could wear glasses even when one had perfectly normal vision. Wearing of glasses was almost a status symbol at that time. It showed that one was doing a lot of reading: volumes and volumes as the students used to say. Some students would even wear empty frames if they found a discarded one, if only to appear learnt. Only Joachim, the son of Dr Onu, one of the three or four doctors in Enugu at the time, wore glasses to school throughout Okoli's days at St Brigid's. It did not mean there were no cases of short, long, or far sight. But where were the optometrists and ophthalmologists to check the eyes of the rest of the pupils? The first time Okoli ever saw a doctor in his life was when he was taken by his uncle to Dr Onumere in Enugu for his medical exam prior to entry into secondary school. Okoli felt as if he had seen God. When he was told to read out the characters from some letters of different sizes mounted on the wall (Snell en's chart), because of fear, Okoli could not pronounce a single word. Even when he was taken so close to the chart, he still could not pronounce the largest characters. Somehow the doctor realized that Okoli was nervous. The medical examination had to be postponed.

Four days after receipt of the admission notice into St Patrick's College Calabar, Okoli's uncle ensured that the money order was dispatched. After a week of the payment of the required £3 (three pounds) deposit, Okoli got another letter from the school that the required deposit had been raised to £6 (six pounds). To ensure that Okoli's place was retained, the additional three pounds was instantly paid. As he came back from the post office where he had gone to post the additional deposit to SPC, Okoli's result to CIC (College of Immaculate Conception) arrived. He passed!

Okoli's uncle was in a fix.

"CIC does better in the West African School Certificate Exams," he said.

"It is rated higher Overall it is a better school. But we have paid to SPC," he said. He did not say more.

That same evening, Okoli contacted Aboni who had then become his best friend in St Brigid's. Aboni, too, had passed to CIC. His elder brother, Seve, had also attended CIC.

A Trip to CIC

Aboni and Okoli took a trip to CIC, which was about two miles away from St Brigid's School. It was like a new world to them. The neat and well-arranged classrooms fascinated the two friends. Every student had a locker and chair to himself (unlike the long forms with no lockers that were used at St Brigid's). The football (soccer) fields were neatly mowed and marked with white paint. The school library was filled with big books neatly stacked. There were individual rooms for the principal's office, vice principal's office, Brother Nubert, Brother Aluosius, and all the other brothers (all Irish Marist brothers who ran the school). They had their names engraved on doors of their offices. Not even the headmaster of the entire St Brigid's School had an office. His table was at the center of the open hall with the different classes spread out in the hall. It was a matter of whose voice was louder when the teachings were going on. It was occasionally like a babel of voices.

Aboni and Okoli then visited the dining room of CIC. It was a large hall with many tables overlaid with water jugs. The school was not in full session, but there were a number of young men strolling about the corridors.

Even though Okoli's fate about CIC or SPC had not been fully decided, he felt he was already a part of CIC. When they got back to school the following morning, Okoli and Aboni found that four other boys from their school had also passed to CIC. The list included Everistus, a very quiet and intelligent boy who lived along Richard Street, almost opposite the school. Everistus was Okoli's other good friend. So six pupils from St Brigid's would make it to CIC. The six immediately became friends, two from Okoli's class and four from the other three classes.

The closing date for acceptance of the offer of admission into CIC and the payment of the £5 (five pounds sterling) deposit was getting close. There was no word of confirmation from Okoli's uncle as to which of the two schools, CIC or SPC, Okoli would attend. Obviously he must have been considering what was best for Okoli. He might also have been holding consultations with Okoli's father in Aba. There was no way Okoli would know what was going on in the minds of the adults. He was not even worried. All he knew was that he was going to become a student and that he was going to CIC, the nonpayment of the acceptance deposit notwithstanding.

It was on a Monday evening, and Okoli had just finished his meals after returning from school. His uncle called him and asked, "Have you decided on your choice between SPC and CIC?"

"I am going to CIC, sir," was Okoli's reply.

"When is the closing date for deposits?" Okoli's uncle asked.

It was just then that it occurred to Okoli that that Monday was the final day for acceptance of admission deposits to CIC. Visualizing the opportunity to get into CIC slipping away from him, Okoli was thrown into a panic, and he started to cry.

Okoli's uncle walked off into his room, and Okoli could hear the call bell ring downstairs. In a moment, Mr Bernard came up. Mr Bernard was the deputy head of sales in the pharmacy store, which was located downstairs. Okoli's uncle handed Mr Bernard five pounds in single one-pound notes along with some coins and told him to go with Okoli to the post office to buy the money order to CIC. Okoli was so full of joy and ran off to the post office ahead of Mr Bernard's arrival. The dream was about to come true.

Okoli is about to become student of CIC, Okoli mused.

The money order was bought and addressed to "The Principal CIC Enugu." It was then sent by registered post to CIC.

It was about 5:00 p.m., and Okoli and Bernard had barely succeeded in completing the money order transactions before the post office closed for the day.

As they took the turn off Ogui Road, leading into their premises, they saw Pius, the office messenger, mounting his bicycle to ride out. When Pius saw Okoli and Bernard coming into the compound, he dismounted and walked towards them.

"Oga say make yu no bai the moni oda again," he told Bernard who proudly held the receipt of the money order with the few pence balance from the commission.

Oga (Master) had sent Pius to tell Bernard not to purchase the money order any longer. But it was too late.

Pius had been directed to hurry to the post office and stop Bernard from purchasing and posting the money order acceptance deposit to CIC.

Something had gone wrong. Did Okoli's uncle change his mind? Did he finally decide that Okoli should go to SPC instead? Cold sweat came over Okoli's forehead. But the acceptance deposit to CIC had been posted. With the acceptance deposit paid, a reversal was not likely.

Bernard and Okoli walked into Okoli's uncle's office. The latter was holding a pink piece of paper in front of him, his large eyeballs appearing to pierce through his thin-framed glasses.

"Did you buy the money order?" he enquired as Bernard held out the receipt and change before him.

Before Bernard could conclude the "yes, sir," Okoli's uncle followed up,: "Have you posted it?" Of course, the money order had been bought and posted. And the post office had closed for the day!

Whatever the situation, my position in CIC had been secured, so Okoli thought again.

Okoli was standing behind Bernard who stood facing Oga (Okoli's uncle). Oga then looked in Okoli's direction and handed the latter the pink piece of paper. It was a telegram and was written in the language of telegrams: very sketchy. Okoli quickly read the scantily worded contents:

"Following the entrance examination and interviews stop. You have been offered admission as a scholar/fee payer into Government Secondary School Afikpo stop. Detailed letter follows stop. Principal stop."

Okoli's full name was then typed below the letter with the word *SCHOLAR* typed in capital letters beside the name.

Okoli could not make much of the letter with all the scanty words and meaningless stops. This was the first telegram that was ever addressed to Okoli. He simply held the letter and was about to leave the room when his uncle grabbed his palm and shook his hands and said, "Congratulations all the same."

Obviously the whole situation was getting worrisome and more confusing for Okoli. First, it was SPC Calabar with the deposit and supplementary deposit paid. That was jettisoned. Then came CIC with the full deposit paid. In under an hour after that, this telegram comes from government secondary school with its terse, inconclusive sentences. For Okoli's uncle, yes, it was a little worrisome. But for Okoli, he had already made up his mind on going to CIC, fee payer/scholar (whatever those meant) and the meaningless stops notwithstanding.

The letter telegram was still in Okoli's pocket the following morning when he got to school. As he entered the school compound, his friend Aboni ran up to him and said, "See, I got admission and scholarship into government secondary school."

He was obviously so happy and was breathing fast. Okoli was unimpressed and wondered why Aboni should feel so excited about that school when the mental picture of CIC with its smooth red brick buildings were making waves in Okoli's imagination.

"Yes," Okoli replied.

"I also got admission, but I did not get scholarship." Okoli then brought out the telegram and showed to Aboni.

The latter ran his sharp eyes quickly through the words and exclaimed, "You got scholarship too!"

"No," Okoli replied. "Where is the scholarship spelt?"

Aboni then pointed at the words *scholar* and *fee payer*, with the word *scholar* underlined, and also at the word *scholar* written in bold capitals under the main body of the letter.

It was then that Okoli understood. Hitherto he had thought that he got the letter with the word *scholar* on it because he was to be the student and that another letter would be sent to his father at Aba with the word *fee payer* since the latter would pay the fees. Okoli had hitherto understood the word *scholar* to mean the person who was doing the schooling.

Aboni then told Okoli that he was certainly going to Afikpo. He said that his father on getting the admission letter quickly contacted Joe, Aboni's elder brother, about the choice between Government Secondary School Afikpo and CIC, and the reply was a two-worded telegram reply from Joe stating thus:

"Certainly Afikpo."

Okoli got more confused.

So people could choose a place right in the bush, its beautiful buildings notwithstanding, so far away from the township, over a place right at the heart of the capital city Enugu a place as beautiful as CIC? Okoli could not understand. He made very little out of the lessons for that whole day as his mind and imaginations kept oscillating between CIC Enugu and Government Secondary School Afikpo. He was so absentminded in class that day that he did not notice when Ms Oneabo, the class teacher, directed a question at him. He was gazing at the ceiling, oblivious of the fact that she was asking him a question. Ms Oneabo immediately sent Okoli out of the class for the rest of the day.

When Okoli got home from school that day, he informed his uncle that he was told that he got a scholarship to Government Secondary School Afikpo. His uncle asked for the letter, and Okoli gave him the same telegram which the former earlier gave him the previous day. It was then that Okoli's uncle carefully read the telegram. He quickly dropped the letter on the table and lifted Okoli up on to his shoulders. Obviously as soon as he saw "Admission into Government Secondary School . . ." so soon after he had paid acceptance fees into two other schools, he stopped reading the telegram further while he initiated moves to see if he could halt the unnecessary expenditure into another school which was likely to be abandoned. Still carrying Okoli shoulder high, he called for his driver (chauffer) and told him to "get the car ready to take everybody to Kingsway stores by 5:00 p.m." that evening.

About 5:00 p.m. that same evening, Uncle took Okoli to Kingsway stores, the biggest department store in Enugu at the time, and bought him a children's three-piece suit, the first and only one Okoli was to have up to the time he graduated from the medical school many years later.

The Coin Box as a Bank

Okoli's uncle and his family and household lived for only two years at the rented apartment where Okoli had met Anayo and Janti. Uncle, as M. O. was often called, had bought land and built his own house along a bigger and more prominent street. The house overlooked the sports stadium. The house was a two-story building, and the occupants could, by standing on the balcony of the second floor, watch events occurring in the sports arena, as the walls of the sports stadium were relatively low. They thus did not have to pay and get into the stadium to watch the matches.

In fact, on certain Saturdays when Uncle traveled out of town or went out with his family, Okoli would allow a limited number of people who could not afford the minimum threepence official gate fee to watch the matches from the balcony for a fee of one penny each, paid directly to him, Okoli. Initially, the latter had contemplated allowing a number of boys (about ten) to come in and watch the matches free. But on one of these Saturdays, the surge was so much at the door that Okoli then had to impose a small fee of one penny per person. Usually the matches would be over before Uncle would return from his weekend evening trips to the nearby Recreation Club, where he played the game of billiards. The matches in the stadium were usually soccer matches, which would be over in an hour and a half. On that particular occasion, however, the match was delayed. It dragged on with extra time being granted.

It was getting late, and Uncle might be back any time. So Okoli told the spectators watching from the corridor to leave. He explained to them that his uncle would cane him if he met them there. They however insisted that they had paid Okoli and that they would watch the match till its conclusion. It was getting to five thirty in the evening, and Uncle usually came back about 6:00 p.m. But the spectators would not leave. The match was heating up. It was the finals of the league championships. Sensing danger, Okoli quickly reached for the Ovaltine container tightly sealed with a slit on the lid just wide enough to enter pennies. That was Okoli's "safe," where he stored all the money he got as gifts and later as "levies" from match spectators. He felt that the best thing he would do to get out the recalcitrant spectators was to reimburse them their money for them to go. He felt it was a better thing to do than to get into trouble with his uncle over the unwelcome guests. Okoli therefore forced the Ovaltine container open using a can opener. The lid had gotten so rusty that the lid could no longer open normally.

Okoli got out ten pennies and offered back to the "pirate" spectators. Only two accepted back their pennies and left. The other eight refused to accept back their money and stayed put. They stood there in the corridor shouting and yelling as the players in the field struggled to score. Okoli pleaded and pleaded with the pirate fans as he held out the pennies which they had paid him. But it was to no avail. He sweated profusely as he pleaded with the spectators to accept back their money, because he knew what lay in waiting for him if his uncle came back and found those strangers in the corridor, especially if he learnt that Okoli charged those people money. After Okoli started crying, one of the spectators came up to him and said quietly, "Give me six pence, and I will leave."

He obviously had seen Okoli when he opened the can, and he knew there were plenty of coins there.

In frustration the embattled, Okoli counted out six pennies and gave to the man. He had thought that the man would leave quietly. But no! The latter walked up to the other seven who were clapping and stamping their feet with every movement of the ball. He brought up the sixpence and holding the coins before one of the others he said, "Old boy, my penny don win sixpence."

His penny had indeed won him six pennies in under two hours!

After that damaging revelation, the man pocketed the money and ran down the staircase and was gone. Seeing a big chance to make money and seeing Okoli still holding the can containing coins on his hand, the other seven young men now came up to Okoli, demanding sixpence each. In fact, one of them said, "Na me last come so my own share go be double. You go give me twelve pennies before I fit go."

He was implying that since he entered last and the earlier entrants were being reimbursed six pennies that he would get twelve pennies. As the tears rolled down Okoli's cheeks, he pondered on whether he should negotiate further. But he soon heard the horn of his uncle's car signaling that the garage door should be opened for him. Okoli could no longer hold the urine in his bladder. With his pants wet with urine, Okoli, in desperation, inverted the coin box on the floor for his "captors" to collect their sixpence each. That was not to be. They noticed the dilemma and like uncoordinated pirates, scrambled for the coins. They took everything except the twopence that rolled off through the hand railing of the corridor to the ground below.

Over two years' savings had been wiped out from Okoli's treasury! The daylight pirates quickly left through the side door with their booty. As they left, Okoli followed them down to pick up the two pennies that had rolled out down through the opening beneath the handrail. He had to quickly wipe his tears before his uncle came in. He had learnt his lesson the hard way. It was a profitable business gone awry. Thereafter, no side spectators ever entered the house again, not on Okoli's invitation.

Pius and the Sweeper Boy

Pius was the youngest staff in the Chemist shop. He doubled as the messenger and the cleaner of the pharmacy premises. His duties also included mixing Mist Alba, a white-colored nasty-tasting laxative which people bought over the counter from the Chemist shop.

Pius's young age and carefree nature made him relate better with Okoli. Most Saturdays while going home from work, Pius would take Okoli with him to Ahia Four, an open minimarket which usually opened about 4:00 p.m. He would usually buy *suya*, barbecued peppered meat wrapped around sticks. He would also buy *kwoi*, boiled guinea fowl eggs used for contest. He would buy about six kwoi and give three to Okoli. The two would then compete about whose eggs would break when the tips were knocked against each other. Which ever person's eggs remained intact after collision would inherit both the intact and broken eggs.

Pius was a jolly, good fellow, and Okoli always looked forward to the weekends because of him.

It was Pius who provided what Okoli considered his very first employment. In addition to Pius's duties as a messenger and a cleaner, he was in charge of washing the bottles with which Mist Alba and other syrups were dispensed. These bottles were mostly discarded beer bottles and empty bottles of creams and balms. These were usually bought from bottle scavengers who hawked these bottles. Ndi olollo, as the bottle hawkers were called, usually carried large jute bags from house to house, striking at an empty bottle with a piece of metal and shouting olollo as they approached each house. People in any household who had any empty bottles to sell would then bring them to the olollo hawker at the front of the house. As many as ten to twelve empty bottles could sell for as little as one penny.

Many olollo hawkers used to assemble on Saturday mornings in front of the Chemist store laden with bags of empty bottles, which they would empty for Pius to choose from. Bottles with chipped edges or those that smelt of kerosene were usually rejected. Okoli used to assist Pius in the selection of the suitable bottles. After the olollo hawkers would have been paid, Pius and Okoli would collect the purchased bottles and immerse them into basins of water so that the bottle labels would loosen. They would thereafter wash the bottles with soap and water and scrub the inside using long-bristle brushes.

As time went on, Pius subcontracted the job of sweeping the pharmacy store to Okoli, who used to sweep the store after he came back from mass serving on Mondays through Saturdays. Okoli did not sweep the store on Sundays as he spent most of the Sundays serving at several masses. Besides, only skeletal services like dispensing of Mist Alba and sale of painkiller tablets (like Aspirin, APC, Codeine Co, and Panadol) were done by Pius alone on Sundays.

For the sweeping of the pharmacy store and assisting with washing of the bottles, Pius placed Okoli on a salary of one penny a week. He later increased this salary to one and a half pence and much later, twopence a week. Occasionally, too, when Pius got his monthly salary and Okoli happened to be around, the former would give Okoli two or threepence. Okoli initially used to keep the money in his schoolbag. Each day he got to school after the amount got up to twenty pence, however, he would be apprehensive about the possibility of Cletus or other big boys discovering that he had money on him. They would certainly provoke an issue that would justify their seizing Okoli's bag. Little did Okoli know that the money he saved from Cletus would be grabbed by some unknown soccer spectators who paid him one penny a piece only to empty his entire savings and leave him with only two pennies.

Okoli had devised the Ovaltine can "home safe" when his earnings from Pius got sizable, as a way of ensuring that he did not have easy access to the money, which would thereby grow with time. It was therefore a big irony that virtually all that he had saved were swept away in one fell swoop. That was a direct consequence of greed, a consequence of the Latin proverb, which he was later to learn in government college, that "amo amandi amondo crescit" (the love of having grows with having).

As his pennies grew, he got greedy and wanted to gather more wealth of pennies until he wanted to fill his can in one day by inviting soccer spectators to pay him a penny each, as previously narrated. Okoli's home safe consisted of an empty tin of Ovaltine, a popular brand of nonalcoholic beverage. Okoli punched an opening on the lid of the empty tin through which he threw in the coins as he earned them. The tin got heavier by the day. One of Okoli's big sources of joy was to shake the coin to be assured that his treasure was multiplying. The harsh sound of the coins in the tin made Okoli happy and gave him a lot of assurance that he was rich.

After the disastrous encounter with the pirate soccer spectators who wiped out his savings of many months, Okoli fashioned out another coin safe. By that time, his salary from Pius had increased to twopence a week. When it was getting close to Christmas, Okoli intensified his savings by now inserting every coin that visitors to the house occasionally gave him. Hitherto he used to save only his regular salary from Pius, and he spent at school on moi moi and *kwuli-kwuli* every other monetary gifts he got. Kwuli-kwuli was a cookie made from blended peanuts molded into a ring and fried in groundnut oil.

Okoli did not have many chores to perform in the house. There were lots of paid domestic help hired by his uncle, who by all estimates was a wealthy man.

Okon was the cook. People used to call him Okon-Calabar, a name that emanated from his town of origin. Okon was a very amiable young man. He must have been in his late teens or early twenties. He occasionally used to throw down some pieces of fried meat to Okoli each time the latter helped him deliver some wrapped items of cooked food to Nkechi, his secret girlfriend who lived across the road. Matthew was the steward. Celestine was the driver (chauffer) while Emeka, who was relatively young, doubled as gardener and general duties man. There was never a shortage of servants in Uncle M. O.'s house.

M. O.'s house was relatively modern. There was constant running water. He did not have to dig a pit to get good water pressure. Electricity supply under the then Electricity Corporation of Nigeria (ECN) was relatively regular. Coal from Enugu was used to generate thermal power from the nearby Oji River, and since there were only few consumers and no heavy industries, supply was adequate.

It was in M. O.'s new house that Okoli saw the water system (water closet system) of toilet for the first time. The first time that he saw a toilet flush, Okoli was both fascinated and troubled. It was about two weeks after the household moved into M. O.'s new house. Emeka, whose duty it was to wash the toilet and bath every morning, had taken Okoli along with him during one of his daily morning rounds. Somehow that section of the house was out of bounds to Okoli since it, being the only toilet in the main house, was adjacent to the master bedroom and was for the exclusive use of Oga and Madam (master and madam), Okoli's uncle and his wife, and their children who were still very young. When Emeka pulled the toilet handle and water started gushing out into the closet, Okoli was initially fascinated. But when the water kept coming, he took to his heels. He fled from the scene believing that Emeka had broken the water pipe and was about to flood the house. He did not want to be accused of having broken the water pipe. When a little later he saw Emeka coming in his direction, he immediately went on the defensive:

"I hope you won't say that I broke it," he started at Emeka, who was often known to argue with Matthew about who broke a plate or a tumbler.

"Broke what?" Emeka asked.

"That pipe in that little room upstairs," Okoli added.

"But no pipe was broken," added Emeka.

It took some time for Emeka to convince Okoli that the former had not broken a pipe to make so much water gush out from that white container. Okoli had to go upstairs again to confirm that the room was not flooded before he could believe that Emeka had not broken a water pipe.

One of the things that amazed Okoli most, the first two weeks after the household moved into the new house, was that he did not ever see his uncle and madam ever come down to use the bucket system toilet and the bathroom, the type in use in Aba. Both of these were in a small house built a short distance from the main building within the compound. Because Okoli was always wary of delaying Papa (as he called his uncle), Okoli always rushed out of the bathroom any time he heard somebody coming to use the bathroom. On one occasion, he just finished applying soap to his body when he heard somebody coming close to the bathroom. Believing that it might be Papa coming to use the bathroom, Okoli quickly emptied the bucket of water over his head and without wiping his body, he opened the bathroom door and rushed out with the empty bucket, clutching the bar soap and his clothes on the other hand. But it was not Papa that Okoli saw. It was Matthew, the steward.

"I thought it was Papa who was coming to use the toilet. That was why I rushed out," Okoli told Matthew.

"No, Oga does not use this toilet," replied Matthew.

"What toilet does he use?" Okoli still inquired rather curious since he was not aware of any other toilet in the house, and he did not fancy a toilet bucket being upstairs in the main house.

If that was the case, Okoli imagined, *how would the night soil man have access to the bucket and its contents, since the night soil men never enter the compound. They operate from the alleys between the different yards.*

"Oga does not go to toilet," replied Matthew with all the seriousness in the world.

"You know Oga is a chemist. He gives himself injection, and the injection dissolves every rubbish in his stomach and intestines including the feces," Matthew continued.

It made sense to Okoli who believed Matthew so completely that he never discussed the issue again nor asked any further questions. He even imagined that Uncle might be giving the feces-dissolving injection to his wife and children also since none of them was ever seen coming downstairs to use the bucket toilet system which Matthew, Okoli, Emeka, Okon, and the Chemist staff used. Okoli even looked forward to the day when he might merit getting that wonderful injection so that he would no longer be subjected to closing his nose to shield himself from the odor and flies of the bucket system toilet. May be if he came first in class again, Uncle might reward him by giving him that wonderful injection, and he could thereafter boast to Aboni, his friend; Ceewai, his cousin and best friend; and all those who would care to listen to him that he had no further need for any smelly toilets since every waste would be dissolved in his intestines by the injection.

It was not until the day that Emeka again took Okoli upstairs and showed him the way that the water system and bath situated upstairs functioned that Okoli realized that Matthew's story was false. It was also that day that Okoli was able to understand the function of the large pipes that descended from the side of the house, as well as the function of the cemented portions of the compound, the septic tank, and soak-away pit.

Okoli's only duty in the house was shoe polishing. After cleaning the bedrooms upstairs, Emeka would usually bring out the shoes to the corridor near the staircase for Okoli to polish. Usually Emeka would bring out all the shoes. With time, however, Okoli learnt to select only the shoes that were recently used, for application of polish and brushing. Initially, Okoli also used to polish Madam's shoes, but these were later moved over to Emeka to polish as many of them were very delicate, and Okoli had on two occasions accidentally cut the strings of which some of the ladies' shoes were made.

Whenever there were visitors to the house, it was also Okoli's duty to polish the visitor's shoes in the morning if the visitor stayed with the family overnight. One of the regular visitors to the house was Mack, M. O.'s cousin-in-law. Mack used to visit on weekends and would usually spend only one night. He was a very pleasant and jovial man, and whenever he would be going, Okoli would hover around since he was often sure to get a penny or two from Mack, perhaps as compensation for the latter's polished shoes. He was always very pleased with Okoli's shoe polishing. The inclusion of unusually long size 11 shoes among the shoes brought out by Emeka on any morning would indicate that Mack was around.

Okoli's room in the new house was one of two at the rear of the ground floor of the house. It was actually the room assigned to Cosi, Okoli's younger uncle. The room had a bed on which Cosi slept. A double-seater cushion chair, a reading table, and a back chair were other contents of the room. A wooden clothes hanger nailed to the wall served as the wardrobe. A small transistor radio on the table was a thing of delight. The radio picked only one station ENBS (Eastern Nigerian Broadcasting Service), and it was entirely battery operated. Okoli's entire earthly possessions consisted of his schoolbag, a tinker box measuring about three feet by two feet, containing his few jumper dresses, two pairs of school uniform, and his coin box. He also had a raffia mat on which he slept at night. Cosi's bed, a metal six feet by four feet Vono bed with tent poles, was shielded from the rest of the ten feet by twelve feet room by a curtain suspended by a string running from one end of the wall to the other. Okoli usually slept on his mat on the floor between the bed and the lone cushion chair in the room. If however there were visitors for his younger uncle, Okoli would usually spread his mat under the bed, and the bed curtain and overhanging bedspread would hide him from the view of the visitors. Sometimes during the harmattan season, the dry, relatively cold weather, when the floor would be cold, Okoli would choose to spread his mat under the bed and roll in there even if there were no visitors in the room. That kept him relatively warm. The location under the bed was also useful for him during the rainy season as it often shielded him from the ever-menacing mosquitoes, which were very plentiful during the rainy season.

It was in Okoli's final two years in the primary school after his younger uncle had vacated his room for further studies overseas that Okoli was "promoted" into having a room of his own. One of Okoli's aunts, Nwomiko, had come to live with the family, and she then "inherited" Cosi's room. Okoli's new room was upstairs adjacent the kitchen. It was an approximately seven feet by five feet cubicle, which was actually supposed to be the kitchen store. For the first time, Okoli had a bed to himself. It was an all-metal four-spring Vono bed. Okoli had a grass-stuffed mattress on it. He still had his raffia mat, and that came handy as bedsheet. It was a big improvement on Okoli's earlier mat-on-floor bed. Okoli felt very proud of his new Vono bed because not many of his peers at school had a bed of their own, not to speak of a room no matter how tiny. One of the rooms upstairs adjacent to Okoli's cubicle was the dining room. It had a wide standard dining table with six chairs and a much smaller dining table with four small chairs. The much smaller dining table was for Uncle's children. Okoli's meals were usually in the kitchen with Okoro and Matthew. Often Okoli would stuff his two pockets with the brown edges cut off while preparing sliced bread for sandwiches. He would pull these "off-cuts" of sliced bread from his pocket intermittently during recreation, and he was the envy of a lot of his peers. He considered himself privileged considering the general standard of living at that time.

Okoli and His Nanny Goat

After the Christmas celebrations before the start of the new school year, Okoli would go to Aba and sometimes from there to Arondizuogu. This was for him to spend some time with his parents. At the initial stages, Okoli's younger uncle would accompany him to the railway (train) station at the Enugu end. His father would usually wait for him at the Aba end. Okoli's father, Ogbuka, never failed to wait for Okoli at the railway station each time the former would return from Enugu. He continued that practice until Okoli was in the senior classes in the secondary school. Ogbuka would always lean on his lady's Raleigh bicycle, looking expectantly at the train coaches for his son, until the train would come to a halt. Under the scorching sun or pouring tropical rains, Ogbuka would wait. As soon as the train screeched to a halt and Okoli alighted, Ogbuka would hug his son and both would trek back to the house, with Okoli's tinker box luggage on the seat of the bicycle. It was usually a thing of great joy for Okoli to be back and to walk in the company of his father. The first thing he would usually announce to his father was his position in class. It was however the word *pass* that Ogbuka often wanted to hear. The class position aspect was more important to M. O. Okoli's uncle.

The train rides were usually very pleasant for Okoli, especially as he was usually stuffed with snacks and given some money for the journey. His ticket was usually half ticket, the ticket for minors, and that was about sevenpence. Uncle however usually provided money for full fare with instructions to Okoli to use whatever remained after ticket fare as pocket money. Each time he traveled, Okoli therefore usually arrived at Aba about seven pennies richer. He usually added this excess into his coin box, which he opened each holidays only in the presence of his mother at Ndiakunwanta. The first time he brought his coin box to his mother, Okoli was rather taken aback by his mother's reaction. He thought she would be very happy with the money. When Okoli brought out the metal can of coins, she initially smiled. She thought it was Ovaltine, a chocolate-based beverage. She had though that Okoli's father or uncle had bought a tin of Ovaltine for the latter for his holidays.

"You won't finish this before you go back, will you?" Eliaba told her son, still believing that the can contained Ovaltine.

"No, Mama, it is for you to buy me a goat with," Okoli said.

"I would want you to buy me a she-goat so that it will have kids, and I will have many goats," Okoli continued.

Ownership of goats and sheep was one of the ways for assessment of wealth. Okoli had always looked forward to the day that he would own his first goat. Eliaba, his mother, had three goats in her stable, and one of these was the nanny goat, which was given by her family during her marriage as tradition demanded. The significance of the nanny goat was that as the nanny goat was expected to have many kids, the woman being given out in marriage was expected to have many children in her new home. Usually a breed of goats that was known to be very fertile is fished out for such occasions. Indeed in parts of Igbo land, by the time a woman delivered her tenth child, a noncastrated he-goat (billy goat) is presented to her in celebration. If she should manage to deliver another four after the initial ten, another two goats will be presented to her. The feast of *eghu ukwu*, as the celebration is called, is usually a cause for big celebration. The eghu ukwu celebrant is usually highly respected in the society. That part of Igbo land was said to have one of the highest population densities in Africa.

Okoli's desire to have his first goat was quite understandable. The coins which he had meticulously saved in the Ovaltine can were his big treasure. He was already fancying how many goats the contents of the can could buy.

"But a tin of Ovaltine cannot buy a goat, assuming you succeed in selling it. So many stores now sell Ovaltine."

Okoli's mother continued as she watched Okoli struggling to open the lid with a penknife.

"Stop!" she said

"If you open the seal, nobody will agree to buy that Ovaltine. Prospective buyers will think that the contents have been tampered with. In any case we can always drink it if nobody buys," Eliaba continued.

Before she spoke more, Okoli had lifted off the lid from the tin and poured out the coins. Eliaba sprang back in great surprise. It was easy to see the worry and amazement in her eyes.

"Where did you get all that money from? Who gave it to you? Is this from Aba or from Enugu? Are your father and your uncle aware of this? No no no no! We don't steal in this family. I cannot have a thief as a son."

The barrage of questions and admonition followed in quick succession as Eliaba ran out of her room towards her kitchen even before her son could explain. In under a minute, she was back with a short whip. It was the first time she ever lifted a whip at Okoli since the latter left home. Okoli was the first of her six surviving children after she had lost her first son at infancy. She was therefore always so affectionate towards Okoli, especially as the latter lived away from home.

"Tell me truthfully where you got all this money from." She lifted up the whip.

"Tell me right now," she yelled almost tearfully.

It took a lot of explanation to convince Eliaba to lay down the whip. Okoli had to explain in great details how he got a salary of two pennies every week, how his uncle gave him excess transport fare, how he had been saving the pocket money given him by his father on his way back to Enugu, how Mack would give some pennies after he polished his shoes. He had to explain virtually every detail in between tears. It was after the detailed explanations that Eliaba got convinced and started to wipe her son's tears with her wrapper and slowly gathered back the coins into the tin.

The following day was Eke market day, one of the four market days in the town. By evening, Eliaba had came back dragging Okoli's first little nanny goat, the latter's first investment property.

Life at Aba

Whenever Okoli was at Aba from Enugu on holidays, most of his time was spent at 121, the house of his uncle Papa 121. The 121 was the house number of one of Okoli's paternal uncles at Aba. The children often called the names of their uncles by their house numbers. Okoli's father was usually called Papa 38. His most senior uncle was known as Papa Nke Ocha or Papa 175. The other uncle at Aba was known as Papa Enugu Street because he lived in Enugu Street, and street numbering had not been effected in Enugu Street at Aba by the time this uncle moved in. The youngest uncle had not gotten a house of his own and was consequently addressed by his actual name.

If Okoli arrived Aba by afternoon, he was likely to be at 121 by evening. The reason for this was simple. That was the house of Ceewai, the closest of his cousins to him. Ceewai was Okoli's best friend in the entire larger family. Most times Okoli went to 121, Ceewai would escort him back to 38, and the two would finally get down to Asa Road midway between 38 and 121, and there they would stand at the spot for hours on end before each would say good night to proceed in their two different directions. Sometimes they would repeat the process two or more times before finally parting for the night. By the following day before noon, they would again be together. There was always so much to discuss. Ceewai would tell Okoli his experiences in school at Aba, and Okoli would narrate his experiences at Enugu, how he often went to European quarters and polo field, and so on.

A lot of times the two cousins would go from 121 to 175. They usually visited Sister Patti at 175. Patti was indeed the mutual cousin of Okoli and Ceewai, but the word *cousin* did not exist in the customary vocabulary. Brother and sister existed and still exist. Patti had one friend who lived across the fence in the next yard. She used to sing together from across the fence with this friend. Okoli and Ceewai never met this friend of Patti's, but they could never miss her voice. Often Patti would shout from across the fence, "HIP"

Then her friend would respond, “Hip”

Patti would add, “PO.”

The friend would add, “Hippo.”

Patti would add, “PO.”

Then the friend would respond, “Hippopo.”

Then Patti would add, “TA.”

Then would come the response, “Hippopota.”

Then Patti would say, “MUS.”

Then Patti’s friend and everyone present would respond in unison, “Hippopotamus.”

It was a very pleasant song for all the children. Sometimes when Ceewai and Okoli came and Patti was not around, Ceewai or Okoli would initiate the song HIP. If they twisted their tongues and their unbroken voices well enough, Patti’s friend would respond with “hip.” But she would soon stop when she realized that it was not Patti’s voice.

The Marijuana Experience

By the time Okoli came back from Enugu on his first holidays to Aba, both Damian and Titus had relocated. Their parents were tenants where they lived close to Okoli, and they were both said to have bought their own houses and relocated with their families. Okoli therefore never got to try to derail any train during his subsequent trips to Aba. Besides, after he became a mass server, he came to regard all attempts at train derailment as a mortal sin even though he often missed those pranks he and Damian and Titus usually hatched. If the latter were still around, it was possible he might have tried one or two of the same pranks again.

Ceewai was a very quiet boy, soft-spoken, and very considerate. He was the one brother or cousin Okoli never ever fought with. Okoli at one time or the other fought practically every one else about his age. Despite his light build, he fought virtually everybody in his class at Enugu, even including his good friend Aboni. The only people he never attempted to fight were Cletus, the bully, and Banto, the muscle man of his lower classes.

Ceewai had one or two friends who were very rough and very mischievous. One of these his friends was called Bob. Bob was very fair. Some people used to call him *oyibo* (i.e., white man). On one occasion, Ceewai and Okoli were setting out from 121 to 175 when Bob came in. The latter then decided to accompany them to 175. On their way to 175, Bob took leave of the other two and said he would join them at 175 later. Some thirty minutes after Ceewai and Okoli got to 175, Bob rejoined them. He was sweating, and his eyes were reddened. He joined in eating the peanuts, which Patti had bought for her cousins. Soon after Patti left the house, Bob dipped his hands in his pocket and brought out a matchbox and a short rolled piece of paper. He tucked the rolled piece of white paper between his lips, struck the matchstick, and lit the paper. Ceewai and Okoli were both surprised. Though Bob's father smoked, Okoli and Ceewai had never seen Bob smoking. Indeed they had never seen anyone their age as much as handle a cigarette. But what Bob was handling did not appear to be a cigarette. It was more like a rolled piece of white paper, and it looked like Bob was merely trying to show off what it would look like, imitating the big boys by lighting a mere rolled piece of paper and smoking same. It might be big fun!

Okoli had met Bob a number of times, but he had never met him smoking cigarettes. Bob must have been a little older than Ceewai and Okoli, but he was obviously much more mature and looked more rugged.

He took a few puffs at the lit paper and offered same to Ceewai.

"It will make you high," he said.

Ceewai declined the offer, obviously looking amazed. Bob then offered the paper to Okoli. The latter had never ever smoked a cigarette before. It was the one vice none of his friends were into. Even Janti, the vicious ruffian and pigeon trapper at Enugu, was not into cigarette smoking. For a moment, Okoli thought of how it would look like being high from puffing at a lit piece of white paper simulating a cigarette. In any case, what was that type of tiny cigarette whose little puff would make somebody high?

He took the smouldering "paper" from Bob, put it between his lips, and inhaled a few puffs. No sooner did he do that when he started coughing spasmodically. He soon felt a little dizzy and started to vomit, expelling all the groundnuts he had eaten. As Okoli started to vomit, Bob snatched the paper from the latter's hands and quickly left the room. A middle-aged lady who lived in the yard came out as Okoli was retching and gave him some water and a spoonful of red palm oil. As Okoli sat on the pavement to recover, he swore to himself that he had tasted cigarette or any simulation of it for the first and last time.

It was many weeks later that Okoli again saw Bob near the market. The latter had a mischievous smile to his face. Okoli narrated to the latter his ugly experience after puffing at the paper, which Bob gave him to smoke, two weeks previously. He then expressed his disappointment at how Bob abandoned him at the latter's moment of difficulty.

Bob was not apologetic.

"You small boys, only two puffs of weed knocked you off," was Bob's reply.

It was then that Okoli realized what Bob had given him. It was marijuana!

GSSA: The Varsity on the River Cross

Okoli arrived at the premises of Government Secondary School Afikpo about five in the evening. It was his first day in the school as a student. He had set out by rail from Aba at about 7:30 a.m. along with many other students from different parts of the southern parts of the country. These were all strange faces to him. The students disembarked at Afikpo Road railway station at about twelve noon to continue the journey by wooden trucks called buses. Those students coming from Aba, Port Harcourt, Calabar, and the other southerly towns were joined by those coming from Enugu and other northerly towns by rail. Some others from Enugu had gone directly to Afikpo through Abakiliki.

There were all sizes and shapes of heads, the thin like Okoli's, and the fat—like the one whom Okoli later got to know who was called Nduke. There was one that was triangular that later got to be nicknamed Talinum Triangulare. There were those thin-legged and a few fat-legged ones. There were those in sandals and a few in shoes like another Okoli later got to know, who was called Donald. There were the very dark and the very fair like Gupta, whom the other students later learnt to be coming from Ethiopia. Most of the students alighted from passenger trucks with wooden benches. Two or three cars were however at sight. They were the cars that brought the ministers' children. These bore the plate numbers ENGS (Eastern Nigeria government service). All the students except the higher school students arrived the same day. The higher school students had arrived a few days earlier.

The vehicles conveying the students arrived through the farther one of the two entrances into the main school compound and parked between Ibiam and Farnfield houses. (Farnfield was said to be the contractor who built the school, while Ibiam was the first indigenous governor of Eastern

Nigeria in which region the school was located. Farnfield House was later to be renamed Okpara House.)

As the students alighted from the vehicles, it was easy to distinguish the new students from the older students. Not only were the majority of the new students generally smaller in size, the timid looks on their faces was an immediate indicator that the majority of them were new to the environment. Most of them were leaving their parents (or homes) to live in a strange place for the first time in their lives. Most of them were meeting for the first time, faces that they had never met before. They were, for the first time, coming to live in close proximity with people from widely different backgrounds, languages, and cultures, as there were said to be nearly two hundred and fifty languages spoken across the vast West African country. A few people like Okoli were more lucky. These lucky ones knew at least one person amidst the sea of heads. Okoli knew Aboni, his old school friend from St Brigid's.

As soon as the students' little boxes were unloaded from the trucks, the students were shown their different houses (dormitories) as had earlier been indicated on the detailed letters of admission. That was a relatively straightforward issue for most of the students. But for Okoli and a few others, it was a bit of a problem. The house designations were detailed in formal letters of admission. Okoli however had with him only the original telegram and had misplaced the detailed letter of admission. He probably had dropped it on his father's table in Aba after showing it to his father. He and a few other new students who had also misplaced their house allocations were therefore asked to wait in the cafeteria for the arrival of the prefect on duty, who would collect the master list of the different houses for these careless students to check for their houses. As the students waited, tired and apprehensive, they observed that one of them, whom they later knew was called Donald, was wearing only one shoe. The other foot was bare. But the boy did not appear to mind. He had probably forgotten the other shoe in the vehicle that brought him and some other boys down to school.

Soon the students all got to know their houses (dormitories). Okoli was assigned to Ibiam House, one of the three older houses which were each two-storied buildings. The other two were Farnfield and School houses. The boy Donald with the one-legged shoe was, like Okoli, assigned to Ibiam House. Unfortunately, Aboni, Okoli's friend, was assigned to another house farther down. His house, Okoli later learnt, was called Charles Low

House. Mr Charles Low, a Briton who migrated to Australia, was the first principal of the school.

As Donald, Okoli, and about four other boys walked to Ibiam House, all carrying their metal boxes on their heads, a series of hawkish-eyed boys passed by them and kept turning towards them muttering the word *or-ings*. On those first few hours at school, that word was so strange to the novices. These were to learn sooner than later the full meaning and the full implications of being an "or-ing." As soon as the novices got to Ibiam House, a group of four boys, those that had walked past them earlier, reemerged.

"Or-ings, why are you looking at us. Or-ings, why did you not greet us!" they yelled.

"You, or-ing"—pointing to Donald—"why are you wearing shoes?" said one.

"And only one shoe," said another.

"Or-ings, you are all very rude," said yet another.

"All of you go on your knees," said a fourth one.

It was all so strange to these new faces who were only a few hours old in school and who had never had any previous contact with these bigger boys not to talk of having the opportunity of ever being rude to them.

Which of the five of us bore the name or-ings? How and where were we rude to these boys? What offence had we committed to merit going on our knees?

These were some of the questions that went through the minds of the new students as they stood gazing at their unprovoked aggressors as these walked menacingly towards them. All the euphoria about transiting from being pupils to being students was fast evaporating. Donald was the first to kneel down in compliance with the orders of these new little masters. And the others immediately followed suit.

That was the baptism of fire, the first welcome to the culture of bullying which the new students were to experience for the next many months. As they knelt, their aggressors stood guard over them for a couple of minutes until they saw one bigger tall, lanky boy appear, and they quickly left. The tall boy, whom the novices later learnt was Etetoha, one of the house prefects, came up and asked Okoli and his kneeling colleagues:

"Who punished you?"

The novices did not know the name of any of the boys.

"Get up," he said as he walked off.

As the novices were pulling their boxes back onto their heads, their apparent messiah looked back and turned to Donald:

"But, you, you or-ing with fat head, why are you wearing shoes in school, and only on one foot? I will give you one run for that." He got out his pen and took down Donald's name on the palm of his hand as the rest of the group hurried away from the scene. It was all so strange.

Over the next couple of days, the novices began to learn the hard way the dos and don'ts in the school. Among these was that one must not wear covered shoes in school. Only sandals were allowed, and they must be brown colored. So it was obvious that Donald committed three "crimes."

First, he wore shoes in school.

Second, he wore multicolored footwear, black-and-white.

Third, he had a shoe only on one foot—improper dressing, the code name of the offence as the novices were to later learn. The house prefect must indeed have been benevolent to have awarded Donald only one run instead of three.

There was no handbook for the dos and don'ts, and nobody had warned the novices that they must not look at class 2 boys or worse still at people in higher classes. Besides on that first day of school, how were the new students to know who was a senior or who like them were or-ings, a name assigned to all novices in the school?

The novices were later to learn about the runs and the detention. A person punished with one run was made to make a timed run from the school water reservoir to the waterworks (the school's water pumping station situated about a mile away down a steep hill) and back. If the culprit did not complete the run within the stipulated time, he would be required to repeat the run. There was the house run, which could be "awarded" by house prefects and house subprefects. There was also the school run, which could be awarded by any school prefect or the school captain. The destination and duration for each run, whether house or school, was the same. Of course, any master (schoolteacher) could award runs even to the prefects. Detention was a more severe form of punishment, which was given for more serious offences. Only school prefects, house captains, and the school captain could give detention to erring fellow students.

Again, of course, any master or principal or his vice could award detention to any student. A total of six school runs in a single week would earn one detention. Repeated detentions in a single term could result in suspension from the school. This latter was a prerogative of the school principal. Detention involved the student having to be condemned to hours of grass cutting using a machete or cutlass on Saturday after the school inspection and parade. Being on detention in the government college was usually not regarded lightly, and it was not expected to be given for flimsy offences. Abuses were infrequent but when reported could be cancelled by a superior appointee or school authority.

In the assigned houses, students were allocated to corners, which consisted of wooden beds with a wooden locker adjacent each bed. Each bed was made from planks of six feet by thirty inches and suspended on two wooden stands. Each student had his personal white bedsheet (cover) and a personal pillow. Mosquito nets were used to cover each bed at night, and the students set their nets at night and would dismantle them by morning. The space between adjacent beds was about three feet. Double-bunker metal beds were not in use in the Government Secondary School Afikpo at that time.

"The School" as the students all proudly called Government Secondary School Afikpo had modern toilet facilities. Water closet system was in use as opposed to the bucket and pit systems that were used in most homes and some other schools at that time. Ceramic wash hand basins were in place.

The school had a central laundry, which accepted a maximum of four dresses a week from each student. There were no washing machines, and all laundry was manually done by the professional washer men, who were full employees of the school. There was a central dining room in which there were rows of benches and rows of tables. Jugs of water were allocated to the different tables.

Each student was expected to come to the dining room with his separate cutlery: a stainless steel knife, a table fork, and a table spoon, as well as his personal cup. The school prefects were provided special mugs by the school, and the college captain (captain of school) had a very special mug provided him by the school. The mugs were distinguishing features for the school prefects in the cafeteria. Also, the house and school prefects sat at heads of tables on stools instead of benches. Other seniors, especially the higher school students, sat at the ends of tables, and the order of seniority decreased to the middle of the tables, which were occupied by the most junior boys.

The food for the different tables was served in basins. It was the duty of the juniors to share out the food into the different plates. Whenever there was an excess of more than one piece of meat to a plate, the surplus was shared out in descending order of seniority starting with the prefects and the higher school students. There was an amazingly high standard of order and adherence to hierarchy in the system, and this was enforced over the years by a just and equitable run and detention system.

Dining hall etiquette was enforced from the first day at school. In fact, the principal himself gave talks to the students on acceptable and nonacceptable standards of dressing and etiquette. No student dared lick the spoon or worse still the knife with his tongue no matter how delicious the food was. Either behavior would earn two runs right away, and the prefects would always look out for such crude behavior. The same applied for holding the table fork on the right hand. Talking with food in the mouth earned two straight runs and refusal to pass down the water on the table when someone called for it earned one run. Calling for water without adding *please* earned one run and if the words *water please*, *salt please*, and *pepper please* were taken for granted. Any junior would omit a *please* at his own peril. By the time he got three or four runs for omitting a *please* while addressing a senior, he would learn.

There was pepperless diet and special diet for students who got letters from doctors indicating need for such diets. Such diets were given to such students at no extra cost.

The dining hall was built in a T-shaped form with all three arms of each T being of equal length. At the junction of the three arms of the T was placed the announcement table. It was from the announcement table that the prefect on duty said the grace (prayers) before meals.

As soon as the prefect on duty rang the bell for the end of any meal, all would stand for the grace after meals, which was said by the same prefect on duty.

"For what we are about to receive, we thank thee, oh Lord, for Christ's sake."

This was followed by a resounding *AMEN* from the seven hundred and twenty hungry young men, whose salivary glands would have been well activated by the impulses from the hypothalamic feeding centers. The sight and aroma from the steaming rice, beans, and stew placed in many large basins was enough stimuli for these centers.

Soon after, the chattering sound of hundreds of knives and forks against the plates would be heard from a hundred yards away. There were fast eaters and slow eaters. But Afikpo had little place for any weak masticatory muscles. One either chewed fast and finished one's food on schedule or the person might be late for the next activity, and the leg and thigh muscles of the slow eater and latecomer will pay the price with a run or two to the waterworks or even a much longer walk to Amasiri town junction, another form of punishment.

After an estimated thirty minutes of mealtime, the dining hall bell would ring again, indicating end of mealtime. All would again stand.

"For what we have received, we thank thee, oh Lord, for Christ's sake."

The end-of-meals prayer from the prefect on duty would again be followed by another chorus of amen. If it was a breakfast on Monday through Friday, the runs for the day would be read out followed by other announcements, and everybody would troop out of the hall. Apart from any food already in one's mouth, further eating during the announcement would attract two instant runs. There was such high standard of discipline almost akin to military discipline. This was not quite surprising since the school had a junior cadet unit to which students from class 4 upwards could enlist.

Soon after breakfast, Monday to Friday, the first bell would ring for morning assembly. This would be followed after intervals of three successive minutes by the second and third bells. By the sound of the second bell, whoever was not yet at the Assembly hall would need to start running to beat the sound of the last bell, which signified "lateness for assembly," whose penalty was two runs.

One or two prefects might be in some undisclosed places with pens and paper at hand for names of latecomers. And by the second bell, the principal would be on his way to the assembly hall. As soon as the third bell rang, he would walk into the assembly hall. Before then, most of the masters would have been seated on the semicircular row of chairs on a raised platform facing the sea of heads of students sitting in the massive very high-walled assembly hall. The principal's high table was located at the center of the semicircular row of chairs. The vice principal had a permanent seat at the number one position in the semicircular row of masters' seats.

Soon after the third bell, the principal would walk into the assembly hall, and all would rise. It was a near-perfect scene. It needed no rehearsals, no introduction even for the first day novice. It was a scene that gave a lifetime sense of nostalgia to anybody that passed through that system. The spontaneity and the uniformity were amazing.

The principal would then announce the first hymn for the morning. It was usually a hymn from *Songs of Praise,* a hymnbook which was placed on every seat in the assembly hall. The organist would strike the tune from the huge organ strategically located close to the principal's entrance door. The masterly fingers of Murah, the ace organist, and in later years Ekeani and Eketa in succession, scanning beautifully across the huge organ's keyboards, would ever-remain green in the memories of all who passed through that system during Okoli's school days.

The first hymn over, the morning's biblical lesson would be read. Then the second hymn, usually from the Psalms, would be sung. Some of these psalms, tongue-twisting as they seemed, while being sung would in later years form the enduring life principles for many who passed through that glorious system. Even the very motto of the school—"Fear God, honor the King"—was taken from one of those psalms.

The singing of the psalm over, the single full prayer was said by all: The Lord's Prayer.

The thing that would strike Okoli on the very first assembly was that after what he had been taught in St Brigid's School to be the last few words in The Lord's Prayer—"And lead us not into temptation but deliver us from evil"—at Afikpo, most of the students and staff continued with the phrase he had not come across before: "For thine is the Kingdom, the power, and the glory, forever and ever."

For a while, on Okoli's first assembly day, he thought these many were making a mistake when they did not just say amen after "but deliver us from evil."

Or was he the person making a mistake? He looked over his shoulders to be certain that he, or some other people, had not gone crazy or had not started "speaking in tongues." But when he saw that even the principal, the vice principal, and the majority of the masters were also muttering those apparently strange words, he felt that he must be the person making the mistake. It was much later that he came to realize that neither he nor any of the hundreds of others were in fact making a mistake.

It was only that while the Roman Catholics would stop the Lord's Prayer at "but deliver us from evil," the Anglicans (Episcopal), Baptists, Methodists, and other Christian religious denominations would continue thus "for thine is the Kingdom, the power and the glory, forever and ever."

The passage of time came to teach Okoli that contrary to what he might have been taught in the primary schools, no denomination nor indeed religion was inherently totally evil when practiced according to the books. He was to realize that no denomination should be considered superior, that practice of one or the other was often an accident of birth, and that the summary of it all was, and remained, that all were children of the same God and that only mutual love, understanding, and respect of each other's views could save humanity.

Okoli was later to discover that many of his friends who came from different denominations or religious backgrounds were really good and trustworthy individuals. He came to recognize that one's denomination or religion did not make the individual inherently good or bad as both kinds of people could be found in any religion. He came to recognize that extremism in matters of religion could only spell doom for humanity and that only by tolerance could humanity progress. This, Okoli recognized, is because violence, religious intolorance, and extremism—not being the prerogative of any religion—could only, if reciprocated by any victims, do mankind no good. Finally, he came to understand that generalizations and stereotyping, in matters of religion, could be very misguided.

The assembly over, the principal would go out of the hall through the same front door from where he had entered. The vice principal and all the other masters on the podium would file out through the door at the back of the podium.

It was then and only after then that the rest of the students, starting with the captain of school (who often sat at the front row with the other school prefects), would move out through the multiple doors opening into the assembly hall. After the exit of the principal and masters and shortly after the exit of the captain of school, it would look like a hive of bees was suddenly let loose, with all the buzzing and the shuffling of feet, as the students moved briskly from the assembly hall to the classrooms. The principal and his vice had their offices in a separate building housing administrative matters. The rest of the masters had a separate large office adjoining one of the classrooms and known as "Staff Room."

Soon after the assembly hall activities, the bell would go for the first lesson to begin. At one-hour intervals, the bell would also go for change of lesson. Break was usually between 11:30 a.m. and twelve noon. *Punctuality* was the watchword in all that was done in Government Secondary School Afikpo.

The last lesson (lecture) was usually over by 2:00 p.m. Lunch was between 2:15 p.m. and 2:45 p.m. By 3:00 p.m., every student was expected to be in his bed for siesta. Siesta was mandatory and talking or even reading in bed during siesta was a punishable offence. Each house was subdivided into sections, and each section had a section head, who was usually a house prefect overseeing between twenty-four and thirty-six students. There were usually four sections in each house. Only the house captain had a private room in each house. The house captain's room was centrally located. Most houses had an additional school prefect, who often deputized for the house captain in the latter's absence.

During siesta, the school would appear to have come to a standstill. One could hear a pin drop. Even a visit to the toilet (restroom) had to be with permission from the section head.

When the bell went for the end of siesta, the school would again come alive. It would be time for games or schoolwork.

On one evening in a week, each house would have schoolwork during which members of the house concerned would cut grass or do some manual work around the school premises. The other houses would be involved in games. For games, there was the upper field lying between the dormitories and the classrooms and administration block and the lower field, which lay across the major road adjacent the gmelina tree plantation. The upper field, which was the older field, was used for athletics, soccer, hockey, cricket, high jump, and long jump. By its northern end was the pavilion, where sports equipments were stored and from where the competitors entered the field. The front of the pavilion also served as the VIP stand from where the principal, other members of staff, and visiting dignitaries watched matches. All other spectators watched the matches standing around the perimeter of the pitch.

Dinner was usually served by 6:30 p.m. By 7:15 p.m., the bell would go for prep. *Prep,* as the official evening study time was called, was the official period for revising the day's work, doing some private studies, and preparing for the next day's classes. Prep was usually taken very seriously. There were special prep monitors for each class as distinct from normal class monitors.

Absence from prep, noisemaking during prep, or sleeping during prep attracted runs, if the names of such offenders were copied and submitted to the school prefect in charge of prep for the week.

At the end of prep period, depending upon the particular day of the week, there would either be school prayers conducted in the assembly hall or house prayers, conducted in the common room of each house.

By 9:00 p.m., the bell would go for junior "lights out." Junior lights out was bedtime for all classes 1 and 2 students. Senior lights out was by 10:00 p.m. for classes 3 to 5 students. The higher school students had the benefit of extended lights out and could usually read till 11:00 p.m. By lights out, all the particular students concerned were expected to be securely in bed under their mosquito nets. There was not expected to be any reading, talking, or snack eating. Each of such actions would attract some punishment. *Cockroaching*, a name given to secret reading after lights out using torchlight or hurricane lantern, was also forbidden. Cockroaching was particularly looked out for by the school authorities, especially around examination time. Around such times, some students devised all kinds of measures to evade detection while cockroaching. Some students would construct "carton and lamp" slit lamps by which a hurricane lantern would be turned low and be hidden inside a closed thick paper box with a small hole made at the side of the box to let out a point of light. The point of light would then be directed at the book being read without anyone else seeing the light from a distance. Using such techniques, some students—especially the very senior ones who headed sections—would be able to read late into the night without being detected by the school masters on duty or even by the principal when the latter chose to go round to check after lights out.

"The School"

Government Secondary School Afikpo was built under the British colonial administration of Eastern Nigeria. It was therefore possibly fashioned after the British educational system. The layout of the school was a planning and architectural masterpiece. The school lay on both sides of the road leading from Amasiri to Afikpo town. On one side of the school lay the principal's house, the classrooms, the laboratories, the technical workshops, the administration block, and the assembly hall. On that side also was the upper field, the halls of residence (houses), the dining hall, and the laundry. On the other side of the road lay the vice principal's house, the other masters quarters, the gmelina tree plantation, the lower field, and the labor line (the artisans' quarters).

Flower hedges and many ornamental trees adorned the entire compound, and the compound was a beautiful sight to behold.

For many of the students, the facilities were the best they had ever seen, especially for those coming from the undeveloped villages. Even for those who lived in urban areas like Enugu, Aba, Port Harcourt, and Onitsha, the buildings and other facilities they saw at Afikpo were the best they had ever seen. For some students like Okoli, though they lived in the cities, they were not used to facilities like the water closet system even when they had seen them before. For those from the rural areas, the water closet system was a complete novelty. In all, it was very uncomfortable for most students initially having to use the toilet sitting down when they had been used to squatting on wooden crossbars or on concrete or wooden slabs placed across blocks for the bucket or pit latrines. Many students therefore, initially resisted sitting on the toilet seats since they could not defecate sitting down. Standing or squatting on the toilet seats often fractured or broke the seats of the toilets or dislocated the ceramic bowls from their bases.

On three occasions within the first week in school, the toilet seats in Ibiam House, Okoli's hall of residence, dislocated and broke when unknown students squatted on them instead of sitting on them. The stories were about the same from many of the other houses and were said to be a yearly occurrence at the beginning of each school year. The culprits were often never caught. A surveillance team was thereafter set up by the house captains of the different houses in the school to track down people who would stand or squat on toilet seats instead of sitting on them. The task of the surveillance team was made easier by the fact that each toilet door was given a clearance of one foot from the floor. The members of the surveillance team could therefore easily detect any student who was using the toilet squatting on the seat. If the legs of the occupant of any toilet were not seen from under the door, then obviously the occupant was squatting on the toilet rather than sitting on it.

Donald was made a member of the toilet-seat surveillance team. He was the class 1 representative in the team, and he was very enthusiastic about the post and the apparent sense of importance it afforded him. As soon as he heard any toilet door squeak open, he would swing into action. He would leave his corner and go peeping under the doors to check for the legs of the occupant of each toilet. Mezoke and Okoli were the first two people Donald caught within the first few days of the setting up of the surveillance team. The two were accused of having been responsible for the three toilets broken the previous week. On Okoli's part, he knew he did not break any toilet seat, but he did indeed squat on the toilet seat. Since the true culprits were not immediately caught, Mezoke and Okoli were made to bear the consequences for the broken seats. They got their first three runs in the school for "barbarism, disobedience, and willful damage to school property." The first count of barbarism was very painful to Okoli since, coming from Enugu which was a city, he had always thought he was one of the elitist students in the school. But the act of standing or squatting on a ceramic toilet seat instead of sitting on it was obviously considered an act of a barbarian. Ignorance was never considered an excuse in Afikpo. Okoli had hitherto felt that only Mezoke should be called a barbarian since the latter said he came from an interior village and had never been to any urban area with electricity. Okoli's hitherto bloated opinion of himself was punctured when his name was announced for barbarism.

The trial was very straightforward:

"You have been standing on the toilet seat while using the toilet," said the prefect to Okoli.

"Yes, sir, but it was only today," Okoli replied in self-defense.

"Don't sir me. Say yes, please," the trial prefect interrupted.

"Yes please, but it was only for today. Today was my first time of squatting on the toilet seat," Okoli said.

"But you broke the toilet seats last week by standing on them," came the second charge.

"No, sir; sorry, sir. No, please, sorry please," Okoli tried to counter.

"But you admit you displayed an act of barbarism by squatting on the toilet seat and breaking them this afternoon, contrary to school rules," the prefect charged.

"No, sir, I am not a barbarian. Yes, sir, I squatted on the seat, please it was only today."

Okoli admitted, trembling and still feeling hurt at being labeled a barbarian, a term which, in Okoli's conceit, should be reserved only for Mezoke and others who came from the villages.

"You don't deny it. You and Mezeoke were caught squatting on toilet seats. So you must also have been the people who broke the toilet seats last week."

Verdict: Guilty as charged.

Sentence: Mezoke three runs. Okoli, three runs.

End of trial.

Tail Cutting

From the second day as students, the novices were being told by the class 2 students that they, the class 1 students, had tails and that their tails would be cut. Once in a while if they passed across the class 2 boys, the latter would say to them, "Or-ings, your tails are overgrown."

The new students had heard stories that tail cutting was a ceremony for initiating new students into the school community. Some of the new students were in fact looking forward to it since they believed they would thereafter be considered full members of the school community. Others among them who heard the whole story however were rather apprehensive about the ceremony.

Tail cutting was fixed for the fourth Saturday after the arrival of the new students. One week prior to the appointed day for tail cutting, however, some overzealous class 2 boys had already started having skirmishes and organizing what they called "mock tail cutting."

On the third Saturday in the school, shortly after supper, a group of four class 2 boys lead by Ebiobo a short but stout class 2 boy cornered about six class 1 boys as the latter were about to leave the dinning hall and ordered them back into the dining hall. They then asked the novices to creep under one dining table. The latter all complied. That effectively hid the latter from the view of passersby. Three of the six culprits were from Okoli's house, Ibiam House: Mezoke, Ugogod, and Okoli. The other three were from some other houses.

Ebiobo the leader of the group then read the charge against the captives, "We hear some of you are carrying bushes around the compound. Yes or No?"

Each of the captives of course denied carrying any bushes about anywhere. Of course, there were bushes around the school compound, but there was no way these new students could be carrying these bushes around the compound. But it was a different connotation of "bush" that

Ebiobo was talking about, one not known to the these younger minds, a vulgar connotation of bush.

"You are all lying, or-ings," said Ebiobo again.

"We shall soon find out," he continued.

"Now pull down your pants and walk over to the other table one by one," Ebiobo ordered again as two of the bullies stood looking fiercely into the faces of the frightened novices. The fourth bully stood guard at the door to look out for any approaching prefect or a more senior boy, or a bully's bully like Abuuzuu, who might come around and stop the exercise or even descend on the bullies themselves.

The novices again complied, each removing his shorts and underwear as ordered. Only their shirts remained on as each walked past Ebiobo to creep and kneel under the adjoining dining table. As the captives walked by, the captors all kept silent until Mezoke walked across. Mezoke was a fairly big boy and was probably the oldest of the class 1 boys in the school for that year. As soon as the latter pulled down his pants and the captors sighted his pubic hair, there came the spontaneous response from all four bullies, "There he is, the bush man." The captors all shouted in unison.

"Get back under the table. You were lying to us. You have been carrying bushes around the compound. Today we shall shave these bushes with broken bottle."

That was the final verdict against the hapless Mezoke.

The bullies then ordered the rest of the captives to scamper (run from the scene).

It was later that the escapees learnt that they had been let off because they had not grown pubic hairs. Ebiobo and his gang of bullies had given the hapless Mezoke a thorough beating for coming to school with pubic hairs, a normal developmental process commensurate with his age. The victim probably only escaped shaving with broken bottle, as threatened by his captors, because before his captors could secure a bottle to break for a tool, the bell was said to have sounded for beginning of siesta!

The victim was not to report the incident; consequently, no charge for barbarism was labelled against Ebiobo and his group even though every class 1 boy got to hear the story.

After inspections on the appointed tail cutting day, and even on the night before the event, the class 2 boys were unusually upbeat. They were all so busy gathering empty cans, charcoal, black paint, mud, rags, brushes, and all kinds of discarded rubbish. It was learnt that Ebiobo and his group had been collecting their urine into empty paint gallons for about one week preparatory to the tail-cutting exercise. The stored urine was to be used as "perfume" for the or-ings during the exercise.

The novices got more apprehensive as the day wore on as they got to realize that the tail-cutting exercise was indeed another form of bullying. They began to wish and pray that the principal or some other school authority would step in to stop what was officially sanctioned as an innocuous tradition, but one which had been hijacked by bullies and converted into a near-barbaric tradition.

Apparently however tail cutting was officially endorsed by the school authority even though it was doubtful if they were aware of the whole extent of the event.

That the event was officially endorsed was evidenced by the school bell heralding the year's tail-cutting event starting to ring about 3:00 p.m. on the appointed Saturday. The class 1 boys were all told to proceed to the lawn tennis court. As they apprehensively walked towards the tennis court situated between Farnfield House and Charles Low House, they kept looking over their shoulders to see if there were some school prefects around so that the potential tormentors could be moderated. They did not see any. On getting to the lawn tennis field, the A and B classes were separated, and the tail bearers were asked to line up in single files.

At the far end of the field, the novices could see Ebiobo, "the Terrible," as the novices had already nicknamed one of their most vicious tormentors. He was at his best that afternoon, mixing concoctions in a bucket, too busy even to notice the arrival of his potential prey. Even Aniobu, who used to sit close to Okoli in Sunday masses and whom many class 1 boys regarded as very mild in the bullying game, was there holding an open paint gallon containing some material with a long paintbrush sticking out from the gallon.

The novices were then ordered to file past the circle formed by the class 2 boys. The order was issued by one of the class 2 boys, one very tiny one called Erim, whom many of the other class 1 boys could squeeze in any one-on-one combat. But Erim was in class 2, and that gave him all the immunity and authority. Class 1A was paraded first. As the group had filed up in alphabetical order according to the class register, Okoli whose surname started with *A* was number three in the row after Abe and Age.

Okoli looked behind him as they were about to commence with the procession. He saw Mezeoke and a few others crying, even before it got to their turn to move. Mezeoke was bigger than most of the class 2 boys, and he was often the target of the worst bullying. The class 2 boys probably often wanted to demonstrate that his size did not guarantee him any immunity. Donald, who used to cry very easily at the slightest threat from the class 2 boys, was surprisingly not crying that day. Perhaps his membership of the toilet surveillance group had given him added self-confidence. Further behind, Nfua, the tiniest boy in the whole class, also maintained a straight face and a stolid look. Okoli gathered courage from these two.

When Abe approached the first class 2 boy, the latter painted Abe's white shirt with black paint. The second boy poured some dirty-looking liquid into the pockets of the latter's shorts; the third urged him on without touching him. It soon got to Okoli's turn. It did not look too bad an experience at first. Okoli moved along, only getting some dirty brushing with all colors of paint on his face, arms, and shirt. He kept looking ahead for when he would get to Ebiobo, "the Terrible." He soon got to Aniobu. He had thought that the latter would just signal him on since he, Aniobu, had always appeared so friendly. That was not to be. Aniobu dipped his brush into his paint gallon, pulled back the collar of Okoli's shirt behind, and stuck the brush between the latter's shirt and his back. The instant irritation was unbearable, and Okoli uttered a big yell. What was it that Aniobu added to the mixture that irritated so much? Could it have been pepper or what?

"Et tu brute!" Okoli started crying as he now hurried past Ebiobo, who merely succeeded in giving him a punch at the back with his fist. He did not have enough time to wreck more havoc. There was no attempt at running away completely though. The or-ings had been warned that any one who ran away would be brought back to undergo the process at a later date.

By the time Okoli got to the end of the circle of class 2 boys, he was dripping from head to toe with dirty, smelly fluids of all colors. The irritation from Aniobu's fluid had luckily been soothed by the subsequent tar and palm oil and perhaps urine which subsequent tail cutters had poured on Okoli. The lone function of the last class 2 boy in the tail cutting circle was to lash the tail bearer with a whip ostensibly to thrash out the tail. This was partly to force the victim to escape fast from the scene, partly to initiate the victim as a bona fide member of the school community. Most likely the hot lash was as a final step in whipping out the long tail, which the victim might have grown in primary school prior to his entry into the noble club of the elite that was the Varsity on the Cross, Government Secondary School Afikpo.

The tail cutting exercise was not to be complete without the victim passing through the hands of Abuuzuu, the highly intelligent and talented class 4 boy who was said to have participated in every tail cutting exercise since his class 2 and who could occasionally bully even the classes 2 and 3 boys if they crossed his path. Abuuzuu stood there like a colossus and appeared to have effectively monitored and supervised the exercise for that day. Even though he held a long whip, he was not seen using it that day. Indeed his presence appeared to have tamed super bullies like Ebiobo, who constantly looked in Abuuzuu's direction as they painted the class 1 boys during the exercise. They themselves might get squeezed if they went against Abuuzuu's unilaterally set rules.

The conclusion of the tail cutting ceremony was one big load off the mind of every class 1 student. The only significant casualty of the ceremony was Mezeoke, who sustained superficial burns to his face and had many blisters at his back, possibly from multiple whippings. After the incident, he kept saying that he would "retaliate on next year's class 1 boys." Luckily, that was not to be because before the following year's tail cutting came on, there were changes in the top administrative machinery of the school, and the new leadership ensured a better supervision of the ceremony to curb the obvious excesses.

Academic and Sports Excellence

Academic excellence was the hallmark of Government Secondary School Afikpo. Next to Government College Umuahia, Afikpo probably had the largest number of graduate teachers in Eastern Nigeria. A good combination of academic excellence with sound participation in sports was encouraged. Thus, there were people like Okonko, who was nicknamed Bob Hayes, Kodumodu, Meriom, and Nokebu—who were all able to combine high class ratings with sports stardom.

Most of the science teachers were Indians, and they were excellent in importing sound scientific knowledge into the young minds at Afikpo. There was one Mr Mathew in biology, Mr Patel in zoology, and two Mr Mathews in physics.

"Fijix is ijii," Mr Mathew senior would always say even when the students found no ease with the speed at which he imparted the knowledge of the subject, physics. Mr Gupta served transiently in chemistry, but the real chemistry star teacher was Mr Vice Principal, a Briton. The latter was so good that hardly would anybody pass through his chemistry classes without falling in love with chemistry. The students used to call him "e-e-qua" because of his emphasis on chemical equations. The dexterity of his left fingers as he ran the chalk on the blackboard inscribing the long chemical equations pronouncing the word "e-e qu-a-a shion" as he concluded made the subject appear so simple.

Mathematics had a pride of place in the school curriculum in Afikpo. The subject was popularized by Mr Oko, whom the students called Mantissa. Mantissa was so passionate about the students mastering mathematics that during the process of teaching the subject, he would often inadvertently smear his face and nose all over with chalk. In between Mr Oko's determined efforts to explain the intricacies of trigonometry, Mtama, the mischievous lanky boy in class 1B who was nicknamed Kpoghilikpo, would shout from behind, "Excuse, sir, I don't understand." Mantissa would now in desperation throw the chalk on the ground and rub more chalk on his nose.

"Echuz chaa, I junt chunjastand," (Excuse, sir, I don't understand) he would say mimicking Mtama.

"What don't you understand? Can't you use your brain?

Better remove the saw dust in your skull and install some brains?"

But Mantissa would again pick up the chalk and restart the explanation. Such dedication as there was in the teachers in Afikpo was hard to surpass.

There was however also a few masters like a geography master whom the principal (and students) did not appear to have so much confidence in. Mr E., as the students often called him was hardly ever sure of where any mountain or desert or river or country capital was situated on the map of the world despite his being the senior geography master. He was actually said to have been a major in another subject but was deployed to teach geography by the Ministry of Education because of the shortage of geography masters. The principal soon got to notice the deficiencies and would sometimes come into the geography classes of Mr E. The former would come in and occupy a seat at the back row.

The principal's presence would make Mr E. more nervous. Mtama would then take advantage and then ask Mr E., "Please, sir, where can we find the Himalayas?" After dashing gazes between the blackboard and the Principal's direction, Mr E. would then run his palm over a map of the United States and Canada! If he felt that the principal did not appear to approve of his guess, he would then reverse his hand and run his fingers from India through Indonesia to Malaysia. A redeployment of Mr E. did not take long in coming.

Even though emphasis was so much in the science subjects, Afikpo had a crop of very good arts teachers. The principal, though did not take regular Latin classes, was a master's graduate of Latin language. There were also two other senior Latin masters. One of them was Mr Merumaka who was nicknamed Cha cha. Before Cha cha, there was Salwe, whose nickname virtually obliterated his actual name from the students' memories. The name arose from his insisting on greeting the students in Latin and the latter responding in Latin whenever he entered the class. From the front door of the class, Salwe would shout, in greeting to the class. "Salvete pueri," he would say.

"Salve magista," the students would reply.

Even when it was said that Latin was a dead language, the students at Afikpo found that over half the students who passed through these dedicated Latin masters spoke fluent Latin, and somehow this mastery of Latin was to help them greatly in their comprehension and use of the English and other Latin-based languages.

In the history class, there were also very sound and knowledgeable and dedicated teachers. The dedication of the history teachers was such that Afikpo, though science oriented like most government colleges at the time, started attracting higher school students in history from other highly rated secondary schools. Many of the private and voluntary agency schools could not afford the high cost of equipment and recruitment of expatriate teachers in the sciences, and so they concentrated in the arts subjects. But Afikpo was able to excel in both the sciences and the arts. Because of the emphasis on the sciences, it was found that most of the students in the government colleges did medicine, engineering, architecture—the pure sciences. That trend resulted in paucity of products of the government colleges in administration, a trend for which a high price had to be paid. Tubia, one of the bright science students, would walk past Ivekwe, who was into arts, and derisively ask him, "When did King Henry die?"

That question implied that since Ivekwe was studying history, he only knew dates of events and that history as a subject was only about the study of dates. But Tubia as a surgeon would later spend the better part of his life performing surgical operations in diverse theaters, only to struggle belatedly to get into administration. But the man who studied when King Henry died would have spent the better part of his life in cozy offices and perhaps would have participated in the formulation of the job conditions under which Tubia would function. Such was the result of undue emphasis on any sphere of life or the wrong impression that any discipline was superior to another even if it appeared to attract higher wages.

Social Deprivations and Their Negative Effects

Mr Ble-gum was newly posted to the school as a history teacher. He must have been in his early fifties but had a very young wife. He was one of the few masters whose residence was on the same side of the road as the student's hall of residence. Indeed his was the only master's house which was situated fewer than three poles from the nearest student's house and on the road through which the students went to classes. It was said that the big boys, the higher school students, were making passes at Mr Ble-gum's young wife from across the flower hedge, as the latter's residence was not properly fenced. Mr Ble-gum soon got to hear of the activities of these higher school students who were said to occasionally stop for a few minutes in front of his house as they appeared to be admiring the flowers.

Initially Mr Ble-gum was a very articulated and dedicated history teacher. But it was soon noticed that he was getting increasingly absentminded while teaching. He would come into class, place his books on the table, and immediately walk towards the window overlooking his residence. He appeared to live in perpetual fear of the possibility of any of the senior students talking to or even greeting his newly married young wife from across the fence.

"Our topic today i-s-s-s . . ."

Mr Ble-gum would then gaze through the window for some seconds.

"Our topic today is-s-s . . . The topic is, hmm, the downfall of the Roman Empire."

Then there would be another long pause and prolonged gazing towards his house across the road.

"What did I say? Yes, the downfall of the Roman Empire. The downfall of the Roman Empire. Yes, I mean, the de-e-e . . . de-e-cay of the Roman Empire."

He could go on repeating the phrase "the decay of the Roman Empire" over and over again until something else would again interrupt him and recall his attention. And as the embattled Mr Ble-gum repeated the same phrases, he would keep stretching his neck through the classroom window in the direction of his house.

With time, the chief mischief maker Mtama would deliberately come late during Mr Ble-gum's classes and on his way pause for a few seconds in front of Mr Ble-Gum's hedge, if only to provoke the embattled teacher. As soon as he knew that Mr Ble-gum was well in class, Mtama would set out from the dormitory, and on reaching the front of Mr Ble-gum's house, he would halt for a few seconds and appear to be arranging his books. Invariably, that would set off increased pauses, repetitions, and neck stretching by the embattled gentleman in the direction of the supposed intruder. Even after Mtama would have left, Mr Ble-gum would still continue his intermittent glances in the direction of his house. Occasionally, he would stand still at the window, only to continue the forward and backward pacing to monitor events around his fence, just to be sure that no intruder was talking to his young wife from across the fence.

It did not take long before the generality of the students learnt that Mr Ble-gum's distractions, repetitions, and constant peeping through the class window was to ensure that some higher school boy did not attempt to take advantage of his absence from home to chat with his young wife. Some eight months later, it was learnt that Mr Ble-gum had applied for a transfer from the school. Such was the result of the activities of some seniors in the school. Such, perhaps too, was the result of excessive regimentation of young adults as obtained in Afikpo of Okoli's time.

In later months, stories were told of some senior boys who jumped the fences to go to labor line in search of girlfriends. The labor line was situated adjacent the lower games field and consisted of a cluster of about ten small houses built for the junior and intermediate staff of the school: the cooks, security men, laundrymen, laboratory technicians, laborers, and so on. Repeated announcements were made during daily assembly restating that the labor line was completely and permanently out of bounds to all students. It did not appear however that the threats of runs and detention were enough to deter the big boy fence jumpers and bound breakers as the number of seniors, especially the classes 5 to upper sixth boys, placed each Saturday on detention for jumping the fence to labor line continued to grow.

By the following term, after Mr Ble-gums's exit, perhaps as a way of diverting the attention of the fence jumpers, the school announced that the higher school students would be allowed to receive female visitors from the school of nursing of the Mater hospital in the town. The visits were restricted to one hour on the first Saturday of each month, and the visitors were restricted to the common room of each house. The school also started to allow exchange Debating Society visits from some selected girls secondary schools. These schools included Queen's School Enugu, Cornelia Corneli College (CCC) Uyo, St Catherine's College Nkwerri, Queen of the Rosary College Onitsha, and Girls Secondary School Elelenwa. These exchange visits were limited to the Senior Debating Society members. The Senior Debating Society thereafter became so attractive that only about 10 percent of applicants could be accommodated each year. The president of that society became a celebrity of sorts.

Any day there was to be a visit from any of the girls' schools to Afikpo, the senior boys would be full of life, polishing their sandals and reironing their shirts and blazers. For the whole of that day, the classes 1 to 3 boys would be confined to the dormitories by the very senior boys. Any one of the latter seen beyond the upper field which separated the class rooms from the dormitories could get as many as three runs at one go. Any such trespasser would be awarded three runs for "enjoying senior jokes" or for "looking at seniors in ways calculated to embarrass them." And, of course, multiple seniors could be simultaneously embarrassed by one single or-ing who for one single wrong look in the wrong direction could gather enough runs from each of the seniors to merit a detention into the bargain.

The Academic Assessment and Leadership Systems in Afikpo

The continuous assessment system that was in use at Afikpo was known as the Form Order System. By this system, the average of the scores in the weekly tests constituted 50 percent of the term's class result. The term's test constituted another 50 percent.

On the last school day of each term, the entire school would gather in the assembly hall for the terms class-by-class result. The process was called "mark reading."

It was usually the day that the academic giants looked forward to. The academically unsound always dreaded the mark reading. All the masters and all the students would gather, and the result and class position of every student starting with class 1B to upper sixth class would be read publicly.

The principal would walk in as on a normal assembly, but this time he would carry with him the compiled results of all the classes submitted earlier in the day by the different form masters to him. The mark reading would thereafter commence. The mark reading and prize-giving day was usually a day of academic verdict as the school principal read out the results:

"Class 1B, thirtieth position out of a class of thirty, is . . . Twenty-ninth of out of a class of thirty is . . . ."

Starting from bottom to top, the names and position of every student without exception would be read. As the tally decreased, unease would begin to grip those who competed for the top positions.

"Third out of a class of thirty . . . Second out of a class of thirty . . ." There would be a dead silence, then, "First out of a class of thirty is Aboni, N." Invariably it was Aboni, N., in the B section of Okoli's class.

Spontaneous clapping and loud cheers would then greet this top person, who would usually stand up to acknowledge the cheers. If it is the third term, there were book prizes for the first, second, and third persons in every class, usually presented publicly after the general mark reading by the principal himself. Competition was thus encouraged.

Students who found themselves at the bottom of the class in any term would not want to have the shame repeated the following term. They would thus struggle to improve in their areas of deficiency. Those who on the other hand found themselves on top of the class would also work hard so as not to be beaten the following term to the second position. In the A class where Okoli was, there was not any permanent first-position holder. Ekunife, Nokebu, and Okoli often jostled for that position. Most often the subjects that determined positions were math and Latin. These were areas where there could be wide disparities in scores. Okoli had topped the class in the very first term in the first year, but by second term, he scored 62 percent in Latin, and Ekunife scored 86 percent. Such wide margins were possible mainly in math and Latin. In subjects like English, literature, biology, physics, chemistry, and the rest, there were hardly wide margins between the high scorers. The bottom positions unfortunately were taken up consistently almost by the same set of boys. This was not because these boys were not intelligent. It was more because they were poor in math, Latin, or physics.

In the B class on the other hand, Okoli's very good friend Aboni, as earlier stated, dominated the class and maintained the first position from year 1 until the set left the school. He in fact capped it all by making seven A1s and one A2 in the school certificate exams, easily the best result not only in the whole school but also in the whole country and perhaps in the whole West African subregion for that year.

The development of leadership qualities was very much encouraged in Afikpo. Right from second year, students were encouraged to attend the Citizenship and Leadership Training Center run by the Man of War Bay. Even from first year, the class master often picked a student who exhibited high leadership qualities as the class monitor. Students were encouraged to join school clubs like the Debating Society, the Young Farmers Club, the Cultural Club, etc. As students got to class 5, they could be appointed to the position of house subprefect if they were found to possess the necessary leadership potentials, and their academic positions were found to be sound. From house subprefect, the student could be promoted to full house prefect in lower sixth (i.e., first year of higher school).

Appointment to the position of school prefect was a prerogative of the principal and the school masters (teachers). Most houses had two school prefects each. One school prefect per house was designated as the house captain, and the latter oversaw the day-to-day running of the house and was responsible for maintenance of discipline in the house.

The highest position of responsibility that the school could bestow on a student was the post of captain of school, usually referred to as school captain. The position of school captain carried enormous responsibility and respect. There was only one school captain in any single year. Among the school prefects, the school captain loomed larger than a mere primus inter pares. The principal obviously must consider many things before appointing anybody as school captain.

Okoli's bosom friend of many years and the greatest academic giant of the time, Aboni, was appointed the school captain in Okoli's set. Two other close friends of Okoli's, Tubia and Meriom, were also appointed school prefects to head New and Okpara houses respectively; Okoli himself was appointed a prefect to head Ibiam House. He was lucky in the sense that it was possibly academics and character alone that influenced his appointment. He did not excel in sports (though he won a few honors in high jump and the on hundred yards sprints), and even in the academics he was not a very consistent top shot like his friend Aboni.

The School Riots

Okoli's set met two sets of principals at Afikpo. Even though their interview for admission was conducted by Mr Mtobo, the sitting principal when they arrived the school was Mr Marriot. Mr Marriot was a very tall man. He must have been over six feet six inches. He walked with a slight stoop. Students used to say that he stooped so that he would not hit the top frames of doors. Students also always said that the doors of the assembly hall were made very high so that they would accommodate Mr Marriot. Little did they consider the fact that the assembly hall had been in existence long before Mr Marriot got posted to Afikpo from Government College Umuahia.

Mr Marriot, a Briton, was a disciplinarian. Students considered him very thorough with his work. He paid attention to details. He would see from a distance that your shoes were not well buckled or that your shirt was not properly tucked in. When he came for sanitation inspections as were done every Saturday morning, he could see tiny pieces of paper that were not picked up between the flower hedges. "Paper, paper," he would keep saying as he briskly walked along the hedges and pointed out pieces of paper, which students had overlooked. He always wore white shorts, white shirt, and knee-length white hoses with brown shoes. Some said he was in the army during the Second World War. That might have been responsible for the militarylike precision that characterized most of his actions.

After the sanitation inspections on Saturday mornings, it would be time for parade. The parades were held around the flag staff near the school pavilion. The students would queue up in order of classes according to their different houses. Every student would be dressed in white shirt and white shorts (for classes 1 to 3) or white shirts and white trousers for classes 4 to upper 6. The school prefects would also be in school ties, which were presented to them on the day they were appointed prefects. The principal, followed by his vice, would then walk through the lines of students, individually inspecting each student as was done in military parades.

Any shabby dressing, funny haircut, or beards would be pointed out and punished for. Sandals and nails were also usually inspected. The exercise was usually taken very seriously. Shorts or trousers that were too short or too tight would attract runs, or if repeatedly worn would attract detention. Okoli's classmate Ijire was once penalized for wearing very tight shorts. The following term, he decided to go the other extreme. He collected knee-length baggy shorts from his father and wore this for inspection. He was instantly put on detention. His charge was "playing the unsuccessful clown and making a mockery of inspection."

Strange as that might seem, there were juniors being punished by seniors for "looking at a senior in a way calculated to embarrass him."

On the other hand, a junior could be put on runs if he looked the other way, for "passing by a senior and ignoring him as if the senior did not matter." Occasionally this latter offence could be labeled as "ignoring a senior." There was no end to the reasons for which a class 2 boy could punish a class 1 boy. If Ebiobo was bent on punishing a junior, he could just, while passing by a junior, utter the meaningless word *mpiringo*.

Woe betide the junior if he did not immediately answer "yes, please" to that meaningless utterance. He could be made to kneel down for hours or creep under the low wooden beds, until released at Ebiobo's pleasure. Before the release, Ebiobo would usually ensure that the offending junior answered "yes please" to all kinds of meaningless and sometimes vulgar utterances from him.

"Or-ing."

"Yes, please."

"Mpiringo."

"Yes, please."

"Utuamiwe."

"Yes, please"

There was no end to what Ebiobo could rattle out as names for the hapless class 1 boy, and the latter would be expccted to respond with a "yes please" to every one of those names, irrespective of how meaningless, vulgar, or offending the utterances might be.

Only the house prefects and school prefects (including house captains and school captain) could place other students on runs. Any other senior who wanted to discipline a junior could either send the junior kneeling down or order the junior to creep under the bed. Creeping under the bed was one very difficult form of punishment that was often dreaded by juniors especially the big-sized juniors. The beds were a mere eighteen inches from the floor and to send a big junior like Mezeoke to creep under the beds entailed his having to crawl along on his belly. If a class 2 boy or a sectional head told another student to "take one round," it meant that the student would crawl on his belly under the twenty beds in that section once. Sometimes the knees would be weeping after several rounds of creeping. And Ebiobo could simply say, "Take five rounds."

There were occasions when a sectional head or prefect could condemn all the students in a section to simultaneous creeping. The reason for such mass punishment as they were called could range between noisemaking or failure to observe lights out.

There were occasional abuses of the punishment and disciplinary procedures at Afikpo. However, whenever these abuses were detected or reported, they were promptly reversed, and the perpetrator might be subjected to the same punishment that he had ordered. Thus, there were occasions when a class 2 boy would be punished not only for excessive bullying (as if bullying was officially sanctioned) or for sadistic behavior.

Unacceptable as these punishment measures might appear however, they essentially instilled a sense of respect for seniority, instituted authority, and they ensured observance of good manners. The student from a government secondary school could easily be distinguished from students of other schools, where good disciplinary measures were not in place.

Mischief Superstars:

There were lots of individual and groups who were mischief makers in Afikpo. Prominent among them was Abuuzuu. He was in class 4 when Okoli first entered the school. Abuuzuu was an extremely intelligent boy. He would hardly be seen reading. He was all over the place. He related well with both his classmates and even his juniors. But he was also a big bully, especially against the "almighty" class 2 boys. The class 1 boys liked him for being the class 2 boys' burden. Whenever anyone in class 1 was under punishment from a class 2 boy, the former would be praying that Abuuzuu would chance around. If he did, he would immediately rescue the class 1 boy and descend on the class 2 boy. He was the last person that class 2 boys—like Ebiobo, Nwambusi, or Hinco—would like to see around while subjecting a class 1 boy to punishment.

Abuuzuu was to class 1 students the equivalent of a Robin Hood. He was tall and lanky with a very light and gentle voice (a voice that could sometimes belie the underlying mischief). He was always within the first three positions in his class during mark readings, ultimately making one of the best grades in the school both in the school certificate and the higher school certificate examinations conducted nationally.

Besides his academic prowess, Abuuzuu also made history by being the first senior boy to be made a bell fag in the history of the school. In many other schools, being the timekeeper was a mark of honor and recognition. In Afikpo, the timekeeper or bell fag usually was the student who had the greatest amount of punitive runs or detentions or who committed the most grievous offence for the week. The bell fag would almost perpetually sit beside the mounted giant school bell from 6:00 a.m. to 10:00 p.m. (with short meal intervals). He would man the bell for all activities, whether it was raining or whether it was blazing hot.

Abuuzuu, for a mischief he had committed in his house, had been condemned to washing the toilets prior to Saturday inspection, a position usually reserved for the class 1 boys. On one Saturday morning, after he had dutifully washed one of the toilets, Abuuzuu had briefly left the spot where he mounted sentry to wash another toilet when Hinco, a class 2 boy in his house, secretly went in and used the freshly washed toilet. Hinco dashed out after using the toilet without flushing it. He had pulled down the toilet seat cover and had shut the door after him. Abuuzuu later came back and took up his position in front of the toilet door, believing it was still as clean as he had left it.

Then came the principal and the prefects on inspection. Abuuzuu confidently opened the toilet door to display the good job he had done on the toilet. He then proudly and confidently raised the toilet seat cover to display the neatness for possible commendation from the principal.

But alas! Some devil had done the unthinkable. Principal, prefects, and even Abuuzuu himself had to jump back from what they saw: a used, completely smeared, and thoroughly messed-up toilet, unflushed after use!

Instant punishment of extended detention with an extended toilet-cleaning week was imposed on Abuuzuu, who could not convince any of the inspectors that he had washed the toilets in the first instance, especially considering his antecedents in mischief making. It was believed that he intentionally had planned to insult the principal and the other inspectors by opening for them the heap of rubbish in the toilet basin.

After the inspection team had left, the justifiably enraged Abuuzuu gathered the few classes 1 and 2 boys that were around and herded them into the toilet, promising hell and brimstone if they did not reveal who the devil was that used the toilet after he had washed it. It was then revealed that it was Hinco who did the evil job.

Abuuzuu there and then grabbed Hinco, who was reputed to have the biggest head among the class 2 boys. Abuuzuu held Hinco by the collar of his shirt, forced down the latter's head into the toilet amidst the tissue paper and feces, held the head there, and flushed the toilet, holding the head long enough to ensure a uniform buttering of the head and face with feces and used tissue. He then let go his victim who, gasping for breath dashed out of the toilet scattering feces, urine, and toilet water everywhere as he ran off. Who ever he ran towards also ran away to avoid being smeared with smelly feces. Hinco was able to find his way to the principal's office where he caused quite some stir with the feces and the swarm of flies following him around his head; among the principal and his staff, everyone tried to avoid the feces and flies that Hinco had come into the office with.

It was an episode never experienced in the history of the school. Abuuzuu had again made history! That type of crime of flushing a fellow student's head in a toilet filled with feces did not exist in the statute books of the school since nobody had ever committed that kind of offence before in the school. That kind of offence did not have a particular name since it had never been committed by any student in the history of the school. The principal and staff were said to have had a hard time deciding what the appropriate punishment for Abuuzuu would be.

Some staff were said to have pleaded for a mitigation of punishment, arguing that the reaction was provoked by Hinco who went to use a washed toilet on inspection morning and failed to flush it thereafter.

At the end, an unprecedented action was matched with an unprecedented punishment. Abuuzuu was placed on multiple detentions and made the bell fag, a post no other senior boy had ever held in the school. Despite the unprecedented punishment, the first position in class 4A at the close of that school term still went to no other person than Abuuzuu! Even with all the mischief and controversy surrounding him, Abuuzuu was simply an academic superstar.

A near replica of Abuuzuu in mischief making was Mtama. Though lacking in the academic ingenuity of Abuuzuu, Mtama was ubiquitous and a person of many parts as far as mischief making was concerned. He was tall, slender, and very talkative. Mtama depicted what the rustic mischievous village boy was. He knew so many tricks. Even though usage of the vernacular was disallowed in school, Mtama would use vernacular language half of the time when senior boys were not around, especially whenever he was plotting some mischief. In such situations, Mtama would descend into his native Afikpo dialect, which was difficult for most other students to understand. He was in the B class, but most of the time in between classes he could be heard from the A class. If he did not want to comply with what other people were doing, he would pretend not to understand what was being said, and then he would start talking in his native dialect. He was not particularly academically superior, but somehow he managed always to pass from one class to the next. Around exam time, he would start warming himself into the company of academic giants like Okoli's friend Aboni, who would often help him through his mathematics revision questions.

As soon as exams were over, Mtama would again make fun of everybody. Most nicknames of the masters in the school were coined by Mtama. It was him who coined the name Imi Oho for the senior Mr Mathew, the physics master, *Imi Oho* meaning the barrel nose (a rude reference to Mr Mathew's very large nose). He also, even only as a class 2 boy, coined the name Egbe (meaning gun) for the new school principal when the latter arrived at the school compound from Umuahia with a double-barreled gun hung over his shoulders as he took a tour of the school compound. Mtama did not spare even his classmates in nicknaming people. Even though he always ran to Aboni to help him out around examination times, he did not hesitate to fashion out for the latter the name Gwongworo (meaning the rugged vanquishing truck), a straight reference to Aboni's all-conquering academic feats. As it pleased Mtama, he would use this name as a compliment (when he needed help) or as a derogatory term when exams were over, and he wanted to make fun of Aboni.

Mtama and Okoli were in the same house. He was not the biggest class 1 boy. In fact, he was a little more than half the size of Mezeoke. But by subtle tricks and intimidation, he managed to psychologically subdue all other class 1 boys in the house, including the big Mezeoke.

Mtama was a very big noisemaker. Most of the time, he was responsible for the mass punishments, which were imposed on the junior boys after lights out. A lot of the time he was under the beds, creeping for one form of offence or the other especially for noisemaking. One day after house prayers when the senior boys were having a meeting with the house master in the common room, Mtama summoned all the class 1 boys in section C where he was. He then suggested that they would have a short meeting of their own. He declared himself chairman of the meeting. He then said that it was not good that everybody should continue to suffer, doing mass punishment for noisemaking, and that one person at all times should accept responsibility for noisemaking and undertake the punishment for all, any time that mass punishment was to be imposed on the class 1 boys in the section. As if to win everybody over, he went philosophical:

"After all," he said, "one person suffered and died for all our sins on the cross."

That feigned religious sentiment appeared to have worked. Everybody nodded in approval of Mtama's idea.

But who would bell the cat? Who would volunteer to perpetually accept responsibility for all noisemaking in the section, all the squeaking after lights out, all the littering? Everybody was silent. Everybody expected that Mtama, being the greatest noisemaker, that he was about to volunteer to accept responsibility for all noisemaking. But that was not to be. Mtama had his plans after nobody was prepared to make that sacrifice. He stood up and asked for suggestions about how a volunteer could be chosen or imposed. No suggestions were forthcoming. Then suddenly, as if he had rehearsed it all, the self-appointed chairman who was Mtama himself, opened the long exercise book he had in front of him and brought out a wooden ruler. Holding the ruler in front of him he declared, "We shall now measure our individual pendulum, and whoever has the longest pendulum will be our chairman for the rest of the term. The new chairman will accept responsibility for all noisemaking to save the rest of us further mass punishment."

Mtama must have known that it was only Mezoke who, among the group, had reached puberty. He was often seen hovering around Mezeoke, whenever the latter was bathing, occasionally peeping through the plastic shower curtain as Mezeoke bathed so that he would have a story to tell about the latter.

After Mtama's suggestion, he instantly pulled down his shorts and quickly proceeded to measure the length of his genitals with the wooden ruler in his possession. He did the measurement by himself and announced the result, the number of inches. He appeared to hold everybody else spellbound, as he pulled everybody's shorts down. After measuring and recording the lengths of the individual genitals with his wooden ruler, Mtama proceeded to announce the results of his "research" as follows:

Okeke, N. = Two and a half inches
Nwosu, T. = Two inches
Okoli, A. = Two inches
Mtama, H. = Two and a half inches
Mezeoke, M. = Four and a half inches

After he had announced the last result, Mtama dropped his paper and ruler on a locker, and fixing his gaze on Mezeoke, he started clapping his hands for the "winner." As if held spellbound, everybody else joined him in the clapping including Mezeoke, who obviously was being indirectly congratulated for having the longest genital. Nobody contested the decision or the result of Mtama's research, as he continued, "From the results therefore, Mezeoke M., will hereafter be our chairman and accept responsibility for all noisemaking and therefore bear the consequences, and the rest of us will continue to pray for him."

More spontaneous clapping followed, but this time without Mezeoke participating in the clapping! The latter appeared either to be ruminating over the enormity of his new duties or to be savoring his new "winnings." Which ever it was that kept him from participating in the resumed clapping, it was certain that Mezeoke was stupefied by Mtama's intimidating ingenuity.

From that evening, Mezeoke dutifully assumed responsibility for all noisemaking after lights out. Even when Mtama would yell and noisily kick on his wooden locker, Mezeoke would assume responsibility if a prefect came in to ask for the culprit. It was not until the following term that the arrangement got leaked to a prefect. Composition of section C was scattered as there was a complete rearrangement of the sections with Mtama being relocated to section A, where mainly the very senior boys were stationed, so that they would have a good eye on him.

The Coming of Egbe.

About one week into the first term of Okoli's second year in school, an event occurred that was to permanently change the history of the school. The new class 2 boys were busy planning how they would conduct the tail cutting exercise on the new class 1 boys. The former were all feeling on top of the world. They had graduated from being or-ings. Nobody would any longer bully them at will as they had assumed the new status of class 2 boys. There was now a new set of novices, or-ings, who could be told to kneel down if they walked past the class 2 boys without saying "good morning please."

Okoli and his classmates now had people whom they could tell to stand on one foot, bend forward pointing the index finger to the grounds till they ached, or hop a hundred times on one leg. There were now new set of or-ings who could be told to creep under the beds in the house when the sectional head was not around. The tail-cutting exercise was to be only a week away.

But the tail-cutting exercise was not to be.

On that fateful Monday afternoon, the very senior boys were seen standing in small groups discussing. The class 2 boys did not know what they were discussing and did not really care to know. All the latter's attention and thoughts were focused on one thing: the impending tail-cutting exercise.

By lunchtime that afternoon, the news was all over the place. The incredible had happened! The school principal had been suspended by the Ministry of Education! The masters were seen pacing up and down going in and out of the principal's office. By prep time, there was no supervision by the prefects. Lights out was not observed that night as prefects in the different houses clustered in small groups discussing.

By the following morning, the apprehension was palpable. The school bell did not ring. Tension was visible even on the faces of the school masters. The principal was not seen at morning assembly, which had to be conducted by the vice principal. It was said that the principal had been summoned to Enugu, the regional capital. The juniors saw the senior boys carrying cans of paint and paintbrushes. Many were busy making posters. Some of the posters read, "Down with Ibiam."

"We want our principal back."

"No Marriot, no school," some others read.

"We stand by our principal."

By midday on Tuesday, scores of posters were all over the place. The senior boys had gathered around the school pavilion. A spontaneous demonstration had started. It was said that the formal radio announcement confirming the suspension of the school principal from office was on air that morning.

The story was that the governor of Eastern Nigeria was to visit Afikpo from around where he hailed. He was said to come from a town close to Afikpo and was a highly respected man, who besides being a physician had done a lot of missionary work in the past. It was said that the principal of Government Secondary School Afikpo was informed of the proposed visit. He was probably expected to pull out the students to line the street to welcome and hail the governor and probably wave flags in jubilation. Apparently, the principal did not see the need to pull out the students for the flag-waving exercise. The governor was said to have visited and driven past the school incognito.

The principal's refusal or failure to pull out the students was apparently seen as a mark of disrespect for the governor. It possibly was also felt that the principal's action or inaction was consequent upon the fact of the governor being an indigenous governor or being African. It was probably reasoned that the principal felt that an African governor did not merit the recognition of being heralded into the town by flag-waving students. It was possibly felt that were the governor the immediate past British-born governor of Eastern Nigeria, the principal, who was a Briton, would have acted differently.

All those were to Okoli and his friends, political and high-browed speculations, beyond the scope of the latter's comprehension. All that mattered to the latter was that the clock should tick faster so that Saturday would arrive for the tail-cutting exercise on the class 1 boys. Okoli and his friends were eager to display their paint buckets and show the class 1 boys that the former were now seniors and that the latter were the new tail-bearing or-ings.

Lunch that afternoon was disorderly. Most students gulped their food and moved to the street, banners in hand: banners berating the government, banners in support of their dear principal. By about 3:00 p.m., virtually the entire school was in the street, marching towards the old district officer's house, the official residence of the highest government official in town. Even the classes 1 and 2 boys, who knew little about the reasons for the demonstration, were all enthusiastically carrying banners prepared by the senior boys. As they marched, the students picked up stones, which were plentiful along the dusty roadside. Some senior boys had cans of kerosene, which they had emptied from their cockroaching lamps. Others had boxes of matches. Very soon the district officer's residence was up in flames. Those who had gathered stones as they marched rained stones on the burning building and the adjacent buildings. Okoli and indeed most of his friends who threw those stones did not even know what they were protesting against. The genesis or the consequences of what had happened or of their actions was far beyond their little imagination. All they wanted was that their principal, who was said to have been suspended, should be reinstated immediately.

The mayhem over, the students marched back to the school compound to have their supper and go to sleep, since there was going to be no prep.

By the time they got back to school, the students saw that the name board bearing Ibiam House had been pulled down by some of their colleagues, and in its place Marriot House was boldly but roughly and hurriedly written across the outer wall of the building. It was later learnt that some senior boys had propped up Keke, the talented school artist, on the shoulders of his colleagues with brush and paint in hand and allegedly unilaterally renamed Ibiam House, changing it to Marriot House.

For several days after the Marriot riots (as the event came to be called), there were no classes. Unknown men, who were later said to be police detectives from Enugu, hovered around the school compound.

About four days after the riots, an averagely built man wearing a low moustache and hanging a double-barreled gun across his shoulders was seen walking around the school premises. He was initially accompanied by another unknown man (possibly a plainclothes police detective). The new man who was later to be nicknamed Egbe (the Igbo word for *gun*) was probably testing the waters. He probably felt it was necessary for him to hang a gun across his shoulders to ward off any students who might contemplate displaying their resentment of the change in administrative leadership of the school. By the next day, the same gun-slinging man was again seen walking around the premises, this time accompanied by the vice principal.

Another principal had been appointed for the school. By the following week, the gun-slinging man had taken up the principal's seat in the assembly hall. He no longer came with a gun, but the name Egbe had stuck, and was to be this new man's nickname for over the next seven years that he would be principal of Government Secondary School Afikpo.

The administrative changes did not bother Okoli and his friends much as class 2 boys. They might have bothered the much bigger boys. All that bothered the former was that the tail cutting for class 1 boys, which the class 2 boys were to perform, had been postponed because of the prevailing events in the school. The paint and brushes, the charcoal and every other thing that Okoli and his friends had been gathering in preparation for cutting the tails of the or-rings had to be put away for a future unknown date. With the arrival of the new helmsman, things began to change. They were never to be the same again.

The New dawn.

As the new helmsman settled down, the very first visible thing he did was to restore the student-changed name of Ibiam House. The inscription, Marriot House, was painted over and obliterated with matching paint. The sign board bearing Ibiam House was fetched from where it had been dumped by the protesting students and reposted against the wall of the building. The school artist, the class 3 student who inscribed the name "Marriot House" on the wall was temporarily suspended from school (an action many considered scapegoatism since other students had carried up Keke and handed him paint and brushes and literally compelled him to effect the name change). Okoli and his friends did not hear of any suspensions for the arsonists of the district officer's house, nor of the stone throwers of which Okoli was one. However, such high-wired politics was beyond the former's scope as class 2 students.

Very soon classes and other school activities were to resume. There were lots of curriculum and other changes. The lower-five program was commenced. It was an ingenious program initiated in Afikpo by the new principal. By that program, which had long been in existence in Government College Umuahia, the best thirty students after the class 1 end-of-year results would be specially prepared to sit the school certificate from class 4 instead of from class 5. Tail cutting was modified for the better and was more adequately supervised. Bullying was clamped down upon (though not eliminated). The sixth form students were allowed more freedom to exercise their discretion in a lot of things. Greater supervision of teaching activities was started; hence, Mr E., the geography master, was observed more closely by the principal. Suspensions from school were commenced for people who misbehaved repeatedly in school.

On the downside however, students started to witness midyear admissions of stray students. Students, especially sons of the influential and politically mighty, were surreptitiously pulled in from lower-rated schools into the government secondary school system. These "stray students," as they were called, often did not measure up academically since they were more or less smuggled into the system out of cronyism. Hitherto strict merit was the basis for admissions and scholarship. And it was on the basis of strict merit that students, like Okoli who had no political connections or the mighty financial background, were able to find themselves in the system and even win scholarships purely on academic merit. Okoli's parents knew nobody in the government, yet under the old system, he and some of his friends were able to come into government college and even earn full board and tuition scholarship communicated to them through the post. Cronyism and favored admission, based on the weight of candidate's pockets, were to assume almost alarming proportions in almost all institutions of higher learning in the system a decade later.

Sports got a big boost with the advent of the new Egbe administration. Sports stars started to enjoy recognition. Sports began to be one of the factors considered for appointment as school or house prefect. Emphasis on church music dimmed even though the Psalms and use of *Songs of Praise* were retained. Etiquette, dress code, and good table manners were emphasized. In fact, there were monthly lessons on the three Ds of a gentleman. Classes on "discipline, decency, and decorum" were introduced and personally taught by the new principal. The art of making intricate knots on the necktie was taught to higher school students. Waltz dance and classical music were also taught to higher school students by the principal himself, all in an honest effort to prepare them for adult life.

Traditional wrestling, which was not originally among school sports, was introduced. Indeed traditional wrestlers were hired from Afikpo and Izii towns to teach traditional wrestling and the drumming that accompanied it. Ace traditional wrestlers in Okoli's class—like Mtama, Akpan, and Nfua—began to shine and get due recognition. Study of Latin language was given a boost. The principal himself was said to be a master of arts holder in Latin language. French language was also introduced as a course in the school.

The use of Latin idioms came into vogue. This was because the new principal being a master of the art in Latin language would hardly make three sentences during assembly or school addresses without including Latin as one of the sentences. It became fashionable for senior boys to address one another in Latin. Phrases like "amicus mea" (my friend). Students started to wonder why it was said that Latin was a dead language. Because of Egbe, the principal, Latin as a language was alive and kicking in Government Secondary School Afikpo. Many Latin teachers were attracted to the school. In fact, at a time there were in the school. It was no wonder that an unprecedented high number of students offered Latin as one of their courses in the West African School Certificate Examinations. Expectantly, many, like Okoli were able to score alphas in the subject in the school certificate examinations. Many of the students began to wish they were also able to study, in addition to the official English language and native languages in the country, some other languages, especially such other widely spoken languages like Spanish, French, German, Russian, and or Chinese.

Much, as Latin which was learnt in school, was not spoken outside the four walls of the school community; the knowledge helped many of the students in figuring out certain difficult English words and certain legal terminologies. Hence, when Afikpo students came across such expressions as "non sequitor" or "delegatus non potest delegare," they could begin to figure out the meaning.

The arrival of Egbe as principal also ushered in such innovations as the introduction of the cadet unit to the school. By that system, some retired military personnel were posted to Afikpo as members of staff to coach the students on certain paramilitary activities. The students learnt that this subject had long been in existence in Government College Umuahia. It took the coming of Egbe to introduce that very useful training program into Government Secondary School Afikpo.

As Okoli and his friends progressed in class and years, the school became more and more the epicenter of their lives. The spirit of competition for academic excellence grew stronger. Every morning the students had a clear picture of what the day's class lessons would be. With the entry of each class teacher, every one would want to grasp as much as possible every sentence that the teacher made. No one knew which one would be useful for the weekly test on Friday. And they knew that the summary of the weekly tests would be the basis for scoring the class position, which would be read out in the open hall on mark-reading day at the close of each term. Nobody would want the mark reading to be started in his class with his name as the principal adjusted his glasses to say, "Class 3A, thirtieth out of a class of thirty is . . . ." The thirtieth and the first position attracted the greatest attention. Just as Aboni always clinched the first position in the B class, a particular student clinched the thirtieth position in Okoli's class for the first three terms of the first year. That was because this particular student, Mananu, being so poor in math and Latin always scored below 40 percent in each of these subjects and always found it difficult to close the failure gap to catch up with the rest of the students. It was not until Mananu dropped Latin after fourth year did he start to improve on his class position.

Mere, another particular student in the class, could not cope with subjects which involved calculations. He was comfortable with English, biology, literature, Latin, woodwork, metalwork, and chemistry (when calculations were not involved). But in math, further math, and physics he would consistently score below 20 percent. A very pleasant and cheerful boy by nature, Mere would always exchange his middle-of-class allocated seat for a back seat in class (seats were allocated in alphabetical order). The students always wondered why Mere would always prefer a back seat when most students preferred to sit closest the blackboard. It was much later that it was noticed that Mere would always take advantage of the back-seat position and stretch his neck to spy on the answers of mathematical questions as written by other students sitting in front of him. By the time he spied and got one consistent answer to a particular question from two or three students, he would straight way affirm that answer as the correct answer. He would thereafter scribble a few figures, juggle them incoherently, and then write down the consistent answer as he had gotten from copying the answers of two or three other students. Multiple-choice questions were not in use at the time. Whenever, therefore the math teacher asked the students to exchange scripts and score the correct answers, Mere would score highly. If however the teacher collected the scripts and read through the calculations that led to the answers, Mere would score almost zero since the teacher would easily discover that Mere merely quoted an answer without the correct calculation. Such were the desperate efforts made by students in Afikpo to ensure that the first name that would be read out on mark-reading day at the end of each term would not be their name. Nobody would want his name to follow the phrase “thirtieth out of a class of thirty.”

“First out of a class of thirty” was more enticing, more rewarding, and certainly much more attractive but more elusive.

All thirteen subjects of physics, math, additional math, English, literature, biology, chemistry, Latin, geography, history, woodwork, metalwork, and technical drawing were compulsory up to end of class 4. After class 4, a student had the option to choose two subjects from add math, Latin, woodwork, metalwork, and technical drawing. Thus by class 5, each student had six compulsory subjects and two other subjects (from the options), making a total of eight subjects, which must be offered for the West African School Certificate. Oral English was also considered a compulsory subject, but it was not considered when checking a student's aggregate score.

In computing a student's aggregate score, the students' best six subjects were utilized. A subject like oral English, which though compulsory did not participate in computation of the aggregate score, was therefore often not taken very seriously by students. The core subjects in Afikpo were regarded as the following: English, physics, chemistry, biology, and math. The others were additional math and literature in English. Unfortunately in Afikpo the emphasis was on medicine and engineering as the students' future professions. Thus, most students had their eyes and ears on math, physics, chemistry, literature, biology, and English. They would then add Latin and additional math if they wanted to do medicine. If however they wanted to do engineering, they would add woodwork or metalwork plus technical drawing. For the high school courses, the medically oriented students would choose zoology, chemistry, and physics while the engineering-oriented students would choose math, chemistry, and physics or math, further math, physics, and chemistry.

It was only after the advent of Egbe as school principal that the arts subjects were brought into the limelight. For the first time in the history of the school, there was a higher school student offering history as a major. Soon, it would no longer be derogatory to ask the question: "When did King Henry die?" Just as Okoli's friend, Tubia, would always ask Ebekwe, the only arts major student in higher school at the time.

English language though classified as an arts subject was greatly emphasized in Afikpo. That was very understandable. Not only was English the official language in the country, it was the language of instruction for all the other subjects. No matter what a student scored in all the other subjects, English was invariably added in the computation of his aggregate score. There were thus situations where a first class student's aggregate would be badly affected by a poor score in English language. Such was the case with a very bright student Gee-Pez, who scored A1 (excellent) in math, additional math, physics, chemistry, technical drawing, and biology. But his poor score in English language P8 brought down his aggregate score drastically. On the average however, it was found that most students who were good in the sciences were also good in the arts. Such was the case with academic giants of the time like Eken, Ocuba, Ekunife, Nokebu, Ekeani, Abuka, Ebeife, and many others. Of course, there was the academic superstar Aboni, who by making A1 in seven of the eight subjects not only exceeded the maximum limit computed with six A1s but also discarded one very useful A1, which would have made a lot of difference to the aggregates of some others, if it were transferable.

The higher school boys were like demigods. At least, so they were, in the estimation of the juniors. There were very few of them. They were scarcely seen as most of them, especially those of them in the newer houses, had rooms of their own. Those in the older houses like Ibiam, Farnfield (later named Okpara), and school houses, who did not have private rooms, had the equivalent of two bed spaces allocated to them. They also had double lockers, and their mosquito nets were left permanently in place so that they did not have to dismantle and reset their mosquito nets every morning and every night.

The average higher school student talked very little and always walked with a dignified stance. Most of them were prefects either at the house level or at the school level. In the few cases where they were not prefects at either level, they could still effectively discipline erring juniors by giving them runs through their own classmates. Their classmates would always ensure that any issues that would entail a fellow higher school boy being punished was sorted out quietly. It was only in very rare situations that a higher school boy would ever be put on open punishment. Such a situation would be very much frowned at. The higher school students were the only ones who could occasionally have their meals sent to them in their rooms. They were allowed to wear trousers (pants) and long-sleeved shirts as opposed to the other students who were allowed to wear only shorts and short-sleeved shirts. They were allowed to dance in the assembly hall with invited female students from certain secondary schools. If any non-higher school student dared to go beyond the upper field during such dance sessions, that person might well be the bell flag for the following week. And when they went to the dinning hall with the female visitors to have lunch, all other students were expected to turn their heads and eyes in the opposite direction as they passed them on the way. If the eyes moved the wrong way, the individual would just hear, as if in a whisper, "You, kneel down there," from one of the higher school boys.

And the junior might have to kneel down in the sun for the rest of the day or till the higher school boy who initiated the punishment happened to pass that way on his way back. The culprit obviously must have been "looking at a senior boy in a way calculated to embarrass him" or he must have been "enjoying senior jokes," and each of these was a punishable offence.

The Teacher, the Master, and the Student

The relationship between the students and the teachers was usually fairly detached. The system had been so arranged by its founding fathers that there was efficient internal organization by the student leadership for the students' day-to-day administration and functioning. Apart from the classroom teaching periods, the masters were rarely seen by the students, especially the junior students. Each house was run in a near-perfect system by the house captain and the house prefects. Conflict resolution was usually effectively handled at the house level. The house masters and the assistant house masters only came in occasionally during the house prayer of the new term and close of term. The house masters often were expected to do minibanking services for the students as each student was not expected to keep beyond a certain amount of money in his possession. During major interhouse competitions also house masters might come to counsel and encourage members of their houses. Beyond these few instances, most students did not in fact know who their house masters were. Houses that were persistently scored low during the weekly sanitation inspections conducted by the school principal also occasionally would have the house master do a prior inspection to correct areas of deficiency before the arrival of the principal.

Enforcement of discipline in Afikpo was almost always effected by the students themselves. There was hardly a single instance throughout Okoli's stay in Afikpo that he could remember being punished by a master. The same was true for most other students. That was because by the time a student avoided all the don'ts enforced by the prefects and by the nonprefect senior boys, there would be no more don'ts to avoid. The prefects' don'ts were enough cleansing crucibles of fire. There would thereafter be no further need to go to purgatory for further cleansing before attaining paradise.

Afikpo like other government-run secondary schools was a nondenominational institution. Students practiced whatever faith they professed. But nobody was allowed to be neutral. One was expected to participate in one form of worship or another. Virtually all the students belonged to one Christian religious group or the other. It was possible there were adherents of other faiths, but they were not very visible.

There were mainly two forms of worship sessions, one jointly for Anglicans, Methodists, Baptists, Lutherans, Adventists, Salvation Army, and all non-Catholic Christian religious groups. There was another for Catholics. The non-Catholics being by far in the majority utilized the assembly hall for Sunday worship while the Catholics utilized one of the larger technical building classrooms. There were no periods or classes set aside for religious instruction as were done in many nongovernment institutions. On the first Monday of every month, however, when Egbe's administration came on board, the reverend father came from town to give religious talk to Catholics, who were preparing for one form of sacrament or the other.

Religious affiliation did not play a part in interstudent relationships at Afikpo. The fact that the pattern of assembly prayers and the songbooks used were more tailored towards the Anglican mode made no difference to the students. The students were all very comfortable with that, and everybody appeared to enjoy the melodious songs from that little book *Songs of Praise*. The melody of hymns from *Songs of Praise* would, for decades after, reverberate in the minds of her products, with a great sense of nostalgia for that great institution, Government Secondary School Afikpo.

As the years wore on and Okoli and his friends attained more seniority and got more mature in mind and body, more and more things at school became routine for them. They got to know what every bell signified. Nobody needed to remind them that they should not place their hands on the walls nor kill (dead) mosquitoes on the walls anymore. Nobody reminded them not to spit along the walkways. They needed nobody to tell them to pick up any piece of paper they chanced upon, as they walked. They needed not to be reminded that they must use the walkways and not cross the field or the lawns. And if one saw a boy flying his shirt or wearing his sandals unbuckled or unlaced or yawning or sneezing without covering his mouth, chances were that that boy did not pass through Afikpo. "Discipline, decency, and decorum" were constantly preached in Afikpo and were to be the guiding principles and the dogmas for the products of that great institution.

The years wore on fast after the first two. Okoli and his friends had virtually all come to recognize what position brackets they all fitted into in class. Occasional surprises for the better or for the worse cropped up, but on the average, most top five students in each class often remained within the top five. After the first end-of-year's mark reading, an additional five students who ranked within the best ten students in class would be awarded full board and tuition scholarship. That was in addition to the best five who had earlier been awarded scholarship from their performances in the entrance examination and interview. Thereafter, the ten college scholars, as these were referred to, were expected to remain within the best ten positions in their classes, or else the scholarship would be withdrawn from any defaulting scholar. It was therefore a swim-or-sink affair for those, like Okoli, who happened to be on scholarship. There was constant threat to their positions by students who were not on scholarship.

In Okoli's class, only one student lost the scholarship for falling outside the first ten positions in class throughout the seven-year-course duration for the school certificate and higher school courses. That student's nemesis was, of course, Latin language. From day one, it was obvious that somehow he could not cope with the simplest Latin declensions and conjugations. Somehow "mensa, mensa, mensam, mensae, mensae, mensas" could not register right in this student's brain.

He was not completely alone. In the second term of the second year, Okoli had scored 36 percent in Latin as opposed to the class average of over 50. That singular incident pulled Okoli's class position to ninth, and that kept him miserable and panicky for the rest of the year. He was only lucky that it was not end of year.

Okoli's school results were usually mailed every term to his uncle M. O. at Enugu since he had filled his uncle's name as guardian. When therefore M.O, received Okoli's result indicating that the latter had dropped from a first position in the class the previous term to ninth position, M. O. was greatly upset. He was aware of the fact that if Okoli dropped beyond the tenth position, he would automatically lose the scholarship which he had been enjoying. For the first time ever, M. O. wrote Okoli an angry letter, rebuking him for disappointing him by the former's "abysmally poor performance." He ended his letter with the following sentence: "Remember that pride goes before a fall."

It was a very worrisome moment for Okoli. But had he really been proud? "Yes," he told himself, "for being in government college and for being a college scholar."

But had he also been arrogant? It was difficult for Okoli to proffer an answer to this latter question. Such feelings often crept in so gradually that the individual might never really notice. The obvious often manifests to the individual concerned only after the crash, Okoli mused. For the first time, the possibility of him losing his scholarship stared Okoli in the face. And it was all because of Latin language. By the following term, which was the third term, Okoli's position had reversed to what it often was, the first position—thanks to his greatly improved performance in Latin. Latin, Okoli's tormentor, had gradually become his darling, so much so that he chose Latin as one of his options for the school certificate, and he was able to score an A.

The Puncture of a Pride

Nothing delighted the senior boys of Okoli's school as showing off to the girls from Queen's School Enugu whenever the Afikpo boys met the girls from Queen's school in the train at Afikpo Road train station. No senior boy would want to experience any situation for which he would be ridiculed by the Queen's schoolgirls who, having boarded the trains at Enugu, would have been already fully seated in the train by the time the students from Afikpo would board the Enugu-to-Port-Harcourt-bound train at Afikpo Road, about midway between Enugu and Port Harcourt. As the proud Mgbomians (as the students from Afikpo were often called) boarded the train, they would often like to be noticed by all, especially by the students from Queen's School Enugu, another highly rated secondary school for girls. Queen's School indeed was the only government-owned secondary school for girls in the eastern parts of the country as opposed to three for boys. That was an era when the education of the girl child was unfortunately not emphasized enough. The girls from Queen's School were often very dignified, and they would often cluster around in one or two couches in the train. They were truly the queens, and they often behaved like true queens, walking tall and dignified where ever they went. Their manners were superb. They talked little, and their dressing was often spotless. Their spoken English was impeccable. They never used an *is* where they should use a *was*, as was often noticed when girls from some less-rated school spoke. Queen's School was the in thing among the girls' schools in the country. It was said that their school authorities used to book the seats in the train in advance for them.

The Afikpo boys as they entered the train would not settle down on any seats. They would patrol up and down the couches until they found the couch where the Queen's School girls were concentrated. They would then try to squeeze themselves into any empty seats, in the same couch where the Queen's girls were seated. Many would even choose to stand even when there were empty seats in other couches, so long as they were close to the girls from Queen's.

It was on one such occasion that Okoli having secured a seat in the couch conveying the Queen's girls, was pressed to use the toilet. Unlike the modern-day toilets in trains, the toilet in each of the couches at that time consisted merely of a compartment with a door and a circular opening of about four inches diameter carved out of the floor of the compartment. The opening exited directly to the rail line. There were no toilet seats or water closet facility as are in use today. What ever waste that emanated from a toilet user dropped directly on the rail line as the train was in motion. Indiscriminate human waste along the rail line was therefore not an uncommon sight. However since these were not concentrated on the same spot, they were often not easily appreciated. The waste randomly dropped along the rail line will rapidly dry up and cake under the scorching heat of the tropical sun. Again, the fact that passengers were not allowed the use of the toilet when the trains were stationary at the train stations made it impossible for the train stations to be littered with waste. Often as the train was in motion, the wind that rushed in through the little opening which was the toilet was very strong. Okoli had finished using the toilet when, on trying to pull back his shorts, the latter slipped off and fell through the open toilet and was of course immediately swept off his grips, through the hole by the strong wind. The shorts easily disappeared into the track as the train rolled on at top speed. As Okoli immediately tried to retrieve his disappearing clothes from the hole, the wind was so strong that he almost found his hand trapped into the hole. His loud yell against the shut door and the loud sound of the coal-powered steam locomotive engine was of no consequence as nobody could even hear him from as close as immediately outside the door of the closed toilet. As Okoli quickly retrieved his hand from the toilet hole, he suddenly realized that not only did he not have the water to wash his besmeared arm, he did not have the short and underwear to put on to find his way out of the toilet. He was literally trapped. He either had to go out naked from the waist, or he would have to stay in the toilet until it was dark! If he decided to stay put in the toilet until night, he would be carried beyond his station, which was Aba. He might be carried even up to Port Harcourt, and even at that, he would still have to walk down the corridor naked. On the other hand, if he came out naked, the Queen's School girls were all seated there, and he would for the rest of his school career be the object of all discussion. He was in a very huge dilemma.

As Okoli stood in the toilet considering what to do, an idea came up in his mind. He would remove his shirt which he still had intact, and tie it around his waist. He would then dash out of the toilet and grab the nearest bag on the luggage rack and rush back into the toilet with the grabbed bag. It would not matter who owned the bag. As long as it was a bag belonging to any Afikpo boy, there was sure to be some spare shorts and underwear in it. After he would have dressed up and come out, the ownership of the bag and clothes could be sorted out. At least he would have gotten dressed up enough to get to where his own bag was. He did not need to give that idea a second thought. It was the best he could do under the circumstances short of remaining in the toilet till nightfall.

Okoli quickly removed his shirt and tied it around his waist. He then immediately rushed out of the toilet and made a dash for the luggage rack above the nearest seat and grabbed the nearest bag that he could lay hands on. The plan had appeared perfect. But the mere opening of the door of the toilet and the emergence of a half-naked individual from inside the cubicle was enough to attract the attention of everybody within reach. Okoli did not have to run far. He had not reckoned with the possibility of the owner of the bag being close by. But there the owner was! Nfua, the tiny little wrestler in Okoli's class who was reputed to have the tactics of falling even Mtama, the mischievous Afikpo boy, was the owner of the bag which Okoli had grabbed. And Nfua was occupying the seat directly below the bag. As soon as Nfua saw a half-naked person dash out from the toilet and snatch his bag, he leapt to his feet and held firmly to the other end of his bag. As Okoli did not want to attract more attention in his half-naked state, he immediately let go the bag and dashed back into the toilet. But the damage had been done even though the Queen's School girls did not have the opportunity of seeing fully the face of the student from Government Secondary School Afikpo who came out half naked from the train toilet. They would tell the story, but luckily they were not able to know the actual person involved as the dash was very transient. It did not last longer than a few seconds.

The dash out of and back into the toilet, though very brief, had however attracted the attention of the train attendants. After knocking at the toilet door, the attendants were able to come to Okoli's aid by locating Okoli's bag and procuring a spare shorts for the latter. On his "release," Okoli decided not to get back to his original seat amidst the Queen's School girls and his other Afikpo friends. The latter action was certain to draw more attention to him. Instead therefore, Okoli briskly walked across to the adjoining couch where the occupants were not aware of what had transpired in the adjacent couch. That way only the people around his original couch could observe what transpired. Okoli, his pride in that instance having been punctured, was careful never to do or say anything that would attract attention to himself when ever Queen's School girls were in the train in subsequent train trips from Afikpo Road. He was always mindful of the possibility of somebody pointing at him and saying, "That was the Afikpo boy who dashed out half naked from the train toilet." He also got very wary of the train toilets and would never thereafter want to use the train toilet even when he was very pressed.

The passage through classes 3 and 4 was essentially uneventful, uneventful in the sense that most things were already routine in the school for most of Okoli's classmates. The only difference for Okoli was at home during the holidays. After his first two years in secondary school, Okoli started to spend most of his vacations at Aba.

Instead of accompanying the vehicle transporting students from Afikpo through Abakiliki to Enugu, Okoli accompanied the students traveling through Afikpo Road from where he boarded the train to Aba. It was usually very exciting especially if the class position was very good for him. The period of wait at the train station at Afikpo Road was usually very exciting. He would stroll up and down buying oranges, bananas, *suya* (grilled, peppered meat stuck on sticks), groundnuts (peanuts), Fanta, and Pepsi. (Coca-Cola came on later). He and his friends would often want everybody to notice that they were the boys from Government Secondary School Afikpo. So they would wear their purple-colored school sweaters over their white shirts even when it was very hot. The very seniors who had college blazers would also often wear them as they patrolled along to be noticed. If there were girls arriving with the train from Queen's School or Holy Rosary College Enugu, the Afikpo boys would be at their best. They would stroll past them several times, adjusting their sweaters or blazers as they passed to draw more attention to themselves, as would peacocks in the sun.

Competitors used to call the Afikpo boys by the name Mgbomians. Mgbom village happened to be one of the villages on whose grounds the great school was built. Initially the Afikpo boys resented the name. With time however, with the repeated successes of the Afikpo boys both in academics and in sports, it became a mark of honor and a thing of great pride to be called an Mgbomian. So much was the beauty of Afikpo. So high was its esteem. So great were the achievements of the products of the great school. So glorious did it become to be called an Mgbomian.

On getting to Aba each vacation period, as soon as Okoli dropped his bag, he would proceed to 121 to see if Ceewai was back. Ceewai was at SPC Calabar. They would both tell endless stories about their school experiences. Ceewai used to call his school "Sparco Varsity," just as Afikpo boys used to call their school "Varsity on the Cross," the cross denoting the River Cross, close to whose banks the school stood, always and for ever a glowing beauty in the morning sun.

The Ventures Beyond

Two of Okoli's most memorable vacations were his visits to Arochukwu and Kaduna respectively. Both visits were in his first and third terms of his fourth year in the secondary school.

Okoli's elder brother Mako, who completed his secondary school education at National High School Arondizuogu a couple of years back, was working at General Hospital Arochukwu. Arochukwu, a historic town from where the early European slave traders were said to have come to abduct and ship their hapless captives, had lost most of its glory after the stoppage of the nefarious and inglorious practice in human trafficking. The first settlers in Arondizuogu claim their origin from one of the villages in Arochukwu called Amankwu village. It was said however that many of the people of Arondizuogu including Okoli's grandfather actually moved in from several towns in present-day Anambra State of Eastern Nigeria. The said movement must have occurred about the middle of the nineteenth century. Affinity between the peoples of Arondizuogu and Arochukwu however remained strong even with the passage of time.

It was usually a thing of excitement for people from any of the Aro communities to be posted to Arochukwu. When therefore Okoli went to visit his brother in Arochukwu, the former was very excited and was anxious to see the legendary *long juju*, a mysterious masquerade with which the Arochukwu people were said to have mesmerized other towns and villages into coming to Arochukwu to pay homage. Such visitors often came to check out on their prospects in life or simply to answer essentially fictitious summons from the long juju and the gods. Arochukwu people were in fact known as and called *umu Chukwu*, which meant children of God.

It was said that some of the supplicants to the long juju would be passed through a tunnel with several diversions, a few leading out back to town, but most leading towards a river into waiting slave ships. For the few that would return, there would be rejoicing from friends and relatives as they were said to have been found clean and worthy by the gods. For the many that might not return the blood of goats or rams deliberately and surreptitiously sprayed down stream would be taken as evidence that they had been "taken up by the gods." The ultimate reappearance of those who would not return (for those strong enough to make the journey) would be some thousands of miles across the Atlantic. Such were the stories Okoli and his friends were told. It is left for history books to confirm or refute.

Okoli felt disappointed at what he saw when he arrived at Arochukwu. From the many stories they had heard about the fame and exploits or notoriety of the town, Okoli had expected to see magnificent edifices befitting of a town so internationally known. What he saw however was a sleepy old town with corrugated rusty brown roofing sheets. The majority of the houses still had grass-thatched roofs. Most roads were untarred (save for the lone major road that ran through the town). There was no running water and no electricity supply to the town. Could it be that Okoli had not really got to the town proper?

He certainly must have been expecting too much. He came from Enugu, which was the capital city, and his father lived in Aba, which was a major urban area. It would have been more appropriate if he had imagined Arochukwu in comparison to his own town Arondizuogu. It would have been a fairer comparison. He would thereby not have expected so much.

Okoli's brother lived in a village called Amannagwu close to a stream from where the townsfolk fetched both their drinking water and the water they used for other activities: laundry, cooking, etcetera. The general hospital where Mako worked was about fifteen minutes bicycle ride from his residence. Okoli had the opportunity of visiting many places of historic interest including the palace of the *eze* (the king) of the town. The Eze Aro, as the king was called, was a very highly respected traditional ruler. The history of the kingdom was said to date back over 150 years.

The people of Arochukwu, Okoli observed, were a very proud people. Despite the fact that the town might have lost a lot of its influence on neighboring towns and villages, the people still maintained their dignity and were very proud of their culture and traditions. Many of the men were polygamists, and the husband would build his house at the centre of the compound and build a single-room reception called *obi,* just at the entrance to his compound. Okoli could see where his own father, who was a strong adherent of cultural values, got the plan of his compound from: a centrally located two-storey building with eight smaller houses each of two bedrooms in a semicircular pattern around the main building for each of the eight wives. The obi was usually a lone large circular one-room house situated near the main entrance into the compound.

Visitors to any compound were received by the head of the family at the obi. One of the wives would bring kola nuts and hand over to the husband, who would then present same to the visitor, who was expected to display the kola to his male companions. The kola nut would then be presented back to the head of the family with the statement:

"Oji eze did eze naka." This implied that the king's kola nut must be back into the king's hands.

The head of the family would, in the absence of any other more elderly person present, pray over the kola nuts, hand over an unsplit one to the leader of the visitors, and proceed to split the rest of the kola nuts. The unsplit kola nut was expected to accompany the visitors back to their home as a testimony of the visit. The split kola nuts would then be carried round to everybody present by the youngest person in the group.

The tradition of kola presentation among the Arochukwu people was very strong. That indeed held true for the majority of the Igbo-speaking people of Eastern Nigeria.

By Christmas holidays of Okoli's fourth year in secondary school, he was invited to Kaduna in Northern Nigeria for his vacation. The invitation was from his junior uncle Cosi. The trip was Okoli's first visit outside of Eastern Nigeria. He had set out from Enugu on the one-and-a-half-day train journey. Having undertaken many journeys from Aba to Afikpo Road and back several times, Okoli had become quite familiar with travel by rail. Unlike the type of train he used to travel with, which used to stop at every station however, the train he took this time to Kaduna did not stop at every station. It was much faster and stopped only at designated major stations.

Okoli was very excited about the expected trip to Kaduna. The only apprehension he had about the journey was a possible repeat of the bad experience he had with use of the restroom when the train was in motion. He had not forgotten how his shorts and underwear were swept off by the wind through the toilet hole in an earlier train journey on a day he and his friends were trying to impress the girls from Queen's School Enugu. After that incident, Okoli had strictly avoided the use of the restroom in the trains. Whenever he was pressed to use the restroom on any train journey, he had always suppressed the urge until the train stopped at a station, where he would dismount to use the restrooms in the train station. The practice was however possible with the suburban trains, which stopped at every station. With the express train, which stopped only at major stations, and with the journey to Kaduna stretching for over a full day, however, Okoli was very apprehensive about how he would avoid complete use of the restroom facilities. In the end, he had to muster the courage to pull it through with more careful use of the train facility.

At the Kaduna end of the journey, Cosi, Okoli's uncle, was waiting for him. As soon as he saw the signposts indicating that the train had entered Kaduna, Okoli pinned down his head against the window, looking out for his uncle who had written him that he would be waiting at the beginning of the station walkway. Okoli could in fact see his uncle from afar even before his coach entered the station's walkway. It was a very happy reunion because Okoli had not seen his uncle since the latter's return from a four-year study overseas.

Okoli was pleasantly surprised by what he saw in Kaduna: the amount of development, the neat wide major roads, and the regularity of power supply. The impression widely held was that only Enugu, Lagos, and Port Harcourt were the well-developed cities. It became obvious to Okoli after his arrival in Kaduna that traveling was a very effective and factual teacher, a very enlightening experience.

Most of the people Okoli came across during his four-week stay in Kaduna spoke Housa, the predominant language in most towns in Northern Nigeria. That was a sharp contrast to the Igbo language, which was the predominant language in Eastern Nigeria, and Yoruba language, which was predominant in Western Nigeria. Even the Igbo people Okoli came across in Kaduna could also speak Hausa. Broken English (an adulterated form of the English language) was however understood by most shop owners, many of whom were either from the east or from the west. Indeed it appeared to Okoli that Kaduna had a greater cultural and linguistic diversity than Enugu, where the latter grew up.

On Okoli's second night in Kaduna, his uncle took him to the cinema to watch a movie. As they were buying their tickets, Okoli observed a very fair boy with a big head, who was conversing in the Igbo language with his companion. After they had gone into the cinema hall, Okoli walked up to the fair-complexioned boy and introduced himself. The boy in turn introduced himself as Ethelbert. He further told Okoli that he was attending Bishop Shanahan College Orlu, a school well-known to Okoli. The two boys sat beside each other for the rest of the show, exchanging school gossips. At the end of the show, the two verbally exchanged addresses in Kaduna and went their separate ways. Little did Okoli know that it would take another twenty years before he and Ethelbert would see again. When they met again, they still remembered the Kaduna cinema and indeed the particular Indian film that was showing that night!

THE SENIOR STUDENT, THE SENIOR CHALLENGES

Before long, the mock school certificate exams for Okoli's class were only weeks away. Events had moved on so fast. Every student was so busy with preparation for the mock exams. Though no certificates would be awarded, part of the results would form the basis for those who would be chosen to do the higher school certificate course in the school. Those who would not be chosen would have to go to other schools, most likely mission schools, to look for placement.

About one week to the mock school certificate exams, Okoli was invited to the principal's office and told that based on his English performance in previous class exams, he had been selected to represent the school in a nationwide essay competition. He was told that the winner of the essay competition would be sponsored to New York in the United States of America. The sponsor of the essay competition was said to be a New York-based newspaper publishing group, which the principal said was being represented in Lagos by another organization. On the appointed day, Mr Oneahala, the English teacher, was appointed Okoli's invigilator for the two-hour essay. Mr Oneahala, whom the students had nicknamed Supra Ingentuum because of his huge size, was very confident that Okoli would win the essay competition. The script was thereafter collected and submitted to the organizers of the contest by the principal.

About a month later, Okoli was again called to the principal's office, where he was congratulated and told that he won the essay competition. Despite the approaching exams, he was told to go home and obtain his parents' consent to travel soon after the school certificate exams. He was also told to get two passport-sized photographs and two full photographs of himself, in addition to the letter of consent from his parents or guardians. He was told that those documents were for the processing of his travel papers. The thought of traveling overseas was so fascinating to Okoli, who had never traveled even as far as to Lagos. So despite the approaching exams, he set out for Aba and collected all the documents and photographs required. He submitted all the documents and photographs to the principal, who confirmed to him the following day that all the documents had been sent by registered mail to Lagos and that he should hope to travel to the United States soon after his school certificate examinations. Throughout the school certificate exam period, Okoli was full of imagination of how he would fly in an aeroplane for the first time soon after his exams. But the latter was never to be. The principal's assurance was the last Okoli heard of that award. It was in the light of later events and observations that Okoli came to believe that anything could have happened to the scripts and documents in Lagos. The principal was to feel so sad about the whole issue when he saw a publication in a national daily that another boy from a Lagos school was flying to the United States on the same competition after his (Okoli's principal's) student had been written a letter officially confirming that Okoli won the competition. Okoli kept carrying with him the letter for several months after the communication was sent to him, hoping, even after the letter got so tattered from continuous handling, that one day he would still be called up to set out on the promised trip. That was never to be, and neither Okoli nor his parents nor even his school principal had "the reach" to investigate the obvious hijacking of that hard-won award. Okoli's solace lay only in committing the whole incident to prayers. He had to assure himself that "God's time is the best." The school certificate came and went by. Repeated enquiries about the proposed sponsorship met with silence. Copies of several enquiries from the school to Lagos about the award yielded no response. Someone along the line obviously must have hijacked the award, a typical situation in the emerging morally deteriorating society.

The school certificate results again showed Government Secondary School Afikpo as one of the best-scoring schools with 100 percent passing result. The school also produced the best individual result. Aboni, Okoli's good friend topped the results in the West African subregion; none of Okoli's class friends went below a grade 2 in the exams. Indeed most came out in grade 1. Okoli himself also made a grade 1 pass. He was very happy with his result, much as he had expected a much better aggregate score than what he got. He and his friends nevertheless all felt very grateful to God for a successful completion of the secondary school course. After the school certificate exams, Aboni, Livi, Donald, and Okoli went out to "the rocks," the rocky hills near the school waterworks and had a picnic, and the photographs which they took there remained with Okoli as happy memories of the good old days at Afikpo.

Okoli and most of his friends were selected for the higher school certificate course. Only Donald traveled out of the country for further studies. Before they vacated for the third term, Okoli was appointed a house subprefect. As they sang the dismissal song that end of term ("Lord, dismiss us with thy blessing"), from *Songs of Praise*, they knew that it certainly had been a worthwhile exercise as they looked forward to the day they would come back in their new capacities as higher school students, wearing no longer shorts and short-sleeved shirts but trousers and long-sleeved shirts.

A Second Chance to Move to the United States

While they were on the long vacation after the school certificate examinations, Okoli's elder brother, who some years before had entered a university in Texas, secured him admission in a junior college in the USA. Okoli had earlier mailed his transcripts and other required documents to his brother. Okoli's father had called him one day and told him that he should make arrangements to travel. He said he had wanted to compensate Okoli for all his "excellent performance in school so far," especially as he was on scholarship throughout his secondary school career. He also said that he wanted to make up for the disappointment Okoli must have felt at the earlier failed New York trip. Okoli was again quite excited about the idea even though he kept feeling that if he left at that stage, he would miss all the fun of being a higher school boy. He was excited all the same, and for the second time in under two years, he started preparing to travel to the USA.

As the family gathered at home during the Christmas, however, Ogbuka (Okoli's father) announced that Okoli would be traveling to the USA.

"But," he said, "no other girls would go to secondary school. Girls belong to other people's compounds, and they should prepare for marriage as soon as they are grown up."

"I will train the girls up to end of primary school, and after that, they should either get married or learn a trade like dressmaking," Ogbuka declared.

He said that the girl's future was in her husband's house and that after all, their mothers did not go to school but were all happily married to him.

Nobody contested Ogbuka's statements, and nobody asked any questions. Nobody ever contested any of Papa's statements or declarations. Neither the wives nor the children ever did. Ogbuka's children were not brought up to question what ever he said. Besides, in the prevailing culture, *di bu uno* (family head) had the ultimate say in all affairs of the family. Ogbuka's decisions about limited formal education for the girl child was certainly not borne out of hatred for any of his daughters. He was only acting based on the culture of his age and time, which unfortunately saw the future of the girl child only from the perceptive of her marital home. Happily it did not take too long after that declaration for the practice to begin to change.

That night of that declaration was one of Okoli's most troubled nights. He felt he was going to be the reason for his sisters not going to secondary schools. How right would it be for him to proceed to the United States of America at the expense of the secondary school education of his sisters?

How justified would it be for him to have his own secondary school education and then be the instrument for denial of that same opportunity to his sisters? How would he have felt if the reverse were the case, where he would be denied an education because of the ambitions of any of his sisters?

Ogbuka had taken his decision. His decisions in matters concerning his family were always final. Okoli would not be the person to counter his father's decision. But if that decision was based purely on the need to satisfy his (Okoli's) ambition to go for further education in the United States, then Okoli felt he should have a right to reject the offer. After all, there were already four universities in Nigeria from where people could get a degree: Ibadan, Nsukka, Lagos, and Zaria. Okoli decided that he would reject the offer to go to America. He was resolved on that. And he decided he would tell his father so. He would for the first time try to counter his father's decision. He felt justified in doing so since he was to be the beneficiary of the project. It was nevertheless a very difficult thing to do, a most unusual thing, a near taboo, for a son to counter the declaration of di bu uno even if the son was to be the beneficiary of the declaration.

Okoli had to grapple with the difficulty of fashioning out the best way to do it, without being taken for a rebel against family tradition. That was because, even though Ogbuka was not dictatorial in his family, no member of his family ever dared go against his orders or behave in any way that was likely to annoy him.

Ogbuka was a benevolent and loving father and an extremely caring husband to each of his eight wives, impartial and forthright. He merited his family's respect in every way. He always referred with disgust to the dictatorial attitude of his friend and neighbor Ogwumike, who always insisted that each of his three wives and fifteen children must salute him and shout *mazi-o-o* (we salute you) when ever he (Ogwumike) passed gas.

Ogwumike would often deliberately pass gas very loudly so that even his wives and children who happened to be some distance away from him would hear it. And all would shout in unison, “Mazi-o-o, mazi-o-o.”

Ogwumike appeared to always take special delight in that salutation any time he passed gas. If there appeared to be any doubt to any member of his household about where the loud sound of his gas-passing was coming from, Ogwumike would lightly stroke his bottom with his right hand to confirm the source. He would thereafter tilt his head to one side as if to hear more distinctly the chorus of “MAZI-O-O-O, MAZI-O-O-O” from every member of his household present. It did not appear to bother him that many of his neighbors, including Ogbuka, did not approve of that oppressive and near-barbaric behavior. Ogwumike always said that it was a tradition that was passed on to him from his father before the latter’s tragic demise, and that it was his right as di bu uno. Indeed, he always encouraged his children to ensure that they continued with the “tradition” any time they got married and had children.

Throughout the night of the announcement of the proposed travel to the USA, Okoli could not sleep. As early as five in the morning, he was waiting for his father in the staircase to tell him that he no longer wanted to proceed with the American trip. The latter’s room was upstairs by the right wing of the building while Okoli’s own room was also upstairs but on the left wing of the building. Of Ogbuka’s forty-six children, only Okoli and his elder brother Mako were allocated rooms in the main building. All the other forty-four children lived in the two room houses built for their respective mothers. Mako was away to the United States. In effect therefore, only Okoli and his father occupied the rooms upstairs in the main building of Ogbuka’s house.

Okoli knew that his father always got up very early in the morning to go downstairs to use the bathroom since the house did not have bathrooms or toilets in the main building.

As soon as Ogbuka emerged, Okoli greeted him, “Papa, good morning.”

He replied and asked what Okoli was doing at the staircase so early in the morning.

“I no longer want to go to the United States,” Okoli said.

“Hmm, is that what is keeping you awake? Did you see demons in the United States in your sleep? Go and sleep, and see me again later in the morning.”

Okoli went back to his bed and was for the first time that night able to catch some sleep. He had, to some extent, unloaded the burden that kept him awake all night.

By morning, before Okoli could wake up, Ogbuka was off for one of his numerous weekend appointments in the village square.

The Man, His Wives, and the Suppers of Many Dishes

About seven in the evening that day, Ogbuka's center table on the first floor of the main building was already lined up as usual with supper from each of the seven wives that Ogbuka had at home at any particular point in time. The center table was a very large oval table made from mahogany wood. It had four large carved feet, between which many of the children whose heights did not reach the level of the table would often crawl as the food arrived in turns from each of the wives. An eighth wife was always at Aba as the rotation dictated. When ever Papa (the name by which Ogbuka was known, not just by his children but also by all his beneficiaries) was at home, each of the seven wives would cook and present a dish of her choice to Papa. Each dish was usually more than the size that would be enough for one person. Indeed, each wife had standing orders to prepare dishes that would feed her, her children, and three extra people. Each wife was therefore under standing orders to prepare a dish that would feed a minimum of seven people. Some would present yam porridge mixed with green vegetables; some others would present *garri* (a cassava product) with soup. Another would present pounded yam, while another would provide breadfruit pudding, and so on. It was usually an endless array of dishes each time Ogbuka was at home, and that was two days every week.

The meals prepared by each of the wives were usually lined on the table in rows and in order of seniority of the wives. Seniority was not based on chronological age but in order of arrival into the family. That way, it was easy for Ogbuka to know at a glance which of the wives was stingy with the dishes. In the event of any indiscretion in the quality or quantity of the dishes, Ogbuka's eagle-eyed gaze would be quick to detect this, and that dish would immediately be waved off the table by a mere movement of *aka nnanyi ukwu* (our master's wave of the hand). The wife that presented the underrated meal would need no further prompting than a wave of Ogbuka's index finger for her to withdraw the dish and rush to her kitchen to augment the dish and present it again before the completion of the family feeding session.

The much younger children often might not know the circumstances surrounding the withdrawal of any dish. Belu, one of the youngest of the forty-six children, often would cry when ever any particular dish of his choice was being so withdrawn. He would soon cheer up again when a larger quantity of the same meal would reappear. The older children often knew and recognized Papa's (Ogbuka's) hand motion to signify rejection of any dish. They were never perturbed when ever any dish was being withdrawn because they knew that it would certainly reappear in a larger quantity or with improved garnishing. The much younger children might also not be aware of the justification for Papa's rejection of any substandard dish. But Ogbuka knew that he always provided to every wife much more than they needed and on a weekly basis.

The soups were usually arranged in a row, while the puddings were arranged in another row. The aroma of the different steaming plates of food was usually ecstatic, a constant source of nostalgia for Okoli in his later years in the secondary school whenever he felt that there was too much monotony in the dishes served at school.

The multiplicity and variety of dishes served in Ogbuka's household was also to affect the attitude of his children later in life. It made it difficult for his children to fit outside of the family in matters of feeding. Bolu, one of Okoli's younger brothers, was once sent to live with his grandmother. He ran back after only two days, citing the presentation of "only one type of food during each meal" as his reason for running back home. When, during the weekdays, Ogbuka was away at Aba, the children of the household always felt free to congregate at the kitchen of any of the wives of their choice. The wife into whose kitchen more children congregated would usually see the presence of the large numbers of children as an honor and as a mark of the acceptability of her dishes. Any of the wives who did not have many of the children congregating for her meals would usually feel some deficiency and would usually approach some more successful cowife for advice on how to improve on her cooking. If the particular children of any wife also deserted her meals, that would be a sure sign for the wife in question to urgently seek advice or go for a cooking course from another cowife.

Each wife regarded the children of the family as *umu anyi*(our children), and the most grievous "crime" that any wife in Ogbuka's house could commit was to discriminate between the children of the family. Any such discrimination would be regarded by Ogbuka as *aru*, an abomination in the household and would only be cleansed by the presentation of a hen, which would be killed, cooked, and eaten by the entire family. The offending wife would further be punished by her being made to be the last to choose when the meat was shared on the *ugbo anu* (meat board), irrespective of her seniority in the hierarchy of wives. Even though the meat so shared was usually very tiny when compared with the quantity of meat consumed in the developed world, each share was of immense significance to every wife and every child in the household.

Some of the much younger children did not bother about the quantity or quality of the different dishes. What they cared most about was the variety of the dishes each of which they could taste, in the wives' individual kitchens whenever Ogbuka was not at home in the village. Very early each morning, Nne, one of Okoli's much younger sisters, about the time she was three or four years old, would usually carry her little plate from her mother's house and make the rounds through each of the other six wives' houses collecting bits of yam, moi-moi, beans, cocoyam, or what ever each wife had prepared for breakfast. Most times she would make the rounds with no dress or shoes on, supporting the little plate on her protruding abdomen. If it was cold during the harmattan period, Nne would clean her leaking nostrils with the back of her hands as she made the rounds. She would usually end the rounds in the corridor of Ebube's house as Ebube usually prepared *akara* (bean cake) for sale, and Nne particularly liked to eat akara.

The aroma from Ebube's *utazi* soup was usually so strong and so sweet that it could lure a hungry passerby into the compound, even from as far away as the road, some three poles away. Ebube was the most senior of the eight wives. Even though she might not have been the oldest in chronological age, she was always conferred with special respect and would be the first to choose whenever food or clothes or other presents were provided in the family. Conversely, whenever work, like the clearing of the bush for farming, was shared out, she would be the person to do the sharing and the last to have a portion to work on, after the others have chosen. The order, harmony, and mutual respect in the family was so amazing. In later years, a number of younger married people who were Christians and whose religion required them to marry only one wife often came to Ogbuka to seek counsel from him on how to have stable homes whenever their monogamous families ran into crises. Ogbuka was expected to know a lot about the art of family stability since he had eight wives and was still able to have peace, harmony, and mutual love and understanding in his family of fifty-five. He was an uncrowned master in the marital arts, marital process, and marital peaceful coexistence.

Ogbuka's advice to those who sought his counsel about marital stress was always simple and straight:

> Don't quit.
> Take control.
> Be just, loyal, and fair.
> Be the lord and master.
> Assume economic command.
> Don't marry two.
> Marry three or four.
> Or, like me, marry eight or more!

"That way," Ogbuka would assert, "there would be minimal jealousy and greater desire for cooperation between the wives. When you have only one wife, you are enslaved to her. When they are two, they will perpetually quarrel between each other and see you to your early grave. But when you have three or more wives, they will compete for your love. They will make peace and cooperate between themselves since they will know that quarrels will be of no use."

"That way," Ogbuka always said, "you will live happy and long."

At seventy-five, he still kicked strong, lived simple, and still rode his Raleigh brand lady's bicycle, with his eight wives to boot.

Ogbuka however never told his listeners whether the converse would also hold true. He never confirmed whether polyandry would also solve the problem where there is constant marital disharmony in a monogamous home.

If the converse was to hold true, and each of Ogbuka's eight wives was to have eight husbands, then Ogbuka might have had to compete with sixty-three other men for the affection of his eight wives. Luckily, for Ogbuka, polygamy, but not polyandry, was permissible and indeed treasured, in the culture of Ogbuka's society.

Ebube's dishes were usually of particular delight to many of the children. Ekuus, Ebube's first daughter, usually told the other children that her mother used to taste the soup a minimum of twenty times to ensure that the ingredients were in the right proportions. She also said that the particular *uzuza* spice that her mother used could only be procured at midnight from the deepest parts of ohia ojii, the thick jungle that separated Ndiakunwanta village from the adjacent Ndiamazu village. It was however known that Ekuus was usually a deep sleeper and was not likely to be awake at midnight to be able to calculate effectively what time her mother would go out at night to procure the uzuza spice from ohia ojii.

Ji-ona, a yellow variety of yam tuber, was a regular dish from Mgoli, the second wife of Ogbuka. Mgoli was known to love peppery diets, and Ogbuka and one of his daughters, Konfo, were always very delighted with the peppery ji-ona diets, which were often eaten with *ncha*, a cream made from boiled palm oil, potash, spices, and dried *asa* fish.,

Eliaba, Okoli's mother, was the fourth wife in the order of arrival in the family and consequently in the hierarchy. She often prepared *abacha*, dried, sliced cassava tuber. The latter she would mix with red palm oil and pepper premixed with *okazi* vegetable and a little quantity of utazi to obtain a tinge of refreshing bitter taste.

Ji abubo, a mixture of boiled yam with fresh green vegetables, red palm oil, and fresh red pepper was a particular specialty of Ezima, the third wife of Ogbuka.

Ochoto, a mixed grill of green peas and yellow corn with green *ugu* vegetables often featured in the dishes presented by Ewelu, who was the sixth wife in order of arrival into the family. Ogbuka used to prefer foods that would be swallowed with soup in a bolus, without being chewed. Foods like *akpu* or *garri* both made from cassava a tropical tuber were often particularly delightful to him. Sometimes he would specifically order for a specific type of food like pounded coco yam with *onugbu* (bitter leaf) soup.

Nime, Ogbuka's seventh wife, was a little more Western oriented. She was the youngest wife for a long time before the arrival of Noneka, the eighth wife. Nime was fairly educated and was the only wife of Ogbuka who was literate prior to the arrival of Noneka, the eighth and last wife. Nime often presented Jollof rice often mixed with chopped beef. She was the only one of Ogbuka's wives who used curry powder and Maggi cubes as spices. These usually made her dishes very tasty and delightful to the children.

Noneka, the youngest and eighth wife, was most of the time resident at Aba, where Ogbuka had his business. The rest of the family did not often have the opportunity of tasting Noneka's dishes except for the two festivity periods of Ikeji and Christmas when virtually every resident in the urban areas would be home to his or her village. Noneka often presented rice and beans with tomato-rich stew. That particular dish was usually delightful to the older children who were in the secondary schools, where that combination was often served.

Every meal whenever Ogbuka was home at Arondizuogu was a feast for the children, and any and every child from anywhere in the village was welcome. It was one of the biggest sources of joy the children had at Arondizuogu, and they always looked forward to the weekends because Papa was home from Aba almost every Saturday to go back to Aba on Sunday evening. Meat and meat products were a rarity. Butter and cheese were never featured. Indeed they were not known of. Snails were occasionally featured especially during the rainy season when there was adequate rotten vegetation for the *nkoto*, the giant snails to feed on. Stockfish was usually plentiful as Ogbuka often loaded these with the regular supply of bags of garri, rice, and beans, which he routinely sent to his wives and children at home, from Aba.

Many people in Arondizuogu were aware of the multiple dishes that would routinely adorn Ogbuka's table each meal time, seven main dishes and many side orders. These were increased to eight main dishes during major festivities when even the wife at Aba would also be home. The suppers of many dishes were usually of very great delight to Ogbuka, his eight wives, and particularly to each of his forty-six children.

Ogbuka was the initial name by which Papa, Okoli's father, was known. He hardly ever used his market-day name, which was Nwankwo. In Ndiakunwanta village, there was hardly any body who did not know Ogbuka, his eight wives, the famed seven or eight dishes, and the fact that all and sundry, irrespective of where they came from, were welcome to participate in the dishes whenever Ogbuka was home. The fact that Ogbuka had forty-six children, twenty-seven sons and nineteen daughters, was also known by everybody in the village. It was a well-known fact that if one was passing by Ogbuka's house around meal time most weekends, there would be seven types of dishes on the center table on his expansive ground floor parlor (living room). Nobody was ever turned away. Ogbuka was indeed usually visibly happy whenever any visitor came in around meal times. The large wooden front gate was perpetually ajar all weekends from about six in the morning till late at night whenever Ogbuka was home.

Whenever the children heard "*kpam, kpam, kpam*" (hello, hello, hello) at the front gate around meal time, they would know that they would have an additional participant at the table.

For every meal, Ogbuka always appointed one of his children to stay at the gate to usher in any visitor. It looked like he always craved for such visitors, who would share in the family's meals.

Could he have been craving for these visitors to show off how wealthy he was? Was he simply so good-natured that he craved for people who would eat out of him?

Any of Ogbuka's children preferring the latter of these possible reasons for an answer might be mistaken for making the answer choice out of patronage for his father. Subsequent events in Ogbuka's life and the anonymity under which he often sent cash, food, and clothing materials to several poor families in Arondizuogu and in Ndiakunwanta in particular would easily confirm the fact of his enduring benevolence and philanthropism. It was some of his children and one or two of his wives who sometimes frowned when they saw too many people come in to share in the meals.

The children sometimes felt that the food might not be enough for everybody if too many visitors came in. Ogbuka would be at his best in such situations. He would immediately call on any of his wives who happened to be closest to him. "Eliaba, go and prepare more rice," or, "Ewelu, get us more garri and soup," Ogbuka would order.

In under an hour, there would be much more food available than all present could consume. The man Ogbuka was simply larger than life. Anyone in Arondizuogu who was around at the time of Madukibeya, as Ogbuka later got to be known, would easily testify to the latter's enduring benevolence.

The issue of Okoli going to the United States vis-à-vis his sisters stopping further educational training was sorted out amicably on the evening of the day Okoli turned down the offer. It was decided that Okoli should complete higher school, and thereafter the issue would be revisited. Happily therefore, none of Ogbuka's daughters had to suspend her education so that Okoli might proceed to the United States. The issue, too, never got revisited because before Okoli completed his higher school education, the Nigerian Civil War had started, disrupting most educational activities in the eastern part of the country. The mere fact that the issue was muted in the first instance was evidence of the sad cultural bias which placed daughters at a disadvantage over the sons of most households, a development which only subsequent mass education and inculcation of more civilized values were to change.

The Aspiration of the Chemist Shop Sweeper

Okoli's days of sweeping the chemist shop for the pharmacy assistant, Pius, and occasionally getting water or helping the latter to hold the funnel with which Pius mixed the Mist Alba in the shop at Enugu influenced in no small measure Okoli's decision to be a medical doctor. In those days when the total doctor population in the whole city of Enugu was probably not more than five or six, very little was known of any functional distinction between a pharmacist and a medical doctor; and the very few pharmacists in town both consulted, prescribed, dispensed, and also performed minor surgeries. The hypodermic syringe in use was the nondisposable glass syringe, and Okoli used to get very excited whenever he saw Pius washing the syringes every morning by aspirating water into them and flushing out the water into the air in a fine jet form. It used to be so much fun for Okoli to watch the syringe being flushed. He often pleaded with Pius to repeat the process several times, and Okoli would often attempt to catch the jet of water as Pius flushed the syringe. The disposable syringes which were later to be taken for granted did not always exist.

Okoli's many years of seeing wounds being dressed, infections being treated, and abscesses being incised and drained left a lasting impression on Okoli and made him decide early in life, even when he did not know the implications, that he was going to be a medical doctor.

Only once did Okoli's resolve waver in his childhood decision to be a doctor. As Okoli spent more of his vacations at Aba during his later secondary school days, he used to accompany his father, Ogbuka, and one of his sisters, Doro, to lodge the proceeds of the previous day's sales into the bank every morning. The bank Ogbuka used for all his banking transactions was called BBWA (Bank of British West Africa). Ogbuka, being an importer and representing many companies in Europe and the Far East, often had goods shipped to him on credit from Britain, Germany,

Holland, Denmark, Hong Kong, and Japan. Sometimes lorry loads of these goods would be so many that there just would not be enough space in the stores (warehouses) for the goods. Virtually every available space in the compound and the front of the house was taken up by wooden cases filled with the imported bicycle parts and tools. Ogbuka had obviously become a big player in the importation business. The man who did not have any formal education—who could barely sign his name, who could read but could not write, who had but one old Voss (and later, an Imperial) brand typewriter—no telephones, and no computers was doing very effective business with multinational companies in Europe and Asia!

Ogbuka's whole office was in one room, adjacent to his bedroom. His secretarial staff only consisted of Hyman, a young man from a neighboring village, whom Ogbuka had trained up to primary school and later had taken into his business. All letters were initially manually written but later after many complaints about occasional illegibility from overseas customers, the Voss brand typewriter was acquired. Typists were initially hired to type the letters, but later one of Okoli's sisters, who studied typing and shorthand, took on the job of typing the letters. Doro, Okoli's sister, became so proficient in typing that she easily got a job with the Bank of British West Africa as a secretary/typist. Ogbuka's one-room office was so stuffed with files from ground to roof that there was often only enough room for table and two chairs. Ogbuka would sit on the one chair reading the numerous letters that arrived every day from overseas and dictating replies to either Hyman or Doro or indeed to any of his sons who was home on holidays from secondary school. If there was nobody available to draft credible letters, Ogbuka would call on any of his younger children still in primary schools to try the drafting. He could read fast and would easily point out grammatical errors from letters even when he could not write the letter himself. It was always so surprising to all, how easily he could detect wrong English grammar and even wrong spellings when he could not write and could only sign his signature with a few upright strokes of the pen and roughly written "O-g-b-u-k-a."

A one-room office, a table and two chairs, a dilapidated typewriter, a hurricane lantern in case of power failure, thousands of files stacked from ground to ceiling—these were the tools that made the waves and generated hundreds of thousands of pounds sterling in annual revenue. These made up the machinery that powered the giant enterprise of the company C. N. Ogbuka and Sons, a company that supplied scores of successful subagents in Aba, Onitsha, Kano, Lagos, and Port Harcourt, the top commercial centers in the country. Ogbuka's children often wondered how some of these subagents would come from Port Harcourt and Lagos to buy from Aba when these good were initially shipped through Port Harcourt and sometimes through the Lagos ports.

Ogbuka often told visiting business partners from Europe, who came to inspect his offices, that his main business office was located inside his head.

"My business office is a whole house, and the house is in my head. And I can tell you the date of my last correspondence with you in Germany, the date of your reply, and the entire goods I ordered," Ogbuka once told Mr Lornz, a visiting business partner from Hamburg, Germany.

Mr Lornz's company based in Germany had done business with Ogbuka for over eighteen years. They had decided to expand the scope of their business with C. N. Ogbuka and Sons, as Ogbuka's company was called. They sent Mr Lornz to come and do an on-the-spot inspection of their business customers in Nigeria. Mr Lornz had lodged in the Catering Rest House, a hotel in Aba run by the regional government. Ogbuka went to visit Mr Lornz at the hotel. Mr Lornz, a very friendly and informal man, decided to come with Ogbuka to visit the latter's house and to commence the office appraisal thereafter. Ogbuka consented to the visit, and after exchange of pleasantries, he decided to go to look for a taxi to convey Mr Lornz down to his (Ogbuka's) house. Mr Lornz, however, declined the offer of a taxi, saying instead that he would accompany Ogbuka in the vehicle with which the latter came.

"Are you sure you can manage my vehicle?" Ogbuka asked Mr Lornz.

"Mr Ogbuka, me Second World War veteran and me can ride on any vehicle car or truck," Mr Lornz asserted in his occasionally disjointed English. Even Okoli, who had accompanied his father to the Catering Rest House could observe that Mr Lornz's English was as poor as his father's own. The children had the belief that all white people spoke perfect English, and they thought that Mr Lornz was speaking bad English so that Mr Ogbuka could understand, since the latter spoke barely comprehensible English but was quick to point out mistakes in the recording of his letters!

As the duo of Mr Ogbuka and Mr Lornz walked to the front of the hotel however, there was no car in sight. Instead, leaning casually against one of the many whistling pine trees in front of the hotel was one old fairly rusty lady's Raleigh bicycle, devoid of carriage behind or sitting frame at the middle.

Ogbuka walked up to the bicycle, his vehicle of over twelve years. He pointed towards the handle bars of the bicycle and asked Mr Lornz, "Can you manage there?"

An obviously flabbergasted Mr Lornz shook his head in disbelief. Would he consent to sit at the handle bars of a lady's bicycle for a two-mile ride on the unpredictable roads of a dusty African city with its chaotic traffic and multiple potholes made worse by the bombings of the civil war? That was obviously not part of the bargain for a German business executive who was on a visit to Africa to promote his company's business!

Mr Lornz eventually arrived to Ogbuka's house in a chartered taxi. He was a very simple-looking man, simply clad in short-sleeved white shirt and trousers. He arrived at Ogbuka's house a little earlier than Ogbuka himself as the latter rode back in his bicycle. Ogbuka was the name by which Mr Lornz addressed Okoli's father since it was the name by which the latter was actually known, as well as its being his business name. Mr Lornz was waiting in the taxicab when Mr Ogbuka rode back, and both men went in together to the upstairs-located family living room. Mr Lornz had a camera with him. He set this up on a stand and took photographs of himself with Ogbuka. He also took another photograph sitting with the members of the family who were present. He was later to develop and print these photographs. He sent copies of these photographs to Mr Ogbuka, who proudly hung them in his living room.

Mr Lornz felt so much at home in Mr Ogbuka's house. Even though his English was not so good, he was still able to communicate with Ogbuka whose English was equally bad. When Mr Lornz and Mr Ogbuka went inspecting the stores and later spent several hours in the latter's one-room office, the household were all wondering how both men were able to effectively discuss intricate business and what they could be saying for so long in such broken and incoherent English since Mr Lornz was German and Mr Ogbuka was Igbo. But the fact that they were occasionally heard laughing out loudly was an indication that their discussions were moving on smoothly.

Ogbuka came out after about three hours of discussions with Mr Lornz and told the family that Mr Lornz had said he wanted to spend a day or two with the family before going back to his hotel room. Everybody was excited. But there was the fear that Mr Lornz might not be able to tolerate the pepper in the family's soup. It was said that white people generally did not like much pepper in their food. Mr Ogbuka always liked plenty of pepper; consequently, the family's soups and stews were usually very peppery.

The other source of worry was whether Mr Lornz would be able to swallow garri, the local staple food stuff made from grated, dried, and fried cassava which was eaten after recombination with hot water. Balls of garri were usually swallowed whole, after being dipped in soup. They were usually swallowed without being chewed. It was also said that white people were unable to swallow hard balls of food without chewing them. It was said that the reason white people did not swallow food whole was because they all had movable teeth and that they were usually afraid that if they swallowed hard balls of food, they might also unintentionally swallow their entire loose teeth. The prototype white man for Okoli's time and age was the Irish church missionary, who had removable dentures. Many of these missionaries often performed "magic" for the village folk by removing their dentures and displaying toothless gums. Okoli had on several occasions seen the white reverend father in his village church apparently pull out all his teeth and display his mouth without any teeth to the children. The children and adults alike would shout with excitement as soon as the "magician" put back all the teeth in place. That "magic," they believed, could only be performed by white people. The African man's teeth, it was believed, were too stubborn to obey such magic.

There were of course no dentists in Enugu or Aba, and nobody ever saw a removable denture.

The worries about whether Mr Lornz would be able to tolerate the pepper or garri soon ebbed. About 5:00 p.m., Mr Ogbuka again came back to where the family and assistants were seated, stringing bicycle cup hubs into chains of tens. The cup hubs were usually shipped in cases, in packets of one hundred per packet but were retailed and sold, stringed in ropes of tens. Ogbuka told the family that after Mr Lornz had gone to use the toilet, he came back and said he could not used the bucket system toilet. Toilet paper was not in general use. Old news papers were an improvement on the leaves that Ogwumike and the other village folks often used at Ndiakunwanta. Mr Lornz obviously must have been horrified by what he saw at the toilet. Ogbuka's family had cleaned the entire house in anticipation of Mr Lornz's arrival. The toilet facility was however the one area they could not do much about, apart from merely cleaning the interior of the room and ensuring that there were enough old newspapers in the room. Everybody only hoped that the night soil men had done their jobs the previous night.

Mr Lornz had decided to go back to the hotel to come back the following day. The Catering Rest House the biggest and only modern hotel in Aba had the water closet system that at that time only very few houses had.

All others had either the pit latrine or bucket systems.

Another taxicab was called to take Mr Lornz back to the Catering Rest House. Ogbuka's family's discussions for the rest of that day were centered on Mr Lornz's visit.

Shortly after eight o'clock the following morning, a taxicab pulled up in front of Ogbuka's house. Mr Lornz had come. Everybody was surprised he came so early. Everybody was expecting him between 10:00 a.m. and twelve noon, even though he had indicated earlier that he would come back by eight the following morning. This time he came clad in white shorts, a shirt, and black shoes.

Everybody had imagined that Europeans would sleep till about noon every day. Whenever anybody developed the habit of waking up late in the mornings, the person would be said to be practicing *ula ndi ocha*, the Igbo translation of *the white man's sleep*. That meant luxury sleep. That was possibly because the British colonial masters were said to always take midday sleep called siesta. Also, they would usually come to work after the messengers and other office workers have reported earlier to open the offices and tidy them up before their arrival. It was therefore imagined that these officers must have been sleeping till late, in their houses.

Everybody was taken by surprise at Mr Lornz's early arrival. They had tried to do as much cleaning up as they could, but there was nothing they could do about the bucket system toilet. Everybody only prayed that Mr Lornz would not request to use the restroom again during that repeat visit. The family just could not manufacture the water closet toilet system overnight. They had mopped the linoleum carpet in the living room, dusted the files in the office, created walkways between the stockpiled cases in the store (warehouse) for easy inspection. They had taken care of about everything they could reckon with. But they failed to reckon with one other thing: the bedbugs, locally called *chinchi*.

About 11:00 a.m., Mr Ogbuka sent Okoli to buy a bottle of Beck's beer for Mr Lornz from a nearby liquor store. Mr Lornz had come with packaged cake and some brown-colored material in short bars (chocolate bars) from Catering Rest House. About noon, Mr Lornz took a break, and the cakes and beer were set out on a side stool for him in the living room. The packaged snacks saved everybody the worry about the pepper in the family's soup and the possibility of Mr Lornz choking in any attempt to swallow the balls of garri without chewing them. Mr Ogbuka went downstairs to inspect the stringing work on the cup hubs.

Just about ten minutes after Mr Lornz had gone to the parlor to have his midday snacks and beer, he reappeared at the corridor upstairs scratching the back of his thigh frantically.

"Mr Ogbuka, ants; ants, they bit me," he kept repeating, "ants, ants, ants," as Mr Ogbuka rushed upstairs to see what was wrong. It was thought that perhaps some soldier ants, which occasionally invaded the premises around, had found their way to the parlor upstairs. Could one of them have bitten Mr Lornz?

"Ants, ants, ants," Mr Lornz continued to shout as he vigorously scratched his thigh.

Mr Ogbuka, Okoli, and Nime, the Aba-based wife at the time, rushed to the parlor where Mr Lornz's beer and cake was not yet half consumed. There were no soldier ants seen anywhere. The three rushed back to Mr Lornz who continued to scratch his thigh furiously and whose color had suddenly turned almost red in the face and on the affected thigh. He had started to sweat profusely, and everybody was worried.

What kind of "ant" could have done this havoc and had disappeared so fast? And the family had done their best to clean up the entire house in anticipation of Mr Lornz's arrival and stay with them.

Mr Lornz pulled up his shorts and displayed his thigh.

It was a terrifying sight! Just beneath Mr Lornz's shorts, the back of his left thigh was very red and severely swollen. Scratch marks were already showing as if streaked with blood. As Mr Ogbuka rushed off to look for *okwoma,* a local balm made from shea butter, the rest of the family mounted a frantic search for the offending "ant." The cushions and pillows on the chairs were ransacked. They then quickly lifted the cushion pillow. Lo and behold! Five blood-filled bedbugs were slowly crawling along the pillows, too fully fed with blood, to run!

How could that have happened? The family had all been sitting on these cushions without any such bites. The family members knew that there were a couple of bedbugs in some of their furniture just as there were mosquitoes in dark corners in the rooms. They had occasionally poured kerosene in crevices in the cushions and chairs and sometimes sprayed DDT and Shelltox insecticides in the rooms to chase out or kill these vermins. At other times they had merely tolerated these bedbugs and allowed them to live like parasites on the blood of members of the family and guests since it had appeared impossible to completely eliminate these tiny animals. But these bugs had never before been such a burden on any one or wrecked as much havoc on any body. So why that day, and why should that happen to Mr Lornz, the treasured family visitor?

"So why now? Why on this August visitor? And why with so much aggressiveness?" every body mused.

Everybody was very worried. The swelling was getting larger even before everybody's gaze. Mr Ogbuka, after applying the okwoma, had also immediately secured a bottle of Mentholatum and started applying it on the rapidly swelling bedbug bite marks. The vigorous massaging appeared to be worsening the swelling as the obviously worried Mr Lornz looked on in bewilderment. Seeing no progress from his unpracticed medical attention to his guest, Mr Ogbuka rushed downstairs and leapt on his bicycle off to Mr Igo, a nearby pharmacist. Mr Ogbuka must have narrated the incident to Mr Igo because in under thirty minutes, both Ogbuka and Mr Igo were back in Mr Igo's car and the now-distraught and visibly shaken Mr Lornz was given two injections, one on either buttocks. He was also given some tablets to swallow by the pharmacist. Further business discussions were of course temporarily suspended since Mr Lornz had to be driven back to the hotel room in Mr Igo's Peugeot 403 car accompanied by Mr Ogbuka.

Two days later, the business discussions between Mr Ogbuka and Mr Lornz resumed, but this time in Mr Lornz's hotel room, far removed from other menacing "ants."

The visit of Mr Lornz boosted Mr Ogbuka's business. Soon after his departure back to Germany, Mr Lornz must have highly recommended Mr Ogbuka, as the latter's imports from Mr Lornz's company almost trebled. Despite his adversities in Ogbuka's living room, he must have made good recommendations of Ogbuka's business to his parent company in Germany. Ogbuka won the sole agency for a number of Mr Lornz's company products. It became even more difficult to find parking space for the ever-increasing number of cases of goods, since the goods stores were already full. As there were no public storages in Aba, the front of Mr Ogbuka's house had to be used as temporary storage for goods.

The Opportunity to Wear a Tie: The Joys, the Burdens

After the initial euphoria of becoming higher school students, Okoli and his friends had settled back to studies in the first year of the higher school, called lower sixth. Okoli had chosen zoology, chemistry, and physics as his subjects for the higher school course. The zoology and the chemistry did not present too much of a challenge to Okoli academically. But higher school physics was certainly not so easy for him. However, he carried on, and with the help of the very good Indian teachers, Mr Mathew and Mr Patel, the students were confident they would successfully sail through with the higher school certificate examinations. Lower sixth did not have any promotional exam. It was the only class in the school that did not require any end-of-year examination for one to proceed to the next class. It was therefore a relatively smooth-sailing year. However, class tests were still held for each of the individual subjects.

The students greatly savored the opportunity of being seniors, with nobody to molest or bully them, wearing trousers (pants) and long-sleeved shirts. They got their college blazers. Above all, they could now participate in the Debating Society sessions with both boys' schools and girls' schools alike. They started receiving the monthly etiquette lectures from Egbe, the school Principal himself. He taught the sixth formers, as the higher school students were called, different dance steps including waltz and fox-trot. He taught them how to behave in public places and large gatherings. He also got the vice principal, a Briton, to educate the students on how the rural and urban British societies functioned and the correct pronunciation of certain frequently mispronounced words.

The vice principal also instructed the students on what was expected of a typical British gentleman. The students were expected to emulate such behavior. They were also given monthly lessons on "how not to date girls" and on how to behave maturely and polished before girls. The latter was a subject which initially the students tended to shy away from since sex education was never taught in schools, and the mere mention of the word *sex* always appeared immoral to students who had all their lives been taught in the mission primary school that boys and girls should not mix up freely and openly. The students were also lectured on leadership and on public speech and on how to ensure accountability in public office. All these were to prepare them for their exit into the larger society, realizing that the next institutions they would get into were the universities where knowledge of these things would be assumed and consequently would not be routinely taught.

At the close of year in lower sixth course, the school authorities, as was customary, appointed new school prefects and a new school captain, who would run the internal affairs of the students for the following year. A total of twelve school prefects were appointed, with the undisputed academic giant of the time and Okoli's childhood friend, Aboni as the overall school captain. Okoli was appointed school prefect and captain of Ibiam House. For two or three weeks before the appointments, there were widespread speculations that another academic and sports star Nokebu was likely to head the entire school based on his combination of excellence in both sports and academics. It was possible Nokebu himself was also expecting this ultimate position of honor. Nobody would have been surprised either if he had clinched it. He probably would have deserved it. But the school authorities thought differently. They decided to bestow the honor on the lone academic superstar Aboni, who was also not lacking in sports participation even though he did not excel in the latter regard.

Like in all human decisions, it was possible the prefectship appointments did not go down well with everybody. It was possible that some students among the upper sixth class did not accept the appointments in good faith. It was possible there were some unrealized expectations even among the appointees. It was even possible that a few members of staff held a different opinion about the appointments. But the fact remained that there could only be one school captain for the whole school, one house captain for each house, and only a limited number of school prefects. No human decision could ever be a 100 percent perfect. Only the most nearly perfect decision could be considered perfect in any particular situation.

For some reasons still unclear to many of the dramatis personae, dissent and fractionalization started brewing within the prefects' body. Some of the prefects and captains, like Okoli, were probably too naïve not to observe what was going on until the dissent and intrigues snowballed into the open. Maybe, because of Okoli's obvious long-standing friendship with Aboni, the school captain, a lot of things were being hidden from him by some of the other captains and prefects. Maybe it was wrongly assumed that Okoli was Aboni's alter ego, and therefore anything that needed to be concealed from Aboni must also be concealed from Okoli. The victim of any plot almost always would be the last to know about the plot. But with the benefit of hindsight, Okoli later began to believe that Aboni must have sensed that some dissent was brewing within the prefects' body. He noticed that the school captain started to personally make more frequent announcements both in the dining hall and in the assembly hall. He also noticed that many of these announcements ran counter to some orders earlier issued by other captains or prefects. The school captain obviously must have sensed some brewing mutiny, or he must have been informed of same.

Unfortunately, neither party made a clean breast of the contentious issues. But, of course, Aboni must have observed the frequent meetings being held in one of the house captains' rooms and sometimes even in a common room. At such meetings, meat and food were often packaged and supplied from the kitchen. Nokebu's nominee happened to be the supervisory officer for students' feeding. The sumptuous feasts that preceded the meetings must have helped win more converts for Nokebu's meetings.

Then, one day the first open giant strike was taken. The school captain issued an order, changing the students' representative in food matters. He immediately replaced him with one Wanoli, a very intelligent and hardworking class 5 student who was known to be very diligent and very honest. That move, even though it might have been merited, was seen by some as a manifestation of nepotism or at best cronyism since the new appointee happened to hail from Aboni's hometown. It certainly was either a preemptive strike or a measure taken to cut off the source of food supply to the meetings of suspected mutineers. That move was the last straw that broke the camel's back.

That same afternoon a group of house captains and some school prefects, possibly the same group that had been holding meetings, were assembled in one of the house common rooms preparatory to a decisive meeting. That meeting followed immediately after the sacking of the food representative. The usual fried meat and chicken were said to be lacking at the meeting since the food representative had been changed. The meeting got to the knowledge of the school captain, who unexpectedly walked into the meeting. As the astonished attendees were still probably exchanging pleasantries, the school captain issued his orders, "Disperse and disband!"

He thundered in unmistakable terms. Then as if his earlier orders were not clear enough, he roared again, "Disperse and disband!"

But the group did not appear to hear. They neither dispersed nor disbanded on those initial orders.

Could it be they did not understand the English, which was simple and direct enough? Or could it be that they were waiting for a counterorder from their leader or leaders. But no leader or leaders stepped forward to issue counterorders. Nobody dared!

There was only one school captain. And he was there in flesh and blood. He needed no arms, no armor, and no bodyguard.

Such was the strength of the chain of command at Afikpo.

Such was the discipline that was in force in the system.

Such was the beauty of Government Secondary School Afikpo, "the Varsity on the River Cross."

As the standoff appeared to linger with no party too ready to back down but with the meeting group not mustering enough courage to openly challenge the authority of the school captain, word quickly spread around the school. Okoli was on his way to his room when Neebbo—his very loyal, intelligent, and trusted aide—ran up to him to inform him of the developments in one of the house common rooms. Okoli quickly ran towards the named common room rallying two prefects who obviously could not have been part of any plot with him.

The people at the meeting must have seen Okoli and the other two prefects coming towards the meeting room. For Okoli, there was no question of sitting on the fence on an issue like this. To him it was a time to take a stand.

From a distance as the three approached the common room, they could hear the school captain say, "I say again, and for the last time—disperse and disband!"

As Okoli and the two other prefects walked into the hall, the attendees at the meeting had already started filing out through the side door.

The captain of school had spoken! *Order* and *discipline* were the watchwords. There could be no counterorders. The statement "Orders is orders" was very frequently quoted in Afikpo, and everybody accepted that the constituted authority needs to be obeyed. Truly an order was an order.

It was all over. Whatever plans that were on the ground had been truncated. The back of a possible mutiny had been broken.

That was the beauty of Government Secondary School Afikpo. That was the beauty of the Varsity on the Cross.

None of the dramatis personae of those events could have prophesized with certainty what the outcome of that meeting would have been if there had been no exercise of the authority of the school captain at that moment of decision. It might just have ended as one of those adolescent pranks, or it might have blossomed into an unprecedented in-house civil disobedience within the student body.

Whatever would have been the result without that order, however, it was obvious that the order "dispense and disband" had diffused a potentially disruptive situation.

One of Okoli's classmates who was one of those present at that meeting later told Okoli that the order issued to assembled classmates and fellow prefects was the most insulting command he had had all his life. He said that the order amounted to a violation of their freedom of association or of assemblage.

Certainly, Afikpo did not operate on the basis of the constitution of any of the nations of the Western world. There was no pretence about its not being democratic. It was better off not being one. That cherished tenet was better reserved for higher politicized terrains. Feathers might have been ruffled, and nerves might have been frayed, but at least the school was able to be kept in one piece by three simple words *disperse and Disband.*

The Coming of the Jack Boot, the Army Coup, and Its Aftermath

When it was announced on a certain January 15 that there was an army coup in Nigeria, little did the students realize to what extent that announcement would affect the students' education. What the military people were doing did not appear to affect anybody until sometime about August when the students were instructed to vacate the school premises. Some of the students were indeed quite relieved at the unsolicited holidays, which they thought would be for a week or two. They packed their few belongings and got them ready for the trucks that would convey them either to Afikpo Road train station or straight to Enugu. Before boarding the vehicles at school, the students had as usual gathered at the school assembly hall and sang from *Songs of Praise* what many of them did not know was to be for the very last time, "Lord, dismiss us with thy blessing." Another of the verses read thus, "Those returning, those returning, make more faithful than before."

Many of them were never to return; consumed by the subsequent war, either in the battlefield, outside of the battlefield, or even by starvation and disease. Hitherto, the activities of the soldiers and their political activities had not fully bothered the ordinary citizens, who essentially carried on with their day-to-day activities. The students only occasionally read in the newspapers about the army coup, the countercoup, and the subsequent killings of soldiers and civilians, especially in the northern parts of the country. The only real feelings about the seriousness of the situation began to dawn on the students when reports of some loved ones being massacred started filtering into the school compound. It was only then that it dawned on Okoli and some other students that the situation was spiralling out of control. It was only then that they had to start checking up the dictionary definitions of *coup d'état*, *pogrom*, and *genocide*. The actual horror was to come when some students started receiving letters with stamps on which were depicted some real pictures of headless bodies, with the inscription "This is genocide." It was then that many of the students began to realize that the situation was truly grievous.

Okoli proceeded from school to Aba through Afikpo Road. There was no threat to Aba from the war at that time. But everybody kept hearing stories of the fall of Nsukka and the fall of Bonny. Later, it was the fall of Enugu. Many of these stories really did not make much meaning to the majority of the citizenry, who had never experienced war or seriously read about wars. Most of the students were still savoring their holidays to some extent and listening to the news about the war over the radio. A number of Okoli's friends and classmates started enlisting in one form of service or the other, especially those who were in the cadet unit at school and those whose homes had been overran by the opposing forces from the Nigerian side of the Nigeria/Biafra divide.

Most of Okoli's days as usual were spent in Ceewai's house. On one of the days while Okoli was in Ceewai's house, he saw Erompekene, his classmate, and as they discussed, Okoli was informed that Tubia, another friend and classmate, was in town. Okoli traced Tubia to the house of the church archdeacon. Tubia was staying with a boy Okoli got to know was called DD as the latter's two names started with *D*. DD was an extremely pleasant young man. Okoli was so surprised at his very gentle manners and at his kindness and humility. He was even more surprised when he learnt that DD was a medical student in one of the few medical schools in the country. After Okoli had consumed the biscuits (cookies) and Fanta, which DD got for him and Tubia, he was reclining on a sofa while conversing with Tubia.

Suddenly the two friends heard the sound of a giant low-flying plane. Aba did not have an airport, and this was not a helicopter. Why should a jet plane fly so low, and in a densely civilian populated area of a town without an airport?

Maybe the plane was about to crash, so Tubia and Okoli thought. They were mistaken. No sooner did they run out of the building to get a better glimpse of the plane when they were shocked to hear several deafening sounds.

Boom! Boom! Boom!

Smoke, ashes, and dust filled the air. It dawned on everybody that Aba was under attack!

That attack claimed the life of one of the most famous medical doctors in Aba.

The reality of the war had finally came right to the doorsteps of the residents of Aba.

Hitherto, people in Aba had not heard the booming of the guns nor of the mortars.

They had not heard the explosions of the land mines nor of the rockets.

That day for the first time people in Aba had witnessed the first actual sounds of war, and it came from the air.

The details of the war, its genesis, its prosecution, the humanitarian catastrophes involved while a good part of the civilized world appeared to look the other way, the allegations of genocide and its rebuttals—all these and their sequelae are for other write-ups and the history books.

The "Goods" that Saved a Family and Served a Village

Okoli had read from storybooks and the history of the First and Second World Wars of how the paper currencies of countries suffered during wars. As soon as he came back from school on forced vacation, Okoli told his father that it might be advisable that the latter endeavored to save coins in preference to paper currency. From the experience of history, there was likely, if the conflict worsened, loss in value of the currency or even a complete change of the currency as an economic measure to impoverish opponents. In such a situation, the paper currency would suffer the most. Ogbuka did not need further persuasion on the issue, and he started saving the largest coin denomination, the shillings. There was no more importation of goods by Ogbuka since blockade of the ports of entry had been effected. But Ogbuka's stores (warehouses) had always been stacked full with goods, and these were bicycle parts and tools, not perishables.

So while further banking was suspended, controlled sales of goods continued, ensuring a steady flow of cash, which was immediately changed into shillings by Ogbuka. It was not long before a section of the stores was stockpiled with bags and bags of shillings, which were later packed into empty wooden cases. So as goods were sold, the proceeds in pounds got converted into shillings, and these were packaged back into the wooden cases from where the goods were previously emptied. So the wooden cases looked like they contained goods of bicycle parts whereas they indeed were fully laden with shilling coins. And since the cases used were those of bicycle cup hubs, which were usually very heavy, the weight of their new content, shillings, raised no immediate suspicion. It was one big ingenuity on Ogbuka's part and was the one big factor that saved Ogbuka's large family of fifty-five, along with their numerous dependents, from the widespread starvation of the Nigerian Civil War years.

As the war drew closer and Aba needed to be evacuated, the scores of cases of goods and coins were loaded in lorries (trucks) and transported to Ogbuka's hometown. Before Aba finally fell, virtually all the warehouses had been evacuated. In a war situation with the full blockade imposed on the breakaway Republic of Biafra, both the goods and the coins were as good as hard currency. This was especially so when Nigeria changed her paper currency, and the breakaway republic was left hard and dry.

By the time Okoli got home, virtually the entire ground floor of his father's main building including the large parlor (living room) was stacked ground to deck with wooden cases loaded with goods and shillings, possibly hundreds of thousands, millions worth of the latter! As stated earlier, this decision of Ogbuka's to save the shilling coin was perhaps the single most important factor that saved them from starvation—his family of eight wives, forty-six children, and scores of extended family members—during the thirty-month-old Nigerian Civil War.

That war better known while it lasted as the Nigeria-Biafra war was surprisingly a little-known war in the United States and in many other parts of the world. That war, judging from its ferocity and consequent humanitarian crisis, if it were being fought elsewhere, or if it were fully and truthfully documented and reported, could be ranked as one of the world's worst regional catastrophes. Only those like Okoli, who were directly affected, would be in a good-enough position to fully and truthfully narrate what went on and the hell through which the fighting forces and the civilians, especially the displaced ones, went through.

History is replete with differing and often conflicting versions of even the same event, but the true position always remains constant despite manipulations of the truth from either or both sides of any divide. It is said that the first casualty in any war situation is the truth. This statement notwithstanding, the one true position always and forever remains constant and that is that the war was one big humanitarian catastrophe, which was completely unnecessary and avoidable.

That the war started in the first place was a direct consequence of the failure of diplomacy. The initial senseless taking of innocent human lives, especially of trusting colleagues, was completely inexcusable and callous. The consequent counterreaction that spiralled into mass killings of other colleagues and innocent civilians was a tragedy. The abject failure of the military class who started it all to conclude their negotiations and abide by their agreements and thereby save the nation from the horrors of war was a much more colossal tragedy. The subsequent descent to a war that must have claimed more than a million lives for a cause that could not be clearly enunciated was a major shame for the players and humanity. That shame would be more so, if the motivating cause for any political or military support for one side or the other in the war could be traced directly or remotely to quest for economic advantage. In due course, history and historians will be able to document more fully and more truthfully the different roles played, and by whom, so that at least humanity will benefit from the revelations.

The paper denomination of the Nigerian currency, the pound, had been changed. Rebel Biafra, as some radio stations often called the secessionist side, had printed its own currency the, Biafran pound, which had legal tender only within Biafra's ever-dwindling boundaries. The Biafran pound, though of very superior physical quality, could not purchase much, as food and other essential commodities were in very short supply. Unlike the pound, the Nigerian shilling coin was not changed, and thus it provided the major means of exchange for scarce commodities like salt, milk, and other foods between an economically blockaded Biafra and the rest of Nigeria.

A few daredevilry youths took on the jobs of buying up any available coins (shillings) from the Biafran side and stealing behind the battle lines on the Nigerian side bought salt, milk, cloth, and cigarettes, which they would sell for huge amounts on the Biafran side. The trade which was extremely risky was called *ahia attack* (attack market). It was a very lucrative trade for those who could defy the bullets and the bombs.

Ordinarily during peacetime, twenty shillings was the equivalent of one Nigerian pound. At the peak of the Nigeria-Biafra war, however, one shilling exchanged for as much as ten to fifteen Biafran pounds. For any, therefore, who had as much as a few hundreds of pounds in the form of shillings, they were the equivalent of millionaires in Biafran currency. But Ogbuka, unknown to any but himself and his son, had hundreds of thousands of these precious metals, the Nigerian shillings, loaded in wooden boxes marked as Hub Cups (a component of the bicycle hub).

When these cases of shillings were being loaded at Aba and off-loaded at Arondizuogu, the cases were so heavy that Ogbuka had a hard time explaining to the muscular job men called *ndi akpu obi* what were loaded in the cases that were breaking their backs. They asked so many questions that at a stage Ogbuka had to employ a decoy. He identified one of the few boxes actually loaded with cup hubs and deliberately pushed it off the lorry to the ground, where the wooden case broke, scattering hundreds of the weighty hub cups on the road. The loaders then saw what they thought was breaking their backs!

The evacuation of the warehouses from Aba to Arondizuogu lasted three days. Despite the huge treasures stored under the deck of his house, Ogbuka never lived ostentatiously. He continued to use the same lady's Raleigh bicycle, which he had used for close to seventeen years. There was absolutely no ostentation in his lifestyle, the extent that would tempt him to buy a car. He even shelved his often-stated resolve to increase the number of his wives from eight to twelve. He hardly ever entered the "goods stores," as the warehouse was called. He handed the keys to his son Okoli and was never personally ever seen around the stores. Whenever a large sum of money was needed, he would call Okoli to the side, and with a show of fingers, he indicated how many shillings the latter should go to the store to get for exchange into Biafran pounds, which were the local legal tender. For every twenty shillings (one Nigerian pound) that he wanted Okoli to get for exchange, Ogbuka would raise one finger. Okoli always understood. He never went into the store from the front door so as never to attract undue attention. Ogbuka dealt with only very few of the ahia attack people and only did small amounts of exchange at a time. Thus, nobody else except Ogbuka himself and his son was aware of the amount of treasures stockpiled in that massive living room under the deck. Even the exact amount stockpiled was not known to either father or son. All that was money that would have been used for importation of bicycle parts from Europe and Asia but which after the imposition of economic blockade had to be converted into shillings and stockpiled over a period of many months.

The ease with which Ogbuka maintained his family, a large extended family and scores of dependants and the helpless, during a stifling civil war when hundreds of thousands of people were dying from starvation did not go unnoticed. The rate at which he was purchasing land in the village raised eyebrows. His readiness to pay off taxes levied on the entire community generated wide discussions. His establishment of free feeding for the destitute in the community was hailed by all. His subsidizing of the Red Cross Feeding Centre was a marvel to all. But nobody really raised much eyebrows especially as Ogbuka continued to ride his eighteen-year-old lady's' bicycle and tie his simple native wrapper cloth over his waist and never wore anything more than a singlet over his body even to social events outside the village.

The zenith was however to come up when Okigwe fell to the Nigerian troops. Okigwe was one of the last major towns close to Arondizuogu to fall to the Nigerian troops during the civil war. Since Okigwe was situated very close to Arondizuogu, Okoli's hometown, people in Arondizuogu could easily hear the sound of mortar shelling into Okigwe. The fall of Okigwe next door to Arondizuogu raised the need for heavy levies in men and material on the adjacent towns, Arondizuogu inclusive. Indeed, part of Arondizuogu was administratively under Okigwe zone, while the remainder was under Orlu zone.

When the war got to Okigwe, therefore, every village in Arondizuogu was required to enlist a certain number of people for digging of trenches for the troops. Cash levies were also imposed on all adult males. After repeated levies, the citizens were getting weary. The young men in particular were greatly at a disadvantage. Their ranks provided the conscripts. Those not conscripted were taxed heavily. Most of them were not employed, and being either in school or under business tutelage prior to the onset of the war, they had neither lands nor money.

During one of the general village meetings for war effort, the amount of money levied on the village was announced. This amount was to be shared out equally between all adult males, and the young men over eighteen years of age were all classified as adult men. The number of men to be contributed by the village was also announced. The older men above forty-five years of age were exempt from the conscription exercise.

The whole village was gathered at the church field. Soon after the announcements, it looked as if a cold shower descended on the young men.

The school field of St Joseph's Catholic School Ndiakunwanta Arondizuogu served a multiple purpose. Officially, it was the school field for sports activities by the pupils of the school. It was also used for church activities, which required open-air facilities like canopies, tables, and chairs for wedding receptions. Being the only open-air facility in the entire village, it was also used for other civic receptions and gatherings that involved attendance by large numbers of people. Consequently, the monthly village gatherings that were held as soon as the town of Okigwe came under threat during the civil war were all held in the school field of St Joseph's School.

When the quota in men and money required of Ndiakuwanta as her contribution to the war effort was announced, the unease among the youth of the village was palpable. Sighs and murmurs rented the air both from the youth, the not so young as well as the elderly. The adolescents were sad because as the numbers of eligible adult males got depleted, it might be their turn to be counted to go to dig the trenches and possibility to go to the warfront, often with only brief training and inadequate armament. The young adult males were sad because they were required to not only contribute money for the war efforts but also to get into physical combat or trench digging. Some of the elderly were sad because it was their sons who, even after they would have contributed money, would still be counted to go into battle, and many would never return, and many would return maimed. None were sad because they did not believe in the justness of the war. All were convinced that it was "a war for survival."

After the sighs came the silence. Where would the money come from? There was hunger in the land. There was starvation. Thousands of refugees that occupied one section of the field in the makeshift tents had no jobs to do even for any pittance. The adult males between the ages of eighteen and forty-five therefore were not only jobless, but most of them (especially those between eighteen and twenty-five) were also required to contribute money for the win-the-war effort.

Speaker after speaker harped on the need for every sacrifice to be made to ensure that money was made available "in support of our troops." But it was obvious that the populace had almost come to the end of its wits, especially in terms of the funds.

After the murmurs and sighs came the silence. It was at that stage that a man walked out from the elders' table. He was the man called Nwankwo, but whose title of Ogbuka had literally become his name. Ogbuka was very well-known in the village as one of the sons of the famed wrestler Obeki, who many decades earlier had done the village proud. Ogbuka was known for his philanthropism. He was also well-known because hc had the largest number of children in the village, forty-six in all, from eight wives, and he had ensured that all his children went to school. Ogbuka was also known by the slightly older folks as the man who had wanted to be a reverend father but who later married eight wives and practiced African traditional religion while maintaining his baptismal name of Cajethan. He was also well-known by all as the man who did not go to school, but who could read all kinds and all volumes of letters, but could not write. He was further known as the semiliterate man who did successful importation business from Europe and Asia from a one-room office, the man who bought cars for people but who had refused to ride one himself, the man who was always seen on his twenty-year-old lady's Raleigh bicycle and who often tied traditional wrapper as clothing around his waist, the man whose dining table in the village served suppers of many dishes and to whose feeding sessions all and sundry were welcome.

It was this man who had stepped forward and requested from the chairman of the occasion for the old battery-operated, hand-held microphone to address the crowd as follows, "Akunwanta Kwenu, Akunwanta Kwenu, Kwenu, Kwezuo nu."

The traditional greetings to call for the attention of the village over, Ogbuka proceeded with the following mystifying declarations, "From this day till this war ends, no young man in this village will pay any more war levies! Nobody, young or old, from this village will again pay any more war levies or taxes!"

There was some palpable stir in the air. When and how did this respected man turn a saboteur of the Biafran cause? If there were Biafran soldiers around, they probably would have immediately shot or arrested him for suspected insurrection. But the man continued, "From today until this war ends, I, Nwankwo Ogbuka, alias Iheanaeboagu, will pay all the money, and I mean all the money levied on this village, and that includes the war levies and all the taxes. The young men do all the fighting and all the dying and maiming. They must no longer be subjected to paying the taxes as well. They must no longer pay the levies. Mr Chairman, sir, I hereby request you to calculate immediately all the current taxes and all the current war levies and all the outstanding taxes and levies, sum them up, extrapolate these for the next three months, and I will pay them all now. And I will continue to pay all the accumulated taxes and levies for the whole village for as long as this war lasts."

Then raising his voice, Ogbuka shouted into the hand-held microphone, "Mmadukibeya! Mmadukibeya! Mmdukibeya!"

It implied that some men are better blessed and are consequently wealthier than others, and that all fingers are not created equal.

After that short and startling speech, Ogbuka handed back the microphone to the chairman of the ceremony. Before Ogbuka could get back to his seat, the crowd had gone wild with joy. The applause and the jubilation could be heard from miles away. Such a measure of philanthropy had never been witnessed in the village. A group had never been seen to go so wild with joy.

As the chairman hesitantly accepted back the microphone in near disbelief, the young men quickly rushed towards Ogbuka and carried him shoulder high, and dancing around the arena, they shouted in unison, "Mmadukibeya, Mmadukibeya, Mmadukibeya."

When the young men finally lowered Ogbuka back to his seat, the latter quickly walked up to the chairman and informed him that he would take his leave to bring money to pay off whatever the total calculated sum for the outstanding, current, and extrapolated levies and taxes amounted to. He did not wait for the actual computation to be completed. He apparently felt very confident that whatever the final figure would amount to, he would be equal to it. Soon after, Ogbuka beckoned on his son Okoli from where the latter was standing, and both rode down on their respective bicycles to the house. Boni, Alex, and Nweke—the ahia attack people who usually exchanged Nigerian shillings for large sums of Biafran pounds—were quickly sent for. Within an hour or two, three sacks of Biafran pounds had been made available in exchange for some thousands of Nigerian shillings. The sacks of Biafran pounds were stacked on the carrier of Okoli's "white horse" bicycle (a gift from his brother Mako when the latter was leaving for the United States). Okoli had a hard time dragging the heavily laden bicycle back to the field of Saint Joseph's School, the venue of the town meeting. Ogbuka followed by his son's side, slowly rolling his old lady's bicycle along with him.

The sight of Madukibeya, as Ogbuka a little earlier got to be called, arriving with sacks of money in immediate fulfillment of his promise raised an even louder round of applause. The sacks of wrapped bundles of notes were emptied on the grass. The backlog of taxes and levies, the current taxes, and levies as well as the extrapolated taxes and levies for three months were paid off; yet so much of those high-quality but minimally valued green-colored Biafran notes were left over. Ogbuka thereupon gave instructions that the excess should be deposited with the Win the War Committee, as security for any future shortfalls.

The Aftermath

The show of financial gallantry and the crowning with the title of Mmadukibeya did not go without their repercussions, notwithstanding the good intentions behind the donation of the money. Not only did the number of destitute villagers who came to feed in Ogbuka's compound triple, the number of people who came to borrow money or to ask for one kind of favor or the other from him, also increased. Most skeptics in the village were anxious to see how Ogbuka would be able to cope with the enormous financial burden, knowing the huge size of his family and the fact that he was no longer importing any more goods from overseas, as the ports had been blockaded.

The suppers of many dishes,
Were expected by many,
To soon get overstretched
Or soon to run out and dwindle.

But the shillings were there.
And were enough to bear,
The toughness of the times
As the war was to bare.

The shilling support base
The extent of which only few knew,
Lay heaped up in mounds
To the consternation of all.

But the doer of deeds
Had known from the start,
That the treasures were there
To last a lifetime of wars.

But it was not all to be without the repercussions. The pomp and pageantry and the riding of the waves were soon to attract the attention of detractors. The disturbing aspect was soon to come. Three weeks after the Mmadukibeya event, as the open field offer to offset the taxes and levies came to be called, three plainclothes security officials arrived at Ogbuka's premises from Orlu, the provincial capital. Okoli was about to ride out to his daily Land Army project, where he was serving in a village called Ohiauchu. The three men drove in, early in the morning at about 6:30 a.m. and closed Ogbuka's huge wooden compound gate behind them. They asked for the man called Mmadukibeya, the name by which Ogbuka came to be known after the field event. Ogbuka came down from upstairs and met the visitors. Two of the men were wielding pistols while the third had a canister of tear gas on one hand and a big bunch of keys on the other hand.

Word quickly went around to everybody in the compound. Two of Ogbuka's wives, hearing of "the invasion," came out crying. The others calmed themselves, but the entire household came out to the front of the main building. Everybody was expecting the worst as everybody believed that the family was under siege from armed robbers, a phenomenon that was surprisingly very rare during the war years. But the man holding the tear gas canister proceeded surprisingly to calm the family members down. He said that they were not enemies and had not come to harm anybody. He further explained that they came on a tip off and had specific orders to search the entire compound. He said that nobody would be harmed as long as everybody cooperated with them and did not obstruct them.

When Okoli looked into his father's face, the latter was so calm that Okoli immediately got all the reassurance that he needed. Ogbuka then asked the men whether they would want any morning kola nuts as tradition demanded for all visitors. When they declined the kola nuts, Ogbuka asked them where they wanted to start the search from. When they pointed to the main building, Okoli's heart sank!

The ground floor of the main building was where all the cases of shillings were stockpiled, along with a few other wooden cases containing assorted bicycle parts and sundry tools. The men obviously must have been thoroughly briefed by a well-informed enemy.

"All our money would go," Okoli said within him. The family might even be branded as saboteurs since people found with large sums of money were often wrongly branded. And the money in stock was Nigerian shillings, and on such unimaginable quantities.

Ogbuka calmly told Okoli to go and get the store keys. But the man with the tear gas canister headed for the front door and using a key from the bunch he had in hand, immediately opened the front door of the ground floor living room. Wooden cases filled with "goods," of course, were stacked from floor to deck in all the rooms. A massive metal safe, which had a coded lock, stood by the right side of the large store. Usually to get to the boxes, which contained the coins. Okoli often needed to climb over several wooden cases containing hub cups, bicycle chains, and other bicycle parts. These other cases of imported goods were mixed up with the other cases of "local goods" (the coins). They were almost uniformly heavy, especially between the coin boxes and the hub cup boxes, and it would require dozens of men who were well fed with *akpu* (cassava fufu) to sift through those heavy cases, even if they worked twelve hours a day for one month.

But these men came with a key that immediately opened Ogbuka's store door. Could they immediately also have come with magical powers, detectors, or other devices that would immediately sift through the heavy cases and detect which ones contained Ogbuka's coin goods and which contained other imported goods?

It was obvious that theses men were surprised at the amount of merchandise that were so neatly stacked in Ogbuka's village home even in the midst of the biting economic blockade.

"What are all these?" one of them asked, obviously in amazement.

"They are bicycle parts, tools, and other goods," replied Ogbuka.

"Where did you get all these cases from?" came another question.

"I imported them from Europe and Asia. I am a licensed and registered importer," replied Ogbuka.

"Do you have the documents with which you imported them?" came another question.

"Yes, I have all the documents," replied Ogbuka.

As they talked, the huge safe caught their attention, and they immediately made for it. The man with the bunch of keys again brought up a key to open the safe. But besides the key, there were two radial-coded locks. The visitors unlocked the safe key and told Ogbuka to unlock the codes. As Ogbuka was selecting the codes to unlock the safe, the three men all turned away their faces. They did not want to see the codes, a rare display of discipline especially for wartime officers and a display of professionalism rare in some of today's men in uniform.

The lower and middle compartments of the safe were filled with property deeds, agreements, titles, and bank documents. Only a section of the upper compartment contained some bundles of Biafran notes about five bundles, which might not be more than fifty thousand Biafran pounds (a relatively small sum because of the low value of the currency). The officers pulled out the entire contents of the safe. They first quickly counted the currency, recorded the amount in their file, and asked Ogbuka to sign for the amount. They then kept back the entire money. They then numbered the files, got Ogbuka to sign again for them, and thereafter they signed two copies of the forms and handed a copy to Ogbuka.

They then turned to the cases. They were obviously overwhelmed. They did not come prepared to open wooden cases and hundred of them too. They asked if Ogbuka had pinchers or cutters. Ogbuka quickly got them pinchers and a cutter. They ripped open a couple of cases. The first two contained bicycle chains. Another contained hub cups, and another large one contained bicycle mudguards.

As they proceeded, Okoli's heart was beating hard.

Should they encounter any box of coins, they might carry them all, he thought within him. *And that would make them want to employ labor to open all the other boxes*.

After inspecting each opened case, they would meticulously close and nail it back neatly. Their discipline was stunning. After randomly inspecting about five cases of goods, it was obvious that their subject was truly and simply an importer of goods. Luck, pure luck, was on Ogbuka's side as the visitors did not encounter any of the cases containing the coins. If they did, the entire scenario would have changed.

When they were done with the goods store, the men proceeded to conduct quick searches on the second floor of the building, Ogbuka's bedroom, Mako's unoccupied room, Okoli's room, and the living room upstairs. Ogbuka and Okoli accompanied them. They turned over the mattresses and replaced them neatly. One of them stacked up three tables and climbed on top of them to look through a manhole into the ceiling as another pulled out the drawers. As they came down the stairs, one of them quietly said to the other, "Another false alarm?"

The other concurred with a nod.

They nevertheless still looked through all the rooms of Ogbuka's eight wives. The pit latrine areas and even the goats' houses and the yam barns were not spared. They checked the kitchens and even the bathrooms. It was a thorough search to a good extent, except that they did not get to the goods, and for Ogbuka, that was really good.

As they were leaving, they told Ogbuka to come along with them in their car. Okoli said he would go with them, but they refused him entry into the car. The family members were all worried because even though these men appeared disciplined, they were armed, nobody was quite sure of the authenticity of the identities which they had presented, and it was wartime, and anything was possible. Sensing the family's anxiety, one of the men brought out his identity card again and showed to Okoli. He said he hailed from Urualla, a nearby town. He further said that they were not going to Orlu, which was farther away but that Ogbuka needed to make some statements in their office at Ndiukwn, a nearby village. To further reassure everybody, they said that Okoli could go through the shortcut footpath and wait for his father at Ndiukwn.

Before Ogbuka entered their car, he called Okoli to the side and told him to go first to inform Nduburuiriro, Ikuegbu, and Mathias—his brother and friends respectively—"just in case." Before they drove off, Okoli jumped on his bicycle; and after sending down one of his other brothers to inform Nduburuiriro, Ikuegbu, and Mathias as directed by Ogbuka, he rode through the footpaths down to Ndiukwn temporary police post,

By the time Okoli got to the police post at Ndiukwn, his father and the officials were not yet there. Okoli was very worried. Could this be a decoy? Could those people have tricked everybody and kidnapped Ogbuka and taken him somewhere else. As he turned to drive through the major road to trace them backwards, there was the white Peugeot 403 car with the four men and his father inside it.

The statement required of Ogbuka at the police post was not to be detailed. It was obvious that the investigating police team had found nothing incriminating against Ogbuka. Within an hour, Ogbuka and Okoli were on their way back through the footpath to their house with all the files intact. Before the duo left the police, post one of the officers (the one who held the tear gas canister and the keys) had escorted Ogbuka to the front door of the two-room station and apologized to him for all the inconveniences he might have suffered. He even offered to pay for the former's transportation back to Ndiakunwanta, but Ogbuka declined the offer and thanked the officer for the outstanding courtesy and professionalism that the officer and his men had exhibited.

Decency and discipline still existed in the system, and Ogbuka did not have to pay a dime as bribe to anybody before he regained his freedom.

It was weeks later that Okoli got information that as news of his father's offer to take over the payment of the taxes and war levies in the village spread, there were speculations that the latter was either minting money secretly or he was being funded from across the border. Nobody doing honest business, especially at that period of scarcity, could assume the name of Mmadukibeya, maintain eight wives and forty-six children, shoulder the bills for endless dishes, and assume responsibility for so many charities and begin to pay the levies for an entire village if that person was not being funded from some sinister sources. So it was believed. They were wrong!

THE WILLING ARMY WITHOUT WEAPONS

As the shortage of food ravaged the population during the war, a special food cultivation unit was formed and was called Land Army. Okoli's cousin and friend Ceewai got to know of this, and he and Okoli joined the Land Army program. Okoli had earlier been enlisted into the Research and Production Unit at Umuahia, where his beloved uncle Cosi worked. He had worked briefly with the RAP as that unit was called and was indeed a reservist with that unit before he joined the land army program.

The nearest Land Army Unit was at Ohiauchu. Okoli and his other Land Army participants were taught how to plant rice, how to dam the streams to divert water into rice fields, how to grow rice nurseries, and how to transplant the seedlings in rows. It used to be very fascinating for Okoli to watch the coaches, many of them a little above his age, who did not have much of formal education, exhibit so much dexterity in planting the rice seedlings. Okoli often spent time simply watching them. They used forked sticks, and clutching the bundles of rice seedlings in their left hands, they stuck in the roots of the seedlings into the swampy rice paddies with such amazing speed that Okoli often spent very long periods of time simply watching their fingers. Those were sixteen—to eighteen-year-old boys who, with little or no formal education and without arms, were contributing by far more than their peers in sustenance of the population at a time when hunger was ravaging the civilians and soldiers alike. They were the relatively unappreciated part of the war effort, in a completely militarized population which often featured stragglers who relished in the display of their officer badges behind the battle lines, while the true dedicated officers often barely made do with only the sign of the rising sun, the then-adored symbol of the breakaway Republic of Biafra.

These young rice-farming experts would first harvest the seedlings and tie them in bunches and immerse the roots of the bunches in muddy water overnight. The following morning, they would wash off the mud and begin to transplant the rice seedlings. One of these coaches called Patrick was so articulate with the stick and seedling that the group nicknamed him Patrick "the planter." Patrick could plant a full row of three hundred feet of rice in under five minutes. He would scarcely stand upright though the entire process. Before Okoli and Ceewai got into the Land Army, Okoli was of the wrong notion that it was only those who were in secondary schools, especially if they were in government colleges that were talented. It was at the Land Army that he met people of his age who probably dropped out of primary schools or who scarcely attended any formal schools that were so very talented and who were in fact contributing more to the development of society than many who thought they were the stars simply because they were attending what they believed were regarded as the best secondary schools. After working at the Land Army for a couple of months, Okoli secured some rice seedlings at one of the weekend seedling sales and started his own small farm near his father's house using a swamp area close to a local stream as water source.

Okoli cleaned the area himself with the help from his mother and his younger sister Fibi, using machetes and spades. He also did the tilling with help from Franco, a teenage neighbor who some years past had taught Okoli the art of fishing, for some cookies and sweets. It was Franco who taught Okoli how to string earthworms on hooks and how to swing out any caught fish out of the stream. Franco who lived permanently in the village was also the one who on one occasion many years back had rescued Okoli when the latter had slipped and plunged into the deep waters in an attempt to swing out a trapped fish caught in his fishing hook.

The actual planting of the rice was done by Okoli himself using the technique he learnt from the Land Army. He had learnt the different species of rice from the Land Army. The species called mass had produced enormous quantities of short-grained rice and was ready for harvesting in about three months. Another species called gina produced long-grain rice with smaller yield and longer duration of about five months.

Okoli concentrated on mass brand, and the yield was enormous. He could not believe the quantity of rice he got from a small farm the size of a soccer field. It was a most successful and rewarding first experience but not without it hazards and a price to be paid.

The Chickens Are Trapped

As he rejoiced at the sight of his planted seedlings picking up, Okoli came up one morning only to see that about a quarter of the farm had overnight been mowed down by bush rats and grasscutters. Okoli had thereafter at different times had to fight the bush rats and grass cutters. He had bought traps and set them up every night. After the first night, he did not realize that he should go to dismantle the traps every morning. By midday when he got to his farm, two native chickens belonging to the neighbors had been caught in his traps. That was a big trouble for Okoli. One of the neighbors reported to Okoli's mother that Okoli deliberately set the trap to catch their chickens in this period of meat scarcity The aggrieved neighbor deposited her dead chickens at the front door of Okoli's mother and demanded a replacement with live chickens of same size. She threatened that if the replacement was not effected before the setting of the sun, she would report to the village council that Okoli was deliberately trapping neighbors' chickens. Of course, Eliaba, Okoli's mother, had to replace the chickens. She did not want to enter into any arguments with Meliza ekwulekwu (the talkative Meliza), as the woman was called. Meliza was reputed in the village to be a big gossip. It was said that she spent the first few hours of each morning going from house to house checking out on what would make good gossip for the day. If there was anything anybody wanted to be widely known, the surest way to get the news disseminated was to let Meliza know the story. The dissemination would be effected without a fee.

Okoli learnt his lesson after the trapping and replacement of the chickens. He learnt to set the traps late in the evenings after the scavenging chickens "had gone to bed." He also ensured he dismantled them very early in the mornings before the chickens would be out to forage for food in the fields.

The traps in Okoli's rice farm, partially true to Meliza's accusation, soon started providing good results. Not only did they protect Okoli's crops, they also started providing good catches of big wild rats the type called *ogini*. At a time, Okoli was catching an average of two big wild rats each night. It soon became such lucrative business that Humphrey, one of the refugees who lived in Ogbuka's house, undertook the contract of setting the traps in the evenings and dismantling them very early in the mornings. Humphrey would gather the trapped rats, roast them, remove the bowels, stretch them out on sticks stuck through the mouth to the waist, add salt, pepper, and palm oil on them, and grill them over hot charcoal fire. The taste was simply super. Humphrey was soon a celebrity among the rest of the young men around for his expertise in the preparation of this newfound delicacy during a war at which people ate lizards and locusts as delicacies.

As Okoli's rice field increased in height, he observed that his traps were decreasing in number. He had a total of sixteen traps, but the number steadily decreased to nine. The disappearance of the traps was initially mysterious to Humphrey and Okoli. Then one morning, Humphrey came back with a very big grass cutter the animal locally called *nchi*. The trapped chi had a rusted old trap on its forelimbs and another trap on its hind limbs. It was obvious that the nchi had sometime earlier been caught by a trap on its forelimbs and had managed to escape from the rice farm with the trap. On this latter feeding session, the unlucky animal's hind limbs got caught by a second trap, effectively trapping the animal and immobilizing it. The double jeopardy made it impossible for the animal to escape from the farm before daybreak. Had it not stepped on the second trap, the nchi might still have managed to escape from the rice field with the first trap. Weeks later, hunters in the village started catching bigger grass cutters and even deer with little traps on their limbs. Those were Okoli's missing traps, which the animals had stepped on, but had escaped with.

As time went by, Okoli had to pay to have two men construct a fence around his farm with sticks. The fence kept off the bigger animals which could not climb over. A strategy by Humphrey also ensured occasional catches of the bigger animals after erection of the fence. At intervals of about twelve feet along the fence, Humphrey would create an opening. Okoli bought a few bigger traps and set them up at those openings. The very first night after the erection of the fence and setting of the big traps, a big grass cutter was caught. There was a big celebration among the children. Even the much bigger members of the family participated in the feast.

The adventure with Okoli's rice farm was not all roses. After exposure to the insect bites and after constant wandering though the rice farms, Okoli started having multiple rashes on both arms and legs and on his face. The mosquito bites in the open fields soon had their toll on him. He developed frequent evening fever, headache, and joint pains. He was soon down with a bad attack of malaria. It was during that attack that he had his first and only encounter with army conscriptors.

The Young Men in Battle Kits "Ajukwu Soja," He Was Labelled as "Freedom Fighter," He Was Hailed

As the civil war progressed, forced enlistment into the army became operational. Much as the will of the populace appeared strong as regards the war, armament was in short supply, hunger was ravaging both troops, and civilians and even the basic army uniforms and boots were lacking. Some troops who returned from the battlefronts looked like skeletons in rags, poorly armed, poorly clothed, and poorly fed. Even with these, the zeal of these young men still appeared unmistakably strong. Okoli came close to tears on one occasion when he came back from his base in the Land Army program. As he took the turn into his compound after the hard day's toils in the field, Okoli listened to a group of these young men with sunken eyeballs, with blisters on their palms, and multiple rashes from mosquito and tick bites in the hurriedly dug trenches, as they marched past. They were hungry and poorly fed, but they were still determined to fight for the common cause. They still chanted as much as their failing strength could allow them with courage and determination in their eyes; an unflinching faith in the cause, in their voices they still sang the melodious and emotion-inspiring song:

> We are Biafrans,
> Fighting for our freedom,
> By the power of Jesus,
> We shall conquer.

If determination, faith, willpower, and dedication to a cause alone were all it took to win a war, perhaps no power in black Africa would (have) subdue(d) Biafra.

But starvation, disease, lack of armament, and other factors, prominent among which were the economic blockade and foreign intervention, were soon to prevail over willpower, belief in the cause, courage, and even faith. The young men of Biafra fought gallantly. They displayed what was unmistakable ingenuity and determination. They were the heroes of a failed cause, which most of the rest of the world either failed to acknowledge or did not believe in. They put their all, goaded to a large extent by the fear of mass annihilation as narrated daily by a very powerful propaganda machinery and aired daily by Radio Biafra. The latter ended its daily news with the caution, "The price of liberty is eternal vigilance.

Biafrans, be vigilant."

Radio Nigeria on its part would also hourly air the rather military statement: "To keep Nigeria one is a task that must be done."

Of course, neither the art of good propaganda dissemination nor the naked display of raw power made for an early end to the war, an unnecessary fratricidal exercise which set the nation back by many decades.

After a while, what was anticipated to have been a swift police action kept dragging on for months. There appeared to be stagnation as the federal troops occupied the big cities and the major tarred roads while the less equipped but certainly more determined Biafran troops occupied the bushes and the hinterland. There were occasions when the contact between the opposing armies would be so close that the troops from both sides of the divide weary of shooting at each other and would merely trade verbal insults against each other from a mere dividing tarred road.

"Nigerian vandals," one side would shout from the bushes.

The spontaneous response of course would follow:

"Kwomotam for kwolta, I gwu-o make yu-u kwazualty and your mama no go know yu-u again."

One would have wished that the whole issue had been limited to verbal exchanges. The nation would have been spared the thirty months of bloodshed and savagery.

Who are there that in modern history of warfare have been able to withstand the combined forces, military and diplomatic, of so many world powers, including one of the superpowers? The dream of Biafra—a child of circumstance, a product of action and reaction, the flag with the rising sun—was thus dismantled or at best put in the cooler or confined to the minds of the proponents and believers in its cause. It would have been good if all the dramatis personae and their successors had learnt their lessons: only in the true spirit of brotherhood as demonstrated by justice and fair play can a mutually beneficial and progressive nation be founded.

That demonstration of justice and fair play certainly does not include overt and covert marginalization of any part of the federating units. It certainly does not include deliberate and systematic humiliation of any group in the system by ensuring that their roads are largely neglected or that their psyche is persistently humbled by ensuring that their qualifying sons and daughters are excluded from certain sensitive positions in the forces. It certainly does not include the deliberate exclusion of their zone from the siting of an international passenger airport even when it is obvious that people from that part of the country do the most travelling. The rest is for the history books.

Suffice it is to say, however, that every cloud has a silver lining, as the saying goes.

Unity, cooperation, mergers, and megamergers are the order of the day, even among the major economic and industrialized nations of the world. There is obviously more to gain from unity than from fragmentation. There is no doubt that a big, strong, and united country pulling resources together has better prospects than fragmented and weakened individual units. The hailed emergence of the European Union is a major example. Besides, there was no guarantee that with time, if the secessionist bid had succeeded, the leaders of the dissenting unit in the Nigeria versus Biafra imbroglio would not metamorphose into worse demons and recreate worse ills than those which they claimed they fought. History is replete with stories of such purported messiahs who ultimately assumed dictatorial powers and began to play god, murdering thousands of the very people they claimed they were fighting for. Even when the populace would rise up asking for a change, such dictators and "messiahs" would turn to bulls in China shops, and it would often take years of patience and tact to ease them out.

Yet, unity having been attained, it would be very useful to realize that the dividends of unity and democracy can only be fully realized if unity is laced with justice and fairness as previously mentioned, and all the federating units are given a sense of belonging as one people, manifesting unity even in diversity. Marginalization in the provision of amenities and denial of merited positions, all in the name of "security measures," many decades after the cessation of hostilities can only succeed in fuelling heightened feelings of alienation, which will not enhance rapid attainment of national growth and aspirations.

Mergers and *megamergers* have become household words. Besides, the ordinary citizens of most warring nationalities really have nothing against each other, except and until incitement with political undertones begins to rear its ugly head both within the military as well as within civilian circles. The different peoples and nations of Africa and indeed the rest of the third world have everything to benefit from unity, understanding, and cooperation between their peoples; otherwise, the destructive and destabilizing effects of the balkanization of Africa can only continue to be fostered.

The Leg that Betrayed the Owner

At a time Okoli was down with malaria after constant exposure to mosquito bites both in the Land Army program and in his rice farm project. Everistus, a pharmacy assistant who was a family friend, was called to give antimalaria injections to Okoli as was the practice in those days. Everistus had just completed administration of the chloroquine injections when one of Okoli's brothers rushed into the room to tell Okoli and Everistus to take cover because conscriptors were around. Conscriptors were groups of soldiers who, when the war situation was getting sour, were periodically sent out (or went out on their own) to villages behind battle lines to forcefully recruit young men who would be given short-term training and sent to the war fronts. It was believed that the biggest casualties of the war occurred among conscripts because they were poorly trained, poorly equipped, and poorly disciplined.

As a member of the Land Army and a card-carrying member of RAP (Research and Production), Okoli was not liable for conscription as he was already a member of one of the essential duties. Everistus himself was a registered member of the Red Cross and was also not liable to conscription. But charged from battle, armed, hungry, and angry, many of these conscriptors, who were themselves often undisciplined stragglers, often simply did not listen to anybody who was not in uniform and arms. They would simply march off any teenager or adult male without arms, whom they felt was fit for battle. Before the passes and other explanations would surface, the victim would have arrived the battlefront. Passes were cards which entitled an individual to leave camp or the holder's place of assignment. Despite their immunity, Everistus and Okoli decided to take cover as advised, as if from an air raid.

Conscriptions were of course only one of the many things one needed to take cover from, during that civil war. One needed to take cover from shells and bombs. One also needed to take cover from air raids. Again, one might occasionally need to take cover from conscriptors even when one was supposed to have a genuine pass, which was supposed to confer immunity in movement as each support group was supposed to complement the others in the execution of the war efforts.

So on that fateful afternoon, Everistus and Okoli, on being told that conscriptors were menacing the neighborhood, decided to take cover under a bed to save themselves the embarrassment of having to answer lots of unnecessary questions from a group that might not even have been authorized to conduct such an exercise in the first place. Everistus was the more vulnerable as he was in the Red Cross, and some of the soldiers saw able-bodied men in the Red Cross merely as cowards, who were dodging enlistment. Everistus had dived in first under the bed and was securely hidden close to the wall. Without enough space under the bed to contain two people, however, Okoli's head and trunk and waist were under the bed, but inadvertently his two legs were sticking out from under the bedcover.

As the soldiers were leaving, after fruitlessly searching the compound and the many rooms therein, they noticed two legs sticking out from under a bed covered with mattress and bedspread. One of the soldiers immediately jumped up and with his boots deliberately landed on Okoli's protruding legs. Okoli felt as if his bones had been fractured. He was yelling out with pain as one of the soldiers repeatedly landed with his boots on his protruding legs and pulled him on both legs and dragged him out from under the bed, exposing Everistus who was stretched out farther in, under the bed. They pulled the latter out too. Luckily for Okoli, his essential duty pass was lying right under the pillow. He was spared further ordeal but with no apologies, especially as the soldiers must have noticed that he was obviously ill with malaria. Everistus was not so lucky. Even though he escaped the boot-stamping and kicking to his legs, he got a few sharp slaps to his smooth and chubby egg-yolk-nourished face from a hungry-looking soldier in tattered uniform. He also got a thorough tongue-lashing, "Big bloody civilian!

Wetin you de hide here for? Na your mama go fight for you? Today you go shit for your pant."

As Everistus tried to explain that he too was on essential duties, a more refined-looking member of the group, who was probably an army corporal judging from the badge on his shoulders, asked him, "You say you be Red Cross. Make we see your pass."

Unfortunately, Everistus did not have his Red Cross pass with him. Besides, Red Cross workers were reputed during the war to be well fed. Everistus looked plump and well fed. While most of the population looked skinny from hunger and malnutrition during the war, virtually every Red Cross worker looked plump and well fed from the unusual meals of foreign-donated egg yolk, stockfish, corn meal, and corned beef which most of them ate daily. The Red Cross workers handled the distribution of most of the donations from the Catholic Relief Organization, Caritas, World Council of Churches, International Committee of the Red Cross (ICRC), and the many other church and other charitable organizations that came to the aid of the war victims. Such aid came even while the home countries of these organizations, perhaps for political reasons, adopted a "wait and see" attitude or actively took measures which aggravated the humanitarian catastrophes. Many of these largely private or semiprivate organizations, like the ICRC, contributed in no small way to the saving of millions of lives during that thirty-month-old war. Some others in conjunction with some countries were kind enough to accept and fly out thousands of ill and starving Biafran children to Gabon and other neighboring countries. That thousands of those children survived remains to the eternal glory of these organizations and donor nations.

The enormous sacrifices in men and materials which many of these organizations made in those catastrophic moments cannot be adequately compensated for. The best that humanity can do to show appreciation for those sacrifices is for humanity to strive to take measures to ensure the avoidance, if not the elimination, of wars and the factors that lead to wars. Even if wars are seen as "nature's pruning hook for the health of the human orchard" (Winston Churchill), and even if the adage holds true that any one who wants peace must prepare for war, the ultimate truth still holds, and that is, that all wars end up at the conference table. Whether the conference is for the handing over of the instrument of surrender or for the brokering of peace between warring parties, the ultimate truth remains that the conference table can and should be used to prevent wars.

The painful thing about wars is that when they break out, it is not the individuals who caused the war who suffer the most from the disastrous consequences. It is often the innocent citizens who suffer and die, while the initiators and perpetrators often escape, flee, and often later resurface in one form or another either get pardoned or on the other hand, if they are victorious, continue to ride the waves of governance, pomp, and pageantry. Many may never want to vacate office thereafter unless and until they are kicked out. There is thus no ultimate punishment for the intransigence and or thoughtlessness that must have claimed millions of lives.

When the conscriptors noticed that Everistus, the pharmacy assistant, did not have a pass with him, they dragged him along with them. The tongue-lashing continued.

"Big bloody civilian," the soldiers lashed out at the trembling Everistus.

"You were hiding under a bed expecting your mother to go and fight for you. Go get your mama. You go see pepper today. All that egg yolk wey you de chop go commot for your yash today."

As the soldiers dragged Everistus along with them, despite Okoli's entreaties, the latter quickly dispatched someone to Everistus's house to pick up the latter's pass while he followed the soldiers and their captive, fully wrapped up in blanket save for his face and feet. About half a mile down the road, they were caught up by the boy who rode down to fetch Everistus's pass. Everistus's release was thus secured, but not before he had gotten a few further verbal assaults for being a "fat bloody civilian hiding from action under a bed."

The Coming of the End, the Picking Up of the Pieces

As the civil war got closer to the Biafran heartland, life got tougher for the generality of people. The refugee situation got worse. Luckily though, the air freight of the children to Gabon and other places had continued despite the dangers of landing planes in Biafra's hurriedly constructed airports.

It was about that time that Aboni, Okoli's childhood friend and schoolmate, found his way to Arondizugu amidst the uncertainty of the roads. It was surprising how he traced his way through the uncertain roads amidst widespread conscription, rockets, air raids, and shells. Okoli was so pleased to see Aboni again after their unceremonious dispersal from school. Aboni followed Okoli daily to the latter's little farm; and amidst the booming guns, overhead bombings, and flying mortars, both friends were still able to tell their stories of St Brigid's and Government Secondary School Afikpo. Not too long after Aboni left back to his base, the signs of the end began to appear.

With the official end of the war, a new phase of life began to unfold for most people on the Biafran side of the conflict. The Biafran currency ceased to be legal tender. No immediate substitute was at hand, and a flat pitiable amount of twenty pounds was given to people who deposited money in banks and who had operated the accounts no matter what amount the individual deposited or withdrew and notwithstanding family size. Those, like Ogbuka, who had coins or goods however were luckier.

While in school at Afikpo, Okoli had opened a post office savings account in which he had one hundred and twelve pounds. When he got to the post office at Enugu to resume schooling in the new site of his school, he was told that the money in the post office was still intact for him. That made Okoli feel like an instant rich man to own over a hundred pounds when even millionaires were being given only twenty pounds when once they had operated the accounts by depositing into the account or withdrawing money from it. The justification, merits, or demerits of that obviously punitive economic policy which made instant paupers of millions of people, again, is left for history to judge. It was nonetheless to the great credit of the victorious side that there was no widespread bloodletting against the defeated side after the instrument of surrender was handed over, contrary to wide speculations. To that extent, the highly publicized "no Victor, no vanquished" declaration held true.

Suffice it is to say however that people bounced back, with an amazing renewed zeal to face the future. Most families sought and found solace in their religious organizations. Sunday attendance to the established religious organizations and churches increased massively, and hitherto unknown churches mushroomed at many uncompleted or abandoned buildings. The prayers and supplications must have paid off as most people were able to weather the storm of the harsh economic measures and picked up the pieces of their ruined economies and businesses.

Ogbuka soon moved back to Aba. His house had been bombed and set ablaze during the battle for Aba. The vibrated block walls however still stood, and the reinforced concrete deck was only slightly damaged. Ogbuka therefore lived in two of the rooms behind the main building, pending the rebuilding of the main building. Sanitation conditions that had nothing to write home about during peacetime became a disaster after the civil war. It was no surprise that widespread outbreaks of diarrhea and infective hepatitis started off soon after the war.

The students were soon recalled to school. When they got back to Government Secondary School Afikpo, the school was temporarily relocated to one building close to the adjoining town called Amasiri. Egbe, the principal, was back there in one room with an old chair and table by himself, taking down names of those that reported back. He was still able to put up a cheerful face despite all that had happened. The students will forever salute his courage at rallying his students back to school. But the school itself was not habitable. The library had been turned into a kitchen by the soldiers during the civil war; all the books were gone. The once-edifying assembly hall had about two inches of cow dung on its floor. It was learnt that it was used as a stable for cows for meat supply for the soldiers, possibly because of its size and possibly because the floors were made with carved polished wooden tiles that would not be too cold for the cattle. All the desks and chairs had disappeared from the classrooms. Of course, all the beds and lockers had also disappeared from the dormitories which looked like shadows of themselves. Many skeletal structures were still standing, and those were all that the students could call the old school, the treasured Varsity on the Cross, what once was the pride of all her students. At that stage however, nobody needed to be told that it was not worth asking the students back at that stage and under those conditions. The school was soon temporarily relocated to Enugu.

THE SCHOOL AS A REFUGEE

The school was relocated to the Institute of Administration Enugu, and Okoli soon moved over to Enugu to get back to school. He shared a room of six feet by eight feet with his two brothers Fab and Chris. The room was at the boys' quarters of his uncle's duplex. The three brothers shared one mat. They slept with their heads and trunks on the mat and their legs on the bare floor. That was because they had to sleep across the mat. Sleeping lengthwise would accommodate only one person on the narrow raffia mat. The three shared one kerosene stove, which worked by manual pumping. They had three small aluminum pots and four metal plates. A kerosene hurricane lantern, a can opener, two bottles (one for palm oil and the other for kerosene), a kitchen knife, a metal bucket, and a metal basin made up the rest of their possessions, furniture, and kitchenware. An open field at a nearby erosion site made up the open-air toilet for the twenty prototype rooms in the boys' quarters. Each duplex had a one room boys quarters allocated to it.

The meals were mainly composed of white bread, garri, rice, and yams for Okoli and Fab. Chris, from childhood, did not eat anything that was swallowed without being chewed. So his meals were mainly bread, rice, and yams. There was always a pot of stew usually prepared by Chris. Fab and Chris were masters in the art of preparing soup and stew respectively. Okoli never rally lived at home for any length of time with his mother except during the civil war, and consequently he did not learn how to prepare any of these dishes.

The three brothers did all their cooking on the floor in that one room. On two different occasions, the kerosene stove had caught fire after being pumped too hard. On both occasions, the brothers lost the entire food being cooked because they had to empty the bucket of water that was usually kept in the room onto the burning stove along with the pot of food that was cooking in order to put out the fire from the burning stove. One shudders to think of what would have happened if, on any of those nights, they had happened to sleep off after the long day's trek to and from school while the pot of food was cooking on the stove. Even though the building was constructed with vibrated hollow blocks, fire in such a building with very little ventilation, a lone window barricaded with fully installed metal burglary proof, and just the one wooden door as an exit would have been disastrous. In a setup where there were no fire-fighting services and no telephones or cell phones, an outbreak of fire in that enclosed little room, where the three brothers slept nightly, would have been very disastrous. It would have been impossible to secure any help, and an escape from the room would have been impossible if a fire were to start from near the only exit, the wooden door.

Chris was attending school at the College of Immaculate Conception, which was about one-hour walking from the residence. Fab and Okoli attended the temporarily relocated government secondary school at the Institute of Administration Enugu. The institute was about one and a half hours walking distance from where the three brothers lived. The breakfast was almost always bread dipped in either stew or water with sugar. That was the easiest meal to prepare if the brothers must not be late to school.

It was exciting, as soon as the students from Afikpo got back to school at Enugu. They were, however, saddened to learn of the loss of some of their colleagues during the war. They were particularly sad to hear of the loss of Orttah and Oyenso. Orttah, a very pleasant classmate of Okoli's, was said to have died defending Post Harcourt during the early stages of the war. Oyenso, a school sprinter and ace footballer, was said to have died defending the school premises itself.

Most of Okoli's other friends and classmates including Aboni, Livi, Erke, Ocuba, Tubia, Agem, Meriom, Kukpai and many more were happily back to school. They were all so happy to be back once again after nearly thirty months of a devastating civil war, a war which, judging from the extent of human suffering, was so grossly and catastrophically underplayed in the world media, perhaps deliberately so.

On the first assembly day at the Institute of Administration conference room, which was to serve as the assembly hall, the students sang again the *Songs of Praise* assembly song:

> Lord receive us with thy blessing,
> Once again assembled here . . .
> Lord again we bow before thee
> Speed our labors day by day . . .

As they sang, the students' minds turned to the scores of colleagues who were no longer there with them, fell by bullets, bombs, or by starvation. For the students that returned,

> Their minds turned solemnly to those many who did not return.
> They discussed them, their former colleagues,
> Great Mgbomians all
> Departed but not forgotten
> As the assembly was over.
> But during the assembly itself,
> There was not a minute silence in their honor
> Not as much as a second's silence to remember them,
> Not even for Oyeso,
> Who died defending the school.
> May be the new school authorities were too afraid to mention them
> Lest they be labeled as collaborators in a lost war.
> These were "rebel combatants" killed in battle
> "Ajukwu Soja" at best, and nothing more,
> Forgotten but certainly alive
> In the minds of their colleagues, as friends for ever.

With the relocation of the school to Enugu came a change in administrative leadership of the school. Egbe, whose name had almost become synonymous with the school, was replaced by another principal, who apparently had been working in the Ministry of Education.

Things were never to be the same again. The principal had been changed, most of the masters were new, the Indian masters were gone, a lot of the other masters had been reassigned to the newly created states, and the orientation of the students had also changed. The highly revered former vice principal and dedicated chemistry master, Equua, was to resurface only briefly at Owerri many years later. His unrelenting zeal and love for his students and the school must have fuelled his desire to return even when he could very comfortably have stayed back in Britain, his home country. But things had greatly changed for the worse. Value systems had been truncated. The people who treasured what Afikpo stood for had largely dispersed. Many of the students had held officer positions in the army. Some had been army captains, army majors, and colonels. Naturally their attitude and orientation towards certain aspects of school life had changed.

It was not only the school that lost. The nation as a whole lost the more. The technology that had been assiduously and meticulously crafted during the civil war by the secessionist scientists had been lost. Though crude and ungainly, these could easily have been assembled and harnessed to the great advantage of the nation.

But no!
These had to be destroyed and destroyed, most were,
Relics and remnants of Ajukwu Soja must go.
Uli and Uga airports, the rebel landing sites
Hastily but efficiently constructed by Biafran engineers,
These and many war laboratories and facilities, ingenuities all,
For thirty months of resistance these had sustained,
The Biafran-made oil refineries, crude as they were,
Institutions that would elude the nation for years,
All these to dust were to go, as to victory we marched
Rebel sources of strength all were to go.
At the end of the day the nation was the loser.
We have won the war, but we lost the war,
As the nation is not the richer for the victory,
Except in volatile oil dollar for now.
The wiser victors in wars of yesteryears
Great talents had preserved and in great esteem had held,
And had utilized the technologies of wars to great advantage in the past,
For necessity the mother of invention always had been,
And preservation the mother of greatness always will be.
A belated attempt at preservation there lately was,
But halfhearted measures no dividends ever yield.
For the destruction, near total had been,
And assemblage of the scientists, insincere to boot.
And we grope in the dark attempting to reinvent the wheel
While our compatriots in other lands to the moon are yearly going.
Chase of oil money our passion will remain
Until our priorities our leaders change
And less emphasis on personal acquisition and materialism bestow.
For our nation once again can be truly great.
We make the waves from far away,
But at home the bug will slowly catch

For stealing and embezzlement as much as we can
To outmatch one another in the game of theft
As the nation bleeds and bleeds to death.
New looters from everywhere surface like ants.
New mansions in our capitals daily rise,
Exotic cars our bad roads daily fill,
Products of volatile oil money most of them are.
From everywhere they multiply by day and by night
Imported technology all of them are.
And the looters of yesteryears their loot daily display.
Little effort is made to punish the looters
And show example to future looters
As the looters of old to governance aspire
With ill-gotten wealth stolen from the poor.
The roads get worse as the funds are stolen.
She dies at childbirth as the hospitals are underfunded.
He dies as a baby because malaria-control funds are embezzled.
He cannot get good quality education because education board funds have been embezzled.
And the teachers go on strike because they will not be paid.
The funds for their wages have largely been stolen.
And the thief with the money buys his way to election rigging.
He comes to rule the people whose development money he had stolen.
Electric power will not come on because the designated funds have been embezzled.
The man who stole the funds will never be punished
He aims at rulership of the very people he has kept in the dark.
The nation is dragged back to the twentieth century
As others march to the twenty-second
And the looters walk tall in the streets for all to see.
They feel very confident because they have covered their backs.
And their would-be accusers have largely been "settled"
And the looters before them have never been punished
And the looter has his men in places high and mighty
And any complainants will languish in jail
And the looter will daily smile to the banks,
Most of which he owns, or through fronts he truly owns.
And millions of the true owners of the wealth will daily groan.

They have no hope for tomorrow as they are economically disenfranchised.
And their children and their children's children will live from hand to mouth
And their leaders and elders are settled from day to day
And silence thereafter they must maintain to keep their price
And there is no public morality left in the system
Even the truth that characterized elder statesmanship is thoroughly gone

For the nation has literally been bought up by looters over the years.
And so will it continue until God's time is ripe
And he sends the nation a messiah at his own good time and pace.

For now the people who have looted the treasury we daily cheer,
As with a small fraction of the looted funds they come to campaign at election time
And the people get peanuts of their looted funds as election incentives
And we clap our hands and cheer them to victory
And little effort is made to stem the tide.
Little effort is made to retrieve the loot
And the little that is retrieved is poorly accounted for
And the cycle on and on must go
And the nation slowly bleeds to death.
The young will daily watch the trend
As no efforts are made with good intents,
The looters of yesterday to nab and severely punish
And the trend will stick and the nation bleeds,
And our people are mocked from far and from near
As a people who cannot, their God-given resources effectively manage,
The first in the world in corruption and in graft, we often are labeled,
We grin as we go and glorify ourselves
As our heroes of yesteryears in their graves will turn
To see their efforts of yesteryears
Besmeared and tarnished by our greed and our graft.

The New School on the Hill

As many of the schools in the newly created East Central State of Nigeria were in ruins, or grossly dilapidated, the few fully functioning ones needed to create more classes to cope with the surge of new students. Class strength was increased from thirty to forty per class. Each stream was increased from A and B to as many as A, B, C, D, and E. Class 1 was particularly overbloated. On one occasion, when after the D class had been filled, the pressure on the principal to admit more and more fresh students compelled him to create a new class E. Okoli had been appointed the school captain after the incumbent Aboni had moved to another institution.

As the school captain, it was one of Okoli's duties to direct the newly admitted students into their classes, on the instruction of the principal. Okoli had earlier invited one of his younger brothers Ody over to Enugu to see if the latter could start school at Enugu. Ody was always so busy helping the mother in the kitchen that Okoli felt that if Ody continued that way, both his physical and academic development would suffer. Ody was always so service oriented. He would offer to cook the food. He would offer to fetch the firewood, fetch the water, wash the plates. He would even offer to surrender his own food if the food was not enough for everybody. He was ever ready to make sacrifices. When other children of his age would be playing, he would sit near the kitchen fire, stoking the firewood to ensure that the fire did not go down, his eyes red and tears dripping down from irritation of the smoke. It was certainly not a healthy situation for a child. Okoli had therefore requested their aunt Nwomiko to accommodate Ody in her one-room residence at Enugu since the little room Okoli occupied with Fab and Chris was already over crowded.

With Ody now at Enugu, the problem of securing a school for him arose. Okoli requested his senior uncle M.O. to use his influence to plead with the school principal to place Ody in one of the newly created classes. As a student, Okoli could not muster the courage to approach the principal on an issue as important and official as school admission, certainly not as a student. That was a prerogative of the ministers, commissioners, permanent secretaries, and other very influential People. Okoli's uncle however could not oblige him, for obvious reasons. The former's predicament was possibly because that same term he had secured admission for his own son through the same principal. He probably would not want to plead again for another admission for his nephew who just arrived from the village. The principal was not likely to oblige him with a second position.

Day after day, Okoli kept escorting newly admitted students to their classes on the instruction of the principal. These admissions of course were not based on any entrance examinations. The major criteria were of course cronyism and on how influential the person seeking the favor was in society. Okoli did not fit into any of the criteria. He was neither a crony nor an influential person. He was school captain no doubt, but he was still a student.

On the third Sunday into the school term, however, Okoli took a decision and said to himself, "Come Monday morning, I will take Ody to the school. I will present the principal with my request. Let him say no to me if he wished. I will accept the denial if it be."

On Monday morning, therefore, Okoli went to school taking with him, Ody. The former trudged on behind Okoli, as they hurried up the hill leading to the Institute of Administration buildings, his tiny feet struggling with his loosely fitting rubber slippers. He would sometimes run to keep up with Okoli's pace, and both were able to get to school ahead of school assembly. As Ody was not yet a student, and having not been brought in a car like almost all the other applicants seeking admission, he had to stand outside of the school, by the roadside.

When assembly was over, the daily admission process which occupied the first thirty minutes of most mornings restarted. The "big men" in their suits and flowing traditional dresses then started streaming from their cars into the principal's office, taking their children or their wards to the principal. As usual, Okoli as captain of school was summoned to receive the students after admission. After taking in the first two students, Okoli went to where Ody was and brought him into the school. The latter, very simply dressed, looked a little different from the other candidates who were well kitted and in shoes. Ody was nevertheless his usual lively and sharp-looking self. It was obvious that intellectually he would match or even beat these others, given the same opportunity. As soon as the principal's bell rang summoning Okoli again to take in another student, the latter grabbed Ody by the hand and walked into the principal's office with the latter. He felt glad his courage did not fail him.

"Sir, I brought my little brother," Okoli started

"Your little brother?" came the immediate question.

"Yes, sir," Okoli replied

"For what?" continued the principal

"For class 1, sir," Okoli continued

There was now a minute's silence, the minute's silence that could not be observed at the start of term for fallen colleagues. Then, staring at Okoli through the top portion of his bifocal eyeglasses, the principal, this time as if with some difficulty, asked again, "For what, who recommended him?"

That was a difficult question for Okoli to answer. But he was sure that these other people did not come with any recommendations, at least not in class 1.

"Nobody, sir; I mean, e-e-m, I did, sir," Okoli answered.

"You mean, you by yourself recommended your brother?"

"No, sir; I meant to say, ye-e-s, sir."

The stare this time lasted longer. It must have been about a minute and a half, but it looked like it lasted an hour.

It was most likely the principal was in a dilemma. There seated on the cushion chairs in his office were the "movers and shakers of society" bringing their sons for admission, people who could help improve funding to the school or perhaps enhance the principal's position too. And here was this unduly audacious student who was only a titular appointee trying to rub shoulders with the dignitaries.

Okoli fixed his gaze on the principal, as his heart beat rapidly. The principal bent his head and started writing on a piece of paper. *Could he be placing my brother to a class?* Okoli mused, as he looked back at Ody, while still holding the latter's hand. The latter too appeared so anxious with his glittering little eyes fixed at the principal.

Then came the break of the silence.

"Send these two boys to class 1E. Bring back your brother tomorrow morning so that we shall check whether there will still be space," the principal said in a low tone.

So at last the verdict has been passed, and it was not in our favor! Okoli mused.

He looked again at the principal. The latter's eyes were fixed on the former, this time with his glasses removed. For the first time Okoli noticed that the principal had unusually big eyeballs with a ring of white encircling the pupils (arcus senilis). As he prepared to leave the room, Okoli turned his gaze on the two men whose sons had just been admitted. His heart sank. He turned to go, still holding Ody by one hand and the piece of paper of class allocation for the other two new students on the other.

"Thank you, sir," Okoli said as he was leaving the principal's office.

Just as he turned the door handle to leave, Okoli heard the principal say, "Wait, Captain, let me have that class admission paper." The principal's conscience appeared to have had the upper hand.

Okoli had even forgotten that the principal handed him the class admission paper for the other two boys who were standing beside their fathers. As he muttered "which paper, sir?" the principal who appeared to have noticed Okoli's confusion and utter disappointment took two steps towards Okoli, stretched out his hand, and collected the class admission paper from the latter. He then bent down over his table, put on his glasses, and scribbled a few words on the paper. He then gave Okoli back the paper saying, "Put your brother also in class 1E."

"Did you say 1E, sir?" Okoli asked as if asking for a reassurance that he heard the principal right.

"Yes, 1E," replied the principal.

It was real! It was not a dream!!

"Thank you, sir, thank you, thank you, thank you," Okoli kept repeating until he left the room.

Just as the school at Afikpo was not quite equipped to receive students after their return from civil war, the Institute of Administration Enugu where the students were temporarily located was not equipped either. The latter did not have labs, did not have an equipped library, it did not have a wood or metal workshop for the technical students. Students in the higher school section therefore started applying to sit the entrance exams for entry into the universities. There were five universities in the country: Ibadan, Nsukka, Lagos, Zaria, and Benin, with Benin being the youngest. There was no joint admission and matriculating board, and so a candidate could apply to as many of the universities as he wanted or could afford. Okoli sat the entrance exams and got admissions to the Ibadan, Nsukka, and Benin. His bosom friend Aboni also, as expected, passed to the universities he sat for including Nsukka and Ibadan. Both friends finally chose Ibadan University Medical School, partly because it was the premier medical school in the country (starting as a college of the University of London) and partly because its facilities in equipment had remained intact since it was not affected by the devastating civil war in the country.

The period between his gaining admissions to the University of Ibadan medical school and his actual entry was the most memorable period of Okoli's entire school career. It marked a turning point in his life. It marked the period of his transition from being a boy to his being a man. He would no longer need bells to beckon him as to when to wake up in the mornings, no bells to beckon him on to classes, no bells for change of lessons, and nobody to supervise his day-to-day activities. It was the first time he would be going to live outside the region. It was the first time he would not have notes dictated, the first time that as a student he would have to take his own decisions about lectures.

Okoli felt very excited because unlike the time when he gained admission into Government Secondary School Afikpo without knowing that the inserted word *scholar* signified that he passed with scholarship, he knew the full implications of being admitted into the medical school: that real hard work, strict discipline, and total commitment were demanded.

Before he finally left government secondary school, his classmates, and the other prefects held a farewell party for him. It was a very emotional event for him. There was very little in terms of speeches. Another classmate of Okoli's and a friend, Ediegwu, was appointed to take Okoli's place as school captain. Ediegwu was a very principled, religious, and decent personality. He was reputed for having the best handwriting in the class right from the students' class 1. His self comportment and manners were as fine as his handwriting, and Okoli was happy he was handing over to such a fine and decent young man who would certainly uphold the very high standards expected of the school captain of Government Secondary School Afikpo.

As he took a very last look at his school on the day he was finally leaving, one thing stood clear in Okoli's mind. He knew that the Institute of Administration was not his school! That was not the Afikpo he used to know. That was a borrowed premises.

> The Afikpo Okoli used to know held promise.
> It was home to all her students.
> It had glamour.
> The Afikpo that was his Afikpo was so well planned.
> It was planned for optimum utility, comfort, and adaptability.

No!
The Afikpo that Okoli knew lay a hundred miles away
It had been looted down to the windowpanes,
It had been left bereft of its old glamour.
Its assembly hall had been adorned with dung
Its library had been turned into a kitchen
And the dedicated masters had gone their way.
Can any replenish those old teaching staff?
Their dedication and commitment was unrivalled.
The tradition was enviable
Bullying though there was,
That had been mitigated
For effective discipline to instill,
And discipline was a major objective,
To produce the best of citizens,
Citizens sound in every respect,
Sound in body, sound in mind. "Mens sana in corpora sano."
As Okoli took a final look
And slowly walked down the hill,
To the high heavens he prayed, and sincerely too,
To have the opportunity even if it be for a day
In his OWN WORDS and in THE FIRST PERSON too,
To write vividly and let posterity know,
The exploits of her products
And the greatness that was
Afikpo, "the Varsity on the River Cross."

Book II

The Coming of Age

The Journey to the West . . . and Beyond

The forty-five-seat capacity bus arrived Ibadan late in the evening. It had not been a very comfortable journey. The bus had been constructed to carry forty-five passengers. But the conductors had added some ten detachable wooden seats on the floor of the bus along the walkway, completely blocking the latter. They called the seats "attachments." The fare for the attachment was slightly lower than the normal fare. The attachment passengers were not given any receipts for the fares that they paid. They were indeed passengers who were fixed up after the buses had been filled up or those who, in order to have much lower fares, opted not to have regular seats. Their names were therefore not contained in the official manifest of the vehicle for the journey. Whatever they paid was not documented and probably not accounted for. It probably went into the pockets of the driver and the conductor for "expenses on the road."

The drivers and conductors often justified their action by claiming that they needed the extra funds "to settle the officers on the road at the numerous checkpoints." Whenever the bus was stopped at a checkpoint, the conductor would jump down and shake the officer's hand. Cash having presumably changed hands, the bus would be waved on. The overloading of the vehicle and the consequent inconvenience to the passengers and the added risks involved in the event of an accident were of secondary, or of no considerations. At the other end, the officer on the road would justify his actions by the allegation that his superior officer would ask him to give account (of his collections) any time he came back from roadblock deployment or from a highway patrol.

It was a truly vicious cycle,
A veritable path to societal decay,
A road to inevitable damnation
For a people so blessed by God
Unless we drop our greed and avarice.

But who is there to sanitize the system,
Who is there to return the society to the path of rectitude?
Who is there to restore the nation to the path of honor and societal decency?

Visitors to our great nation watch with disbelief
As we denigrate our self-respect on the highways and airports
And sell our nation's honor for peanuts.
And our leadership appears to turn the other way
As our nation's image is dragged to the dust
And we expect the respect of the civilized world,
Simply because we are what we are
The giant of Africa, the world's biggest black nation.
As if these alone entitle us to all the honor
Or exempt us from what is expected of civilized and decent behavior
Even if we daily abuse ourselves
With ill-gotten wealth and filthy lucre.
And our youth watch and they copy,
The leaders of tomorrow, we thus corrupt.
And the cycle goes on and on, till doomsday halts the drift
Or till the inevitable comes to pass:
A sanitization that may be all consuming
As the many that are good will go with the few that are bad, powerful and depraved
Unless we change the system now,
And toe the path of rectitude for a change.

I had left Enugu very early in the morning to Onitsha and boarded one of the Ibadan-bound buses at Onitsha, the big commercial city at the banks of the great River Niger. It was the very first time I went beyond Asaba, a relatively smaller city on the other side of the River Niger.

The journey from Onitsha to Ibadan took us through Ore, the junction city we heard of so much during the civil war. I was so amazed at the thick bushes, large trees, and dense forests that we met around Ore. I had never imagined that such natural reserves existed in my country. I started imagining that if such vast forest reserves existed in Nigeria and are not very much mentioned in the geography books, then the Amazon Rainforest must be truly wonderful to behold.

At Ore we had our first meal for the day. The roadside hotels were so many, with passengers from Lagos and so many other places disembarking for a meal. The meals were served steaming hot. I saw several types of dishes ranging from one that was deep brown to black in color called *amala*, to pounded cassava, and pounded yam all very inviting. Stockfish—which was in such short supply during the civil war except for the supplies from Red Cross, World Council of Churches, and Caritas International—was being served generously. The catering services at Ore were so brisk and efficient that one wondered how the hotel owners managed to keep up almost all day and all night long.

The city of Ibadan was so vast. The trip through one section of it to the university did not ever seem to end. At a stage, I started to wonder whether the bus driver was simply driving us around the city. But every section provided new sights and some peculiarities. A number of similarities however struck me. The roofing sheets were almost uniformly rusty brown, probably depicting the age of the ancient city. There were very large numbers of people on the roads at every turn. There was so much street trading that the center of the city looked like one huge open market.

The change in the mode of dressing was so strikingly different from what obtained in the eastern parts of the country. Whereas most men wore shirt and trousers in the east, most men in Ibadan (and the west in general) were more traditional and wore loose-fitting trousers with long loose flowing robe and cap. Ceremonial dresses, as I was later to observe, also differed. The women in the east tied one inner wrapper and another outer wrapper (long sheet of cloth) on top of the inner wrapper.

Conversely I observed the nonuse of the smaller outer wrapper in the west. In each of the two cultures women covered their head with the head tie. In Ibadan the head gear was more loosely bound.

As we got towards the city center in Ibadan, we began to see periodically large microphones mounted on some houses, beaming messages in the vernacular. I later learnt that those were mosques. I then began to confirm what we had learnt in school that the population in the far north of Nigeria was mainly Moslem, the North Central and west mainly mixed Christian and Moslem, while the eastern parts of the country was mainly Christian. The diversity was very fascinating. The unity that had existed (baring the thirty months of civil war) amidst the diversity was even more fascinating and a great credit to the ingenuity and political and religious resilience, tolerance, and social engineering wizardry of the founding fathers of the republic that emerged after the country attained independence from Britain. Perhaps if the men in khaki and underarms had been well schooled in those virtues, we might have been spared the gruesome and senseless massacres that were initiated by these men, culminating in a more gruesome and senseless civil war that only succeeded in setting the country many generations back, almost destroying the mutual confidence and the economic, academic, and social values that the country had inherited from the many years of British colonial rule.

The main gate of the University of Ibadan was so very simple. It consisted of one small decked gatehouse sitting between two simple inlet and outlet gates. The gates led into a dual carriage way stretching about half a mile and ending at a central clearing behind which stood the university's hallmark structure, the Trenchard Hall. The Trenchard Hall housed the university's main tower clock.

The driveway between the university gate and Trenchard Hall had beautifully mowed lawns lying on either side of the dual carriage way and between the two roads, the inlet road and the outlet road. On the right side of the dual carriage way, approaching from the gate, were a few staff houses, while on the far left and close to Trenchard Hall was Queen Elizabeth Hall (called Queen's Hall), which was the only female hostel as of the time. At the right side of the Trenchard Hall were the University Library and Mellanby Hall. At the distal right of Trenchard Hall lay Tedder Hall while Kuti and Sultan Bello halls lay at the proximal left and distal left ends respectively. Farther down, left of Trenchard Hall were the Postgraduate (Balewa) Hall, Azikiwe Hall, and Independence Hall. So much were the halls as we got to know them. The Clinical Students' Hall, which we later got to know about, was situated some five miles away at the University College Hospital site.

The lecture halls, the laboratories, thc University Library, the vice chancellor's residence, and the other staff residences lay farther down the road. Abadina quarters, the two Christian churches, and the mosque all lay farther down towards Abadina at the Mellanby Hall end. Such was the sketchy outlay of the great University of Ibadan the, first epicenter of university education in Nigeria.

The vehicle that brought us to Ibadan from Onitsha finally stopped us in front of Trenchard Hall and I easily found my way to Mellanby Hall which was to be my residence for the subsequent two years. I was soon checked into my room by the porters on duty. As I was disembarking from the vehicle, my mind immediately went back to my experience many years back when I disembarked at Afikpo, on my first day in secondary school.

How immensely the years change everything
How maturity and differentials in life situations dictate the patterns
How different the situations between childhood and adulthood.
How wide the differences between the "college student"
And the true college student,
The university undergraduate,
The secondary school student, and the university student.

We were now men,
And the men welcomed us into the hall of residence.
The porters were there all to assist.
Courtesy was the watchword,
And like the slogan on the popular soda Sprite, in Nigeria,
"The difference is clear."

I was given the key to my room. I was also given the schedules for laundry, rules and regulations, as well as my meal ticket package for one month. The room which was on the second floor had two beds, two reading tables, two office chairs, and two wardrobes. It had a patio overlooking the flower gardens. My roommate must have arrived earlier because the second bed had been occupied as was evidenced by the books and clothes on it. Later that evening I was to meet my roommate, Sule, for the first time.

Sule was a very polite tall lanky young man. He was in his second year in the university and was a political science major.

Supper time was very exciting. The bundle of meal tickets contained coupons for breakfast, lunch, and supper, a strip of three, for meals for each day of the month. The meals were very good. They appeared commonplace and routine to the old students, but to me, they were so special, especially coming from a background of a devastating civil war characterized by hunger and starvation. The most fascinating aspect of the dining hall to me was that tea, coffee, and Bournvita (a cocoa-based beverage) were being served from the taps. That meant one could drink as much as one wished. I had never seen that kind of thing before. Initially I thought that the machine had a way of knowing who had earlier taken a cupful or for recognizing a cup that had been used before. So even though I loved Bournvita and would not have minded helping myself to a second or even a third cup, I was afraid of going for a second round of serving, lest the machine might detect me. Coco-based drinks had been my addiction right from secondary school.

My nickname, Chico, in secondary school was based on a coco-based beverage called Chico. I enjoyed Chico so much that I used to lick it in its unreconstituted dry form, from its container. On one Saturday morning just before the principal came into the dormitory for inspection, I had stuck my head deep into my locker to lick a few spoonfuls of dry Chico. Just as I started licking the Chico, the principal came in with his inspection team, and I had to hurriedly withdraw my head from the locker, spilling the Chico granules on my white shirt and staining it badly. As the principal walked past me, he quickly observed the thick brown stains on my white shirt. Of course, I immediately got two runs as punishment "for wearing Chico-stained shirt at inspection." Till this day, many of my friends like Tubia, Davidson, Frank, and others still call me Chico.

Much as I loved coco-based beverages, I always limited myself to one serving, because of that belief that it was one serving per meal ticket that students were entitled to. It was not until about our third day during breakfast that I observed a man sitting opposite me on the table help himself to a second cup, and then a third cup from the tap. I did not see him pay any extra money, nor did I see anybody stop him. I thereafter got to know that it was permissible to drink as many cups of tea, coffee, or Bournvita as one wished. So I quickly gulped my first cup, got up, and rather timidly, at first, went for a second, looking anxiously from side to side as the cup filled to see if anybody would stop me or ask me to pay extra. After that day, I would eat sparingly and fill up with two or three cups of Bournvita.

The registration for courses at Ibadan was very smooth. It looked so strange. Nobody compelled anybody to do anything. The first time I woke up in the morning as an undergraduate student in Ibadan, I expected I would hear some kind of bell ring signaling the time for breakfast or time for lectures. I had been so used all my life through primary and secondary schools to being guided and reminded about classes and other events by bells. But not anymore. This was a university, and the students were treated appropriately as adult men and women; men and women who were or should be expected to know what they wanted and how to get about them—only being guided by handouts, bulletins, timetables, and lectures. There were people who would stick to the timetable and attend all the classes and events on schedule. But there were others who might decide to sleep all day or play music all day in their rooms. The only television set in the common room of each hall of residence was free for any student who wished to watch television till late into the night. This was a sharp contrast to my days at Afikpo where there was neither a television set nor the freedom to enjoy any such luxury.

The lecture sessions were brisk and to the point. They were initially difficult to follow since they were neither being dictated nor were they available for copying from the boards as was the case in the secondary school. They however very soon became interesting and easy to follow. Participation in sports activities was optional, unlike in our secondary school where it was mandatory so long as the student was healthy. The equipments were much more sophisticated. There were no form orders and no mark readings. Those were the two academic issues that used to keep us on our toes at Afikpo. In the absence of these weekly tests, we initially thought that university life was all a bread-and-butter affair, especially as we always saw so many posters of social events and so many social clubs being advertised. We were soon to find out and I easily remembered the Shakespeare's verse that we had read in secondary school about all that glittered not being gold.

Our first year courses of zoology, chemistry, physics, and organic chemistry were more like our higher school courses. They were however much more oriented to medicine, and there was a lot more emphasis on the laboratory work. Organic chemistry was a tough one for most of us, but the environment was much more conducive to studying, even though the multitude of chemical structures was always a scourge.

I was so amazed the first day we were introduced to the University Library. It was so very fascinating. I found that our entire school library at Afikpo was more like a grain of sand in a beach when compared to the volumes and volumes of books, journals, publications, and all that were in the University Library. I began to appreciate the appropriateness of the Igbo language word *mahadum* for university, which when translated means *know it all*. Obviously, that gigantic building called the University Library with all it contained must know it all. The assistant librarian who took us round on our "introduction to the library" tour was so patient, so diligent, so thorough, and certainly so very knowledgeable.

During our first year, which was appropriately called "preliminary medicine year," we had exactly the same courses with the science major students. We also took the same exams. Some of the science major students had actually applied at the time of the entrance examinations to do medicine but did not make the cut-off marks required for the course. They had therefore settled for science as a second choice. Many of them still had the intention of switching over to medicine if the opportunity should come up. Those of us who were doing preliminary medicine were therefore specifically warned that if any preliminary medicine student should score below 50 percent in any of the three major subjects of zoology, physics, and chemistry, the place of that student would be taken up by an aspiring preliminary science student who scored well above 50 percent in each of the three major subjects.

Our preliminary medicine year was therefore a rat race, a kind of a dogfight between the incumbent preliminary medicine students and the aspiring science major students. That scenario made our preliminary medicine year in the university particularly dicey. It was akin to the "publish or perish" theory, which we were later to hear our lecturers talk about in relation to their academic publications vis-à-vis their prospects of advancement in rank in the academics.

The Fear of Failure and the University Riots

The ever-constant fear of dropping off the medicine list (as the list of preliminary medicine students was called) made our first year in the university quite uncomfortable. The constant fear of a science student taking up one's position was like a sword of Damocles hanging over our heads. There were lots of very brilliant science major students, and some of them addressed themselves as "medical students waiting in the wings." It was an extremely difficult year, akin to those years at Government Secondary School Afikpo when, as government scholars, we were to perpetually struggle to stay academically ahead of the nonscholars if we were to keep our scholarship.

The practical chemistry classes, especially the ones involving titration, were particularly intriguing. One tiny drop of water or other reagent from a pipette could make all the difference to the end point. But we had very dedicated lecturers without whose patience and understanding our stories would have been different. Father Foley of practical chemistry in particular was so dedicated to the subject and greatly simplified what would otherwise be an insurmountable hurdle for many of us to cross.

When the final exam results for the first year were released, most of the medical students were able to successfully sail through. It was such a hectic year for most of us. It was so hectic that after the first week in the university we scarcely thought of anything else apart form the classroom, the laboratory, and the library. We called our three destinations "the triangular path for success."

A few weeks into the second term of our first year in the university, an event occurred that was unprecedented in the history of the university. That event was to a large extent to change the history of the university forever.

The students had for some time been complaining about the quality of their meals. As earlier narrated, for many of us who were just emerging from the horrors of war where rats, lizards, and locusts occasionally formed our only sources of protein, the meals could not have been better. Having meat and stewed chicken in the dining room and unregulated cupfuls of tea and Bournvita from taps made the university feeding system look like "Alice in wonderland" for those of us the east. For me, in particular, that situation where I could have as many cups of Bournvita as I wanted, oozing into my cup in the dinning room, and at no extra cost to me could not be any better. The complaints nevertheless went on, snowballing into a demonstration by the students around the university campus. The students carried placards demanding improved feeding conditions and the removal of the university's head of catering services. For those of us who were freshmen to the university, we knew nothing of "how good it used to be." We had no yardsticks for measuring any differences. Most of us joined the demonstrations as these, if nothing else, offered a diversion and a welcome relief from the monotony of book work.

At a stage during the demonstrations, the police were called in by the university authorities. Unfortunately the police were said to have come with live ammunition, perhaps not having been properly drilled on the art of mob control. The demonstrating students were mostly gathered in front of Trenchard Hall, the epicenter of the university. The police were assembled some distance opposite the students toward the Queen Elizabeth Hall end of the university. It was said that some students threw stones at the police. Shots soon rang out from the police end and a student was felled. The dead student was said to have been hit in the head. It could have been any of us. The killing of this student, a most unfortunate incident which shocked the whole nation, sparked off massive protests from many quarters including the media. A very protracted tribunal of enquiry was set up at Ibadan. The student body was very fortunate to have representation from one of the most talented young attorneys in the land. The mere stories of that attorney's legal sophistication during the entire duration of the tribunal kept many of us back at Ibadan even when the university was forced to close down temporarily. The said attorney was said to have meticulously represented the student body at no cost during the protracted tribunals that followed the demonstrations and the subsequent killing.

The tragedy of Tunji's death certainly was a sad event that will never be forgotten in the history of the university. The sad event and the ensuing tribunal of enquiry were of course to bring about major changes in the way that catering and administrative services were organized in the university.

The Second Year

The second year of medical students in the university was known as the first preclinical year. The subjects studied were anatomy, physiology, and biochemistry. The anatomy studied was entirely human anatomy and involved the systematic and painstakingly detailed dissection (cutting) of cadavers preserved with formalin. The cadavers selected for preservation were usually those that were whole and not mutilated in any way so that the students would be able to cut open the different parts, organ by organ, to identify the different muscles, blood vessels, and nerves. The different organs like the brains, kidneys, intestine, lungs, heart, gall bladder, urinary bladder, reproductive organs, bones—indeed every single structure big and small in the entire human body—were dissected out, and their course from beginning to end traced. Even after we had heard stories of the experiences of earlier students on their first day in the anatomy room, we still had a mild drama.

We all looked smart in our white laboratory coats as we walked from the halls of residence to the anatomy laboratories positioned some distance off the Seat of Wisdom Catholic Church. We all felt proud to have scaled through the preliminary course year. We wanted to be noticed as future doctors in our lab coats even on that first day of preclinical course. Even though those were dead bodies we were going to cut up, we felt as if we were already going to see patients and/or perform surgery. Each of us was clutching his dissection set containing the dissection knife (scalpel), the probes, and magnifying glass. We also each had a copy of our *Grant's* (or *Last's*) *Atlas of Anatomy*. Some of us even carried with us our copies of the massive *Gray's Anatomy*. We had assembled in front of the Anatomy Building, which stood innocently amidst the other equally big Biochemistry and Physiology buildings, innocently, in spite of the initial scare their contents were to give the new students.

One of the instructors (who were called demonstrators) came out and addressed us briefly. He merely told us that we would be assigned "four to a table, two on each side of a cadaver." May be the instructor had got so used to the "horrors" of the dissection room and the irritation and smell of formalin that he did not remember to prepare us for the sights we were going to behold. On the other hand, it was possible that he wanted us to learn from experience.

The double swing doors to the very expansive dissection room were laid open. We were ushered in, in alphabetical order, and I was number four in the list. The first student in alphabetical order was fortunately or unfortunately a lady. As she stepped in, she pulled to the side. The second person, Yeti, was the most massive boy in the whole class. He ironically pulled the drama. As Yeti stepped into the air-conditioned chill of the dissection room, he yelled, "My Jee," and he sprang back with his eyes looking as if they were popping out after a sight of ghosts. Luckily the girl who entered first was still inside, close to the door, though too scared to go fully in. The third and fourth students followed in quick succession. There lying stiff—completely naked and many with complete set of teeth, displaying as if in ghostly grins from retracted lips, and lying all supine—were over forty male and female cadavers. It was the most scary sight I had ever beheld all my life, as of that day. I pulled towards Bimbo, the lady who entered first, as if to draw some inspiration from her. Some eight demonstrators (instructors) were scattered in different parts of the expansive hall doing business as usual, oblivious of the enormous fright that had caught many of us. The other students followed, all lining themselves along the walls as if to seek protection even when the numbering on the slabs indicated which dead bodies we were supposed to go to. Soon we could see Yeti, the fleeing big, boy reenter to find his way behind Bimbo, whose petite structure was not big enough to hide Yeti from the "view" of the "men and women" on the slabs.

All the arrogance and bravado we had displayed on our way to the Anatomy Building had oozed off. The chill in the large hall, the "mocking grimaces" from some of the cadavers and the eye irritation from the formalin had all jointly brought home to all of us the futility and vanity of our arrogance and the reality of the true situation that we needed to face up to.

Soon the professor was to walk into the room. Simply dressed in a long white lab coat, he briefly welcomed us into the Anatomy Department and told us of the need to ensure we mastered every single structure in the human body since according to him, our written exams and vivas (oral exams) could come from even the tiniest structure. He emphasized the need to combine the physical structures that we would see in the dead human body with what we would read in the text book. He thereafter wished us good luck in our study of human anatomy, and then he left the room.

I was assigned along with another person to the right side of a male cadaver, a hefty middle-aged man. He must have been a very muscular man. My partner and I started with the thorax and abdomen while the duo on the left side started with the lower limb. According to our instructors, while my partner read out the directions from the anatomy workbook, I dissected. After some time, we would reverse roles. The first few cuts I made were with immense trepidation. After that, I was more confident. After the first day of dissection, the subsequent ones were more routine for us. We were no longer afraid to look at the faces of the cadavers as we dissected. I could still however see two slabs on which faces of the cadavers were covered with handkerchiefs while dissection was going on. It was possible the students were initially afraid of the grinning faces of the bodies they were dissecting.

As the weeks and months progressed, we moved systematically from one region of the body to the other: the head and neck, the thorax and abdomen, the pelvis, the upper limbs, and the lower limbs. The attention paid even to the minutest details was amazing. The most intriguing aspect of the two years posting in anatomy was when we did the brain. When, later in the week we were to link the microscopic study (histology) and the mode of functioning (physiology), one could not but marvel at the endless and infinite wisdom of the hand that crafted and, of course, coordinated all that. One could not but humble oneself before the Almighty and give glory and honor to the maker of the universe, whose infinite wisdom alone could have made all that coordination possible.

Physiology and biochemistry postings were almost equally intriguing. A few tracings were provided by the Physiology Department for demonstration purposes, especially during the experiments on muscle twitch and the stretch reflexes. We compared our carbon paper tracings during experiments, and they were all interesting.

The histology posting was a mixed grill of excitement and near fantasy to some of us. Initially the microscopic appearances of many of the organs appeared all so similar. When initially we were presented with slides of the spleen, the pancreas, and the liver, they all appeared to look the same—mere sheets and sheets of cells. It was not until much later that one could pick out obvious distinguishing features and could almost at a glance distinguish between different structures—the skin, the kidneys, the liver, the gut, the vagina, the urethra, the brain, the testis, cartilage, and various characteristics—that distinguished one from the other. The Indian professor Fendan, who headed the histology unit made it all so interesting. He was so very knowledgeable, so funny, and ever so ready to help with apparently difficult slides. He would come in breathing fast, "armed" with boxes and boxes of slides. He told us that he had three lobes of his lungs removed at surgery and that with only two lobes remaining, coupled with his chain-smoking habit, he would live only two more years. Then, he would add, "Ven I jai, juu can juuz my lungs for muo jilaids."

But Professor Fen, as we called him, did not get to *jai* (die) nor did we get to *juuz* (use) his lungs for *muo* (more) *jilaids* (slides) throughout our stay in the medical school. Indeed he lived well beyond our clinical years in the university.

Professor Burore, who headed physiology, took us on two lectures a week. It was said that he was a practicing physician, a gastroenterologist, for a long time before he joined the academic community. He would come in, in his three-piece suit. (Some said he used to come in straight from the clinic.) With both hands in his two-trouser pockets and with his head turned upwards towards the ceiling, he would ask the class, "Where did we stop the last time?"

Someone would hazard a guess which Professor Burore would not verify. From there we would learn the entire clinical presentations of a particular disease and how we would manage same. It was all very interesting to us as most of us wanted to go to the clinics as quickly as possibly. Nothing fascinated us as much as being seen with stethoscopes sticking out from the front pockets of our lab coats even when what we still had to contend with were dead bodies in Anatomy Department and the twitching muscles of toads in physiology as well as the all-elusive biochemistry. Professor Burore was very particular about our early masterly of the different heart sounds. He would place the stethoscope on the chest of someone and then ask, "Now you there tell me, is this heart sound regular or irregular? And if it is irregular, is it regularly irregular or irregularly irregular?"

That was a time when we scarcely knew what the whole thing was all about. But those early challenges greatly motivated us to work harder to learn which heart sounds were regular and which were irregular; which ones were regularly irregular and which were irregularly irregular.

Biochemistry appeared "all Greek" to most of us, at least at the initial stages of the course. The biochemistry building itself looked as uninviting as the course itself, standing there bereft of flowers and grace with its worn-out paint appearing to say to us, "Come in to me, and I will show you pepper."

But we had to like it, or we would lump it. There was no running away from it.

We had to learn the mandatory twenty amino acids. We had to learn those which became essential if some others or some other factors became unavailable. We had to know their names. We had to know their chemical structures, their interactions, the consequences of their deficiency in the diet, and so on.

Biochemistry constituted a waterloo for many a medical student. Professor B, the first letter of whose surname also happened to be the first letter of the department which he headed, had no ambiguity about this.

"You have to step up with biochemistry, or you have to step down from the clinics," he would often state amidst a lisp. In the end, three students had to step down from the clinics because of biochemistry.

To ensure we kept up with biochemistry, Professor B instituted monthly examinations which were to constitute 50 percent of our final score for the end of the course. Those monthly biochemistry exams constituted the biggest scourge for any preclinical medical student. The first year medical students took the same monthly exams with the second year biochemistry major students.

In the very first test that we took, not a single student, in a class of one hundred and forty-two students, scored up to 50 percent! My own score of 37 percent made me so miserable that for a long time, to the extent, I started to doubt myself and my capability to continue with the course. My misery was confounded by the exit soon after of my friend and confidant Aboni. His excellent academic credentials with the best school certificate result in the West Africa coupled with his excellent higher school certificate/general certificate in education results must have attracted the attention of some of the world's renowned universities. He soon left for a university in the United States.

With our initial travails with biochemistry and histology, not withstanding, we soon found our way around. We learnt to memorize a whole lot of names and structures. We learnt to recognize histological specimens by repeatedly studying slides. About forty-six of us succeeded, from the class of one hundred and forty-two, in scaling through the second MB examinations at first attempt. The second MB was the name given to the exam taken at the end of the second year of anatomy, physiology, and biochemistry in the preclinical school. It was the hallmark exam for medical students. Only those who passed the three subjects at the first or second attempt would proceed to the clinical years. A single subject failed would be repeated after six months. Failure in two subjects would involve a repeat of all three subjects after six months. Failure of any one subject at second attempt after six months would mean loss of a full year. Another failure in any of these subjects for any student repeating the year would involve a withdrawal from the course, a disaster for any medical student.

The Move to the Clinic

Having passed the second MB examinations, we were now ready to move on to the clinical years. The clinical training aspect of the medical school was located at the University College Hospital which was some five miles away. UCH, as it was called, also provided accommodation for the medical students, the nursing students, and the resident doctors. Moving over from UI (the University of Ibadan) to UCH was what every new medical student looked forward to. It was believed that any medical student who passed the second MB exams would ultimately be a doctor; it was just a matter of time. Until one passed the second MB, however, the course could still be derailed by even a single subject. Having passed the second MB, we could now hang our stethoscopes around our necks. Hitherto, we had them in the pockets of our lab coats, occasionally feeling for them to make sure they were still there, occasionally feeling a little shy or hesitant to bring them fully out, until we were certain that biochemistry would not hold us back or even see us out.

Although the main campus of the university was separated from the University College Hospital, where the clinical medical students lived, buses shuttled routinely between the University of Ibadan (UI) and the University College Hospital (UCH). The rides were completely free, and plying hourly from about 7:00 a.m. to 11:00 p.m., the shuttle ensured close contact between students in UI and the clinical students in UCH.

We looked forward to the first day when we would have our first introduction to UCH. On the appointed day, we were all so smartly dressed in our new lab coats. All types of stethoscopes were on display, ranging from the simple single-stranded ones to the sophisticated single—or double-stranded ones. The most popular was the Littman brand, which was said to be very sensitive. It had the light and heavy versions. As we entered the buses in batches to go to UCH, we felt an unusual sense of fulfillment, primordial doctors about to transit from dealing with toads and dead bodies to dealing with live human beings.

The tension of the preclinical years had been enormous. The apprehension occasionally reached breaking point. We scarcely knew what else was going on in the university community except the classrooms, laboratories, and dissection rooms. When we went hunting for toads for dissection classes, we would occasionally encounter the other students especially the social science students coming back from parties, especially at the weekends. These merry fellow students in other faculties used to sing for us a derisive song which ran thus:

Medical students are a funny lot.
They pass through the university all,
But the university does not pass through them at all.
With the benefit of hindsight, one may now add,
"How true!"
The average medical student from what I could see was a little self-conceited.
He almost lived in a world of his own with a narrow circle of friends.
He was close to being a recluse.
Faced from his first day in class with the threat of dropping out of the course,
He would withdraw to his books.
Threatened from day one with the possibility of being beaten at the prelim medicine exams by the science major students,
He had no peace of mind.

At the end of the day
What was the prize,
For the doctor and his labor,
What was the gain?
Near utter seclusion all to himself
In a consulting room, lab, or operating theater,
He would find himself,
A fat paycheck and cheers,

Though he may find
But when all is done,
One would then ask,
"Is it worth all the trouble
In this day and age?"

"Yes," one would say,
For his self-esteem
For his initial vain glory all to achieve,
But no, another would say, in the truth of the matter,
For when all is done, all is in vain,
Except to the service of humanity,
All is routed.

THE UNIVERSITY COLLEGE HOSPITAL THAT I KNEW

The University College Hospital was a beautiful sight to behold. The approach view of the hospital was enough to instill confidence and hope in any patient coming to the hospital for the first time. The dual-carriage driveway led up through a semicircular ramp, which opened directly to the administrative offices and to the wards of the right and left sides. The Emergency Departments were directly under the ramp, while the Laboratory Departments were to the left side under the ramp. Apart from the main entrance were some two other entrances through which vehicles and pedestrians that did not have to do with direct and immediate treatment purposes entered or exited.

After some weeks of introductory sessions, we finally moved into the UCH Medical Students Hostel. It was initially called Clinical Students Hostel and later Alexander Brown Hostel (ABH). The third year, fourth year, and final year medical students lived in this hostel.

Alexander Brown Hall had about the same pattern with the four older halls in the main campus of the University of Ibadan (UI). Most rooms as in UI, housed two students except for the rooms in the A wing, where the final year students lived. Those rooms housed one final year student per room. The general administration of the hostel and the dining hall facilities were essentially as in the main campus of the university. The students were, however, much more mature. There was not the usual noise and shuffling of feet as would be noticed in many corridors in the main campus. Also, there was much more courtesy between the students in ABH and the environment was generally better kept with well-trimmed flower hedges. Like in UI, there was steady water and power supply. Indeed, I cannot remember one single day that we had any significant water or power disruption either in the main campus of the University of Ibadan or the University College Hospital. Thrash collection was so efficient that we always wondered whether the thrash collectors worked round the clock in these two institutions.

Our first day at the ward round with our consultants and professors provided the very first contact we had with live patients. We had earlier been briefed by a couple of senior residents, the registrars, and senior registrars. We were instructed on how to check patients, how to take medical history from them, how to do physical examination of the patients, how to comport ourselves before the patients, and how to do case presentation at the ward round before the consultants.

We were assigned patients whom we were to take history from and whom we were to follow up as they were being medically managed. Even though it was physically tasking, it was nonetheless fascinating. The fascination was however to go for only as far as the medicine and surgery postings were concerned.

We had thought that we were done with dead bodies in the anatomy dissecting rooms, having passed our second MB exams. We did not reckon with pathology which, for purposes of our pathology posting, comprised of pathology (morbid anatomy), microbiology, parasitology, immunology, and chemical pathology. We had been told that pathology encompassed the whole basis of diseases that afflicted man. Yes, we were happy to learn about the whole basis of diseases that afflicted man. We knew we had to learn about these diseases; otherwise, we would not be able to treat for them as doctors. But we did not reckon with the fact that even after all we had gone through with, in human anatomy at the preclinical school, we would again have to watch or participate in the cutting through of dead bodies—this time mostly freshly dead bodies, sometimes decomposing bodies, and sometimes disjointed body parts brought for autopsy for certification of the cause of death. The major difference for us as medical students was that unlike in the anatomy room—where we did the dissection to follow the courses of blood vessels, nerves, and muscles—in the pathology room, the cutting was done mainly by the pathologist to determine the cause of death, not its course. It was not aimed at redefining death as a biblical curse for sin to mankind.

The part 2 MB exams involved pathology and pharmacology. Pharmacology—even with the very many drug names to be memorized along with their modes of action, side effects, bioavailability, toxicity and all—was quite interesting. For me in particular, pharmacology always reminded me of my days in my uncle's pharmacy at Enugu when I had to help Pius, the pharmacy assistant, to mix Mist Alba for a fee. At that time, many of the names that were mentioned by patients who came to purchase medicines were the trade names of the medicines. A few of the medicines were however sold in their generic names.

Of the subjects lumped under pathology, the most abstract to most of us was immunology. As of the time in question, the acquired immune deficiency syndrome had not become the scourge it was later to present as, and the subject of immunology had not assumed its present almost all-encompassing dimensions. For our purpose in the tropics much as an all-round medical education was insisted upon, tropical diseases had the emphasis, and infectious diseases and their treatment, rather than cardiovascular diseases, featured prominently.

Having been lucky to be among those whose numbers appeared on the board as having been successful in both pathology and pharmacology, I began to humble myself with every passing day, realizing that it did not all depend entirely on how hard one read or solely on the number of hours one spent in the wards. As one progressed in the medical school, as I began to see it, one needed an element of luck in addition to hard work and careful planning. Hardly any two situations became exactly the same anymore. The clinical case that student A might encounter might not be the same as student B would encounter. There, therefore, arose the joint need for hard work and prayers. As we began to encounter the different kinds of diseases that cut across all age groups, from the newborn with congenital abnormalities to the octogenarian with the diseases like Alzheimer's that may come with ageing, it was obvious that no one was completely immune to any kind of disease or indeed to any possibilities as far as living, ailing, or dying was concerned. Attending to the sick and the dying and realizing that one did not pay any special price to be healthy and strong was enough cause to be humble and grateful to God.

As we commenced our pediatrics and obstetrics/gynecology postings, we were now virtually living in the wards. For each of these postings, we needed to be signed up by the attending residents (nonconsultant doctors) for specific number of procedures. We needed, for instance, to be signed up for the number of EBTs (exchange blood transfusions) we did, the number of scalp vein infusion lines we set up, the number of cut downs we did for establishment of intravenous fluids, where it became impossible to obtain a vein elsewhere.

And in obstetrics, we were to be signed up for a specific number of baby deliveries which we took. Out of these deliveries, a minimum number were expected to be vertex deliveries (headfirst deliveries) and a minimum number of breech (buttocks first). Some of theses were signed up by the attending resident doctor; some others, like in normal deliveries, were signed up by the matron or staff nurse/midwife on duty at the time the delivery was taken. A minimum number of deliveries were required of the medical student before he would be allowed to sit the qualifying obstetrics/gynecology examination. Where it was impossible to secure theses cases and signatures in the University College

Hospital, the student would be expected to scout around other nearby hospitals like the Adeoyo State Hospital or Oluyoro Hospital for these cases.

It was a very good and very effective training program for us, and with the benefit of hindsight, one cannot but commend the planners of the program and only hope that unguarded proliferation of medical schools or the cankerworm of admission frauds that appear to have permeated the system of university admissions do not in future drop standards for medical school enrollment below acceptable levels, thereby undoing the commendable work that the founding fathers of that great medical school had done.

The gynecology postings were not as hectic as the obstetric counterpart as we had more than enough cases both in the Outpatient Department and in the theatres to necessitate our having to go scouting outside to be signed up. The cesium sessions that were in use for cancer of the cervix at that time were the ones we had to take our turns to observe as there were not enough radioactive cesium therapists then, possibly because not many people wanted to train in that field.

As we sailed through the pediatrics and obstetrics/gynecology (part 3) exams, we then moved into the sixth and final year of our medical school training. The final year involved the final three postings: preventive and social medicine (PSM, now called community medicine), medicine, and surgery. Theses courses had earlier been taught along with the parts 2 and 3 courses (pathology, pharmacology, pediatrics, and obstetrics/gynecology), but exams in them were taken only in the final year in which year they were the major courses taught.

The final year of medicine, surgery, and PSM (preventive and social medicine) was one of extreme hard work coupled with apprehension, expectations, and careful planning. By that time, the average medical student was already making up his or her mind about what he or she intended to make in life, in terms of field of specialization, place of internship, plans for national service, and all such issues which were expected of the young doctor, including social ties like marriage.

Most medical students, because of the very hectic nature of the first three years up to the end of second MB year did not form any strong social ties with the opposite sexes. There would hardly be any free weekends for any meaningful relationships. By the first year, the medical student would live in perpetual fear of dropping out or being replaced by a science major student. By the second and third years, he or she would still be living in mortal fear of anatomy, physiology, and biochemistry.

By the time he or she extricated himself or herself from the "conspiracy" of these three monsters, the other "one-eyed Cyclops" of pathology and pharmacology would be threatening. For the male medical student, much as he might be the object of a lot of eyes from female students from Queen Elizabeth Hall (female hostel) or the closely situated School of Nursing Hostel at (ABH), pathology and pharmacology would make him essentially unavailable. The female medical student in the same vein would be so engrossed with *Gray's Anatomy*, Guyton's *Physiology*, and the Medusa-headed biochemistry to have time for any dating. By the time she moved to the Clinical Students Hostel, she would have gone "above reach" for the average UI student, who in any case already had plenty of choices in UI. The best chances for the average female medical student once she came over to the Clinical Students Hostel therefore would be with the senior clinical students who, themselves, would still be burdened with threats from pediatrics, obstetrics/gynecology, medicine, surgery, and PSM. The "available" ones might also be turning to UI or the school of nursing for younger and more "pliable" girlfriends, leaving the major alternatives for the average female medical student with the male resident doctors. These male resident doctors themselves were usually few in number, and many who had remained single up to that moment were likely to remain single for a long time.

For me, there was no question of getting into a relationship in the midst of a precarious struggle for academic survival. Right from the first week of lectures in zoology, physics, and chemistry when we learnt of the possibility of losing our slots in medicine, it became an all-out battle not to fail. That done, the second MB potential debacle came into focus. It was a swim-or-sink kind of situation. A few soft-worded letters were written to acquaintances of the opposite sex. Many more were received conveying even much softer words, but amidst it all, one thing was clear:

one must either distinguish one's self in one's chosen career, or one would join the "crowd of chorus singers." And there was one sure way of doing the former: to concentrate and read one's book.

It was all so very tempting to go for weekend "jumps," the all-night dancing parties. There were so many of such parties popularly called *owambe* parties. A couple of guys from our class braved it. Some, even often, in our fourth and fifth years attended such parties in far-away Lagos from Ibadan, a journey of about two hours with the chaotic traffic situation. A few got away with it and still passed their examinations. However, the majority who were very regular at such parties paid some price. If they attended the party the previous night, the chances were that they would be late for lecture or ward round the following morning. Invariably though most, having gotten to that stage, would still become doctors, they were bound to suffer some delay.

There was in our class the case of Big D, who was often away at weekends for those parties. He would often join the ward rounds late, coming straight from those parties sometimes very late and shabbily dressed and unshaven. One Monday mornings, he again joined the ward round late. The professor, who had on many occasions warned him, this time was mad at him and had to use the rather strong admonition.

"Big D, or whatever they call you, listen to me! Medicine is not for drunks and irresponsibles. You are probably in the wrong profession, and as long as I am in this department, you either have to reform your ways, or you will never be a doctor through me. And if you continue this way and happen to graduate outside my charge, I will never be your patient."

With these apparently harsh words, he sent Big D out of the ward rounds.

As expected, Big D did not graduate with his set. But while the professor was on vacation, Bid D graduated six months later. Having been rejected for internship in the teaching hospital, Big D went to a general hospital elsewhere for his housemanship.

As fate would have it, the professor was said to have been involved in a road traffic accident and was rushed in an unconscious condition to the nearest general hospital. The doctor on duty was Big D.

Resuscitative efforts through Big D were successful.

And when the professor opened his eyes, after regaining consciousness there was Big D to cheer him up.

THE FRIENDS AT UCH

I had a large circle of classmate, personal friends while in the medical school. Apart form Tubia and Ukubasi, who were originally my friends from Afikpo, there were very other close friends like Dele, Dave, Hilary, Obi, and Ade. Dele was in the same Mellanby Hall with me. A very pleasant personality, he was always so plain and unassuming. He came into UI from one of the prominent secondary schools around Ibadan, and so he knew so many people. Dele would not read much but would most often still scale trough exams, which people like me had to "swot" through the nights to pass. Dele a fast-talking young man, was so generous, and the textbook exchanges I had with him were so very helpful in my making the exams first time throughout the course. Unlike Dele, Ade was the hard-reading type. Unlike Dele too, he was on the quiet side, much more calculating but definitely a very pleasant person.

Dave and Obi shared common background with me, in the sense that we all came in from post-civil war situations. We used to spend our little free time discussing about the greatness of our respective Government Secondary School Afikpo, Government College Umuahia, and King's College Lagos. We would debate our school's respective exploits in the academics, in soccer, in cricket, and in hockey. Then in our fifth year during relatively less stressful interval between parts 2 and 3 exams, our discussions often shifted to our respective female friends. We succeeded in making our friends to also become friends between themselves.

Lulu, a very close family friend, was on a visit to a cousin of hers at the main campus of the University of Ibadan. She stopped over to see her cousin at the University College Hospital, and I offered to accompany her to the university. That was after our part 2 (pathology and pharmacology) exams. That interval between part 2 and part 3 exams were usually regarded as the golden period of the average medical student's life in the university. That was because it was the only period that there were no serious exams. One could therefore afford to spend some hours on visits since most of the clinical work remaining for most students were revision work. Lulu and I disembarked from the UI-bound bus at the gate of UI to purchase some fruits, which Lulu intended to use as presents to her cousin at the Queen Elizabeth Hall. Having purchased the fruits, we decided to walk the rest of the distance between the UI gate and Queen's Hall. About midway between the gate and our destination, Lulu's eyes caught two girls approaching from the opposite end. Oblivious of us, the two approaching girls kept walking towards our direction. Suddenly Lulu stopped, a few yards away from the approaching duo.

"Agie! Agie! Is this Agie that I am seeing?" The girl in question, who apparently did not earlier believe her ears, immediately rushed towards Lulu and embraced her.

"Lulu, Lulu, you are here. Where are you coming from?" The expressions of joy and surprise went on for some time. The four of us—Lulu, Agie, and the girl who accompanied Agie, and I—headed down to Queen's Elizabeth Hall, ending up in Tinwe's room. Tinwe was Lulu's cousin, whom the latter actually came to visit. The rest of the evening was uneventful, save for the cookies and Fanta (soda) which Tinwe treated us. The rest of it was girls' talk, which did not very much fascinate me as I spent virtually all the time reading through a news magazine that was on the table. I soon left to catch the 6:00 p.m. bus back to UCH. Little did I realize that the chance meeting of that evening was later going to create a permanent impact that was going to shape my life for ever.

The Student Politician

Our day-to-day activities as medical students continued in UCH. Having passed our part 2 (pathology and pharmacology) exams, it was almost certain that we were going to be doctors. Even though parts 3 (pediatrics and obstetrics/gynecology) and 4 (PSM, medicine, and surgery) were not bread-and-butter stuff, passing them for any student who had got to that stage was only a matter of time.

It was at this stage that I decided to take a shot at university politics. The posters had come up on walls and on the notice boards all over Alexander Brown Hall about the student union and Student Representative Council (SRC) elections. These were the equivalents of the legislature for the Central Student Body of the university. There was also the domestic Student Administrative Body, which was headed by a hall chairman. The seat of the Student Union Body was situated in the main campus of the university and was headed by the president of the students' union.

It was often felt that medical students scarcely participated in the central union activities either in the executive branch as headed by the students' union president or in the Student Representative Council (SRC), which acted as the legislative arm. It was further believed that a medical student participating in the SRC activities was likely to fail in his or her medical education pursuits. I did not however believe that the latter should necessarily be the case. In my penultimate year in the medical school therefore, I decided to run for office as a member of the Student Representative Council. Against the advice of many of my friends (who advised against this in good faith), I joined the race. I campaigned mainly outside my circle of friends not because my friends would not wish me well, not even because I was assured of their votes (since they did not even support the idea in the first place) but because there were eight other contestants who came from outside my circle of friends. I felt that if only I could break into other fora, I could extract support from the majority who, in an effort not to hurt any of their own who were also contestants from the same regional background, were more likely to support a neutral candidate like me, if only I made the necessary approach.

I thereafter won the highest votes and thus emerged as first member of the Students Representative Council often addressed as "first member."

It was a very useful experience that was to help me in later life in my brief stint in party politics and ultimate involvement in leadership of my professional body.

The debates in the SRC were so lively. Most of the debates centered on students' activities and issues concerning the welfare of the larger student body. Other issues pertaining to relationship between the university authorities and the generality of students featured prominently. University policies which were considered inimical to the generality of students were often debated exhaustively.

My primary responsibility as a medical student involved duties in the wards, in the theaters, in the in-patient and out-patient clinics, and in attendances at the classrooms. These overwhelming requirements did not allow me to participate as actively as I would have liked to in the students' union activities. That was more so in view of the fact that the biweekly meetings were held in the students union's chambers in the main campus. Besides, the meetings often lasted well into the night, and on many occasions when I waited in the chambers till conclusion of the debates, I missed the last buses that would have taken me back to the UCH about 10:30 p.m.

The ultimate joy of my tenure as first member of SRC was that contrary to general belief that participation in student union activities would lead to inevitable failure in class, I did not fail in a single class, before or after the SRC position—thanks to prayers, determination, and hard work.

Second Meeting with Agie

The Easter season had just commenced and with it the period of Lent when Christians celebrated the risen Christ. I had gone to the main campus of the University of Ibadan to join in the Good Friday stations of the cross, the march that symbolized the tribulations of the Lord before his crucifixion. We started the march from the Catholic chapel, Our Lady Seat of Wisdom church, past Mellanby Hall, and Tedder Hall through a torturous course that ended at the cross post at the elevation between the Catholic and Protestant chapels. As we knelt facing the cross, I realized that my shoes were touching the dress of the person kneeling directly behind me. I turned round and apologized profusely and moved forward. But I realized that the person I was apologizing to was a familiar face. At the final *amen* of the We Fly to Thy Patronage Prayer, I finally got up to go, and looking back again, I realized that the person I was apologizing to was the same girl that I had met some months previously in Lulu's company, who had accompanied us from near UI gate to Tinwe's room. I had forgotten her name, but the face was unmistakable. There was no missing the complexion nor the slim figure nor the little scar on her left cheek. There was no missing the big bright eyes nor indeed those perfectly innocent looks.

"Hello, were you not the person that Lulu and I met sometime ago?" I started.

"E-e-m, yes, along the road and then to Tinwe's room," she remembered.

"So how are you finding UI?" I continued.

"So, so-o, no problems," she replied.

"You mentioned that day in Tinwe's room that you and your friend that we met you with were still expecting your school certificate results. I learnt that the results are now out. Have you got yours yet?" I continued.

"Yes, I learnt that the results are out, but I have not got mine. I hear the admissions office has copies of all the results, but I have not gone to check," she continued, not looking or sounding worried.

For a while I did not talk again, as we walked beside the university bookshop towards Trenchard Hall in front of where I would take a bus back to UCH. I wondered within me what kind of a girl this was that did not appear worried enough about her school certificate result when it should be obvious to her that her continued stay in the university was, at that stage, completely dependent upon her passing with a minimum of five credits in the school certificate exams. Could she be so naïve as to appear to be enjoying UI so much and in the process she overlooked going to confirm her eligibility?

But I kept my anxiety and concerns to myself. I merely asked her to remind me of her name.

"But you have not told me your own name," she replied, smiling but looking me straight in the face.

Wa-o-o! I thought.

Was this girl not afraid? Just four months in the university and not being shy of me who would soon be a doctor! She was so lucky this was not my Secondary School at Afikpo. An or-ing, a novice dared not look a senior boy in the face at Afikpo, I kept musing.

But of course that was not Afikpo, and besides, that was a girl. I then suddenly realized that I should have mentioned my own name before asking for hers.

The girl's boldness nevertheless surprised me and subtly impressed me.

"Oh! My name is Okoli. My friends call me OO, some others tease me with a nickname Chico," I corrected.

"Sorry if I appeared discourteous, my name is Agie, but I am usually called AC," the girl replied, still smiling.

The UI to UCH bus was waiting. Just before I boarded, I stretched out my hand and said, "OK, Agie, I will be going. I wish you a very happy stay in UI. But remember to check your school certificate results after Easter. Happy Easter in advance." She shook my hand with a smile and left.

As we drove back to UCH, my mind kept turning back to this girl whom I had met only twice and only very briefly. The feeling was like no other.

I had really never had any serious relationships in my life. I dared to say, I had never had anybody I could call my girlfriend. Prior to my teenage years during my school days at Enugu, it was a triangular path for me: from my house to the church where I served at mass, to school, and back to the house.

At Aba, whenever I went on holidays during my early teenage years, it was always between my house and 121 to Ceewai, except for my occasional visits to Hyman, my father's assistant for many years. And in the first four to five years of university life, the situation was even more tight in terms of social life with the constant struggle not to fail and the continuous efforts not to drop out of the course. As it was for me in the medical school so it was for most of the medical students, many of whom consequently were either introverts or were outright social misfits. The formation of medical students-only social clubs like the Les Amis to which I was a member were good and bold attempts to ameliorate the self-imposed seclusion by medical students.

I got back to UCH and back to my books, the ward, the outpatients clinics, and the operation rooms. But, for the first time in my life, the thought of a girl, this girl I had met only on two informal occasions, never left my mind. I had met and interacted with so many girls in my life, at school during Senior Debating Society outings, in parties, during NFCS (National Federation of Catholic Students) meetings, and indeed at so many other formal and informal gatherings. I had written and reviewed letters from many of these, after these meetings.

I had, several times over supper or lunch at weekends spent hours with my friends Dave, Obi, Hilary, and others discussing girls, occasionally conjuring fascinating exploits to boost our ego. But never for once had I really given any serious thought to any such meetings, letters, or discussions immediately after they were over. But this time, in this particular instance, let me not even imagine that I was persuading myself to fall in love.

NO! Not with a girl I had met her only twice, a girl I had not spoken with for longer than a full hour, somebody whose background I did not ev1en know, worse still somebody whom I was not even sure that she would continue in the university since she had not even had the wisdom to go and confirm her eligibility to continue with her course in the university. So it must be all infatuation, a foolish dream which I must get off my mind. I started to get angry with myself. But like most self-reprimands, this anger did not last.

In order to get this issue over with, I decided, instead of fruitlessly fighting the issue, to take a positive step, so that if for nothing else, to pass the burden over. I went to the hall tuck shop and bought an Easter greeting card and inserted *Agie* above the prewritten message and then inserted *from Okoli* after the message and put the card in the envelope. I boarded the next available UI bus and went straight to Queen's Hall to drop the card.

At the porter's lodge in Queen's Hall, I suddenly realized that I knew neither the surname nor the room number of this girl. Without these two pieces of information, there was no way I could correctly address the envelope. This realization then confirmed to me how foolish I had been. I turned to go back.

But No!

I bent down over the porter's table and addressed the envelope "Agie, Care of Tinwe" and then added Tinwe's name, surname, and room number. I hoped there would be only one Agie known to Tinwe at that material time. I hoped the card would be correctly delivered. But if it didn't get delivered, at least I had taken a giant step, an unprecedented one to satisfy my curiosity. I hoped the thought of this girl would not disturb me again. Sure, for a long time it didn't, as I neither got a confirmation on whether my poorly addressed Easter greeting card was correctly delivered or not. Serious class work again soon took over my thoughts.

Preparations for my part 3 examinations were under way. The examinations were in pediatrics and obstetrics and gynecology. The failure rate in part 3 were usually not very high as most of the students must by this time have become very accustomed to the pattern of life in the clinical student hostel, the hospital, and the usual pattern of clinical examinations. Having gone through the examinations without trauma, my attention became focused on the approaching Christmas holidays and my final examinations, which were to come on the following May through June.

The month of December came on with the usual frenzy of greeting card purchases. Hitherto, I had not often found the need to send cards to any beyond my parents and my close circle of school friends and friends in the two clubs I belonged to: Les Amis Club and the NFCS (National Federation of Catholic Students). Sending of cards to a girlfriend or to girlfriends had never featured among my priorities even though I had occasionally exchanged letters with girls that I had come across at the interschool debates. Nonprioritization in this regard did not come as a puritanical aspect of my life. There was no doubt that the moral standards set in my earlier years of service as a mass server and monthly attendance at NFCS seminars had impacted on me and must have played a role in my attitude to life even at that stage. The major restraining factor at that stage must have been the pressure of academic work and the constant fear that if I derailed, I might fail, and that if I failed, the efforts I had put in so far might be in vain. Besides, the shame for failure, even if I were to have a second chance, might have been too much for me. It was possible that Government Secondary School Afikpo had instilled such high ideals and even a sense of near academic invincibility that any thought of possible failure scared us to the death.

The Christmas season of my final year in the medical school was very different. That year, I had bought a pack of Christmas cards instead of merely picking up some cards singly. That year I had to tabulate the names of the people I would send cards to, instead of merely picking up a few cards in a bookshop, addressing them there and walking straight to the post office to post them. That year, unlike in previous years, the first card that I addressed was to somebody I had known for less than two years, somebody I had not met more than a couple of times, somebody whose surname I had only recently known. That somebody was Agie.

Again, of all the cards that I addressed, there was only one that I chose to deliver personally. That card was to that same girl, the same girl who had looked me straight in the face and demanded to know my name before she would tell me hers.

I got to Queen's Hall about 4:30 p.m., and after signing the necessary visitors' papers, I went in for the first time to see this girl. I was clutching the Christmas card and clad in the characteristic shirt and tie which clinical students in UCH were known for. (We were often told in UCH that as future doctors, we must always dress well, and the emphasis on dress code was often put into maximum practice when medical students visited the female hostel.)

I was lucky on my way to have met Vec, whom my friend Aboni had made friends with prior to his departure to the United States. It was to Lulu, Tinwe, and Vec that I owed gratitude for all my initial successes with this girl, Agie. It was Vec who redirected me to Agie's new room to which the latter had only recently relocated. I probably would have gone to the wrong room and possibly would not have met her that day. To that extent and more therefore, I shall always remain grateful to Vec.

Agie was indoors with her roommate, Calo, who happened to be girlfriend of an old schoolmate of mine, Okiy. I recognized Okiy's photograph mounted on Calo's reading table immediately as I entered room G8. There was no photograph mounted on Agie's reading table.

My knowing Okiy provided an excellent opening discussion and made a soft landing of my visit as the discussions started with my days at Afikpo with Okiy.

I presented the Christmas card to Agie and added.

"I will bring my own photograph for you to mount on your table also."

Agie looked at me, smiled, and thanked me for the Christmas greeting card.

She was silent on the proposal to mount my photograph on her table.

I reckoned that was a smart way of my asking if she already had another boyfriend whose photograph she was reserving the space on her table for.

"How is UCH?" Agie asked.

"UCH is OK," I said, "and how are you coping with academics?"

"We are trying our best, but the lectures move on so fast, and there is two much backlog of work to do," Agie said.

"I believe you must have now checked on your school certificate result and that it was OK?" I added rather cautiously.

"Yes, everything was OK, I made a grade 1 pass," Agie added without any emphasis, as if it did not matter.

"Congratulations, you must have been very confident about the results," I added as I stretched out my hand to shake Agie's.

Could this eighteen-year-old girl have been so certain about her result that she did not bother to check as soon as the results were released, or was she simply carefree about something as important as a result that was to determine her continued stay in the university? Either way, I was beginning to feel that this must somehow be a very spectacular girl.

Much as I was initially very concerned about Agie's school certificate result, the discussion about UCH and academics was not actually the direction that I wanted to direct my attention at that time.

I was yet to get a response on my subtle proposal to get my photograph to be mounted on Agie's table. With the benefit of hindsight, I now realize that I was being too naïve. There was I, asking a girl I had known for such a very short time and who had indeed not known me well enough to mount my photograph on her table, a de facto acceptance of me as her sole boyfriend to the exclusion of others.

I did not hide my feelings.

"What size of photographs of mine do you want me to bring, that size?" I said pointing to the six-inch-by-six-inch photograph of Okiy on Calo's table.

There was initial silence. But as I kept looking at Agie, obviously waiting for and answer to my question, Agie said, "I do not mount people's photographs on my table. But if you wish you can bring one. You may bring any size of photograph."

All I needed to hear was the last bit of that statement. The earlier part might as well not have existed. I did not wait for any further concluding statement, which nevertheless came on thus: "provided it will fit into my photo album."

That was a million-dollar statement.

"Provided it will fit into my photo album" did not give me any special place. But what I wanted was a mounted photograph of mine on Agie's table, just like Okiy's on Calo's table. It was possible I had a bloated ego of myself.

Throughout my life, I would not say I had encountered any failures nor indeed any deprivations beyond what obtained for my peers. My family background, the primary and secondary schools that I attended, the positions that I had held at school, the course I was doing in the university which we, as medical students, (wrongly) believed was the ultimate, the zenith, all these combined had possibly planted in me that false belief that I could get anything I wanted, including a pride of place in a woman's heart, as epitomized by my mounted photograph on Agie's table. But I had been proved wrong. My ego had been punctured. I might have to accept to eat the humble pie and have my photograph in the photo album and not mounted on the table.

I sat on the chair on Agie's reading table, debating within me on the next thing to do, on how best to change the topic so that I would not out of inexperience behave like Koki, the imbecile in my village. Koki was the only son of a wealthy fabric merchant in my village. He was well beyond the average age for marriage when his parents decided that they must get a wife for him in spite of his imbecility. They had taken Koki to the introductory meeting with the family of the proposed bride. Koki had been told as soon as the party set out that the trip was with a view to getting a wife for him.

The visitors had all taken their seats. Then, as soon as the proposed bride was called out to greet the visitors, Koki, sighting the proposed bride, jumped up from his seat, threw his arms around the proposed bride, and started kissing her to everybody's embarrassment. He already assumed that the proposed bride was his wife as of right, even before conclusion of all formalities. My name was Okoli, not Koki, but I probably was already assuming too much, almost behaving like Koki.

"Can I look through your photo album?" I now requested, thoroughly subdued. At least it would be a good thing if I should see which other person or persons I might have to compete with for a pride of place in this girl's photo album, since I could not secure a place on her table.

As I flipped through the pages of the photo album, Agie sat by the edge of her bed and introduced the different people that were in the photo album. The photographs of the parents were there, her only brother, the classmates at school, different baby and childhood photographs of hers. All that interested me were three photographs of young men, one of which featured more prominently. We had flipped rather hurriedly through them when the photographs of family members were being introduced.

"This is Felix, that one is Waky, and that one is Tim," Agie had said

"Is Felix your cousin? Where is Waky? Who is Tim?" I could not conceal my anxiety as I asked these questions, more like an unduly jealous husband. I wanted to keep hearing, "Felix is my cousin, Waky is my cousin, and Tim is my cousin." That would have satisfied my anxiety and reassured me that I was still to be the dominant male even in spite of my very recent arrival into the scene of events.

But it was not to be.

"Felix and Waky are my cousins, and—" She didn't conclude before I followed up.

"And Tim too," I concluded for her, eager to be assured that I was in the picture of a monopoly.

"No, Tim is a family friend," she corrected.

Family friend, I mused.

Could she have meant boyfriend? I further mused.

I stopped for a while and then continued flipping through the photographs, with the thought of this Tim still in my mind.

Soon I was through with the photographs. Calo soon excused herself and went off to the library. Agie got some crackers for me. As I ate the crackers, my mind kept going back to that lone photograph of the grinning young man, whose photographs appeared in three different places in Agie's photo album. I grabbed back the album and turned the page to where Tim first appeared. I later turned to his second photograph. Agie was in the meantime flipping through a campus magazine. She must have been a very sharp girl. She was obviously watching me through the corners of her eyes.

"Is Tim still in the university, or has he graduated?" I asked rather feverishly. I was very eager to hear that this fellow called Tim had not been able to secure admission into a university or that he was doing one irrelevant preparatory course somewhere.

"Oh! Tim is still in teachers training college somewhere around Nsukka," Agie said.

Thank God, I silently heaved a sigh of relief. At least Tim was not around Ibadan. Secondly, he was in a teachers training college, which was ranked lower than the university. Thirdly, this guy Tim was "still in a teachers training college somewhere around Nsukka." To me the word *still* meant that Agie had ranked Tim well below her status academically and that was enough to disqualify him. Again, the phrase "somewhere around Nsukka" to me implied that this girl was not sure specifically where Tim's teachers training college was located, which must have been a sign of lack of interest.

I was quiet for a while as I kept analyzing the resume of a potential competitor, whom I had never met. But this sharp-witted girl was quick to notice:

"Are you thinking about Tim? He is a nice guy, but he is, unfortunately, not quite academically superior. He was good in the arts subjects, and he will probably make it as a primary school teacher, and that is where he chooses to be."

There was another sigh of relief. Even if this Tim was or planned to be the boy friend of this sharp-witted girl, he was not likely to maintain that position for long. He had been declared academically inferior. Finally, the limit of his ambition would not meet up with the possible heights which this girl was likely to climb up to, with those sharp wits and with her being in the university. He simply would not be able to make it as a possible or sustained boyfriend of this girl. I immediately, silently declared myself the winner, a dominant male in that unilaterally declared war with an imagined adversary, a victory I had claimed, laced with arrogance and conceit on my part.

For the rest of the evening, my discussions with Agie were centered on plans for the Christmas vacation, where she would spend hers and where I would spend mine. She intended to go straight to Nnokwa, her hometown, and I planned to go to Aba. I was beginning to truly enjoy the discussions especially then that I began to get quite convinced that there was no other really serious man in this girl's life. And, of course, there was none in my life either. I was already beginning to feel that at least I had found my very first girlfriend. I was beginning to wish that the clock would tick much more slowly for the rest of the evening so that the visiting time for Queen's Hall would not come fast enough or would not come at all.

Then, all of a sudden, from the ground floor walkway outside of the window, we heard a loud call, "G18, visitors still in your room?"

The menacing half question and half command was twice repeated, I was still trying to come to terms with the question when after about two minutes, the final warning came, "G18, you are warned, visiting time is over."

It was obvious that neither Agie nor I had wanted the time to be so short. As I got up to go, I immediately remembered part of the poem we had learnt in school which stated that time is too long for those who wait, but that "for those who love, time is eternity."

I began to wish that for the duration of my stay in that first visit to Agie's room that time would be endless.

I soon realized that, try as hard as I did not to acknowledge it as I repeatedly fixed my gaze on Agie's face, I was beginning to fall in love.

As Agie escorted me to the porter's lodge exit of Queen's Hall that evening, we agreed to book into the same vehicle from Ibadan to Onitsha from where we would board different vehicles to Nnokwa and Aba respectively. On my way back to UCH in the university bus, I slowly recounted the events of that evening. I felt an unusual sense of fulfillment and gratitude to God. I felt that my patience had finally paid off. I slowly recited in my memory one of the Shakespearean verses, which we had learnt in school, which again read in part (as a father's advice to his son), that

> If you can keep your head when all about you,
> Are losing theirs and blaming it on you,
> And that,
> If you can trust yourself when all men doubt you,
> But make allowance for their doubting, too . . .
> Yours will be the earth and all that is in it,
> And what is more, you will be a man.

I then quietly tried to recollect in my mind the concluding part of that same poem which stated inter alia that if you satisfied all the stated conditions, yours would be the earth and all that was in it; and that what was more, you would be a man.

We had recited in school the relevant Shakespeare's piece ever so often, even when we did not always get the sentences right that it almost always reverberated in our ears.

> I felt that finally my time had come . . .
> I had always prayed to God for the best.
> I had always tried to do my best
> Always leaving to God the rest.

I had over the previous two years kept to the habit of composing my own prayers in writing. Indeed, I had kept up with a target of one full reporter's notebook of composed prayers and poems for each examination I had since after my second MB examination. I knew I was a sinner, not a saint. Could my prayers have yielded a rich reward for my patience?

Would mine and Agie's hereafter be the earth and all that was in it? And would I thereafter be a man? I quickly recalled myself from that short dream, reminding myself of the biblical foolish rich man who, having filled his barn with a rich harvest, exalted his soul to "rejoice and be merry" since he thought he had gotten all the riches of the world. He was only to be told, "You fool, this night your soul will be taken from you." I had no intention of playing the foolish rich man. I reckoned I was neither foolish nor rich.

The Lovers and the Robbers

About eight days to Christmas, Agie and I sat side by side on a bus bound for Onitsha, the commercial city east of the River Niger, from Ibadan, on our way for Christmas vacation.

There was a long delay at the Asaba end of the bridge leading into Onitsha. When the bus crossed into Onitsha, the traffic jam was even worse, and the driver asked those who wished to disembark and continue the journey to the park on foot to do so, since it would be faster that way. Some passengers, including Agie and I, disembarked.

I had two bags, and Agie also had two. We were walking beside each other feeling on top of the world. It was about five in the afternoon. We were heading towards the town from where we expected to take other transport to Aba and Nnokwa respectively.

We had not walked up to six poles from the bridgehead when three boys aged between sixteen and eighteen approached us from one of the numerous makeshift stalls on the sides of the jam-packed road. The smallest of the three boys approached me and said in pidgin English, "Oga, you don' come again.

You don' de wicked us every time you pass here. Wetin we do you, e-eh? We bin warn you make you no de harass us again."

He was implying that I had come again and that I had been harassing them every time I passed there and that they had been warning me to stop harassing them.

But I had never set my eyes on the young man, and I had never had cause to ever stop at that part of Onitsha, not to talk of harassing the young man. I was still trying to figure out what the young man was up to when suddenly the young man bent down and quickly gathered sand with his two hands and immediately emptied the sand on my face, into my eyes! As I raised my left hand (which held the smaller bag containing my money and other valuables) to try to clear the sand from my face and eyes, I felt the smaller bag snatched from me. With the free hand, I now held tightly to the other bag, which my attacker made no effort to snatch. I felt a burning sensation as if pepper had been poured into my eyes. It was possible the young man also had ground pepper in his palms.

The pain and tears were unbearable. I immediately dropped the larger bag from my right hand as I shouted, with both eyes tightly shut, "My god, my god."

I could also hear brisk movement on my left side, where Agie had stood, and I also heard her shouting and wailing. There was still full daylight and in the full glare of other human and vehicular traffic, about five in the afternoon! As I staggered and groped with fully shut eyes, I could feel a hand grab me and lead me away from where I stood. I was being led away to the side of the road where I had earlier observed the presence of lots of makeshift stalls. I felt water being poured unto my face by someone I did not know.

As I now shouted "Agie, Agie" in agony from the peppery pain in my eyes, I could also hear a female voice shouting from a distance, "O-O, O-O, where are you?"

It was certainly Agie's voice! I was thoroughly distressed, and my worry was more about Agie. I thought they abducted her and were leading her away.

I could hear the voice of the person washing my face shouting, "Some one please get me some oil, oil, quickly!"

Something soothing was briskly rubbed over my face and eyes. I later found from the red color on my shirt was palm oil. I could then partially open my eyes.

As I kept shouting "Agie, Agie," the man washing my face apparently feeling angered by my apparent ingratitude shouted back at me in Igbo language, "Mechie onu gi" (Stupid boy. Keep quiet. Save yourself first before you think of woman. Na woman make them rob you so).

He was of course implying that I was robbed because I was marching with a woman. A spontaneous apology and forced appreciation followed from me, "Yes, sir, I am sorry, sir. Thank you, sir. Please thank you, thank you, sir."

I could now see Agie at a distance. Someone was also washing her face a short distance away. I could also see the heavier and bigger of my two bags at a distance. Some of the books in it were lying scattered on the dusty roadside. Our assailants probably found the bag too heavy to make away with and had merely unzipped and ransacked it. Apparently after they found that the bag contained only books and a few shirts and trousers, they had abandoned it. They escaped with the smaller bag, which contained some money, documents, and other valuables including photographs. One of Agie's bags had also been taken away along with her sunglasses and wallet. The heavier bag containing her books was lying near where they were washing her face.

I started wondering why those apparent good Samaritans allowed those miscreants to operate so close to where the former were doing their legitimate business of buying and selling from the roadside kiosks. Could the good Samaritans have been in some kind of collusion with the bad boys? Whatever their alignment was however, those good roadside traders had been of immense help to us. It obviously must have been their presence that saved us from more assault than we had. We might have had black eyes into the bargain if it were not for the latter's presence.

The man who washed and oiled my face finally removed my shirt and wiped my face with it. He then gave me back the shirt and said with a wry smile on his face, "OK, young man, you can now go and rejoin your woman. Next time hold on more firmly to your bag rather than to your lover. And be more careful and shine your eyes when you come to bridgehead. And make sure you two don't cross here again holding hands. It may be worse next time. You hear me so-o?"

I was no longer sure whether this good Samaritan (or good Nigerian in that case) was sympathizing with me or reproaching me. Certainly I was not holding hands with Agie. Our two hands were each carrying our bags, and firmly too. Besides, I had never before stopped or disembarked at bridgehead Onitsha nor had I ever set eyes on the young man who accused me of provoking him before pouring sand and pepper into my eyes and snatching my bag. I was completely innocent of all the accusations from both attacker and my rescuer.

I thanked my rescuer profusely. He did not ask for any fees for his services. He quickly went away back into his shed, which was one of the stalls along the refuse-littered roadside.

When I got up to where Agie's face was being washed, I saw that her eyes were red, and there was a lot of sand on her hair. On the ground beside her was one of her bags. The other one had obviously been taken away by our attackers. About six onlookers were there watching while her face was being washed. The man who washed her face was a little more sympathetic than my own rescuer.

"Oga, make una sorry, but make una hurry commot from here."

The man was expressing his sympathy with what had happened to us but was urging us to hurry out of the vicinity. We thanked the man and grabbed what was left of our luggage, two bags now left for us out of our original four.

As we hurried away, some young boys who were standing as onlookers but who had made no effort at pursuing the attackers repeatedly said, "Oga, so una no go give us something?"

Agie's primary rescuer asked for nothing nor did my own, but the young boys who stood as onlookers were the people asking for money. That was even when they saw that we had been robbed in broad daylight, and they had made no attempt at countering or pursuing the attackers! They might even have been part of the robbery team. The situation however did not warrant our waiting to rationalize. It was good enough that we escaped without more bruises. It could easily have been worse. As we hurried away, we kept wondering why the traders at that spot had not taken measures to flush out those miscreants from where they were doing their businesses.

Away from the danger zone which we later learnt was called "no-man's-land," we started to count our losses. Agie's bag containing all her money and most of her valuables was gone. On my own part, only one of my two bags, the one containing my books and few dresses, was left. The only money I had on me was the change I received after buying food at the road junction town of Ore. I had luckily kept that change in my shirt pocket. I had avoided keeping my wallet in my trouser pockets for fear of pickpockets. It was obvious after the robbery that my wallet would have been safer in my pocket than in my traveling bag.

It soon became obvious to us that we were stranded. There was no way we could continue with our journey. Cell phones were not yet in use in the country. The few land telephone lines were very unreliable and literally unavailable. Communication with any friend or relation was not possible, and it was getting quite late in the evening. Our fear was that since we still had one bag each, we might still face another attack which under full darkness might be more vicious.

We quickly considered many options: one was to look for the nearest police station. Another was to look for the nearest church, while another was to look out for the nearest school where we would explain the situation to any porters on duty and at least stay the night with them until morning.

Whichever option we had to choose however, we knew that we needed to dispose of or abandon our big bags, which were liable to expose us again to another possible attack. Our experience of the previous hour or two had led us to the wrong conclusion that any person we passed by along the street in that part of Onitsha about that time could be a potential robber. The tears from occasional irritation in my eyes were continuous reminders.

Just as we were about to choose the school option, I suddenly remembered that one of our seniors in UCH, Dr Ebuono, was said to be doing his housemanship (internship) at one of the hospitals at Onitsha. Ebuono was one of our most brilliant students at Afikpo. He had also been a house captain in his set and had been known to be a very kind prefect who would award only one run instead of two to any culprit who was caught crossing the football field.

We took a quick decision to seek out the general hospital where I remembered Ebuono was said to be doing his internship. We decided we must get to the general hospital even if it meant discarding our remaining bags for personal safety and trekking whatever distance it was.

Leaving Agie with the two bags at the roadside, I walked a little distance to the side street and enquired about the direction to the general hospital. I was given the direction and an estimate of the taxi fare per person. I checked my shirt pocket for the amount of change I had there. It was a little short of the required fare for the two of us plus our two bags.

We nevertheless decided to try. At the worst, Agie could go with the taxi and then inform Ebuono of our predicament. Ebuono must have a car since all house officers were routinely given car loans wherever they were serving. It was one of the incentives for attracting house officers who were in very short supply at the time.

As soon as I got back to Agie, we flagged down the next available taxicab. The taxi was already carrying two other people whose load filled the boot and a sitting space inside the car. Agie and I offered to carry our loads on our laps if only the taxi would agree to carry us for the incomplete fare which we had. I looked at the face of the girl occupying the front seat of the taxi. It was red, and her hair was sandy. The more elderly man sitting behind appeared unhurt and unruffled. It was most likely that those two earlier passengers in the taxicab had suffered a similar fate as we did. But at least it looked as if their luggage was intact. And luckily too the elderly man did not appear to have been attacked. As we sat inside the taxi, our two bags and the third bag belonging to the earlier passengers on our laps, I heard the elderly man telling the girl sitting in front, "I told you to leave that bag for those boys. You should not have struggled with them. Your mum will not be happy with you. How much was it you had in that bag after all."

It was obvious that the father surrendered his bag and was spared. But the daughter held tight to her bag and was given sand and pepper.

The taxi driver had added, "For next time make una no drop for dat danger spot. Ibi no-man's-land. Me sef, I no fit stop to pick passenger dier."

He was implying that the place where the man and his daughter had disembarked was so dangerous that even he, as a taxi driver, dared not stop there to pick passengers.

Neither Agie nor I narrated our own experience. We merely looked at each other but kept mum until we were safe at the gates of the general hospital.

As we got off the taxi, the driver was still blaming the daughter and father, "Dat place we-e una drop, dem fit kill man dier. Doose agbulu boys, dem too dangerous. Ifin police no de like go dier."

Agie and I were very lucky we got only sand and pepper. We might even have gotten some beating into the bargain, since even policemen were wary of that spot, according to the taxi driver.

We waited in front of Dr Ebuono's apartment until he returned from the hospital call about at 10:00 p.m. By the following morning, we had clearer eyes and were driven down by our friend to the park where we boarded the vehicles to Nnewi and Aba respectively, with our fares paid by our friend Dr Ebuono. Agie was to proceed to her hometown via Nnewi, and I was to proceed straight to Aba from the park. This time we had some money in our pockets, again courtesy of Dr Ebuono.

THE JEALOUS LOVER

The bridgehead experience tended to cement the bond between Agie and me. We did not continue to narrate our story to many people. Everybody we earlier mentioned it seemed so familiar with bridgehead that we looked foolish for disembarking there in the first instance, especially at that time of the evening and around Christmas when pickpockets, robbers, and all kinds of thieves were often on the prowl for money with which they would show off in the villages. But we had seen a few other people disembarking but did not know whether they all suffered the same fate. Perhaps those young men had a way of knowing who was new to the place.

When we were back from the Christmas vacation, I visited UI more regularly about every other weekend. Occasionally, I would wait till lunch so that if Agie would want to go for lunch in some other hall than theirs, I would go with her. During lunch in Mellanby Hall on one of my visits, one man from Postgraduate Hall, who was on the queue in front of Agie, paid for his own food and paid for a second plate while pointing to the cashier the girl who was standing behind him. When Agie, who was queuing in front of me, collected her meal and I stretched out my hand to drop two meal tickets, the cashier told me that the man in front had paid for her. I collected back my extra ticket. But I kept pondering within me who that man was, who was paying for lunch for *my girlfriend*. I was so jealous that I could not wait long enough after lunch to ask Agie who that man was. She merely smiled. I could not make much meaning out of it. All said and done, I went back to UCH a little confused. Still not settled in my mind about it all, I felt I deserve more answers.

Could that man who paid for Agie's food that evening be my competitor? Why did she not refuse the offer? Why would I not get more explanations? Was I merely fooling myself, playing the deluded "reserve guy" when there was a "main guy" closer by, especially as I lived far away in UCH and that other man in Postgraduate Hall was living just close by? When one is jealous, everything points towards a confirmation of one's worst fears.

I rode back to UCH that evening with a full heart and a more confused head. The following morning, not able to contain my anxiety and doubts any longer, I fired a note to Agie and dropped the note through another medical student who was going to UI for pharmacology lectures. In the note, I demanded to know "who that man was, who paid for your meals." For days, there was no reply. Then by weekend, I followed up with another letter. This time the response came instantly via a short brash mail:

I can't understand all this.

After all, we are only friends.

For me, those two sentences constituted a bombshell. They were laden with multiple possible meanings.

I remembered my secondary school mathematics master Mantissa, who in response to mischievous Mtama's statement that he did not understand what was being taught, would always reply, "What don't you understand? Was my simple request for a simple explanation too complex?"

I mused, *Was I not specific enough in my note?*

And, as regards the statement "we are only friends," who constitute the "we," and who were the "friends"?

Was I only a small part of a multitude of suitors?

And if no, was I not entitled to benefit from the adulterated dictum "Thou shall have no other (friends) before me"?

All these questions boiled up in me even during the ward rounds. For the first time in my life, I found myself playing a role of a jealous lover. It took me a while to come to terms with the fact that Agie was neither engaged to me nor was she my wife. What right therefore did I have to dictate to her?

I was able to absorb the shock by "soaking" myself back into my books. I reactivated the "fear of failure" mentality by which I constantly convinced myself that I would fail if I derailed by pursuing girls. It was that fear which had always glued me to my books even when most of my classmates were out for "October rush," the term commonly used in the University of Ibadan for the rush by male sophomores for female freshmen at the early weeks of each new academic year.

I convinced myself that there was a need for me to stop going to UI if I wanted to pass my finals at first attempt.

I further convinced myself that it was because I did not have a girlfriend who would distract me that I had never failed any exams.

I finally convinced myself that girlfriends including Agie were distractions and that I was better off without any.

I then remembered the story we were told in school where the fox, not being able to secure an apple from a treetop after several attempts, declared that all apples are sour. That "all apples are sour" dictum helped me brush off the doubt, anxiety, and anger that had started to build up in me for nearly a full week.

I revived my daily prayer writing which I found I had suspended for a couple of weeks. I was still writing a verse when a gentle knock sounded at my door. For a while I thought it might be Dave or Obi or Hilary. But I knew that Dave, Obi, Hilary and I were never that gentle when we knocked before entering each others' rooms. And it was never usual for any of us to wait that long before opening the door of each other's room.

"Come in if you are good-looking," I said (as we usually said) in response to knocks at our doors. The door handle was turned, but the door did not open. I suddenly realized that I had locked myself in to have sufficient privacy to ruminate over my woes and to meditate.

"I am sorry," I apologized as I moved to unlock the door.

"Ah," I uttered as I beheld the beautiful smiling face of the girl whose two sentences had kept me on my toes for a full week.

As Agie sat down on my single reading chair, which I turned over to her, I felt all the doubt, anxiety, and anger that had built up in me suddenly disappear.

"I am sure you must have misunderstood me," she said, smiling.

"I believe I did. So what is the correct interpretation?" I said, now playing the tough guy.

"How many are we in this game?" I continued.

Agie starred me in the face reminiscent of the day she demanded to know my name before she would tell me hers.

"OO," she said.

"Believe me, there has never been nor will there be any other but you," Agie said.

I wanted to confirm I heard her right.

The last two words, *but you*, impressed me the most, but I was silent.

Agie then added, "You can verify what I have just said. I was brought up under strict Catholic principles, and I have always upheld those principles."

I did not require further assurances. At last, I had finally met my match, the principles I had always treasured; the principles I would want to uphold.

I got up, took her right hand, and kissed the back of her palm.

We spent the rest of the evening discussing our family backgrounds, our social values, and how we were raised up.

Agie told me that she came from a family of four, that both parents were teachers, and that she had one other sibling, a brother. She further told me that her parents insisted on daily morning prayers, daily morning mass, daily communion, grace before and after meals, and daily family night prayers. She further told me that from a Catholic primary school, she went straight to a Catholic secondary school in Onitsha. She said the school was run by Catholic nuns and that she entered the university straight from the Catholic secondary school immediately after her secondary school certificate examinations. The university, she told me, had been the very first place where she had to take independent decisions. In taking those decisions, she said she did not intend to deviate from those principles under which she had been brought up. For the first time, as she spoke, I noticed the finger rosary on one of her fingers, the tiny beaded ring that devout Catholics in my part of the country often wore on their left middle fingers.

In narrating my own background, I told Agie that I might be considered a pagan compared to her. I came from a family of one father, with eight wives and forty-six children. I was the third of the forty-six children of my father. My father, I told her, was initially baptized, but after an unfulfilled wish to become a reverend father, he abandoned his Catholic faith and embraced the African traditional religion (ATR), which acknowledges the existence of one Supreme Being called Chukwu, Chineke, Olisa, Obasi, or Oseburuwa in the different Igbo dialects. The religion also recognized the existence of lesser gods subservient to the almighty power of the one Supreme Being. This religion also espoused the belief that the Almighty being assigns to every individual a guide called *chi* (guardian angel) who could be good (*chi oma*) or bad (*chi ojoo*).

The religion which my parents practiced, I further told Agie, believed in the reverence of our forefathers who, having passed on, could still intercede for us before the Almighty Being and could also help us in difficult situations and abandon or punish us in certain circumstances. Finally, my father's religion believed in reincarnation, whereby the soul of a dead individual could reenter the body of a future individual and be born again to one or different individuals. The individual's fortunes or misfortunes in the reincarnated state could be dependent upon whether his or her antecedent being lived a life of wickedness or a clean and worthy life. In my father's African traditional religion, symbols—wooden, metallic, carved, or painted—could be used to represent the Almighty Being.

The chi or our ancestors were all represented by these symbols or paintings, and it was expected that libations should be poured on these symbols during ceremony or during periods of festivity. Despite the fact that Christianity was spreading fast in the community, my father, a former Christian, was not a worse man for his African traditional religion, I told Agie. In fact, I emphasized that my father's African traditional religion required and indeed compelled him to comply with certain social norms among which was the avoidance of anything that was rejected by the community as evil. The recognized evil practices in my father's society included maltreatment of widows and orphans, murder, stealing, maltreatment of strangers and visitors. Others were victimization of the helpless, abortions, rape, uprooting of planted crops even during land dispute, as well as such other practices as reverence of some species of snakes like the eke ogba, which did not bite human beings but could swallow chickens and chicken eggs.

These forbidden practices were called *alu* or *ihe ana na aso nso*, that means a practice that is rejected by the land. Violation of any of these rejected practices attracted sanctions that ranged from fines of chickens or money.

Agie listened with rapt attention as I disclosed my background. I also told her about my mother, the best mother that I know. I informed Agie that my mother was never baptized up to the time I left home, and she never had the opportunity to go to school. The most caring, most loving, and the most intelligent people I ever knew, my parents, as I narrated to Agie, would go to any lengths to make their children comfortable. I narrated to Agie how, despite our large numbers in the family, fifty-five in the immediate family, we had lived in near-complete harmony to the amazement of neighbors. I narrated to Agie how we survived the civil war, how the family of fifty-five usually ate communally from dishes prepared by the different wives, and how the extended family system with the multitude of cousins, aunts, and uncles had been put to best advantage by my larger family. I narrated to Agie how we treasured our suppers of many dishes and how my background of communal living had influenced my life and my general attitude to people and made me a people-oriented human being, unassuming, friendly, and ready to share whatever I had with others.

Agie also listened with wrapped attention as I narrated to her the story of my life so far, my brief stay at Aba, my mass-serving roles in the primary and secondary schools, and finally, how I entered the university. Unlike her, as I concluded, I had been very vociferous about imaginary exploits in discussions within my circle of friends, but like her, I had in reality never ever had any girl who was so dear to my heart and whom I could call my own. And that was only until I met her.

It was time for supper, and Agie and I proceeded from my room to the Alexander Brown Hall dining room for our very first meal together in Clinical Students Hostel. Sitting beside each other in the bus as I accompanied Agie back to her hostel in UI, we scheduled to meet again the following weekend.

The Passing on of a Future Father-In-Law

The proposed meeting as scheduled between Agie and me was not to hold. Four days after Agie's ABH visit to me, I was told by a porter that I had a visitor waiting at the lodge to see me. When I got to see the visitor, a middle-aged man who looked tired, the latter informed me that he was sent from Nnokwa (Agie's hometown) by Agie's mother to see me. He had instructions to see me first before going to see Agie. He announced to me that Agie's father died in an accident along the road as he drove to school in his vehicle the previous day!

It was a devastating news. I had met Agie's father only once when Hyman, my father's former assistant, drove me in his car from Arondizougu to Nnokwa. It was a very brief visit that barely lasted one hour as we arrived at Agie's house on an early Sunday morning amidst the family's preparation for mass. We had accompanied the family to Sunday mass and left from church immediately after the service. But for that informal visit to Nnokwa, I might never have had the opportunity of meeting Agie's father in life.

Agie must have talked to her mother favorably about me for her to trust her only daughter to my care at that period of utter grief.

My final examination was only three months away. Most of the final year medical students were very busy with the revision classes at that time. The revision classes were on, and every working day of the week mattered. Only the weekends were relatively free. Clinical cases of examination importance were being assembled, and every student would want to attend as many outpatient clinics as possible to stand a better chance of familiarizing himself or herself with some possible clinical cases. That therefore would be the worst time to travel out of town, or to be seen to be absent from revision theory or clinical classes.

But the father of my first and only girlfriend had just died. The information about the tragedy had been passed through me for communication to the latter. It would be the most uncharitable thing to abandon Agie at that stage no matter what happened. It was not a question of not going. It was only a question of how best to handle the situation so as to minimize the shock to Agie and to reduce any academic trauma that my absence might entail on me.

Agie was in UI, but the message bearer had come straight by night bus to me at UCH. I agreed with the message bearer that Agie must not be told the full story immediately. We were only to tell her that her father was seriously ill and needed to see her. I got dressed, gathered few dresses, and informed Davidson and Anyanyo, my friends, and set out for UI with the message bearer.

When we arrived UI, I first sought out Flossy, Agie's friend and told her the full story. I also told her that I was going home with Agie. She also immediately offered to accompany us.

Agie received the mitigated news with astounding courage. The four of us set out from Ibadan by a commercial Peugeot 504 station wagon bus via Onitsha. There was no problem at the bridgehead. Indeed, as we passed the site where we were robbed a few months earlier, a narration of our ordeal to our other two companions provided a welcome diversion from the great apprehension and grief in our minds.

We changed vehicles at Onitsha. As we got to Nnobi, the neighboring town to Agie's town, Nnokwa, I felt it was time to let Agie know the full story before her getting fully into her house. She broke down and sobbed as I unfolded the full picture of the fatal accident that had claimed the life of her father as earlier narrated to me by the harbinger of the news. But she was able to be controlled on her seat in the vehicle. As Agie sobbed in the vehicle, the driver of the vehicle kept saying, "Sorry-o-o, Sorry-o-o."

He knew the famous schoolteacher who died in a vehicle accident two days previously.

It was a very sad moment when we alighted from the vehicle at the city center, where the vehicle had dropped us. The half-mile walk from the city center to Agie's compound seemed to last hours. The emotions when I met Agie's mother for the second time ever were so sad. The wailing when Agie entered the compound was profound and sad. But everybody was controlled. Flossy and I stayed with Agie for a total of five days. Three days after the internment, Flossy and I went back to Ibadan. Agie was to stay a minimum of ten days, as tradition demanded, before she headed back to the university.

I put in extra hours of study when I got back to UCH to make up for the lost time. Soon Agie came back to Ibadan. She visited me in UCH. She wore black earrings as a sign of mourning. I tried to console her as much as possible. She soon fitted back to her studies.

My final examinations were soon on. After two weeks of very strenuous oral, written, and clinical quizzes, I was done. Prayers, good luck, and hard work combined to guarantee my resounding success in all courses at first sitting. I rushed down to the chapel after seeing my result and thanked God for his mercies. From the chapel, I headed straight to Agie's room to inform her. The swearing-in ceremony and the traditional administration of the physicians' Hippocratic oath was observed by Agie from the spectators' gallery. At the postswearing-in ceremonies and the cocktail parties, Agie and I took a lot of photographs. Happily, too, I was one of the new doctors selected to do their internship at the University College Hospital, a privilege which most young doctors looked forward to.

The Medical Student the Night Before, the Doctor the Morning After

The transition from being a student to being a doctor was so dramatic. For a while it did not seem real. When I woke up from bed on the first morning after the swearing-in ceremony, I was a little confused. I was not exactly sure of what roles were expected of me as an adult man, as a doctor. It was the very first time I would no longer address myself as a dependent student. Prior to that time, not many responsibilities were thrust on me. I had been so full of hopes and plans, expectations and zeal. But that first morning as a doctor, it initially appeared to be an anticlimax.

The sun still rose from the east.
The winds still blew.
The birds still sang from the tree branches
The sound of passing cars still disturbed the calmness of the morning
It was still the same me,
Nothing had changed
Except perhaps for a nominal appellation change, mister to doctor,
Nothing else had changed.

I knelt down in prayers beside my bed asking for God's direction. As daylight broke, the horizon for me appeared brighter. As I went for breakfast, I felt as if a very heavy load had been lifted off me. Shouts of "congratulations!" rented the air for all of us who were lucky to make it at first sitting. Luckily and virtually, all my friends also made it that first sitting: Davidson, Anyanyo, Bede, Maranzuh, Hilary, Dele, Martin, Idowu, Ukobasi, Ade, Tobias, and a host of others. Our joy knew no bounds.

Lucky was however the key word, for one needed lots of luck in an examination called *viva*. The internal examiners and the visiting professors varied widely from candidate to candidate. In those examinations, therefore, sound clinical knowledge played a major role, but good luck also contributed significantly to ensure anybody's success since there was no way any particular candidate, no matter how versatile, would know every thing in a field as wide as medicine.

The oral examinations in particular could be so treacherous. One's memory or composure could easily fail him or her. I remembered that during my surgery viva (oral quiz), I suddenly went blank at a stage when a visiting professor held up a urethral catheter and asked me how many milles of fluid I would use to inflate the catheter to secure it in the urinary bladder. A procedure in which I had very often participated during my urology posting suddenly went blank from my memory at that moment of stress. It was only the intervention of my internal examiner, whom I had often worked with and who knew that I had often participated actively, Professor Solanke—that great surgeon whom I shall always hold very dear all my days, of blessed memory—that saved the situation for me at that moment of temporary amnesia. That sort of situation could easily occur to anybody under intense fear.

It was at the breakfast table that we started getting a clearer picture of the results of the final examinations. We were sad to hear of two relatively bright students who had failed in surgery. Such was the uncertainty that could surround any of the clinical examinations in the medical school.

The signing-on ceremony for housemanship (internship) at the University College Hospital was smooth. We had a seven-day interval before commencement of work. It was the only free moment I had experienced for many months. I was always counting the hours for it to be evening so that I would board the bus to go to UI. Virtually all my suppers those seven days were at the Mellanby Hall cafeteria. All were with that girl who had looked me boldly in the face and asked for my name before she would tell me hers, the girl who turned out to be the first love of my life. All were with Agie.

The Doctor, His Patients, and His Pains

The new doctors accepted for housemanship soon moved into the House Officer's Residence (HOR). These were single suites of a bed, a reading table and chair, two single-seat chairs, a balcony with railing, and a bathroom with bathtub, shower, and hand wash basin. There was no attached kitchen. A subsidized cafeteria was provided for the hospital staff.

The duties of the house officer were rigorous but exciting. It was an extension of some of the activities we carried out as medical students during our postings in medicine, surgery, obstetrics/gynecology, and pediatrics. The major differences were the levels of participation and the degree of responsibility. Another difference of course was that the house officer was a paid employee of the hospital and was answerable for his actions and inactions to the hospital while working under a consultant (attending). The medical student on the other hand was, as implied by the name, simply a student who would not be held directly accountable for any activities or inactivities concerning the patient and the hospital.

The house officer was the least in the ladder of the medical team. But he was also the most visible officer in the team. He would do the initial documentation of the family and medical history of the patient's illness, a procedure called *clerking*. He would also do the initial clinical assessment, collect blood and other specimens for routine laboratory examinations, and do a detailed presentation of the patient during the consultant's ward round. He was allowed to participate in the minor and sometimes major surgical procedures depending on the number of other senior residents in the team. Where there were many senior house officers, registrars, and senior registrars in a team, the duty of the house officer might be limited to retraction of tissue during surgery, and running on errands or adjusting of the surgeon's mask or glasses. My first opportunity of handling the scalpel (surgical blade) was offered by a Russian-trained resident obstetrician during an emergency caesarean section. I was quite clumsy initially while cutting the skin, but as we proceeded through the fascia and muscles, I became much more confident.

The *amenity patients* were reserved for the consultants. These were cases where the consultant had indicated in writing on the patient's folder that he must personally take charge, either because the cases posed particular potential risks or (as the story often was told) there had been a special "inducement" to the consultant to pay particular attention. The case files of such amenity patients were often marked boldly with KEEP ME INFORMED. Even senior residents were often very wary of such cases where it was felt that the consultant had special interest. The senior residents often faced double jeopardy with such cases: if they intervened, and if anything went wrong, they would be blamed for "overenthusiasm" or acting beyond their capability. On the other hand, if anything went wrong while the consultant was being waited for, the senior resident could again be blamed for "not intervening fast enough." In a sense, therefore, the "keep me informed" patient could also suffer a disadvantage, since the consequential exercise of extra caution could be a disadvantage, as a "long spoon" was often required in such cases.

UCH, being the first major teaching hospital in Nigeria, was a major collection center for difficult cases. Major ailments which could not be handled at the community hospitals, private hospitals, and government general hospitals were often referred to UCH (and the other teaching hospitals). There were often therefore large collection of terminal cases and serious accident cases in UCH. The death rate in some of the wards was consequently higher than might be seen in many hospitals where less serious cases might cluster. The quality of care was, of course, undeniably much higher than could be obtained in other neighboring hospitals.

As we rotated through the four clinical departments, we were signed off by the department heads or consultants (attending). The signing off was necessary before the house officer could obtain his certificate of Full Registration as a Medical Practitioner. The latter certificate was usually issued by the Medical and Dental Council of Nigeria, MDCN, which was and remains the statutory highest regulatory body for the practice of medicine in the country.

The housemanship year though rigorous was also a year of intense social activity for most young doctors. Anytime we did weekend call, we had the next full day free. We had no lectures to attend and no examinations to take for a full year or two since the year after housemanship was spent doing national service. The house officer was therefore "as free as air" any day he or she was off duty. With a brand-new car and a *Dr* before his name, he was a very eligible bachelor. Many girls who had earlier shunned him would now fall for him, as he would no longer be said to be a failure. It was usually said that the house officer had "scaled the poverty bar." As expected, that bloated feeling of self-importance often led to reckless living by many house officers. Road traffic accident rate was said to be highest among house officers as many of them cruised at high speed in their new cars with little driving experience. There were so few of them that demand for them was very high. Many hospitals, especially general hospitals, queued up to recruit them, offering all kinds of incentives ranging from brand-new car loans, fully furnished apartments, to free catering services.

Most of my free evenings were spent in UI. I would park my brand-new fully air conditioned car at the car park of Queen's Hall, on mutually free evenings waiting for Agie to complete whatever she needed to do in the hall before we would drive out. As I leaned against the sparklingly clean new car, I would swing the car key on my index finger to confirm to any passer by that I was the owner of the car. Of course, I would always have a necktie on to confirm my status, even when the weather conditions did not so warrant.

Our usual resort was the prestigious Premier Hotel, and our usual spot was the swimming pool area with its exquisitely beautiful adjoining gardens with swing chairs. We would sip fruits with crushed ice from the straws while we sat on the swinging chairs. The drink that I enjoyed most was the one they used to call Chapman. It was a mixed fruit drink with a little wine and cut lemon sticking out from the large glass cup. We would order for chicken parts, and amidst the glass of drink and chicken, I would recite to Agie the many poems that I learnt in school and those that I composed myself. I loved poetry, and I used to compose quite a number of poems. Agie was not much of a poetry lover, but she would listen to my recitations with rapt attention. She would always remind me that she attended postwar school, where academic and other literary values had changed tremendously. I always wished that I could infuse those poems into her sharp brain so that we could recite them together. Occasionally, I was afraid that I might bore her with too much poetry.

It was during one afternoon prior to my graduation that I went to Lebanon Street, a popular street near the Dugbe Market in Ibadan. I had made up my mind that I was going to propose to Agie that weekend. I knew I needed an engagement ring if it was to be formal. All I knew about rings was that they were ornaments that people wore on their fingers to indicate either engagement, wedding, religious inclination as in finger rosary, or simply as an ornament. I knew neither the quality of rings nor their different designs. At Lebanon Street, I saw where they displayed rings in a glass case. It was being hawked about by a man who was temporarily taking a rest from the scorching sun under a tree shade. I was fascinated by one ring that looked sleek and had a well-trimmed glass stone at the center. I asked the hawker which of his many rings were engagement rings.

The man ran his hand over the entire lines of brilliant-looking rings in the glass showcase:

"E bri thing here," he said

"All na good one. Por engagement, marriage, e-e—bri thing. All na good one. E-e go vit madam well, well," The man said.

The hawker had implied that all the rings were suitable for engagement, wedding, and socials. He had also asserted that the rings would fit madam well. The nondistinction between the different designs and the lack of specificity for use made me a little uncomfortable. But the one I had pointed to looked good to me. I enquired about the price. It was within the range of the money I had in my pocket, a part of my little pocket money since I was still a student hoping to graduate in a couple of months. I immediately paid for the ring. The hawker packaged the ring into a small white envelope for me, and I proudly put the packaged stuff into my pocket and walked off to the nearest bus stop back to the hostel in UCH. I was going to have my private engagement party, and the thought of that filled my head.

During my outing with Agie that evening, I informally suggested to her that we should get engaged before my graduation. I had felt that the early engagement was necessary just in case I passed my final examinations but did not get selected for housemanship at UCH. The engagement would then ensure that we kept to each other no matter where we were. When Agie without hesitation consented to the engagement, I immediately brought out the envelope containing the ring from my pocket and presented it to her. She accepted the ring and looked it over. She appeared to have admired it greatly as she inserted it on her ring finger beside her finger rosary. For the first time ever, I was honored with a kiss from my future wife!

It took Aruisa, a flamboyant social science student who was Agie's next-door neighbor in Queen's Hall, to point out to Agie that the engagement ring which she was wearing was not original. Aruisa had scrutinized the ring and asked Agie where she bought it from. She, Aruisa, had added that the ring was beautiful, but that it was not original. When Agie told her that it was her engagement ring from her boyfriend in ABH, she had ridiculed her, telling her that if her boyfriend bought her a cheap engagement ring even as a student, then he would buy her cheap wrappers when they marry. Agie's explanation that her boyfriend was still a poor student did not mitigate the ridicule. Both Agie and I felt very proud about the ring, which she continued to wear throughout my student days, oblivious of its price worth which we neither knew about nor even bothered much about. That incident was later to remind me of the popular song by Dolly Parton about the "coat of many colors."

My father and my sister Doro attended my official graduation ceremony at Ibadan. It was a very memorable occasion. Agie met my father for the first time. Unlike the situation between Agie and her mother, I had never mentioned Agie to either of my parents. It was only my sister Judith who knew. Judith was the closest of my sisters to me, and we often confided in each other. She had experienced strong opposition from our father about the person she wanted to marry, and the marriage consequently did not hold. Fearing I might experience a similar opposition as Judith did, I kept my plans about the girl I wanted to marry from my father.

The Secret Wedding, the Undisclosed Pact

To ensure further that nothing stopped our marriage proposals, Agie and I decided to marry secretly in a court registry. We effected this without informing anybody and secured our marriage certificate which we hid from everybody, including our closest friends. Even though we were officially married, we could not yet live together nor behave like husband and wife because the Catholic doctrine of which Agie was a strong believer forbade such association before church wedding. Even though I was a retired mass server, my morality was not as strong as Agie's, and I would not have minded moving in with the girl who was then officially my wife, but I had to fully respect her religious beliefs, about the need for a church wedding before her moving in with me.

Agie was preparing to travel to her home for the Christmas vacation. I therefore applied for my annual vacation to coincide with her trip. We therefore drove to the east together in my car. It was my first visit home since my graduation and the first time I was to drive a long distance of well over two hundred miles. It was Agie's first visit to my house at Aba. From Aba, Agie traveled down to her home at Nnokwa. It was during that visit home that I formally told my parents that I wanted to marry Agie. That of course was in spite of the fact that we had earlier concluded a secret marriage at Ibadan. My mother was indeed very excited about the proposal.

My father had his reservations because he said that my elder brother Mako should marry first since he was the first son. It was later that I found out that my father had commissioned extensive investigations about Agie's home background through his business partners at Onitsha before he approved of the marriage. That was of course after I was made to obtain a dispensation from my elder brother, confirming that he did not mind my marrying before him.

The presence of my father and/or some elders from my family were of course required before we could perform the traditional marriage ceremony called *igba nkwu*, which was and still is the recognized marriage ceremony in Igbo culture. The igba-nkwu ceremony which was considered as the main traditional marriage consisted of the conveyance of palm wine in jars and calabashes by the family of the bridegroom to the family of the bride and the public sipping of the wine between the celebrants. The church marriage was for the church while the registry was for government. The foregoing is the belief in my culture.

Prior to my father's blessing for my marriage, I was afraid that he might disapprove of my marriage and therefore refuse to go for the traditional marriage ceremony with me. He had told me sometime that his children must marry in order of seniority. He had said that my elder brother Mako must marry before he would approve of my marriage unless I obtained that dispensation from Mako. Mako easily granted the dispensation and in fact assured me that he would attend the traditional marriage ceremony at Nnokwa from his base in Asaba, a town not too far from Nnokwa, Agie's hometown.

I was not sure I would be able to obtain the required dispensation very readily since my elder brother did not live at home, and contacting him might delay events for Agie and me. For fear that my father would refuse to attend the traditional marriage ceremony with me if the dispensation was not granted, thereby casting doubts about eligibility before my proposed in-laws, I secretly arranged with three of my colleagues—Obi, Tubia, and Hilary—that each of them would import elderly men from their homes and come along with them to the traditional marriage. They themselves would also grow their beards and also attend, wearing elder's dresses. They would thus provide a good number of elderly people (or elderly-looking people) who would accompany me to the ceremony should my folks decide not to accompany me if my elder brother failed to grant a dispensation. Elderly people from my home would of course refuse to accompany me if my own father refused to approve of my marrying before my elder brother. I was however able to get my elder brother to repeat the consent before my father, before the latter consented to the marriage. I thereafter had to send down word to my friends to discard the idea of importing elders or turning bearded overnight elders themselves.

The Bride Price in the Back Pocket

I was told that bride price (the money paid by a suitor to the parents of a bride) was usually high in Agie's town. I learnt it could be a high as five thousand naira. Naira, the local currency, was at that time much stronger than the U.S. dollar as one thousand naira then equaled about one thousand and five hundred U.S. dollars. My monthly salary as a house officer was about four hundred naira, and after all kinds of taxes and deductions, the best I could take home was about two hundred and fifty naira. I proceeded to the east for the traditional marriage with a total of about six hundred naira. That was my total savings over several months. After expenses for palm wine, beer, soda, and Schnapps (a popular hot drink), all I had in an envelope tucked in my back pocket for the bride price was four hundred naira. My father had helped with hiring the bus for conveying visitors as well as in payment of the traditional dancers and the masquerade that accompanied us.

I knew of course that my father was more than financially capable of paying for every dime for the ceremony. But it was not usual nor manly that a man—a doctor, that is—should expect his father to finance his marriage after he was sponsored through medical school. Besides, when I indicated to my father my intention to marry soon after my housemanship, the latter had initially reminded me of the Igbo proverb: "Atulu ya epu mpi, ekwo kaa ya."

When translated, that meant that the sheep that intended to imitate the ram by bearing horns (for fighting) should ensure that it had very strong and well-developed neck muscles. That implied that I should ensure that I was financially capable of financing a marriage and married life before embarking on the project. I was therefore quite grateful that he sponsored certain aspects of the traditional marriage ceremony.

It was not mandatory that the full amount of whatever was demanded as cash for bride price should be paid en block. I had therefore resolved that no matter what Agie's folks demanded as bride price, I would simply drop on the table the four hundred naira, which was about all that was left with me. The rest of the money which I had on me, which indeed was all that I had, was under forty naira, and that would be for my petrol (gas) back to Ibadan.

The ceremonial drums which we came to Nnokwa with were beating. The masquerades were dancing. The compound was filled with people. Some were inside the building on the first floor. Others were on the second floor. Many more were outside. The whole place was in intensive festive mood. Soon the *iqwe*, the traditional ruler of the whole town, arrived amidst a thunderous ovation. He was said to have been a good friend of Agie's late father, who was one of the igwe's red cap chiefs.

The formal welcome speech was soon made by the master of ceremonies over the battery-operated, hand-held microphone. The leader of our delegation, my father, as empowered by my eldest uncle and head of the larger family Papa Nke Ocha, was asked as tradition demanded to announce the subject of our visit. After series of proverbs which my father was very well versed in, he announced that Arondiznogu people were there at Nnokwa and in that particular compound because they found "something good which was hiding in that compound." He then cleared his throat and continued thus. "It is this something good that we have come after," he said.

In response, the leader of Agie's family, the host family who was the eldest in Agie's compound, then welcomed us formally with kola nuts.

"We welcome you all to Nnokwa," he said.

"We are overjoyed that you have found something good from within our midst. We at Nnokwa are reputed for producing good things. You people of Arondizuogu are today lucky to be the beneficiaries of one of the many good things we have here at Nnokwa."

He then loudly cleared his throat and gently but deliberately looked from side to side for one second or two and then added in a low voice, "However, em, em-m, everything good has a price."

He then asked us to bring forward the five people who would go inside with five people from their own side to discuss the price for "this good thing." So, my father, my eldest uncle Papa Nkeocha, who had delegated his leadership position for that particular occasion to my father, and three elderly men from my place were invited upstairs. I was also invited to accompany them even though I was not expected to say anything during the discussions. A goat's skin was placed on the floor, and the negotiation of the bride price started.

The hosts' spokesman spoke at length about how well they had trained their daughter and said that millions of naira would not be enough to compensate for the "treasures" they were about to hand over to us.

"However, we are asking for a modest one million naira as a token for our daughter's bride price, a very modest price since we are not selling our daughter," the spokesman added.

My heart missed a few beats at the mention of that said amount. I became very apprehensive in spite of the fact that I knew and understood that bride price was highly negotiable. My father did not appear disturbed. In response, he thanked the hosts for their "modest" demand. He said that any girl is a treasure and that "a beautiful young girl who has gone to university is an unquantifiable treasure." He then informed our hosts that in Arondizuogu, where we came from, the highest bride price that could be paid by anybody was twenty-five naira.

"However," he added, "since we are not in Arondizuogu but at Nnokwa, and in appreciation of the goodness of what has brought us to Nnokwa, cloupled with the sound education and training you have given to your daughter, we are going to pay you double what we ask for at Arondizuogu."

"Therefore," he said, "we are going to pay you fifty naira, considering that this is a channel for cooperation that is being opened up and not a sale of a commodity."

I heaved an audible sigh of relief, prompting everybody to look in my direction.

The leader of the hosts then thanked my father, and after three further stages of negotiations as tradition demanded, an agreement was arrived at.

"We totally agree with you that we are not selling our daughter. Therefore pay us whatever you came with, since bride price is a continuous exercise and must not be concluded in a single sitting."

With that statement from the leader of the hosts, the issue of bride price was settled. My father then asked me to get whatever money I came with. He all along was clutching a large purse under his armpit. I was later to learn from one of my sisters that my father indeed had come with thousands of naira in that purse ready to pay any amount that our hosts insisted on should I prove unable to provide enough money. But he wanted me first to play my own part. I immediately drew the envelope from my pocket and placed the entire contents of the envelope, which was four hundred naira, on the table. Papa asked me how much it was, and I told him it was four hundred naira. He took up the money from the table and holding it up with both hands as if it was a very weighty load, he announced, "We are paying you two hundred pounds!"

There was loud clapping of hands from both our hosts and members of our team. Two naira was once equivalent to one British pound sterling, and there was a habit among more elderly people to continue to use that exchange rate nomenclature even when the rate had greatly changed in favor of the pound sterling.

I was not sure what exactly the hand clapping was for, whether in praise or in sarcasm. A man was asked to pay one million naira, and he succeeded in paying only four hundred naira, and there was a loud ovation and clapping of hands. Whichever way it was however, all I knew was that I had paid some bride price, and that was it.

Downstairs, when we rejoined the rest of our delegation, Agie was told to walk through the crowd of men and women to identify her husband, holding a cup filled with palm wine. The culture demanded that carrying a cup of palm wine she should search through the entire crowd and be able to identify and isolate the prospective husband from where the latter would be hiding among the young men who occasionally were similarly clothed. When she found the prospective husband, she would then kneel in front of him and offer him the glass of wine. The prospective husband would then accept the wine and take a sip from it and give to the prospective wife to signify unity between the two. He would thereafter pull up the wife from her kneeling position and embraced her, signifying complete union. The remnants of the wine would thereafter be handed over to the father of the bridegroom or who ever stood in for the latter.

I had been tucked within the crowd of men in the visiting team. It was relatively easy for Agie to find me because I wore my signature tune tie which I always went to Queen's Hall in. With the finding of the bridegroom and the payment of the bride price over, all that remained was the fulfillment of some rites. The first was the *igba ndu* rites by which a goat would be killed, and both families would dip smoked meat from the neck of the goat in oil and salt and eat the meat jointly to signify complete unity and complete trust between both families. In Igbo land, it is believed that palm oil is a very soothing balm and therefore in-laws during the igba ndu rite were required to dip the meat from the neck of a goat into oil and salt and eat same jointly, signifying that both families could henceforth entrust their necks to each other without any fear of the neck being hurt in any way, and that thereafter the respective families would eat and enjoy all dishes from each other's household without fear.

After the igba ndu rite was concluded, the traditional handing over of gifts and entitlements to the mother of the bride, the bride's age grade, the young men of the village, and the grandmother of the bride or her representative was done. These entitlements were usually clothes or tobacco or soda (soft drinks) or beer. They could be provided physically or could be paid for in cash. The list of requirements was given to us, and my father settled them in cash. I had indeed not reckoned with that latter aspect of the culture, and if my father had not come with money, I would have been stuck at that stage since the remaining money with me was barely enough to cover my gas costs back to Ibadan. There was eating, drinking, and dancing thereafter.

Since we came from a long distance, activities were hastened up for us, and in under four hours, we were on our way back to Arondizuogu.

Ije, Agie's childhood friend, accompanied us to Arondizuogu in conformity with the tradition of Agie's people, which required that the closest friend or sister of a bride should accompany her to the bride's new residence for the first night. A large crowd of well-wishers was already gathered in our compound at Arondizuogu by the time we got home that night from Nnokwa. There was eating and drinking and merriment throughout the night to welcome the new member into the family.

Ije, Agie's friend, stayed with us till the following morning before she left back for Nnokwa.

As early as six in the morning of the following day, other visitors from the village and my parents' many friends had started gathering in our compound "to see our new wife." In our culture, the arrival of a new wife is a very special occasion in the village. The arrival of a new wife usually attracted large crowds. Our large compound gates were opened all night as people thronged the compound to rejoice with us. Food and drinks were provided in abundance by my father as a fresh round of cooking was resumed very early in the morning.

As large as my father's compound was, with the centrally located main building of two floors and separate houses for each of his eight wives, virtually every available space was taken up as early as seven o'clock the following morning. Some people who accompanied us to Nnokwa had stayed back through the night. Some others who were awaiting our return from Nnokwa also stayed the night to be joined by the scores of others who were trooping in from far and near as soon as it was daybreak. Each group that came in demanded to see "our new wife." At a stage I was afraid that Agie might be exhausted presenting herself to be embraced and welcomed by hundreds of family members, neighbors, visitors, and well-wishers. Every group would make a speech and say some prayers wishing her good health and "as many children as possible." One group, after offering prayers, reminded Agie that as the first daughter-in-law of Mmadukibaya (the name which my father was conferred with during the war), the least that was expected of her was to ensure that she got at least half as many children as Mmadukibeya. I was not sure whether the man meant what he was saying or not until he repeated the wish. I started wondering whether that wish was a blessing or a curse considering that Mmadukibaya had forty-six children, and the man's wish when translated would mean that Agie should have twenty-three children all by herself! I thought the man was drunk, but I heard him make other sensible statements confirming his sanity.

Three days after the traditional marriage, we were back to Ibadan. We had planned to follow up that traditional marriage within one month, with the church wedding. That was not to be as I had exhausted every penny that I had. We were barely able to fuel our car back to Ibadan. Agie's pocket money had sustained us until I got my paycheck at the end of the month.

We scheduled the wedding date for two months after the traditional marriage. We had initially proposed to have it one month after the traditional marriage so that I could still be in occupation of my room in the house officer's residence. By the new date, I would be in the mandatory National Youth Service Corps orientation camp, where I would have no room of my own. Rather I would have a bed in an open hall with the other National Youth Service Corps members, a compulsory one-year national service for all fresh university graduates. Only medical doctors, lawyers, and pharmacist who needed to do internship or law school for one year after graduation were given a year's grace before they would go for the national service. All other fresh university graduates were drafted for national service after graduation unless they were above the age of thirty.

A corps member could be posted to any state in the country. Not being sure where I would be posted to and being newly married, I feared for what would happen to my wife, who had earlier lost her father and who just turned twenty years old, should I die during national service. Even though the service was not a military service, we learnt that military men conducted the orientation drills and that a corps member could be posted to a very rural community with hardly any postal or telephone service. I therefore took up two life insurance policies from two prominent insurance companies in Ibadan.

Luckily I was posted to Oyo State for my national service, the same state where the University of Ibadan is situated. The orientation exercises for the national service were scheduled for a teacher's college in Oyo town about fifty minutes driving distance from Ibadan. The duration was to be about a month, and unfortunately the date that Agie and I had fixed our wedding fell within the orientation period. We had much earlier printed and distributed the wedding invitation cards, making it untenable to reschedule the date. The location was to be the Seat of Wisdom Chapel near where Agie and I had met on a Good Friday and where we occasionally went to pray together. The reception was to hold at Mellanby Hall cafeteria, the cafeteria of my first hall in the University of Ibadan, the same hall where I first had my first experience of unlimited cups of the cocoa-based drink Bournvita. The invited guests were mainly Agie's mother and relations, my mother and numerous relations, and our respective classmates and friends. My father did not come. It was either that he did not believe in church wedding, being deeply engrossed in African traditional religion or that he felt that the marriage ceremony had been perfected, with the conclusion of the traditional marriage. One of my consultants at Ibadan and his wife, the Ibziakos, graciously agreed to be our church wedding sponsors. This couple, indeed, about one month to the scheduled date of the wedding, had made a generous gift of fifty naira to help us, quite a big sum at the time where a tin of condensed milk of the peak brand sold for only ten kobo, one-tenth of a naira (about ten cents). That fifty-naira gift was a very big boost to our finances.

I had completed my housemanship and moved out of the house officers' residence by the scheduled date of the wedding. Agie on her part had by that time passed her part 1 bachelor of dental surgery (BDS) exams and moved into Alexander Brown Hall in the University College Hospital (UCH) for the clinical part of her training. She was indeed admitted into University of Ibadan as a science major student in prelim year, but after preliminary (first year) science examinations, her excellent score secured her a place in the newly established bachelor of dental surgery (BDS) program in the faculty of medicine.

My being out of the house officer's residence and Agie's being in the hostel meant that we had no residence of our own, not even a temporary accommodation. We had therefore requested a friend from Arondizuogu, Madam Nko who lived in Ibadan, to allow Agie to dress up and set out for the wedding from her house. On my own part, I was to set out for the wedding straight from the National Youth Service Corps orientation camp!

Madam Nko had also graciously allowed our two mothers and other relations who had traveled down long distance from the eastern part of the country to stay the night in her house. They all spread themselves on large mats all over Madam Nko's house. There was no way we would have been able to afford hotel accommodation for anybody.

My sister Comfo did a fantastic job cooking for the visiting family members. My sister Judith put up with our friends the Osujis. It was tremendous sacrifices they all made to attend our wedding. Agie's friends Jooke, Etam, Flossy, Yonyiade, and many others kept so close and were so supportive of her throughout the very busy period. Her childhood friend Ije had even traveled from the east despite a very busy schedule just to attend our wedding. Most of my friends were already scattered around the country in youth corps orientation camps but friends like Obi, Hilary, Martin, Okey, and my best man Davidson were still able to travel down.

On AWOL to Wed

On the eve of that September wedding day about 11:00 p.m., I had secretly driven my car out of the orientation camp and parked it along the road some distance from the camp. The camp rules were quite strict, and I suspected I would not have been allowed to leave the camp since I had earlier fully utilized my maximum two-day official pass. There were stories of people who in the past were detained at the camp gate when after being denied passes, they had attempted to steal their way out of the camp. I did not want to take the chance of applying for a pass only to be denied. It would have been disastrous. Again there was no question of rescheduling the wedding because most arrangements had been concluded before the announcement of the orientation dates. And arguing in English language with the army corporals and sergeants at the gate was not the most advisable thing to do on somebody's wedding day. Many of the soldiers who conducted the orientation exercises detested people who appeared to unnecessarily display their knowledge of English language.

About 4:00 a.m. on that memorable day even before the morning tattoo—the military trumpet summoning members of the service corps to morning marching, salute, and exercises—I dressed up in my drill (outfit, khaki trousers, shirt, canvas boot, and cap) and avoiding the main gate and side gates sneaked through the barbed-wire fence demarcating the college compound and headed for my car, removing my cap and long-sleeved shirt for disguise purposes as soon as I was on the road. I had earlier loaded my wedding suit and entire earthly belongings in bags into the boot of my car. I drove off almost at breakneck speed, lest I be easily followed, towards Ibadan, constantly scanning my rear mirrors to ensure I was not being trailed. My biggest fear, which perhaps was unfounded, was that officers might notice my absence or get information about the wedding and somehow come to Ibadan to disrupt it.

I had "escaped" successfully from the camp. My other friends in the camp were however not as lucky. About four of them were caught at the side gates of the camp as they were "breaking bounds" to attend my wedding much later in the morning. They had thought that they would elicit the sympathy of the guards if they explained to them that they were caught while actually attempting to attend the wedding of a fellow member of the corps which was holding that morning. Under intense interrogation, one of them had apparently given out the name of the bridegroom corps member who had thought he had successfully escaped notice. Luckily the officers did not follow the bound breakers to bring the principal bound breaker back to camp in his wedding suit. It was possible the strict camp rules did not extend that far. But other reprisals waited for me. That day was "principal assignment posting" day, the day that the principal places of service for each corps member would be posted on the notice board. There were favorable places that people clamored for. There were other places that were not considered favorable that most people dreaded. Most corps members wished for places like Ibadan, Oyo town, Ogbomosho town, and so on. During the early days of orientation, those who were familiar with the state knew about some places which were prone to communal clashes and where many corps members loathed. A corps member who was annoyed by another corps member would threaten him thus, "I will report you, and they will post you to Igettu." Igettu was thus rightly or wrongly taken as a symbol of punitive posting.

As soon as I drove into Ibadan, I cleared by the roadside and changed from the camp drill dress into my wedding suit. I then proceeded to check out on a few final preparations. Agie was being dressed up in her wedding outfit at Madam Nko's house. I checked out on the proposed reception hall, on the caterer, and on the photographer among others. There were no cell phones, and thus every contact had to be physically effected. Traffic hold ups made movement unduly difficult.

About one hour to the scheduled wedding time, I dropped my car and was picked up by my friend and best man, Dave. He had picked me up in the car of his friend Emeka since his own car was busy elsewhere conveying materials and family guests. We were approaching UI when just three cars ahead of us and about three minutes drive to UI, the gates of the railway crossing got closed to make way for an approaching train. The weeding was for 10:00 a.m., and it was about 9:30. Ordinarily the railway crossing would not remain closed for longer than a couple of minutes. The first five minutes passed, then ten minutes, then twenty, thirty. I started sweating profusely from anxiety. The gates did not open even after the train had passed! The traffic built up behind us for poles and poles away. On the opposite side, impatient commuters, jumping the queue from behind not knowing that the gates were closed, were blocking the road completely against oncoming traffic. Ten o'clock was my wedding time, and it was 10:15 a.m., and I was still on the road with little hopes of the traffic clearing. About 10:25, the railway crossing was mechanically opened by knocking off the jammed hinges. But the traffic would not clear. We were seeing the buildings in the university from where we were, stuck in the traffic but walking distance could take up to another half hour. I became very jittery, sweating profusely.

Cell phones were not yet in use in the country then, and there was no way we could communicate with the people who were waiting for us in the church. My best man too was speechless. We both removed our jackets, our shirts soaked in sweat from the scorching heat and blazing sun. The guests would all be waiting in the church. The officiating minister, Reverend Father Monoz who had been so kind to us, would be waiting. Above all, my bride would be waiting (she told me after the wedding that at about 10:30 a.m. the reverend father had jokingly asked her whether her bridegroom had absconded). By the time we finally reached the chapel at 11:02 a.m., my best man and I were virtually looking like harassed ghosts from outer space. It was a worse experience for me than the daylight robbery, which Agie and I had experienced at Onitsha bridgehead, some eighteen months previously. We were just lucky that no other weddings were scheduled in the same chapel that day and that the officiating minister was not otherwise engaged and that he exercised all the patience to wait for us.

The sigh of relief was palpable in the church when the best man and the bridegroom finally entered the church. There were audible murmurs and whispers of "thank God" all over the room. Some had feared that we might have had an accident on the way, while for some weird imagination some feared that I might have run away. The "search party" that had been dispatched to look out for us had got stuck at the other end of the traffic and did not return until we were well into the actual wedding mass.

The early photographs of the wedding thereafter obviously portrayed the confusion and anxiety on our faces. But we soon got over that and settled down to enjoy the wedding, the most memorable day we ever had.

Homeless on My Wedding Day

The wedding ceremony over, it was time for the husband and wife to proceed on their honeymoon. We had no residence of our own, no house, no hotel room. Agie lived in a hostel with a roommate in UCH. I had no residence that I could call my own. All my earthly possessions were packed in the boot of my car. Our wedding presents plenty of them, from our family members and school friends, were stacked at the backseat of the car. Our initial plan had been that after the wedding, I would quietly slip back into the youth corps orientation camp. Agie was to get back to her hostel in UCH, pending the time I would get my permanent youth corps posting, which I had hoped would be in Ibadan or its environs. I had not reckoned with any punitive postings. I had not anticipated that my AWOL from camp would be detected.

Straight from the wedding, we drove off to the youth corps camp, my temporary open hall home, to check on the notice board for my posting since corps members could proceed to their primary assignments once after that day's posting. Some corps members who arrived later to the wedding told us that the postings were being made as they were about to depart the camp that morning. But they did not check (my) posting, they said. May be they wanted me to discover by myself. When I got to the camp notice board, a "good wedding present" was waiting for me: my posting was to Igettu, the rich marble-mining town which nobody wanted to go to at that time. The posting must have been considered an appropriate punishment for my escaping from the camp to wed, without the necessary permission to leave camp.

I stood still for a while but soon recollected myself. I must not tell Agie the stories we heard about the place. It was said that there used to be recurrent communal riots in the town. But I must not tell Agie about those stories which in any case might have been exaggerated. I must not spoil her joy on her wedding day. It was better we proceeded to the place to see for ourselves. So long as there would be a room for us to lay down our heads, we would brave it. We would make the best of it. We must not complain.

We sought for directions and drove off to Igettu. It was a long journey from Oyo, and it was getting late. We had earlier spent some time at Ibadan to say farewell to our family members and other guests who had traveled long distances to attend our wedding.

As we veered off from Ogbumosho town, the road became very narrow. It was tarred but was very narrow. Indeed, it was barely the width of a lane in any highway in the western world but certainly more uneven. I was wondering whether it was constructed when the colonial district officer (DO) was the only person who drove a car into, or out of the town. Since he alone drove a car, there might not arise the need for another car to overtake him or another car coming in from the opposite direction.

I was just praying that no vehicle might come in the opposite direction. Indeed none did, through the nearly seventy-mile journey from Ogbomosho to Igettu. The road was so lonely that at many points along the road we encountered where people had spread out grated cassava and sliced yams along the road for drying. If there was anticipation that cars or trucks might soon drive past along the road, the villagers would certainly not have risked drying their food materials along the tarred public highway. Fat goats and chickens roamed freely along the road, and we did not observe the presence of many people as we drove along.

It was already getting dark when we got into Igettu. From a distance, we could see some hills. We could also see some flickers of light clustered around a place some distance by the right side of the road. As we approached the cluster of lights, our headlights shone against the prominently planted signpost showing the inscription General Hospital. That was my place of primary posting. We turned in. There was a beautiful wide gate which was wide open and unmanned. The entire place was so quiet. There were fairly nice buildings scattered all over the place. We saw no cars nor ambulances. At first, we thought the facility had not been put to use. We drove towards one of the buildings and noticed some movement inside the building. As we pulled up in front of the building, a man in his early thirties wearing a nurse's uniform came up to meet us.

I came out of the car and introduced myself. I said I was the new National Youth Service Corps doctor posted to work in the hospital. The man leaned forward and touched the ground with his fingers and greeted me profusely in the traditional way of greeting.

"E-elee, sir," he said. : "We are very happy." He introduced himself as Staff Sadiq and said that he was the staff nurse on duty. I had never before then encountered any male nurses. I only knew that there were male nurses during the Second World War because we had a highly respected veteran of World War II in my village who was said to have been a nurse during that war. In the University College Hospital where I trained and where I did my housemanship, we had only female nurses at all cadres. We had learnt that there were some male nurses in the general hospitals. Staff Sadiq said he would take me to the NS.

"NS, lived at the other quarters," he said, pointing a slightly larger house three blocks away from where we were standing. As we walked along towards the house he told me that the "NS" would take me "to the doctor's quarters." Staff Sadiq kept referring to the "NS" in virtually everything he said. I did not know what *NS* meant, but since it was assumed I should know, I felt we could keep going for the time being. All I really wanted at that time was any opportunity to lay down my head after "escaping" from the camp early in the morning, having a wedding and driving such a long distance.

Before we got to the larger house, a smart-looking middle-aged man had come out of the house and started coming in our direction. He must have seen us from a distance. The staff nurse said in a low tone as we approached the middle-aged man, "That is the NS."

"This must be our new doctor?" the middle-aged man said, smiling very broadly. Again as he got to us, he bent forward and touched the ground with his right fingers in the traditional greeting style and mark of respect. I had never encountered such spontaneous politeness and unreserved welcome coming from a background of a very large cosmopolitan hospital like the University College Hospital. The NS then introduced himself. (I later learnt that *NS* stood for nursing superintendent). He said they had been expecting me since morning. "The ministry promised several months ago that a doctor would be posted to the hospital by September." It was then that I understood why he felt that I must be the new doctor. But I did not quite grasp the implication of the wordings "a doctor would be posted."

I then asked the NS to take me to the medical director. I had wanted to report my presence before settling down for the night. "That one is the doctor's house," NS said, pointing to one gigantic building, a double-storied building with gable roofing, standing dignified at the extreme end of the compound.

"Can we go to see him now?" I asked NS, expressing my desire to go and see the medical director first.

"You mean the doctor's house," NS said.

"Yes," I said, "I just want to say hi to him before I go to rest." I continued still expressing my desire to greet the medical director, my boss, first.

NS seemed a little confused by what I said, but he continued, "Should the driver bring doctor's car nearer, or can we be walking down while Staff Sadiq tells driver to follow us with the car?"

It was my turn to get a little confused. NS had seen somebody in the car from the dim lighting. He could not make out because of the dimness that the occupant was a woman and was not on the driver's seat. He taught a chauffer drove me down to the place and wanted the staff nurse to tell the chauffer to drive down to us and pick us up to the doctor's house. I was too tired to walk farther.

"Let me bring the car down," I said. "You can be walking down to the medical director's house." I imagined that if the NS and the staff nurse accompanied me to the car, there would be no sitting space for them since the backseats were all filled up with wedding presents.

I got to the house first in the car before NS and Staff Sadiq arrived.

"This is doctor's house, sir. I will immediately send for Jericho, your steward. Jericho had been playing truancy since former doctor left," NS said, as soon as they got to the house.

As soon as NS saw the inside of my car fully loaded, he said, "Oma se! (What a pity!) It looks like you carried some of your load inside your car and drove yourself with madam. Is doctor's driver coming from Ibadan with the main load this night?"

Most of the things NS was saying initially sounded out of place to me. He had been so used to expatriate doctors on contract coming to work in Igettu Hospital (since many indigenous doctors would rather work in urban hospitals). These expatriate doctors always were chauffer-driven and came in with large loads from the ministry for their comfort. Their load was often transported in separate trucks distinct from the cars in which the doctors were driven down.

NS tried the handle of the front door of the house, but it was locked. He then asked me if I did not want to drive into the open-car garage attached to the building. But I said, "No, let me not block the medical director."

NS looked at me in bewilderment.

After we stood in front of the house for a while I asked, "Is the doctor not at home?"

More bewilderment followed. I had kept referring to a nonexistent medical director oblivious of the fact that there was no other doctor in the hospital, and that all the talk about doctor's house actually referred to my house.

There was light in only one room on the ground floor of the large house. All the rooms upstairs and the other rooms on the ground floor were dark inside.

As we were still talking, we saw a young man running towards the house.

"That is Jericho coming. Stupid boy!. He always wants promotion to senior steward, but he won't stay in the house," NS said, pointing to the young man who was panting from the sprint.

"Sorry, sir, I just go to Jibowu him house," the young man said as he brought out a bunch of keys and opened the front door of the expansive house.

"Quick, quick, make you begin bring down doctor's load," NS said using Pidgin English so that both Jericho and I could understand.

As Jericho opened the back door of my car and started unloading my belongings, I had to ask, "Am I going to live with the medical director?"

It was at that stage that NS, a very intelligent man, said, "Doctor, this is your house. Dr Morsi left four months ago and is not coming back. He has gone finally back to Egypt. Jericho is your steward. His real name is Oluwaseun, but Dr Morsi nicknamed him Jericho because he could not pronounce his name, and everybody now calls him Jericho. Jericho will help you with everything you need for this night. By tomorrow morning the gardener and other staff will be here. I will then introduce you to the rest of the hospital staff." He wished me good night and very politely took his leave with Mr Sadiq.

I stood for a while in amazement. So I was going to live in this massive house alone and manage this massive hospital. I had no administrative experience whatsoever. I had very limited surgical experience, no experience in human resources management, and except for the limited period I was house captain and school captain at the government secondary school, I had never been in a position to direct human behavior to any measurable extent. But there was I, suddenly thrown into a very massive rural hospital which, as I was later to learn, was located at Igettu when the regional minister of health came from that area.

Agie and I got into the fully furnished house and sank into the sofas in the ground floor of the living room. After evacuating the backseat of the car, Jericho requested for the key to the boot. He looked so smart and was so confident and so precise in his every move. It did not take him five minutes to boil hot water for us to bath within the bathroom upstairs. By the time we came downstairs, there was already a big bowl of boiled rice with stew and dried bush meat on the dining table. He had set out the table with full cutlery well arranged, with serviettes sticking from the glass cups and fresh flowers adorning the table.

We gulped the food and were almost falling asleep on the dining chairs when we heard sharp knocks on the door. Jericho opened the door, and a nurse came in with many hospital cards.

"Doctor, we have emergencies! Some of them are too bad, and we sent them back. These ones are still alive but bad." With this statement, he handed me six cards with bloodstains on them!

"Waoo, this was what I needed least at this particular time. Why just today and just now, in under four hours of my arrival," I was saying within me. Sadiq, the night nurse on duty, had obviously informed the other staff that a new doctor had arrived, and coincidentally these emergencies had cropped up that same night.

I thought it was a road traffic accident. Nothing else, I thought, would be able to wreck so much havoc at once. I immediately remembered the narrow road through which we drove down to Igettu. I felt convinced that the narrow winding road must have been responsible for that accident. So I thought.

Outwardly I put up a straight face and a confident look. I must not be seen to be afraid of emergencies. *Executive privileges go with executive responsibilities. I must muster strength and courage. I must be equal to the challenge to the best of my capability,* I mused.

I had always worked under supervision as a house officer in a large teaching hospital. I always had senior house officers, registrars, and senior registrars supervising whatever I did. In addition to the resident doctors, there was always a big boss, the consultant. But that night, my very first night in Igettu, the big medical challenge had come, and on my wedding day!

It was a baptism of fire—a rich gift for a promising honeymoon.

"What happened, Staff?" I asked the staff nurse, forcing a confident look on my face to mask my apprehension. My "man o' war bay" training while at school in Government Secondary School Afikpo had taught me to be my best in moments of great challenge. My experience as a captain and as a school and college leader had prepared me to handle situations with confidence when others looked up to me for guidance and direction. I must not be seen to be unsure of my footsteps. I must not be seen afraid.

"They fought again. These minerals are tearing the community to pieces. This one is very bad," the nurse said.

I went upstairs and changed into simpler shirt and trousers and went off to the hospital with the nurse. It was a horrible sight. Lacerations puncture wounds, broken bones, pools of blood on doorway, couches, stretchers—everywhere.

It was no time for detailed history taking as we used to do in UCH. We needed to start acting immediately, at least to save those that we could still save.

We moved into the theater where the nurses had already set up the surgical trays complete with appropriate sterilized instruments. We were in the operation theater till the early hours of the morning: suturing deep cuts, debriding wounds, doing the most of immobilization of broken bones that we could. We lost one of the patients that night due to absence of blood for transfusion as there was no functional blood bank. By the following morning, we referred two to the University College Hospital.

It was later the following morning that I got the details of the probable cause of the mayhem. The feud was said to be over the mining rights which were said to be granted to a mineral prospecting company. The deal was said to be favored by one section of the community who were said to be enjoying the royalties, to the exclusion of the other section. The disadvantaged section was therefore fighting back. The communal fighting was said to be a regular event. It therefore appeared that nature's blessing was turning out as a curse to the community.

Within a week at Igettu, I had got myself familiar with the hospital. I had also been taken around the town by the NS to places of interest, including a visit to the traditional ruler of the town, the *oba* of Igettu who himself was said to be aligned to the group that favored the mining rights.

I took Agie back to Ibadan after a week at Igettu since their classes were still in progress.

The potentials of the hospital at Igettu were much. The limiting factor was the lack of coordination and continuity. The security situation occasioned by the communal crises at that time was poor, and that, as of then, tended to scare away meaningful development including residence of health personnel. Otherwise, Igettu was a very beautiful town with beautiful hills and a hospitable population.

I suddenly found new maturity by the enormous responsibility imposed upon me by being the physician in charge, the administrative head, and the chief accounting officer of the hospital. There were usually so many papers to sign, so many vouchers, local purchase orders, sick leave certificates, police reports, leave authorizations—so many intricate things that I had hitherto taken for granted for the one year that I had worked in a large establishment like UCH.

The difficulties which I experienced at Igettu as the chief executive of the relatively small hospital made me appreciate the enormous work which those who administered megainstitutions like the UCH were doing to keep services functioning smoothly. Hitherto we were prone to incessant complaints and criticisms when little things went wrong. We were even ready to carry placards in condemnation and protest even over small lapses. My experience during the service year taught me better to appreciate other people in positions of high responsibility. I learnt basic administrative functions from the nursing superintendent and even from the other staff of the hospital, experiences that I would otherwise never have acquired.

After the first few days of my work at Igettu General Hospital, I found that there was no functioning clinical laboratory in the hospital. As a consequence of that, it was not possible to investigate or confirm fairly simple medical problems. In the absence of a clinical diagnostic laboratory, medical diagnoses of the clinical ailments were based almost entirely on the physical signs and symptoms without laboratory diagnostic confirmation. The only laboratory investigation that could be carried out in the hospital was simple urine analysis using a dipstick. Even the simplest blood glucose monitoring machine was not available. We could not ascertain any patient's electrolyte and urea status. We could not even stain any blood specimen and check for malaria parasites even in an environment where malaria was endemic. There were neither the necessary staining materials nor even a light microscope. For me, coming from a background where many laboratory investigations were routine for every newly admitted patient, the situation was almost intolerable. I started to wonder how the hospital had been operating for so long without these basic facilities.

The nursing superintendent was very helpful to me in making necessary contacts. Within the first six weeks of my arrival to Igettu, I was able to secure a microscope and a few laboratory reagents from the Ministry of Health in Ibadan. We also got blood glucose monitoring machines, a centrifuge, a hemoglobinometer, and a hematocrit counter.

There were three rooms at one end of the outpatient's buildings that were simply not being put to any meaningful use. Checking through these rooms I found that one of them had shelves in it and that another had tables and office chairs and two stools. The third room had drawers and a ceramic sink and a nonfunctioning tap. It was obvious that that part of the hospital was meant to be a laboratory. In the absence of effective use, dust, empty cartons, and lizards had taken over the possession of the rooms.

Within two days of their "discovery," the rooms had been converted into a side room laboratory, and we put a bold door sign of LABORATORY across the front doors to serve as a permanent reminder that a laboratory was there and only needed equipping and staffing. We then commenced the necessary letter and legwork to persuade the Ministry of Health to get the laboratory fully functional. For a while, I functioned as physician, surgeon, obstetrician, and laboratory technologist. We took photographs of the new laboratory and sent to Ibadan with some of our equipment and personnel requests. By the end of the third month in Igettu, a fully functional medical laboratory was at the general hospital, and a qualified laboratory technologist, a youth corper, had been posted to the hospital. I was thus able to publish an article in the *Youth Corps Journal* with the title: "A Laboratory Is Born." A combination of these and other humble efforts at the Igettu General Hospital and in the community were later to win me many letters of commendation and a commendation from the State National Youth Service Corps.

The Stone Which the Builders Rejected

My one-year sojourn at the Igettu General Hospital was very memorable. I learnt a lot, and I also imparted quite some knowledge. With the excellent cooperation I got from the nursing and other staff, we were jointly able once again to get the place "alive." I believe the hospital must have been set up with lofty ideas in mind by its founding fathers. Years of neglect and an unjustified and morbid fear and perhaps exaggerated gossips about the town scared doctors and other professionals from the place despite the obvious hospitality, which I observed, the community accorded to strangers. During my short stay at Igettu after my initial tour to the oba, the traditional ruler of the community, I made several visits to the headmasters of the schools.

I visited the leaders of the Christian and Moslem communities. I visited leaders on both sides of the political and economic divide. I visited the German-born chief executive of the mining company and his wife, both very amiable individuals. Indeed the chief executive's wife and my wife became great friends, and the couple often visited us whenever my wife came to Igettu. They had a very big dog which they had trained so well that it was able to go on little errands like shutting the door and bringing some newspapers and news magazines from the living room to the patio. I was always so amazed at the intelligence of that dog which Mr and Mrs. Stan named Alp. We all took several photographs together, and those photos remain regular reminders of my days at Igettu.

As I visited different leaders of the community, I preached to them the need for peaceful coexistence. In a very humble, detached, and casual way, I discussed with them how God had blessed their community with such massive and widespread treasures hidden directly under the ground. I told them that my own native community was not so blessed. I subtly urged them to make peace, to unite, and to cooperate with one another so that they could benefit maximally from their God-given resources. I was neither a politician nor a religious leader nor a businessman, I told them. I was only a simple nonpartisan visitor who was in their midst to play my little role, serve out my time and go my way. I told them that it was only them who had the capability to heal their community. External intervention was only likely to be partisan, either in the immediate or in the distant future. I made my visits to the different groups most informal.

Initially I was afraid to visit alone, out of fear of what I had heard in the camp. But soon I found that most of the horror stories of hostility to strangers as peddled in the youth corps camp were false or at best exaggerated. I found that the people were really very friendly and that the perceived animosity between the two warring factions was most likely being fuelled by divisive elements, for possible maximum exploitation of the rich solid mineral resources. I did not make the visits too frequently so that they would not be boring. With time, I would stroll down alone without my car and visit one or two of the villagers. On one of these visits, as I was discussing with one of the community leaders in his house, we heard the sound of an explosion in a distance. The man's countenance immediately changed as he bent his head in one direction as if to discern more accurately the direction from which the sound was coming.

"You hear dat, Dokita? Na so dem de blast and steal our wealth."

He was drawing my attention to the sound of the blasting of the marble rocks and complained that people were again blasting and stealing their minerals. The distant sound of marble stones being blasted was a welcome sound to the group receiving royalties, but to the opposing side, it was a rallying call to arms.

I told my guest that he should regard the booming of the explosive as a clarion call for him and his faction to realize that it was time to meet with the opposing faction and make peace in the interest of their mutual community. He did not look convinced. But I believed that he was at least pacified to the extent that he was not further incited into increased rage.

My initial problem was a nonmastery of the language. I had lived in Ibadan for seven years, which time was enough for me to fully speak the native Yoruba language. Being in an academic community where English was routinely spoken throughout my stay in Ibadan, I did not get much exposure to the language even with Dele, Doyin, Bayo, and many of my other friends being Yorubas. I spoke and understood Yoruba only scantily, but not enough to communicate fluently with the natives at Igettu.

I therefore occasionally went out with two members of staff of the hospital, whom I made sure were not from Igettu for the sake of neutrality. I further made sure that one of them was a Christian and the other a Moslem to reflect the near-equal Christian and Moslem population strength of the town, even though religion was not the issue in contention.

The impact of my little peace moves during my one-year stay in Igettu is not for me to judge. The horror of broken bones, blood, the dead, and the dying during my first night in the hospital was scaring enough. But it was not long before I won the confidence of both sides through completely informal unrecorded visits and discussions. I could only estimate the impact of those nonpublicized humble efforts by the observation that from the time those rounds of discussions started (precisely my second month in Igettu) till I left Igettu nearly one year later, there was no longer a single recorded incident of communal clash that occurred in that community.

I did not and do not attribute the peace to our little efforts. Many other factors must have played significant roles. The fact however remained that for the first time in many years, somebody was able, by casual friendly and nonpartisan one-on-one discussions, to bring foes together. The villagers were quick to notice that we did not take sides with either side of the initial divide. They knew we were not there to stay or to exploit. Besides, what we told them made sense: that their economic destiny and their destiny as a people lay squarely in their hands. It was little wonder therefore that by the time I was leaving Igettu some eleven months later at the end of my service year, there were massive outpouring of emotions by the hospital community. Several groups in the town made me presents of wood carvings. The oba (traditional ruler) too was not left out. He invited me to his palace and in the presence of his chiefs gave me his royal blessings. Mr Stuan, the German chief executive of the mining community, requested for my permanent address. He did not inform me he was making me any present. He merely told me during my farewell visit to him that he and the mining community were very appreciative of my efforts and that I "would be hearing from them." By the time I got to my house at Aba at the end of my service year, one hundred bags of pure white marble chips each weighing twenty-five kilograms (about fifty-five pounds) were stacked in the open space between the main building and the goods store in my father's house. My father told me that a Mercedes Benz 911 truck had delivered them two days earlier with a letter for me. When I opened the letter, it simply read my name with the following words: "In appreciation of your honest and untiring efforts and impartial role in our community."

Under that inscription was the signature of the chief executive of the mining company, Mr Stuan.

It took me quite some time to believe that it was not a dream! That was the greatest material possession I had ever called my own. I tried without success to recount what particular exceptional role I had played to merit all that largesse. I was still marveling at the lavish party and many presents that the hospital community had organized and made just before my departure, and the many framed photographs and native dresses they presented, not knowing that the greatest was yet to come from the marble industry. It was simply far beyond my wildest expectations.

My posting to Igettu which many, and even I, believed was a punitive measure for my going on AWOL from the camp to wed turned to be a blessing, both for me and for the community of my posting. The many photographs I took with many of the groups I met at the Igettu remain as happy reminders to this day. The youth corps directorate had published the story of the laboratory which I founded in the *Youth Corps Journal* and had posted a laboratory technologist to the hospital to run the laboratory. The article was titled "A Laboratory Is Born." It had also awarded me a certificate of commendation for my services to the community and the hospital.

Igettu, the stone that the builders rejected, had become the cornerstone.

A Father in the Field

It was towards the last quarter of my posting at Igettu that my younger brother Fab, who by then was a medical student at the University of Ibadan, came to see me at Igettu. He brought me the happy news of the delivery of my first son at the University College Hospital. The baby weighing 2.8 kilograms (6.2 pounds) had arrived some two weeks before the due date. Both Agie and the baby were reported to be doing well. Since Agie went to the maternity room straight from her Clinical Students Hostel residence and I had no place of abode in Ibadan, I had to leave immediately for Ibadan to see Agie and the baby and to make arrangements about accommodation into which mother and baby would move in upon discharge from hospital and into which I would join them at the end of the service year. I was overjoyed to meet Agie and the new baby in good health. A father in the field had come to see his baby.

I was lucky to rent a two-bedroom apartment at a place called Agbowo directly opposite the gate of the university. I could only stay with Agie and the baby for two days before heading back to the hospital at Igettu. Two weeks after the baby's birth, Agie sat her part 2 pharmacology examination and was still able to pass with an A score.

At the end of my service year, I rejoined the University College Hospital for a postgraduate diploma program in anesthesiology. The program was run by the University of Ibadan Postgraduate School but the practical training was done at the University College Hospital.

I had initially intended to specialize in ear, nose, and throat surgery (ortho-rhino-laryngology). I was always fascinated by the dexterity of ENT surgeons, especially in dealing with troublesome foreign bodies in the throat and in the nose. I was often most thrilled when coins swallowed by small children and pebbles inserted deep into the nose by small children were removed. The instant relief to both the affected children and their apprehensive parents greatly impressed me.

Much as I was thrilled by ear, nose, and throat surgery, it had always been my wish to devote some reasonable time in the rural areas. The difficult health problems and the almost complete lack of good medical facilities in the rural areas like my town of origin made me resolve at the later part of my medical training to start considering going into general medical practice after my graduation. My experience at Igettu where I saw a very beautiful medical facility being so grossly underutilized, understaffed, and unduly underrated because of absence of a steady medical doctor made me change my mind about what to specialize in.

I began to see anesthesiology as a field that would prepare me for dealing with a cross section of the other disciplines in medicine, especially as regards being able to handle urgent resuscitative measures especially cardiopulmonary emergencies. I also considered the need for me to be able to have a patient ready for carrying out minor surgical procedures, which I might like to handle in an urban or rural setting where I might not be able, in general medical practice, to secure the services of an anesthesiologist.

Hence, I applied for and got accepted into the program in anesthesiology. We were four in the program for the year: a Ghanaian, an Indian, and two Nigerians.

About midway into the program, it became a little more encompassing than we had envisaged as courses in acupuncture and some aspects of Chinese medicine were touched upon. I had imagined that we would only deal with cardiopulmonary resuscitation and pain management, employing the various local and general anesthetic agents by spraying, infiltration, injection, or inhalation. We found that we had again to go through the principle of various surgical and obstetric procedures, which I thought I was already done with. The principles behind going through these procedures, of course, was that the anesthesiologist should be able to envisage the principles of the procedure that were to be performed so that he or she would be able to prepare for the anesthetic technique required for each procedure. I thus found that I had to be away from the house for very long hours, sometimes up to eighteen hours at a stretch. Those were very difficult times for my very young family, especially considering that my wife, with a baby who was still breast feeding, still had to grapple with her medicine, oral surgery, and dentistry postings. We were lucky that my mother-in-law, Agie's mom, soon arrived to help us out through those difficult days. Her presence made more time available for Agie and me to concentrate on our studies, and hence, I was able to pass the anesthesiology exams at first sitting.

I got employed in the department, and after some months I was given a higher position by the Ministry of Health in my home state.

The practice of anesthesiology in the University College Hospital was quite fascinating. It gave me the opportunity, as I expected, to be familiar with a cross section of procedures spanning through the entire surgical, obstetric, and some medical subunits.

Nothing gave me as much satisfaction as the cardiopulmonary resuscitative aspect of the practice. At the early stages of the training, tracheal intubations appeared so challenging to me, but with practice this, as well as getting the tiniest visible vein even on a day-old baby, became so very easy for me. It was all so fascinating even though anesthetizing for very protracted neurosurgical procedures sometimes lasting twelve or more hours at a stretch could be very challenging. The aspect of the practice that I did not like were the few situations where we worked with an unnecessarily pompous surgeon or gynecologist who would feel that everybody else working on a particular patient was subservient to him or her, simply because he or she was holding the scalpel. Such self-conceited surgeons would tend to bark orders at their subordinates and, sometimes, in a display of arrogant and unprofessional anger would throw instruments on the floor and bark insults when the wrong instruments were handed to them by their assistants. Some of these were often people who managed (sometimes after series of attempts) to scale through their medical school courses and were consoled with being "buffered" into certain departments. These were essentially colleagues who wrongly believed that one specialty was superior than another, but who easily forgot that the colleague they might be bluffing for easily and always beat them in all the courses that they did together. We had a few of such unfoundedly arrogant practitioners who chose to forget that specialties were more often a matter of choice, much as some specialties were more popular and consequently more competitive.

On two different occasions, I encountered such arrogant colleagues who failed to know the bounds beyond which they should not go with other colleagues in their chosen specialties. In each of these situations, I found it so easy to puncture these bluffs which were of course without merit. The ignorance was so badly punctured on each occasion that the "peacocks" could not any longer open their mouths or throw foolish tantrums whenever some of us were around.

Mr Peacock, as one of these surgeons was nicknamed, was in the habit of coming late for scheduled surgeries, and whenever he came in, he would start verbally bullying the nurses and other theater workers. He failed to realize the fact that someone liked nursing and choosing to take nursing as a profession did not necessarily mean that the person was not capable of doing medicine if he or she so desired. The fact that the nurse and other theater staff had succumbed to his bullying tendencies for so long had probably emboldened Peacock until he went overboard by attempting to extend his conquest to his colleagues in other departments including mine. Right from secondary school, I had always known that bullies were often cowards. There was no question of giving a bully any time to consolidate. You cut him down to size at his fist bullying attempt. Thereafter, there would be mutual respect between all the different cadres of staff. And that worked perfectly well in that particular instance to the utmost delight of the staff who had hitherto suffered in silence.

The Minor Reversal—Going Back East

It was not long after a vacation trip to Owerri, the capital of my home state, that I received a letter from the Ministry of Health offering me the post of senior registrar in anesthesia "as a result of my successful application and interview" for the post. The fact of course was that I neither applied for nor did I attend any interview. I was later to find out that the State Ministry of Health had many surgeons and obstetricians in its employment at its several general hospitals. Because of the absence of a qualified anesthesiologist, certain procedures that could have been performed had to be referred out to the teaching hospitals.

The Ministry of Health had therefore engaged the services of a retired professor of anesthesiology from one of the teaching hospitals on contract to establish a formal Department of Anesthesia. The contracted professor, a highly experienced and revered practitioner, worked with nurse anesthetists to cover the anesthetic needs of the hospital. They covered the theaters as well as other areas of the hospital where pain management and intubations were called for, including the intensive care unit (ICU). The ministry probably felt that, since the professor was a contract senior officer, they needed to survey for and seek the services of a more permanent doctor in that discipline, hence the letter of offer "after successful application and interview," was sent to me—without a formal application and interview. I had, during an earlier visit to Owerri, accompanied my friend Dr Igo to the health management board when the latter went to see the chairman of the board. In the process, I got into discussions with the chairman about my field of specialization. The board chairman had casually asked me whether I would like to join the State Ministry of Health on an accelerated-promotion basis. Even without giving much thought to it, I had replied in the affirmative. That was all the application and interview that was needed for the offer of employment a few weeks later.

Despite the fact that I had literally dug in at the University College Hospital with furnished two-bedroom apartment, a wife, two lovely toddlers, and a wide array of friends, I saw the offer in my home state as a call to service. I saw the need to go and let the people from my particular area of origin benefit a bit from my training, especially as Ibadan already had quite a number of anesthesiologists while there was near-complete paucity in my state. The fact that there was such scarcity of qualified personnel in a field that serviced several crucial areas of medical practice made it more mandatory that I should go to offer services. Besides, my acceptance of the offer would bring me close to my old school friends and members of my larger family. The opportunity for a faster rise in rank was also there for me since virtually all the positions were still vacant, and my step of entry was slightly higher than what I had at the teaching hospital. Finally, my going would offer me the opportunity for fulfillment of a childhood ambition: to have a business of my own, render beneficial service to my home community, and derive some satisfaction from the realization that one's training made a positive impact on the society.

As I considered the possible positive results of an acceptance of the offer, I was not unaware of the obvious negative impacts of my movement at that stage. My wife was still in the university pursuing her degree in dentistry. My first son was under two years old, and my second son was six months old. I had never trained myself to cook, and I had no delusions about the difficulties I would encounter living with very young children even with Nanneka, Agie's cousin whom my mother-in-law had brought down to live with us. Nanneka herself was still a child, barely eight years old, and on several occasions I had seen her and our older boy jumping up and down the dining tables and climbing over the cupboards with none controlling the other. The first week that she was with us, she had turned on the tap of the filtered water machine in the living room and flooded the house by the time we were back. She had come to help take care of the two younger kids, but being so young herself she often needed to be taken care of too.

To Go or Not to Go

Going back to the east was a very difficult decision to take in view of the fact that I was already quite comfortable in my position at the University College Hospital. I had made many friends, and I had a fairly comfortable accommodation. I still had a very young family, and my wife was still in school. The choice appeared to be between a secure present and an uncertain future, between the known and a possibly precarious future. Prayers and mere weighing of the options did not initially appear to provide a solution. But we needed to take the bull by the horns.

Finally, Agie and I decided that I should go.

Agie was to move into a one-bedroom apartment with her good friend and classmate Flossy.

I was to set out with Nanneka and the two boys to take up an appointment in a state public service system, which we though offered better prospects for advancement in one's career but turned out to be neither as well funded nor as well organized and disciplined as the system we used to know.

Agie accompanied us to Owerri and stayed with us for two days before going back to Ibadan. The Ministry of Health checked us into a hotel. The chairman of the board that oversaw the state hospitals had told me when I reported to him on my arrival that I was going to be checked into the state-owned hotel, which as of then was the best hotel in town. I was asked to meet the chief finance officer for the authorization paper for movement into the hotel. The chief finance officer appeared a little edgy when I presented him with the chairman's note which read as follows: "CFO, please check this officer into appropriate hotel."

I did not know the works of the civil service system. I did not know the interplay of vested personal or group interests at play in the system, especially in the financial system.

When the chief finance officer collected the chairman's note from me, he read it and stared steadily at me for about a minute, as if to size me up. He then asked me, "Are you familiar with the hotels in Owerri?"

I told him I was new to Owerri and did not know the hotels. He smiled wryly, scribbled something on a piece of paper, signed it, and put his official stamp on it.

He gave the paper to me without uttering another word. I collected the paper, thanked him, and left his office without reading what was written on it.

When I got outside of his office, I saw that the paper bore the name of a hotel quite different from what the board chairman had told me and had the words *full lodging and accommodation* with the signature, name, and stamp of the chief finance officer.

Outside the office, and sitting on a stool with a small rough-looking table with some old newspaper on it, was Sammy, a tall slim middle-aged man. As soon as the man saw me coming out of the chief finance officer's room, he beckoned on me.

"CFO him don check you in?"

I said, "Yes." I greeted the man and walked out towards where I parked my car under a tree shade. I did not know how the tall lanky man who turned out to be one of the office messengers managed to know that I was being checked into a hotel room since I had never met him nor talked with him.

As I was about to enter my car, I saw the tall lanky man walking up towards me. As he hurried up towards me, he kept looking behind intermittently.

"Oga," he said, "which hotel CFO check you into?" I pulled the CFO's paper from my shirt pocket and called out the name of the hotel. The man shook his head and said, "Oga, make I tell you, that hotel e-no good. Na the CFO him hotel. Na him own am. E-no good. Make you go tell chairman. Say, you wan go Imo Hotels. That one na better hotel. Na him better pass that CFO him hotel. The hotel wey CFO write for dat paper no be better hotel. Na so dat man de do."

All that implied that the CFO had checked me into a poor-quality hotel which belonged to him, contrary to the directives of the chairman which was that I should be checked into Imo Hotels, which was the "appropriate hotel" for me as a senior officer. I immediately remembered that the chairman had mentioned Imo Hotels when he was talking to me. Apparently Imo Hotel was the best hotel in town at that material time.

I was in a dilemma. I did not want to start making trouble from my first day in the ministry. I felt I should first go and see the hotel that the CFO sent me to. If it was good enough, I might as well accept it irrespective of its ownership.

The messenger had hurried away after he had advised me. He did not want to be seen long with me.

I asked my way down to the hotel where the CFO had referred me to. As soon as I parked beside the open gutter in front of the hotel, I saw the CFO driving through the badly rusted metal gate leading into the hotel premises.

The hotel itself was one dilapidated old building with rusted mosquito gauze on windows and a few broken glass panes. The old paint on the outside walls was begging for retouching. It was located very close to the noisy daily market, and everything about it was uninviting.

I did not need to enter. I needed no further confirmation of what the messenger had told me. It was obvious that the chief finance officer had vested interest in the hotel and had referred me there contrary to the instruction of the board chairman.

I entered my car and drove straight back to the premises of the hospitals management board. The board chairman was walking towards his car when I arrived back. His chauffer had already reversed the car to face the road. As the chairman, a benevolent-looking senior citizen, saw me he said, "Doctor, you did not check in again?"

"I came back to confirm, sir, which hotel you wanted to check me into," I said.

"Imo Hotels, of course. Didn't the CFO tell you so?" the chairman said.

"No, sir, it looks like there is some little mix up," I said.

The chairman then went back into the building but came back within a few minutes.

"The CFO is not on seat, but it's no problem. Go to Imo Hotels and check in. We shall straighten everything tomorrow morning," the chairman concluded as he entered his car and was driven off. I felt relieved that I had not been instrumental to any row at that stage. I was however resolved in my mind that if I stayed in that system long enough, I would certainly be instrumental to puncturing such nasty practices that could only lead to a putrefaction of our society. Much as I laid no claim to being a social crusader, I was fully conscious of the old saying that goes "Bad men thrive when good men choose to maintain their silence."

I also easily recalled an article written by an internationally respected Nigerian writer and which I had read in a newspaper while in secondary school which had warned, just prior to the Nigerian Civil War that a compromise with blatant evil practices would only lead to a putrefaction of the nation.

I branched off into the general hospital to collect my family, whom I had dropped in the residence of my friend while doing the board rounds. By the time we got to Imo Hotels, we saw the chief finance officer waiting outside the reception. He walked up to me and said, "Doc, I have come to check you in. Do you have that paper I gave you in the office?"

Without uttering a word, I brought out the paper with which he had referred me to his personally owned hotel and gave it to him. He put it into his pocket and said, "This is a very nice hotel."

I was not sure which of two hotels he was then referring to as "very nice hotel," his own badly dilapidated hotel, into which he had surreptitiously wanted to check me, or the one in which we were.

There were no further apologies and no further discussions.

It was later that I found out that the CFO, after failing to let me in to his hotel, had driven back to the board and was told that I was seen outside the office discussing with the board chairman. The latter information probably prompted his change of gear, and perhaps, his rush to Imo Hotels to attempt to set things right.

My family and I were checked into a newly completed part of the hotel behind the front building. It was very neat. The air-conditioning system was very good, and other facilities worked, and for the first night in many days, I had a sound sleep and a very good meal. I was told that I was entitled to the accommodation for two weeks and that whatever food that we ate was also taken care of. Any drinks consumed were however to be paid for, by me.

At the end of the two weeks allowed, I found that I had made no progress with securing accommodation in town. That was in spite of the fact that I had informed a lot of people to help me look for any accommodation I could rent. The buildings to be rented were simply not available. The state was only recently created, and most of the available buildings had been taken up by civil servants who had moved in first from the parent state from which Imo State was carved out.

After the expiration of two weeks in the hotel, I was given a note to inform me that the official duration to be paid for by my employers was over, "unless it was officially extended." I went to the ministry to complain that I had not yet found accommodation. I was referred to the chief finance officer who told me that nothing could be done about the situation. He offered no solutions, no alternatives. May be there might have been a solution if I had agreed to stay in his hotel. He obviously was about to extract his "pound of flesh" for my refusal to stay in his hotel. I was in another dilemma. I could not pay for the hotel from my pocket for even up to one week. I even started considering the possibility of going back to my former job at the University College Hospital Ibadan since I still had up to two weeks safety period to change my mind.

I mentioned my dilemma, on my way out of the CFO's office, to that benevolent messenger who had by that time become my friend.

"Make you go tell chairman," Sammy advised me.

"Him fit extend it for you," he said.

The messenger's advice that I should appeal to the chairman was very helpful. Luckily, too, the chairman was "on seat" in his office. I walked straight to him. As usual, he was very understanding. He told me that the period allowed "by state" was two weeks. He then said that he would extend it by two weeks for me under "special considerations" as allowed. He again gave me a note to the CFO who this time immediately endorsed it to Imo Hotels without a word.

My first day at work at the general hospital was a bit of a nightmare. I was probably expecting too much. I had come with the background of the premier teaching hospital in the country where virtually everything worked, from the personnel to the equipments.

I had never imagined that an officer could be absent from his duty post for several days at his whims without his subordinate staff knowing where he or she was and when he or she would report for duty. I had never imagined that subordinate staff could have unrestricted access to documents and confidential materials to the extent that they could sit over other people's personal files and entertain themselves by comparing comments by their superior officers on their files. I had never imagined that duly scheduled cases that had been fully prepared and wheeled in for surgery could be offhandedly wheeled off the theater at the whims and caprices of a doctor for reasons other than medical or ethical. I had never imagined that an operating theater would be functional without adequate changing places for the staff working in the theater and with toilet facilities so unkempt, and most people would accept same as normal. There was no sitting room for the doctors, nurses, and other staff. In between cases, the doctors and nurses would either crowd in one tiny sisters' office or stand in the corridor.

I had reported my assumption of duty to the administrative head of the hospital addressed as the chief consultant surgeon in charge. He appeared a highly principled gentleman who spoke sparingly. He stammered a bit as he spoke and that was probably why he chose not to speak much. He also appeared to have time consciousness. I got to his office a little before 8:00 a.m. By 8:00 a.m. the chief consultant surgeon was in the office, a most unusual thing for a chief executive in the local situation, where it was not unusual for the chief executive to be in the office as late as 9:00 or 10:00 a.m. on a routine basis. The reasons often proffered for the executive lawlessness was that the messengers and cleaners needed time to get the offices ready before the boss would be chauffeured in.

The chief consultant surgeon in charge (CCS I/C as usually abbreviated), after interviewing me having read the letter from the board chairman, wrote minutes on my file and sent me to the chief consultant anesthesiologist.

For four consecutive days, the chief consultant anesthesiologist was "not on seat." Rather I was referred to the principal nursing superintendent who appeared to be deputizing for him. Apparently the department boss and his nurse deputies were quite comfortable at how things got on in the department without an additional doctor in the department. That was understandable since each allowed the other maximum time to carry on as they wished. A new doctor in the department was likely to come to work daily and might disrupt the comfortable equilibrium that prevailed, albeit to the disadvantage of the end users, the patient, and the system.

The other nurse anesthetists, too, appeared to loathe the presence of another physician in the department. The only doctor in the department before now was the head of department himself, and since he was almost always "not on seat," he did not bother the other staff in the department. But another physician might present a problem, especially if he was a younger officer who might want to come to work daily. People were not paid by the number of hours of work done, but merely on the basis of the staff having his or her name on the payroll. The salary would come whether the individual worked or not, whether he or she spent three quarters of official time in private pursuits, or did not even report for duties regularly.

The tardiness was called "not on seat."

The principle was called "government work."
The team leader was called *oga*
And oga was a boss, not a servant
Attention from oga was a favor, not a duty
His loyalty was to himself, not the people
His service must be personally appreciated, or it may not be rendered
His official car for him is personal property.
Say what you like, it must take him to socials.
Feel how you may, it must chauffer him to church.
Write what you may, it must drive him to friends
The people, the true owners of the property, can go to hell.
You are said to be jealous if you complain.
The man at the top may not be any better.
He looks the other way as his subordinates ruin the system.
His own can of worms he must protect.
His erring subordinates his failings know.
He must not "offend" them, or they blow the whistle.
At the end of the day, the nation suffers.
At the end of it all, we all will suffer,
As the iniquities pile up and themselves compound,
Until the day of reckoning which will surely come.
But when it does eventually come,
It is easy to forget.
And the man who besmeared the system
Is regarded as a victim
And the man who tries to sanitize the system is regarded as draconian.
But the day of reckoning for the spoilers will surely come
And the anger of the people will be fully justified.

I had never before my arrival at the general hospital worked with nurse anesthetists. In fact, prior to my return to Imo State, I had never seen one. The University College Hospital where I worked operated a system which utilized only physicians as anesthetists, but the General Hospital Owerri operated the system that trained and utilized nurses in handling anesthetic cases, under the supervision of physician anesthetists.

I remembered some seminars of anesthetists we had while I was at Ibadan. There was trading of verbal punches between the participants from the universities that utilized physician anesthetists only, and the lone university hospital that trained and utilized nurse anesthetists. The former had accused the latter of starting the nurse anesthetist program out of the desire to lift from themselves the responsibility and burden of the often tasking job of carrying out and supervising all anesthesia-involving theater procedures. They further accused them of shirking their professional responsibilities and compromising and violating ethical standards. The lone university hospital that trained and utilized nurse anesthetists had countered the allegations by accusing the physician-anesthetists-only university hospitals of bigotry and selfishness and of not being in compliance with current trends that opens up doors and disseminates information. They further accused the former of relishing in, capitalizing on, and contributing to the nationwide shortage of trained anesthetists. For the surgeons and obstetricians that attended that seminar, the direction of their sympathy understandably was with the lone teaching hospital that trained and utilized the services of nurse anesthetists. One urologist at the seminar in his contribution to the discussions almost spoilt the case for the lone teaching hospital by concluding his presentation with a note of gratitude in these words, “If for nothing else, we the surgeons, thank you, nurse-anesthetist trainers, for providing us with a ready and cheap source of anesthetic coverage.” The statement tended to create the impression that the only reason for training nurse anesthetists was to provide cheap labor without due regard for quality and standards.

Coming from a background of physician-anesthetist-only hospital therefore, it was initially difficult for me, especially without proper directives, to know where I fitted into the equation. I also found that over 95 percent of the surgeries that were carried out at the hospital were those that could be carried out using spinal anesthesia or epidural anesthesia. I was not sure whether the limitation was consequent upon limitation in anesthetic coverage or whether it was a consequence of limited surgical competence. Anesthetic-coverage limitation one could understand, due to irregular presence of the contract anesthesiologist. Surgical incompetence was difficult to comprehend because many members of the surgical teams were highly trained fellows of renowned British professional bodies. The only reason I could adduce for the predominance of cases like appendectomy and herniorrhaphy over the major surgical cases that were often referred off to the teaching hospitals was the tendency towards quick returns (on investment) or a gradual loss of skills due to protracted lack of practice.

Such cases as were often left for the registrars and junior residents in the teaching hospitals were often the mainstay of the surgical lists of the most senior surgeons in the general hospital. Of course, one would not expect a professor of anesthesiology to spend whole days, five days a week giving spinal anesthesia. He would rather, with a clear conscience, train nurse anesthetists to carry out these. In any case what would he be doing at the hospital all day long with no research material and no academic challenges? Again, even if he wanted to engage in research, where were the equipments and the funding?

Two dilapidated Boyle's anesthetic machines, cylinders of oxygen and nitrous oxide, and some bottles of halothane, packs of lignocaine, ketamine hydrochloride, atropine, a few worn-out endotreacheal tubes and one adult-type laryngoscope were virtually all the tools available to him. I remembered how I had to run to the boot of my car to get my personal pediatric resuscitation set—a pediatric laryngoscope, pediatric Ambu bag, pediatric-sized tubes, and all—on the first day I was faced with a pediatric emergency case that needed immediate intubation. I started to wonder what had been the fates of similar cases in the past in the absence of these tools which ought to be routine accompaniments of any hospital emergency pack. Subsequent appeals to the hospital to provide these relatively inexpensive tools did not materialize up the time I left the establishment.

It was obvious from the beginning that my boss, the head of the anesthesia unit, was not quite sure what roles he wanted me to play. The system was already comfortable with a titular head of the department, who for the reasons earlier adduced was rarely present in the hospital despite the fact that his office was much more expansive than that of even the overall head of the hospital. Only the head of the Dept. of Anesthesia and the overall head of the hospital had private offices. All the other consultants only ad a table and a chair in the General Outpatients Department (GOPD) as their offices. I learnt that the provision of an extralarge and well-furnished office was one of the conditions under which the professor appeared to have agreed to take up the contract appointment. The office had different compartments including a miniclass room and a common room for the nurse anesthetists. It was never envisaged that another doctor would join the department, and hence no provision had been made for an expansion. It was therefore understandable why there was some form of resentment in the department for another doctor.

I joined the department as a senior registrar, a senior resident, and it was only the following year that I became a consultant.

Because the system had, as it were, stabilized, it was a little difficult for either the head of department and more so the surgical team to accommodate a young doctor who was enthusiastic to work and who, coming from a well-known teaching hospital, might not take dictations from them as would most of the nurse anesthetists. The surgical team appeared quite comfortable not having any physician anesthetist, even if the absence of one limited the scope of the surgical procedures that could be carried out. Nobody really appeared to care. Unlike the teaching hospitals, there was little or no research work going on in the general hospital, and as long as the teaching hospitals would continue to take the "difficult" cases referred to them, the good times could continue, with the appendicectomies and herniorraphies. These could remain the mainstay of the listed cases.

A new doctor in the Department of Anesthesia might not succumb to the whims and caprices as might be in place and might insist on certain things being done according to the rules. Such practices as rushing in a cold case straight from some private practice somewhere right into theater for anesthesia and surgery without proper preanesthetic laboratory investigations, documentation, and preparation would of course not be tolerated under a qualified anesthesiologist. This could be forced upon the nurse anesthetists, sometimes with disastrous consequences. Situations like that were not likely to be accepted by this new young doctor. The surgical team appeared happy and comfortable with the head of anesthesia not being regular at work. They could therefore order the nurse anesthetists and more or less bully them into accepting cases that were not quite fit for anesthesia. Occasionally, the latter could be placated or favored by having some of their private cases attended to surgically, through the back door. The population not being fully aware of their rights would simply accept casualties as "an act of God," even when disastrous consequences resulted from such negligent practices which obviously were "acts of men." A new doctor in anesthesia who was likely to show presence was not likely to be an "advantage," especially as most of the cases were what were referred to as bread-and-butter surgical procedures, which might not even require the presence of a physician anesthetist.

The only consultant neurosurgeon in the hospital had resigned about two months prior to my arrival. Some said he could not stand the deficiencies in the system. The other five consultants in surgery including the head of the hospital were general surgeons. There were also four obstetrician/gynecologists; one ear, nose, and throat surgeon; and one dental surgeon, who routinely used the main operation theater and consequently the services of the Anesthesia Department. The emergency room and the intensive care unit also utilized the services of Anesthesia Department.

Since there were no challenging cases that would necessitate careful planning, my initial deployment entailed getting into the theater and administering spinal anesthesia. Only once in a long while did the need arise to utilize inhalation anesthetics. After sometime, the cases became so routine that having to go to the theater daily to repeat the same thing on the same type of nonchallenging cases started becoming boring. I began to see why the professor was not usually around. Perhaps I was expecting too much. Perhaps I was becoming unduly elitist in trying to compare a general hospital with a university teaching hospital.

As time went on however, the type of cases began to change. Maybe it was a coincidence or maybe my occasional teasing of some of the surgeons as bread-and-butter surgeons encouraged them to start taking more complicated surgical procedures. Possibly, too, the presence of a resident anesthetist beefed up the confidence of the surgical team to start taking on cases they might not have liked to take without physician anesthetic coverage. The practice started becoming more interesting. I was not unaware of the resentment from a few members of the department who probably felt that my presence diminished their relevance. That was only a natural feeling in a situation like that, and I felt that the best one could do in situations like that was to ensure professionalism and steadfastness. A few applied different types of threat and blackmails trying to employ their closeness to the administrative leadership of the establishment to force my hands into accepting certain things.

On two occasions, after threat and blackmail had failed, the offers came to me to state my percentage if only I would allow the passage of certain cases which might not have met with the required criteria for safe administration of anesthesia. It was a double-edged sword. If I should succumb to that most unprofessional and obviously dangerous temptation, patients would be put in obvious jeopardy. On the other hand, if I should stick to my principles and turn down such cases till the required tests and other preparations were made, then I would be accused of obstructing essential surgeries and impeding progress in the work of the hospital. Should the latter complaint get to the ministry, the chances were that with the numbers and influence of the surgical team, I would be somehow said to be at fault, or at best told to "cooperate with the surgical team."

It was so tempting since it was alleged that "everybody was doing it." Everybody doing it, of course, meant that everybody was taking money privately from patients before consenting to put them on the list for surgery, a practice that ran contrary to the regulations at that time and more so to my conscience.

There might be nothing ordinarily wrong with a patient paying the surgeon for a surgical procedure if the payment was made officially, without coercion and within the bounds of the law. If such payments were officially permissible, then, of course, I as anesthetist would willingly and officially fix my own fees. After all, intramural private practice was being practiced officially in some Western countries from where we took our cue. But the prevailing law did not make room for a patient to be stealthily pulled in from some undocumented private facility after being privately billed. Therefore where corners are cut to get the same patient into the operation list in a government hospital where the official fees will again need to be paid, there would be no moral justification for accepting an unofficial percentage. One would indeed be hard put to accept such smuggled patients for anesthesia except if it was a genuine emergency. Again, where there were grounds for an anesthetist to be paid a fee for a procedure in a public facility, such an anesthetist should have his fee paid in his own recognition and as of right. The fee should not come as a percentage of any surgeon's fees.

I did not see much of my head of department. Indeed, I do not think I saw him more than four times during the eight months we worked together. I saw him in the operation room only on two occasions. On both occasions, the surgeons taking the cases appeared so nervous that I started wondering what was amiss. It was either the surgeons were intimidated by his mere presence, or they were not so confident and feared the criticism that his wealth of experience might bring. As soon as he left the theater on each of the two occasions, and the nurse anesthetists again took over, the surgeons again brightened up and started cracking jokes. He obviously towered well above the institution being a professional senior to all, including the administrative head of the institution.

Homeless the Second Time

After a total of four weeks of my stay at the board-sponsored hotel room, I was informed that further stay in the hotel would be at my expense. I needed to pack out since I could not afford the cost of even five days stay. But I had not found accommodation. I was about to experience a second period of homelessness, two years after my wedding day's state of homelessness.

I had sent messages round to all the people I knew that came from Arondizuogu, my hometown, informing them of my plight and requesting that they help me find accommodation. The messages paid off at least temporarily. Two days to my final stay in the hotel, Injoma, a very amiable senior civil service employee from my town, visited me in the hotel room and informed me that I could temporarily move into a house that he was acting as a caretaker in. The house was newly completed, but power had not been connected to it. I moved into the house with my little family of three, two young sons and the nine-year-old young girl looking after them. My wife was back to school at Ibadan.

The house was not furnished, no chairs, no tables, no window blinds, just a freshly completed and freshly painted empty house. I went to the market and bought three mats. The mats were made from raffia, the type that could be rolled. I also bought four small pillows and three mosquito nets. I set up the three mosquito nets using strings tied to the window burglary proofs on one end and two hollow blocks which I picked up from within the compound at the other end. The mosquito nets thus sloped from a height at the window to the ground. The mats were spread under the mosquito nets.

It was a big anticlimax, moving from the comfort of a cozy four-star hotel to a ramshackle dwelling devoid of all comfort including the very basics. I chose to see it as a jamboree but for the discomfort of the terrazzo floor with only a thin sun-bathing raffia mat covering it. That night, I and my little family had bread, corned beef, and Ovaltine (a cocoa drink) for supper. I tried to enjoy the "fun" of eating from the floor. The children appeared to enjoy the fun having so many empty rooms to run around in, as opposed to the enclosed one room in the hotel. I saw the situation reminiscent of the immediate postwar period at Enugu when I shared a mat on the floor with my two brothers Fab and Chris.

The following morning after moving into the temporary accommodation, I thought of purchasing some furniture, but I was not sure yet of the type of apartment I would eventually secure. Besides, I wanted to wait until I collected my first month's paycheck, which I had calculated would have been available. Besides, it made sense to conserve whatever funds I had since I was not sure how much would be required to pay as down payment for house rent.

That afternoon I went to the accounts office in the board offices to ask for my paycheck since I had completed a month. I was shocked to be told that no payments would be made to me until after about three months!

The deference of payment of salary was a complete deviation from what I had been used to in the University College Hospital. The deference was not an official policy but was apparently an internal practice. It was said that it was a way for the top financial managers to benefit from new employees' salaries by fixing the first few months of such salaries in deposit accounts and collecting the interest up front. Since most of the victims would still be studying the system, they would not complain too much.

The temporary residence into which I moved in with my young family did not have a gate nor a compound wall as did most of the other new buildings in that newly developing area of Owerri. The car garage was however attached to the house and had good doors, and the windows all had burglary proofs. I had gone to sleep on my mat after the hard day's job of packing out from the hotel room. I must have had a very sound sleep since I did not get up at night, not even to visit the bathroom. Neither of my little boys also got up as they occasionally did.

At about half past five in the morning, however, I noticed the rays of the streetlights shinning not only through the windows, which were devoid of curtains, but also through the doors which I found ajar. I called on Nanneka, the little girl who looked after our little boys, and reminded her that she should always remember to shut the doors after her at night to prevent entry of mosquitoes. She however told me that she had not gone out of the room since the night. I started to wonder whether I could have forgotten to shut the door the previous night. That was not likely because the rays from the streetlights would have reminded me. I then tried to shut the door only to find that the tongue of the lock could not catch. The door opened back after me. I took a closer look at the door and found that the door lock had been forced open and destroyed! It had rained the previous day, and the grounds of the compound were still wet and muddy since they were not yet cemented.

I needed no further proof to be assured that someone had broken into the house while we were asleep. Further proofs were there! Looking out through the door I could see large footmarks, large toes, not shoes! Leaning against the wall by the window, I saw one broken fluorescent tube that was not there the previous day when we moved in. Even though the house had not been connected to the public power supply service, the lightbulbs had been installed. These must have been common unsophisticated burglars. They saw nothing else worth stealing, and they had to unscrew and steal lightbulbs and fluorescent tubes. Or maybe they were not aware that the light had not been connected, and they did not want to risk having the lights accidentally switched on while they were on their little "operation." They or their informants must have noticed our car drive in the previous day and fancied that the new occupants of the building must have moved in with a lot of very useful properties worth stealing. They must have felt terribly disappointed seeing one wretched man and three young children, who could not even afford a bed, lying on the hard floor with a raffia mat with only an old mosquito net over them. They must have taken pity on us and had chosen to leave us alone, as one of their own, the wretched of the earth.

It was not the era of car stealing, and so the car parked in the garage did not attract the burglars. The garage door was not even opened. I was scared. I really was, not because of what the burglars might ask us to bring. I was scared for our personal safety. There had been stories about victims from whom robbers could not extract enough valuables. There was the story of the popular attorney who had these nocturnal unwelcome visitors. After they could not get enough cash from the attorney they called him "a big for nothing lawyer" and gave him the beating of his life before leaving the house.

After inspecting to ensure that the car was not broken into, we contacted our friend Injoma and some other colleagues who advised us on security measures which we had to put in place. We lived in the building for a further three weeks before we were able to rent a three-bedroom apartment that was being vacated by an old friend Mr Nchebe. One year advance payment was required for the apartment, but we were able to afford only six months payment which the landlord was kind enough to accept on concessionary grounds.

I was at the end of my second month into my new appointment but still had not been paid any salary. The money I had at hand was running out. What I was left with after making an advance payment for six months in my new apartment would barely last my little household for one week. While we were at the University College Hospital, children one—year old and younger were given free supply of tinned powdered milk twice a month, two tins every two weeks. We therefore did not have to spend money on milk for supplementation of breast feeding for our little baby. At Owerri both sources of free milk were not existent, and so we needed to purchase powdered milk. For the first time, I felt the financial impact of lack of free baby feeding. One of my brothers Jike had come from Aba to stay with us at Owerri. I did not know that Jike had heard me lamenting aloud one day that I was running short of money even for our feeding. By the following morning, my smart brother told me he wanted to go to Aba. By evening, he was back to Owerri with the huge sum of four hundred naira from my father. That sum was equivalent to about two hundred dollars at that time, a sharp contrast to the value of the currency barely two years earlier when I went to Nnokwa to marry. Jike must have told Papa (our father) the extent of my financial plight. I was later to learn that Papa had told him that he would not be alive and see his son and his grandchildren starve, be they doctors or night soil men. The money was worth more that a million dollars to me. It was about half of my month's salary at the time, and it was able, with prudent spending, to last me the entire month and up to the time I got my bulk three months' salary.

About eight months into my joining the general hospital, I arrived to work and was informed that my head of department was no longer working for the hospital. No one that I spoke with was sure of the reasons behind his exit. Some people said that he revoked his contract with the ministry. Others said that the ministry had refused to renew his contract since, among other reasons, another doctor was then in the department and that the ministry saw no reason for continuing to pay so heavily for a contract officer. I did not have the honor of being made aware of his impending exit. Even though we did not see each other more than a couple of times and did not relate with each other as well as I would have wanted, he was my boss and colleague, and I would have loved to have the opportunity to say a sincere farewell to a senior colleague and boss. The only official confirmation I had of the exit of my boss was a new heads of departments list, which I saw posted on the notice board with my name as head of Department of Anesthesia. It was most absurd, as were a lot of things and procedures which were happening around the system at that time. There was no official handing over, no discussions, no formal introduction to the inventory and other matters concerning that department on which many other departments depended for their smooth functioning. There was no formal farewell to a colleague who had served the department and the hospital for so long no matter how inconstant he might have been. It was simply absurd to me and certainly should not have been the case, not with such a highly placed officer who must have made quite some sacrifice to come into that system and set up the department. I felt that whatever might be said about his regularity in the hospital or whatever opinion any body might have about his services or his person, the fact remained that the credit for the setting up of the Department of Anesthesia in that hospital would always be his.

The keys to the massive office of the head of Department of Anesthesia were handed over to me by one of the nurse anesthetists. For the first time, I had the opportunity of getting around the rooms which were so well kept and furnished. The office indeed looked more like a residential apartment than a mere office.

About two weeks prior to my appointment (by notice board information) as head of Department of Anesthesia, I had received a letter from the board informing me of my promotion to the position of consultant in the department. Two of my three other classmates in the course had much earlier in other states attained that position. My own promotion probably had to wait due to lack of vacancy at the time. The fourth one among us, the Indian, had relocated, and we lost track of him. In the letter communicating the promotion to me, it was stated that "a copy of the letter was being forwarded to the head of my hospital." I had expected that the hospital would have written to congratulate her staff for that big elevation, as was done elsewhere under similar circumstances. None came. My new designation was however reflected in all subsequent communications with me from the hospital like in circulars and hospital bulletins. It was not as if my promotion receiving the pleasure or blessing of the leadership of the hospital really mattered very much to me. To me, what mattered, and that I was positive about, was that I merited the new position, that I would uphold the dignity of that position and serve creditably, and that society stood to benefit from the whole exercise.

It was obvious, that the rather uncoordinated way that cases were often conducted in the theater, with no doctor on the ground to ensure compliance with conventional standards for the administration of anesthesia, all benefited some people, who consequently would want maintenance of the status quo. A consultant anesthetist who was likely to be present to enforce compliance with these standards was not likely to be the darling of some members of the surgical team even if the former was quite efficient and professional in his actions. That was probably one of the reasons for the initial coldness and lack of enthusiasm about my promotion. It was not long however when it became widely accepted that it was in everybody's overall best interest that things were done professionally and in compliance with well-recognized standards.

At the height of the disagreement, as to procedure between the surgical teams and the anesthesia team, a peace meeting was summoned by the chairman of the health management board in the latter's office. The meeting was sequel to a complaint by the surgical teams as represented by the consultants in surgery and obstetrics/gynecology that the Anesthesia Department was impeding their work and consequently the smooth running of the hospital by insisting on certain "unusual conditions" before accepting patients for surgery. There was also the subsequent countercomplaint by the anesthesia team as represented by the consultant in anesthesia (that was me) that the surgical teams were trying to legitimize unethical and unprofessional behavior by not complying with accepted principles of professional practice. There was also the countercomplaint that the surgical teams were smuggling private patients through the "back door" and were thereby endangering the lives of the patients who were not properly investigated for fitness for anesthesia before surgery. At the hearings which was chaired by the board chairman who had earlier called the meeting a "peace meeting," all the consultants in the surgical teams were on one side of the large oval table. I was alone on the other side being the only doctor from the Department of Anesthesia. The chairman of the board was at the head of the table with his secretary behind him. The allegations and counterallegations were tabled and argued.

Instances were cited. Names had to be mentioned with dates where applicable, of various malpractices, and unprofessional behavior. One comical aspect came up during the peace meeting when I said that I would not bring up any case against one particular consultant "even though he too was an accomplice." That, I said, was because that particular consultant did me a favor when I was a prospective medical student, and he was a doctor practicing in the government general hospital at Aba. Pressed to expatiate by everybody present including the doctor in question (a very amiable senior), I narrated how the doctor had given me back the "one guinea" (one pound and one shilling) which he had privately collected from every student who had appeared before him for "medical exam" prior to his agreeing to issue the certificate of medical fitness. During that medical examination, the particular doctor saw from my form that I was about to enter into the university as a medical student, and he immediately congratulated me and gave me back my one guinea. I was so very overwhelmed by the kindness, and I never forgot it when many years later I again met that same doctor as a colleague at the General Hospital Owerri. He had forgotten that incident, but the incident was still fresh in my mind. I had very great respect for that doctor whose comportment of himself and his practice was always very moderate and distinct from what almost generally obtained in the system. Despite the serious business on the ground, that senior colleague received a standing ovation from every body present for his demonstration of esprit de corps, and for his being, as the board chairman comically put it, "the least bribe taker."

At the end of the peace meeting, it was mutually accepted that we should bury the hatchet and that each should turn a new leaf. We all embraced each other at the instance of the chairman. It was emphasized by the chairman of the board that progress could only be made by adherence to what was right and proper and that we must all respect each other and ourselves. The chairman further stressed that we needed each other and that the ultimate goal of everybody should be to strive for the ultimate good of the patient and the hospital. I had prayed very hard for God's guidance and protection before that meeting since I had figured how difficult it would be for me to stand alone against so many colleagues, most of whom were very much my senior both in age and in the profession.

There were obvious changes for the better after the meeting, in the relationship between the surgical teams and the Department of Anesthesia, and the patients coming on for anesthesia and surgery were definitely the better for it.

I wrote thereafter to commend the chairman for his excellent handling of the meeting without which tempers might have flared and the system would have been the worse for it.

It was also possible that some of the other participants also wrote to commend the chairman.

One big positive impact of the peace meeting was the establishment of order and discipline in the way patients were presented before surgery. The lists of the patients for surgery were thereafter well presented and submitted in advance so that proper anesthetic ward rounds were carried out. Major cases started to feature more regularly on the operation lists either because of better commitment by the surgical team or because of greater confidence by the surgeons that there would be more efficient anesthetic coverage.

After the meeting, there was much better understanding between the surgical theater users.

With my appointment as a consultant and head of department, there were more responsibilities for me in the sense that I would then be prepared to be accountable for any lapses in the department. I lessoned the burden on me by letting the most senior nurse anesthetist continue to make the roster for the nurse anesthetists. That way any objections to the roster by his colleagues would still be directed to him. It was only when there were unresolved problems within the department that I would intervene. Since I could make my own schedule, I could plan out my time more effectively.

It was about that time that a prominent private hospital in Owerri approached me to cover one of their newly established hospitals on a part-time basis, after official work hours. After inspecting the facilities and discussing with the medical director of the hospital, I started putting in some hours of coverage every week in the hospital. The remunerations were quite attractive, and the practice afforded me the opportunity of keeping myself busy during my free time without contravening the law on private medical practice by government-employed doctors as was then in force, especially as I did not own the private hospital. I alternated duties at the private hospital with a Filipino lady doctor who was really very good and dedicated to her job. I used to tease the latter about her name which was Jesus. She never went to church despite her name.

With the added revenue I got from the private hospital, I was able, for the first time, to start making a positive balance in my bank account at the end of the month.

With my added revenue came added problems because of my being more often on the road. One evening, on my way back from evening preanesthetic rounds at the general hospital, a drunk driver rammed into the back of my car at high speed. Luckily no one was seriously hurt, but the car was wrecked. The boot was squashed into the backseat, which luckily was unoccupied. The drunk driver emerged from his car, vomited on the tarred road, and collapsed. After he was pulled to the side of the road and ventilated, he got better and after negotiations, signed an undertaking to bear the full cost of repair if I would not press charges or involve the police. He had no insurance. One of his relations who happened to be my teacher in secondary school was sent for, and the latter signed as our joint witness.

The car was towed to a mechanic's workshop. For about one week, I was walking to work as public mass transit systems were nonexistent. When my father learnt of the accident, however, he sent me down his sixteen-seat-capacity van which he had bought only a month before for the transportation of his large family. The arrival of that van helped me a great deal until my friend Frank told me of how I could obtain a bank loan to buy a car with my salary as collateral. I then took a four-thousand-naira loan (about $2,000 at that time) from the bank and purchased a Volkswagen beetle (bug car) and then sent back the van to my father.

The man who smashed my car ultimately defaulted on the agreement, renegade on his written undertaking, and abandoned the car in the mechanic's workshop. It took me several months to be able, at personal expense, to get the car repaired since the insurance company kept dragging their feet with the opposing party having no insurance. Eventually, my insurance agreed to pay some of the cost of repair. The car was however never the same again thereafter as the damage done to it was so extensive.

The Private Medical Practitioner

My ambition after graduating as a doctor had been to go into full-time general private medical practice. The fulfillment of that ambition was the major reason why I opted for anesthesia in place of ear, nose, and throat medicine which I had initially wanted to do. Much as I was enjoying my new position as a consultant and head of department, the fulfillment of the ambition of going into private medical practice full-time was not lost on me. The part-time attachment to a private hospital in Owerri afforded me the opportunity to test the waters. After my third year at the General Hospital Owerri, I started mapping out strategies for going into full-time private practice.

Agie had completed her bachelor of dental surgery program at the University College Hospital and had started her housemanship with a dental center in Ibadan. There were no dental hospitals in the eastern part of the country accredited for housemanship in dentistry.

I needed to purchase my equipments for setting up a private hospital, and after drawing up a comprehensive list of what I required, I decided to travel to Britain for the purchases. My mother-in-law, who was a schoolteacher, had to come to Owerri to stay with our two sons. We had fixed my trip for the holiday period, and my brother Jike was very helpful at that period, especially in caring for our second son, Chibu, who as a toddler was very fond of crawling under cushions and other obscure places. The relationship between Jike and Chibu became so close that the latter came to associate every white van he saw around our house as "Jike mmotto" (Jike's car), since Jike often drove our father's white van while he was with us.

The success of my equipment-purchasing trip to Britain opened up another chapter in my life. With my full set of medical and surgical materials, lab equipments, and other essential hospital necessities ready, I disengaged from my job at the private hospital and from my primary job in the Ministry of Health. I then rented an apartment a short distance away from my official residence and set up a full-time medical practice.

Agie by that time was at Owerri, having been posted for her national service in the state of residence of her husband as allowed by law.

Setting up a full-time private practice was not as easy as I had imagined. I had thought that all that was required was the building and the equipments. I did not quite reckon with the administration aspect of it all. To meet up with the registration requirements of the Ministry of Health and the all involving commitment since, unlike the part-time private practice of one who was employed elsewhere, all the revenue accruing to the full-time private practitioner will have to come from his or her practice. To register my hospital, I had to disengage from my job. I needed to run my practice. And to run my practice, I needed to have it registered.

The Ministry of Health was dragging its feet with the necessary inspections and approval procedures. Getting the ministry to acknowledge receipt of my duly completed applications or to fix a date for the inspection proved a Herculean task. My personal visits and appeals to the ministry made no difference. While I was trying to comply with the requirements and abide fully by the regulations, other doctors who were in full-time government employment and many others who were on their own and did not bother to even apply for registration were running their full hospitals and clinics happily. It then seemed to me that complying with the regulations was then a disadvantage. People who disobeyed the regulations and paid none of the necessary application fees or filled the application forms were apparently being rewarded.

Should I sit back and see my family starve because I wanted to comply with the law which I saw was not being enforced? Should I be made to suffer because some overpampered and overserved civil master, who sat in a public—maintained air-conditioned office, would want me to go on my knees before he or she would do the work for which he or she was being paid. With the discipline which had been instilled in us in government secondary school, I decided to make one final effort. I sought audience with the director of health services (popularly called DHS) fully armed with all my application documents and evidence of payment. After filling all kinds of visitors' forms and being made to wait for over two hours, I was told that the DHS was leaving for a meeting and that I could not see him.

I left the office of the DHS disappointed and dejected, disillusioned with a system which tended to punish people who sought to comply with the regulations, a system which appeared to reward lawbreakers. Twenty-four hours later, I mounted my hospital signboard (which had already been prepared) and threw open the doors of my new hospital, in a forced defiance of the regulations. Obeki Clinics was born albeit under factitious circumstances. It was a Thursday morning.

About 11:30 a.m. on the following Monday, my temporary receptionist came into the consulting room, where I was examining a patient, a motorcycle accident victim, and told me that a man who introduced himself as "ADMS of the Ministry of Health" wanted to see me immediately. The receptionist had not quite completed her statement when a man clutching some files opened the door and stormed into the consulting room:

"This is an unregistered hospital and must close down immediately. This is . . ."

The man started. He also muttered some other words about legality and illegality which my furor did not give me time to listen to. It did not appear to bother this visitor that an accident victim was lying there on the examination couch. He appeared to have thrown all courtesy to the winds as he appeared so consumed by a desire to accomplish a mission for which his superior officer in the ministry had apparently sent him.

Something came over me which I could not control any longer. Here was I, a qualified medical practitioner trying to make my legitimate living after several thwarted attempts to comply with the regulations. And there was this official whose office had deliberately frustrated all my attempts at complying with the law and who, for reasons best known to him, had persistently turned a blind eye to the activities of many others who were openly flouting the regulations.

Taking the law into one's hands was a wrong thing to do, and an attack on a government official on duty was even a worse thing to do. But indignation at the apparent injustice and double standards overwhelmed me.

A long and pointed letter opener lying on the consulting room table got into my hands, and a chase of the "intruder" followed. The chase got up to the gate where the intruder dashed into a chauffeured waiting car and was driven off. It was a most unfortunate incident. I had allowed my anger at the tardiness of the ministry at attending to my application for registration and their prompt reaction at my opening of my clinic to becloud my good sense of judgment. The indignation was accentuated by the feeling that the ministry officials had deliberately ignored the action of their colleagues in government who were operating illegal clinics and had only beamed their searchlights because a private individual had opened shop. I had acted as if responding to a wrong with another wrong would correct the first wrong.

I was wrong.

By Tuesday morning, I was told that I would be charged with "aggravated assault against a government official" and with "operating an illegal clinic."

By the same evening after my statement and countercomplaint and after I had distributed all the relevant documents and receipts to everybody that mattered about the several attempts that I had made to comply with the regulations and how my efforts had been deliberately thwarted by officials who chose not to be "on seat," the charge was dropped.

It looked like the overwhelming weight of evidence of dereliction of duty on the part of some ministry officials would land some senior officers in trouble if the matter was pursued. By Thursday morning, four months after my initial application for inspection and registration, exactly a week after my failed effort to see the elusive director of health services and three days after the unwelcome visit of the assistant director of health services, the formal inspection of Obeki Clinics for registration was under way. It was so unfortunate that it had to take some measure of involuntary rash action and incivility to effect an action which was one of the primary functions of that arm of the Ministry of Health. The latter appeared to be in the habit of deliberately putting obstacles on the path of private medical practitioners wanting to register their clinics while glossing over their statutory functions of regulating quacks and curbing other illegal acts associated with operation of hospitals.

Agie was nearing the end of her national youth service year. The Egyptian dentist who was heading the Government Dental Center had concluded her contract and had left back for Egypt. Agie was made the acting head of the center. It was our intention that she should go fully private after her service year, so that joining me in my practice, we could decide to set up anywhere we wished. We had planned that we would set up in the rural areas and serve there for about five years before coming back to town. That was actually one of the promises we had privately made in the medical school while we were praying and studying for our exams. The major problem we had was the prohibitive cost of setting up a dental hospital. The alternative would be that Agie would serve as my assistant and manager of the hospital. But it was obvious that that course of action would make her lose her skills over time.

The story of my encounter with the assistant director of health services had made waves all over the Ministry of Health. It was said that after the circulation of the story about the purported "attack on the ADHS" and the subsequent detailed and widely circulated counterstatement narrating the apparent deliberate frustrations being imposed on private medical practitioners, files started moving faster, and the "not on seat" phenomenon got less. Obviously, the commissioner for health must have started looking more closely into the office of the DHS, and that must have made everybody sit up.

The encounter also obviously drew some necessary or unnecessary attention to me as a private medical practitioner married to a dentist. I once heard myself being described as "that troublesome anesthetist" by two ministry officials who did not know the identity of the very slim man in a long necktie who was sitting next to them in the waiting room of the commissioner's office. They did not conclude their story about me before I was called in to see the commissioner. It would have been interesting to listen a little further about the gossips about me, a humble and harmless practitioner who stood on nobody's way and who was only trying to survive.

The Birth of the Dental and the Rural Medical Clinics

Two weeks after the encounter with the assistant director of health services, the chief pharmacist of the Ministry of Health who happened to be from my town and who knew me personally invited me to his office to introduce me to the representative of Siemens, a reputable Lagos-based German firm. Siemens was introducing some of their dental equipments. There were no private dental clinics in the whole of Owerri, even with the latter's status as the state capital. The only dentist in the Government Dental Center was Agie, my wife. I would therefore make a good prospective customer for Siemens. I was willing to, but I did not have the cash. After some lengthy negotiation, however, Siemens and I arrived at an agreement whereby I would make some bulk deposit of about 50 percent of the cost of the products necessary for a fully equipped dental hospital. The remaining 50 percent was to be paid over a period of two years with interest.

Within three weeks of the negotiation with the German firm, Obeki Clinics became the first private hospital in the whole state to have full medical and full dental facilities under one roof. The Siemens team moved down to Owerri from Lagos with their technicians and the equipment in crates and cartons. The speed and efficiency of those technicians was amazing. The whole setup—glittering parts, brand-new—was a beauty to behold. I felt proud, fulfilled, and grateful to God.

The installations were completed on December 11. On December 18, our daughter was born, and on Christmas day December 25, Obeki Medical and Dental Clinics had its first dental patient, a case of fractured lower jaw in an eighteen-year-old young man who was involved in a fight during a Christmas party.

Obeki Medical and Dental Clinics grew rapidly in popularity. Besides it's being the first combined medical and dental facility in the state, we brought in revolutionary changes whereby a sick patient did not have to pay a card fee, the fee paid before a sick patient would be registered to see a doctor. At Obeki, a patient would be registered without a fee and would be examined by the doctor and only pay the actual cost of treatment with a minimal professional fee. We put in all the dedication that we knew. The appreciation of the populace and the response was enormous. The establishment grew in leaps and bounds. We were happy, but we had our fears. Our major fear was that we might lose sight of our promise during our years of struggle in the medical school and UCH. We had promised to put in at least five years in a poor rural community, before coming back to the urban areas. The success of our practice and the fame that came with the former were about to have the greater part of us and becloud our good sense of judgment and humility. It was so tempting to renege on our promise. One Sunday night we took a decision, Agie and I. I must make a move to the village before the success of the practice got too much into our heads.

On Monday morning we loaded portable medical equipments and a few medicines into one of our two cars. All morning medical cases on Mondays, Wednesdays, and Saturdays were shifted to the evenings. Emergency cases on those days would be referred to the general hospital.

I drove off to Azondizuogu to start off an unplanned prescription and dispensing clinic. The expansive ground floor living room of my father's main building which used to house the scores of cases of goods during the civil war and which had long been cleared of the goods was converted into a medical clinic.

Word quickly spread round that a "hospital" had been opened in Madukibeya's compound. It was a free clinic, no card fees, no medication fees, no prescription fee, no professional fee—completely free. And it remained completely free for three months. The gains from the Owerri clinic paid for the medicines. The equipments were our own and the waiving of professional fees cost us nothing. Agie used to accompany me on Saturday mornings and treated minor dental cases and later did simple tooth extractions. The response was so overwhelming that after the first three weeks, we scarcely could attend to more than one-third of the cases that turned up to the clinic at any sitting.

Many of the cases were so bad that they desperately needed hospital admission. Some of the dehydrated cases who were put on dextrose saline or normal saline infusions needed to be monitored, and we occasionally needed to leave a nurse behind to monitor the infusions, as we drove back to Owerri.

It was obvious that we could not continue to handle cases with that "fire brigade" approach. Something is needed to be done, and urgently too. We needed to build a hospital in that village if the little effort we had initiated would have any lasting meaning. I approached my father and intimated him with our plans. He was so very happy about it. He pointed to the wooded land adjacent his compound a place called Ikpa Ayo. He said that that land belonged to him and his two brothers, his immediate elder and his immediate younger brothers. He advised me to approach them individually and request for the land from them and that if they consented that I should build the hospital there. That same weekend, I made the requests to Papa Nke Ocha and Papa 121, my uncles, and both readily consented. They were very happy that I was about to bring development to Ndi Akunwanta, our village.

By the following Friday, I had hired a bulldozer from Owerri and roughly four acres of land had been cleared and leveled. The Owerri clinic was yielding quite some money, and building materials were cheap. A tipper load (ten cubic meters) of white sharp sand cost seventeen naira (about six dollars at that time). A fifty-kilogram (110 pounds) bag of Portland cement cost about four naira. Daily labor cost was very cheap, under five naira. We also bought stones, wooden planks, and rods and moved down to site. A long batcher (wooden makeshift house) was constructed for the hundred bags of cement and rods. Water tanks were bought and transported to the site, and within a week of commencement, the whole site was a beehive of activity. But it was not to be all smooth sailing.

When I got home by the third week of work on the proposed hospital site, I was told that one other family in the village had hoisted palm fronds at the building site, indicating that they had an interest in the land. I learnt that the said family had said that the people from whom my father and uncles said they purchased the land had also sold a portion of the land to their father. A member of the protesting family was said to have emptied one of the water tanks, everting the tank, in protest. They were said to have threatened that they would be there every day to ensure that work on the hospital site did not continue. My eldest uncle, Papa Nke Ocha, was said to have been so infuriated when he heard of the actions of the protesters and the damage that they had done to his nephew's property that he rushed to the site with a large sharpened machete and threatened to "deal" with anybody who dared interrupt work on that site again. Sometimes such disputes were "settled" that way, since ownership was often neither documented nor always certain.

Papa Nke Ocha was at that site every day thereafter from morning till evening; and work resumed without interruptions until the main building was completed, painted, and furnished. A main hospital block of ten rooms and another smaller block of four rooms for toilets and stores behind the main building had been completed. We moved in equipment and material from my father's living room and supplemented those with more newly purchased equipment from Owerri.

The first hospital ever had been born at Ndi Akunwanta. Patients came from far and near. Electrical wiring had been done on the building, but we did not have an electricity generator, and there was no public power supply at Ndiakunwanta. On a regular clinic day, we would run outpatient clinic all day and do surgical operations sometimes till as late as 3:00 a.m. using gas lamps and large battery torchlights. The success of the project and the smiles on the faces of the recovering patients gave us all the stamina and courage that we needed during those days. My normal working day on Mondays, Wednesdays, and Saturdays started at 9:00 a.m. and ended about 3:00 a.m. the following morning. Snack breaks were between 2:00 to 2:30 p.m. and 7:30 to 8:00 p.m. On some days we had up to eight surgical cases per night of surgery. I used spinal anesthesia, local infiltration, and ketamine hydrochloride for most of the surgeries. I did not employ inhalational anesthesia.

I lived in one of the ten rooms of the hospital building, and that made it possible for me to quickly respond to any emergencies, arising either de novo, or to any of the surgeries performed during the night. Most of our surgeries were herniorraphies, appendectomies, hydrocelectomies, ganglion removal, lipoma excision, torsion of the testis reversal, immobilization of fractures, evacuations in incomplete abortions and retained placenta, a few cases of emergency cesarean sections, and lots and lots of accident cases, falls, ruptured ectopic pregnancies, and many other minor to moderate surgical and gynecological emergencies. Many were quite far beyond my surgical competence. There were many neurosurgical cases that I dared not even attempt, and many cases came that we could not effectively refer out as we had no ambulance, and the patients had no means of transportation. There was nothing as saddening as watching a patient go down simply because he could not be transported, and I did not possess the surgical skill or the tools to help him or her.

As time went on, it became very necessary to expand the hospital. A comprehensive architectural drawing had been drawn of which the original ten-room building was a part. We started assembling the materials: stones, trips of sand, rods, and blocks. Suddenly Papa Nke Ocha took ill and died a few months later. The transition was a very big blow to the entire family as he had been, even in sickness, the patriarch and emblem of strength and authority for the whole family. As we were busy with the burial ceremony of the head of the larger family, a member of the family that had laid claim to part of the hospital land went back to the hospital site and started causing trouble again. My larger family's reaction was to confront the men both with full physical force and by force of law. It was felt that they were taking advantage of the demise of the patriarch of our family.

I felt however that it was possible that the opposing family had some genuine case because there were instances of double sale of the same property by some unscrupulous people, especially in those days where there was little or no documentation. There was no doubt that the complainants were capitalizing on the death of my uncle. I nevertheless advised that we approach the opposing family to arrive at a peaceful settlement with them.

After the burial ceremonies of my eldest uncle, we scheduled a meeting in the opposing family's house as represented by the eldest of the five cousins and brothers who were causing the havoc. The entire five claimants were present at the meeting. On our own side of the meeting were my father, my eldest aunt, my eldest sister, my brother Fab, and I. Both sides arrived at the conclusion that since there was no documentation at the time the purchases were said to have been made and that since the project was for communal good, the opposing side should state the amount of payment that would be made to them for them to completely withdraw whatever claims they had to the land. They consulted behind closed doors and came up with an amount. What they mutually agreed upon was indeed not a very large sum. What we had which was over 90 percent of their demand was paid to them on the spot in the presence of the ten people present. The amount was handed over to the eldest of them, and we all shook hands. The remaining 10 percent was paid the following morning in the presence of a witness, Mr Mat. I had requested for a receipt for the initial payment, but the consensus of opinion was that since the original purchases were undocumented and the protesters had made no documented protests that the whole issue should be regarded as a gentlemanly agreement between both families and that there would be no further disturbance at the site by any of the protesters. Three of the members of the host family escorted us to the gate as we left. It was all so cordial.

The negotiations had dragged on far into the night. I had forgotten my torch by the side of the chair on which we sat. When we got to the host's gate, I had to go back to collect my torch from the host's house. I saw the eldest family member and one of the other members in a fierce argument. The words *ego*, *ego* (money, money) was repeatedly mentioned during the portion of the hot exchanges which I heard.

It was obvious there was some disagreement over the custody of the money paid to the protesting family just a little earlier. I told my father what I observed when I went back to the house to pick up my torch. He said that we should let them sort out the problem between them. Events were later to reveal that they did not sort out the issue amicably. The eldest member of the family, Donny, was said to have kept the entire money to himself, prompting a reaction from one of the other four brothers.

People in the village were so happy at the apparent peaceful settlement of the hospital site issue. Work continued at the site with molding of more and more blocks for the expansion of the hospital. Small retail and grocery store businesses started opening up around the hospital premises. Electricity-generating plants had been brought down to the site which was brightly lit every night. The villagers had renamed the hospital site as Ikpa Ayo London. We had named the operating theater Eneanya Theater after the name of the very first person who was operated upon in the theater under the glow of a gas lamp. The lady in question happened to be the eighty-two-year-old lady who had midwifed my birth using plantain leaves as mat, nearly three decades earlier!

About a month after the payment of compensation to the family contesting the hospital site, it became common knowledge that there was a serious disagreement over the modalities of sharing the money paid to the family.

We learnt that the eldest member of the family to whom the money was handed had refused to share the money with the other members of his larger family. He was said to have given the entire money to one of his sons who was a rice farmer in a town called Abakiliki, either as a gift or as a loan, to help the later develop his rice business. Three of the brothers who were financially comfortable were said not to have bothered their eldest brother about the money. One of the five, however, the one I saw arguing with the eldest Donny on the night the bulk of the payment was made, was said to have insisted that his own share of the money must be given to him. He was said to have insisted that half of the entire sum should indeed be paid to him since he said that he alone came from a different father who was the acclaimed first son of their grandfather, the purported purchaser of the disputed portion of land. The other four were said to share the same father, and the "recalcitrant" contender said that those four brothers from one father were jointly entitled to only half of the entire money paid for the land. The contention of the "recalcitrant" contender was said to have infuriated Donny, the eldest of the brothers, and he was said to have threatened that he would expose the true paternity of the father of the recalcitrant contender, if the latter did not withdraw his claim.

He was said to have referred to the father of the latter as "a bastard," a statement which most villagers said was unproven since no paternity tests were ever carried out. The insulted brother decided to seek legal redress and sued his elder brother to court over the hospital land. However, instead of limiting his suit to his brother who had seized his share of the paid money, he also joined the party who was said to have benefited from the land, and that was me. Thus a measure which was initiated as a humanitarian venture became an issue for litigation, and I found myself embroiled in a legal tussle over an issue whose origin I knew nothing about and from which I stood to gain absolutely nothing materially. The womenfolk of the village demonstrated their solidarity with me during the hearing and were at the courthouse every day for the duration of the hearings. The menfolk maintained a dignified silence, a wait-and-see attitude.

Since the village hospital project was more a charitable venture and was beginning to be a contentious issue, I told my father that I was going to shut down the hospital and pull the facilities back to Owerri. My father said that instead of pulling the hospital completely from Arondizuogu, he would arrange to secure land from his uncles at Ndiawa for movement of the hospital to Ndiawa so that the town as a whole would not suffer a complete loss of the noble objectives of the projcct.

A larger piece of land was secured from my father's uncles at a relatively swampy area at Ndiawa. The arrangement involved payment of cash for the land and a compensation for cassava and other crops to be uprooted during the construction. These were paid and receipted for, and a formal agreement with an irrevocable and perpetual power of attorney was then signed and registered with the relevant civil authorities, as we did not want a repetition of our past unpleasant experiences. The hospital was thereafter relocated to Ndiawa, where it became possible to put on the ground the full potentials of what we had planned for Ndiakuwanta. A massive structure that could accommodate as many as eighty hospital beds was constructed. It had separate blocks for junior staff quarters, an expansive doctor's quarters, a power plant block, a maternity block, four underground water storage facilities with overhead tanks, and stands for water distribution. An oil palm plantation was raised at one section of the expansive compound, and electricity power was stepped down from the national electric power line.

The hospital was easily registered with the State Ministry of Health. The inspection and registration exercises were quite smooth as the new administration of the relevant Ministry of Health appeared more efficient and much more cooperative than their predecessors. A beautiful, well-planned, and well-organized hospital was born. The hospital, named after our only daughter, grew to become the fulfillment of our dream for a rural medical facility which we had planned to run for five years and hand over to another management before moving back to the urban area for the education of our children. The hospital which, like its predecessor at Owerri, had full medical and dental facilities was the envy of our friends and the pride of the family.

I shuttled between Ndiawa and Owerri for a while before we decided, in the interest of the family staying together, to shut down the facility at Owerri and relocate everything to Arondizuogu. We were later to discover that the practice of dentistry was more of an urban practice in our environment. We were to discover that were it possible to get a dentist to run it, it would have been better to retain the dental clinic in Owerri to let it remain in use as its utilization at Ndiawa was not up to 10 percent of its installed capacity. We nevertheless accepted that no amount of financial or other considerations would make us compromise the family's need to stay together, especially in those formative years of the children's character and education.

The need to ensure sound education for the children again drove us after two years to relocate the dental clinic to Okigwe when the state-owned university was moved to Uturu Okigwe, a town some thirty minutes drive from Ndiawa. The university had a staff primary school which was said to be very good. We had hitherto hired private teachers to supplement the classes offered in the local public school at Ndiawa into where we had enrolled the children. As soon as the children (our first and second sons) were enrolled into the university staff primary school at Uturu-Okigwe, we had to rent an apartment at Okigwe where we relocated the dental clinic.

In terms of economic returns, the relocation was a minimal advantage over Ndiawa. It however made it possible for Agie to drop the children at school and stay in Okigwe clinic till the close of school to bring back the children to Ndiawa. Whenever I remember Agie's daily shuttle on that lonely stretch of road with two young kids to and from school, it makes me shudder. The memory of the very winding road with no protective railing from the deep stretches of hillside gulley which my wife and two sons had to go through daily still sends shivers through me. The sacrifices nevertheless paid off as the children were both able to pass into the highly competitive federal government college at Okigwe where they attended initially from home as day students. They however later had to move into the boarding facility as the cost and risks associated with daily shuttle from Ndiawa increased.

We had planned to serve for five years in the village. We found ourselves stretching over ten years. We felt we "had paid our dues" as was the saying. It was time to move back to Owerri. We had however invested very heavily at Ndiawa and made quite some friends. We therefore initiated plans to lease out the hospital management. Not many doctors however wanted to serve in the rural areas. Our success at Ndiawa was a big surprise to many people, but many would not want to experience it.

We acquired some property at Owerri and rented an apartment for the dental clinic which we again relocated from Okigwe back to Owerri from where I had started. The cycle had been completed. Agie moved over to Owerri, and I visited Owerri at the weekends from Arondizuogu.

After running the dental clinic in a rented apartment at Owerri for about two years, we decided to build a full hospital. We acquired property in two different locations and started building a hospital in one of the locations. While the construction of the estimated twelve-bed hospital was going on, I still ran the hospital at Ndiawa and operated an outpatient-only clinic at Ndiakunwanta. It was not easy to coordinate all these practices. Even though the revenue was good, I was no longer getting the fulfillment that I cherished from the practice when I had so little, when I found joy and fulfillment in that little smile and the gentle "thank-you" that came from a recovering poor villager who had paid me nothing. It became increasingly obvious to me that it was not all about money, as I found that I had more peace, more joy, and more fulfillments during those years at Ndiakunwanta when the poor recovering old lady would, from her hospital bed, look up and say, "Thank you, Doctor, thank you."

I appeared a little happier when I was a little poorer.

I began to realize that true happiness did not come solely from the weight of one's pockets.

It became increasingly obvious to me that a greater sense of fulfillment came from service, especially when it was rendered to the poor and helpless.

The Armchair Critic or the Active Politician: The Difficult Decision

The military had been in power in the country for close to ten years. They had been hailed initially when the populace felt that the politicians were corrupt and were grinding the economy of the country to a halt. A massive outcry against military rule and a yearning for return to civil rule soon followed what the populace saw as colossal failure of accountability and flagrant abuses of human rights by the men in uniform. A timetable was soon set up by the military for return of power to civilians. As the preparations were on for a return to civil rule, many people who felt that they could help make positive changes in the polity decided to join one of the two political parties that were ordained by the machinery setup by the military government.

One of these parties was called National Republican Convention (NRC), and the other was called the Social Democratic Party (SDP). A brilliant academic political scientist was appointed to oversee the formation of these parties and to conduct the elections with the perceived view of transiting from military to civilian rule. There was widespread enthusiasm among the populace as people trooped out to register to join the political parties whose ideologies were said to be "a little to the left" for one and "a little to the right" for the other. Constitutions and manifestoes for each of the two parties were drawn by the military-appointed federal electoral commission. I joined the Social Democratic Party from the simplistic appeal that the words *social* and *democratic* conveyed. Many other people joined one or the other of the parties mainly because they admired the people in those parties or that their friends or relatives were there. There were not much of ideological considerations. For me, much as I had held positions of responsibility both in the secondary school and in the university, I had never really participated in party politics before then.

The military authorities had declared a ban on politicians who had served in certain positions in previous civil dispensations, from participation in activities of either of the parties. The ban was of course not completely effective as many of those so called "banned politicians" were either very wealthy or were the darlings of their peoples and remotely were dictating the pace, direction, and activities of the "new breed" politicians. It was also widely believed that the military government in power while professing its neutrality was secretly funding directly or through those banned politicians the activities of some of the new-breed politicians.

It was fun attending those political meetings after the day's clinic. It provided some relaxation from the many years of almost round-the-year consulting room and theater work. Most of the time during the meetings was spent strategizing on how we would recruit more credible and popular people into our camp. The initial stages were spent on how to outmaneuver the opposing camps which soon developed even within the same party, each camp trying to gain control of the party machinery by having her followers elected into executive party positions. There were four levels of executive functions in each of the two parties. These were the ward, the local government, the state, and the national levels. The first task of the federal electoral commission was to elect officials into each of these party levels.

It was obvious that whoever was able to control the largest number of ward executives in any state was likely to control the local government executive and hence the state executive. And of course whichever "strong man" was able to control the largest number of state executives was likely, in a fair election, to control the national executive. The battle for the wards was therefore stiff and in some cases bitter. We did not see much external intervention in my ward as were reported from many other wards. That was possibly because we already had one strongman, a so-called banned politician, a very friendly and principled gentleman who was already rich both from his family background and from his personal resources. He was never present at our meetings since he was officially banned, but he remotely controlled the ward leadership.

On the morning of the elections for the ward executives and the state, local government and national delegates, both the office seekers and the party members, had assembled in an open field. It was an ingenious form of open-ballot system by which all office seekers would stand in front, and those party members who supported any office seeker would queue behind the office seeker. The system was called "option A4" and was supposed to be a rigging-proof system because all results would be glaring as the winners' queue would elongate and wind round in curves while the losers' lines would be very short. The numbers of the people queuing behind each candidate would then be counted, recorded, and publicly announced. The results were supposed to be transparent to everybody. The only way a result could be rigged was where the returning officer, as the chief election official at each location was called, would deliberately record a wrong result after announcing the correct result. Even at that, each candidate or his or her representative was expected to endorse the results recorded if they were correct. But again there were said to be instances where fake papers would be presented by a returning officer for signing by the agents only to be replaced later by the genuine papers bearing forged results with forged agent's signatures.

I had for so long complained about the bastardization of governance in my country. I had written articles condemning the state of affairs of the polity. I had in private discussions with my friends always decried the deterioration of our society and social values. I had for so long remained an armchair politician, virtually criticizing about everybody and everything in the running of the system. The lifting of the ban on political activities therefore presented a unique opportunity for me to stop complaining and to participate in the politics of the country. I was determined that if the opportunity arose, I was going to make a positive difference in the outlook to politics. And I realized that opportunities were rarely handed out to people. Opportunities are seized. And they did not come very frequently. How and to what extent that was possible to seize the opportunity, I was not sure of. But for a start, I decided to run for office as a state official of the party of my choice, the Social Democratic Party. To do that, I first had to contest as a state delegate from my ward. I also encouraged Agie to contest, and she won as a national delegate, and it was they who later went to Abuja, the national capital, to elect the national officers of the party.

On the morning of the proposed ward elections for state delegates of which I was one of the contestants, I had to deploy vehicles to go round the different villages in the ward to convey party members to the venue of the election. I also had to deploy paid canvassers who would sit in the vehicles and convince people to vote for me by queuing up behind me. It was serious business for me as I did not intend to lose to my opponents in the other camp. Sometimes cash had to exchange hands between the canvassers and the prospective voters. Many of the prospective voters needed to close their shops for the day to come to queue up behind the contestant. Some would therefore ask for compensation for their lost day's business for coming to queue for a candidate. I had the particular advantage that very many people who had benefited from my humble services in the past not only turned up on their own to vote for me but also voluntarily became vote canvassers for me. The display of goodwill and solidarity was overwhelming.

When I turned up at the election venue, there was a spontaneous rousing welcome for me. That was mostly from many of my former patients, and I was very humbled by their spontaneous show of solidarity with me even in that event that was likely to keep me away from them a good part of the time. But then something happened that almost threw me off guard. Just about one hour before the start of the elections, we saw luxury buses arriving to the election venue filled with young men. One of my workers recognized some of the young men as students of a nearby institution of higher learning which was situated outside the jurisdiction of the ward under which the election was being conducted. One of my opponents had secretly gone to recruit those students to come to vote. We did not know how they obtained the party cards. I was thrown into a panic.

My chief strategist and adviser however was soon able to obtain assurance from most of the students that if we were prepared to exceed what these students had been given by our opponent, they would switch loyalty en mass to my side. They were said to have explained that their contract with my opponent stated that they would "come to the election venue in support" of my opponent. By coming to the election venue in the vehicle hired by my opponent, the students said they had supported my opponent and that for whom they stood behind was not part of the contract. The contract did not specify that they would queue behind any candidate they said. It then became clear that it was a "cash and carry" affair. Success would go to the highest bidder. We needed to act very quickly. A lot of cash was needed, and very quickly too. I did not have enough cash on me for so many people. But the local bank which I utilized was only a short distance away.

I quickly had to send for my checkbook from the house. In under an hour, one of my assistants was back from the bank with bundles of money all in twenty naira denomination (about five dollars at that time). The money, having exchanged hands, made the loyalty of the occupants of the buses switched. It no longer mattered who conveyed the students to the venue for the day's event. What then mattered was who "settled" them on the spot. Within another three hours, it was all over. The battle was lost and won.

My queue elongated and curved three times laden with both appreciative young and elderly village folks who had benefited from my free medical services as well as fierce-looking and belligerent young men who dispersed and left back into their buses soon after they were counted on the queue. They threatened to manhandle the bus drivers who brought them down and who, on the orders of my opponent, had refused to convey them back to their campus. The students were accused of breaking a contract. When they started chanting war songs and started banging fiercely on the body and on the windscreen of the vehicles after boarding, the frightened drivers had to acquiesce to their demands to convey them back to their campus. It was obviously a rather crude way of winning an election, but to me it was a lesser evil than the original act of hijacking or forging party cards for use by imported voters.

A Doctor in Politics?

Obviously my work had suffered during the period of electioneering. But I believed it was a necessary sacrifice if I was to participate in reshaping the political landscape upon which even the health care policies of the populace was dependent. So I had reasoned.

Immediately after the official announcement of the results, alignments and realignments started to shape up. The big moneybags and political godfathers started maneuvering to lure in as many of the delegates as possible into the camps which they controlled. If any of them was able to have majority of delegates, then he or she would be in a position to control the party machinery and thus be in a position to dictate who would run for executive office either at the local government, the state, or at the federal level. Series of meetings of the elected delegates were summoned by the emerging political godfathers who were mostly rich or old politicians or rich businessmen who aspired to political power or the not-so-rich but charismatic aspiring political big players.

The major qualifications and characteristics for being a political godfather were big mansions with many well-furnished rooms for guests, very large compounds and parking spaces for scores of cars, large expansive in-built halls and conference rooms for entertaining political guests, multiple chauffeured cars for self and staff transportation and for transportation of party chieftains and "party stalwarts" (a name used for for party thugs in some instances), in-built large kitchens and bars that would churn out food and drinks to assembled party men and women, all these, and of course a near-inexhaustible or perceived inexhaustible purse that should be able to churn out cash to delegates after each meeting. The prospective godfather should of course be able to talk big, talk tough, dress lavishly or impeccably, and sometimes hold a swagger stick. He may sometimes need to display a pot belly to confirm than he was not "a hungry politician." Politicians or their cronies or dependants flying abroad for "tummy tuck" (liposuction) was not yet in vogue.

At one time after attending a meeting summoned by one aspiring political godfather, I momentarily deluded myself into believing that I, too, could even be a political godfather: I had a big compound, I had a number of old cars and a bus, a big house at Ndiawa, I could talk big and tough if I so desired. But then, I did not have the tons of money, and, of course, I did not have pot belly and would certainly look hungry in the midst of other godfathers. I quickly retreated from the delusion.

It was soon time for the local government party executives elections. Our group had our own candidates for the different posts ranging from local government party chairman to local government party ex officio members. The other group within the party, which had her godfather outside the local government area, had their candidate too. We went from the ward in the local government, campaigning for our candidate who was known to be a very honest and reliable man. He was however not as educated as the candidate of the other group who was a well-educated professional. Being a novice in the slippery political terrain, I had believed that we were unanimous in our support of the candidate officially backed by our group. Being a state delegate, I was not a delegate to the local government elections. Though we had campaigned hard for our candidate, I was only a spectator from a distance on the election day.

During the delegate's election at the local government level for the local government party chairman, we learnt that a number of delegates from our group, whom we had at our expense conveyed to the venue of the elections, had suddenly switched camp inside the voting hall and had thrown their weight behind the candidate of the rival group. There was no way we would know whether it was another case of victory for the highest bidder or victory for the best candidate.

As the date for the state and national officers' elections got closer, realignments and mergers began to occur. My group merged with one of the other prominent groups to become the dominant group in the party. The factionalization that had occurred in the party was however so deep that it was certain to rob the party of victory if unresolved.

At the state party executives elections, we won a clear victory, and I was elected the state publicity secretary of the party. My victory, I believe, was due in part to the influence of the group to which I belonged and partly because I was quite visible in the party, and many believed I could speak and write well and thus would be a publicity asset to the party. Besides, the fact that I was a medical doctor must have added to the credibility, even though that was not a sole criterion as there were many other professional men and women in the race.

We were soon to go to Abuja to elect the presidential candidate for the party. What I witnessed was a massive display of political maneuvering, intrigues, and jockeying. There was a massive trading of delegates and seemingly and hitherto respectable men and women, making political whores of themselves. The actual elections were very transparent, but what transpired the night before was nothing short of political prostitution and banditry. It looked as if people came from different parts of the country only to stuff their pockets with cash all in the name of electing political flag bearers.

Delegates from different states were camped in distant hotels from the election grounds in Jos, a town in the central part of the north of Nigeria. My own delegation was camped in Bauchi, quite some distance from Jos. We had traveled in convoys of long buses throughout the night with an initial brief stop at a hotel on the outskirts of Onitsha, a prominent commercial city in the southeastern part of the country. We sang as we traveled, finally arriving Bauchi in the early hours of the morning. To ensure that the opposing group did not buy over our delegates, access was made near impossible by our delegates being camped in a luxury hotel on the outskirts of the city. The pockets of the delegates were lined intermittently through the night with cash, as sacks of money were emptied in bundles in open view of everybody. Some smart delegates who knew the terrain well made sure they broke bounds after collecting from our group and found their way to the camp of the other group and also lined their pockets. All they needed to have on them to be admitted to the venue of the cash distribution was the delegate's badge, which had earlier been distributed by the party administrators at the states. On election morning, people who had traded their consciences throughout the night all came up again looking like innocent little angels but with pockets bulging with ill-gotten political money. At the entrance to the convention grounds, the first shocker came: bags of money and pockets stuffed with money would not be allowed into the convention ground. It was announced that any delegate who was found having an excess of two thousand naira (about five hundred dollars at that time) would have the excess confiscated. That was possibly to prevent a further sharing of money inside the convention venue or a strategy by the people who had dished out the money to subtly collect some of it back. People had to start off loading their loot and a few delegates turned themselves into temporary banks and stayed behind outside convention grounds to guard their own and their colleagues' loot, all stacked in little labeled bags of all shapes and colors! Some others decided to convert the cash they had into dresses, shoes, caps, and anything that had a price. The front of the convention center soon turned into a huge supermarket. The hawkers in the city may never again make such brisk business.

When the convention was over, the spending spree continued as people who had not often saved as much as five thousand naira at any particular time in their lives now found themselves controlling scores of thousands of naira overnight. They began to buy about anything within reach if only to travel a little lighter in terms of cash.

The Political Jobbers and the Highway Robbers

On the morning after the all-night elections, we trooped to the motor parks as the buses that brought us had all disappeared. As in the character Melanthius in the popular film *Sinbad and the Eye of the Tiger*, we had played our roles, used and discarded. My mind flashed back to the riotous student voters during the ward elections that my opponent had transported to the election ground, only to have me hijack them with some bait. Those students had not quite fulfilled their contract with my opponent. But I justified my hijacking them on the grounds that an irregularity had already been initiated. In the case of the Jos delegates, however, many of the voters who collected "pocket money" from one camp remained loyal to that camp. Only a few "smart" ones went to several camps that same night. Abandoning the loyal voters after the voting was over, therefore, was like condemning the good with the bad. But as succinctly demonstrated in Shakespeare's *Macbeth*, in that political arena, it could be said that "fair is foul and foul is fair."

The delegates had been ferried through some five hundred miles to cast their votes; after which, there was no further need for them, and they needed to make their individual arrangements to find their ways back to their respective destinations. In any case, many of us deserved the desertion which we got. Many had succumbed to the monetary inducements, and many others, which excluded me, had traded their votes through the night, collecting money from both sides of the major political divide. Unlike in the case of the students who had been imported to vote at the ward elections, the drivers of our vehicles were not even available to be threatened. They had been paid to drop their "wares" and to go their way.

We were all guarding our heavily loaded pockets as we trooped to the Bauchi motor park after the voting, which had stretched till the early hours of the morning. Little did we realize that the park thieves were watching as the unusual heavy human traffic streamed into the park. The commercial minibuses that we boarded took off in groups of three.

Not quite fifty miles on our drive from Jos, the rear bus speeded past our bus which was at the middle. The driver and conductor of the speeding rear bus kept pointing to a fourth unidentified vehicle following closely on our heels. The driver of our vehicle tried to speed up, as the "ghost vehicle" followed in hot pursuit.

The highway robbers were after us! That vehicle must have been trailing us right from the park. Ill-gotten wealth must have a way of putting intense fear into people. Many people started trembling. Some started removing bundles of money from their briefcases and stuffing them into their shoe stockings. Others started hiding bundles of money under the seats of the minibus. Some others started stuffing their own money into their underwear. We soon lost sight of the other two buses ahead of us as they appeared to have accelerated off much better. It was possible they might have branched off the road or docked into the bushes. Our own driver kept speeding off, but when it became obvious that the robbers' vehicle was accelerating much faster, the driver took a sudden turn off the road towards a lonely abandoned building by the side of the road. It must have been an old building used for a road camp.

As soon as the minibus suddenly veered off the major road and came to a halt in front of the roadside building, we all scrambled out of the bus and made for the adjoining bushes, each person clutching tenaciously to his or her bundle of money. We ran in different directions. The pursuing vehicle had not anticipated the sudden diversion at the road junction and had speeded past the junction. But it was soon to make a U-turn and return. We could hear it stop close to where our own vehicle had suddenly discharged us to facilitate our escape from the rampaging robbers. It was like the biblical saying "To your tents oh Israel," as we scrambled off the bus with nobody directing. As the driver of the vehicle screeched to a sudden halt, I could see him leap out from the driver's seat into the thick bush. The bus conductor had followed in a different direction, both without a word of direction. The rest of us, the passengers, left on our own, all scrambled into the bush to safety. There was no time for any body to direct the other. Even during my man o' war bay drills in school, I had never witnessed any such thing. It was as if it was in a dream.

I did not want to run too far into the bush for fear of some other dangers. I did not know the terrain. I did not speak the language; I was not sure of possibilities of wild animals. I might be escaping the devil for the deep blue sea. I must have meandered my way for about six poles into the thick bush before stopping for fear of being completely lost in the bush.

I lay flat in the bush behind a tree, not even raising my head from the ground. I started wishing that all the money would go if only I lived to get home to see my wife and children. I started cursing myself for getting myself into that mess. I was fairly comfortable as a medical practitioner. I was well respected in my community.

What would my many patients back in my home say if they were to see a photo or video of me dashing out of a minibus clutching my loot into the bush? How would I look telling the story? Did I truly believe that my entry alone was going to change the political terrain of the country, or was I simply being greedy, or wallowing in self-delusion. What if I got shot by those robbers in that thick bush? What would I say that I was pursuing in Bauchi? Occasionally I would pinch myself to confirm whether it was a dream or whether I truly was in a thick jungle five hundred miles from the comfort of my home, perhaps in pursuit of uncertain fame.

At every moment, it seemed to me that the robbers might decide to comb the bush. What if they got angry at not recovering any money in the vehicle and decided to shoot randomly into the bushes, knowing that their victims were hiding there and that they all had a lot of cash?

If they shot us there, our bodies might never be recovered. I prayed to God to let the whole money go if only I would be allowed to get home alive. I promised God that I would not touch "politics money" again. I had always complained about the worsening rate of corruption in our society. But there was I participating in a situation in which money was distributed to delegates as "pocket money." Was that pocket money not a kind of inducement for the delegates to vote in a certain way? Even though it was not spelt out and even though some delegates went from one camp to another and people were free to cast their ballots in secret, the mere acceptance of any form of monetary gift was, in my opinion, an inducement. And I had participated in the process despite my complaints. Even though I tried to justify my participation by convincing myself that I would vote according to my conscience, the fact that I did not speak out against the process at that period in time was in itself a de facto approval!

When I raised my head amidst the silence and the rotten mousy-smelling vegetation, I could not see nor hear anybody. I could only see the top of our vehicle where it was parked near the old empty road camp house. I lowered my head again and lay still. I was prepared to stay in that position for the whole day. Then suddenly I heard a voice from near our parked vehicles.

"Dem don commot. Them thief politicians!" the voice said.

That implied that the political thieves had all escaped.

Sure the robbers were on our vehicles.

The thieves were saying that we were thieves and that we had escaped. The thievish politicians had escaped. I hoped and prayed that they would allow us to escape, at least to give us the opportunity to repent and make amends. I promised God that if only I escaped from that bush alive, I would make amends. I only wished that that promise would not fizzle away as soon as the ordeal was over just like a lot of promises made in moments of dire distress.

But did we really steal any money? Would it be right to classify me as a politician? I was only a medical professional in politics. But the delegates had been given money to induce them to vote in a particular way. As earlier stated, some had received money from two opposing groups of political godfathers. But they would not vote in two opposing ways. They had voted in one particular way. Who then were the guilty ones, the givers or the takers?

I tried momentarily to justify my position by saying that; after all, I paid money to the hired student delegates who had been brought down in buses to vote at the ward elections and all that. But two wrongs do not make a right. Besides, if delegates received pocket money from candidates to vote in a particular way during elections, what ground would these delegates have to complain when any of the candidates in victory decided to loot the nation's resources in the name of the same pocket money? We certainly deserved whatever those robbers might do to us. At worst, it would only be another case of two robbers, one stealing from the loot of the other. But I still prayed fervently that the robbers would spare our lives.

Even among thieves, there should be some honor, at least some mercy. I was not sure whether thieves observed esprit de corps! We were all guilty. The political godfathers had stolen or embezzled the people's resources to reinvest in politics. The delegates, by accepting pocket money from the political godfathers, were indirectly stealing part of what had been stolen from the people. Finally, the highway robbers, by stealing from the delegates, were only "recovering" into their pockets only a small part of what was stolen from the people. To that extent we were all guilty and should only plead that in the name of esprit de corps that the robbers should spare our lives. We should indeed all have left behind our bags of pocket money in the bus before escaping into the bush. That way we would have made the loot go round and compensated the robbers for their pain and suffering for taking the pains to pursue us for so long from the motor park in Bauchi. We would have had a better story to tell our families on our return to our respective bases. We would thus have successfully replayed another version of the biblical Job, by saying, "Naked came I into Bauchi, and naked shall I return."

We must have stayed hiding in the bush for two hours. Most of the time I hid my head buried into the leaves behind a tree so that if the robbers should get angry and start shooting wildly, they would not hit me on the head. After some time, I started to hear people talking. I cautiously raised my head and saw some movement of people. I did not quite hear what they were saying. I could not see their faces. It was not easy to be sure whether these were our friends or our foes, the attackers or the attacked, the political jobbers or the armed robbers.

But it was not likely that the robbers would want to wait for so long.

We must have hidden in that thick bush perhaps long after the robbers must have left. Then the horn of our vehicle started to sound intermittently. I could then distinguish Zorro's voice as he spoke with a stammer. Zorro was the massive heavily built semiliterate stammerer who often undertook the physical assault for any group that hired him. He was said to have been a motor park tout, a bouncer, who gradually assumed some refinement and got elevated by a political godfather to the status of a national delegate, a status by which he found himself in the midst of doctors, lawyers, and other fairly successful businessmen and women. By his elevation, perhaps for a favor he had done for a political godfather, he would directly participate in selecting the presidential candidate of the party. Many of us initially protested Zorro's inclusion as a national delegate on the grounds of his image, his rashness, and his past. The counterargument was of course that we might need Zorro if there was the need for physical fighting with an opposing camp. That argument made sense.

Zorro bellowed as he spoke, and as he spoke with a stammer, his voice was easy to distinguish. He was one of the occupants of our bus, and since he was out of the bush, it meant that the robbers had left. He too had scampered into the bush for safety despite his size and reputed physical strength. Having heard Zorro's voice, I mustered the courage to stand up amidst the leaves and grasses. There, sure enough was Zorro and a number of my fellow delegates clustered around our minibus. They were discussing something.

As I got up and walked out of the bush more confidently, I saw a few other delegates coming out of the bush from different directions. That included Ode, the reverend minister who was also a national delegate. Ode was always very reserved. He was ordinarily a nice guy and was often called upon to say the prayers at the beginning and at the end of the meetings. He did not wear his cleric's collar that morning. But his briefcase also appeared heavy, most likely with "inducement allowance" from our group or from both groups. Whichever way though, it was certain that Ode must have voted according to his conscience, as he always advocated we should do.

We were soon back into the minibus heading back to the eastern part of the country from where we came. Ode had led us in prayers soon after we got back into the bus. This time we sang church hymns as we traveled. We ought to have said special prayers of repentance for the sin of accepting pocket money in the first instance. Every one of us knew it was a kind of inducement, even though we chose to say that it was "compensation for our pain and suffering." We had chosen not to acknowledge that the man or the people who financed the compensation for the pain and suffering would, in victory, turn around to recoup their "investment." In the end, accountability and good governance would be the victims.

Nobody had been hurt during the stampede and dash for cover. Only one delegate, Mr Obia, a retired teacher, had lost or forgotten his briefcase containing his money as we ran from the van for cover in the bush. It was possible the robbers had "harvested" the briefcase as their sole loot. The rest of us except Zorro, however, agreed to contribute five thousand naira each to help offset Mr Obia's loss. Zorro, in refusing to contribute, argued that since the retired gentleman who lost his briefcase knew that he was not strong enough to run from robbers and did not have the strength to hold strongly enough to his wallet, he should not have come to Jos as a delegate in the first instance.

"This business no be for woman, na only strongman vit come. Me, I no vit give my moni to any woman," Zorro had insisted, implying that only strong people like him, not weaklings, should participate in politics and that he was not prepared to part with any bit of his money to a weak person. Knowing Zorro's background, it was no surprise that he held that view and that he spoke so disrespectfully of the female gender. He did not go to school. He understood only politics of violence, and according to him, who ever did not have the muscles for a fight should not participate in the game of politics.

When challenged by Mr Obia on why he too ran away from the robbers since he believed he was a strongman, Zorro got aggressive and declared, "Na only mad man w-e-e go see fire go jump inside-am."

Then opening his eyes widely as if gearing up for a fight, Zorro continued, "You w-e-e de talk, you vit fight Zorro?"

He was implying that only a mad man would see fire and jump into it. He followed that latter statement with a challenge to anybody among us who felt strong enough to fight him.

Everybody was of course familiar with Zorro's bellicose stance whenever he was faced with realistic arguments. He had once again succeeded in intimidating everyone else. In any case, nobody would want to get into further argument with Zorro, not after all we had gone through. Everybody decided to leave the strongman alone.

We got back to Owerri early the following morning without further incidents.

The Sage Returns to His Ancestors

My father had often enjoyed very good health for as long as we knew him. Only rarely did he have malaria, which was very common from the bites of the ever-present mosquitoes. The only occasional ailment he complained about was cough. He said he smoked quite a bit during his youth. That must have been responsible for the chronic bronchitis which he was later diagnosed with. Papa had on a number of occasions received treatment either from Dr Moue or from my brother Dr Fab or from me. On one occasion, he was hospitalized in the hospital where Dr Fab worked. When he relapsed some months after discharge, I had to admit him in my hospital at Ndiawa. He recovered and enjoyed good health for some time. Our friends Dr Frank and his wife Dr Suzi were of much help during the period of Papa's hospitalization.

The relapse that came on later after Papa's discharge from hospital took a turn for the worse, and we found the need to refer him to our good friend and schoolmate who was the most renowned cardiologist in the state. Despite all efforts, however, complications supervened, and our beloved father suffered the fate of all mortals. It was a most shocking incident. Even though, from the medical point of view we knew the ultimate sequelae of cor pulmonale, we did not expect that the end would come on so soon. When one is directly involved, however, the disbelief is always there. We would always believe that our own case or the case of our loved one would be different. We would always believe that somehow, the best would turn out. We would always remain optimistic till the end. The sorrow and disbelief gave way to anger at how and why this was possible. It was so easy to forget that as humans we would each one day or another inevitably toe the line and go the way of all mortals.

In a matter of days, we had to accept the supreme decision of the Almighty. We had to accept that the icon—Iheanaeboagu, Ogbukanwafor, Ebolebo Egbunam, Onyegaeguzuniru ekworo, Madukibeya, our hero, the legend of our time—was no more! We had to accept:

Though the tears welled in our eyes
And our hearts sank in confusion and near despair,
And our fingers and legs trembled in uncertainty,
And we felt like sheep without a shepherd
We had to stand.
We had to stand up like the men that we were
Sons and daughter of a truly great man
Forty six in all, we were,
We had to stand.

Though the tears still fill my eyes as I write,
And emotions tend to take over the better part of me
I know we had to stand.
And stand we did, to live up to his words,
In absolute gratitude for the lifelong love he had bestowed on
us his children,
And in obedience to the plea he made to us while he lived,
To give a befitting burial to our hero
The greatest dad of all time,
Our dad.

And we gave glory even in the midst of grief
To God who giveth and taketh away
For the good life dad lived while he was with us
A worthy life in the service of others
And I, even only as the third of forty-six,
Knelt in total submission and gratitude to God
For giving to me such a dad
A dad that I would for all time treasure,
Till the day that it will be my turn,
To bow with reverence,
And take my leave with pride.

After two preliminary family meetings in our village home, the larger family met several times to plan for the funeral. Elaborate arrangements were made and fine-tuned.

Great in life, Madukibaya appeared even greater in death. His core family of eight wives and forty-six children, the larger family of over four hundred, hundreds of friends from far and near, thousands of sympathizers and business associates from all over the globe thronged to Ndiakunwanta to pay their respects. It was like a carnival. I am yet to witness another like it. The line of vehicles extended for miles from both ends of the narrow dusty road leading to our compound. Despite the elaborate arrangements and the presence of peace officers, it was impossible to control the crowd. At a time we feared there might be chaos.

There just were not enough seats despite the mopping up of chair rental facilities in town and around. There wasn't even enough standing space. The crowd had stretched beyond my house behind my father's house, beyond my brother Chris's house, our neighbor's houses, and the old hospital building to the road. Special sitting arrangements had been made inside the compound for traditional rulers, the clergy, and the very elderly; but as the day wore on, and the numbers increased beyond our expectations, most arrangements started to dislocate as some orderlies of some politicians and some of the so-called very important personalities (VIP) sought to install seats along walkways and corridors for their principals and masters, thereby blocking access and exit.

The viewing of the body dragged on till about 4:00 p.m. well beyond the 1:00 p.m. scheduled interment time. It had to be halted with the queue still stretching down the road.

Just before the final closing of the casket, an unfortunate event occurred. There arose an argument among the children about which cloth should be included and which should not, among the in-laws, according to tradition. A rather trifling issue grew into a big disagreement, and one of my brothers got angry and banged his fist on the glass casket. The sound of shattering glass set off a pandemonium in the crowded room. People in the adjoining corridor heard the sound and thought that the casket had blown open, and they started to run. As they ran out, they bumped into other people, starting off a cascade of pandemonium.

Someone from the crowd shouted that Madukibeya had blown open his casket and had got up. That increased the pandemonium through the gate which was jammed with people. Younger people within the compound who could climb started scaling across the compound well to escape. Even some of the reverend ministers started scaling the wall. The leader of the congregation of reverend brothers to which one of my brothers belonged got suspended on the wall as his white cassock got caught against a metal spike on the wall, as he was climbing over the wall, leaving him suspended on the wall as he tried to scale over during the pandemonium. A good Nigerian had to run up to release the reverend minister's robe from the spike before the reverend gentleman could continue his race for dear life. It was a most unfortunate incident, which almost ruined the elaborate arrangements that had been made.

Even after we had peacefully resolved the issue of the cloth acceptance procedure inside the room, we could still see and hear people running outside. Some were running towards their cars. Others were simply running away not even knowing what they were running from. So much was the awe and myth that surrounded Madukibeya both in life and in death. He truly lived his name even in death.

The funeral ceremony continued uninterrupted for fourteen days well beyond the ordinary three days for most funerals.

After our father's death, we settled down to take stock and reorganize ourselves as a family. The tidying up of Papa's business, his assets and liabilities, his commitments, and many more was one big task that remains not fully resolved. For a man who was larger than life in most things, it was not easy for any person to fit into his shoes. He died intestate by choice as he had always told us that he would not make a will. He had always stated that if we, his children, wanted to destroy ourselves over his assets after his death, we were free to do so. For most of us though, the rich legacy of his humanity and the goodwill he generated in life were much more important to us than any millions he might have left in assets both locally and overseas.

The Heating Up of the Polity

The political scene had heated up. The local government elections had been scheduled for a particular date. The two political parties were pitched against each other. It was obvious that the Social Democratic Party (SDP) had the upper hand in my local government area. It had a much greater following not just because it had greater "grass root support" but also because its stated constitution was more people oriented. There was equal government funding of parties, but the SDP appeared to be better funded by individuals, the so-called moneybags in the state. In my local government area, the SDP easily won the elections. The story was expected to be the same at the state elections to produce the state governor.

A recently retired academic and personal friend of mine was being groomed to vie for the post of governor. He had visited me at my Ndiawa home soliciting my support. Even without his asking for it though, I would have given him my full support. Not only had we known ourselves for some time, his wife and my sister were very good friends at school. After his official presentation as the candidate of the party in the state, my wife and I had visited him twice at his Owerri residence to present our little material support to help him in his bid for the number one position. During electioneering for the party primaries, it had been difficult for me explaining to the locals why I chose to support someone from a distant local government in preference for another contender for the same position who was from the same local government area with me. It was argued that charity should begin from home. The truth of course was that the other guy had been my friend, and my family and his knew each other so well. I could more or less predict him, and his principles were largely known to me. It was therefore a question of "the devil you know" being preferred to an unknown angel.

My support for my old friend was to cost me dearly during the former's electioneering campaign in my local government area. My friend had left Owerri in a blue Mercedes 230, the same brand and color as I used. He was scheduled to address party supporters in an open field at the local government headquarters. I set out from my home for the reception site in my blue Mercedes 230 car. Three other cars were heading for the field behind me, and the four cars had looked like a convoy. I did not know that some overzealous supporters of the other candidate were waiting at the roundabout close to the rally field, armed with stones. We knew that political thuggery was not an uncommon event in our elections. But since I was not a candidate, I did not consider myself in any danger. Little did I reckon with possibilities of mistaken identity. As my car took a turn at the roundabout towards the field, I experienced the unexpected. Heavy stones rained down on my car from the roadside, smashing the rear and side windscreens and the rear lights. I had to drive off at breakneck speed to avoid further onslaught. They obviously had mistaken my car for the car of the opponent of their candidate.

It was an obvious case of mistaken identity which could have been more disastrous if I had made the mistake of stopping or even slowing down. The intended target had to come through another route after word was sent down to his convoy that some political thugs were lying in waiting for his convoy; since it was obvious, the assailants must have later realized that they had attacked the wrong person.

Polls were not usual in Nigerian politics, but the massive support as shown by numbers during our rallies pointed to the likelihood that we would win the governorship elections in the state.

Just a few days to the elections, however, the military government at the center issued an order disqualifying some governorship candidates around the country. One of those affected was my friend on whom we had staked so much and who had been tipped to win the elections in the state!

Some people described the sudden disqualifications as a deliberate way of destabilizing the system for some ultimate political ends. We were virtually coasting to victory.

The candidate of the other party, who did not appear as popular, was not affected by the *purge*. He thus had an uninterrupted campaign. His robust campaign machinery coupled with his maturity in age and politics were completely undisturbed. Again the inability of my group to resolve the rivalry between it and the other faction within the party militated against our chances as the splinter group was said to have lent their support to the obviously less popular party's candidate.

We had quickly reorganized after the disqualification of our flag bearer. We substituted another candidate in place of our disqualified candidate, but it was too late. The new candidate, though a vibrant young man and a former local government party chairman, had very little time to campaign. I remember that the boot of my car and the entire backseats were laden with bundles of posters of our new candidate for distribution just a day to the election. Despite our gallant fight, victory went to our opponents.

It is noteworthy that the very next day after the disqualification of my friend from the governorship race, I went with my wife to visit him to commiserate with him on the very sad decision of the military administration. What we saw surprised us greatly. The gate of his house that used to be manned by four strong guards to keep out surging supporters and well wishers was widely open and had been completely deserted. The surging crowds had disappeared overnight; the cars of the visitors that lined both sides of the street the previous days prior to the disqualification were all gone, and the party stalwarts and multiple advisers had all evaporated into thin air! The fair-weather friends were all gone. Only the turkeys, which prospective office seekers might have brought as gifts, still roamed the compound. The long wireless telephone antenna that made the telephone buzz all day still stood, a sad reminder of the heydays of possibly the best governor that we never had. I found my friend alone in the living room into which we walked with no ushers directing. Just the previous day it would have been an uphill task seeing him. The swift disappearance of the multitude of fair-weather friends so soon after the announcement of the disqualification brought home to me the truth of the old saying in my community: "Success has as its companion, a thousand cousins, but failure is an orphan."

My friend described his disqualification as "a decapitation." But I was happy that after our long discussions, he picked up his spirits and told me that he was confident that his stars would shine again someday. He further said that the events of the previous forty-eight hours had made him know his friends in need, his true friends. He had concluded by saying that if his stars ever shone again, that he would "form a think tank" with me in charge. I was happy that we were able, even at those sad moments, to put a smile on each other's face with a few jokes about the campaigns.

After we lost the governorship race, there was a big lull in the activities of the party at the state level. Soon however the preparations kicked off again for the presidential elections, frequent dillydallying and policy changes dogged the presidential elections. Validations, invalidations, revalidations, qualifications, and disqualification became so regular and commonplace that at a time it became impossible to say who would or would not contest, or more correctly who would be allowed to contest or who would not be allowed to contest. With the eventual emergence of a definite candidate for each of the two political parties, however, it was felt that the stage was set for credible election s and installation of a comprehensive civilian government in the country. The presidential candidate on either side was a multimillionaire in his own right even though officially the parties were government funded. Each of the two candidates was a businessman. Each was a Muslim, and each appeared to be a friend of the military administration. None of these made any difference to the generality of people in the intense desire to have a civilian administration in place.

The major differences between both candidates were that one was much better known than the other; the better-known one had been a big spender especially in philanthropic issues. He was also chronologically older and appeared to be more pragmatic and had been very outspoken in certain sensitive international matters like the issue of reparations. He also appeared more visibly people oriented and, prior to his quest for the presidency, had overlooked political, ethnic, and religious divide in his association and philanthropy.

It was little wonder therefore that when the elections came and the latter was a candidate, the response across the country pointed to one direction. According to press reports and the results of the electoral commission, the much that were allowed to be released, the results were overwhelmingly in favor of the latter.

Even when further release of results was halted and the elections subsequently annulled, one thing was clear in everybody's mind—that there was a clear winner in what had come to be regarded as the freest and fairest election in the history of the country. The rest of course is history.

Suffice it is to say, however, we had crisscrossed the county in quest of a genuine democratic dispensation for the world's largest black nation. And as an elected publicity secretary of the party that was acknowledged to have won the election at the centre, I personally felt greatly robbed when the annulment of the elections was announced. I had never been a quitter. I had always believed in fighting issues to their logical conclusion. But in my opinion, no sane man should go to make a fist against a man with a loaded gun. I did not see any light at the end of the political tunnel for free and fair elections in the country unless and until something drastic happens. Not being in a position to effect that drastic change, I found only one honorable choice: to quit party politics for good.

THE RETREAT FROM PARTY POLITICS

I retreated into my professional practice and tried to dissipate my energy and satisfy my burning appetite for leadership opportunities by running for leadership positions in my professional body, the Nigerian Medical Association. I soon got elected as the vice chairman of the Nigerian Medical Association in Okigwe zone, the third largest zone in the state after Owerri and Orlu zones.

The enthusiasm, activism, and leadership qualities which I had always cherished as school prefect, as house captain, and later as school captain in government secondary school and later still as first member of the Students Representative Council in the university, representing the medical students in the University of Ibadan, and later still as state publicity secretary of the leading political party in Nigeria were now to be turned to the advantage of my professional body, the Nigerian Medical Association, NMA.

My zonal chairman, one of the most decent and disciplined gentlemen I am yet to come across, was himself a silent achiever. As a former commissioner in the state, he was known widely as Oku na Mmiri (that is, light and water) for his untiring and highly successful efforts in ensuring that electricity and pipe-borne water supply reached every nook and corner of the state. Under his leadership as the zonal chairman of the medical body, we succeeded in reactivating the zonal branch of the association, doubling attendance at meetings, and generally rekindling enthusiasm and esprit de corps in the zone. We began to rotate the venue of the meetings to the homes of willing hosts. That enabled us to know each other better. Where the host's clinic was close by, we visited the clinic after the meetings, and that enabled us to constructively criticize and advise the practitioner on necessary areas of improvement. We got to know our members very closely, and despite the distances and bad roads separating our homes and clinics from each other, we learnt to act as a family. Under our leadership, Okigwe zone regained its pride of place as one of the three big zones in the state branch of the Nigerian Medical Association.

To further boost the image of Okigwe zone, I once undertook to single-handedly host the whole state when it became impossible at a stage to secure a host for the state under Orlu zone. To accommodate the expected large numbers of doctors, I had to knock down a solid block partition wall to connect the living room and another room, a modification that stands till date, a perpetual sign of commitment to an association that I loved. Even though the state later deferred the hosting, the glory of the offer and the readiness for it is still recorded in favor of Okigwe zone. It was our successes in the leadership of Okigwe zone of the Nigerian Medical Association that many years later set the stage for my taking a shot at the highest office in the state branch of the Nigerian Medical Association, the position of state chairman of the organization.

My planned five-year sojourn in the rural areas had dragged to ten years and four months. There was so much that we had developed that was enough to make us stay back permanently in the rural areas. Regular water supply from our extensive underground storage facilities and overhead tanks was present. Also provided were regular electricity supply from our two power-generating sets and from the National Electric Power Authority (NEPA, now called Power Holding Company of Nigeria, PHCN), the latter with a substation and transformer located within the estate. We also set up a fairly extensive palm plantation with improved palm seedlings which I procured form the state Ministry of Agriculture, fruit tree orchards, a well-planned eighty-bed hospital building, and a very comfortable expansive two-storied residential complex. All these with nice flowerbeds and a nice, quiet secluded environment were enough to make anybody want to stay back. But we had fulfilled our plan of setting up a facility in a rural community which only needed personnel to continue. Our personal presence was not a sine qua non to this continuation. Even if it was interrupted for a while, it would spring back to life with time.

With time, therefore, we were able to complete and register a modern hospital complex in an elite area of Owerri. We continued to run the Ndiawa and Owerri facilities concurrently for sometime while we looked for a doctor that would run the Ndiawa facility on a full-time basis.

Deterioration of public facilities was setting in fast. The roads became increasingly nonpassable, public power supply almost ground to a halt, letter communications through the state-sponsored postal services became almost nonexistent. Telecommunication facilities were nonexistent. Public servants were being owed many months of backlog of salaries, and thus services began to stagnate at all levels. The only things that worked appeared to be the fleet of vehicles and the sirens that heralded the movement into and out of the government houses, of the ruling military administrators along with their wives and cronies. It was thus almost impossible to get a doctor to live permanently in the rural areas. My consistent use of myself as an example of living in the rural areas for ten years and four months no longer persuaded any young doctor to take over from me and run the extensive facilities that we had at Ndiawa. We nevertheless endeavored to maintain the registration of the hospital from year to year to ensure that its rejuvenation with time would not present any problems.

Over time, I discussed with my cousin, a reverend minister, about the possibility of getting the mission to run the hospital. We had an extensive tour of the facilities, and under him a German-sponsored team ran the hospital for about four years. A number of difficulties beset the arrangement which had initially held much hope and promise. These ranged from the absence of a permanently resident doctor, inexperience in private hospital administration and management, and the said demise of the expected expatriate financier and proposed medical director of the project in an accident.

With the collapse of the management or takeover arrangement, the search continued for some credible personnel or organization that will be able to fill the vacuum and help sustain the objectives or similar objectives for which the project was initially created.

It was relatively easy to fit back into practice at Owerri. My exit from party politics afforded me the opportunity to concentrate better on my clinical practice and on affairs concerning my professional body. I was soon elected the state secretary of the Association of General and Private Medical Practitioners of Nigeria (AGPMN). Poor attendance at meetings and generalized apathy characterized the activities of the organization whose members were estimated to constitute over 75 percent of the doctor population of the state.

There was a sharp contrast in interest and participation between the Association of General and Private Medical Practitioners (AGPMPN) and its parent body the Nigerian Medical Association. That was possibly because the parent body embodied the entire medical doctors in the state, both those in public and those in private employment. Ironically, at the regular meetings, attendance was higher among the private medical practitioners, the same group that found difficulty strengthening their own association.

Most of the doctors in public service appeared more involved with their affiliate bodies like the Association of Resident Doctors (ARD), the Medical and Dental Consultants Association of Nigeria (MDCAN), or the Guild of Medical Doctors in the state government service (the Guild).

It was found that members of these affiliate bodies of the parent Nigerian Medical Association (NMA) mainly attended meetings when they had problems with their employers or when they had issues bothering them. There was therefore the tendency for the leadership of the state Nigerian Medical Association to be composed predominantly, year after year, until recently, of doctors in the private sector. That was not a very healthy situation because the strength of any organization depended greatly on the numbers of active and participating members. Also, for decisions arrived at during meetings to be representative of the views of a cross section of the members, it was necessary that there should be widespread participation. That was the message I started preaching as soon as I moved back to Owerri and noticed the poor attendance at the association meetings.

I felt that, as I had tried to do by participating in party politics, I would be better positioned to effect positive changes and put into practice what I had preached by being involved in the actual running of affairs of any organization. In other words, I felt that I would be in a better position to contribute by being "a doer of deeds" rather than a "preacher of deeds." Experience had shown that armchair critics hardly achieve meaningful results. Results are produced better by actual participants as espoused by the saying "*Factis non verbis*," implying that action speaks louder than words. Again, we had been taught in the secondary school, the speech from America's president Theodore Roosevelt which ran thus in part:

> The credit belongs to the man who is actually in the arena,
> whose face is marred by dust and sweat and blood,
> who strives valiantly;
> Who errs, who comes short again and again . . .
> Who at the best knows in the end the triumph of high achievement,
> And who at the worst, if he fails, at least fails while daring greatly.

It was in the light of the above and with the conviction that I had something to offer that I had in the first instance joined in the political race some years earlier before the annulment of the elections instead of sitting idly and criticizing what was going on. It was again in the light of that belief that I had something to offer that I decided to contest for higher office in my professional body, the Nigerian Medical Association Imo State.

My decision to contest was borne out of the conviction that there was work to do in the leadership positions of that body. It emanated from a conviction that I had experience, the zeal, the steadfastness, and the selflessness to serve the association with all my strength. I felt that if there was anybody who had something to offer the association in terms of wealth of experience in leadership, it was I (the way most politicians think). I was aspiring to the association's leadership with the aim not of taking but of giving my time and talent and if need be, my treasure. I aspired to lead the association to newer heights, to broaden its follower ship base, to increase the zeal of its membership, and to use the wealth of experience I had developed over the past years in building construction to elevate to the greater heights its secretariat project, which my two immediate predecessors had started on. Besides, I wanted to elevate the respectability of the office of the chairman of Nigerian Medical Association to one that was absolutely incorruptible irrespective of the level of the temptation or the magnitude of the offer. Above all, I wanted to reestablish the respectability and esteem of the doctor to its pride of place and hoist it once again to the number one position which it once was, and which, by virtue of the caliber of the men and women who got into that profession, it should, as of merit, continue to be.

In campaigning for the office of the chairman therefore, I would not claim to be the only one with good qualities, but I would claim to be the best, and I would demonstrate beyond all reasonable doubt that I was the best. As the election date for the new executives approached, two senior colleagues had casually indicated to me that they would also run for the post of chairman. A third colleague, a former officer of the association, had already publicly declared his intention to run for the post too.

For the first two colleagues—who were also consultants, much as I did not wish to underestimate their capabilities—I doubted if they would stand the stress required to crisscross the zones and be humble enough to request to be given audience by younger colleagues. I doubted if they had the charisma and patience to address groups of doctors and stand before them to hand out their manifestoes on election day. I doubted if they would not flare up in anger when the inevitable derisive question of where they had been all these years would be thrown at them by one of their resident doctors. I did not write them off because from experience I knew that the election ground was a very slippery ground and that the political terrain, even for professional politics, was like quickstand. But I knew that if either or both of them came out to contest, I would, even with all due modesty, be very ready, willing, and able to defeat them.

For the third aspirant, a former officer of the association, however, I had my reservations about the ease with which I could beat him. I knew he was a hard fighter, quite intelligent, and pragmatic. However, I believed that in addition to possessing those qualities, I had the advantages of experience and integrity; and I believed that people who knew me well enough would attest to my resoluteness, incorruptibility, humility, and the capability to fight to the end, any cause I believed in.

Even though I had been making personal contacts about my intentions for some time, I did not kick off my formal electioneering until one month to the actual day of the election.

The process of campaigning for elections into the state executive committee, unlike what we had in political parties, did not involve rallies. The association was simply a professional body, and for the joy of one feeling that one was being of service, there were absolutely no remunerations. That probably accounted for the lack of enthusiasm by many people who would wish to associate. It was certainly not for people who would wish to tie every service with material remunerations. For those who had the enthusiasm to serve, however, the competition for the opportunity to serve was nonetheless very keenly contested. The campaigns consisted of individual contacts and group contacts between the contestants and the doctors during zonal meetings or affiliate body meetings. A new dimension was added when one or two contestants rallied some doctors in an office in the health management board and in the doctor's common room of one of the health institutions and entertained them with soda and cookies while selling his manifesto. By and large, however, unlike in political rallies, the campaigns were very decent as there could never be a question of inducing a doctor to vote in a particular way. These were largely principled and fairly economically comfortable people who were sufficiently informed as to know well who would represent their group interest the best. Based on the forgoing premise, I made my rounds to the zonal meetings of the association's five zones. I also campaigned at the meeting of the association of the resident doctors of the local federal medical center. I made repeated phone calls to as many of the doctors, whom I had access, as much as possible. I then made personal visits to those doctors whom I knew were in a position to influence one way or the other the decision of other doctors. I concentrated in this regard on those doctors who owned medical institutions that employed other doctors and those that headed public or voluntary agency hospitals where other doctors worked. I distributed copies of my manifesto to the heads of these institutions as well as to the individual doctors.

In my manifesto, I chronicled the different roles I had played in furthering the cause of the Nigerian Medical Association. I narrated the role I had played as the assistant secretary of the association even as a house officer in the University College Hospital. I mentioned my role as the zonal vice chairman of the association. I narrated how I had, at great cost to myself, single-handedly undertaken to host the whole state branch of the association in my house when there was no one else willing to host. Finally, I narrated my constant presence and active participation at virtually all state meetings of the association. I then went into great details to marshal out my plans to lead the association to greater heights if I was elected the state chairman.

I concluded by making a firm promise to work out a formula for remodeling and reconstructing the thoroughly run-down, dilapidated, roofless building which the association had secured from the state government and which, overgrown inside and outside with bushes and inhabited by rodents and reptiles, we had hitherto used for our meetings. The incumbent chairman, in a very courageous move and to ensure physical occupation, had prepared an arm of the complex for the association's bimonthly state meetings. I also had promised that if elected chairman, I was going to fight at the center to bring the NMA national body to Imo State, to draw attention to the potentials of the state, to boost tourism, and hence to position the state for greater things to come.

I arrived at the venue of the election on election day along with my wife and two assistants, fully laden with bundles of my manifesto. Even though we were about thirty minutes early for the meeting, a time when ordinarily not even the officials would have arrived, we saw the venue buzzing with cars and people, including doctors whom we had never seen before at our meetings. Cars including SUVs were seen dropping off a number of doctors from the rural areas. Also already present were scores of house officers from the local Federal Medical Center, colleagues who though they were entitled to be members were not registered with us and who, not being financial members, were not eligible to vote. I was also shocked to find that the pillars and walls around the venue were littered with posters of some of the candidates, an unprecedented event in the history of our association. Two of the candidates vying for positions in the elections that day were also already there, shaking people's hands and patting them at the back. They also had multiple canvassers who went around convincing other doctors. And there was I, arriving with just my wife, two assistants, and not even a single poster. I just had copies of a typed manifesto. It was no time to start ruminating over our obvious lack of foresight in preparation. We quickly parked our car and grabbed our manifestoes and started distributing, panicky at first at our lack of color and luster. But we soon picked up confidence. We put up a smile as we went from person to person. We were unwilling to let our faces betray our amazement at what we saw nor to convey any acknowledgement or acceptance of the superiority of our opponent's physical and innovative state of preparedness. Two of my ardent supporters approached me and quietly whispered into my ears, "Doc, it may be a sad day. This other guy has imported a lot of ghost doctors."

"No," I replied, "these are pointers to our superiority. We shall see."

"What do you mean?" my friend asked.

"These ghost doctors will not vote, trust me," I all but boasted, mustering all the confidence I had in me.

The little hall being used as the meeting room was filled beyond capacity. Doctors of all age groups were there, including many whom we had never set our eyes upon, people who did not even know that we had a state secretariat. We only assumed they were all doctors partly because they had presented themselves at that crucial doctors' meeting and partly because some of the contestants at the venue seemed to know them.

As we filed into the hall, one of my cousins who was working in one of the rural hospitals approached me and told me that he was conveyed down to the meeting by one of the vehicles hired for that purpose by one of the contestants. He also gave me a few hints about the strategies of some of my co-contestants at the election. Those revelations confirmed my earlier suspicion that most of the strange faces that surfaced on that election date were nonregistered and, hence, ineligible voters in that day's election.

The biggest mistake my team would make therefore was to allow a situation whereby people would vote simply because they were doctors or simply because they had arrived to the election venue. The constitution of the association was clear on the issue: "Eligibility to vote, or to be voted for, at the association's elections was based on the individual being a financial member in good standing." Even my cousin told me that he himself was not current with his dues. He then told me that I should insist on accreditation and clearance by the state financial secretary, who had a list of all current financial members. That was of course the basis of my earlier statement to my friend: "They will not vote."

After the preambles, the major agenda of the meeting was called up: the state elections. We did not want to take any chances. Time was of the essence. A beating about the bush might be disastrous. After the valedictory speech from the outgoing chairman, the old executive was dissolved, and a returning officer was appointed. One of my assistants who had been deliberately positioned in a different location from me in the hall, as earlier directed, immediately raised a point of information. One of my opponent's assistants, recognizing my assistant and fearing that whatever the former was about to inform the house would not be to the candidate's advantage, immediately sprang to his feet.

"Objection, Mr Returning Officer," the latter said. "We do not need any information today. We are here for an election, and we must proceed."

Of course, the objection was overruled, and my assistant was allowed to continue.

"I wish to inform the house that there are many ineligible voters in this hall and that the constitution of this association is very clear on the issue of eligibility and ineligibility for elections. We must therefore clear the hall for proper accreditation and determination of financial eligibility of the prospective contestants and voters."

Against all protocol and decorum, one of the contestants sprang to his feet.

"The last speaker is not the financial secretary. How does he know that there are ineligible members in the hall? Returning Officer, please let the elections proceed," he said.

That statement was a disaster coming from someone who wanted to lead an elite association like the Association of Medical Doctors. Any one who would not encourage an adherence to the tenets of the association's constitutions certainly would not hope to succeed in the association's elections.

Other points of information, points of correction, and points of order followed.

But the constitution was very clear on the issue. The returning officer, a very composed and disciplined gentleman, read out the relevant section of the constitution and immediately thereafter ordered that the hall "be cleared." Everybody had to move outside. The secretary's membership list and the financial secretary's list were used to readmit eligible members. Over half of the former occupants of the hall were found to be ineligible. Even one of the contestants for the secretary's position was disqualified.

From inside the election hall we could see and hear some of the previous occupants of the hall either driving off in their cars or asking hired drivers who brought them to take them back. A few others remained outside the hall, grumbling loudly. My cousin and a few of my men who failed eligibility were of course outside—ready to counter any attempts to disrupt the elections. But there were no incidents. These were doctors. These were disciplined gentlemen.

The situation was getting clearer, fast crystallizing in my favor.

I was getting increasingly confident that a comfortable number of the doctors who remained in the hall were people who would vote with their heads based on reason and not emotions. The formal nominations followed, and one of the most critical aspects of the campaign was brought up: the candidates' address to the members and the reading of their manifestoes. Even though the written manifestoes had been distributed, each candidate was, just before the actual election, expected to publicly address the voters to finally expatiate on why the vote should go to him or her and not the opposing candidate.

The two most hotly contested positions were the post of the chairman and that of the treasurer. The tossed coin gave the first-speaker position to my opponent. That was sheer luck for me, because of the obvious advantages in speaking after the speech of one's opponent.

My opponent was an obviously powerful speaker. He was also a very dedicated and hardworking gentleman. He had been an official of the association at the state level before, and so he knew quite a bit about the problems associated with running the association. He tapped extensively from that experience. He was quite articulate but dwelt too long on his many trips as an officer of the association. Again he referred too often to the numerous points which he had jotted down on sheets of paper, and that tended to divert the attention of his audience to his hands and gesticulations rather than his words. Finally, his points-and-time distribution was not well coordinated, and by the time he was prompted that he had only two minutes remaining, he had not quite mentioned his areas of priority as chairman of the most elite association in the state. The two minutes prompt appeared to slightly destabilize him, and he spent another minute trying to prioritize his points. At the end when the gavel sounded three times to indicate that his time was up, the chairmanship aspirant kept listing. "I will . . . if elected chairman." He had to be prompted a second time that his time was up, and it took only the continuous clapping of hands and murmuring by the audience to halt what was otherwise a very beautiful speech.

My previous experiences as the school captain of an elite secondary school, as a first member of the Student's Representative Council of the nation's premier medical school, and as a state publicity secretary of one of the two existing political parties were very useful to me when it became my turn to address my colleagues on why I felt I was a better qualified candidate to be their chairman.

The "relaxed mien, gentle smile, occasional jokes, and point-by-point approach to the problems in the association and (my) intended solutions to them," I was later told by my assistants, won me immediate admiration by my listeners.

I first briefly welcomed the voters and thanked them, "who like me had been regular at our association's meetings." In three or four sentences, I rattled my previous activities in the interest of the association. I then briefly but comprehensively narrated some of the problems of the association and proceeded in a little greater detail in a pincher style to proffer my executive's solutions to those problems. From secondary school, I had been a compulsive student of the speeches of that great president of the United States of America, the late president John. F Kennedy, and I tried to tap from his style of positive thinking. I shunned the *I wills* and headed for positive-style deadlines:

> In three months from today, there will be a roof over this secretariat.
>
> In six months from today, plumbing and all electrical work will be over with, in this secretariat.
>
> In one year from today, this secretariat will be completed and commissioned for use, to the glory of God, and the pride of you all, my colleagues.

> And before eighteen months from today, this secretariat will stand tall, as the biggest in black Africa.
> And it will, I promise you, host the doctors from the entire thirty-six states of the Federal Republic of Nigeria. These much I promise you, and more.

In conclusion I had stated the following:

> My antecedents speak for me, my dear colleagues,
> I am not just a doctor.
> I am also a builder, and you can check this fact out.
> I come from a very large family.
> The third of forty-six children of one loving father.
> And this background has taught me the use and value of numbers, and of teamwork.
> We used to eat together in the family, the forty six of us and more.
> And those dinners of many dishes taught me in more ways than one,
> The art of cooperation and the need to share joy with others.
> And I intend to put all these to the advantage of this Association.
> I pledge on my honor to build the NMA, structurally, morally, and in membership.
> I have never before failed any group that I led and will not fail the one Association that I hold so close to my heart, the Nigerian Medical Association.

The ovation was tremendous, and as I took a bow in three directions—left, center, and right—the gavel sounded for my reminder. I voluntarily forfeited the remaining two minutes. The counting of the votes cast by the constitutional secret ballot system followed. The result was unmistakable. I won with a near landslide.

My opponent was gallant in defeat, and I was magnanimous in victory. We approached each other, shook hands, and embraced each other.

"We'll work together," I told him

"Congrats, Doc," he replied. "That was a good job." There was no doubt that my opponent was a disciplined and a hard-fighting colleague.

The NMA Executive and Its Accomplishments

My executive set out to work soon after the elections. There was not much in the association's coffers by way of finances to start work with. We therefore had to make personal financial sacrifices to get started. We first got laborers to clear the grass that had virtually overgrown the entire premises. We thereafter set up a system whereby people who donated certain amounts towards some aspects of constructing and reconstructing the building or who personally undertook to do the construction themselves up to a certain amount be honored with plaques of bronze, silver, gold, or platinum. Projects between ₦25,000 and ₦49,999 were categorized under bronze plaque; ₦50,000 to ₦99,999 got silver plaque; ₦100,000 to ₦249,999 got gold plaque while ₦250,000 and above got platinum plaques. The plaques were to be engraved in marble to be mounted permanently on the building when completed.

Sponsorship of these plaques was to be open first to doctors and later to any friends of the association who chose to participate. The project was given wide publicity, and a date was scheduled for the formal launching.

Handbills, posters, and banners were made; and the event was advertised both in the radio and television, and we traversed the entire length and breadth of the state to ensure that practically every medical facility manned by a medical doctor in the state received an invitation. It was to be an epoch-making event, and we ensured that the photograph of the complex overgrown with tall wild grass adorned the back of the invitation card as a big challenge to the doctors and any well-meaning individuals who would want to participate in the realization of our collective dream, which was to actualize the building of the biggest medical secretariat in Africa.

We started off the day with a church service. The response was so spontaneous. It surpassed our wildest imagination. Doctors and their families filled up an entire wing of the expansive Assumpta Cathedral.

Camera men were so busy, and the pressmen were all over the place from the church to the venue of the launching. It was the largest gathering of medical doctors the state had ever witnessed.

All the past chairmen of the association were present; a representative of the state governor was there, state commissioners, some traditional rulers even the young doctors who scarcely attended meetings including those who were unable to vote during the election day for the incumbent executive. The presence of the young doctors was particularly gratifying to me since it was a confirmation that there were no ill feelings. It was like a carnival.

During the opening formalities which included the opening address, I passionately challenged the doctors to demonstrate their claim of being primus inter pares among the leading professions by putting up a secretariat which was to be truly primus inter pares, first among equals. I challenged past chairmen there present to demonstrate their desire for maturity of the baby they had midwifed, the NMA. I challenged the government of the state whose logo at that time was “Land of Hope” to demonstrate that the state truly had the strong hope to be the best by donating to a worthy cause. I challenged every doctor in the gathering that afternoon to immortalize his or her name and have something to show his or her children and grandchildren about his or her participation in his or her professional body, by having a name engraved in the annals of history of the association. Finally, I challenged our visitors and other friends of the association, the Bar Association, the Union of Journalists, the Association of Engineers to support us so that their members, too, would see the need to aim as high as we had done in embarking on that gigantic venture.

I rested my case by placing the project on the doorsteps of the doctors, with the following admonition, “Colleagues of the medical profession, this is your project. Make it succeed and accept the glory or let it fail, and we all fail together! The choice today is yours, not mine.”

After the applause, there was silence in the hall for about a minute. It was as if the participants were trying to digest what was said. The interval was perhaps also necessary for people to make up their minds and act responsibly instead of pledging on the spur of the moment only to renege later.

Experience had shown that after such calculated lulls, it would be necessary to jump-start positive action by calling on known people who commanded respect and who would be willing and able to move events forward, to open up the day. This is in contrast to throwing open the floor where money is involved, only to be greeted by protracted silence. The latter might be devastating to a fund-raising event as every person would be looking up to the other person to start up with a donation.

I therefore once again picked up the microphone and headed for the high table. I handed over the microphone to the pioneer chairman of the association, a highly intelligent, highly successful, and very hardworking colleague, a renowned physician who had always been very willing to share the secret behind his success with the generality of the doctors. It was a good thing I made that choice for a start. In one fell swoop, we got a confirmed pledge for the roofing of the main secretariat building, the construction of the main hall, and the construction of the library by the Emeritus chairman and his wife. This almost defied our categorization as it was far in excess of our imaginations for even a platinum plaque. The applause was deafening, and morale was boosted, beyond expectation. Other pledges followed in quick succession. My former chairman at Okigwe zone took a gold. Other gold, silver, and bronze plaques followed. Even the very young doctors who had not been participating in the affairs of the association were so motivated that some of them took on bronze plaques, amounts which were almost half of their month's salaries. By the end of the day, we got close to half of what we would need to do the job we had mapped out to do.

We were resolved on fulfilling or even exceeding our election promises. We wanted to demonstrate that unlike what obtained in our political party setup, election promises were supposed to be covenants between the electorate and elected officials and were supposed to be fulfilled to the letter. Before our first year in office, we had completed and were ready to commission from what information available to us the biggest medical association secretariat in the continent of Africa.

On the following physician's Sunday, about one year after we got into office, the state secretariat of the Nigerian Medical Association Imo State was commissioned "to the glory of God and the pride of the doctors."

The success of my executive was hinged on the mutual cooperation between the members of the executive, especially from the vice chairman, the state secretary, and state treasurer. We were able to fulfill the pledges we had made on our election day. Indeed in some cases we were able to virtually beat the deadlines which we had given for certain projects, thanks to the unprecedented cooperation we received from the members of the association. These latter saw the diligence, commitment, financial transparency, and accountability and the humility which we put into all that we did and bent over backwards to complement our efforts. Some doctors—who were initially skeptical based on some previous disappointments and unfulfilled promises, perhaps even from outside the medical circles—upon seeing the dedicated work on the ground decided to chip in their own bit. It was a big success story.

The Dark Days of the Struggle

Our first tenure in office was not all a bread-and-butter affair. After our first year in the association's executive, issues cropped up between some affiliate bodies of the association and the state government. These were to severely put to test our steadfastness and integrity as individuals vis-à-vis our duties as doctors and as elected officials of the association entrusted with the duty of loyalty to the association and its members who put us into office. These events also almost tore to shreds the unity, mutual trust, and friendships which had hitherto existed between individual members and between some members and the association itself.

Prior to these events, the association had no axe whatsoever to grind with the state government. We had functioned like every other professional body, an association committed to the welfare and good of our members and as a watchdog for the public on health matters. The association and our individual members never failed to air our views on matters that might affect the well being of individuals and members of our association. We had also on certain occasions alerted the government on certain matters that might impact adversely on or impede public health and public good in general. At no cost to Government we had enhanced the Government programs in ensuring good health of the populace by free public lectures, seminars, and sometimes school visits. Some of our affiliate organization like the Medical Women's Association had often organized seminars and lectures on such issues as sickle cell anemia, breast cancer, and HIV screening. Those lectures often increased public awareness and lifted the burden off the shoulders of the government.

Also, as a demonstration of our goodwill and solidarity with the government, the executive of the state Nigerian Medical Association had paid a courtesy visit to the state governor in the government house within the first three months of the executive's coming into office. During that visit, we had wished the government well and advised on certain vital issues which we believed would enhance the good health of the populace, improve on health education, and increase the availability of medical personnel in the state. It was in the above regard that the first in the list of our suggestions to the governor during the executive's first visit to the governor was the urgent need to establish a medical school in the Imo State University. That, we had pointed out, would provide places for the hundreds of well-qualified medical school applicants from the state who could not secure places in the federally run and other state-run medical schools in the country due to the quota system that often excluded hundreds of our state-born young men and women. It was also on record that we had pointed out in that address to the governor the great relief which the expected teaching hospital of the proposed Imo State University Medical School would offer to our young doctors who would have the opportunity to do their housemanship in the institution. We had in that address passionately appealed to the governor to consider the issue of the Imo State University Medical School as a priority in view of the very severe stresses that our sons and daughters were undergoing in their quest for medical school education. We had also advised on the need of lifting the embargo on employment for more doctors by the health management board.

That maiden courtesy call on the governor was very cordial and very successful. The state deputy governor, the speaker of the Imo House of Assembly, and two other state commissioners including the health commissioner, and the head of service of the state were in attendance with the governor when he received us in his office. Among the doctors' entourage, I had included all past chairmen of the NMA, the head of the Federal Medical Center, members of my executive, and my old friend and best man, Dave.

The governor was quite appreciative of our visit and had thanked us for our useful suggestions. He responded quite positively on most of the issues we had touched on. He, however, had said that the issue of medical school in the Imo State University would be considered a little later when the finances of the state improved. He promised to keep the issue in constant view.

A few months after our cordial and successful visit to the governor, the Guild of Doctors in the service of the state government wrote a complaint to the state NMA informing the parent body that the state government had failed to implement the salary increase for doctors in the state service as was previously agreed between the doctors and the government. That agreement as a matter of fact was between the doctors in service of the federal government and the federal government itself. It had however been presumed that it was binding also on the state governments, as many state governments had started implementing the agreement soon after it became applicable at all federal health institutions. The Nigerian Medical Association at the national level had of course expressed the view that all doctors in government service throughout the country ought to benefit from the salary increase.

When the state NMA got the complaint from the Guild of Medical Doctors, we wrote to the state government requesting it to implement that salary increase since the earlier nationwide strike by all the doctors in the government service was called off on the promise that doctors would be paid those allowances irrespective of the government level at which they worked. Our letter did not get any response. We had followed up the initial letter with another letter before we got a letter from the office of the head of service indicating that whatever agreements that were reached at the center were not binding on the state government. Inquiries made by the Guild of Doctors and the state NMA had however indicated that many state governments across the federation had started implementing the salary and allowance agreements. We had to provide documented evidence to confirm that the new salaries and allowances were being implemented elsewhere, but these did not seem to make any impact.

It was not until the Guild of Doctors threatened to go on strike that a meeting was summoned by the office of the head of service to discuss the issue. The meeting was attended by the chairman of the Guild of Doctors in the service of the state government along with the state NMA secretary and me. It was not a fruitful meeting as it looked more like a meeting summoned to let us know what the state government wanted or did not want, rather than a meeting to examine facts and resolve issues.

Three weeks after that fruitless meeting, the doctors in the Guild had communicated to the NMA their resolution to go on strike if nothing more was done to address their plight. I had to summon an emergency meeting of the state Nigerian Medical Association to look into the issue. The Guild, being an affiliate body in the NMA, the parent body, was duty bound to consider any matter affecting the latter as one affecting the parent body.

The meeting of the state NMA was attended almost en masse by the doctors who were members of the Guild including some veterinary doctors who allied themselves with the Guild of Medical Doctors for purposes of that action. With their preponderance of numbers, the Guild members were able to sway the vote in their favor that the NMA would call the Guild doctors out on a statewide strike action if the state government failed to address their salary and allowance issue after a certain date.

Since I considered a strike action inimical to the general good, I had to address a letter to the state governor, warning about the consequences of allowing the doctors in the state government service to go on strike by a failure to address their genuine demands. I also intimated the governor on the possibility of a future sympathy strike action by the parent body of the Guild of Doctors, the state Nigerian Medical Association. When no response came from the government house and the Guild of Doctors was getting restless, I wrote another letter to the governor, enclosing copies of the resolutions of the guild and those of the parent body, the state Nigerian Medical Association. After about ten days of my second letter, I got a letter from the principal secretary to the governor inviting the state executive of the NMA "for a meeting with His Excellency, the governor in government house."

On the appointed day and at the appointed time, I was in government house with the association's state secretary, two past chairmen of our association, and the chairman of the Guild of Doctors in government service. Two hours after the appointed time for the meeting, we had not been ushered in. One of the past chairmen left in frustration. I went in to see the principal secretary who had signed the invitation letter. I was ushered in to see the principal secretary after a further one-hour wait. On sighting me, the latter asked, "Is that the Lawyers' Association?" He was not aware of any meeting with the doctors! When I produced the letter signed by him, he glanced at it and asked me, "Who sent you that letter?"

"But that is your name, sir?" I said

The principal secretary took a closer look at the letter and said "His Excellency is in Abuja."

There was no indication of when His Excellency would be back. There was even no indication that the secretary himself remembered scheduling the meeting, even as he did not dispute the fact that he signed the invitation letter. After looking through his manifest (as they called their list of appointments), he said he could see only the Lawyers' Association as scheduled to see His Excellency sometime that day. But I had the original copy of the letter signed personally by the secretary. He did not contest the authenticity of the letter, but that made no difference. There was not as much as an apology nor a regret for pulling us off our work for the day only to be told after a long wait that we were not scheduled to be seen. It was perhaps expected that we should even prostrate in gratitude to the secretary for his mistake of allowing us come to take a glance at the four walls of government house! Such arrogance was not an uncommon event in the new civil service setup, where every public servant had turned into a monstrous and overriding public master treating every other citizen as trash and regarding his or her paid duties as a favor to the public. It was not even unusual for inducements to be expected or even frankly demanded before some of such duties would be performed.

We left the government house more confused and more frustrated than ever.

On getting back to my office, I wrote a protest letter addressed to His Excellency, the governor, protesting the shabby treatment meted to the executive of the Nigerian Medical Association. I also enclosed copies of the two previous letters we had written to the governor and the letter of invitation which we had received from government house for the abortive meeting.

A letter arrived a few days later, scheduling another meeting between the association and the government in the deputy governor's office. There was no reference to the previous meeting which did not hold. It was difficult to get some of our members to accompany us to that meeting in view of their previous experience. I still felt that everything should be done to avert a strike action which would be to no one's advantage and which was bound to divert our attention from our development targets for the association.

Again at the appointed date and time we were at the waiting room of government house. This time the team comprised of the state secretary, five senior members of the association, and me. As usual, we had to wait for about two hours in the general reception room, after the scheduled time of the meeting before being directed to the deputy governor's conference room, a bungalow to the left of the main building. We warmed the seats in the deputy governor's conference room for a further one hour before somebody came in to tell us that the deputy governor would be coming to see us soon. It was then about 1:00 p.m. The scheduled time for the meeting was 10:00 a.m.

It took another one hour before some officers filed into the hall from an adjacent room. We felt relieved thinking that at last His Excellency, the deputy governor, would be gracious enough to see us. That was not to be, as the harbingers were two commissioners and a principal secretary.

As the door closed behind the officers without His Excellency, there were audible sighs of disappointment from my colleagues, many of whom were experiencing for the first time what I had experience twice before. The government officers took their seats on the opposite side of the large oval table. His Excellency's seat at the head of the table remained vacant.

About thirty minutes after their entry, one of the officers went out to take a call from his cell phone. He soon came back and left again in company of a second officer. Shortly after they left the room, one of the officers came back and beckoned on one of us from the window. I thought he was beckoning on one of his colleagues, but he kept pointing in my direction. When I pointed to myself, he nodded his head. He was standing on the corridor outside. When, from inside, I walked towards him at the window, he told me that I was wanted upstairs in the governor's office. I was a little worried at why I should leave the negotiation room to go for another meeting upstairs, alone. I nevertheless whispered to one of the members of our team the message I got and my apprehension. The colleague, a distinguished medical practitioner, assuaged my fears and said I should still go but that I should remember that the rest of them were waiting.

As I entered the beautiful, nicely air-conditioned office upstairs, I could not but observe the heavy and thickly built steel doors which were shut by remote control as I got in. The permanent secretary who ushered me into the room left the room as soon as he showed me in. There were only three of us in the room. If there were other secret eyes, secret monitors, or secret recorders in the room, there was no way I was to know.

I realized that the real meeting was about to begin. The expected meeting in the conference room in the other building where my colleagues were waiting was only cosmetic. The rest was supposed to be very confidential, but I was politely reminded that the big labor leaders at the center did not make their way to economic stardom by being stubborn or recalcitrant, or by sticking too tenaciously to principles. I understood. But must I toe that line?

My heart pounded hard within me. There was not much time for any detailed prayers. But as I left the room about thirty minutes later, I thanked God with all my heart for giving me the strength to uphold some cherished principles and for that steadfastness not to betray the trust reposed in me by my colleagues, some of whom were waiting patiently in the other building. It was so easy, so very tempting to negotiate away one's conscience for selfish reasons. It was so easy to fail. I began to see why so many labor leaders betray their organizations for short-term personal gains. I could equally see why so many steadfast ones, like the Imuodus, succeeded for their unions and got their names immortalized thereafter. The choice is always there for one to make.

As I walked back to the conference room in the deputy governor's office, my knees were wobbling, and my legs were trembling visibly. I was visibly shaken, but I succeeded in maintaining a straight and cheerful face. His Excellency, the deputy governor, later surfaced in the conference room soon after I reentered the hall. There were all kinds of unanswered questions from my colleagues, who were waiting in the hall. Even to this day, I have kept mum to those questions, and so will it remain since an answer or an explanation would make no difference. So long as my integrity remained intact and I had to do the duties for which I was elected, in absolute loyalty to the organization and people who had reposed so much confidence in me, to the full satisfaction of my conscience, and in consonance with the religion which I practiced, it made no difference. I might have appeared the poorer for my *recalcitrance*, but I sincerely believed, and I still do believe, that I am the richer, at least in spirit, for the steadfastness.

The negotiations had failed upstairs and were therefore bound to fail downstairs. What followed downstairs was only a verbal bullying of "the recalcitrant doctor who, leading a small body of doctors, thought he was powerful enough to pull down or discredit the government." Those were the words with which I was to be described some four months later, at the height of the inevitable strike action. If I had succumbed to the spoils of office, a small nonexecutive office of a mere professional body, I probably would have earned a better description, at least from the powers that were. But who knows where I would have been thereafter.

I might for a short while have been heavier in my wallet or my bank account and perhaps for a short time been a friend of government. I might perhaps for an even shorter time have participated in feeding at government house on the funds of the people at the numerous government dinners or perhaps have gotten chauffeured in a government vehicle as a board chairman to visit my friends to demonstrate to them that I "had arrived." But beyond these, would I have been able to hold my head up as I can do today anywhere I go? Would I have been able to wipe from my conscience that sense of guilt which I would forever have felt at a betrayal of the trust of a group that had reposed so much confidence in me? That feeling of guilt would have trailed me for the rest of my life.

But today I can walk tall and hold my head high among my colleagues in the medical profession. Today I can relish that award of the highest honor in the medical profession, the award of Distinguished Medical Practitioner (DMP), which my colleagues in the state Nigerian Medical Association conferred on me in absentia two years after I left office as chairman, even while I was six thousand miles away across the Atlantic Ocean. I feel fulfilled.

Nothing can be more satisfying. Nothing can be more rewarding. I would not exchange that honor for any amount of tons of gold nor dinners nor diamonds; no, not for any position, not on this planet. I feel fulfilled.

After the drama during the failed negotiations, another emergency meeting of the association was summoned to update the members about the "progress" of the negotiations. It was obvious from subsequent events that rather than pay the doctors what was due to them, the powers that were had chosen subterfuge, blackmail, false allegations, and a divide-and-rule attitude towards the issue. To us it did not matter whatever unwholesome tactics were being employed. As far as we were concerned, there was only one issue on the table: pay the doctors what was due to them, and every other issue would be over.

At the emergency meeting, it became obvious that some of our members were already being used against the interest of the association. Two distinct views became obvious at the emergency meeting: the view of "friends of the government" and the view of the Nigerian Medical Association as dominated during that meeting by members of the Guild of Doctors in government service. I was not a friend nor a foe of the government; I was not a member of the Guild of Doctors in government service. I was only an elected chairman of the state Nigerian Medical Association. It was therefore my duty to play a completely neutral role. After heated debates which almost degenerated into physical combat, I felt it would be necessary to call for motions reflecting the different views. We would then vote to arrive at a resolution. There were moves to block the proposed voting. Tempers rose to fever pitch. It looked like some people felt that their jobs might be on the line if a motion that was not favorable to government sailed through. At a certain stage, a statement which was later withdrawn even accused the chairman of working for an opposing governorship candidate.

Of course, I knew that my only commitment was to the association which I was elected to lead. I was committed to no man, and at that particular moment my only interest was the good of the organization which had reposed confidence in me by its members electing me to lead them. Any other consideration was of secondary or no consequence. For me there was no other consideration.

I therefore rose and called for the motions and countermotions. The voting that followed witnessed the ascendance of a motion that called for a total and indefinite statewide strike action by all doctors in state government service if by a certain date the government failed to implement the agreements reached at the center between the doctors and the federal government. Even before the ultimatum was officially communicated to government the following morning, all kinds of anonymous threatening phone calls started coming to me. I had to switch off my phones throughout the night. It was obvious that the resolutions of the doctors had already been unofficially communicated to the government most likely by the government-sponsored "ears" within our ranks.

By the following morning, the official decision of the Nigerian Medical Association was communicated to the state government nonetheless. We deliberately did not copy the press at that stage believing that the issue could still be resolved.

What transpired between that day of communication to the government and the end of the two weeks' deadline by way of phone calls, personal calls, and threats from unknown quarters was unimaginable. Some of our members who probably felt very disappointed at having failed to perform their "duties to avert the passage of the motion" felt a deep sense of anger. I was warned by more than three different people to be careful about my personal safety. At that stage, I started wondering what it was all about. Couldn't the advisers of the powers that were simply advise the government on the simple straightforward reasonable thing to do—pay the doctors? If they did that, and we did not call off any impending action, then they would be justified to brand us with whatever accusation they desired.

Perhaps they had committed themselves too strongly and perhaps had promised more than they were capable of accomplishing. In such situations people are wont to be desperate, and a desperate man is capable of overreaching himself.

There was no way that we would know of the genuineness or otherwise of any moves being made by some of our colleagues since, as succinctly demonstrated in Shakespeare's *Macbeth*, there was no art to find the mind's construction in the face.

All said and done, one thing was clear: a strike action by doctors resulting in disruption of health services would be to nobody's advantage. Besides, the most vulnerable in society, the poor people, were likely to suffer more as they would not be able to afford the high cost of private medical services. Again, no matter how we viewed it, the image of the doctors and their association, the Nigerian Medical Association was bound to suffer when the inevitable casualties of any such action would start tumbling in. Many people would not go into as much as to ask about the intricacies of what the real causes of the work stoppage were.

It would simply be said that the doctors callously let people die just because they wanted more money. Only few people would say, "Why didn't the government give the doctors more money if that was what was agreed upon?"

It was therefore necessary to do everything possible to avert the strike action. That was the direction in which we were thinking; at least that was the direction in which I, as an individual, was thinking. With the deadline for commencement of the strike action approaching, therefore, I wrote another letter to His Excellency, the state governor, passionately imploring him to use his good offices to stop a statewide industrial action by all medical doctors in the service of the state government. I also pointed out the possibility of a sympathy work stoppage by all other doctors in the state, if the grievances of the doctors in government service were not addressed. I finally reminded His Excellency that we all owed it as a duty to ourselves and to our people to protect them from all harm including, by omission or commission, the harm of illness and disease. I emphasized on the urgency of the situation and advised that the issue be given the urgent attention it deserved.

I tried to ensure that other prominent citizens joined in the fray to advice His Excellency rather than the few professional advisers around the corridors of power who might indirectly be benefiting from the withholding of the funds that would have been used to offset the doctors' demands. I sent copies of the letter to many prominent and respected people and organizations in town including the chairman of the Council of Ndieze (traditional rulers), the chairman of the Bar Association, the bishops of the Catholic and Anglican cathedrals in Owerri, and the chairman of the Union of Journalists. I requested all these people to kindly intervene in that issue which I knew would have far-reaching consequences for us as individuals and for the generality of our people. Three of the people that the letters were addressed to phoned to acknowledge receipt. But there was no word from government house. I came to know however that subterranean moves using the mighty powers of the government were being called into play to forestall whatever the doctors were about to embark upon. All was being done, but the one thing which was the crux of the matter: the payment of what was due to the doctors was not being addressed.

Based on the information that we got, I had to move out of my house two days prior to the day of the press conference that was to announce the commencement of the strike action. Unwelcome phone calls flooded my telephone lines, most of them threatening hell and brimstone and "dire consequences" to my person if I dared even show up at the venue of the proposed press conference. I thought of reporting those calls to the police. But in a situation where the issue involved the government, I doubted if such a move would yield any positive results in a third world country where even court orders were often shunned by the executive arm of government. Any reports to the police that tended to implicate the government or its agents was almost always shunned by the police. Besides, I did not want to sensationalize the issue, and I was not equipped for the "did you" or "did you not" and the "come today, come tomorrow" that was bound to characterize such a report when the issue at stake involved the government of the day. The individual is thus almost always left helpless when issues involved the government or its agencies.

I doubted if indeed the chief executive of the state was fully aware of all that was going on, because knowing him as an individual, I did not think he would have sanctioned any of these. I was aware that a lot of things could be done in the name of a chief executive without the latter's knowledge or approval. It was even possible that none of our letters or entreaties ever got to the knowledge of the chief executive. But like in all things, the buck stopped at the doorsteps of the man in charge.

I knew I might be stopped on my way to the NUJ press center, the venue of the proposed press conference. I suspected that other more sinister measures might even be attempted, not necessarily on the orders of the state's chief executive whom I had come to respect as a principled and disciplined individual. But certain unorthodox things might be initiated by other less disciplined, overzealous lieutenants even if only to make good their promise to abort the proposed action.

Very early on the morning of the proposed press conference, therefore, I drove out in near disguise and in a borrowed car to a site very close to the press center and got into the expansive premises much earlier than the scheduled time of the press conference. If therefore there was to be an attempt at my abduction or some other unorthodox action, let it be in full view of the public and the press. I did not intend to show up at the exact time of 10:00 a.m., but it was necessary not to let the pressmen and the doctors including members of the state executive who showed up to disperse.

Many days prior to the proposed press conference, many local and national newspapers were already awash with news of the impending strike action. Even the widely read Catholic Church newspaper in the state carried a prominent article on it. We had hoped and prayed that all that publicity would make the government change their mind. Again even if the lieutenants of the state's chief executive were concealing our letters from him, we believed that the governor would have read about the impending doctors' strike action in the press. Certainly he was not like some African leader who relished in the affirmation that he did not read the national newspapers. Certainly the chief executive would not like to play the role of Nero who played on the harp while Rome burnt.

At about 10:20 a.m., I entered the hall of the press center. The seats were almost filled to capacity. Indeed, when I did not show up at the appointed time, it looked like the leadership of the Guild of Doctors had concluded arrangements to go solo and proceed with the press conference, even though I had kept copies of my speech close to my chest. A number of our colleagues were aware that there were strong moves by the powers that were to divide the ranks of our membership and ensure disloyalty to the association in order to disorganize the strike action. There was therefore great relief when I walked into the fully packed hall. The chairman of the Guild of Doctors—a great, highly intelligent, and dedicated young man and a meticulous organizer—had fully arranged every detail of the gathering and ensured that virtually all the prominent national service news media were represented at the press conference. After I was introduced to the gathering, I immediately proceeded to read my prepared statement. The statement chronicled the genesis of the industrial dispute and how the state Nigerian Medical Association had made all efforts to get the government see reason in paying the doctors to no avail. I therefore announced that "consequent upon a resolution of the association," I was "calling out the doctors in the service of the state government on a total and indefinite strike action until the issues in dispute were fully addressed."

It was a most painful and most unfortunate decision and one that had been forced upon the doctors. Even up to the last minute before that press conference, I wished at every moment that I could get either a letter or a call from the state Ministry of Health or from government house to the effect that the government had accepted to pay the doctors. Much as I did not fear it, I did not want it to go down in the history of the NMA that I led a doctor's strike that paralyzed or even disrupted medical services, a strike that would inevitably lead to pain and suffering and even some deaths to the populace especially when I knew that most of the people who would suffer were not the people who caused the problem, but the people at the lower ladder of society. These were the people who mainly patronized the government-owned general hospitals. These were the people who could not afford the nonsubsidized bills of the private hospitals. These were the people who could not afford to pay or have their ways paid for medical treatment to Europe and or the United States of America and Canada. It was to avoid that scenario that I had to hesitate for so long. Yet I knew that in conformity with the resolution already taken by the association which I headed, and whose constitution I had sworn to uphold, that I had to, against my personal wishes and desires, declare the strike action. The consequences were bound to be grave, but it was a necessary evil, a strong furnace that was necessary to make the finest steel. If the doctors in the state government service felt so dissatisfied with the pronounced disparity between their pay without the amendment and the pay of their colleagues in the neighboring federal medical center, there was no way they would be expected to produce commensurately good services. The long-term effect of a corrective strike action was obviously better than a protracted period of silent dissatisfaction.

Dissatisfaction expressed by public protests and demonstrations for instance would be preferable than bottled-up anger. A blowup of the latter could often have disastrous consequences. These were some of the arguments which I used to pacify myself and my conscience and justify my being the principal instrument a reluctant one for the commencement of what turned out to be the longest-lasting strike action in the history of medical practice in the country, an action that was to last seven months and four days!

I drove straight to my house after the press conference with a clear conscience and the realization that even if I was arrested, abducted, or harmed in some other ways, it was already too late. As I drove down, my heart pounded heavily in my chest. What if I had an accident on my way and I needed to be rushed to the nearest government hospital where there would be no doctors as a result of the strike action which I had just announced? What if I was attacked by robbers or even hired hit men, and I needed to be rushed to the government hospital? Would I not be orchestrated by the government press as "the foolish physician who shot himself on the foot"? Would I expect any sympathy from anybody except perhaps by the few who truly understood the plight of the doctors and the justness of the cause for which we fought?

Subsequent days witnessed the influx of press men and women into my office in the association's building and in my private office adjacent to my clinic.

We had not envisaged that the strike action would last longer than a week or two before the government would call for meaningful truce by paying the doctors what was due to them or at least making a commitment to pay at a future date. Maybe that would have been the case if we were allowed access to the state governor on any of the occasions we had applied to see him. Perhaps we would have been able to explain firsthand to him what the actual situation was. I still believed that being a good man but one who had what many people believed was not the best of lieutenants, assistants, and advisers; if he got to know the true position of events, he would have taken personal charge and would not have allowed the strike action and the undesirable aftereffects to commence in the first instance.

By the time that preparations for the national general elections got into the second month, the efforts to break the ranks of the NMA membership had greatly geared up. Instead of efforts being channeled towards addressing the grievances of the doctors in the government service for which the parent body, the state Nigerian Medical Association, called a strike action, efforts were dissipated in propaganda and blackmail. Virtually all that were friendly with me on personal basis were detailed to come to persuade me to call off the strike action. It was amazing how people who were my schoolmates, personal friends or even blood relations were fished out and detailed to persuade me "to see reason." Some were to tell me that I was being silly by failing to take my cut while I "still had the opportunity." Others were to tell me that the people I was fighting for were only using me and would soon abandon me "as soon as they were settled." Others still were detailed to use subtle blackmail by telling me that the government had information that I was being sponsored by rival political parties. Even my closest friends, except two, were to desert me to one extent or another. My biggest fear was that my personal family cohesion was being stretched to breaking point and might crack under the enormous pressure.

"Tell your husband that he is playing with fire."

"Tell your husband that he is playing the fool."

"Tell your husband that he is not being a Nigerian."

"Tell your husband that the government is monitoring him."

"Go, warn your husband that . . ."

Oh, I was almost being driven crazy by the mounting pressure and blackmail that was daily dished out to people who were dearest and closest to me. And that was for a mere leadership of a professional body, a position which was by no means an executive position or a political appointment.

On one occasion during Corpus Christi Church service in an open-field service, my wife and I had joined the queue for Holy Communion when a text message vibrated into my cell phone. Thinking it was an emergency message from the hospital, I pulled aside to read it. The text read, "We'll get you on your way." There was no name to the text.

The previous day, I had two messages from two friends who advised me to be more careful about my personal safety. With the anonymous message then supposedly bluntly telling me that they would get me on my way, I felt convinced that the threat was becoming real. My fear was especially heightened by the fact that there were many unresolved murder incidents in the state about that time. My fear was not that any officials of the state would be out to physically hurt me for something as small as a professional body's industrial action. I did not believe they would descend so low. But then, in every such situation, there could be some mean and overenthusiastic hit men and hangers-on who might want to unconventionally deal with people whom they might feel were inconveniencing their masters and threatening their "sources of chop money." It was such people that I was apprehensive about, indeed fearful of.

My heart pounded heavily in my chest after I read the text message, but I did not show it to my wife. I rejoined the queue and continued for Holy Communion; after which, I showed the message to my wife. We quickly left the church service just after communion, and with our son and daughter who were at church service with us, we drove off in a different direction from our house and left town. It was later that night that Dr Ndu, my good friend, phoned to tell me that he and his wife waited for over half an hour in front of our gate after they failed to see us at the road junction on their way to the village. It was only then that I remembered that I had earlier that morning spoken with my friend and that I had told him that I would be at the junction on the road to my house about 1:00 p.m. on my way from church service.

That incident brought home to me the extent of misconceptions and wrong judgments which people could reach, even in unrelated issues, when they were under severe stress and in fear. We felt so stupid when we started driving back to our house from our hideout that I even started questioning the correctness of some of the very actions that we had taken so far based sometimes on what we might have misjudged.

As the strike action got more protracted without the government budging, the Guild of Doctors in government service sponsored a successful motion calling on all the other doctors in the state to embark on a sympathy strike.

As a date for the two-day warning strike action approached and the national elections were approaching, it looked that the powers that were got apprehensive of the possible consequences of a sympathy strike action by the doctors in both the private sector and those in the federal medical center and in voluntary agency (mission) hospitals.

A hitherto unknown association calling itself Committee of Senior Doctors wrote a letter demanding that I summoned an emergency meeting to stop the strike action. The committee which was unknown to our constitution sent a letter which unfortunately was purportedly signed by a hitherto highly respected member of the NMA and another doctor. The letter indicated that the purported authors had copied the letter to the state government which to me, rightly or wrongly, was an indication that the authors one way or the other were only trying to please the powers that were without taking time to address the plight of their colleagues who were being denied what their counterparts with equivalent qualifications were receiving. It therefore became necessary for me as chairman of the state body to inform the members at the subsequent routine state meeting that the association in question was not known to NMA as an affiliate body and was consequently unconstitutional. At best it was a private initiative for good or for ill, and since its stated mission was at variance with the documented resolution of the general house, it could not be said to be conforming with the decision of the general body of doctors.

So many other sources of pressure were mounted by different interest groups during the seven months that the strike action lasted. Since however the decision to embark on a strike action was not a personal decision of the state chairman nor the state executive but the general body of the association, its being called off was not expected to be a personal decision no matter how uncomfortable we as individuals might have felt about it. It was possible the authors of the letter were acting in good faith. There was no way I or indeed any other person would know. The fact remained however that the doctors were being owed, and all that was being carried out were discussed on the floor of the association's secretariat and were documented. Besides, a resolution was voted on and passed, and at least one of the authors was present at one of the botched efforts at a peaceful resolution of the impasse before the declaration of the strike action.

The statewide sympathy strike action by private, voluntary agency hospitals, and the Federal Medical Center was not total. Provision was made to maintain services for patients already on admission. Emergency cases were also attended to. The maintenance of those skeletal services was a good thing because all said and done, strike action by doctors and indeed other medical personnel was an ill wind that would blow no one any good. Medical care is like mercy in Shakespeare's *Merchant of Venice*, which blesses him that gives and him that takes.

The mere fact that virtually all the hospitals in the state had gone out on the forty-eight hours "warning strike" albeit for outpatient cases only, I believed was of significance. I believe that it was a pointer to the powers that were that despite efforts at instigating disharmony within the association, there was need for it to accelerate arrangements to meet the legitimate demands of those doctors. It had became increasingly obvious that the orchestrated propaganda stunt that the state chairman of the NMA or any functionaries of the association was working against the government or had any hidden agenda was untrue. I repeatedly circulated letters affirming the commitment of the NMA to call off the strike action the very minute there was a commitment by the government that the new salary scale and allowances would be implemented. Anybody who had a hidden agenda or who had in any way committed himself or herself in any way would not make those statements. In any case, what inducement would anybody commit us with? Was it money or position, houses or cars? What exactly could the price be? One might not have all the silver and gold, but those items truly meant very little to many of us and, with all humility and modesty, to me in particular.

It probably was a realization of the futility of any of those inducements after the failed meeting in government house that made some of the functionaries resort to some degree of blackmail, which I did not in any case lose any sleep about. I was sure that like other measures before it, blackmail was also doomed to failure. And it did meet with failure.

THE PHYSICIANS COME TO TOWN

In fulfillment of one of the election promises we made during the campaign for chairmanship, I offered on behalf of the Imo State NMA that the state would host the whole nation at the Annual General Meeting (AGM) Delegates Conference. The hosting of that conference if taken in turns would come to any state and the federal capital territory only once every thirty-seven years. It was usually a very major decision for any state to take since the burden was usually heavy, both physically and financially. Virtually any state NMA that would host the AGM must be certain of backing from the relevant state government. But there was Imo State NMA, at "war" with the state government over doctors' salaries, offering to host the AGM of the Nigerian Medical Association where thousands of doctors from all over the country and companies from all over the world would participate.

As soon as we won the hosting rights for the conference at a meeting held in Abuja, the nation's capital, my eyes were opened to the reality of the situation and the enormity of the burden we had taken upon ourselves.

Without the financial backing of the state government, where were we going to get the money to host thousands of doctors and the scores of other national officers and their office staff? My colleagues at the state had been made almost donation weary from the demands of the state secretariat to which the incumbent government contributed just a hundred thousand naira (about one thousand dollars).

The hosting of the conference was going to cost millions of naira, and our pockets were virtually empty.

Rather than rejoice over the winning of the hosting rights, the right of that victory turned out to be a nightmare to me as I tossed round my bed in my hotel room pondering on whether I had bitten more than we could chew. My apprehension was attenuated the following morning after I spoke with Chidy, the state secretary.

Chidy to whom I owe a great deal of whatever successes we might have achieved during our tenure, simply told me, "Will is way."

I believed Chidy. Back to Owerri, the state capital, I called up Amaze, a very articulate, loyal, and hardworking chairman of one of the zones of the state NMA. Amaze had been one of the pillars in our struggle for the rights of the government service doctors. He was the only zonal chairman who sponsored a room at the state secretariat when it was under construction. Again at a stage during the struggle, when we did not have either association or personal funds to sponsor a press announcement at the national network, he had come to the association's rescue. I knew Amaze was somebody I could trust to handle the all important project of overseeing the hosting of that national conference. I knew the implications, the burdens, and the rewards. It was a big burden, but I knew Amaze was capable of handling it. I equally knew that he would be rewarded when we succeeded by gaining national prominence. I informed Amaze of our success in winning the hosting rights, and I offered him the position of coordinator of the local organizing committee. He hesitated for a while after the offer. He knew of the enormous burdens involved since he had once been a state officer. He then accepted. I knew by his acceptance that we would succeed. I was happy.

It was enormous work for us all. The chairman of the state hosting the NMA was usually the chairman of the local organizing committee (LOC). In our instance, however, Amaze was appointed the coordinator, the de facto chairman. He set to work immediately. Thousands of letters had to be written. Hundreds of personal visits, phone calls, and piles of mails were needed to be made and attended to. It was an enormous job. But in the end everything all tied up well. The state government because of the industrial action did not contribute a dime to the conference. Other state governments in similar situations of hosting would shoulder up to seventy-five percent or more of the overall cost of the conference which would be seen as a big honor to the state. One of the state governments in one of the states in the northern parts of the country was known to have written off the total cost of hosting when an earlier hosting right was granted to the state NMA. Besides, such a conference would directly and indirectly boost the image of the state and open up doors to tourism. My state government saw it differently, in its great wisdom. Even the normal request for a courtesy call on government house by the visiting national executive of the association was denied.

When it became obvious that the state's chief executive would not be available even to declare the conference open as was usually the practice, we succeeded in getting a visiting federal minister, who was a doctor, to perform that function. The state health commissioner later showed up though and was appropriately ushered to the high table. It was a highly successful conference, and we got the national chairman of the NMA to commission another wing of the association's state secretariat, which was opened during the conference.

The success of the Annual General Meeting without government financing coupled with the impending general elections into executive positions in government possibly combined to compel the powers that were to see the compelling need to pay the medical doctors in the government service what was their due. It was possible also that after seven months of futile blackmail and concealment from the state chief executive of the true situation on the ground and the true reasons for the strike action, the powers that played around government house and others who were angling to have a role finally opened up to the chief executive the full picture. At a very unexpected moment and in a situation akin to a big anticlimax, I was informed from government house that if we called off the strike action, even if momentarily, the government would "approve the full implementation of ALL the demands of the doctors." The condition was that I should announce a suspension of the strike action first before the government would announce a full acceptance of all the conditions for which the doctors had been on strike for seven months. The "condition" appeared to be a face-saving measure. It was to emphasize that the government was not forced by the strike action to acquiesce to the justified demands of the doctors. But it was not to us a question of a victor or a vanquished. After all, we did not just embark on a strike action overnight. We discussed, pleaded, complained, warned, and gave ultimatum before ever we took the only remaining option. We never for once contested the enormous powers of the government nor did we aim at flexing muscles with the government which we knew had the powers of persuasion and coercion. It was therefore not a question of who would be said to be a victor or who would be the vanquished. It was not a question of who would blink first. If the government had done the right thing ab initio, there would never have been the need for any complaint nor indeed any strike action. We were prepared at all times to call off the strike action if the government gave an undertaking that they would pay the doctors. Indeed, if ab initio there was a promise from the government that they would pay the doctors, there might not have been the need to have embarked on the strike action in the first instance. In any case, if we called off the action and the government reneged on its promise, we could very easily resume the action. By then it would be more obvious to any doubting Thomases that the government was not being sincere.

On getting the call from the government house therefore, I summoned an emergency meeting of the NMA, and we immediately suspended the strike action “temporarily.” By the following afternoon, I got a letter signed by His Excellency, the governor himself, channeled to me through the Ministry of Health indicating the acceptance by government of all the demands of the doctors.

The unnecessary battle was over.

Over, more surreptiously than it began.

And who was there to count the cost in men and materials?

Nobody!

The constitution allowed me a two-year tenure. At the end of the two years, I had wanted to get back to my clinic. The position of the state chairman of the medical association and the intense efforts I had put in to ensure that I fulfilled the projects I had in my election manifesto had told adversely on my practice. I found I was no longer putting in enough time into my practice, and my patients were quick to notice that. It is easy for a physician to believe that a patient does not notice when the physician is not putting adequate time to the practice. And I knew that it would be unfair to my patients if I took them on but did not give them all the attention. I therefore decided to take only scheduled patients and referred most of the others to my other colleagues. I therefore had wanted to go back fully into my clinic after my first tenure. I however later changed my mind when it became obvious that what we had put in so much effort to put in place and the sacrifice and the struggle that we had shouldered were just waiting to be pulled to dust. The enormous pressures from well-meaning colleagues especially our colleagues in government service who felt that a new administration might not fight as doggedly for actualization of the promises that we had got came to bear. I therefore consented to run for a further two years as allowed by our state constitution. The Guild of Medical Doctors, whose cause was being fought, and many well-meaning members of the association were very instrumental to my decision to run for a second term. It was a hazardous position to vie for at that time considering the overriding interest of the powers that were to sponsor someone who would dance to their tune. Indeed the final thing that made me decide to run for a second tenure was when I got information from someone, who was being sponsored to oppose me should I decide to run, about the plans that were on the ground. That friend had approached me and confided in me that his decision not to be used against me was because "you do not change a winning team." After that very patriotic and friendly information, I made up my mind that there must be something that made those powers that were not to want me around. That particular thing certainly could not be in my best interest nor in the best interest of the association. I resolved to fight back, not necessarily to make a point, but rather to ensure that all our efforts would not be in vain or get reversed so soon after successes were achieved.

As my friend declined the sponsorship against me "in the interest of NMA," a replacement was quickly substituted by the powers that were and their cronies.

Unlike in the first tenure, the election for the second tenure was virtually a noncontest. All the doctors that the powers that were had approached to pick up the candidates ticket to oppose me had declined. Some had come to inform me of the approach made to them. The consensus opinion and slogan were later to become "You don't change a winning team." The administration on the ground was credited with giving "a new sense of direction and a new lease of life to the NMA," hence the massive support. Those did not of course impress the powers that were since they would prefer puppets who would "cooperate with government" even if that "cooperation" was to the detriment of the doctors or even of the population.

It was therefore no wonder that on the scheduled election day, all the doctors who had learnt that the powers that were had concluded arrangements to sponsor for the chairman's position, a doctor who had earlier picked up and returned a completed nomination paper for the post of assistant secretary, they thronged en masse to see how the apparently sponsored candidate would succeed.

This colleague had neither picked up nor completed the nomination paper for the position of chairman as required. He was apparently picked up for sponsorship by the powers that were, at the last minute, when everyone else had declined the sponsorship. He had also apparently been provided the resources and the assurance that all senior government doctors who were in management positions had definite orders to support him. He also probably had instructions to stir trouble and scuttle the election process if he found that he could not muster enough support during the elections. Unfortunately most of those who had been detailed to spearhead the crises to scuttle the election did no turn up, knowing how unpopular their move would be among the rest of the doctors.

The orders were that since they knew they could not beat the incumbent, they should scuttle the election so that an interim executive, whom the powers could manipulate, would be appointed. That would give the government the opportunity, with the incumbent out of the way, to groom a relatively acceptable candidate other than the incumbent chairman. The arrangement leaked shortly before the election, and the rest of the Guild members and the rest of the well-meaning members of the NMA geared up for the challenge to ensure that a puppet executive was not manipulated into office for the doctors by the state government. It was for these reasons really that I decided to run again despite my earlier resolution to retire back to my clinic.

After the dissolution of the executive, a returning officer was elected. The elected returning officer, who was thus charged with the responsibility of conducting the elections, was a gentleman to the core, a man who would not be manipulated, a man who stood his ground against government-sponsored agents at that election, a man who as commissioner had ensured that power and water supply got to many nooks and corners of the state under a previous administration in the state, a man who was my former zonal NMA chairman. He took control. He resisted pressures by highly placed government doctors, a handful of puppets, to postpone the election. The principled ones among the group had stayed away. These few, who showed up, employed all kinds of tactics in an effort to disrupt the elections. Insults were deliberately hauled at the returning officer to provoke him into losing his temper and acting irrationally. He called for nominations for the post of chairman. There was only one documented candidate, and that was the incumbent chairman. Suddenly someone raised his hand and said he wanted to contest too. Apparently in their last-minute arrangements, the sponsors forgot the procedure for nominating a candidate. The candidate could not nominate himself. He had not filed nomination papers. Even at that, and perhaps to avoid rancor, the returning officer waived the paper nomination rule and asked the "candidate" for his nominee. All were silent. Then a government agent sitting behind picked up courage and nominated him. A supporter became another problem until another reluctant agent put up his hand while looking to the ground as if to hide his face to voice his support. They found themselves between the wrath of their fellow doctors for being obvious "sellouts" and the later wrath of their masters in the government.

Two nominees for the post of chairman thus emerged. One was the established and documented nominee who had submitted his photographs, resume, and nominee, as stipulated by the election guidelines; the other was an emergency nominee, who was reluctantly nominated on the floor of the house without any prior documentation. Then the time arrived for the financial screening by the financial secretary who was called upon to give the financial status of the emergency nominee, since the later had not earlier undergone financial clearing as required by the regulations. The emergency candidate was not a financial member of the association. He was found to have paid the immediate past three years dues only the previous day. He did not pay for four years prior to the immediate three years. It was obvious that he was communicated only the previous day that he should go and oppose the incumbent, and he had gone to make emergency payment of dues for the previous three years. According to the constitution, those payments were to be applied to the years from the time he joined the NMA, which left him with a four-year debt. That debt of course meant that he was not in good financial standing, and he was thus not qualified to contest the election.

Even though it had became obvious from their actions that many of our colleagues who were in big positions in government or who held brief for government had orders to support that last-minute candidate, the returning officer with his characteristic courage immediately disqualified the "emergency candidate." I was thus returned unopposed for a second tenure as state chairman Nigerian Medical Association. There was Spontaneous jubilation in the Hall. Unlike during my first-tenure election, there were no shaking of hands between the winning and losing candidates. Technically there was no losing candidate.

The rest of the election went on smoothly, and both the prospective candidate and the rest of the main body of doctors were able to cooperate thereafter for the overall good of the association. This cooperation of course confirmed that though there were disagreements; there were no traitors whatsoever to the cause for which we all fought. The powers of coercion and even arm twisting of their employees could be quite pronounced by governments in many countries of the third world. It is not limited to my part of the world.

In my postelection speech, I had called for "unity among the doctors for the good of the public and the doctors." I empathized with our colleagues who were obviously under orders to work against what we all ought to have been working towards. I knew they had little choice since in our type of democracy, the government had almost limitless powers, a sad reminder of the many years of unfettered military dictatorship during which the word of the military commander in chief was law.

After the resolution of the doctors' pay issue, our relationship with the government became at best tolerable. There was no bitterness nor undue sense of hilarity and chest beating on our part realizing that we only succeeded in doing our duties. An unfortunate incident, however, came up which had tended to restart another round of agitations. That was an incident between the chairman of the Guild of Government Doctors and the government, emanating from series of apparently unpalatable letters, which the former was said to have written against the governor and some high government officials.

The government had purportedly issued an official query to the Guild chairman and subsequently prematurely retired him from service. It was the view of the guild chairman that the actions taken against him were a punitive measure for the role he was said to have played in the seven-month-old strike action by the government service doctors whose chairman he was, at the time of the strike action. The chairman of the Guild of Doctors had requested the NMA to prevail on the government to reverse its decision since it had been understood that no member of the Guild of Doctors would be punished for his role in the strike action. In my mind, too, I believed that the action of the government might not have been directly or indirectly unconnected with the disappointment that people in power or the corridors of power felt at the success of the doctors' action and their inability to intimidate the NMA or bully her members into submission in a matter in which the association felt fully justified. I nevertheless tabled the letter of the guild chairman before the state executive and also sought the opinion of our legal advisers on the issue.

The matter was then tabled before the general meeting of the NMA. It was the general view of the members that the letters written by the guild chairman even after the settlement of the matter between the government and the NMA were too far-reaching and touched on matters outside the scope of the issue for which the NMA was fighting. It was felt that the issue was not a personal war and that the NMA as a body should not bring itself to ridicule by threatening another strike action over an issue, which though it involved one of its members had been almost so personalized, according to the view of a number of the association's members, to the point of slander.

Meanwhile the guild chairman, apparently feeling distraught at the apparent nonresponse of the NMA, had started firing letters accusing the NMA of abandoning him. He went almost to the point of insinuating that the NMA chairman failed to act in his defense because of the routine Christmas pack of candies, bathing towel, Christmas card, and a bottle of nonalcoholic beverages all wrapped in a big woven basket, which the state administration yearly sent to chairmen of the major professional bodies in the state: The NMA, the Bar Association, the Nigerian Society of Engineers, etc., for that year was routed through the state secretariat because of the lack of cordiality between the state chairman and the administration.

The feeling of the guild chairman was of course natural in the circumstances in which a supposedly disciplinary action was taken against him so soon after a protracted strike action that might have embarrassed the powers that were. There was, however, absolutely no justification for the indiscriminate and ostensibly wild accusations against the leadership of the NMA, which had staked so much in defence of the organization which the Guild chairman led. All said and done, however, I personally greatly sympathized with the situation of the Guild chairman and wished there was a way that one would have been of personal help to rescue his position. Otherwise, he, like some of us, should only seek solace in the realization that despite the obvious discomfort to our persons, he, like the rest of us in the NMA state executive, had successfully fought for a just cause; and that when the history of the state NMA gets to be written, his name would be in letters of gold. He, as the guild chairman, was a fearless and dogged fighter, an incorruptible and courageous leader who had sacrificed so much for his colleagues even under threats and in circumstances where many would have capitulated.

As we wound up our activities in the leadership of the doctors, my executive and I found much to feel fulfilled about. We considered what we met on the ground when we took up the mantle of leadership and compared that with what we had put on the ground and into the psyche and self-esteem of the average doctor in the state. We considered what impact our honest and humble recommendations and suggestions had made to the development of health in the state, especially as regards the establishment of the Imo State University Medical School. We felt satisfied and could not but beat our chest with joy and satisfaction. We found satisfaction in the realization that, even with all due modesty, we had succeeded in printing our humble footsteps on the sands of time.

Whatever hardships we had suffered, whatever pains we might have gone through, whatever transient "enemies" we might have made, and whatever friends we transiently might have lost, were only, in my opinion, necessary prices we had to pay in the process of the fight for a worthy cause. And we felt that if one were to borrow words from the Winston Churchill's "this was their finest hour" speech, we might proudly say that if the NMA Imo State lives a thousand years, it would still be said of our executive that "this was their finest hour."

The Board Member: An Insight Into the Dirt and the Decay

About the middle of my first term in office as the chairman of the state NMA, I was appointed a member of the board of the Federal Medical Center Owerri. The appointment, which was made at the recommendation of the national executive of the Nigerian Medical Association, was "at the pleasure of His Excellency, the president of the Federal Republic of Nigeria." So was it written in the letter communicating the appointment to me. It was interesting reading those high-sounding phrases and clauses which I often heard politicians quote ever so often as a means of uplifting their ego and sometimes as an excuse for embezzling government funds as if the mere mention of His Excellency's title was one big justification for the colossal breaches of public trust which we ever so often witnessed. Sometimes I wondered whether the use or misuse of that word *excellency* contributed to our failures in governance in the third world when the leadership of even the world's greatest power would feel satisfied at merely being addressed as Mr President. Could there be an element of inferiority complex on our leadership that would necessitate the compelling need for ego-boosting titles and appellations? Or could there be an inverse relationship between that appellation, *excellency,* and the actualization of excellence in selfless governance and incorruptibility? I, too, to a great extent must have been guilty by association, because I know that I displayed that letter of appointment "at the pleasure of His Excellency" to a number of my friends, probably to demonstrate that I too "had arrived."

The board had a membership of ten people from various parts of the country since it was a federal establishment. It comprised of a chairman and nine other members from various professional backgrounds, but more were from the medical profession. It was the inaugural governing board for that institution and was supposed to be the policy-making body of that federal institution.

The board position for the first time offered me the opportunity of seeing the way that public office holders in the country viewed and handled their positions. For the first time I was able to see firsthand why things did not work right in the country and why they may never work right unless the whole concept of public office appointments is overhauled to connote dedicated service rather than the sharing of the "national cake," a cake which many of the sharers did not, and would not, contribute to the baking of.

From what I could see in the board, for as long as board appointments are considered political patronage rather than civil responsibility, accountable positions of trust, for that long would we continue to drift as a nation, for that long would our abundant natural resources be wasted and misapplied, for that long would overbloated political jobbers continue to be paid fat emoluments for sitting around and performing little, simply because they represented certain political interests, for that long would the morale of genuinely serving and hardworking public servants be diminished, seeing waste and indolence being so richly rewarded. So would the ground be made more fertile for the cankerworms of corruption and ineptitude, which appear to overwhelm the polity.

It would be difficult and indeed scandalous to document fully one's experience in the nearly two years that one served in the board. When upon enquiry, I was told that what were obtained in both the center that we were supposed to be overseeing and in the overseeing board itself were just tips of the iceberg and mere reflections of the general trend in most government institutions, my heart bled for my country.

A situation in which public trust and public funds and resources were flagrantly and brazenly abused and or misapplied left such a sour taste in the mouth. Grossly abused executive privileges, inflated contracts, unlimited cronyism, wanton and arrogant misapplication of funds, and more appeared to be the order of the day. The rest of the staff watched helplessly as the resources that were supposed to be applied towards improvement of facilities and personnel were literally carted away.

To whom would they complain when a good percentage of the loot went into the "settlement" of whoever would receive the complaints? The complainant in such a situation could easily turn to become the accused after cash and other favors would have exchanged hands.

A situation in which less than wholesome actions were carried out in the names of very highly placed officials of state, who were supposed to be the watchdogs against such actions, would make every patriotic citizen elsewhere weep for the polity. It was easy to see why the roads were so bad, why public utilities that are taken for granted elsewhere would not work, why utterly unqualified people were placed in positions of responsibility, why merit was largely thrown to the winds, and why mediocrity thrived. At a certain stage, I remember I had to reproduce and distribute to the board members and all who cared to read copies of a lecture titled "Merit Enhancement, a Veritable Tool to National Development." I had earlier the previous year delivered that lecture to the members of the Rotary Club of Owerri at the president's night of the Rotarians, an event which was held at the prestigious Modotel Owerri. I had to reproduce and distribute copies of that lecture to see if it could make a difference in the way we as a team conducted ourselves and our assignments, especially as regards the way hospital personnel were hired and/or promoted.

It did not make a difference.

While serving in the board, I had also submitted a detailed memorandum to the then federal minister of health suggesting ways in which I felt medical services, especially at the tertiary level, would be improved. Needless to say, most of these efforts yielded no fruitful results. I was, however, happy that if my tenure did not make significant impact, it would not be for want of trying.

When I learnt that the board had been dissolved after about two years of its existence, it was a big relief. Of course, other boards would be appointed, and the cycle would continue or even get worse.

Nothing had changed.

Nothing would of course change.

Again, for as long as appointments to top management positions are made purely on the bases of patronage, and for as long as ulterior motives are the guiding principles and as long as merit and accountability are thrown to the winds, Nothing will change.

A river badly polluted from source would scarcely be expected to be clean so soon downstream. It was usually so disgusting whenever positions were advertised for appointments and ten times the number of people would turn up to fill up the positions and over half of them would be clutching letters from highly placed government officials ranging from the country's top office holders at the center to the members of the state assembly at the state level all requesting or directing the board chairman to "oblige" as the holder of the letter was the relevant officer's "candidate." In one particular occasion, one single position had eight candidates clutching letters from eight "Excellencies"! The center being a federal institution, these "Excellencies" came from both the federal and state levels and included two Excellency's wives, who of course were also Excellencies. It was a big dilemma for all the board members. I had suggested a tossing of the coin between pairs of Excellency's candidates to see which Excellency's candidate would prevail in the end. As we were still debating on ways to get out of the quagmire, it was pointed out to the board members that one of the Excellencies was from the state house in the federal capital. That letter "from the presidency," whether true or faked, presented by the management saved us further deliberations as that Excellency immediately prevailed over the "minor Excellencies." Even in that little board room, there were powers and superpowers, Excellencies and super-Excellencies!

I was later to learn that what obtained in the medical center and in the board which was overseeing it were only child's play when compared with what obtained elsewhere in the public service of the country and in the political arena in general. Would it therefore be surprising to anyone that we are ranked among the top two most corrupt countries on the planet? The situation brings great pain to all discerning and patriotic citizens who find themselves powerless to ameliorate the condition.

From the airports to the seaports, from the offices to the schools, the story is the same. On the highways one does not know who to fear. If one escapes the unofficial nonuniformed armed robbers, one may yet, until recently still, encounter the official uniformed armed robbers. The most distressing often are the other men in uniform who are officially paid to ensure road safety but whom everybody knows have turned the roads into "fishing grounds," preying upon the very road users whose safety on the roads they are paid to ensure. Drivers' licenses for a fee are issued to people who have never undergone any tests whatsoever or who have never handled the steering wheel. Renewal of licenses to genuine drivers is deliberately made almost impossible unless an inducement is made or unless one goes through touts and other agents of the road safety officials. The issuing officer will either be "not on seat" or the laminating machine will break down. Even when one has paid the official fees, the official receipt booklet would have exhausted. One has to pay a special fee to be issued an official receipt for a payment duly made. If the individual fails to "cooperate," he or she may have to call multiple times at the office before an official receipt will be issued for payments duly made. Another special fee may be required to have the documents posted to Abuja or Lagos. And the hapless citizens are deliberately subjected to all forms of hardships until they comply. And the big *oga* hides himself in his office and waits for the "returns." At the end of each day, the boot of his car is loaded with sacks of cash—ill-gotten cash fleeced from the public. And the higher oga in the higher office waits for his own "returns." This he will again share with the much higher oga in the much higher office. And more mansions are built by the officer who develops potbelly. And the man whose total life income has not exceeded five million naira yearly buys or builds mansions each worth more than one hundred million naira. He works in customs, ports authority, one of the forces, or more lately road safety. Some agency of government "has made him rich." He is hailed as progressive. And the image of the nation suffers. And our youth will watch as the pattern is entrenched. And the rest of the world watches with dismay as humanity's most populous black nation totters and continues to paint a picture of shame for us all.

And the traveler at the airport is treated no better. In full glare of citizens and foreigners alike, the officer lies in waiting. The traveler, his prey, is not worth any courtesy. He must buy the courtesy with dollars or naira tucked into documents for examination.

And the big oga at the corner looks the other way
As his subordinate officers the public fleeces,
And the "noncooperating ones" are made to suffer,
As there will always be a reason for which they will be delayed
Or one way or another denied free passage,
And our visitors shake their heads at the shame of the nation,
And we expect the respect of the rest of the world
As the perpetrators of our shame wallow in filth
And accumulate their billions to contest elections,
And the filth is carried into government house or into parliament
And the cycle goes on and on
And there will be nobody to break the cycle
And critics are muzzled or sent to jail
And the nation putrefies and bleeds without reprieve
And our youth watch and accept this as the norm.
Who then will break the cycle, and who will stem the tide,
Or shall we remain thus until doomsday comes?
Unde habere nemo inquit,
Sed necese habere est.

That again was part of the Latin we learnt at school. One's source of wealth is never questioned in our unfortunate circumstances, so long as the wealth is acquired. The end justifies the means. That officer whose total salary in five years would not fetch more than a four-bedroom house and who puts up chains of duplexes, gas stations, and hotels is only conforming to a pattern in the system, a thoroughly depraved system that daily cries for a radical overhaul. Such an officer is said to be well positioned. He is said to understand his environment. He is said to be smart. But if he completes his service and keeps his hands clean and his conscience clear, his friends and family members would hold him to scorn. He is said not to understand his environment. He is said to be a *mu-mu*, a foolish man. He will never have a chieftaincy title conferred on him. He will forever remain a "mister," and his reward will only be in heaven. But we all want our rewards here on earth.

It would not matter if after that, the roads don't get done. It would not matter if public power supply and water supply become nonexistent. It would not matter if our public school system degenerates below acceptable standards or if our roads are taken up by heaps of refuse or if our open gutters are completely clogged up. So long as there is still space for the tires of the chief executive's SUV (collectively called jeep), the looting can continue.

If one is a "mister," one is a nobody. And one does not become a chief, or a high chief empty-handed. It does not matter if the resources with which one became a chief or a high chief came from being a thief or a high thief of public funds.

FROM THE BOARD TO THE COUNCIL

At the end of my tenure as state chairman of the Nigerian Medical Association, I was appointed a member of the Medical and Dental Council of Nigeria. The council is the highest regulatory body for medical and dental practice in Nigeria. The appointment was made by the federal Ministry of Health on recommendation from the National Executive Council of the Nigerian Medical Association. The council is charged with the registration of doctors after graduation from medical schools, the accreditation and reaccreditation of medical schools, as well as the approval of medical curricula. It is also charged with ensuring sound medical practice in the country and the investigation, trial, and discipline of erring doctors and dentists among other functions.

The council was a much more disciplined and seasoned body than the board. Unlike the board, which cut across professions, the council was composed of essentially medical and dental professionals, and that probably accounted for the finesse that was easily visible. These were deans of faculties of medicine, provosts of colleges of medicine, directors of medical services in the States, professors in various medical specialties, and other doctors and dentists who have distinguished themselves in various fields in the profession.

Discussions were much more mature, and it was obvious that there was greater adherence to certain accepted principles of public and professional behavior.

In the council, I was made a member of the investigative panel which was charged with investigating deviant behavior on the part of doctors and dentists as either reported to the panel or council or as observed by panel or council. After investigating, this panel had the responsibility of establishing whether or not there was a prima fascie case against any individual doctor or dentist. On establishment of the prima facie case, the panel would refer the case to the tribunal of the council which, having the powers of a high court, would summon the doctor or dentist to appear before it. I was also appointed a member of the medical education committee, which was charged with the duty of inspecting medical schools and determining whether they met the standards for accreditation or not.

I was particularly thrilled by my appointment into the medical education committee since I felt it would afford me the opportunity of advising the Imo State University Medical School on accreditation matters, having been the person who, on the floor of the NMA Owerri, moved the motion for the NMA to pressure the establishment of the medical school many years back. I had also led a delegation of doctors as NMA chairman to the state governor, requesting for the establishment of a medical school in Imo State University Owerri. I had also served in a committee set up by the chairman of the governing board of the university many years back to draw up the agenda for establishment of the medical school. Furthermore, I had, as chairman of NMA, on three occasions led teams that inspected and advised on the facilities at the preclinical section of the medical school at its inception.

I therefore felt I owed it a duty to help in any way I could to see to a materialization of that project which was so dear to us, seeing how much our young men and women were suffering before they could secure admission into medical schools in other state universities, even when they were fully qualified for entry.

My tenure in the council was quite exciting and educative, as every case had to be studied in details if one were to do justice to every case as a lead writer. Much as one felt very enthusiastic and would have liked to participate fully in all case discussions and decisions, there were occasionally situations in which one found the need to abstain and be at best an observer. There was for instance the particular sensational case of a colleague from my part of the country, in whose case I found the absolute need to stay completely out of, since both the accuser and the accused were well-known to me. Besides, I found that I might not be completely fair in my contributions since I appeared to have some background knowledge of the situation, which could only lead to bias, or perceived bias, if I were to participate in the discussions and decisions. Such situations were, however, few and far in between.

I could not, however, complete my tenure in the council because for family and other reasons, it became necessary for me to be out of the country for long periods of time, a situation which made it impracticable for me to be an effective council member. I therefore wrote to inform the council and the relevant appointing authorities of my inability to continue.

The Threat to the Life of My Family The Dog as an Instrument for Our Survival

We got the siblings Jimmy and Terry as three-month-old puppies. We got them as presents from our friends Lulu and her husband, Tony. They were mixed-breed dogs, a native mother and a foreign-breed father, the exact breed name which I did not know. Jimmy and Terry were very playful dogs and made very good companions for our children, especially to our daughter, Som. We unfortunately lost Terry, the female of the siblings, from an unknown illness about eighteen months after we got the pair. Jimmy grew up to become a very strong and medium-sized dog, brown in color, with flapping ears which curved forwards as if to cover the external ear canal. Jimmy was very friendly to all the members of the family but would bark very fiercely at any intruders at our gates. Jimmy would usually stick out his nose through the space between the gate and the pillar carrying the gate. The sight of Jimmy's nose through the gate usually frightened passersby who dared to walk too close to the gate. If any such passersby did not notice Jimmy, the latter's deep and loud bark often scared such people off their feet. Jimmy's senses of smell and hearing were so sharp that most times if passersby leaned against our walls who stood at a road junction, Jimmy could detect their presence from the other end of our large compound, even without seeing them. In such a circumstance, Jimmy would start to bark loudly and would run towards the exact direction where the passerby was leaning outside the block, walled fence. If we went upstairs to look outside the wall, we would invariably notice that somebody was standing close to or leaning against our wall at the exact site outside of where jimmy would be barking from.

About one o'clock in the morning, sixteen days after I had addressed the press conference calling the government doctors out on a strike action, we heard Jimmy barking fiercely in the direction of our gate. It was one of the many dark nights occasioned by the failure of power supply from the National Electric Power Authority, NEPA. (NEPA was often nicknamed by people as "Never Expect Power Always" and later "Never Expect Power At all" when the power supply situation worsened. They were later to be labeled as "Power Withholding Company of Nigeria" when their name was changed to "Power Holding Company of Nigeria," PHCN). Everywhere was in pitch darkness as we had switched off our small diesel-power-generating plant for the night to save gas. Jimmy was about five years old then,1 and we had lived with him long enough to understand from his bark when he was barking at mere passersby or when he was barking from real anger as he would do if people were standing directly at our gates. Most times such fierce barking would not last longer than one or two minutes as the intruders would readily leave the gates at the first few barks. But on that particular night, Jimmy had barked fiercely and persistently for over fifteen minutes. He barked so fiercely and persistently that I was afraid he would lose his voice.

I got out of bed. I told my wife that something amiss must be going on. I felt my way to the second floor living room with my torchlight at hand but switched off. We had learnt that in such situations of uncertainty, one should not move around the house with the torchlight on. By avoiding to switch on the light, one would not give away one's position in the dark to a lurking robber who might be armed.

When I got to the living room, I heard Jimmy give out one sharp shrill cry, this time from the far end of the back of the house. He did not bark or cry again thereafter. Such sudden cry followed by protracted silence was most unusual for Jimmy. Whenever it barked for long at the sight of danger or in severe anger, it would continue to growl for a long time thereafter, even if it retreated to a quiet corner. It hardly ever gave up completely until a member of the family showed up. But this time it had uttered a shrill cry and was completely silent thereafter. Something had obviously gone wrong, but what it was, I was not sure of.

I then saw from the staircase the rays of a torchlight in the dinning room which was situated adjacent the kitchen downstairs. It was obvious that we had intruders within our compound, most likely within the ground floor of our house. I had not made a noise nor did I shine my torchlight. The rays of torchlight moved in different directions as if the intruder was scanning the walls and windows of the building. As was, and still is, the practice, because of the security situation, virtually all doors, windows, and vents in most buildings have metal burglary proofs behind and often also in front of them. The asbestos ceiling boards are sometimes also burglary proofed as some daredevil robbers have been known to climb through the ceiling of the eaves projection to descend into bedrooms. Some have also been known to break through block walls with sledge hammers since they know that the doors and windows would be more difficult to go through.

When I saw the moving torchlight dancing from one end of my wall to the other, my heart pounded so fast that I though I would collapse as my feet wobbled under me. I had heard of armed robbers and hired assassins murdering people in their bedrooms. I had once encountered mobile armed robbers on the Okigwe-Owerri road one afternoon on my way back to Owerri after my wife and I had gone to visit our son at Federal Government College Okigwe. In that particular instance, it looked like those roadside robbers were after cash and Mercedes Benz cars and did not care for my Volkswagen Santana car which had my hospital name boldly written on both outsides of the front doors. In the instance in question, the robbers who intercepted us in three (perhaps stolen) Mercedes Benz cars and a Toyota SUV had let us go after searching us. One of them who had a dead discolored incisor tooth had jokingly and brazenly pointed to his tooth and after asking for which of the two of us was the dentist told my wife that he would visit her at the dental clinic to have his tooth fixed. They had seen Hospital and Dental Clinic boldly written on our car. They had no masks or any other form of disguise. They let us go unharmed even though my trembling fingers for a while did not allow me to insert the ignition key into the keyhole amidst the "go, go now, go, go" order from the robbers as they flagged down an approaching Mercedes V-booth car.

The particular one o'clock attack in my house was completely different. The road robbers might be after the money, valuables, and car. But an attack right inside my house might have been after my very life. At such an unholy hour of the night, what else might a robber come looking for. In the relatively easy banking era, people hardly kept large sums of money in their houses. It was therefore likely that the attackers were after the persons of the household owners. The cars parked downstairs were untouched. The electronics in the living room were not touched either. The government-doctor crises had sapped so much of my physical and mental energy that only those few hours of sleep each night were what comforted and refreshed me.

I often said Jimmy, my dog, saved my life. On the surface, that was what could be said because that was the aspect we saw and heard. But certainly it was the hands of the Almighty that made it all possible for Jimmy to bark, for me to wake up, for the courage to step out to the living room; otherwise, how else could I have seen the torchlight, and how else would I have known that the attackers were already inside my house.

Until perhaps they would be in my bedroom
And the slaughter would perhaps take place,
And the killers would never be found,
If at all the murders would ever be investigated.

My fear, thanks to God, soon gave way to anger.
"A man's house is his fortress," the saying goes.
Where else would I run to?

I dashed back into the bedroom and told my wife that the robbers were right inside our house. We spontaneously knelt down and said a very brief prayer. We were not sure whether it would be our last. Then I suddenly remembered that Chu, our youngest son, was sleeping in the adjacent room. If they held him hostage, we would be compelled to surrender. Chu hardly ever woke up until we banged hard on his door. But that night he woke up at the first knock on his door:

"Chuchu, robbers are in our house. You must get up and out now," I whispered through the key hole.

A sleepy "yes, daddy" had greeted us as Chuchu got up and unlocked his door, robbing his eyes with his hands.

He probably did not fully comprehend the severity of what I had just told him. He certainly would have panicked if he understood that the situation at hand could spell death to all of us if mishandled.

I ushered Chuchu into my bedroom. With my eyeballs almost popping out from a mixture of anger and fright, I mustered the last courage in me. Should I simply hole myself up in our bedroom with my wife and son and let the robbers or assassins mow down the door or the block wall knowing that they would not be challenged at 1:20 a.m. by some sleeping idiot with his wife and son? Or should I, knowing how helpless and vulnerable we were, hazard a few words to let whoever were there know that their victims would not go down like cows waiting to be slaughtered. If we kept mute and the assailants got us in our bedroom, the chances were that we would all be dead in minutes.

There were precedents in the recent past. The chairman of the Bar Association who was said to have been critical of government in an adjoining state was dragged out from his car and brutally slaughtered along with his pregnant wife. Their assassins were never found, even though there were widespread accusing fingers. And that was in broad daylight. Even an attorney general was mowed down in his house, even with all the security details that were supposed to surround him. Not as much as comets were seen, almost paradoxically conforming to the old Shakespearian saying that "when beggars die, there are no comets seen."

And to all intents and purposes the attorney general was far from being a beggar.

If such calamitous situations could befall people at such heights with such relative ease, how much less would the story be for the likes of insignificant people like me.

I looked at the clock on the wall. It was 1:20 a.m. I needed to act in seconds. I grabbed the cell phone and began to dial the number of the Operation Fire for Fire, the police rapid response equivalent of 911, which was supposed to be operational at that time. When the number rang about four times without any response, I suddenly remembered the last time I called Operation Fire for Fire That was the night about a year earlier when from my bedroom window I watched robbers tearing down a section of a club building. I had immediately phoned the Fire for Fire people. That was about 2:00 a.m. By the time the latter arrived at about 4:10 a.m., the robbers were already done and gone.

I dropped back the phone. Every second was vital.

The biblical Samson was said to have had his eyes plucked out by the Philistines. But he was said to have prayed for the restoration of his strength. He was said to have died with his enemies.

I was not Samson, but I decided that it was better to die with my assailants if I had to and if I could. It would be better that the enemy's bullet should hit me at the front of my chest with me fighting than that the bullet hole should be seen at my back with me in cowardly retreat even when I knew there was nowhere to run to. If the end result would be death, it was nobler that I died fighting than that I should be slaughtered hiding between my wife and my son. I knew that no sane man would want to come out empty-handed at 1:20 a.m. to face possibly fully armed robbers or assassins. But then no reasonable man would willingly surrender himself to the same robbers to be slaughtered. The instinct of self-preservation would be too strong for the latter. It was necessary at least to let the intruders know that their proposed victim was awake and that he did not intend to die without a fight if he could. I reasoned that if I did not fight, it would be death, but there was a slight chance that I might succeed in scaring the attackers if I let them know that their victim would not simply give himself up in his own house.

I reached under and grabbed whatever crude and primitive weapons of self-defence as I could lay hands on. I went down on my belly and crept out to the second floor living room after tucking my wife and son in what I had considered a safer corner of the house. Flat on my belly and tucked away from view of anyone approaching from the heavily fortified staircase and in a final desperate effort to scare or to warn, I then shouted on top of my voice, "Whoever you are, whatever weapons you have, and whatever numbers you may be, half of you will be dead before I die. Be warned that I too am armed. My family and I are waiting. You may advance if you dare."

My voice almost failed me before I could complete the last sentence. My laryngeal muscles and vocal cords were almost going into spasm as I uttered the last words of that warning. It was the very first time in my life that I was to experience that degree of extreme fright and extreme forced courage, both at the same time.

It appeared to me as if a large lump was wedging in my throat. My vocal chords went into momentary shutdown. I was afraid I would choke.

For a while there was silence. The torchlight went off, and the sound of obvious hacking and barring at the heavily built and fortified front door stopped. I was gladdened. I expected to hear stampede from escaping robbers.

But no!

There was silence. May be the "robbers" had quietly fled. I was just about to stand up from my prostrated position when I heard loud footsteps on the slopping roof of the barricaded patio. Then in through the upstairs corridor leading from the patio came the dazzling beam of torchlight. The beam barely missed my pronated position just off the corridor. They might have fired some shots if they had seen me. The searchlight then went off. A deafening bang then came against the metal barricades of the patio.

"That was it," I said within me.

These were not mere robbers. They certainly had come with other missions, most likely a mission to kill. Otherwise, what amount did they hope to get from the house of a privately employed medical doctor to warrant the risks they were taking, even after they knew we were awake and ready to offer some resistance before being killed, I mused.

"Lord Jesus, I am yours," I kept on saying within me.

With the metal barricade of the patio down, there was no more barrier between me and my attackers. The only saving grace was that it was dark, and the attackers did not see how close they were to their victim. If light and vision were able to go directly around corners, the attackers would easily have pumped red-hot lead into me, lying as I was on my belly under sixteen feet away from them. I sprang up to my feet and made a quick dash across to the bedroom, banging the door and pulling on the security devices as I entered and again crept rapidly towards the hiding position from where I could see my little family, kneeling and clutching at each other. I then changed my mind and decided that it would be better to be killed defending my family instead of being mowed down in the corridor. Crawling would be a very slow process. I sprang up to my feet again still clutching at the crude "defensive weapon" in my possession. I then dashed across the corridor into the relatively secure section of the safe room into where I had heralded my wife and son earlier. I found Agie and Chu-chu on their knees saying the Rosary. They appeared too engrossed in prayers to even notice my entry or to ask any questions. In my dash, I had bypassed the bedroom and did not collect the cell phone, which I had dropped on the bed earlier.

As I entered the safe room, I pulled Agie and Chu-chu to the side and left the door halfway open. I then took up a position behind the metal barricade of the door, silently daring any person to walk in. That was my final fortress, and I was fully resolved to chop the head off from whoever came in first. The accomplices could then feel free to finish me and my family off thereafter if the decapitated head of their colleague would not be enough to scare them off. That would be my own little way of replicating a local Sampson. I felt that it was the best I could do under the circumstance.

Leaving the door halfway open was a decoy. My earlier shouting at the assailants had made no difference. I felt that leading them into a trap was a better option. And a partially open door, I guessed, was a better trap. That appeared to have worked. It most probably was simply God's work. The robbers were soon at the partially open door who now came ramming against the metal barricade with a loud bang. I had hoped that the sound from the latter would attract reactions from neighbors. But that was not to be, and understandably so. My residence was in a low-density area. Besides, the natural reaction from a population so persistently mauled by sieges and stories of sieges was to resort to defence of self and family in situations like that. They might have been enthusiastic to help, but they too wanted to live. The best they could do in such circumstances was to barricade themselves and family in. A call for help from Operation Fire for Fire was often futile. Even if Fire for Fire came, their fire might be inferior to the fire from the assailants. A situation had played up sometime when attackers robbing a bank were said to have mounted roadblocks at strategic road junctions including the government house road junction, and using loudspeakers (microphones) the robbers had warned people not to come out. In another occasion, a neighbor's house was being robbed at night, and another neighbor had opened fire to scare off the robbers. The robbers used a microphone to inform the neighbor firing that he should save his bullets because they were coming to him when they were done with their present victim.

As a dozen footsteps made towards our bedroom from the corridor, it was finally time to act. The rest was all God's work. The loud firing from where the robbers had fruitlessly rushed triggered a stampede.

This was certainly not a suicide squad. Their mission obviously did not include a resolution to succeed or die. The robbers obviously treasured their own lives. The stampede was accentuated by the triggering into action of the multiple alarm systems which the robbers never expected to exist in the house when they were lured into the decoy and allowed to tear down the patio barricades unchallenged. As said earlier, it was all God's work because some security and defence systems had been known to fail when they were needed the most.

Luckily for the robbers and for me, no head dropped, because if one did, even in situations where people had in the past acted in self-defence, the system that had failed to protect them had turned around not to vindicate them or, worse still, had sometimes outrightly condemned them.

Within ten minutes of the forced entry, it was all quiet as the security systems that had been triggered into action all acted in unison. The retreat was faster than the approach, and the roof of the patio was the worse for it. The aluminum roofing sheets of the patio were so badly dented that by morning it looked as if a ball dance had been staged on it. The expertise with which the metal barricades and the thick metal gate were disabled was amazing.

Experience had taught one to never rush out after an incident like that, to take stock of possible casualties. One might in the process turn a casualty after escaping the major assault. I therefore remained in the safe room still with the door partially open till about five in the morning, when I ventured out to collect my cell phone. I immediately called Frank, my friend and neighbor. Unfortunately Frank was at Ikot Ekpene, a town some three hours driving distance away. He, however, helped reach his friend who was a special assistant to one of the big guys in government. It was this last gentleman who, using his governmental position, then rallied the police who at arrived my premises about 6:30 a.m. That special adviser and some of my colleagues including my good friend Felix, whom I also contacted, trooped to my house in sympathy. The police had asked me for any suspects I could think of. I did not shy away from mentioning a number of suspects, some of them strong suspects. Like most of such things in my society, however, nothing else happened after that, except that the residents of the area where I lived were asked to contribute money "for the fuel and police vehicle for increased and improved security in the area."

Later in the morning, we found Jimmy whose loud and persistent barking had aroused us from sleep. Were it not for Jimmy's bark, I might not have lived to tell my story.

As my friend Felix and others who had gathered stood miffed at the site of entry and daredevilry surrounding the break-in, one of the members of the law enforcement team that had arrived at the site had asked me, "Oga, na you own this big house?"

As I answered in the affirmative, expecting some sympathy, he followed up with the question, "How long you don live for here?"

"Many years," I replied.

Then the bombshell came.

"Many years, eh? But you never know say we station near this place? Na only now wey dem wan kill you, na him you com remember say we dey?"

He was chiding me for not "recognizing" their presence near my residence prior to the attack, possibly implying that I had not been coming to pay my "tithe" by way of homage for the "protection" which they were offering. The chiding might have degenerated into something worse for me had my friend Felix not intervened.

"But I have been seeing you people regularly," my friend chipped in.

The man looked at Felix for a while then said, "Y-e-a-s, I recognize you. No be you wee live for yonder. But I never see dis man."

I was stupefied. A man who had just narrowly escaped being murdered was being chided by a peace officer for not coming to pay "homage." My mind immediately went back to the renegade conscriptors of the civil war years whose apparent sole mission was to comb the areas behind the front lines and exact maximum intimidation and harassment of individuals who did not actively bear arms, no matter how equally important the latter's roles were to the war effort. The hate and anger in the looks of the young officer as he chided me was most intimidating. It was most unprovoked. It was most unkind. It looked every inch like a war situation.

But we were not at war. Yet we were "at war"! And the worst kind of war is one in which the enemy is unknown, one in which the enemy may be one standing directly beside you with ostensible arms to protect you but with arms that may surreptiously turn against you even with as little a "provocation" as "not cooperating" in the highway or elsewhere.

At wartime, you knew your enemy. But a peace in which your enemy is unknown or one in which your potential attacker may be your paid protector is a peace of the beast. It is the law of the jungle where might is right. It is worse than the peace of the graveyard.

Luckily, however, the leader of the team, obviously a more disciplined senior officer, stepped in, changing the topic.

"Was it you who made a report at the office this morning?" the officer asked me.

"No," I said.

"One man with gray hair was at our office early this morning to report this before we got a phone call from the oga there. That man who came must know something about this attack."

I had my guess about the man he was talking about. But I knew it would make no difference even if the attack was traced to him. Similar reports in the past about the man in question had made no difference. He had always boasted that he was a friend of every top officer. If he was the culprit, he might have been acting with his group de novo, or he might be acting on behalf of some interested parties.

To the best of my knowledge, nothing further by way of investigation was heard about that attack. If my family and I were slaughtered, as I suspected was the objective for the attack, the incident would at best make the local news for a day, and that would be the end of it.

It was after the police and my friends, who had called in, had left that I could make my way to the back of the compound in search of Jimmy, the dog that God had used to save my life and that of my family. Those persistent barks and relentless attempts to ward off the aggressors as they made their way through our metal gates were the sole instruments that woke me up and kept me from sleeping off again. Had Jimmy shied away at the sight of the attackers, my family and I might not have survived that attack.

I found Jimmy lying on his abdomen with his tail tucked between his legs, a most unusual position for him. He did not run up to greet or lick or jump on me as he usually did at his first sight of me in the mornings. He merely uncoiled his tail and wagged it gently from side to side. As I approached him where he lay there in the electricity generator room at the far end of the compound, I noticed that his eyes were red but there were no visible signs of trauma on his face, neck, head, or body. It was only after I had walked up to him and stroked him at the back that he stood up and actively began to wag his tail. We could not exactly determine what the attackers had done to Jimmy or how they subdued him and got him to the electricity generator room. It was possible the attackers had sprayed some drugs over his face or that their numbers simply overwhelmed him. Whatever it was that they used to subdue Jimmy was immaterial at that stage. The very pleasing thing was that he survived and that he did his job at the time of the greatest need, a most useful dog, a very trustworthy friend.

The attack brought home to us the extent of our vulnerability and the porosity of our gate and walls. It also highlighted the weaknesses of some of our security arrangements and devices. Most importantly, it reemphasized to us the nakedness and unreliability of our public safety system, a system where the citizen may need to provide his own water supply by boreholes system (deep wells), his own electricity supply system by electricity generators, and may also be expected to provide his own police by hiring chains of private security guards. The citizen may also need to arrange his own school systems by his hiring of private tutors. He may even be expected to construct his road network making the citizen begin to wonder what the role of government is. A situation where the security to life and property is not guaranteed the individual makes the citizen begin to wonder what the real essence of governance is.

We had to begin to reinforce our security system, the best we knew how, changing the gate, changing and reinforcing the antiburglary devices, alarms, retardants, and all.

Those were the best the average citizen could do. Some of the strong suspects, as earlier stated, had always boasted openly about their links with law enforcement agents. The ease with which these people were let loose after arrests for overt criminal activities in the past tended to give credence to their claims. Would these sort of people be the ones to be reported to the police? Where obvious and brazen violation of the law is not investigated, how would one expect a mere suspicion of criminal involvement to be investigated? Where evil men are allowed to literally ride on horsebacks waving flags and announcing their criminal exploits, how would law-abiding citizens be expected to walk the street and feel safe? In situations like the above, the statement often repeated comes to mind: "If you can't beat them, join them."

But one does not successfully practice to be left-handed in old age, as the African proverb says.

Besides, the training and discipline imbibed into one in the Secondary School at Afikpo would not even allow one to deviate into the absurd, the disorderly, or the unconventional later in life.

Fear of the unknown is the worst form of fear.

It makes one unsure of one's paths even when such paths are familiar paths.

And to live in fear in one's own home makes nonsense of existence.

To unlock the front door of one's house in the morning needed a prior peep through the glass window. An unwelcome guest might be lurking around to say good morning when he intended the morning to be bad for the owner of the house.

A cry for help, should the "guest" pounce on you,
Will be largely unheeded,
Perhaps even by the law enforcement people, should they get
your call.
There either would be no vehicle, or there would be no gas.
There may even be no paper to take your report,
Or no pen to scribble the statement.
The madam in the nearby kiosk sells the paper and the pens.
You either purchase, or you may stay the day.
You may request to see the chief,
But you stood a chance of being labeled the thief,
As situations change so rapidly without the right connections,
And the right pockets!

But before you begin to blame the officer, you must blame the system. The officer may be "on seat."

He may even be a pious, morally upright man. But the man who put him there expects daily, weekly, or monthly financial "returns"; and the poor officer must meet the target, or he may get transferred to a less lucrative station. He may even be forced out of the system completely. And he has a duty to feed himself and his family. And even against his personal wishes and desires, he has to send his men to the streets and highways. These poor fellows' salaries may not have been paid for many months, and like the scavenging renegade soldier of the civil war years, he has to scavenge for food—clutching his gun on one hand.

The upright and modest ones may be polite and courteous.

At the end of the greetings he requests for some "cold water." And if scores of vehicles keep passing without any "cold water" emerging, the anger may be turned against the next road user. And would you blame the poor fellow with the gun in his hand, especially as his oga sits watching every move from a command vehicle parked in the low bush nearby? And this oga himself, pius as he may be, has to satisfy the expectations of the bigger oga in the office, who has to satisfy the other bigger oga in the bigger office, and this latter has to satisfy the bigger oga in another bigger office until the cycle ends in *kabruuja*, where powers meet the superpowers.

The biggest oga on seat is shielded from the scenes.
His ears are plugged with pegs, and he does not hear the moans.
His eyes are padded with steel, and he does not see the rot,
He does not see the extortion, the ripping off of the nation, the mayhem on the highways, the seaports, and the airports,
Scenes of shame for a nation so blessed.
And we pretend that all is well.
We protest when we are classified as one of the most corrupt in the world.
But the cycle goes on and on and on.
And even "leaders" whom people had believed were tailored by providence to redeem the situation, having been rescued from the jaws of death themselves, soon forgot.
Having tasted the honey, they craved for more.
And the nation moans.
The nation bleeds.

The people cry for help.
But nobody hears their cry!
Your next-door neighbor will be largely unhelpful even if he would like to help.
His own high walls laced with barbed wire against the thieves
Might not offer enough protection should the thieves later turn against him.
Your neighbor adjacent may be the enemy.
He makes no disguises about his antecedents.
He boasts to everybody about his exploits,
His exploits laden with theft and possible blood.
And yet the law does not catch up with him.
The law cannot catch up with him.
The law would not want to catch up with him.
He is said to understand his environment.
An environment almost dominated by crooks:
Crooks in public service.
Crooks in private enterprise.
Crooks in governance.
Crooks in school at all levels.
Crooks even in purported "houses of God"
Crooks in traditional institutions
Crooks everywhere.
Where does one turn to for redemption and for hope?
I see no light at the end of the tunnel.
The vice is called "the Nuggeram Factor."
It is glossed over, and the cycle continues. You are said not to understand your environment if you do not toe the line.
Dishonesty and cheating are eulogized, and there is little or no punishment for embezzlement of public funds.
Where the machinery is on the ground for detection and enforcement of such punishment,
"Red tapism" is entrenched to thwart the progress
And the culprits soon get off the hook
The theft of public funds has gone so widespread
That enforcement against it becomes so ineffective
Five hundred million dollars will be voted
For a public road project that will cost five hundred million naira,

An amount over a hundred times in excess, that is.
The excess is embezzled and stashed away.
The project gets poorly done or is not done at all.
The ministry's engineer certifies it as well completed
The project money is drawn and shared between accomplices.
The ministry's engineer draws his millions
The chief executives are not left out of the plot
They build their mansions and increase their fleet
Their girlfriends smile to the banks and drive posh cars
Ditches and deep potholes take over the road.
Dark nights reign in the nation as electricity dollars are stolen
The embezzlers get potbelly and still ply the same road.
At best they buy their jeeps and sit at the backseat of the car.
Their townsfolk sing their praises as they wallow in filthy money.
They understand their environment, and must be honored.
Their traditional rulers make them chiefs and hang on them some garlands.
They assume new names that match their wealth.
Their source of wealth is not the question.
They have made their money, and that is the answer.
The pain of the nation is not the question.
The weight of their purse is all that is the answer
Unde habere nemo inquit,
Sed necesse habere est.
The source of wealth is not the question,
All that is essential is to acquire the wealth.
How true this is, for most underdeveloped nations
But how sad it is for the nations in question,
Unfortunately, including my own.

The embezzler chief winds up the tinted glasses of his limousine and tries to avoid the sight of the heaps of garbage. He has now become a political king maker, a chief thief. If he so desires, he may aspire to displace his poorer traditional ruler. Where that fails, he may fund the creation of another autonomous community for himself. The powers that be are ever ready to oblige him. The makers of the law are at his command. So long as he rolls out tons of cash, his wish is their command. The chief's community gets balkanized at his discretion. A new autonomous community is created for the thief.

There he becomes a king and multiplies his kind.
When his tummy aches from overfeeding, he boards the jet
He flies to Europe, America, or more recently to India.
There the roads are better and the potholes are fewer
Medical facilities are better as the funding is provided.
But soon the bubble bursts, and the chief longs for home.
He has not stolen any money for the duration of his absence.
His second in command at home might be trying to "outdo" him in the grabbing game.
That was why the chief for years refused to go on vacation,
Lest someone else steals, for a month or two,
What for years the thief had stolen to become a chief.
"Working leave" is the name of the game
Lest some other thief should outsmart the chief,
And so the deputy watches and bids his time,
He beats his chest as his chief's tummy grows,
And he knows for sure that the time will come
For the chief to proceed ashore for the tummy tuck that is sure to come.
But the tummy-tuck procedure will not last forever.
The chief survives and yearns for home,
He had been missing the servants he left at home,
All that will daily mill around him at his command.
The thief's jet back to the country, "a hero" coming home.
The airport is filled to capacity with songs and dances.
Scores of official cars in the entourage hold up traffic from both ends of the airport route.
"Oga is coming back from an official visit to London,"
So the official statement will steadily say.
Banners and oga's photographs adorn the streets.
Oga alights from the plane amidst cheers and drumming.
His tummy tuck had been done and that with perfection.
He waves and smiles as he is ushered into a waiting car,
A bulletproof replacement for the one before.
Oga is driven through the same bumpy road whose reconstruction money he had embezzled
He will soon order special shock absorbers for the car of his choice,
So that he will no longer feel the same bumps that are meant for the poor,
The type that lesser mortals, his subjects, endure.

Such is the environment under which the crooks will thrive
Such is the situation under which the crime rate will rise.
Decency and decorum are thrown to the winds.
Mediocrity thrives and con men have a field day.

Science and technology are not encouraged
Research is neither funded nor is it encouraged
And where officially funded that will be on paper,
The funds are embezzled and critics are muzzled.
As long as the oil flows nobody really cares.

The university don finds himself left behind in the race.
He cannot change his car nor can he own a home.
His student of yesterday, a politician's child,
Owns a jeep and sprays the don with pothole water
As the latter waits for a ride at the side of the road
His broken-down car in the garage he had long abandoned.

Disgusted and embittered, the don joins the fray.
"Publish or perish" as a slogan for him has failed.
He must now make the money, or all will perish.

He publishes some pamphlets and begins to sell grades.
The student must buy the professor's "book," or he will not make an A.
A clerk is put in the office to sell the book
Names of buyers are recorded for the professor to see.
You do not buy the book, and you will not make the grades.

The money is made, but that is by the way.
Contentment has shifted to newer heights
Other "fringe benefits" must follow to compensate for the spray.
The male students with cartons of wine their way must pay,
Christmas dress must follow for the professor's wardrobe.
The female student herself must hire the room,
And the goodies must be there as the professor desires.
The professor must be invited, or a failure score will follow.
Sexual harassment is hardly in our list of crimes.

The truth may be bitter, but they must be told.
It may be inconvenient truth, but it must be exposed.
The bad may be few, but they smear the rest.
The ones that are bad will thrive and blossom.
The many that are good are left to rot.
The good are not rewarded for the system is rotten.
A cleansing must be done, but who will bell the cat?
The innocent are surely there, but who will hear their cry.
You must change the system
Or you must withdraw your child.

At the end of the day
The nation is the loser.
We cry in despair for a redeemer for our nation,
None may be at sight, but the day will surely come,
And the judgment of God,
Is sure to come.
Manifestation of his wrath
May be slow to come
But whether it will come,
Is never in doubt.

A Nation Thoroughly Blessed

A glance at the natural and human resources of the country makes one wonder whether there are other nations of the world that are as richly blessed. From the mangrove swamps in the deep south to the most northern fringes that are savannah or semidesert, all kinds of mineral and agricultural resources abound. The finest grade of crude oil abounds in huge reserves in the deep south, extending to the bordering continental shelf. Gas reserves abound in trillions of cubic tons. Bitumen, coal, gold, iron ore, bauxite, zinc, aluminum, and virtually all kinds of valuable minerals abound as one moves up from the delta to the north. Timber and virtually all kinds of tropical trees adorn the forests. The ground is fertile right from the riverine areas to the far north, providing potentials for cultivation of a wide range of products from timber to cereals.

The climate is hot, warm, or cool all year round, depending upon the location, providing a situation akin to an all-year-round summer.

The savannah provides wonderful grazing grounds for cattle, goats, sheep, and other kinds of livestock.

The environment is stable, and natural disasters are extremely rare: no land tremors, no earthquakes, no hurricanes, no volcanic eruptions, and minimal proneness to flooding.

The population is largely hardworking and innovative, friendly and highly hospitable to visitors. Tourist attractions abound in virtually all corners of that potential El Dorado. From the striking mangrove trees to the Ogbunike caves, from the awe-inspiring Olumo rock to the Obudu cattle ranch, from the Argungu fishing festival to the long juju of Arochukwu, the nation possesses enough attractions to make her live on tourism resources. Virtually all the potentials that go to make for greatness abound in the nation.

But the largest black nation on the face of the earth still totters. The country was said to have exported the oil palm nuts which largely contributed to the establishment of the oil palm plantations of one of the South East Asian countries renowned today for palm oil exportation. But today my beloved country imports vegetable oil products. The palm plantation miracles of the 1960s are today's thing of the past, overgrown and not replaced or rejuvenated. The once-thriving cocoa industry that built the Cocoa House in Ibadan and sustained the subregion's most pragmatic economy is largely a shadow of its old self from lack of due attention. The once awe-inspiring groundnut pyramids of the nation's vast north have vanished. All these are largely due to the wind of crude oil craze. The discovery and exploitation of oil has taken its toll, as all attention is focussd on the black gold, a diminishing resource. But despite its purported vast reserves, the crude will one day run dry and, the upcoming generation will read the history of the hundreds of billions of dollars that the oil yielded. They will see the ecological devastation and ask some questions. Where did the billions go, and what do we have to show for it? The fact that the country is said to be about the seventh largest exporter of crude oil in a world whose economy is largely controlled by fluctuations in crude oil prices has made little difference either to the price her citizens pay for refined crude or to the general standard of living of the largely distraught and economically and politically disenfranchised population.

The nation's leading position in cassava tuber production has also made relatively little difference to its position in world economy or to the socioeconomic position she occupies in the world. Her over one hundred and twenty million human population, which ordinarily should have been a big advantage, does not seem to have boosted her position. Countries like India and Pakistan, which at one time or the other were under British colonial rule like Nigeria, are now world powers of sorts. But the country, my beloved country, that is often called the giant of Africa still totters, recognized almost only on the basis of the number of con men or international web fraudsters that claim the nation for their nationality. The root cause of all the drift of course is corruption, a cankerworm that appears to have eaten deep into all aspects of the nation's fabric—eroding all that is noble, all that is patriotic, all that should be treasured by any self-respecting nation.

And the people who have benefited massively from this cankerworm daily walk the streets, smiling and displaying their ill-gotten wealth. And the young and the old who know the source of all the wealth of the politicians and the men in uniform before them watch with suppressed anger and indignation as they travel under the scorching sun on the dusty roads or under the heavy tropical rains. They travel largely on auto bikes as most reliable cars are outside their reach. They travel sometimes clutching their bags on their heads or strapping their babies behind their backs. As they travel, they are every now and then chased off the bumpy roads by the regular siren-blowing vehicles of the big ogas, the new masters, or of their wives or girlfriends or of their cronies.

The ever-present motorbikes meander through the congested traffic with neither rider nor passenger wearing a protective helmet. The riders often narrowly miss falling into the open gutters or colliding with one another. The impoverished passengers ever so often fall off the motorbike as they try to hold tight to their babies or to their other belongings. The broken bones and fractured skulls from the latter daily flood the orthopedic units of the few well-equipped and well-staffed hospitals.

Driving the motorbike taxi called *okada* or *inaga* is the ready source of occupation for all cadre of the unemployed, ranging from the illiterate tout to the unemployed young graduate. They are angry at the system that has condemned them to that fate. They curse at short notice and are ready to fight at the drop of the hat. They are in solidarity with one another and are prepared to fight any system. Woe betides you if you hit them with your car or if they hit you with their "machine." Either way, you will face the wrath of their colleagues. They will descend on you in droves from everywhere. Whether they mistakenly hit you or you mistakenly hit them, they will besiege you, and you must repair their vehicle and may compensate them for their mistake. They feel that society is responsible for their lot, and they take it back on society at the slightest opportunity. The police avoids them as much as they can. The ubiquitous traffic wardens loathe them as they will some hot potato. The government pampers their unions lest they would react. They are prepared to go to jail if the need arises. There they meet their colleagues, and that makes a party. It makes no difference if you take them to court. He that is down needs fear no fall.

But is that the type of generation that we aim to succeed us? How can we grow if we do not improve their lot? The strength of the chain is its weakest link. We must improve their lot before we can claim to be improving.

But our country is very rich. And the oil daily flows, and exotic buildings daily erupt, and exotic cars daily make their debut on the dusty roads outside of the capitals. And the millions of rural and urban poor, the real owners of the wealth daily watch, and their hapless young are daily corrupted, knowing fully the source of all the wealth, all the affluence, all the splendor.

It is not all that are successful that are sourced from corruption and from graft. There are a few who through sheer hard work have made their fortunes. But these are few and far between. And the people may be poor, but they are not entirely blind. They can distinguish the genuine from the fake. They can distinguish the merited from the stolen. Even when they have been economically and politically disenfranchised, the grey mater of their brains is still intact. Even when they have been made to lose faith in the ballot box as a means of effecting political changes, many of them are still very intelligent. And a few of them are aware of the famous statement of the late Robert Kennedy, that "those who make peaceful change impossible make violent change inevitable."

These few who are aware fear for my part of the world. And they pray that our leaders learn from past events, and indeed from events of the recent past especially from events in many parts of the vast land mass hitherto known as "the dark continent."

Luckily we have lately witnessed the emergence of an educated apex leadership, a leadership that at least appears to have some respect for the rule of law. The emerging leadership will hopefully read the national dailies (unlike a few of their predecessors) and at least feel the pulse of the nation and wipe the tears of the people as they cry.

The horizon appears to hold some initial hope.

The Youth and the Embracement of Fraud: The Cankerworms

The ingenuity of our youth which in the past was renowned worldwide in the academic circles is diverted from scientific and cultural creativity to discovery of new computer scams baiting their potential victims with stories of millions of dollars of purportedly "abandoned" money in banks and other financial institutions. They then seek "cooperation" for the recovery by requesting the potential victim to deposit an advance fee. The scam has assumed such enormous and embarrassing proportions that the term "419," which represents the criminal coding of the crime, has become a household word in the country. This has gone on to the extent that even the primary school child will describe every deceitful behavior by his playmates as "419."

Before the partially successful clamping down on this scam, it had almost become fashionable for the youth to claim that they were "419." That was because the "419 people" were recognized as the successful people in the society, as they patrolled the streets in their oversized SUVs and other exquisite and exotic cars to the awe of the rest of the citizenry and the dangerous corruption of young minds. The situation got so bad that many schoolteachers reported that when they asked their pupils what profession they would like to pursue in the future, many of the pupils often innocently replied that they would "like to be 419."

It came to a stage where many Nigerians overseas had to claim that they were from Ghana or the Cameroon to avoid extra scrutiny or ostracism at gatherings. It was perhaps as a result of the embarrassment that the nation's envoys and politicians faced abroad on the mere mention that they were from a certain country that prompted measures against the scam at home. Irrespective of the factors that prompted the action, nonetheless, it is a big credit to the powers that be that measures are on the ground to curb that dangerous trend.

The crude oil flows more heavily, and the prices soar by the day. But the infrastructure at home deteriorates. The roads get worse especially the federal roads in the so-called marginalized parts of the country. The power situation despite repeated promises of improvement remains unreliable. Billions of dollars were said to have been sunk into the power sector. But there is hardly anything on the ground to show for the billions.

And the looters walk the streets.
They flaunt the loot and the rest of the nation watches.
Immunity or extended immunity will always be there to shield them
And crimes against the society are thus overlooked.
New looters are encouraged as there has been no probing of the past;
No punishment for the previous master looters
Except for a few smaller flies who may be the scapegoats.

The educational system totters, and the once highly revered Nigerian university degree is now often held suspect as having been bought or forged. And even when proved to be authentic, the quality is still held suspect. The world is now a global village, and hardly any event can be effectively fully concealed. The rest of the world now knows that our university entry can be largely bought. They know that our grades can be largely sold for cash or other favors. The grades of our graduates are held as guilty until they can prove themselves as innocent. That is the price we have to pay for our unfettered corruption, for our streams that have been fouled from source.

Our young men and women graduate from institutions of higher learning without any hope of finding jobs for years. In the past, graduating students sought exemption from the National Youth Service Corps on any available grounds, because highly paying jobs were readily available to university graduates. Today, young graduates pray to be posted and are happy if the posting can come as early as six months after graduation. Many have to wait much longer periods. Some pray that they will have their postings extended if only they can continue to be paid the meager sustenance allowance. They may not find jobs for years after discharge. The joy of graduation turns sour, and the chances for realization of the expectations grow dimmer.

The universities proliferate but the standards get more questionable. Admission process into the universities witness the biggest and most dangerous fraud, for when admissions are bought and the unqualified flood the system, they drop the standards and proliferate their kind. The university campuses deteriorate fast and scarcely get the necessary face-lift. The infrastructural facilities get poorer where existent. The morale of honest and dutiful members of the academic community sags by the day while the crooked ones among them appear to wax stronger.

A recent visit to the chemistry laboratories of one of our universities almost made me weep for our dear country when I compared what I saw with what we had even at my old school Government Secondary School Afikpo some three decades back. A situation where ordinary test tubes were scarce and running water was irregular in a university chemistry laboratory certainly have not been tailored to make us join others to the moon any time in this century.

Virtually all our problems stem from corruption and greed and the lack of the will to fight these cankerworms. It is not that the nation is not rich enough. It is not that the citizenry are not intelligent or hardworking enough. It is simply that we as a people have allowed ourselves and our values to be so hijacked by that bane of humanity called greed that there is complete eclipsing of the recognition of the near-complete vanity of human acquisitions. Thus, we watch and see those who had in the past looted the treasuries of nations die, leaving behind their loot. No looter's acquisitions have ever been known to be buried with the looter.

The looted nation may be left bereft of the looted riches, but the looter gets to the coffin and the grave, alone, and in some cultures and religions, naked or scantily clothed. And yet new looters do not learn. On the other hand, we see perpetual adoration and merited honors being bestowed, in life or even long after their deaths on selfless leaders like Abraham Lincoln, Winston Churchill, Mao Tse-Tung of China, Mahatma Gandhi of India, Nelson Mandela of South Africa, and even our own justifiably revered Tafawa Balewa, Sir Ahmadu Bello, Nnamdi Azikiwe, Obafemi Awolowo, Michael Okpara, Ladoke Akintola, Sam Mbakwe, Murtala Mohammed, and Joseph Tarka. People like Shehu Shagari, Yakubu Gowon, Tai Solarin, Wole Soyinka, Gani Fawehinmi, Odumegwu Ojukwu, Lateef Jakande, and Balarabe Musa deserve special mention too. These are citizens and leaders who no matter what contrary opinions one may have about them are highly adored by most of their people for having placed the interest of their people and other ordinary citizens before self. Many of these people acquired little for themselves in life. Others spoke out loud and clear against social injustices, and are leaving or have left treasured legacies for the people that they led or fought for.

We choose to ignore the lessons of history and crave for the loot of the nation's treasuries and stockpile what even our children's children cannot exhaust, impoverishing the rest, stifling development, and corrupting the future generation. At the end of the day, we still go the way of all mortals and are reduced to dust. But the havoc that we must have committed persists. The billions of dollars that we have stolen and stashed away in foreign bank accounts will not be buried with us. The fallout of our corrupt leadership endures, and the nation putrefies. And we expect a place of honor in history.

To Stay or Not to Stay, the Big Question

Against the background of insecurity, disgust at the inexorable drift towards social Armageddon and the need for respite and sanity no matter how transient, it became necessary to survey other options since we have only one world, and we have just one life to live. Even with the relative comfort of home with its widely acclaimed situation of one belonging to the club of "those who have made it," the need arose to seek to experiment even at the later stages of life to survey new grounds and test new waters. Knowledge of only one pathway may amount to knowledge of no pathway especially at the end of the day when the sun goes down, and the known pathway begins to dim.

There sure can be no abandonment of the motherland, the land that has given us milk, the land that we love and cherish. There, sure can be no abandonment of the friends that we have made, of the family that we have known and grown up with, of the establishments we have founded, or of the Foundation for the Poor that we are funding. These are too dear to our hearts to be relegated, whisked away, glossed over, or discarded.

But before the confusion about what was right and what was justifiable enmeshed us all, before the need arose to be helped on board a flight because of age or infirmity would arise, the need to act became imperative.

It was not a very easy decision to arrive at. Besides, it was like sailing an uncharted sea. As different from the many occasions when one took four to six weeks off in the year to go on vacation to Britain or the United States, a quest for an immigrant status in God's own country was to be an all-involving affair. It was not to be simply fun. It was not to be a bread-and-butter affair. It was to be seen as serious business, commencing with the interviews and clearances, with subsequent visa issuance at the embassy.

I knew it was a decision of a lifetime. I was not unaware of the implications to me, my practice, my friends, my larger and immediate family. It was certainly a painful but necessary decision to take, especially in view of the circumstances that I had been faced with since after my leadership of my professional body. But we were often told in school that "a good soldier fights today to live to fight another day."

The American Embassy "Business Center"

The sea of heads at most Western embassies in Nigeria gave the impression of a nation in flight, a mass flight of the youth in particular. A visit to the American embassy in Lagos in the late 1990s and early to mid-2000s would reveal intense activities at the entrance gates commencing as early as 2:00 a.m. By 4:00 a.m., the queue of visa applicants would have stretched to the road and taken many turns.

Many young men and women would come as early as twelve midnight and take up positions in the queue well ahead of the official queueing time of about 6:00 a.m. Many of these would be genuine visa applicants while others would be touts who would later towards 6:00 am sell their positions in the line to other people who arrived late and who desired to enter the embassy building early. Prior to the full implementation of the appointment system, not everybody who came for visa interview would be attended to on any particular day.

Touts therefore took advantage of the situation and did brisk business, selling their positions in the line for as much as the equivalent of fifty dollars. When a tout who had a number one position in line sold that position early enough, he could again secure a sixtieth or seventieth position, which he could again resell to somebody who otherwise would only have been in the two hundred and fiftieth position. So, on a good day, simply by standing on the line in the American Embassy in Lagos, a tout could earn in a day what a senior business executive in the country makes for working a number of days.

Besides the line-trading touts, there were also many other types of touts. There were the seat touts who offered seats outside the embassy to visa seekers or the people who escorted the latter to the embassy. Each seat on a long bench cost fifty naira, which was then a little under fifty cents, and the contract for the seat was only for the duration that the individual waited outside the embassy for the interview for the day. There were other forms of brisk business makers in front of the embassy building. There were the passport photographers and hawkers of all kinds of snacks and drinks including bottled drink and "pure water," this latest being water that was sold in sealed plastic bags which despite the name might not always be so pure despite the good job being done by the regulatory agencies. The passport photographers made particularly brisk business at the embassy "business center." It did not matter how apparently conforming the passport photograph that one came with was; he or she was likely to be told that the photograph would not be accepted. Apparently only the passport photographs taken by the embassy "business center" photographers appeared to be acceptable.

When the visa issue was done with, the tidying up of the handover presented new problems. Those done with, as best as we could, we were soon airborne, emigrants from the land of our birth, the land that had been our home for half a century, the land that had not really failed us in any way except for that sense of constant physical insecurity and that constant disgust at how individuals, many of who should know better, are daily ripping off the rest of the populace and consistently corrupting the polity. That corrupting influence has escalated to the extent that unless something drastic happens to sanitize the system, the future generation may no longer be in a position to distinguish between what falls within the bounds of social decency and what falls outside of it.

Our young men and women are watching. They are learning. What they see is what they learn. And should they begin to practice what they see us do today, then, the nation is in trouble. Nothing, absolutely nothing, by way of reformation of the system can be achieved until very drastic and determined measures are taken to wipe out the twin-headed octopus of bribery and corruption. Every other thing will fall in place thereafter. It certainly will require very drastic and perhaps painful measures. A kid glove treatment will only amount to a postponement of the evil day.

The situation gets more painful when one realizes that one is completely in no position to help to ameliorate the system, which though it is not salvaged by quitting or absconding yet would have held more promise if there were some light at the end of the tunnel. Some of our "leaders," people who had suffered under a bad system and got rescued and consequently appeared to have been appointed by fate to reform the system, got bitten by the bug of human personal ambition and greed and blew the godsent opportunities. They failed to learn from leaders like Nelson Mandela of South Africa who suffered under a bad system and were able through perseverance and selflessness change the system for the better and quit the stage.

Our own leaders appeared to have felt differently. They corrupt the system and would not want to quit, even when their tenure is over. They leave only when they are forced to.Thus did our nation slip back into the dark ages during their reign and may remain so for a long time, until it pleases the Almighty to send us a redeemer.

Nobody advocates the Jerry Rawlings style of "sanitization," but sometimes only the hottest fire makes the finest steel, and radical surgery may sometimes be required for complete excision of some troublesome ailments. As the nation bleeds under the hydra-headed octopus called corruption, the rest of the civilized society waits and prays for the day when the world's most populous black nation will get a true messiah.

The Flight and the Resident of the United States

My wife was sitting to my immediate left and our teenage son to my far left. It was a little before midnight, and my mind suddenly drifted back to that night some months back when at about 1:00 a.m., the three of us had knelt together at the rooftop of our house, with me clutching at a crude defensive weapon while we waited for possible death at the hands of our attackers.

As much as the seatbelts of the plane could allow us, and as we took quick glances at the haphazard areas with electricity and the other areas of pitch darkness in what was once our dear nation's capital city, the three of us held our heads together, and together we prayed for God's guidance in our journey, with a short prayer for God's direction for our nation, as soon as the wheels of the plane finally got lifted off the tarmac.

By the time we were well into the clouds, our little son Chuchu made his first sentence since we set out for the journey.

"So we are finally on our way," he said.

Finally was indeed the word for him. The attack along the Owerri-Okigwe road and the more recent near deadly attack on our residence must have severely mauled his psyche. He had since then been craving to continue his studies outside the country, preferably in the USA. He was twice denied student visa. The reasons given on both occasions as stated on the slip he was given after each denial was that every visa applicant in his category was regarded as a potential immigrant. After the interview at the first denial to which I had escorted him to the embassy, he felt very dejected. He remained speechless throughout our return journey to our home. I repeatedly had to comfort him and remind him that "God's time is the best."

Finally, therefore, in God's good time he was in the air to fulfill his academic and other dreams, not on a visitor's visa, not even on a student visa, but as a permanent resident of the United States.

We arrived in the United States after a six-hour flight from Lagos to Amsterdam, and another eleven hours flight from Amsterdam to Los Angeles. It was a relatively familiar trip for my wife and me since we had on more than one occasion spent our annual vacations both in Los Angeles and in New York City. For our teenage son, however, it was his first trip out of his home country.

As we stepped out of the plane at the Los Angeles International Airport, the prayers that reverberated in my lips were, "Here we come, Lord. Do with us what you will."

It had been about a generation since I turned down the offer of my father to sponsor my education in the United States. It had been every inch a most fulfilling period through my studies, through my married life, and through my working experience. I had, by the special grace of God, succeeded in every venture I set my efforts into. The only venture I would say that did not quite succeeded was the aborted stint in politics, where my aspirations to contribute my quota towards a change of our society for the better were thwarted by the annulment of the June 12, 1993, elections in Nigeria. Even after that, I found fulfillment in channeling my efforts into my professional practice in medicine and in the contribution of my little quota during my leadership position in that profession, culminating in appointment as a member of the Medical and Dental Council in Nigeria, the highest regulatory body for the practice of medicine and dentistry in Nigeria. That was after I had served the constitutionally maximum four years in two successive terms as the state chairman of the Nigerian Medical Association, as earlier chronicled. I therefore regarded myself, especially after we successfully set up our dream project, Foundation for the Poor, with all humility and gratitude to God, as a completely fulfilled man, both familywise, publicwise, and professionally.

The move to reside in the United States was for me another phase of life. I dare say that I had indeed found fulfillment in my earlier life in the country of my birth. I experienced no major disappointments in the land nor in my people. If I did, I considered myself outspoken enough to have voiced it loud and clear. My one concern and that was a major concern for me was the near total collapse of those tenets upon which those of us who were lucky enough to have been brought up in the government secondary schools, especially my own school at Afikpo, were raised: the principles of patriotism, honesty, justice, and fair play and above all, unfettered self-discipline. Living in a corruption-ridden society where one would not want to give bribes would spell disaster for any individual. Operating in a system where one finds things going wrong and discovering that one is almost completely hamstrung and voiceless or that one's outcries would make absolutely no difference could be one of the most distressing situations for any politically aware individual.

In either situation, it might be more advisable to move, either permanently or for a while, if for nothing else, for one's sanity and peace of mind. Besides, a situation where an individual's personal safety is constantly under threat seems to make nonsense of existence. But it must be emphasized that such a move must not be construed for a flight from or a condemnation for one's country. For unless faults and shortcomings in a system are recognized and pointed out, there may never be moves to correct such faults. It is often the painting of favorable images of excellence and the shielding of the realities on the ground from our leaders by their political handlers and praise singers that convey the false message of infallibility and the consequent "the king can do no wrong" message to those "Excellencies." Hence, corrections can hardly ever be effected. Instead, we tend to sink further and further into corruption and ineptitude.

The American Dream: The Fancy Homes and the Homeless

We had arrived to the first of the first world, the acclaimed best of the best in most aspects of human endeavor, a free nation, the nation where the action really is, the melting pot of cultures, the acknowledged land of endless opportunities, the land that is said to be truly "God's own country."

It was after one of our previous vacations that my wife and I, after a careful review, decided—even in spite of patriotism for one's country—to train our children in the educational system obtaining in the USA. That decision was to assume wider dimensions later as a result of subsequent events in our lives, culminating in a decision to seek and obtain residency.

Having spent all my childhood and a good part of my adult life in another culture, the fascination of an entirely different culture, values, and general attitude to life was for me very enermous.

When in the past we had come spending our annual vacations, it was for us more of visiting places of tourist attractions. We never really had the opportunity nor the need to move into the society and mix with people. We never worked nor rented a home. We either stayed with our brothers and cousins (and these were many in the USA) or with our two other sons, whom we had earlier sponsored over to the United States. On one occasion, we had spent some time in London, and after landing in New York, we had traveled the breadth of America to Los Angeles by Amtrak, a journey that took us three fascinating days, the most fascinating three consecutive days of my life so far, all expenses paid, courtesy of one of my younger brothers, Omeninyo.

But we had this time come in, in a different capacity. We needed to plan. We needed to make a living. We needed to work. One of my brothers and one of my sisters each owned a nice home in California. Our two other sons who had been studying in the United States prior to our arrival lived in the city center. Each of these three groups—our brother, our sister and our sons—would not mind having us with them, but that would be decent and reasonable if it was only for a while. So on our very first day of arrival as residents in the United States, one of the first things I had asked my brother Ody, as he drove us from the airport to his house, was how we could buy or build a house of our own, no matter how small. I had always loved bricks and mortar, from after the time that I built my first house in my home village many years back. I had imagined from my home background that the money we came with which was, by all Nigerian standards a large sum, could straightway buy us a small home into which we could move in, after a few weeks' stay with my brother.

It was at this enquiry that I got my very first shock. I was told that unless I was prepared to pay all cash, home purchases and home loans were based on "credit standing," income, and many other factors necessary for financing, and that the loan approval took many other factors into consideration. Those statements were all like Greek to me. In the system from where I came, credit cards were not in use. If one wanted to own a house, the person would either purchase one already fully built and pay fully; or the person could purchase land, buy the materials, draw the building plan, satisfy the local building requirements, hire a builder, and get the building job done. Ninety five percent or more of home owners owed nobody a dime. All the talk about "credit check, prequalification, preapproval mortgage payments," and so many other related issues were largely not obtained. You bought your house if and when you had money to do so and you moved in. You could go to sleep thereafter without one bank or other lending institution hounding you around. Otherwise, you could rent a place and pay your monthly house rent. In the unlikely event of your not being able to pay your rent, you could always move in with another family member even if he or she had ten or more other family members or friends already living in the house. No landlord would bother a tenant or start dictating to the tenant the number of "brothers or sisters" who would occupy the room, apartment, or house with him or her. The latter action would be considered unnecessary meddlesomeness. Unless a tenant was known to harbor people of questionable character, no landlord would be so nosey as to start bothering how many extended family members occupied a room or an apartment. And in the extremely rare circumstances where somebody got so financially distressed and so hopeless that he or she could not find a relation or friend to move in with, such a person could always report to his or her town meeting who invariably would find solution to the problem. Every one was his or her brother's keeper. At the very worst of situations, the individual could always move to the family home in the village.

There is nobody, absolutely nobody, who does not have a village home to which he belongs, a family home which can always provide shelter to even the most distant cousin. My native language, Igbo, does not have any word for cousin. Your relation is your *nwanne*, and that word extends from your direct brother or sister to the most distant cousin. Indeed the word translated directly means "the child of your mother," and that translation summarizes the extent to which the Igbo people treasure the extended family system. No matter how distantly related you are to somebody, you are that person's brother or sister. There is no half brother nor quarter brother, whatever, in my native Igbo language. There is no cousin either. Indeed, village neighbors who are not related by blood are often regarded as brothers and sisters especially when they meet outside the village setup.

A popular Igbo idiom states, "Agbata obi onye bu nwanne ya" (One's neighbor is his or her brother or sister). This idiom consolidates that tradition of fraternity. I have never all my life known of any sane Igbo man or woman who is said or known to be homeless in his native land. Even for the lunatic who walks the street, there is the saying that "Nwanne onye ala ka ihere na eme" (The shame of the wandering lunatic belongs to his brother or sister). That statement epitomizes the traditional belief and assertion that nobody, not even a mad man, should be homeless.

My first sight of a homeless man on the streets of Los Angeles was a big surprise to me. And I was to see scores of them more within a few weeks, even in the tourist spots of Downtown Los Angeles. Many of these were able-bodied men who wheeled all their earthly possessions on carts, with their clothing, blankets, and eating materials wrapped in large polythene bags of all colors. I could not but wonder at why and how such a situation should still exist in "God's own country."

I did not believe that God, who most of humanity recognizes as "all loving," would want any body to be homeless in his own country even if that person was a drug addict, a lunatic, or simply one who had fallen on bad economic times and consequently could not pay his or her rent. Allowing such a situation to continue should have been regarded as the shame of any nation and ought, at all costs, to have been remedied as a matter of utmost urgency.

Having been involved with quite a few properties in the place that I was coming from, I thought it would be a simple and straightforward process to own a home. Besides, I had been told that part of the widely acclaimed American Dream was a situation where the individual or family would own their own home. Again, I felt that the wealthiest and most powerful nation on the planet—the widely acclaimed "only surviving super power" nation—would do everything possible to ensure that every individual family owned a home of their own, except where the individuals were for some reasons of some physical or mental disability declared incapable of maintaining a home, for shelter is one of the acclaimed basic needs of man. I did not in my wildest imaginations believe that there could be people in the United States who would be homeless not out of desire or by reasons of insanity but purely because they lost their jobs or because of other vagaries of the system, a sad situation which I had not seen even once in my third world country of origin.

It was in the light of the foregoing that I had my first big surprise to learn that I could not just purchase a home or make a deposit for where I could live with my family until the different hurdles which were narrated to me were scaled.

When one of the two basic needs of man, food and shelter, is not readily available to God's own people, even in God's own country, then man cannot be said to be fulfilling the desires of God in his own country.

As we drove through the California's six-and-more lane superhighways, the fact of my previous visits did not daunt my continuous admiration of, and consternation at, what the hands of man had constructed.

To people who ply these roads daily and the millions of others who were born into the system or who grew up seeing these things in place, these structures and highways may seem so ordinary. They may become so very easily taken for granted. Such people, God bless them, may not fully appreciate what they have. Such people are obviously robbed of the fascination which people like me are wont to enjoy, born on the floor on banana leaves with assistance from an illiterate elderly traditional birth attendant using a rusted knife for the cutting of the umbilical cord, reared in an emerging city in the third world amidst the gangs of children stealing mangoes from European quarters, and let into twenty-first-century America with its pomp and splendor as adults. People outside my circumstances obviously miss the fascination which people like me enjoy, seeing the marvelous handiwork of man, a mere mortal.

The sun was fast setting as we cruised between Los Angeles International Airport and our destination in Rancho Cucamonga. The sea of vehicles each cruising at an average of sixty miles per hour along the CA 210 San Bernardino Freeway, the orderliness, and the complete absence of even one smoking vehicle amidst the tens of thousands that we saw playing the route were another source of fascination for me.

During my previous visits, I did not quite pay attention to the pattern of vehicular movement on the roads because I knew I was only visiting and would not need or be allowed to drive. That day along the road, I took particular interest because I knew I would soon have to drive myself since I would have no chauffer here. A chauffer which many medical directors and other chief executives would consider routine in Nigeria could be one of the biggest luxuries and indeed a near aberration here except for the likes of top CEOs and the very top political bigwigs on strictly official functions.

In contrast, a third world country which often requests for financial aid and possibly debt forgiveness from the world's richer creditor nations can afford the luxury of tens of thousands of able-bodied men whiling away millions of man hours every year waiting on as chauffeurs for some chief executive who is in no way physically disabled even while the latter is on unofficial outings.

The government minister will have a couple of chauffeurs; his wife will have some assigned to her from the pool of "oga's drivers." Of course, there will be one or two whose only daily duty will be "to drop oga's children to school and to bring them back."

The duty of Madam's driver may be to take the latter for shopping and to bring her back.

The duty of "oga's spare driver" may simply be to carry oga's briefcase into the backseat of oga's car and thereafter to follow oga's car behind in a spare car.

Each of "oga's special assistants" will of course have a chauffer. So may each personal assistant and so may each assistant to the special assistant. So will the count continue down the line. The retinue is repeated at the state level where every commissioner, every special adviser, and the assistants as well as the assistants to the special assistants, including the advisers and the assistants to the advisers, almost ad infinitum, will all have chauffeurs assigned to them. The directors at the multiple ministries and perhaps the assistants to some of these directors are not left out. All these are of course at government expense. If they are not paid for directly, their salaries and allowances are "monetized" and paid to the officer concerned. And these cars, of course, are 95 percent of the time used for private pursuits, either for shopping, clubbing, attendance at Sunday worship, or attendance to village meetings and all sorts of activities unrelated to the officer's official duties.

The local governments are not left out. The roll call of honor (or dishonor) is repeated down the line as each local government chairman would also like to play the role of a local Excellency. It was a mild drama on one occasion when a siren-blowing "local czar" was driving in one direction along a dusty major road in his ill-maintained and thoroughly ripped-off little "empire" when his convoy encountered a larger siren-blowing convoy of a state czar of an adjoining state, approaching from the opposite direction. The outriders of the state czar easily chased the siren-blowing convoy of the local czar into the bush. The rest of the road users who watched the drama at least had some fun watching the drama between a local power and a local superpower. The greatly enraged and thoroughly humiliated local czar thereafter swore that he would "do everything possible to get to the state level." Of course, he would have to embezzle much more to accumulate the funds to bribe or rig his way through to a future election "victory."

Then the electoral chief executives will grow richer. The local czar will steal more. The public office chief executive will get younger in his official age as the years progress. The latter must not be seen to be approaching official retirement age lest some younger deputy steps into his shoes and begins to get potbelly with embezzled resources, just like the boss has enjoyed over the years. And the rest of the enlightened populace watch with suppressed indignation at the rape of the polity and the pollution of young minds. The unenlightened in the system hail the perpetrators and resign themselves to their fate: the wretched of the earth in a land blessed by nature with milk and honey. They can only pray that their children can grow to be successful 419 practitioners since most doors to legitimate economic ascendance in the system appear to have been shut against him. Alternatively he can also pray that his children can develop strong muscles to fight their way through as chief party thugs to some political godfather, whose bouncer they will be and whose political and social dirty jobs they will perform. In the latter position they, like Zorro, may get rewarded someday with a position as important as being a national delegate. They may thereafter be able to go to Kaabruuja to participate in electing the political leaders for the nation and come back to their base with tons of money. That is, if the highway robber does not successfully trail them from the motor park!

In the midst of all the rot, the callous waste, and misapplication of material and human resources, how can the nation make progress? How can we hope to join the rest of the civilized world to successfully build a just and egalitarian society and be able to transform from "developing" to "developed" in the next generation? How can we begin to reeducate our youth, the future hope of the nation, and reorient their socially battered psyche away from what they have seen, right from their toddler years, at school, and outside of school: corruption, cheating, embezzlement, and all forms of social vices. How do we begin to convince them that there could be nobler goals in life than the mere acquisition of tons of money, even if the acquisition is at the expense of the nation and the deprivation of the downtrodden in our society.

Nobody will of course begrudge "His Excellencies" the entitlement of being chauffer-driven. Security and protocol alone would definitely warrant this. But the convoy of vehicles which would accompany each "Excellency" or each "Her Excellency," the official wife of His Excellency, on every routine trip would leave even the presidents of the world's richest nations gasping for breath. It is easily forgotten that we once had a head of state, who even though he was a military ruler, would drive to work in his private vehicle. Even though that particular leader was later mowed down by an assassin's bullets, his legacy will continue to live for as long as the entity called Nigeria exists. His image which is not measured by material wealth will continue to outshine the totality of the worth of all looters before and after him. Again, too, it is easily forgotten that the mayor of one of the world's most cosmopolitan cities, who himself is by no means a poor man, goes to work using the underground rail system just like every other mortal, his subjects. And yet the annual budget of this mayor's office is hundreds of times more than the annual budget of even our central government.

Even then the list of Excellencies is not yet exhausted! A "daughter Excellency" the first daughter of the original "Excellency" for whom a special office was once contemplated, must also have an assigned chauffer, all paid for from state funds. Of course, down the line the chief executives of the "government parastatals" and all equivalent government agencies must not allow themselves to be cheated out of the largesse, and thus every office will have scores of near redundant able-bodied men milling around waiting for oga's orders.

It is not just that billions of taxpayers' money would be wasted each year to pay redundant staff, but by far the greatest damage is done by the spoiling silly of many of these chief executives by encouraging a lifestyle which they cannot sustain on their retirement paychecks. To sustain their princely lifestyle developed while in public office therefore, these depraved top politicians or public service barons will have to steal the country dry while still in office since they would have gotten so spoilt and so lazy in office that they cannot last a couple of months outside of office on their legitimate paychecks. They therefore would begin to manipulate the system or try to change the constitution of the country to enable them elongate their tenure or even to remain in office for life.

Another fallout of the bogus lifestyle of top public servants and top political office holders at public expense is that it makes government so attractive that people are prepared to go to any extent to win or rig elections that there is a complete loss of confidence in the electoral process on the part of the electorate. Constitutional and peaceful change of government, of course, become a near impossibility. And when the latter occurs, the way is more easily paved for a fulfillment of the earlier quoted statement by Robert F. Kennedy that '"those who make peaceful change impossible make violent change inevitable."

A direct consequence of violent change of course is instability which most nations of the third world can ill afford.

I came from a background of cities where numerous smoking vehicles were allowed on the roads, where smog tests were nonexistent or were not enforced, where the thick black smoke from the trailer in front would completely obscure the view of the driver behind, and where traffic indiscipline and near anarchy prevail on the well-funded but poorly built and poorly maintained roads (stemming from massive and unchecked embezzlement of project funds). I therefore could not but continuously marvel at the very high quality of the roads as we drove along the road from Los Angeles International Airport. The road quality and discipline constituted a big fascination for me. I once in later months encountered one of the very rare occasions when there was failure of a traffic light. I was greatly amazed at the order with which the drivers approaching from each of the four directions carefully took their turns, allowing a stream of vehicles from one direction to pass before another stream from another direction would follow, thereby spontaneously avoiding chaos. In my native situation, if the traffic light failed, as it often did from failure of the public power company, or where there was no traffic warden at a road intersection, there would be anarchy. Sometimes the arrival of the traffic police or the traffic warden at such a period of momentary anarchy would make no difference or might even worsen the situation as the latter might arrive with a combative wooden baton or a horsewhip called *koboko*. By the time two or three drivers are whipped, chaos might result from the panic and confusion. Traffic could be held up for hours by the simultaneous convergence of vehicles from all four sides of the road each struggling to pass first.

The citizens are not born with indiscipline. It is rather the failure of leadership that hands the baton of indiscipline down the line.

The fact that the system works in the developed world may be taken for granted by the people who have the advantage of having been born into this system. The same goes for those who have lived here all their lives and for whom the sight of very good roads no longer holds any fascination since they have not seen any really bad roads to be able to appreciate the beauty of what they have.

The fact that power supply was steady and the fact that the taps never ran dry no longer were fascinations for me. That was in spite of the fact that the society that I came from did not enjoy these luxuries. My previous vacations had made me take these for granted whenever I stepped out of my native country. Besides, the advent of deep wells (locally called "boreholes") and extensive use of private power-generating sets (simply called "generators") had made it possible for some lucky ones like me not to feel the full impact of near collapse of public utilities in the world's seventh largest oil exporting country, my dear native country. But once in a while, especially whenever I happen to fly into or out of Los Angeles at night, I cannot but marvel at the unappreciated wonders and technological wizardry that there must be, in powering the hundreds of millions of lighting points in the greater Los Angeles County alone, when one takes a view from the air.

Looking like millions of stars on a clear starry night as one would often see up in a December night in the land of my birth, these man-made "little stars" would often remind me of that anonymous popular poem we had been taught in early primary school years and which every little child was familiar with, the poem which runs thus:

> Twinkle twinkle little star,
> How I wonder what you are
> Up above the world so high
> Like a diamond in the sky.
> (Anonymous)

Often in an unconscious effort to comfort myself and hold brief for the power inadequacies that abound at home, I would turn my mind to those starry nights that I spent at Ndiakunwanta, my native village. I would then persuade myself that what we lost on the ground at home by way of electricity supply we gained in the sky by the quietude and tranquility and the millions of stars that glittered naturally in the clear and unpolluted skies of the home that I knew and still hold so dear.

The hills in Rancho Cucamonga, California, were quite majestic and nothing excited me more on the first few mornings after my arrival than standing outside of my brother's house before the sun came up to gaze at those hills. Their rolling nature in dips and spikes made me marvel at them the more. The white specks of snow at the peaks of the hills on certain mornings in January were very fascinating for me. I would begin to compare them with the Udi Hills in the city of Enugu in Eastern Nigeria, where I grew up. The clearness of the latter with the all-year-round summer and relatively small vehicular traffic in the vicinity contrasted greatly with the frequent smog, seasonal snow, and massive vehicular traffic around the former. Both share the same quality in the beauty they confer to the respective cities that they surround.

The thing that would strike most first-time visitors to "God's own Country," as indeed to all Western countries that I have visited, to me is the order in the system. We were always told in school that "order is the first law in heaven."

Whether this nature's law holds true, in my society of origin it is questionable. And if truly order is the first law in heaven and if by extrapolation or inference disorder holds sway in hell, one can safely say of my roots that "we are in hell."

> In "hell" despite the ever-flowing "petro-dollar"
> In hell despite the ever-springing exotic cars and mansions

Man-made hell,
A hell that need not be,
Hell in a land so blessed,
A land that Mother Nature made
To flow with milk and honey,
But a land near polluted
By man's greed and insatiety.

Fortunately or unfortunately, this situation, as defined in Shakespeare's *Julius Caesar*, is not in our stars, but in ourselves.
It can be reversed.
It indeed should and must be reversed. We certainly can do better.

Courtesy and discipline in public places are often thrown to the winds in most of my root's circumstances, especially the higher that one has climbed up to in the society. This is a sharp contrast to what obtains in more developed societies. I believe we can do better. We indeed should do better.

While other drivers would queue behind and take their turns when there is traffic hold up, there invariably would be one or two, most often those who believe they have money or power, who would choose to jump the queue and form a parallel queue. A fresh and illegal line of vehicles would follow, as many other drivers would immediately queue up behind the miscreant driver thereby obstructing traffic flow from the opposite side. As the situation gets compounded, it might become difficult for any traffic officer who arrives the scene later to know which was the original correct line of traffic and who were the offenders. Sometimes three or four lanes of traffic are formed on a one-lane road in the same direction, completely shutting down traffic flow from the opposite side. Where a similar situation obtains from the opposite side, there could be complete and chaotic traffic hold up for hours on end.

A traffic officer or a member of the armed forces escorting his oga (master) in a siren-blaring vehicle may soon arrive the scene. The officer would alight from his vehicle, wielding a live weapon and often a horsewhip. He does not know which vehicles started the problem. He starts shouting at the drivers to clear the road for his master. But the roads are completely blocked on both sides, bumper to bumper. The officer gets angry and starts hitting the bonnets, the roofs, or boots of the vehicles with the butt of his rifle. Occasionally he may fire a shot or two into the air to confirm to all and sundry that he has a loaded weapon.

The innocent driver who was originally on the correct queue and who might have been partially edged out of the line may become the victim. In extreme situations, his headlight may be smashed or his windscreen may be battered. He may even be given a red eye or some "dirty slaps" for the crime he did not commit, while the culprits may be spared.

I had once suffered this fate at the hands of the escorts of a bullion van. In that particular episode, my side mirror was smashed, and I had a butt blow to my left shoulder even as I sat innocently in the original correct lane in my vehicle. And in a situation like that, there is nobody to complain to. One can only lick one's wound and quietly curse the system and the people that had virtually legitimized indiscipline in our system through a systematic denigration of the fundamentals of a decent and civilized society because of their insatiable thirst for illicit wealth and loot of the public treasury.

The Siren-and-Police-Escort Mentality

There is an increasing craze for now to go with police escorts. The vehicles of "who is who" in the society are fitted with sirens. Efforts at limiting the abuse in the past did not appear to have been heeded. It has become a status symbol, the mark of "arrival," for the politically well connected in society and a few economically well-placed ones to go with sirens and police escorts. Leaders of governments and their cronies and lieutenants at various levels would go with the siren and a police escort sitting at the front by the side of the driver, while oga occupies the backseat and peeps out through the wound-up glasses as the wretched of the earth, the rest of the citizens, are chased off the roads. The police escort often would clutch a service pistol and a horsewhip. Even King John of evil fame was not reported to have a pistol while chasing his subjects off the streets. Maybe pistols were not yet discovered. But our modern-day czars and their cohorts hold not only horsewhips, but also something more lethal, pistols, or sometimes submachine guns! The people who "elected" them into office or who elected their ogas and friends must be chased off the road whenever they are on the road. Whether they are on important missions of government or they are on evening missions to visit their girlfriends is irrelevant. Convoys of vehicles with siren and policemen must accompany His Excellency, Her Excellency, Daughter or Son Excellency. Friends of the Excellency must not be left out. A reason can always be adduced to drive through the streets with the siren blaring. All manner of elected and unelected personnel, so long as they have the slightest connection with people in power can always be allotted government vehicles with which they move through the roads blaring sirens. Sometimes it looks so ridiculous, and one cannot but sympathize with a system that has degenerated to the levels where things that are supposed to be taken seriously are so flagrantly abused, simply because someone wants to show that he or she "has arrived."

Cassius in William Shakespeare's *Julius Caesar* had described the latter thus: "He doth bestride the narrow world like a colossus."

If Julius Caesar bestrode the world like a colossus, he probably merited it to a good extent considering his exploits for Rome before and during his five-year reign. One is at a loss to say what exploits, what sacrifices, what contributions some of our modern-day local czars have made to our society to justify the strangleholds they hold on the society in our little part of the world, except perhaps that they had been selected by some perhaps equally despicable tyrant against the election-day wishes of the people. Of course, where people are so selected rather than elected, they owe little or no allegiance to the electorate.

Again, like King John of evil fame, who we were told used to overfeed and sitting on a mounted horse would ride around town and whip his subjects on the streets, these selected "leaders" can afford to mount blaring sirens and chase people off the roads into some open gutters which they fail to maintain. Where they do not physically and personally whip the people, their escorts in uniform will do so on their behalf.

Recently a new dimension has been added to the escort-and-siren mentality, whereby any body that can pay the price is provided with police escort who sits on his or her front seat as the latter drives around town or through the highway. Of course, large sums of money must be dished out before such a service is provided. And the officer so assigned, of course, will inevitably like to go the extra mile to please his oga, even if it be to the disadvantage of the rest of society and the rights of the people. It thus boils down to the situation where those who really would need police protection cannot get it because they cannot pay. And, of course, the service does not come cheap. Sometime ago one of my brothers traveled home, and because it was getting late in the evening, he went to seek the services of a police escort to travel safely home. The amount of dollars (not naira) which he was told to pay was so unreasonable that he decided to brave the journey without an escort. He paid much more dearly. He nearly lost his life on the road.

For the over twenty-eight years that I was privileged to travel to the developed world, I cannot remember a single day that elected officials no matter at what high levels were seen on the roads with sirens and police escorts chasing people off the roads.

A situation where the pomp, pageantry, and largesse associated with public office are seen to be the main motivations for such offices rather than the genuine desire to serve and make positive contributions leaves much to be desired. When the siren is heard on the street, the chances are that it is neither the fire service nor an ambulance conveying the sick or personnel on other emergency duties, nor the police on emergency duties. Chances are more than one in two that it is either one politician or his crony, or it is an "ambulance" conveying a long-embalmed dead body.

It may be a very good thing if our law enforcement agents are once in a while sponsored on retraining courses abroad to see how the other parts of the civilized world function. That way it will be appreciated that even law enforcement agents obey traffic regulations. That way, our system will gradually develop; otherwise, the word *developing* attached to our part of the world will never transit to *developed*, not even in the next one hundred years. We may, instead, degenerate back to that word *underdeveloped*, which our leaders had protested about in the past.

Indeed, even with all the patriotism in the world, even at the risk of being misinterpreted, misquoted, or misrepresented from what one witnessed in the past couple of years, from the educational sector to the political, we appear to be regressing and indeed deteriorating. A situation where no credible elections nor credible censuses can be conducted, where educational assessments are based on the weight of one's wallet or "cooperation" rather than on the quality of a candidate's actual performance, where honesty and morality in public office are derided and the crook extolled, we may not be too far away from the inevitable fate that awaits all godless nations—the path of disintegration, decay, and destruction. The latter will be an ill wind that will blow nobody any good. We as a nation need to pray and work hard on our values and retrace our footsteps if we must survive the fate that awaits all nations and peoples that throw public morality and accountability to the winds. It is possibly God's love and the persistent prayers of the poor masses that have helped to sustain us despite our colossal failures and inadequacies in just governance and accountability. Even one of the past military rulers of the country once wondered aloud what it was that was still sustaining the system,

It is probably only the oil and other natural resources that still hold us together. But these are all diminishing resources and are bound to exhaust someday. Unless we as a people begin today to retrace our footsteps as adults and begin to retrain our young ones in rechanneling their thoughts towards honesty, hard work, patriotism, and unity built on justice, equity, and fair play, no amount of armored cars can shield our leaders or the hapless citizens from the crime wave that will emerge in the next generation. Not even a price tag of a thousand dollars for a barrel of oil will save us from the impending socioeconomic disaster that will be sequel upon the current emphasis on "money, no matter from where," a clear manifestation of the saying that the end justifies the means.

We have an energetic and hardworking population. Our youth are sharp witted and quick to learn. Nature has blessed our nation in virtually all things that any nation can desire. It is only selfless and dedicated leadership that is required to galvanize the efforts for maximum effect. The choice is ours.

Most of our leaders are certainly not demons. Some of them indeed might mean well initially, but as soon as they get into office and surround themselves with cronies and boot lickers, they soon get shielded away from reality and the expectations of the very people they are supposed to be serving. The ones at the federal level will no longer see the ever-present potholes and death traps on the roads as they will no longer travel by road. On the few occasions that they will have cause to travel to the states to commission some "completed projects," the potholes along the short distance through which they will pass after alighting from the nearest airport are hastily patched up to last for a couple of weeks. The boss from Kaabruuja must not be given the impression that the boss at the state level is "not performing." The billions of naira coming into the state from the center must be seen to be doing some good job, and this includes patching up the death traps on the roads which the federal government is supposed to be maintaining.

The jets and helicopters will of course always be available for use by the big Kabruuja boss, and before the big bosses left office they ensured that they embezzled enough to purchase private jets and private helicopters for themselves so that they can maintain the same unfathomable tastes that they had sharpened while in office. But they are blind to the fate that visited previous dictators and embezzlers before them. They always believe that their own situations will be different because they are smarter. But they are wrong.

If the long arm of the law completely misses them with time, certainly the normal arm of nature, be it Karma (for those who so believe) or otherwise, will certainly catch up with them. It is only a matter of time.

We certainly can do better, but,

It takes a good leader
To produce a good team.
It takes a good team
To produce good results.
It takes a good teacher
To train out good students.
It takes good students
To produce good results.
It takes a good home
To turn out good children.
It takes good children
To build up a good society.

Again, a stream that is clean from source will certainly give good water at some point along its course. But when a stream is polluted at source, it can hardly give clean water downstream.

The success of any nation is largely dependent upon its leadership.

An Igbo language adage states that "when a nanny goat chews its food, the kids observe very attentively."

When therefore the leaders of any nation display honesty in governance, their appointees are likely to be honest, and the rest of the nation takes a cue from there.

Corruption and ineptitude are not the birthmarks of any leader, any official, or any people. These are acquired characteristics and hence can be decried or rejected by any leader who wishes to succeed and hence lead his or her nation into the path of rectitude. One of the governors of one of the southeastern states of Nigeria was sometime said to have been aided to rig his way into office, but while in office, he had so transformed his state into a near El Dorado, and had built so many good roads and schools that his people who had protested his coming were virtually pleading for his continued stay. That was a clear manifestation of the fact that nobody is inherently or totally evil.

Of course, subsequent good governance after the rigging of an election would by no means justify the initial rigging of the elections. But for a people who have been so repeatedly mauled by successive generations of politicians, all is well that ends well. Any politician, civil or military master who could tar their roads, give them good drinking water, provide steady power supply, or provide reliable health facilities for them and their dependents would be very welcome.

People, no matter how they emerged into prominence, can still reform and transform their communities and nations. It only takes the moral courage, and often the self-denial. It must start with reformation of the leaders' self and the team. The rest of the nation will inevitably fall in line. A precedent exists. Two army generals were once in power in Nigeria. Military dictatorship was decried and will rightly continue to be decried no matter how benevolent. But those army generals had preached and practiced a program which they called "war against indiscipline." It did not take long before the rest of the populace fell in tune. People began to queue up to be served in public places. Civil servants reported early for work, corruption issues began to be seriously addressed ("don't give, don't take" became the vogue), and even in the face of the administration's alleged human rights abuses, order in the society was slowly being restored. It did not take long after the administration's collapse for all the previous vices to reemerge and indeed multiply.

We certainly can make it as a nation if we try, but the leadership must set the pace and take the lead.

Adjusting Into a System

When I used to visit, I did not have the need to drive myself around. The public transportation systems and members of my family drove me to wherever we wanted to go. One or the other of the many members of the larger family in the USA was always available to guide or transport me around, whether I was in New York, in Texas, or in California. It was one big dividend that emanated from coming from a large family, one of the forty-six children of my core family and one of the four hundred and eight children of the larger family. My friends in the United States found it difficult to believe the numbers. They need to visit Africa with me to believe. Even our numbers in the United States alone speak for themselves.

Who says polygamy does not have its advantages?
It may be illegal in some places, but it has worked for us.
Without it, perhaps I would not have been born.
Every cloud has a silver lining, we hear,
And every silver lining has its rough edges for sure.
But certainly each rough edge has its own glitter,
And each glitter radiates its love and care.
Especially for a family that has been taught to care.
From the cradles we had been taught to share.
Even tiny little chickens that were available to share,
And with persistent mutual love we had learnt to fear,
Whatever little quarrels that might bring us a tear,
To the cherished family unity that had been nursed with care.
But father and mother, a man must leave
And cling to his wife and both must be
One spirit in Christ, the holy book says.
So let it be, for those who cherish,
The tenets of monogamy as a way of life,
To love and to cherish,

We are told to say.
But to put it right,
There is a prize to pay.
Or, till divorce do us part,
It may turn out to be.

Settling down presented no problems to us. The entire larger family in the United States was of immense support. We were once again privileged to witness the joys of coming from a large family, a united family, and the wisdom of our parents who insisted on giving their children a good education. We saw the gains on the insistence of our father that we ate together. We saw the foresight of our parents who, even when there was only one chicken to share, insisted that every one of the forty-six of us together with a father and eight wives took a share from the same wooden meat chopping board. We saw the wisdom of the larger family maintaining the same name and constantly involving our married aunts and sisters along with their spouses in the larger family's annual festivities.

On our arrival to the United States, we received an average of two calls each day during the first two weeks of our stay from our brothers and sisters as well as friends from all over the United States.

Settling down as permanent residents certainly differed substantially from visiting. We soon began to realize that we needed to start afresh with whatever certifications we had had in our native country, starting with our driving licenses. We had a free gift of a car from a family member within our first week in the United States.

We had thought that, being adults and having each driven for over twenty years especially in a country that also drives on the right side of the road as the United States does (unlike in Britain where they drive on the left), we might only be required to simply validate our driving licenses and thereafter renew them when the renewals of the validated licenses fell due. That was, however, not to be.

We were required to take the full written tests and undergo the eye tests and pass both before issuance of the temporary (learner's) permit. Thereafter, we had to take the full practical driving test and convince the examiner that other road users were safe with us on the driving seat on the roads. There was no shortcut to it no matter how long we had driven in our native country. We must not incur any "critical error" nor make more than a certain number of mistakes for us to pass the exam. There was absolutely no cutting of corners. The professionalism of those examiners in the Department of Motor Vehicles was spectacular. I had wished that I could lift the setup and infuse same into the motor licensing system in my country of origin.

At first though, I had seen it as an unnecessary punishment, subjecting someone who already had evidence of many years of driving to those written physical and practical exams. It was after I had gone through the DMV handbooks that I became convinced that there was great wisdom in the authorities' insistence on most foreign-licensed drivers taking the tests. Not only did it ensure uniformity. It also ensured that all claims were true and that the foreign-licensed driver would not constitute a danger to himself and to others on streets, avenues, boulevards, and the extensive freeways of California. Indeed, a relaxation of the rules could spell disaster, judging from the discipline, courtesy, and attention exhibited and required on the roads here in contrast to the background of anarchy and indiscipline that I came from. After being lucky to scale through the tests at first sitting, my apprehension about driving on the freeways needed to be put to personal test (since freeway driving was not included in the practical test). Prior to my driving on the freeway, I was initially apprehensive about and amazed at the number of vehicles on California's freeways. Nothing on any of my native country's roads compared even narrowly to the new experience. Not even a drive through the third mainland bridge in Lagos came close to that experience. It is a completely different world.

The Housing Situation

The housing conditions and the real estate sector in general bore a few similarities to my native country, but only as regards certain aspects of tenancy and ownership. The conditions, covenants, and restrictions (CCRs) as well as adherence to the rules of tenancy are, however, much more stringent here. The background checks before someone can rent an apartment or a house here are much more thorough and much more stringent than what obtains anywhere in my native country. To start with, the credit check of the prospective tenant here is enough to screen off the individual. The move-in and move-out checks as well as the number of occupants per apartment are closely monitored as different from the situation where a tenant can literally bring in his entire village to live with him so long as there is sleeping space on the floor.

Security, of course, is another factor that makes the former situation very essential. I remember that after two weeks of stay with my brother, my wife and I went to stay with our son in his rented apartment.

After a week of our stay with our son, the resident property manager surfaced on the eighth night to query our son about who were the extra two persons staying with him. Explanations with family photographs to explain to the manager that we were the parents did not placate the manager, who insisted that we must move from our son's apartment within seventy-two hours. I felt rather indignant at the manager's apparent lack of due consideration, especially as we came to know that there were four other similar situations in the property which the manager chose to ignore. It was felt that the manager displayed some element of discrimination in ignoring four cases of six or more extra people occupying a similar apartment and picking on two parents who were visiting their son. It was nevertheless the manager's prerogative to choose which nonconformity to pursue. Indeed I applauded his diligence and vigilance much as they were not uniformly applied.

We quickly returned to my younger brother's house and had to make immediate arrangements to rent our own apartment. We would have loved to buy one no matter how small since from my experience in my native country, I was aware of the advantages of buying as opposed to renting. However, much as the money we had at hand would have done for a down payment of 5 to 10 percent of the cost of a small apartment, there was no way we would have been able to sustain the mortgage since we were not earning any salaries. In any case, no lender would have easily preapproved us without evidence of adequate income and good credit, neither of which we had. We could see before us the invisible inscription: "Welcome to the American Socioeconomic Setup."

THE EXAMS AND EMPLOYMENT

We needed to start working. But we needed to sit the exams and be duly licensed before we could practice our professions or indeed any other profession. But there, the conflicts came on. I would want to practice my profession since it was the only thing I had formal training. But my real interest, which turned out to be a hobby, even during the time I practiced in Nigeria had always been in real estate. That was the reason I invested quite a bit in real estate before my movement to the United States. Indeed my first real property was, as earlier narrated, as early as when I was in secondary school, from retail trade of cigarettes during the Civil War.

I used to hawk cigarettes for some time during the civil war. One of my regular customers was Kehin, who was an acknowledged chain-smoker. I used to carry the packets of cigarettes in my side pocket and sold the sticks by retail trade to any body who was prepared to pay cash for them. The only exception to the cash payment rule was Kehin, who could buy any number of sticks he wanted and pay every Sunday morning. I gave Kehin the privilege of credit payment because he bought so many sticks every day and never defaulted with his payments. After some four months of regular purchases, however, Kehin struck a deal with me for monthly, instead of weekly payments. But at the end of the first month, he had consumed close to four rolls of cigarettes on credit. He almost made me run out of supplies. When it was time for him to pay, he requested for one week of grace. I was reluctant to oblige him at first, but I had to yield when Kehin offered to pay double the price for sticks smoked during the grace period. I felt it would be good business.

When, however, I approached Kehin for the payment after a further two weeks into the grace period, he got angry at first but later placated me by offering to smoke free for an extra two weeks in exchange for a plot of his land which was situated behind my father's compound. I had rejected the offer at first but later accepted on advice from my mother. That property, an empty piece of land at that time, still stands and houses my resort in the village of my birth. I always took pride in telling my children that I bought my first real estate property as a teenager while I was still in secondary school and with the money which I earned by myself. Even though I know that the situations are not similar, I often use that "feat" as a challenge for them to learn to invest as soon as they can.

Practice of my profession would entail a three-year residency program and a further upwards of two years of specialization, a minimum of five years assuming I would pass the medical licensing exams on schedule. If all went well, then the earliest I would expect to settle down to practice independently would be six years. It would be a good idea since the pay packet would be heavy thereafter. Then I would proudly add MD and an American-awarded medical fellowship to my name after my original MB, BS, and DA. Great, great idea, and I was already beginning to savor the idea in anticipation. But then I also considered the cost, the time involved, and how effective and happy I expected to be thereafter, assuming all went well. It was not all about the money alone, even though I would like to have the latter to pay my bills and solve some problems and more importantly to sustain the charity we had set up but would that be the style of life I would like to live at this time? Would I really want the confinement and the restriction that starting virtually afresh would entail?

Could I stand the physical stresses that the residency program would entail? Would I want a complete severance from all one had set up over a period of a quarter century if I must give a hundred percent of my available time to the new pursuit? Would it be fair to the causes I had championed if I should at this stage of my life start to get fully engrossed in the consulting room or operating theater in a situation where any half measure or mistake, no matter how trivial, might meet with enormous litigations? Would I truly be happier, even if I was making the money assuming I succeeded in getting back into practice as an anesthesiologist? What, apart from the higher remuneration, would make me choose a fresh start in medicine over my longtime interest in real estate and my passion for writing and poetry, including "my time on my hands" which the latter would afford me—a situation which I had enjoyed for a quarter of a century as a private medical practitioner?

And assuming I succeeded in scaling the hurdles, would I be able to devote my full time to the practice and still make out time for visits to ensure the running of the small charity we had set up many years back?

Would I be able to muster the same strength that I was able to plough in when I started my first group of hospitals many years ago?

It took me quite awhile to make up my mind. The indecision initially made me read simultaneously for both Exams, the United States Medical Licensing Examination and the California Real Estate Exams. As expected, the latter was the easier.

One may sometimes succumb to ego-inspired pressures to go on a course of action against one's wishes. The drive for the actualization of an ego pursuit may prevail and compel one into an ill-prepared decision to attempt those medical professional examinations. In a situation where one's head and heart are in one direction and one's ego is in another, the resultant catastrophe can only be expected when one succumbs to the latter. When one had thought that one was academically invincible and that one had never accepted and would never accept a failure in any Exams one should never call one's self a fool until he or she jumps into the medical licensing exams halfhearted, ill prepared, or purely for ego-boosting purposes. I was a thorough example of that self-conceited fool who only learnt my lessons in humility when the results came tumbling in the mail, and boldly written poor results stared me in the face. It was obvious that even if I wanted to work with them, those results would not secure me any worthwhile position.

"Wha-a-at? Me-e-e?" I initially exclaimed.

Yes, it was me.

How are the mighty fallen? I seemed to ask myself. It served me right. I was so used to winning and passing Exams big time, that I had begun to assume an invincibility which I neither had, nor indeed deserved. It was a big lesson in humility, one which I certainly needed for me to make a realistic move in a new direction, another worthwhile direction, a more enduring and perhaps more reformist-oriented direction.

I opened my eyes wider to reassure myself that it was not a dream. Initially, I had all but taken the whole thing as a joke, being propelled more by my ego rather than by a genuine desire to go the whole hog of a new residency program and confinement in the clinics. But when the big guys in the examinations council now told me that I was ill prepared, I started wishing that I had taken the whole thing more seriously rather than bluffing through it. Even if I had not made up my mind to practice, I still would have preferred that it was not that I could not practice but that I did not wish to practice. I jokingly told my wife, "Now you see, it is not that I do not wish to practice. It is rather that the gods have decreed that I should be spared the ordeal of another thirty-six months of residency."

I needed no further persuasion to make a hurried retreat and turn my full attention to that other passion of mine, bricks and mortar, and more importantly that other aspect of my life which I had missed for so long: writing. I could readily have persevered with the USMLE and perhaps made it better at another attempt, perhaps with a more humble approach. If for nothing else, I would have liked to reassure my ego that I was not quitting because of exposition of an ill-conceived ego of invincibility which I had developed from my secondary school days. But would my aspirations have been so satisfied? Would I, in embarking on another professional residency program, obtain the fulfillment and flexibility in time and freedom to look into my other interests across the Atlantic, especially as regards the charity foundation that we had started? Would I in all honesty be happier even if the uncertain dollars were to come rolling in? What new grounds did I expect to break? It is never too late in any day to start, no doubt, but at a certain time in ones life a realistic approach needs to be made and pertinent questions would need to be addressed realistically.

At the end of the day, the balance tilted in favor of that area of my passion and longtime interest. Yet often and again, the nostalgia for medical practice reared up its head. I consoled and further convinced myself by reassuring myself that I was already basically a qualified doctor and an anesthesiologist by specialization. I could always, albeit, with more grey hairs, restart from where I stopped. Of course, I know deep down within me that the latter would be a tall order. I had crossed the Rubicon as the saying goes, and it was more realistic to burn the boat! With the former consolation and self-reassurance therefore, I proceeded to read for the real estate licensing exams, which luckily turned out well at first attempt. Thereafter, I applied for and obtained my license.

The Doctor as a Realtor

The arrival of my state real estate salesperson's license marked a new phase of life for me. Hitherto, albeit in my home country, I had been combining professional medical practice with part-time practice of real estate, buying land and putting up houses. The latter required no special training and no licensing in my country of origin. It was more of an "all comer's game" and was neither fully regulated nor did the practitioners have a well-organized association. Any one who could make the contacts and could bring seller and buyer together was free to practice the trade. Consequently there were so many con men, so many frauds, and so many litigations. The land title insurance as is known in the United States did not exist in the area from where I was coming.

So much as real estate matters had been my area of interest, it was only a hobby. Full-time practice as a realtor, a member of the National Association of Realtors, was a different kettle of fish. But I was so happy and so fascinated to discover that the National Association of Realtors into which I had been accepted was a very highly disciplined and well-organized body in California. I felt quite impressed the day I went to their regional office for registration and enrollment. The high quality of the subsequent seminars and lecture sessions far surpassed my expectations. I was even more impressed when I started reading through the regulations and bylaws, and I felt fascinated the day I received the realtors metal badge, realizing that I could once again, even as I did as a medical practitioner, walk tall, realizing that I belonged to an association of disciplined men and women committed to abiding by certain commendable ethics in the practice of their profession.

I was excited to explore new grounds in a relatively new field. Variety being the spice of life, I felt rejuvenated. I, however, had no illusions about the difficulties that I would face being both new in the profession and in the community where I lived, especially realizing from my training that success in the practice depended to a large extent on who you know and who knows you.

The many ideas and occasional conflicts coming up in my mind prompted a constant need in me to recite the old-school anonymous poem taught us in our first year in Secondary School at Afikpo by our English literature master, Mr Guorge, which ran thus:

All that you do,
Do with your mind
Things done by halves
Are never done well
One thing at a time
And that done well
Is a very good rule
As many can tell.
(Anonymous)

Mr Guorge was unfortunately killed by a cow, some four months after he taught us that poem. He did not live long enough to see his students put the wordings of that poem into practice.

A very articulate and dedicated school master, Mr Guorge taught us in class most of the poems we knew. He insisted that every one of us his students must learn three new poems every week, and it is to his credit that most of us, his former students, learnt and could recite fluently over one hundred poems each. Many of those poems we still remember. Mr Guorge it was, who also taught us to compose our own poems.

Long-hoofed cows sharing the same roads with human beings had pulled off Mr Guorge from his motorbike as he tried to drive past them. They reportedly flung him high into the sky and repeatedly trampled over him as he landed, killing him on the spot!

Herds of long-hoofed cows still use the road past my house in Owerri every morning and evening, and whenever I encounter them, I sorrowfully remember Mr Guorge and quickly wind up my car glasses. It is certainly easier to deal with the heaps of dung that they deposit on the road than to deal with their long hoofs should they get angry and decide to attack you at the roadside where you have parked your car to allow them to pass. The municipal council apparently collects a lot of taxes from the herdsmen, and therefore the health menace and danger can continue.

The Care Manager

As I was pursuing the professional licensing in my original profession and in real estate, I realized that it was necessary to take on a job so that I would be able to pay my bills which rolled in, in leaps and bounds irrespective of how one tried to control them. The house rent needs to be paid. The telephone and other bills must not be paid late if they were not to attract penalties. The good thing was that the services were provided, unlike the situation elsewhere, when the bills would roll in without the services being provided. The many other utility bills were there in addition to the car bills and the relevant insurance and parking expenses. And should I get parking tickets, the problems would be compounded.

The first ticket I got was the day I parked my car facing the opposite direction from where the other cars faced. That was two weeks after I got my driver's licence. I had seen a parking space on the opposite side of the road as I drove past. Without making a U-turn, I simply reversed into the left side of the road where I found the parking space. I took up the space with my car still facing the direction towards which I was driving from the opposite side of the street. It was an obvious deviant parking, but that did not immediately strike me as wrong since I felt I was not physically driving the wrong way.

When I came out of the car I had checked thoroughly to ensure that my tires were no more than six inches from the curb. I felt satisfied. But it did not strike me that every other car on the side of the road where I parked was facing the opposite direction. I left, only to return after about an hour to find a red ticket for a fine of thirty five dollars for "wrong parking"! That was my baptism of fire on the streets of Los Angeles. I read the parking limit signs over and over and felt convinced that I parked within the correct time limits. I kept wondering for the next half hour where and how I had gone wrong. It took another driver to call my attention to the fact that I was facing a different direction from every other person who parked on that side of the street. I added that experience to my list of learning for the day.

Close to where I lived, I took on a part-time job in an Alzheimer's unit. It was a very good and well-managed center, the closest I could get to attending to the sick, a nostalgia which I still had in spite of my excitement about my new profession. Even though a part-time job two days in a week, the unit was in no way related to professional medical practice; it afforded me the opportunity to study firsthand certain manifestations of this problem which is related to ageing. I felt very happy for the first time to witness working from the other end of the cadre spectrum from what I had been used to. It made it possible for me to be of direct help to the physically helpless, and I felt very happy about that experience. Above all, and I really felt grateful to God for this, it afforded me my second opportunity of taking orders rather than prescribing them. My first opportunity of taking orders was during the Nigeria-Biafra war when I worked as an assistant in a rice farm. I had thereafter occupied the position of issuing orders in varying capacities from my very first job as a doctor on internship posting, through my national service, to my various positions in the postgraduate school, as a consultant in a government hospital, to my last held position as a medical director and chief consultant in a relatively well-known hospital. Honestly, on every occasion I bent down to help a resident with a task or something else, I came to closest terms with the utter vanity of human pride or arrogance, realizing that those helpless residents of today in that fairly high brow center were once the stars and perhaps the minigods of yesterday either as world champions, top business executives, or movie stars. But there they were in the sunset of their lives tucked in away from their mansions, yachts, and fleet, even with all the comfort and care in the facility, living from day to day, oblivious of their past, the present, and the future, awaiting the end of time. I began to come to terms with the fact that unless a cure for Alzheimer's is found in our lifetime, some of us would end up that way if we lived long enough. The oft repeated question therefore arises: Why should the spirit of a mortal be proud?

Again, from the few hours I put in two days a week in that facility, the verse in Shakespeare's seventh stage in "the seven ages of man" succinctly called to mind:

> . . . In second childishness and mere oblivion,
> Sans teeth, sans eyes, sans taste, sans everything.

I was so fascinated with the care—medical, social, and physical—which I saw being extended to the residents of the center in question that I made a formal written request to the chief executive of the conglomerate to grant me a franchise to open a similar center in cooperation with them for people with similar problems in my native country. I had offered to donate some of the facilities required for the actualization of that project. Even though a response to that request was yet to arrive, I still felt hopeful that someday that kind of cooperation will be made possible. This is because with growing urbanization, it would only be a matter of time when we will find that our elderly, especially those with age-related impairments, may no longer continue to benefit from the current and very commendable close family care as we know it today. I could already see it coming on fast especially with expected worldwide increase in life expectancy.

Much as one would not want close family care to yield place to institutionalized care, as currently being obtained in the developed world, there are bound to be a few inevitable cases that would require institutionalized care. Measures should therefore begin to be put in place to handle such emerging cases even in cultures where close family ties and noninstitutionalized family care currently exist.

My worry, though, is whether the provision of such centers in our increasingly fragile extended family setup would subtly encourage or even frankly facilitate the collapse of our very closely knit family ties and values. A number of people who might have collected their aged or ailing parents or relations to live with them might begin to take the easy way out and dump them in such institutions, where they will go to visit them only once in a long while. That will be a sad day for our very treasured and hitherto very helpful traditional values, and I would not want to be part of the dismantling of our treasured family values. To my mind, family care should always be encouraged except where it is impossible to obtain same, or where such care is found to be grossly defective.

I soon started to learn the terminologies of the real estate industry in greater detail. I had studied enough of it to pass the state exams. The practical aspect of it was much more interesting and much more demanding than mere buying and selling of houses and lands and/or helping sellers and buyers.

I was to find out that being a realtor required one to abide by a very comprehensive code of ethics which, in conjunction with the existing laws, makes the practice of real estate as disciplined and as professional as what I had been used to in my many years in the medical profession. I was to begin to see the realtor as a disciplined and well-tutored professional and not just as another tout who would want to talk one into buying or selling a property. I was to realize that a very strong and highly structured organization existed in the board of realtors which I enrolled into, for continuing education courses, seminars, and workshops for her members. The first of these seminars which I attended was so fascinating, so elucidating, and so professionally organized that most of us, the participants, were so amazed that it was at no extra cost to us, even with all the resource persons in attendance. The financial requirements for membership may appear a little daunting on the surface, but I believe that the benefits definitely outweigh those costs.

With the arrival of my state license, I readily joined one of the prominent real estate companies in California, one which also has a very good national spread and presence. On my first day at the branch office of the company which I joined, I was received by the team leader of the branch, an extraordinarily versatile and amiable gentleman. The team leader's duties as I was to learn later included the general organization of the place, including the organization of the teaching sessions which were to surpass all my expectations.

It did not take more than two weeks of lectures from the team leader and a number of other lectures for me to disavow myself of the long-held belief that practitioners of my primary profession were the sole repository of intelligence and versatility. I got so humbled by so much that I did not know and I came to start respecting every professional as a worthy specialist in his or her field. I had hitherto, even right from my secondary school days, come to believe that those of us who did zoology, chemistry, and physics or math, chemistry, and physics and who were thereby heading for medicine or engineering were the only gifted ones in society. The others who did the arts and humanities, we assumed, were the lesser mortals, the leftovers. That was partially because of the overriding emphasis on science in my school in my days in school. It was possibly also because those who were good in the sciences also excelled in the arts and humanities.

Now I know better. Indeed I now realize that even in the true understanding of what life is all about, many of us celebrated stars of yesterday are indeed very defective in other ways, especially when removed from our narrow cocoons and academic empires of conceit. I now realize that indeed even when it comes to living life to its fullest, we, who hitherto regarded ourselves as the superstars because we are in the medical profession, are indeed very greatly disadvantaged and indeed marginalized iatrogenically as we perambulate around the hospital complex, our little empires, oblivious of the fact of the much wider horizon of the other more people-oriented professions. Indeed I would recommend that once in a while people should switch professions even if it be only for a while. That way they would be better educated and better positioned to appreciate other professionals and people. My worry is that if the latter is tried, there may be a massive drift from the hitherto acclaimed elite professions, the huge-pay packets of the abandoned professions notwithstanding. The major rewarding aspect of the medical profession, of course, remains—that inner joy which comes with seeing one's patient recover. The disappointment and sadness that often accompanies the loss of a patient whom one has attended to for sometime can never, on the other hand, become routine. Even after long years of medical practice, I still found that, that late-night call informing me of a gasping patient continued to be ever painful, irrespective of the patient's age and circumstances. Conversely, the gentle smile from a recovering patient was often worth more to me than all the silver and gold. That of course is the major loss I will suffer in being off medical practice for a while. But since a complete severance is not implied, nor contemplated, the respite and the opportunity to do something new will certainly offer a new lease of life and offer the opportunity to serve in other ways and expand one's horizon in another exciting field.

The team leader of the group that I joined was so articulate and well grounded with the different topics that he lectured on that I felt that his talents would be largely wasted to the industry if they were not recorded for the benefit of other students and even other practitioners in the industry. He possessed the uncommon talent of being able to interlace the teaching of serious business with lighter commonplace events that got his listeners glued to the subject. The topics got so simplified when he discussed them that his listeners were often wrapped in attention through the duration of each of his lectures. He never failed to remind us that he once dropped out of college before he was able to fall back on track. Like those other very richest men in the world who were said to have dropped out of college before they made their fortunes, I could see only one reason why this former guy dropped out: he probably knew too much.

My initial four to six weeks as a real estate practitioner were the most difficult moments for me. Even with my new awareness, I still battled with myself as to whether I was not being naïve in "putting in the cooler" the profession in which I had trained and to whose peak I had to all intents and purposed reached. Was I being realistic, just because I love bricks and mortar and had taken a fancy for seeing new buildings come up, getting them bought, buying them myself, or getting them sold jettison my training and experience of so many years for romance with a profession in which I was just being schooled? I began to tell myself that since they use more of wood here for construction, and that if my fancy got fuelled merely by bricks and mortar, then I was in the wrong place. Besides, I told myself that I would not have ready money since I was a private contractor, who would still need to pay his bills irrespective of the state of the property market and the volume of business.

I started asking myself whether I had permanently ditched the thousands of people who, six thousand miles across the Atlantic, had reposed so much confidence in me by lending themselves to the services of my professional practice for close to a quarter of a century. I started asking myself whether my newfound love, my new professional orientation, would spell boom or doom to the charity, Foundation for the Poor, which my wife and I had founded and funded for many years and whose yearly recipients still looked up to us. Those doubts and calculations cropped up in my mind every now and then during the first six weeks of my registration and commencement of work. It took quite some self-convincing and one lecture on powerful mindset for me to finally resolve those issues and accept that whether as a doctor or a realtor, I could still offer my full role in service of humanity. Again, I convince myself that as far as the people I served was concerned, those two roles were not mutually exclusive since my continuous physical presence did not make all the difference as long as the institutions we founded remained functional. I reassured myself that it would be more fulfilling to have my time on my hands to do what I love to do and to serve God and humanity by being exemplary in the practice of my new profession. I was also playing a positive role. I resolved to maintain the part-time care service which I was involved with, even if it be, with time, on a volunteer basis. I wrapped up my resolution with a silent recitation of the short verse which we often recited in secondary school:

> Honor and shame on no conditions lie,
> Act well your part, there all the honor lies.

When I got home that day, I told Agie of my final decision, and despite her reservations about my decision, we celebrated the resolution over two glasses of cold apple drink.

From a Nigerian Knight to an American Knight

One of the things that impressed me most in the United States, even right from the time I used to visit, was the courtesy and the willingness to help whichever people irrespective of their ages often exhibited. On the other hand, I was always so disgusted when I saw teenagers and adults alike kissing on the streets and in public places. I was beginning to feel that public morality in general and sexual morality in particular had been thrown to the winds and that the American society, as I saw it, was fast degenerating into a godless society as far as sexual morality and marriage were concerned. I had almost come to the conclusion that the family as a sacrosanct entity was fast falling apart in this system. Of course, I now realize that those observations were more of exceptions rather than the rule. It is generally easier to observe an exception from a pack of monotony, especially for someone like me who came from a background where so much pretence and taboo are attached to matters of sex and sexuality where such discussions in public are regarded as taboos. Again my family background, where communal living was the rule rather than the exception, played a major role in my arriving at the former conclusion. Besides, the happy memories and nostalgia for those suppers of many dishes, those tiny little chickens we used to share between fifty-five people and more, and the love and cheer that radiated on the faces of our loving father and mothers as we shared, tend to make me feel that the society that I see is an aberration of what life and living should be.

But every society and age has her peculiar romances and her own abhorrences consistent with the social norms existent at the time and place. Extrapolations may constitute unfair comparisons and are bound to lead to wrong conclusions.

Certain things that would be regarded as taboos in my society of origin were readily, to my mind, easily glossed over, tolerated, or even subtly encouraged in my new society. Mine happened to be a much stricter society in terms of being more puritanical when it comes to public display of love and affection; and our social values, parentage, relationship between the sexes, tolerance of certain rights, and family life in general are much more strict than elsewhere in the Western world. Whether this display of puritanism in the society of near equal numbers of Christians and Moslems from where I come translates to an equal display of public morality when it comes to fiscal accountability and embezzlement of public funds as well as adherence to civilized social behavior in general is another matter.

It therefore becomes a question of deciding who is less godly and who is more satanic. Is it the man who kisses in public but who lives a more upright private life and holds public trust as sacrosanct, or is it the other man who makes the sign of the cross at every available opportunity in a public gathering or seeks out the direction of the sun to venerate and pray five or seven times a day publicly but in either situation abuses himself or others and betrays public trust by embezzling funds meant for development of his community or nation in private?

As I began to integrate more into the society in the United States, it became more obvious to me that much as the society appeared more permissive with issues that concerned the individual, certain basic tenets like telling the truth, courtesy, discipline in public places, and reverence for public trust are much more highly respected and revered in the American society. On other issues like the sanctity of marriage, the extended family system, and strong family ties, the background from which I come appears to certainly come stronger. When we marry for instance, we marry for life. Divorce hardly comes into the picture as practically every in-law would come into the picture to ensure that a marriage in whose traditional ceremony they participated does not break up. Even in the rare and extreme instances where an adulterous relationship leads to the birth of a baby, the man almost invariably takes back the wife and resultant baby after an atonement called *igwa ekwu* is performed by the wife. That situation in the Western society of course could be seen as worse than an "irreconcilable differences." The foregoing, which of course is extremely rare, only goes to show to what extent my native society could go to forgive in matters of marriage while not necessarily condoning promiscuity, if only to ensure the sustenance of a united family. That probably explains why polygamy was able to thrive, giving the forgiving, caring, and sharing attitude that was an invariable accompaniment of the large family units. That goes to explain how despite our large numbers, forty-six in all we were, we managed to make it even through the most difficult of circumstances, falling upon each other's shoulders for support in periods of utter stress, and relishing in our weekly suppers of many dishes, even in those times and ages when meat supply was so scarce and the toe of a chicken might be all that one might expect for his share from the wooden chop board, as we fixed our gaze with our little eyes on the board, as the sharing was done.

I soon got admitted into the Knights of Columbus, the biggest lay Catholic organization in the world. I had belonged to a similar organization in my native country, the Knights of Mulumba. The fundamental tenets of service and charity which both organizations espoused perfectly fitted my goals and aspirations, much as my nondenominational and indeed nonsectarian background right from secondary school does greatly impact on my receptive attitude towards religious diversity and people from other denominations and indeed faiths. This liberal attitude I hold, with the full realization that most people's religious beliefs stem largely from the background of their upbringing. Most indeed are "accidents" of birth, since we are all children of the same God. Certainly, our society and indeed the world in general would be a much better place if we all can begin to see the face of God on one another's face every day of our lives. Whether that face that we see appears beautiful or ugly, whether it is black or white, and whether it belongs to a Christian, Moslem, Hindu, Jew, or a Gentile would become immaterial.

I also had joined the relatively small but highly effective group of families from my hometown, Arondizuogu, living in California. Through these various organizations and groups, I looked forward to integrating better into the society with the ultimate aim of fulfilling my obligations to my new society, my nation, to my God, and to my family.

I was soon able to establish contacts with some old boys of my beloved School Government Secondary School Afikpo in the United States. I understood there are hundreds of them out here. I earnestly looked forward to the day when I shall be able to meet some of them in a group. No experience will be more memorable than when we can sit together and reminisce over those happy days at school. We may be able to meet some juniors whom we can call "or-ings," and we may also be able to meet a few senior boys who we can answer "yes, please" to, even before they conclude a sentence, even if the sentence ends up ordering us to kneel down.

Luckily there will be no beds to crawl under, no frog jumping to do, no *amaseri* walk to be punished with, no runs to do, and happily no detentions to be put on, and no grasses to cut either.

But certainly we shall be able to remember many of those masters that made the school great, those dedicated staff that were to shape our future forever for the better: the Equas, the Egbes, the Mantissas, the Lapels, the Matthews, the Nwigwes, and others both living and dead—too many to mention.

Then perhaps, if we can still fully remember the verses, we may be able once again, albeit from six thousand miles away and until we are able to arrange a physical trip to the true alma mater—the true caring mother, the gentle craftsman of most of our commendable social values—to Afikpo, the Varsity on River Cross, to once again, together, happily sing,

> Lord, receive us with thy blessing
> Once again assembled here.

Finally, with each passing day I search the Web, listen to the radio, and watch the television, I pray; and I eagerly look forward to the day that I will get the news from any of the media announcing the firm decision of the leadership of my little part of the world to deal decisively with all forms of corruption on the highways, at the ports, in offices, and in governance. That action will enable the good and hardworking people of that part of the world to join the rest of the civilized world to see people do the jobs for which they are paid without fleecing the society. That feat has been achieved elsewhere in the world. It certainly is not beyond us. It only requires a firm resolve on the part of the top leadership and a realization that acquired wealth is only a transient thing and serves the particular individual for only as long as he or she lives, and that will certainly not exceed six scores at the most. Wealth wrongly acquired at the expense of other individuals or the polity can only incur curses covert or overt; if not now certainly in the future, and if not from the present generation because of muzzled speech, certainly from the future generation. This is because strive however hard we may, we can never for all time blot out the judgment of history.

We can make it as a people, if we really want to.

Without the elimination of bribery and corruption, however, there is no way reasonable progress will be made, and the world's largest black nation will still totter despite her enermous human and material resources. Nothing will give one more joy than living to see that day, since I believe that with the hydra-headed monster of embezzlement, bribery, and corruption eliminated, every other good thing will gradually fall into place. It is only by so doing that, our youth, the true hope of any nation, will once again begin to decipher between what is wrong and what is right, what is real and what is fantasy.

Criticism of social ills must never be mistaken for lack of patriotism. It is only by seeing clearly where we have gone wrong that we will be able to make correct moves about how we can go right. It is only by leadership by example that a demonstration of the true tenets of patriotism can be made, and it is only by a strict manifestation of the latter that *the labors of our heroes past shalll never be in vain.*

EPILOGUE

SUPPERS OF MANY DISHES

As the horizon clears after the rains
We look up to the bright blue sky,
And our hearts feel gladdened
Not with what we see around us
For it is mostly rot that we see,
As the many that are good
Are eclipsed by the few that are bad, rotten, and depraved.

But since the sky that was dark and gloomy with the rains could clear
So we know that the horizon too will surely clear
For all, who the widely spread rot, today their abode do claim.

For as the day always follows the night
So shall sunshine and laughter will surely come
To a people who have known most of their lives,
Nothing but rot, decay, and deprivations
Even in the midst of God-given riches, strength, and plenty.

And all our days of pain and suffering
With the dawn of reformed leaders will surely be compensated
For no people have been known to suffer for all time
No, not when they have atoned enough for whatever their sins might be,
As the people in this picture surely have done.

Index

N

O

P

R

S

T

U

W

Z

www.ingramcontent.com/pod-product-compliance
Lightning Source LLC
Chambersburg PA
CBHW020616310726
48979CB00008B/1512/J

* 9 7 8 1 9 4 0 9 0 9 0 6 6 *